WILLIAM

STAR TREK®

ODYSSEY

THE ASHES OF EDEN
THE RETURN
AVENGER

with
Judith Reeves-Stevens
and
Garfield Reeves-Stevens

POCKET BOOKS
New York London Toronto Sydney Tokyo Singapore

These titles were previously published individually.

POCKET BOOKS, a division of Simon & Schuster Inc.
1230 Avenue of the Americas, New York, NY 10020

This book is published by Pocket Books, a division of Simon & Schuster Inc., under exclusive license from Paramount Pictures.

ISBN: 0-671-02547-3

First Pocket Books trade paperback printing September 1998

10 9 8 7 6 5 4 3 2

Printed in the U.S.A.

STAR TREK®

THE ASHES OF EDEN

So delicate—that's her.
So dignified—that's him.
Handsome, winsome, graceful—that's them.

Judy and Gar Reeves-Stevens

and

An inspiration to my perspiration,
My muse mused suffused.

ACKNOWLEDGMENTS

My thanks to these fine individuals
without whom this show would not have gone on:

Kevin Ryan
Richard Curtis
Carmen LaVia

PROLOGUE

Seventy-eight years after history reported him dead, James T. Kirk's journey had come to an end.

He was going home.

For the final time.

On a mountain slope, far above the simple cairn of rocks that was Kirk's grave, a lone figure stood in meditative silence, a sentinel keeping faithful watch.

His elegant black robes shifted in the twilight breeze of Veridian III. Their intricate embroidery spelled out the timeless principles of logic in metallic threads and Vulcan script. Those principles shimmered in the dying light of sunset.

The sentinel's gaze remained fixed on the battered Starfleet emblem that rested on the grave. In his expression, there was no betrayal of emotion, until his meditations were at an end and proper decorum had been observed.

Then a single tear welled up in the corner of his eye.

Ambassador Spock didn't fight it.

That battle between his two halves—Vulcan and human—had been fought and won decades ago.

Three weeks before this day, Spock had never known of this planet's existence. Yet now he knew he would never be free of it.

For history now recorded that it was on this world that James T. Kirk had reappeared, only to die again.

Spock's second grieving for his friend was far, far worse than the first had ever been.

What logic could there be in that?

Far below Spock, the setting sun drew long shadows from the modest pile of rocks he watched over. In the air above those shadows, five points of light sparkled to life.

Spock looked on as the transporter beams resolved into five Starfleet officers.

One he knew—William Riker, late of the Starship Enterprise. *Elsewhere on this planet, that vessel's shattered wreckage was being dismantled and removed by a team of Starfleet engineers under Riker's command. In accordance with the Prime Directive, no trace of advanced technology could remain behind. Should the future inhabitants of Veridian III's sister planet land here, they would discover nothing. Not even Kirk's body.*

The four others with Riker formed the honor guard that would travel with Spock back to Earth, for Kirk's official interment. A hero's funeral.

For all that Kirk had meant to the Federation, that honor seemed trivial to Spock. Yet what more could be done to assuage the sorrow of those Kirk had touched when his spirit had fled?

Spock had passed through that last veil himself. But because of Kirk, he had returned.

"You would do the same for me," Kirk had told him, long ago on the summit of Mount Seleya, when Spock had been reborn.

Now the tear grew in Spock's eye because he knew he could not. Though against all logic, he desired nothing else.

At least, he knew, Kirk had not faced whatever lay beyond his moment of death unaware of its coming.

Spock knew his friend had confronted his fate and reconciled himself to it, in that time between Kirk's return from Khitomer and the launching of the new Enterprise *which had sealed his fate.*

Spock took comfort from that knowledge. He found it to be most logical.

On the horizon, Veridian set and the stars shone forth from the gathering dark. The day at last was done.

The honor guard waited at attention by the grave. If all proceeded according to schedule, at this moment, far overhead, a starship would be shifting orbits, preparing to lock her transporter on the remains beneath the stones.

There could be no Mount Seleya in Kirk's future. Logic, therefore, directed Spock to seek solace not in what might lie ahead, but in what had gone before.

The tear slipped down his cheek. Spock watched it fall to the dust of this world. Swallowed as if it had never existed.

Except in his memories.

So to his memories now he turned, to the final adventure and the revelations of those last days he had spent with his friend.

When the journey of James T. Kirk had been ending—

—but was not yet over . . .

ONE

Kirk didn't look back to the past—he slammed into it running, diving, hitting the volcanic ash of Tycho IV shoulder first, rolling to cover by Ensign Galt behind a jagged boulder.

But the boulder hadn't been good cover for Galt. The ensign was dead. Skin blue-white. Body locked in a final contortion of pain.

Kirk faltered. He was twenty-four years old, a lieutenant three years out of the Academy. Ensign Galt had been only nineteen. On his first mission. He had looked up to Kirk, and Kirk hadn't protected him.

The communicator at Kirk's side chirped and reflexes took over, freeing him to act. He snapped it open.

"Kirk here."

"Where are those coordinates?"

It was Garrovick. Kirk's captain hadn't beamed back to the *Farragut* when he had had the chance, before the transporter coils had overloaded. He had stayed with the wounded. Waiting for the shuttlecraft. Still ten minutes away.

"Scanning now," Kirk said. He forced himself to his feet, exposing himself to whatever lay beyond the boulder. Whatever had attacked the *Farragut*. Whatever dwelt among the ashes of Tycho IV and was now picking off the *Farragut*'s crew, one by one.

Kirk held his bulky tricorder before him like a shield. His eyes darted from the readout to the surrounding terrain and back again. Tycho Prime was setting. The horizon blazed with the color of blood. But there were no readings.

"Captain, there's nothing out there!" Kirk's voice betrayed the tension he felt.

But the voice on the communicator remained calm. "Stay put and keep scanning, Lieutenant. You've got forward fire control till the main sensors are back in operation."

"Aye, sir," Kirk acknowledged. In standard orbit above him, the *Farragut*'s weapons were at his command. With no sensors to guide them, Kirk was now their targeting system. Somehow, the weight of that responsibility felt good.

A distant scream cut through the dusk, ending too abruptly. High-pitched. A woman.

Kirk held his position, heart hammering. He fought the urge to throw down his communicator and draw the laser pistol at his side. Garrovick had given him his orders, and there was nothing Kirk wouldn't do for his captain.

Garrovick was that kind of commander. That kind of man.

A figure ran for Kirk's boulder. It was nothing more than a red-tinged silhouette against the sunset. Kirk quickly checked his tricorder. The figure was human.

Androvar Drake.

The young lieutenant slid into position beside Kirk, out of breath, laser drawn. His short, bristle-cut blond hair was streaked with black volcanic ash. He glanced at Galt's body, but he showed no more reaction to it than a Vulcan might.

"That scream," Drake said, "it was Morgan."

Even as Kirk felt the shock twist through his chest, he saw the flicker of a smile on Drake's face. Faith Morgan was the *Farragut*'s weapons officer. For the last three months she had shared Kirk's quarters. As his lover.

Kirk wanted to grind Drake's smirk into the rocks of this place.

But he had his orders. Garrovick's orders. Starfleet orders. There was nothing more he could do for Faith Morgan, but the crew of the *Farragut* numbered four hundred. At least it *had,* when the ship had first entered this system.

Kirk waved his tricorder into the gloom. Still no readings. He felt angry tears sting his eyes, but he fought them back.

Before anything else, he was on duty.

Drake clicked through the power levels on his weapon, twisting the stubby barrel completely around to its highest setting.

Kirk reached out to stop him. "Lasers don't work on it." One of the sentries had managed to gasp that into her communicator before whatever it was had snuffed out her life.

"The creature can change its molecular form," Drake argued. "Maybe lasers can work on one form but not another."

Kirk rapidly changed the settings on his tricorder, scanned again, looking for a target. "Garrovick says *phasers* will do it." Phasers were the newest weapons in Starfleet's arsenal.

Drake gestured dismissively with his laser. "What does Garrovick know?"

Kirk slapped his communicator to his side, grabbed Drake by his collar, shoved him hard against the boulder. "He's the *captain,"* Kirk hissed. "He'll know how to get us out of this." As far as Kirk was concerned, that was what starship captains did. They were invincible. They had to be.

Drake looked amused by Kirk's emotional outburst. He smoothed his tunic where Kirk had crushed it. "He didn't do so well in orbit, did he?"

Kirk flipped open his communicator again, to keep his fist off Drake's jaw. Drake wasn't worth it. Kirk had found that out at Starfleet Academy. Their final after-class fight in the antigrav gym had cost Kirk two demerits. Kirk had won, barely. But the greater satisfaction had come when Kirk had edged out Drake by two percentiles and drawn first star duty in their class.

"Something caused a temporal shift in the sensor grid," Kirk said. It was the only explanation for how Garrovick had been taken by surprise.

Kirk had been on duty on the *Farragut's* bridge when it had happened. The sensor boards had lit up as the ship had been invaded by . . . something—a gas cloud, a creature? At the time there had been no way to be certain.

Garrovick had ordered shields to full strength. The creature responded by somehow vanishing from the sensors' sensitivity range. At the same time, an impossible temporal phase shift overloaded every key circuit in the *Farragut.* It might even have been a defensive move on the creature's part. But whatever had caused it, for a breathless hour it had seemed the ship might not be able to hold her orbit.

Garrovick had ordered the evacuation of all but a skeleton flight crew. Then he had saved the ship. Invincible.

But by then the creature had found the evacuation camp on the surface of Tycho IV. And it *was* a creature, there could be no doubt about that now. A creature that fed on the red blood cells of humanoid life-forms. Like Galt. And Faith. And all the others already cut down.

On the surface, the creature methodically probed their defenses. It overpowered their emergency forcefields. Withstood whatever the laser cannons could send into it. Enveloped everything with a sickly sweet smell—the smell of death on an already dying world.

Immediately, Garrovick had beamed down to the heart of the action, organizing the withdrawal of his crew. Fighting at their side.

Then, suddenly, halfway through the boarding process, the ship's transporters had stopped functioning. Too strained by the temporal overload and the first evacuation.

Garrovick had called down the shuttlecraft.

No one believed they would make it in time.

But Kirk never doubted that Garrovick would save them. Somehow.

He was the *captain.*

Something spiked on the tricorder's display.

Kirk fine-tuned the reading. Di-kironium. It meant nothing to him.

But then an unwelcome fragrance reached out to him. Too sweet. Overpowering.

"It's coming back . . ." Kirk said.

"Lieutenant!" Garrovick transmitted. "Where are those readings?"

Something moved out by the distant rocks.

No—not *moved—billowed.* Roiled forward against the scarlet sunset like a storm front from hell.

"Kirk?!" Garrovick repeated.

It was at this moment, in another time, another life, that Lieutenant Kirk froze. Faced with certain death, weighed down by the responsibility of his duty, he hesitated.

But not this time.

"Kirk to *Farragut!"* he shouted. "Target bearing thirty meters due west this location! All phaser banks *FIRE!"*

Instinctively Kirk charged Drake, forcing him down to cover as well. A heartbeat later, the heavens of Tycho IV were ripped open by twin lances of blue fire.

Kirk felt the ground shake as the eerie harmonics of phased energy tore apart the atoms of everything in its beam. He smelled burnt dust, heat, the tang of ozone released by atmospheric ionization.

The barrage ended.

Kirk peered past the edge of the boulder. A cloud of dust was lit from within by the glow of superheated rocks.

The creature was gone.

"We did it," Kirk exulted. He brought his communicator closer. "Captain Garrovick—we . . ."

A wispy tendril of white vapor twisted from the dust cloud like a tornado forming in reverse.

Kirk stopped talking.

The vapor stretched up from the ground, spinning faster, rising along the ionization trail left by the phaser beams.

Rising up to the *Farragut.*

"Dear God . . ." Kirk whispered.

He looked at Drake. Drake's eyes gleamed in the final trace of light from the sunset. His expression was unreadable.

"Kirk to *Farragut!* The creature is on an intercept course! Get out of there!"

Garrovick broke in on the transmission. *"Farragut!* Break orbit! Maximum warp! *Now!"*

The *Farragut*'s science officer responded, her voice breaking up in static.

". . . shields down . . . coming in through . . . antimatter containment is . . ."

A new star blossomed directly overhead.

"Farragut?" Garrovick said. *"Farragut,* come in . . ."

Nothing. Not even static.

Kirk stared up at the flickering pinpoint of light. Two hundred crew. A Constitution-class starship. Reduced to one dying star among so many.

Now obscured by a slender coil of white vapor. Spiraling down from the heavens.

Coming back to claim them all.

Drake laughed beside Kirk. "Great instincts, Jimbo. See you in hell."

The descending cloud creature was almost on them. Kirk had run out of options. There was only one thing left to do.

"End program," he said.

Then the creature and Drake and Tycho IV dissolved into a holographic haze, back to the past where they belonged . . .

. . . and Kirk no longer did.

* * *

"Was the suit too heavy, sir?" The young Starfleet technician waited respectfully for Kirk's answer as Kirk slipped off the bulky encounter helmet he had worn during the simulation.

In the cavernous room in the subbasement of the Cochrane Physics Hall of Starfleet Academy, massive banks of machinery hummed. The unpainted, generic blocks and platforms that had recreated the rocky terrain of Tycho IV dutifully reset themselves into yellow-gridded walls.

Kirk's eyes ached where the visual input encoders had pressed against them. His back ached from the weight of the servo drivers that controlled the feedback web enclosing his body. The entire holoenvironment encounter rig *was* too heavy.

But Kirk wasn't going to be the one who complained about it.

He made a conscious effort to stand straighter, move his arms more quickly. He flashed a smile at the technician. "Felt fine," he said lightly. "Almost as if I were back in my old uniform."

The technician grinned, impressed. As if all he ever heard were complaints. He started disconnecting the feedback web.

"You know," the technician said as if Kirk were a familiar friend of his, "someday it should be possible to do away with the suit entirely. Use focused tractor beams. Microgravity control. Maybe even build some props with transporter matter replication."

Kirk groaned inwardly as he kept a patient smile on his face. In addition to its weight, the suit chafed in places he didn't want to rub with an audience around.

He let the technician babble on happily about the wondrous abilities of his gizmos and gadgets and the future of holographic simulations.

He hoped the technician would think the sweat streaming off his subject's forehead was the result of the encounter suit's skintight fit, and not the exertion that had left Kirk close to exhaustion. Or the pain in his shoulder not letting him forget the way he had hit the simulated ground and rolled behind the simulated boulder.

He thought it was too bad Starfleet engineers couldn't simulate the feeling of indestructibility he had had in his youth, when he could hit the real ground on a roll five times a day and never feel the consequences.

"Think of it," the technician continued with innocent enthusiasm. "Just walk into an empty room in your ordinary uniform and *zap!* Instantly you're surrounded by a holoenvironment so realistic you can't tell the difference between it and reality."

Kirk flexed his hands, remembering the weight of the old-fashioned tricorder he had carried during the simulation. The way the fabric around Drake's neck had compressed in his fist. All of it an illusion.

"Trust me. It's very realistic now," Kirk said. He meant it.

"So you can be sure that's what would have happened."

Kirk didn't understand. "What would have happened?"

"If you had fired at the cloud creature right away, instead of hesitating the way you really did."

Now Kirk understood. But he didn't want to talk about it. He hadn't thought about Faith Morgan in years. But he had never forgotten her. He would never forget any of them.

"You see, by not firing the phasers right away," the technician persisted, "the creature only attacked those crew members on the ground. The *Farragut* and everyone on her were safe. But if you *had* fired right away—based on the computer's reconstruction of the cloud creature's abilities, it would have returned to the *Farragut,* destroyed her, *then* finished off everyone else on the ground as well. So you did the right thing the first time round."

And Garrovick had died because of it, Kirk thought grimly. He changed the subject. "It should make for a wonderful training device."

The technician gave him a bewildered look. "Training? I guess. But how about for entertainment? The gaming possibilities alone are endless."

Kirk kicked off the heavy feedback boots that had made him feel as if he had crunched across volcanic soil. "You programmed all this for 'entertainment' purposes?" he asked.

The technician retained his puzzled expression as he retrieved Kirk's feedback boots, balancing the entire suit in an awkward position across his arms. "Sir, we've programmed almost *all* your early exploits into the system."

"*My* exploits?"

The technician nodded ardently. "This encounter with the cloud creature of Tycho IV, and your destruction of it eleven years later on stardate 3619.2. And stardate 3045.6—remember? Your encounter with the Metrons and hand-to-hand battle with the Gorn. And 3468.1—when you escaped from the alien on Pollux IV who claimed to be the Greek god Adonais. We've almost got them all, sir. More coming online each day."

Kirk felt rattled. He couldn't recall a single stardate from his first five-year mission on the *Enterprise* if his pension depended on it. "But why?"

The technician stared blankly at Kirk, as if he couldn't understand why the question had been asked. "Sir . . . you're a hero."

"Oh." *That again,* Kirk thought.

"Don't you feel that way, sir?"

Kirk hesitated. He didn't want to say the wrong thing. This young man had gone to a prodigious amount of effort to re-create an incident from Kirk's past in Starfleet's prototype holographic encounter suite. In incredible detail, as well. Even Kirk had forgotten the laser sidearms that used to be standard Starfleet issue.

He had, he admitted to himself, forgotten a great deal from those days.

He smiled at the technician, trying to soften the blow. "Those . . . 'exploits,' " he began.

"Yes, sir?"

"They were just my job," Kirk said simply. "A job I did a long time ago."

The technician regarded Kirk blankly for a moment, as if unsure how to respond.

"It was more than a job, sir. To us." With a nod he indicated his fellow technicians in the control room overlooking the encounter suite. Men and women, they were all the technician's age. Younger than Kirk could ever imagine having been. And all of them were lined up against the viewport, watching Kirk's every move. It was disconcerting to be under that close scrutiny.

Kirk could see the dawn of disillusionment in the young technician's eyes. "We'll never forget, sir."

With that, the young man turned and walked back to the control room.

Kirk held out his hand to stop him. He wanted to say something, anything, to erase the youth's disappointment.

But he didn't know how.

It wasn't the first time, either.

The problem was with expectations, Kirk knew. For all that it mattered to others, his past held little appeal for him. He had always looked toward the future, toward new challenges, not past accomplishments.

But his future was running out.

He was a starship captain without a starship. Unable to look back, unable to go forward. Trapped in the present. Pent up. Frustrated. Ready to go nova.

It was an intolerable state for James T. Kirk. And he knew he had to do something about it soon. Otherwise, he would have to give up. And giving up had never been an option for him.

He'd rather die first, and Kirk was not yet ready to face that final moment.

Though in time, he knew, even a starship captain must die.

TWO

No one knew who had built the Dark Range Platform.

The seemingly haphazard supports of the immense space station stretched out like demented spiders' webs. Coiled around a confusion of life-support spheres and cylinders installed by a dozen races over the platform's millennia of service.

Once, it might have been a transfer point for vast flotillas of starships. Some, perhaps, belonging to the Preservers themselves. It was that old.

But now it was a backwater refueling stop. A starting point for dreamers seeking fortune among the stars. A lair for the smugglers and cutthroats who would steal that fortune from them.

Alone, it drifted in the dark between the stars. At relative rest in the hinterlands of the Federation's frontier and the Klingon Empire's Old Regions. As telling testimony to the station's true worth, neither the Federation nor the Empire claimed it.

No one knew who had built Dark Range. What's more, no one cared.

But for Pavel Chekov on stardate 9854.1, it was the most

important thing in his life. Because the grime-covered walls of its access corridors might well be the last thing he would ever see.

The cold tip of the disruptor's emitter node dug deeper into Chekov's temple.

The leather-gloved hand tightened against his windpipe. It was impossible to breathe.

That was the point.

Kort, the one-eyed Klingon, breath reeking of bad *gagh,* leaned in closer, finger tightening on the trigger stud, counting down.

". . . hut . . . chorgh . . . soch . . ."

In seven seconds, Chekov would be a cloud of disrupted subatomic particles. His only thought: *What would the captain do?*

". . . jav . . . vagh . . ."

Chekov struggled uselessly against the Klingon's thickly muscled arm. "I vanted to get on with my life!" he gasped.

Kort stopped counting. Narrowed his one good eye at his captive. Infinitesimally lessened the tightness of his grip.

"That is why you *punched* an admiral?" Kort asked. His disbelief was evident. "Destroyed your career?" The deep ridges in the Klingon's heavy brow furrowed all the way down to the duranium plate that covered his useless eye socket.

"Vat career? Starfleet had nothing more to offer me." Chekov looked sideways along the barrel of the disruptor. Kort's breath made him want to gag. But he had the Klingon's attention as surely as the Klingon had his.

"Thirty-three years I had given them," Chekov continued. "And for vat? I vas still a commander—a *commander!* Always having to do vat the brass told me to do." The words came easily to Chekov now. He wasn't even aware of the disruptor's tip easing away from his temple. " 'Readings, Mr. Chekov.' 'Run a sensor sveep, Mr. Chekov.' Alvays in someone else's shadow. Never a chance for *me.* To show vhat *I* could do."

Along the length of the disruptor's barrel, Chekov met Kort's icy one-eyed gaze. Held it. The weapon's ready light pulsed silently, fully charged.

"I vanted to let go of it. I didn't vant to be angry anymore."

At last, Kort pulled the weapon back. But still held its aim on Chekov's head. Still kept his hand on Chekov's throat. Water dripped somewhere. The slippery decks rumbled with the comings and goings of cargo shuttles from the nearby bays. Chekov counted heartbeats. Waiting.

Kort shot a glance across the shadowed corridor. To where the two Andorians held Uhura.

One delicate blue hand was clamped over Uhura's mouth. A ceremonial dagger precisely indented the skin under her jaw. The blade's silver sheen was marred by a pinprick of red blood. Human blood.

Kort nodded once.

Uhura tensed.

With great reluctance, the bulky Andorian in the fur vest took the dagger away. The slender Andorian in chain mail removed his hand from Uhura's face.

It was Uhura's turn to gasp for breath.

But still she couldn't move. The Andorians kept her pinned to the bulkhead.

"Is it true?" Kort asked Uhura.

Uhura's eyes darted to Chekov. Chekov saw the same thought hidden there. Knew what she was thinking.

"Don't look at *him!*" Kort shouted. His deep voice echoed along the twisting corridor of pipes and conduits. Was swallowed by the distant thrum of jury-rigged air purifiers and gravity generators.

Kort jabbed his disruptor back into Chekov's temple. "Is . . . it . . . true?" he repeated.

"Yes," Uhura said evenly. "For both of us."

Chekov counted ten heartbeats. An eternity.

Then Kort reholstered his weapon. Motioned to the Andorians to release Uhura.

Their antennae dipped in disappointment, but they did as they were told.

Kort grabbed Chekov by the shoulders. "So, even fabled Starfleet is no different than the Empire's navy. Step on a worm often enough, and even the lowliest will evolve wings!"

Chekov didn't bother trying to follow Kort's idiom. He only braced himself as the Klingon crushed him in a bear hug.

Ten more heartbeats passed. Chekov felt dizzy.

Kort released him. Gave him a pat on the cheek that was more an open-handed punch.

"They'll call you a traitor," Kort boomed.

Chekov rubbed the side of his face, trying to lessen the stinging. Unused to the stubble of beard that grew there. "They have called me vorse."

Kort looked at Uhura. "And you, the same."

Uhura flashed a savage smile. Chekov could see Kort's nostrils flare with interest.

"I've called *them* worse," Uhura said.

Kort reached inside his belt and pulled out two identity wafers.

"How unfortunate you didn't see the errors of Starfleet's ways a decade ago," the Klingon growled. He returned the wafers to Chekov and Uhura. "Then, by now, perhaps it would be the Empire gathering to gnaw at the Federation's bones."

Chekov slipped his forged identity wafer into a hidden pocket on his coat. For all the wafer had cost, it had been useless. Kort had been able to determine his and Uhura's true identities in less than ten hours—effortlessly discovering they both had left Starfleet under less than ideal circumstances six short months ago.

"I do not look upon vat ve are doing as gnawing the

Empire's bones," Chekov said. He adjusted the somber civilian clothes he wore. Uhura did the same.

Kort clamped an arm around Uhura's shoulder, drawing her near. "Of course, the law of the juggled." He managed to look almost wistful as he spoke. Not an easy task for a Klingon. "Eat or be dinner." He frowned at Chekov. "Yours is such an awkward language."

Chekov shrugged. "Vat happens now?"

Kort gave his new human friends a final painful squeeze and then released them roughly, causing both to stumble back into the Andorians.

"Now," Kort said, "we do what we came here to do. *Business!*"

He began to stride down the corridor, heading for Dark Range's habitat levels, his Andorians at his side. Kort's heavy, metal-shod boots clattered with each step. Chekov and Uhura took rapid double steps to keep up.

"Weapons-grade antimatter," Kort began, counting off his merchandise on his thick, hairy fingers. "Photon torpedoes—still in their crates. Disruptor cells. Warp cores." He suddenly stopped and spun around to leer at Uhura. "Dilithium crystals!"

"Vorthless," Chekov said.

Kort looked astounded.

"Ve can recrystallize them now."

Kort shook his shaggy mane in wonder. "Oh, brave new planet . . . how many times were our forces held back from dealing you a decisive blow because we had no dilithium?"

"Who cares?" Uhura interjected. "So far, all you've told us about is low-level matériel we could get from any two-credit smuggler. You told us you had access to *generals.*"

Kort grinned at Uhura. Chekov winced as he saw the twitching tail tip of a single *gagh* worm still caught between two of Kort's stained and yellow teeth.

"In your language, the Empire is having a going-out-of-business sale." Kort looked at Chekov. The grin vanished. "You also say: You get what you pay for."

"The people we represent are vell funded. If they vant veapons-grade antimatter, they can get it from their own contacts, direct from Starfleet."

Kort waited. Uhura didn't disappoint him.

"What we want is hardware," she said.

Kort gestured broadly, making a joke of Uhura's request. "But of course. A Bird-of-Prey? Maybe two?"

"No secondhand Romulan junk," Chekov snapped. "A cruiser."

"*K'tinga*-class," Uhura added. "Maybe two."

Kort's remaining eye widened.

"Of course," Chekov said coolly, "if that is beyond you . . ."

Kort grabbed Chekov's arm as if to keep him from walking away. "I had no idea," he said quickly. "When I found out your documents were forged . . . that you were Starfleet . . ."

"Ex-Starfleet," Uhura corrected.

"I thought this was, in your language, a stung."

"Sting," Chekov said.

"A cruiser?" Kort asked.

"Ve know there are generals who are . . . making them awailable."

Kort glowered. As if even a Klingon criminal had standards. As if somewhere beneath his avarice, his willingness to deal in the debris of his collapsing Empire, there still beat the heart of a patriot. Someone who still believed in his flag and his ruler.

Chekov wondered how much this transaction was really costing the Klingon. What price could there be on lost dreams?

But this was not the time for sentiment.

"Vith dilithium reserves so low," Chekov continued, "how much good does a powerless cruiser do the Empire, anyvay?"

Kort nodded. A serious expression clouded his dark face.

"Bones to be gnawed," he said. "With the Federation the vulture for once." He glanced at the Andorians. Chekov could sense that he had reached a decision.

"Cargo Bay Twelve," Kort briskly told Chekov. He held up two fingers. *"Cha' rep."*

"Two hours," Chekov agreed.

Kort nodded once to Uhura, then turned and clanked off down the corridor. His two Andorians hurried after him.

Uhura rubbed at the tiny scratch under her jaw. "Still think this is a good idea?" she asked.

"I enjoyed punching that admiral," Chekov answered with a shrug. "Besides, ve might end up vith a Klingon battle cruiser of our wery own."

Uhura put a hand on her hip and frowned at her co-conspirator. "And just what do you think you're going to do with a Klingon battle cruiser?"

Chekov smiled winningly. "A man can dream, can't he?"

Uhura shook her head and patted Chekov's cheek. "You keep dreaming, Pavel. That's what you're good at."

She glanced up and down the corridor. They were alone.

"Come on," she said. "We've got two hours to get our credits together."

But Chekov didn't move.

"What?" Uhura asked him.

"When Kort was getting ready to kill us . . . I saw vat you vere thinking. In your eyes."

Uhura waited.

"You vere thinking: Vat vould the keptin do now?"

She nodded, smiling. "The bluff worked, didn't it?"

"Da. But I vonder vat the keptin *is* doing now?"

Uhura pulled her cloak tighter around her. "If he's smart, he's trying to find an admiral of his own to punch."

Chekov was surprised. "And leave Starfleet?"

"And get on with his life," Uhura said. "Which is what we should do."

She started up the corridor then, not waiting for Chekov.

Chekov hung back for a moment, trying to think of Captain Kirk no longer being part of Starfleet.

It was easier to think of the Earth without the sun.

But still, after all that Kirk had accomplished in his career, what more could he want from Starfleet? What more could he expect?

A man could dream. But what dreams were left to a man who had already captured so many of them?

Chekov hurried along the corridor after Uhura.

He hoped never to live so long that he ran out of dreams.

He wished the same fate for his captain.

THREE

Despite the best efforts of human mind and machine, it still rained without warning in San Francisco.

Kirk liked that.

Throughout the worlds of the Federation, Earth was hailed as some ethereal fairyland. Home of perfection. Free of want. Of need. Of disease. Of crime.

By the standards of the twentieth century, perhaps it was.

But every time some aspect of that perfect order broke down—even something as inconsequential as a late-summer thunderstorm arriving unannounced to thwart the Bureau of Weather Management—a part of Kirk rejoiced.

Who wanted to live in a perfect world?

He had seen too many of them in his voyages.

Perfection meant there were no more challenges.

It was as good a definition of death as Kirk could imagine.

He idly rocked the glass in his hand. Making the scotch swirl. The ice cubes clink. Blending with the soft patter of the raindrops on the window.

Spock could probably make a poem out of it, Kirk thought. The soft sounds of a sleeping city—San Francisco spread out below him, distant lights shimmering in the rain, fading away to nothing in the 3 A.M. mist. Now and then the slowly moving running lights of a flying car, or a shuttle, floated past like a firefly on an Iowa night.

But poems weren't Kirk's way.

He gulped a mouthful of scotch. Felt it burn his throat—ice cold and fire hot at the same time. That was his poetry. Sensation. Being alive. Imperfection in all its glory.

The gray clouds above flashed with inner lightning.

Kirk closed his eyes, waiting for the thunder to reach him. Dreading it.

Because it wasn't lightning. It wasn't thunder.

She was calling to him.

From up there.

Bound in spacedock. Awaiting the order that would turn her into scrap.

The thunder came. Rumbled past him. Made the window rattle.

Kirk saw the face of a horse he had cherished, lifetimes ago.

The look in the creature's eyes as it lay beyond the help of twenty-third-century veterinary science.

As Kirk's uncle had raised the short barrel of the laser rifle.

He couldn't remember how old he had been. Eight? Ten?

All he remembered was the horse's eye. Seeing in it the knowledge of the oblivion to come.

The horse had kicked feebly. Tried valiantly, heartbreakingly, one more time to stand. Knowing somehow that if it could just stand up one last time, then the man with the rifle would leave and everything would be as it was.

Tears streaming down his face, young Kirk, little Jimmy, had pulled on the horse's bridle, trying desperately to make it stand up. One last time.

But the horse couldn't stand. Jimmy's aunt pulled him gently away. He heard the soft pop of the laser. The last soft whisper of the horse as . . .

More lightning. More thunder.

The *Enterprise* called out to him. Beyond the clouds. Among the stars.

One last time.

Stand up.

The man with the rifle.

The knowledge of oblivion.

Alone . . .

"Come back to bed, Jim."

Kirk's eyes flew open. A flood of adrenaline shot through him. He hadn't heard Carol come up behind him. He had forgotten she was here.

He made himself smile before he turned around to face her.

It was her apartment, after all. Where he always returned.

His safe harbor. His spacedock.

Carol Marcus slipped a hand around Kirk's waist, snuggled under his arm, watched the city with him.

Kirk could see their reflections in the window. The smile became real. Starfleet's heroic starship captain and the Federation's best molecular biologist, nothing more than two middle-aged civilians in terry-cloth bathrobes. He wondered what the young virtual-reality technician from this afternoon would think.

Then, in a sudden flash of lightning, he saw himself and Carol as they had been when they were the technician's age. So full of dreams, of promise. As Spock would say, so full of *possibilities*.

But as quickly as the lightning faded, their youth fled once again.

Kirk sighed. His shoulder hurt from the holographic simulation this morning. He felt tired. He felt . . . old.

Carol hugged Kirk to her. "Thinking about the farm?"

Kirk shook his head. He had forgotten all about it, actually. The advocates handling his parents' estate were after him to decide what to do with the Kirk farm. His nephews had no plans to return to Earth. Kirk was the only family member left who might have an interest in maintaining it. But the demands of the paperwork associated with the decision had been incessant. Upsetting. Pushing any desire to deal with it out of his mind.

"They don't need a decision till the end of the month," Kirk said.

They stood together in silence for a minute more. Far away, the air-traffic warning lights on the Golden Gate Bridge pulsed weakly through the mist.

Carol nuzzled his shoulder. His bad one. Kirk winced.

"It's all right," Carol said. "Really."

Of all the troubles he faced in his cluttered, planetbound life, Kirk knew what she meant. He didn't want to discuss it. He drew away from her. Swallowed the rest of his scotch.

Carol misunderstood his action. His silence.

"It happens, Jim. To every man. Sooner or later."

Kirk could feel his cheeks burn. He knew his anger wasn't right, but it didn't change the way he felt.

He wasn't every man. He couldn't be.

"Jim, I don't know what we are to each other after all these years. More than friends. Certainly—" Carol reached out to turn his face to hers. "—certainly lovers. But I do know we've been through too much together for you to stand there . . . sulking."

"I am not sulking."

Carol's hand fell away from his face.

"Getting up in the middle of the night to drink scotch and stare out at the rain isn't my idea of having a good time."

"I like scotch. And rain. Especially when it isn't programmed."

Carol shook her head. Moved closer. "Come back to bed," she whispered.

She moved her hand inside his robe, pushed against the tie that held it in place, let it fall open.

"We'll try again." She kissed his neck. "As many times as it takes."

She took him in her hand.

But all was as it was before.

The fire had fled as surely as their youth.

Only ashes remained.

"Carol, don't." Kirk pulled away, tied up his robe. He turned away from her tears, unable to deal with them.

"Why do you keep doing this to me? To us?" she asked, voice breaking. "Why do you keep coming back?"

Kirk stared out at the storm. He had already asked those questions of himself. He had no answer.

"What do you want?" Carol asked—*demanded.*

But Kirk was too cold, too tired, too *old* to answer.

Lightning flashed. The thunder would come.

She cried out to him.

One last time . . .

"What do you want, Jim?"

The thunder arrived, enveloped him. He tensed. Waiting.

But it carried him nowhere.

"I don't know," Kirk said. A voice of defeat. He faltered as he heard it come from him, but could do nothing to temper it. "Not anymore."

Carol went back to her bedroom. Closed the door.

Kirk poured another scotch. Turned a chair so it faced toward the window.

The rain lasted all night.

Tears he couldn't shed.

FOUR

Chekov shivered. The cavernous Dark Range cargo bay was that cold.

There was no forcefield to hold in atmospheric pressure and heat. Only large metal doors—uninsulated, obviously—a hundred meters across. All the air would have to be pumped out of the hold before those doors could be opened.

There were no tractor beam nodes in the splotched and flaking walls, either. Four shuttles were docked here—each older and bearing more hull patches than the next. Each would have to maneuver by station-keeping rockets or impulse power to leave under manual control. One misstep, and a bulkhead could be punctured, a door thrown out of alignment.

Chekov studied the welded panels and mismatched, frost-covered sheets of hull metal lining the hold. It appeared such missteps were not infrequent.

Disturbingly primitive, he decided. But then he remembered how old the Dark Range was. It was surprising that anything aboard it still worked at all.

Beside him, by a stack of modular cargo crates marked with Romulan warning symbols, Uhura pulled her collar up around her neck. For a moment, her teeth chattered. Her breath hung before her. One of the few working overhead lights caught it perfectly, a pale vapor ghost glowing against the hold's deep shadows.

But their "banker" showed no sign of the cold. The

compact, young human woman stood three meters away with her flight jacket open. As if ten degrees below freezing were her body's natural setpoint.

She noticed Chekov looking at her, returned his gaze. Attractive, Chekov thought. Finely drawn features. Dark complexion. A strong intelligence in her eyes. But a mouth that was not used to smiling.

As for her hair, that was hidden. She wore a tight flight hood favored by pilots who spent too much time in microgravity but didn't wish to shave their scalps.

By now the banker's expression had become one of challenge. Chekov had looked at her too long.

"Is there something you want?" she asked.

Her code name was *Jade*—the only designation Chekov and Uhura had been given. But Uhura had dubbed the woman "the banker" early on. An old Earth term, Uhura claimed. From the days when Earth had relied on money for financial transactions.

Chekov thought the term fitting. This far out on the frontier, where the Federation's massively complex economy had yet to be established, archaic institutions like banks had reason for existing.

In Jade's datacase were computer wafers holding enough exchange credits to buy a small planet. To say nothing of a Klingon battle fleet or two.

Chekov and Uhura had come through with their part of the bargain. Now it remained to be seen if their Klingon smuggler would come through with his.

And Kort was late.

Chekov looked at the time readout on his chronograph—a small pocket model with a few built-in sensor functions—the closest the civilian market could get to a decent tricorder out here. "Perhaps he is not going to show."

Jade's dark eyes burned into him. "He'll show," she said. "Even if he doesn't have access to battle cruisers, he won't be able to resist making a grab for this." She held up her datacase.

"I hadn't thought of that," Chekov muttered softly to Uhura.

"Maybe you're not cut out to be a criminal," Uhura said.

"Did *you* think of it?" Chekov asked indignantly. He felt very much the criminal type, given all he had been through in the past six months since leaving Starfleet.

Uhura answered by pulling her cloak open long enough for Chekov to see the full-sized phaser II pistol attached to her belt.

Chekov was surprised. "That's illegal," he hissed. Not to mention unsafe.

But Uhura rolled her eyes. "So's buying Klingon military hardware."

Chekov had left his own phaser—a palm-sized type I—in his quarters. With Kort's insistence on searching them at every meeting, it was the simplest thing to do. But he was regretting the decision.

Jade raised her hand and motioned to Chekov and Uhura to be silent.

Uhura heard it first. A communications expert's trained ears. As exceptional as any Vulcan's.

"Footsteps," she whispered to Chekov.

Chekov didn't hear them. He hadn't even heard a personnel door open into the hold. So how could there be anyone else here?

Unless someone had set up an ambush.

"Reach for the *Hovmey,*" Kort thundered from behind him. "And turn around. Slowly."

Chekov sighed. He was getting tired of this. Six months.

He turned with his hands held high. Uhura did the same beside him.

Kort and his two Andorians stood five meters away, all with disruptors drawn. Kort's metal-shod boots were wrapped in packing foam and made no sound against the deck. A banged-up Tellarite ore shuttle was directly behind them. The blackened phaser streaks on her side suggested she had hauled more than just ore in her day.

"I thought ve vere going to do *business,"* Chekov said. He didn't have to feign annoyance.

"Shut up or put down," Kort barked.

"Put up or shut up," Uhura corrected. "Maybe you should think about buying a Universal Trans—"

Kort's disruptor beam bubbled the deck plate metal just in front of Uhura's boots.

Then he aimed directly at Uhura. "Prove to me you can afford to buy what I have to sell."

"Wery vell," Chekov said. He began to speak over his shoulder. "This is . . . our banker . . ."

But there was no one behind him.

Jade was gone.

"I have no time for Terran games," Kort snarled.

"She vas just here," Chekov stammered.

"Who?"

A phaser whined. The large Andorian to Kort's side suddenly arched back. Burst into a blaze of blue energy.

Chekov was appalled. The disintegration could only mean that Jade was still here, and she had set her phaser to kill.

Kort and the thin Andorian fan-fired their disruptors to either side. Chekov hit the deck, rolling behind a Romulan crate.

Uhura's voice rang out in the cargo bay. "Don't even think about it, mister!"

Chekov peered around the crate.

Uhura held her phaser on Kort and the Andorian.

So Kort and the Andorian held their disruptors on Uhura.

"Two to one," Kort said. "Even a Federation *Qtalh* like you can figure those odds." But he kept glancing about. Still not sure of the source of the first phaser blast.

"Then I'll take one of you with me," Uhura said. "And I'm not aiming at the Andorian."

Chekov saw the Andorian's antennae prick up with interest.

Kort took a step sideways and behind the Andorian.

The Andorian moved sideways, exposing Kort again.

Chekov calculated the trajectory he needed. He lobbed his chronograph to the top of the Tellarite shuttle. It disappeared nicely in the dark shadows, out of sight, then clattered on the shuttle's hull.

Kort and the Andorian spun, disruptors firing against the shuttle's hull.

The Andorian fell to the deck as Uhura's phaser stunned him.

"The odds just evened," Uhura said.

"You led me into a trap," Kort hissed.

Uhura's aim was unwavering. "You drew first."

Chekov edged out from behind the crates, trying not to make a sound. Whatever Jade was up to, he couldn't wait for her. If Uhura could just keep Kort talking . . .

"And why shouldn't I?" Kort exclaimed. "Starfleet Intelligence agents everywhere. The Empire's own internal peace forces turning on their own. It is not an easy time to be in business for yourself."

Chekov moved carefully, quietly. He could hear the growing sense of unease in the Klingon's voice. Uhura wasn't his only adversary. He had to know there were at least two others in the hold with him—Chekov, and whoever had fired the fatal phaser blast.

Chekov peered past the glaring lights at the docked shuttles. Deep shadows stretched between haphazard stacks of crates. Still no sign of Jade. Chekov didn't understand her tactics. But he didn't waste time trying.

Right now he had to disarm Kort before he could fire at Uhura. Or before Jade could kill the Klingon.

Unless one of the wild bursts Kort and the Andorian had

fired had managed to kill Jade instead. That could explain why she hadn't fired again. It was easier than believing she wanted Chekov and Uhura out of the way.

Chekov eased between two large crates labeled FREEZE-DRIED STOMACHS in Klingon script. He didn't even want to *think* what they might be for.

All he could think of was Jade's datacase. Filled with credit wafers. Enough to buy a small planet.

A man *could* dream, Chekov decided.

He squinted around the edge of a crate.

Kort was one stack of crates over, backing up to the Tellarite shuttle.

He was near the pilot's hatch.

Chekov understood what Kort was planning. Saw his chance.

"I suggest we withdraw," Kort shouted to Uhura. "Begin negotiations again. By subspace."

"Negotiations end here and now," Uhura answered.

Kort's free hand came up behind him, feeling for the shuttle's hull. Found it. Moved to the hatch controls.

Chekov tensed. Muscles coiled.

Kort pressed the activate control.

The hatch puffed open.

The Klingon couldn't help himself—at the sound of the panel opening he *had* to check with just the barest movement of his eye. The slightest diversion of his attention.

Chekov sprang forth screaming—to startle Kort and to warn Uhura not to fire.

Somehow it worked.

Kort swung his disruptor toward Chekov. But Chekov plowed into his gut, bashing him backward.

Chekov felt something crunch in his own neck as Kort's massive body collapsed by the shuttle. He heard the Klingon's heavy head slam against the hull with a clang, the disruptor hitting the deck and clattering away, Uhura running forward.

He heard the *snick* of a coiled knife springing to life.

Knew what it meant.

No Klingon ever carried just *one* weapon.

Chekov also knew Uhura would never close the gap in time. He braced himself for the bite of the knife as it pierced his back. Thrusting for his heart, as he knew it must.

He wondered what his captain would do.

He was disappointed as he realized that this would be his dying thought.

But he didn't die.

Kort grunted.

Chekov opened his eyes. Looked up past Kort's bulk to see Jade—crouched beside Kort, a phaser jammed against the Klingon's thick neck, taking the uncoiled spring knife out of his glove.

Chekov got to his feet. Grimaced as a sharp pain from his wrenched neck flashed down through his arm. But he was alive, and Uhura was beside him.

"Vhat vere you thinking of?" Chekov yelled at Jade. "Vaiting so long?"

But the young woman just stared coolly at him, then swung her datacase onto Kort's chest. She popped it open, letting Kort see the credit wafers it held.

Kort strained to look into the case, almost comical.

"You know I could kill you," Jade said. Her words formed puffs of vapor. They swirled around the Klingon's shadowed face.

Kort coughed, then nodded once, as best he could under the pressure of Jade's phaser.

"But instead, I'm showing you more credits than you could earn in a dozen lifetimes."

Kort nodded again. His one eye strained to look up at his captor. His brow glittered with sweat even in the space cold air.

"What does that tell you?" Jade asked.

"B-business," Kort croaked. "You want to do business."

"Very good. And some people say Klingons don't have the brainstem of a mugato."

Kort's eye bulged at the insult, but he did nothing more.

Jade had accomplished what she had set out to do. Proven she was in control. She pulled the datacase back, flicked it shut, rocked back on her feet, stood up.

She motioned her phaser at Kort to stand as well.

Chekov didn't like it, but Uhura's eyes told him not to interfere. They were merely intermediaries here. Now that contact had been made, it was Jade's operation.

"No more small talk," Jade said to Kort. *"K'tinga*-class battle cruisers. How many can you get me?"

Kort rose painfully to his feet. He staggered toward the Tellarite shuttle. The stale smell of dried Tellarite ceremonial mud wafted from the shuttle's open hatch.

Kort eyed the datacase on the deck. More credits than he could earn in a dozen lifetimes.

He eyed the phaser in Jade's steady hand. Groaned in defeat.

"That . . . I cannot provide."

Chekov and Uhura exchanged a look of shock.

"Cannot . . . or will not?" Jade asked.

Kort seemed to shrink in stature. He could not meet Jade's eyes. He swallowed hard.

"Cannot."

Jade stared at the Klingon with unblinking intensity. Her face revealed none of the thoughts that Chekov knew must be spinning through her mind at warp speed.

The time that had been wasted locating Kort. The credits expended. The risks taken. And for what?

Without taking her eyes off the Klingon, Jade spoke to Chekov and Uhura. "Leave." She adjusted the setting on her phaser. "I don't want any witnesses."

Chekov froze. True, he wasn't used to thinking like a

criminal. But killing an unarmed prisoner? Such an act went beyond any bounds he was prepared to accept, even in this new life.

But before Chekov could object, Kort did. Shockingly.

"Please," the Klingon begged. He was so abject, so lacking in Klingon spirit, that Chekov had to wonder what atrocities Kort had encountered to lose his warrior's resolve and training so absolutely.

Klingons never begged.

At least, a decade ago they didn't.

Neither did they sell off parts of their Empire for quick profit.

Times were changing and Klingons with them.

"There are other goods I can provide," Kort pleaded, hands held together in supplication. "Weapons-grade antimatter. Photon—"

"Battle cruisers," Jade said implacably, repeating her demand.

"Surely . . . surely there is something more, out of all the mighty works of the Empire . . . ?"

Chekov couldn't believe it. The Klingon was groveling.

But Jade was like a statue. Her phaser arm unwavering. Her expression unchanging.

"What else could something as miserable as *you* know about the Empire's mighty works?" she said.

The deck creaked, responding to some slow temperature change. A flurry of ice particles slipped off one bulkhead and rattled across the side of a shuttle in a far corner of the bay.

To Chekov, Kort wore the expression of someone who had sunk to the deepest level of Klingon hell.

"I was a . . . datakeeper." Kort's rough voice was barely audible. "For the Imperial Forecasters."

Chekov saw Jade's cheek flutter as she tightened her jaw. Just once. A strong reaction for her.

"What level?" she asked.

Chekov didn't understand the question. He had never heard of the Imperial Forecasters before. They sounded like Klingon meteorologists.

"Crimson," Kort said wearily.

For the briefest instant, the corner of Jade's mouth flickered up.

"What is the path of the fourth-rank watch dragon?" she asked.

Kort reacted to the question in astonishment. "You know the code?" he blurted in shock.

"Answer me. If you wish to live."

"By Praxis' light, in seasons still to come." Kort intoned the phrases as if reciting poetry.

"I believe you, datakeeper. Now tell me, and I will ask only once, what was the secret in your Crimson Level that will make me spare your life?"

Kort tried to square his shoulders, but failed.

"Chalchaj . . ." he whispered, two soft guttural exclamations. To Chekov it sounded like a death rattle.

"Louder," Jade ordered.

"Chalchaj," Kort repeated. *"Chalchaj 'qmey."*

Chekov glanced at Uhura. Since the voyage to Camp Khitomer, she had labored hard to improve her spoken Klingon. But she looked puzzled. "Something about the sky and children," she said under her breath, answering Chekov's unspoken question. "But an odd construction."

Chekov glanced back at Jade. It was his turn to be astonished.

She was smiling.

It was as unnatural a sight as if he had seen Spock do the same.

"You know of the *Chal?"* Jade asked.

Kort nodded without taking his gaze off the deck.

Chekov instinctively knew that whatever the Klingon had revealed to Jade, it had cost him the last scrap of his honor.

But it must have done its job, because once again Jade adjusted the setting on her phaser.

Chekov wondered what secret the Klingon had just surrendered. He wondered how far he himself would have fallen, what secrets he might have been tempted to reveal, if he had been in Kort's place.

Chekov knew Kirk would have found a way to cheat death. Somehow. But was there a price that couldn't be paid, shouldn't be paid, even to escape annihilation?

Then, with a sudden rush of fear that matched exactly the startled grip Uhura took of his arm, Chekov realized he would never know the answer to that question.

Jade was aiming her phaser directly at him.

"No witnesses," she said, the horrible smile still on her face.

The blue beam was blinding.

Chekov's last thought was to wonder what his captain would have done.

A grime-covered wall of Dark Range Platform was the last thing he saw.

FIVE

The first time Kirk had entered the Great Hall in Starfleet Headquarters, he had been a lowly lieutenant. Still two years from his captaincy.

He had been able to admire its grandeur then, uninterrupted. The soaring cathedral of its ceiling, hundreds of meters high, its immense dining floor, its raised orchestra balcony framed by the Seal of the Federation—a mosaic of stones indigenous to the founding worlds of that great undertaking.

But most of all, Kirk had been able to gaze undisturbed at the Mural. There was a long-winded, bureaucratically inspired plaque on the wall that gave its real title. But no one ever called it by that name. Let alone remembered it. Because no other name was needed.

The Mural swept wondrously around the Great Hall's curved walls, tracing the evolution of humanity's journey to the stars. From Icarus and the Montgolfier brothers, through Apollo, Pathfinder, Cochrane's *Bonaventure,* to the first joint missions with Vulcan vessels.

The Mural ended yet didn't end with the *U.S.S. Constitution,* the ship that had set the design standard for Kirk's own *Enterprise.* There was still room for many more vessels past that one, but the Mural itself was deliberately unfinished. Its last fifty meters faded to the white of the artist's blank canvas.

The message was clear.

Humanity's journey, like the artist's painting, would never be finished.

Kirk couldn't remember what had become of the artist, though.

But he had no time or opportunity to reflect on the significance of that thought now. Two thousand dignitaries filled the Great Hall this evening, and all of them knew him.

Or thought they did.

He had never gotten used to it.

It had begun slowly enough, this rise to celebrity. At its earliest stage, he would walk into a bar on a starbase, and a suddenly waving hand would rise from a table filled with gold shirts, beckoning him over.

It was fellow officers who recognized him then. They had

seen his face on his edited logs, circulated throughout the Fleet for general reference and review.

That's Kirk of the Enterprise, they'd say. They'd buy him a drink. *What was Elaan of Troyius* really *like? What sort of maneuvers did that Romulan vessel make out by the Neutral Zone?* The questions were unending, and at its earliest stage, he was flattered.

But then his recognition had moved beyond the Fleet. Civilians began approaching him, asking the same questions, seeking more details. Always details. After the incident with V'Ger, the floodgates had opened. All Earth claimed to know him. Most of the other worlds, too.

Now Kirk couldn't go anywhere without detecting the unsettling flash of recognition in strangers' eyes. All the more intense because, unlike the sudden recognition awarded a new sports star or politician, people had come to recognize him over decades of his career.

He was filed away in their brains with other long-term acquaintances, the same memory slots given over to family members and lifelong friends. So that's how they approached him now. People like the young technician who had grown up seeing his face in the news updates, reading of his adventures—his job. They felt they knew all about him. He was their friend. Their uncle. Their inspiration.

Kirk would be the first to admit he was in their debt. By their support of Starfleet and the Federation, they made what he had done possible. And for that he would always be grateful.

But the truth was, to Kirk, they were still no more than strangers.

After the millionth question had been asked about Elaan, after the millionth question about some Romulan commander, his reticence at appearing in public had little to do with the fact he could think of nothing new to say. It was more the feeling that there was nothing lonelier than a man with a million friends. For how could he ever return that true, yet false, debt of friendship?

It was a no-win situation, and Kirk had learned painfully that the best way to deal with those was to avoid them at all costs. Even if it meant that some of those strangers who once thought of him as friend now thought of him as enemy.

He had first paid that price long ago, and knew he would continue to pay it as long as people knew him.

Or thought they did.

At least at a formal Starfleet reception, his stature was not unique or remarkable. Indeed, there were many whom Kirk himself recognized from having seen their news updates and read about their exploits. The mutual recognition they shared with Kirk was a secret signal of shared commiseration. They were members of the same exalted and beleaguered club, unable to voice their complaints about public adulation without appearing spoiled and unworthy.

Kirk wondered if the others in the club knew the answer to the question that plagued him now. He wondered if there were any among them he could ever ask.

But, of course, there were.

They approached him now. One who looked even more uncomfortable in his formal uniform than Kirk felt. And the other who wouldn't look uncomfortable in an Iron Maiden with rats chewing at his toes.

Spock and McCoy.

For an instant, Kirk felt a wave of relief wash over him. Here was friendship he both understood and could return.

"Good evening, Captain."

Kirk grinned at Spock's greeting. So formal. So typical.

"Hiya, Jim. Quite a spread, isn't it?"

McCoy's smile was wider than Kirk's. And for good reason from McCoy's standpoint, Kirk knew.

The reception *was* a wonder to behold. The national costumes of Starfleet's guests, along with the rainbow hues of their skin—and fur, and scales, and feathers, and what-have-you—were an explosion of color. Matched only by the kaleidoscopic extravagance of the banquet tables laden with the bounty of uncounted worlds.

The only thing McCoy liked better than a good time was seeing others having a good time, too.

"Very impressive," Kirk answered. "Wouldn't you say, Mr. Spock?"

"Indeed," Spock admitted, with typical Vulcan detachment.

McCoy shook his head. "The biggest party to hit Starfleet in ten years. The top ambassadors from the Federation *and* the unaligned worlds. The Lunar Philharmonic up on the bandstand. And all you can say is, 'Indeed'?"

"What would you have me say, Doctor?"

McCoy gave full vent to his exasperation. "That you're having a good time."

"That would be—"

McCoy chimed in. "Don't say it. Illogical. I know."

"Perhaps there is hope for you yet," Spock observed.

McCoy rolled his eyes. "Don't count on it."

Kirk caught Spock studying him. "Are you well, Captain?"

"Isn't that my line?" McCoy said.

Kirk held up his hand to quiet the doctor. Trust Spock to see right through him.

"I didn't get much sleep last night."

Spock nodded. "Yes. The rain was unprogrammed."

"It wasn't the rain," Kirk said. He felt his mood sour as even the thought of last night reawakened the feelings he had wrestled with.

McCoy seemed to understand what might have happened. "Wasn't Carol going to come tonight?"

Kirk shrugged. Not much to say about that.

McCoy did understand. "Why don't I get us some drinks," he said.

"As long as you're prescribing."

McCoy started off through the crowd.

Kirk took a breath. Preparing himself for what he wanted to say to Spock. To try out the waters.

But Spock beat him to it.

"Captain, I will be leaving Starfleet at the end of the quarter."

Kirk opened his mouth. Said nothing. That was going to be *his* line.

"I will be joining the Vulcan Diplomatic Corps."

"Ah," Kirk said, still containing his surprise. "The family business."

Spock nodded thoughtfully. "I will be working with my father on a number of initiatives. Though the Romulan question is what I shall direct most of my efforts toward. It was a topic of considerable interest at the Khitomer conference."

"The Romulan question?"

"Unification," Spock said. "Vulcans and Romulans have been apart too long."

Kirk stifled a laugh of amazement. "Spock, that could take . . . decades. If not a century."

"I hope so, Captain. It would be interesting to see the process concluded in my lifetime."

Those simple words were like a slap to Kirk. Spock's Vulcan heritage meant he was barely at the midpoint in his life. Another century of full productive life was not out of the question.

Spock regarded Kirk with penetrating eyes. No secrets lost between the two friends.

"You had something to tell me?" Spock asked.

"I'm . . . thinking of leaving Starfleet, too." Kirk regretted the words as soon as he spoke them. They sounded foreign.

"I was wondering how long it would take you to reach that decision."

"Then you think it's a good idea?"

"It is not up to me to pass judgment on your plans."

"So . . . you're saying you think I should stay?"

Spock hesitated before replying. Choosing his words carefully, Kirk knew.

"Captain, wherever your future happiness lies, it will not be found in the pronouncements of others. Only you can make that kind of decision."

Kirk frowned. "You're not making this any easier."

"Such decisions seldom are."

McCoy barreled back through the crowd. "What decisions?" He held two tumblers of thick blue liquid. Shoved one into Kirk's hand.

McCoy waited expectantly.

Kirk stared dubiously at his drink.

"Bones, I swore off Romulan ale a year ago. You were there, remember?"

McCoy narrowed one eye. "What decisions?"

Spock looked innocently neutral. An expression he excelled at.

Kirk swallowed a shot of the ale. Surprised he had forgotten how intensely it burned the gullet.

"I've been think—" he began, then coughed. "I've been thinking—"

"CITIZENS OF THE FEDERATION AND ALL EXALTED GUESTS!"

The amplified voice boomed throughout the Great Hall, instantly stopping each conversation.

Kirk, Spock, and McCoy turned to the stage as did all the others. A ten-meter-tall hologram of the Federation Council president was projected above it. The president's holographic arms stretched out to encompass everyone.

The real president standing beneath the projection was a small figure, almost obscured by the assembled heads and other topmost limbs and protuberances of the guests standing in front of Kirk. He was recognizable only by his long mane and mustache of white hair.

Kirk was surprised to see a few Klingons in dress armor near the stage as well. There appeared to be no end to the Federation's attempts to reach out to the Empire.

"ON BEHALF OF THE FEDERATION COUNCIL, I BID YOU WELCOME."

The president then began to repeat his greeting in Vulcan.

McCoy whispered into Kirk's ear. "This should be good for the next half hour. *What* decisions?"

But Kirk didn't want to talk. Another figure was moving on stage to join the president. For now, he was just outside the focus of the holographic projector.

But Kirk saw the figure's burgundy uniform jacket and didn't have to see the admiral's bars on it to know who it would be. Though at this distance he couldn't tell which admiral it was.

"Shhh, Bones," Kirk said. "That's got to be him."

"Of course it is," McCoy said without shushing. "That's what this whole wingding's for."

Kirk sighed. "Well, I want to see who it is."

"You mean you don't know? It's got to be the worst-kept secret in Starfleet."

"Bones . . ."

". . . GREAT PLEASURE TO ANNOUNCE, WITH THE UNANIMOUS APPROVAL OF THE COUNCIL—"

The president had switched back to Federation Standard. He moved to the side. His hologram motioned to someone to join him.

"STARFLEET'S NEW, SUPREME COMMANDER IN CHIEF—"

The admiral stepped into the holographic projector's range. His ten-meter-tall projection took shape like a giant invading the hall.

Kirk felt his stomach twist as he finally recognized the admiral. It couldn't be true.

"ADMIRAL ANDROVAR DRAKE!"

The Great Hall thundered with applause.

Kirk was stunned.

The rival he had sworn never to forgive had just achieved an impossible position. On the same day Kirk had decided to give up the fight.

McCoy's voice betrayed his interest in Kirk's obvious discomfort. "You know him?"

"In the Academy," Kirk said, struggling to sound offhand. "Then on the *Farragut.*"

Kirk closed his eyes, saw Lieutenant Drake's sneering face on Tycho IV, laughing at the death of Faith Morgan. Kirk saw his own son, David, so innocently led into danger.

"Is something wrong?" McCoy asked.

Kirk knew everything was wrong. "If that's what's going to run Starfleet," he said, "then I was right. It's time for me to leave."

SIX

Chekov's first impression of death was that it was colder than Siberia.

He wasn't impressed.

It also smelled like a Tellarite mudbath.

That was when he decided he wasn't dead after all.

But he couldn't move. And he couldn't see. And his body ached with the all-too-familiar pains of a high-intensity phaser stun.

"She didn't kill us," he said aloud. His voice was dry, raspy, weak.

"Thank you, Mr. Obvious." That voice was as weak as Chekov's, but only a few centimeters away.

"Uhura? Vhere are ve?"

By now, Chekov had recovered sufficiently to know he was flat on his back on an ice-cold surface. His hands and legs were expertly bound, immovable. Gray shapes began to melt out of the darkness at the corners of his vision. Somewhere, however dim, there was light.

"Listen," Uhura said.

Chekov forced himself to concentrate on something other than the pounding of his heart. At first he heard the thrumming sounds of laboring equipment that told him he was still on Deep Range Platform. That was a good sign.

But there was some other sound there. Coming from above. Directly above. Almost random. A faint clicking or tapping. Getting stronger. Getting softer.

He heard a muffled snort.

The sounds made sense.

Hoofsteps.

Chekov moaned.

He and Uhura were under the Tellarite ore shuttle in the cargo bay and its crew was on board. He could hear them walking around in the shuttle's cabin.

"HELP!" Chekov yelled. His eardrums rang. The shuttle's lower hull was less than a handsbreadth above him.

"Forget it," Uhura said. "They're Tellarites. They'll never hear us through the hull plates."

Chekov's mind raced with potential strategies. "Can you hit the hull?" he asked. "Or kick it or *something?*"

"I can't move," Uhura said. "Can you?"

Chekov strained. It felt as if his legs and arms were bolted to the deck.

"Vhy has Jade done this to us?"

"She said it herself. No witnesses. But it's clear she needs bodies."

"Da," Chekov sighed. It *was* clear. When the time came for the shuttle to launch, whether or not it used maneuvering rockets or impulse engines to lift off the deck, he and Uhura would be scorched or irradiated to death. Presumably, whatever was holding them to the deck would be vaporized. And whatever passed for law enforcement on Deep Range would have two easily identifiable bodies. Death by misadventure. Freeing their erstwhile partner, Jade, to pursue her purchase of . . .

"Vhat was it the Klingon said to her?"

"Chalchaj 'qmey," Uhura said. "I still can't figure it out. Probably a code name of some kind. Maybe a type of experimental Klingon weapons system."

"Then it makes no sense Jade has done this to us," Chekov protested. "That's exactly vhat ve vere supposed to be buying."

"Not 'exactly,' Pavel. Otherwise we wouldn't be here."

Chekov didn't say anything. He listened for the Tellarites above him. They had stopped moving around the cabin. A bad sign. It meant they were strapped into their seats.

Preparing for launch.

"At least I figured out what the captain would do in a situation like this," Uhura said.

"Vhat?"

"Have a backup plan."

Chekov sighed. "Jade *vas* our backup plan."

A hum began. It came from the shuttle. Systems coming online.

"At least," Chekov said, "vhatever propulsion system they use, it vill be quick."

A new noise began. Closer, louder. A pulsing roar from beneath the deck.

"Wrong again, Pavel."

Air pumps.

The cargo bay was being depressurized.

"Vonderful," Chekov said. "Suffocation and *then* incineration."

"At least she's thorough."

Chekov grunted as he suddenly strained every muscle against his bonds.

Nothing gave.

He gasped for breath after his exertion.

"I'll miss you, Pavel."

"It's not over yet," Chekov said.

His gasping intensified, quickened. The hum from the shuttle became muffled as the air pressure diminished.

"The keptin vould never give up!"

He fought once more against his bonds. He heard Uhura do the same. The sounds of their struggles seemed to move farther and farther away as the air grew thinner.

Chekov's lungs ached. Black stars flared at the edges of his vision. But he wouldn't give up either.

He hated the idea of dying twice in one day.

Next time, he told himself, he'd be sure to have a backup plan.

And then there was no more air to breathe.

SEVEN

In the end, Kirk had not left the reception and dinner for Starfleet's new commander in chief. That would have been admitting defeat. And Kirk *never* admitted defeat.

Instead, he had had three Romulan ales, effectively changing the rules of the game.

He simply no longer cared about Androvar Drake.

After three Romulan ales, it was difficult to care about anything.

Or so he told himself.

"Bones, you're supposed to be talking me out of this," Kirk said.

McCoy sat back in his chair, arms folded. The circular table was littered with the remains of the coffee and dessert course. Most of the guests were on the dance floor or talking in groups by one of the bars. But Kirk, McCoy, and Spock still sat together. Unspoken evidence of their knowledge that the times when all three of them could share their company this way were finite, and counting down.

"Why'd you join Starfleet?" McCoy asked.

Kirk grinned. Closed his eyes. Said the words so familiar to every cadet. "Why did anyone? 'To seek out new life and new civilizations . . .' "

McCoy pushed back on his chair, making it teeter two-legged, then rocked back with a thump. "And what are you doing for Starfleet now?"

Kirk's grin faded. "Teaching. Consulting. Chairing committees."

McCoy's gaze fixed on Kirk. "And you *want* to be talked out of leaving?"

Kirk didn't know the answer himself. Spock replied for him. "I believe the captain is undecided at the moment, because he has not yet determined what it is he should do upon leaving Starfleet."

"You 'believe' that, do you?" McCoy replied.

Kirk poured himself another cup of coffee to take up the fight against the Romulan ale. Hearing Spock and McCoy go at it was like listening to a live version of the debates he had been having with himself.

Sure enough, Spock took up the baton. "Do you know what *you* shall do upon *your* retirement from Starfleet, Doctor?"

"Who said I was retiring?"

Spock angled his head thoughtfully. "A man of your years—"

"Hold it right there! I might not have any of your damned green blood in my veins, but sixty-seven isn't what it used to be. I look at what passes for sickbay design in the new ships on the drawing boards and I tell you, I'm not leaving Starfleet till they carry me out. There's no heart to what they're thinking. No thought given to what goes on between patient and doctor. Someone's got to care about that part of it. And it looks like I'm the one who's got the job."

McCoy paused for breath. He saw that Kirk and Spock were both watching him carefully.

"Sorry," the doctor said tersely. He reached for the coffee. "I tend to get a bit passionate about Medical's policies."

Spock folded his hands together. "Which clearly accounts for your decision to remain in Starfleet. There is still a job you can do for the service which is useful, necessary, and for which you feel passion."

Spock looked then at Kirk.

Kirk didn't have to hear him say it. It *was* that obvious.

But Spock said it anyway. He was good at that. "In this case, Captain, passion *is* the most logical answer to the questions you are facing."

McCoy rolled his eyes. "Now I've heard everything, Jim. We're being lectured to about *passion* by a *Vulcan.*"

"Doctor, once again you remind me how little you know about the true nature of my people."

Kirk stared off across the Great Hall as Spock went on to tell McCoy how Vulcans really did have emotions and simply chose not to allow them to rule their lives.

McCoy, of course, rose to the bait, hotly disputing Spock's definitions.

They could go on for hours. On occasions, they had.

Without paying attention to the familiar arguments he had heard over the years, Kirk was struck by how much just the sounds of their voices brought an ease to him. As if he were a child again, sitting at the table in his mother's kitchen for a holiday meal, listening to his parents, grandparents, his brother, aunts and uncles, and the cousins. Their competing words raised in the noisy confusion of long acquaintance. The bonds of family.

That's what Spock and McCoy had become to him.

Family.

He was glad to have such friends in his life. Yet he knew there *had* to be more. . . .

Spock went on about Surak's teachings as McCoy snorted dismissively.

Kirk's attention wandered to the dance floor. A group of Klingons stood off to the side, unsuccessfully trying to hide their disdain for what passed as dancing on Earth.

Kirk had been to a Klingon dance once. McCoy had ended up giving him three protoplaser treatments to make the scars fade.

Klingons took the act of cutting in very literally.

Then Kirk saw that familiar flash in one of the Klingon's eyes. The Klingon recognized him, nodded at him—a sign of respect. Kirk returned the gesture, marveling how the day had ever come when he actually felt respect in turn for a Klingon.

But the events surrounding the attempted assassination at Camp Khitomer and the growing peace movement between the Federation and the Empire had changed many minds. Including his.

Kirk supposed he should be glad that he was not totally set in his ways. That he could still entertain new thoughts, new ideas.

Before Camp Khitomer, when Spock had told him that the explosion of the Praxis moon meant the Klingon race might perish, Kirk's first reaction had been to blurt out, *Then let them die.*

Almost at once he had realized how wrong those words were. How hurtful. How unfeeling. But once spoken, there had been no way to take them back, to soften their impact.

He regretted those words still.

Decades ago, he might have been unseasoned enough to have said those words and meant them. But not now. His voyages had not just been about making discoveries for the Federation. He had made them for himself, as well. And change had come because of what he had encountered, and what he had learned.

Kirk dreaded the day he would stop learning. Stop changing.

His gaze continued to sweep the room as Spock and McCoy companionably argued on in the background. He reflected on change. On passion. Other people on the dance floor caught his glance. Most smiled back at him. A few looked momentarily startled, as if they had never expected to see so notable a figure in the flesh. Kirk was used to all their reactions, had seen them all a thousand times before.

But then he found one person who was already looking directly at him before he saw her. It was Kirk's turn to be startled.

But he didn't know why.

Perhaps it was her eyes, he decided at first. Heavily lashed, dark and enticing . . . if he had been a twenty-year-old cadet he'd have been by her side in fifteen seconds. Ten seconds if he wanted to beat Gary Mitchell to asking her to dinner.

Then he was startled again as he suddenly realized those haunting eyes belonged to a Klingon. Her dark hair, dramatically swept back for the reception, revealed the ripples of her high-ridged brow. Though, oddly, it was not as pronounced as most females' he had seen.

He understood why when he saw her ears.

Pointed.

Klingon *and* Vulcan.

That was reason enough to be startled, Kirk decided. Just as people sometimes took a few seconds to place his identity after realizing that they recognized him, he decided his scrutiny must have taken in the young woman's unusual features, sensed the inherent contradiction of them, and then paused just long enough for the facts to come to the attention of his consciousness.

Which meant he was doing to her exactly what he disliked so much when it happened to him.

He was staring.

But she didn't seem to mind.

In fact, she smiled at him.

Not the giddy smile of someone recognizing a celebrity.

But a smile of success. Of finding something lost.

Kirk knew he shouldn't keep staring, but he couldn't *not* stare.

The smile transformed her face. Worked some magic that he couldn't comprehend.

Until his brain finally fought through the fog of Romulan ale and spoke plainly to him: *She's gorgeous. That's why you're staring. She's the most beautiful woman in the Hall. And she's letting you stare at her like a shuttle pilot who's been on solo duty for the past two years.*

Kirk's mouth suddenly felt dry. He felt the faint rush of

what had been a familiar sensation when he had been a twenty-year-old cadet and the whole galaxy lay waiting for him. A lightness in his chest. A thrill of anticipation in his stomach.

His brain kicked in again, like his own personal Spock offering observations untinged by emotion: *You're thinking as if you're twenty again, and she isn't even that. You're old enough to be her father. Hell, you're old enough to be her* grand*father.*

A dancing couple moved across his line of sight. The instant she was gone from his vision, Kirk shook his head, as if a spell had been broken.

"Don't you agree, Captain?" Spock asked.

"If you do," McCoy countered, "I'm through giving you advice."

Kirk had no idea what his friends had been discussing. "I think," he said cautiously, "the answer lies somewhere in the middle."

Spock and McCoy exchanged a look of surprise.

"Fascinating," Spock said.

But McCoy narrowed his eyes in disgust. "You didn't hear a word we said, did you?"

The music ended. The dancing couples on the floor began to drift back to their tables. Kirk put his hand on McCoy's arm, nodded out to the floor.

"Bones, that young woman over there. In the long dress . . ."

Kirk saw only a flash of her glittering gown moving amid the crush of people. His heart actually fluttered. She was moving in his direction.

"Where?" McCoy asked. "The one in red?"

"No," Kirk said. "You can't miss her. She's half-Vulcan, half-Klingon."

"A most improbable combination," Spock said.

McCoy frowned at Spock. "Look who's calling the kettle black. Or in your case, green."

Kirk turned to Spock. "She's right over there. Klingon brow. Vulcan ears."

"I see her," McCoy said brightly. "She's stunning. I wonder whose daughter she is?"

"Klingon-*Romulan* would be a more logical conclusion," Spock said.

Kirk could barely keep up with the doubled conversation. "Romulan?" he asked Spock. "At a *Starfleet* function?" He turned to McCoy. "What do you mean, 'daughter'?"

"Starfleet did invite several high-ranking Klingons to this reception,"Spock said. "Undoubtedly invitations would have gone out to the Romulan diplomatic missions as part of the ongoing move toward openness."

"She's very young, Jim," McCoy said. "Probably some diplomat's child."

Kirk's heart sank. "She's not that young." But he knew she was.

"Perhaps some diplomat's consort," Spock suggested.

Kirk's heart hit bottom.

McCoy gave him a quick look of understanding. "Oh, ho. About to add 'cradle-snatching' to your list of crimes against the Klingon Empire?"

Kirk felt his cheeks start to burn. "I was pardoned," he said. "So were you. All I was saying was that I thought she was . . . exceptionally lovely. And I wondered who she was. That's all. Completely innocent."

McCoy pursed his lips to keep a grin from spreading across his face.

Kirk scanned the crowd. Whoever she was, she was gone.

"If, indeed, she is a child of joint Klingon and Romulan heritage, her beauty should come as no surprise," Spock said.

"Is that so?" McCoy retorted. "In addition to passion, you're suddenly an expert on beauty?"

"The perception of beauty in most cultures is connected to symmetry of features. Symmetry of features indicates that an individual has not succumbed to any one of a number of diseases which affect growth during childhood and adolescence. Therefore, beauty equals symmetry equals robustness. And hybrids generally take on the most positive attributes of their parents, becoming, as it were, exceptional specimens."

"Such as yourself," McCoy stated dryly.

"As always, Doctor, the depth of your logic impresses me."

McCoy couldn't tell if he had just been tricked into complimenting Spock.

Kirk knew he had been.

Then the woman appeared in the crowd, only a few tables away, heading in Kirk's direction.

"Bones, Spock—there she is."

Kirk stood up as her eyes met his.

She moved so gracefully, it was as if he were watching a dancer perform.

She was slim, lithe, but despite McCoy's speculations, clearly a woman. No mere girl.

For a moment as he rose to his feet, Kirk almost forgot how old he had felt recently. He wanted desperately to know why she was coming over to him. He wanted to hear her voice, know her name. Know everything about her.

Spock was right. Passion *was* his answer.

But two tables over, she stopped.

Her entrancing face clouded. Her delicate brow ridges became much more pronounced, almost as if she were scowling.

Kirk started to hold out his hand.

But another hand came down on his shoulder, hard enough to surprise him. Kirk turned just as he saw the woman do the same—turn away.

"Jimbo! Glad you could make it to my little party!"

Kirk was face to face with Androvar Drake.

His new commander in chief.

"Admiral Drake" was all he said. He *loathed* "Jimbo."

He glanced back over his shoulder.

She was gone. Again.

Drake poked him in the stomach.

"Spending too much time behind a desk, Jimbo?"

Kirk concentrated on not making his hands into fists. Drake still kept his now white hair in a military bristle cut. His sharp features had filled in since the years he had been in Kirk's graduating class. The extra lines there, deeply etched, were kept company by a thin ragged scar over his right cheekbone. A protoplaser could take it away in a month. But Drake had earned it in battle, the story went. He had taken out a Klingon battle cruiser just before the Organian intervention. That scar was his badge of honor.

Or a relic from a bygone day, Kirk thought.

Drake put his fists on his hips. "We've both come a long way since the Academy, eh?"

Kirk didn't want to get drawn into anything with Drake. What had happened between them was long passed. David was at rest and nothing could bring him back.

"Congratulations," Kirk said simply.

Drake took that as an opportunity to pump Kirk's hand.

"Ever wonder what might have happened if you hadn't taken the *Enterprise* out again?"

Kirk shook his head. As captains, both he and Drake had taken out starships on five-year missions. Both had survived, returning as heroes within months of each other and receiving immediate promotion to the admiralty. And then, after V'Ger, Kirk had been unable to resist the siren call of the stars. He had turned his back on a career in Headquarters and had gone back out.

But Drake had remained.

Now, twenty-three years later, Kirk was a captain again. And Drake was still Drake. Even if he was commander in chief of the entire Fleet.

Four Romulan ales, Kirk thought, and I could probably get away with belting him. No matter what his rank.

But instead, he said, "May I introduce my friends—Captain Spock, Dr. McCoy."

Drake shook McCoy's hand. Then he respectfully raised his hand and gave Spock the Vulcan salute, instead of committing the faux pas of attempting to touch a Vulcan. Drake had obviously learned well during his years climbing the ladder at Headquarters.

"Know them well," Drake said enigmatically. "Always followed your career, Jimbo." His lips tightened. "Always impressed you were able to accomplish so much, after . . . well, you know." He laughed with a tone of calculated, hollow, camaraderie.

But Kirk didn't respond, by word or by gesture. He could sense McCoy's glance of curiosity. He knew Spock would be equally intrigued by Drake's statement, though of course he wouldn't show it. But the past was the past.

Drake was running Starfleet now.

Kirk had never wanted the job. But he knew in his heart that it had always been a possibility. He *could* have been commander in chief. If he had stayed behind as Drake had. Played the political games at Headquarters as well as he played the games of life-and-death on the frontier.

But Kirk hadn't chosen that path. It was no use thinking of what might have been.

"Can't stay long," Drake said.

"Pity," Kirk replied.

"But thought you might like to know—reviewed the Fleet status logs. The *Enterprise.* Decommissioned next month."

Kirk nodded, like hearing of a friend's terminal illness. "I know."

"Going to use it for wargames."

McCoy frowned. "Starfleet hasn't fought wargames for years."

Drake shrugged. "An oversight I intend to correct." He clapped Kirk on the shoulder, far too familiar. "The *Enterprise* will be a target ship. Try her out on a couple of the new photon torpedoes. Mark VIIIs. Twin vortices." He winked at Kirk. "Should go out in a real blaze of glory." His eyes were cold. "Thought you might like that, stuck behind a desk and all. At least something in your career will go out in a blaze of glory."

"Waste not, want not," Kirk said lightly.

Drake laughed. "Good one." He started to go. "See you at the decommissioning ceremony?"

Kirk shook his head. "I'll . . . be off planet."

Drake winked again. "I'll see that they save you a piece of her. Put it on a plaque, mount it over the fireplace. Tell the grandkids about—" Drake suddenly took on an expression of feigned sadness. "Oh, sorry, Jimbo. Forgot about your son. David, wasn't it? Klingons killing him, and that. There won't be any grandkids, will there."

With that, he was gone, swallowed into a crowd of well-wishers.

"What the hell was that all about?" McCoy sputtered.

"We go back," Kirk said. "Too far." He sat down again, more tired than when he had begun the evening. He looked for the young woman, but she was gone, too. As he knew she would be.

As the *Enterprise* would soon be gone.

As all things must go.

Passion among them.

McCoy and Spock exchanged a look of concern.

"You want another drink, Jim?"

Kirk shook his head. "I've had enough." It was late.

He would never hear the sound of her voice.

He would always remember Drake's.

"I've had enough," he said again.

He didn't mean Romulan ale.

EIGHT

The outer doors in Cargo Bay Twelve opened before the straining pumps had removed all of the atmosphere.

A sudden storm of ice crystals plumed from the growing gap between the moving doors.

Inside the bay, loose debris swirled into empty space. The shafts of light from the ceiling fixtures faded without dust and moisture to define them.

On somc of the cargo pallets, sealed drums and crates bulged in the absence of air pressure.

But there were no squeals of metal or plastic to accompany their deformations.

There was only the silence of vacuum.

Of space.

Of death.

The Tellarite ore shuttle in the cargo bay brought its maneuvering systems online.

Four thrusters on its battered lower hull vented pinpoint streams of hyperaccelerated plasma to lift the shuttle against the Platform's artificial gravity.

Any organic material within range of that plasma was only seconds from being carbonized.

The Tellarite shuttle rotated. Its nose pointed toward the open doors and the stars beyond. Its impulse ports glowed briefly, pushing it forward.

The plasma jets left blackened streaks on the deck plates.

The shuttle launched.

The doors ponderously closed behind it.

Nothing lived in Cargo Bay Twelve.

Pavel Chekov clenched his eyes shut to prevent the moisture coating them from sublimating in the vacuum. He gasped desperately for a last lungful of oxygen.

Air flooded his lungs so easily, he was shocked into opening one eye.

"Hikaru?"

Captain Hikaru Sulu grinned down at his friends. He offered both his hands to help them up.

Chekov and Uhura slowly got to their feet. They were on a transporter platform.

Uhura's face tightened in confusion as she looked around. "The *Excelsior?"* she asked.

Sulu's laugh was deep and genuine. Then he took on a serious expression. "I'm sorry. I know I shouldn't . . ." He grinned at Chekov again. "But the expression on your faces . . ."

Chekov didn't share Sulu's good humor. He was still shivering with the cold of space. His lungs still ached with the effort of trying to breathe vacuum.

Chekov's voice was coiled as tightly as a Klingon spring knife. "How long have you been tracking us?"

Sulu's smile melted in the force of Chekov's withering stare. "Pavel, calm down. You're safe now."

"How long?"

"Since the beginning of your mission," Sulu said.

Chekov could hear his heart thunder in his ears. He couldn't tell if he was shaking from the cold or from outrage.

He hit his open hand against Sulu's shoulder. "So each time ve faced a disruptor, each time ve were scared to death someone vould catch on to us, you vere out here ready to snatch us to safety?"

Sulu's eyes grew wide. He took a step back.

But Chekov grabbed Sulu by his uniform jacket. "You bastard!" he shouted.

Sulu pushed at Chekov's hand, trying to disengage.

"Pavel, take it easy!"

"Take it *easy?* Six months undercover! My friends and family thinking I'm a criminal! *Living* vith *Klingons!* And you want me to . . ." Chekov's outburst choked off in rage.

There was only one way he could continue this conversation.

With a roar of anger he swung his fist into Sulu's nose.

Sulu grunted and stumbled back, completely taken by surprise.

A gout of blood exploded across his upper lip.

Chekov kept his grip on Sulu's jacket. Held him up.

"Vhat vere ve to you? Chess pieces to be moved around? To be sacrificed?"

On that last word, Chekov let Sulu have it again, this time releasing his hold so Sulu fell back against the transporter console.

Uhura tugged at Chekov's arm, trying to hold him back.

"Pavel! That's enough! Hikaru saved our lives!"

But Chekov straight-armed Uhura out of his way.

"Ve nearly died because of him!"

He swung at Sulu again.

But Sulu was ready this time.

He brought up an arm to deflect Chekov's wild swing. Leaned in with his shoulder to keep Chekov's center of gravity moving forward.

Sent Chekov over his back to thud against the deck.

Now Sulu grabbed Chekov by his jacket, leaned over him.

"Listen to me, Pavel!" Sulu hissed. "My orders came from Intelligence Oversight. Even the brass were excluded. If you knew you were being monitored by the *Excelsior,* and any of your Klingon contacts had used a mind-sifter to question your stories about quitting Starfleet . . ."

With the end of decades of military tension between the Federation and the Klingon Empire, the Klingon armed forces were falling into disarray. Weapons inventories were no longer secure. This section of the galaxy was especially vulnerable to the possible entry of Klingon armaments into the open market.

So Chekov and Uhura had sacrificed six months of their Starfleet careers and brought shame to their friends and families, who could not be told the truth. All to create a false background establishing them as illegal weapons dealers with extensive Starfleet connections.

"Oversight had nothing to do vith leaving us there—freezing to death—until the last second!"

Chekov kicked up and caught Sulu on the back of his leg.

Sulu let go of Chekov to jump away before he could lose his balance.

The two men faced each other, half-crouched. Chekov looked for an opening like a barroom brawler. Sulu turned sideways, hands positioned for the Vulcan *sal-tor-fee* defense.

The two men circled each other warily. Sulu tried again. "Pavel—you're overreacting. While you were on Dark Range, I had to keep the *Excelsior* at forty thousand kilometers, right at the transporter's maximum range."

Chekov swung. Sulu parried.

"I had to keep our sensors on their lowest setting so Kort wouldn't detect them."

Uhura tried to move between them again.

"Stop it, Pavel. Listen to him."

Sulu used Uhura's intervention to advance his argument. He spoke rapidly over Uhura's shoulder. "Sensors showed you two and Jade meeting with Kort and his Andorians in the cargo bay. They showed the phaser emissions. But it wasn't until the others left that I knew you were remaining behind. And even then, because I was picking up life signs from you, I couldn't be certain it wasn't part of some plan you'd put together. Until the bay doors started to open."

"You see?" Uhura asked Chekov.

Some of Chekov's murderous rage began to diminish.

But not all of it.

"I had my orders," Sulu said. "I could only interfere if I thought you were in immediate danger of being killed."

Uhura put her hands on Chekov's shoulders, holding him back. "He got us out, Pavel. He got us out as soon as he could."

"We're on the same side," Sulu said. "Someone tried to kill you. Let's do something about it."

Chekov couldn't speak. He wanted to punch a hole through a bulkhead.

"It was Jade," Uhura said.

Sulu looked stunned. "But this was her operation. She's supposed to be one of the top agents in Starfleet Intelligence." He wiped at the blood streaming from his nose. His face betrayed his surprise at how much there was.

"Kort offered her something she couldn't refuse," Uhura said grimly. She pushed Chekov back. "Take a couple of deep breaths," she advised him.

Chekov unclenched his fists. Felt his whole body tremble. For six months he had believed that Uhura and he were living on the brink of instant death. All because Sulu had his orders.

He remained silent and sullen as Uhura told Sulu about the enigmatic exchange between Kort and Jade in the cargo bay.

When she had finished, Sulu walked around the transporter console, carefully giving Chekov a wide berth. He hit a control.

"Computer: Identify a Klingon organization designated 'Imperial Forecasters.'"

Without an instant of hesitation, the computer's distinctive voice responded from a console speaker.

"The Imperial Forecasters were a division of the Klingon Strategic Operations Bureau."

"What were their responsibilities?" Sulu asked.

"Using advanced wargaming and simulation techniques, they forecast probably outcomes to military scenarios."

Chekov shrugged. "So, they vere military planners. The Klingon Empire is a military culture."

But Sulu wasn't finished. "Computer: In the context of the Imperial Forecasters, what is the significance of the Crimson Level?"

"That classification corresponds to Starfleet's security classification, Ultra Secret."

Sulu glanced at Chekov and Uhura. "Now it's getting interesting." He addressed the computer again. "What aspects of military planning were the responsibility of the Crimson Level?"

Again, the computer didn't hesitate. "Doomsday scenarios."

Chekov heard Uhura's sharp intake of breath. He started to pay attention to what the computer was saying.

"Define," Sulu said.

The computer complied. "Scenarios concerning the effects of interplanetary famine, plague, and natural disasters on the ability of Klingon colony worlds and protectorates to support the Empire. Scenarios concerning the effects of political upheaval on the ability of the High Council to govern the Empire effectively. Scenarios concerning the effects of the military defeat and subjugation of the Empire by its enemies, on the ability of the Klingon race to survive."

"Definitely high-level material," Uhura said. "I don't think I'd like to know the Klingon response to the defeat of the Empire."

Sulu tapped a finger against the console. "In this context, what significance do the following phrases have: 'the path of the fourth-rank watch dragon,' and 'by Praxis' light, in seasons still to come'?"

"They are lines from the death poem of Molor."

Before Sulu could ask another question, Uhura said, "That

poem was in my upgrade courses. About fifteen hundred years ago, Kahless the Unforgettable defeated the tyrant Molor to found what became the Klingon Empire. It's considered a classic."

Chekov walked over to the console. He felt drained. He chose not to look at Sulu. "Kort referred to the lines as a code," he said.

Sulu did not respond to Chekov. He looked across the console at Uhura, instead. "Uhura, give the computer the Klingon phrase Jade found so interesting. I'll never be able to pronounce it."

Uhura cleared her throat. "Computer: Translate the Klingon phrase *chalchaj 'qmey."*

The computer complied at once. "Literally, the phrase translates as an archaic form of 'the sky's offspring.' "

"That's close to what I thought," Uhura said.

But the computer kept speaking. "In the context of the death poem of Molor, the phrase translates as 'the children of heaven,' referring to those who would inherit the lands destroyed by Molor during his final war against Kahless and his followers."

Sulu shook his head. "More code words?"

Chekov frowned. The *Excelsior's* captain was missing the point. "Computer: Vhat does the phrase 'children of heaven' mean in context of the Imperial Forecasters and the Crimson Level?"

This time the computer hesitated.

"That is restricted information."

Sulu gave Chekov a sardonic smile. "Computer: This is Captain Hikaru Sulu. Confirm voiceprint identification."

"Voiceprint identification confirmed."

"Security access code Sulu alpha-alpha-omicron-alpha. Identify the phrase."

Another hesitation. "That information is restricted."

It was Chekov's turn to smile. Sulu stared at the console in indignation. "Computer, I'm a starship captain. I have a level thirteen security clearance."

"That information is restricted to security clearance level seventeen."

Sulu looked up in amazement. "I thought there were only *fifteen* levels of clearance in all of Starfleet."

"That is restricted information," the computer replied.

Sulu unconsciously prodded his nose in thought. Chekov was pleased to see it seemed tender.

"A Klingon who was once involved in planning doomsday scenarios for the Empire . . ." Sulu said, thinking aloud. "Offers to share something so secret it's classified at one of Starfleet's highest levels . . . to what he believes is an illegal arms dealer."

Chekov stated the obvious, wondering why Sulu didn't see it. "It must be a veapon."

"Something exotic," Uhura added.

Sulu nodded. "And so terrible it would only be used in the event the Empire was defeated."

Chekov didn't like the implications. "There are those who vould say that given the current state of the Empire, it already has been defeated. Not by its enemies, but by history."

Sulu's scowl showed he didn't like the implications, either. For the first time since their fight, he looked at Chekov.

The tension was still thick between them.

"You're saying that someone might be deciding to use this weapon? Whatever it is?"

"I think that's obvious, gentlemen," Uhura said, trying to keep the two men from making matters personal again. "Whatever kind of weapon the 'Children of Heaven' is, it was enough to make a top Starfleet Intelligence agent willing to kill two other agents, so she could get the secret for herself."

"A renegade agent vith a Klingon doomsday veapon,"

Chekov sputtered. "This is far beyond the objectives of our mission."

"I agree," Sulu said. "You two will have to deliver a full report at once."

"Take us to a secure communications station," Chekov said. He began to walk toward the transporter room's doors.

"No," Sulu said.

Chekov turned to face him, ready to fight again if he had to.

"Vhat do you mean, 'no'?"

Six months of living like a criminal had had an effect on him.

Sulu remained calm. "Not by subspace. I think we have to assume that a Starfleet Intelligence agent like Jade has full access to current codes. It might be best for her to think you two really are dead. Otherwise, she might take extra precautions to make certain Starfleet can't find her."

"You want us to report in person?" Uhura asked.

"I don't even want to consider what a Klingon doomsday weapon might be capable of," Sulu said. "Their standard armaments are bad enough." He toggled another control on the console. "Captain to the bridge."

Sulu's science officer answered. "Bridge here, Captain."

"Lay in a course for Earth. Maximum warp. And maintain a communications blackout. I don't want anyone to know we're coming till we're there."

The science officer acknowledged her orders. "Bridge out."

"That serious?" Uhura said.

"That serious," Sulu confirmed. "We're going to have to take this to Admiral Drake himself."

"Admiral *Androwar* Drake?" Chekov repeated. "Vhy him?"

"He was just appointed commander in chief, Starfleet."

Chekov glared at Sulu with incredulous disgust.

Sulu's voice revealed he'd been unprepared for Chekov's

reaction. "Starfleet needed a new C in C to take over from the acting chief who replaced Cartwright."

Chekov headed for the transporter console and leaned against it for support. This changed everything.

Needing a replacement for Admiral Cartwright was old news. Because of Captain Kirk and his crew, Cartwright had been arrested at Camp Khitomer. He had been part of a conspiracy to restart hostilities between the Federation and the Klingon Empire.

In the aftermath of that arrest, Starfleet had been shaken to its core. Cartwright had been considered one of its ablest leaders. For someone of his reputation and stellar accomplishments to have been promoted to a position of absolute authority, while at the same time working against everything the Federation and Starfleet stood for, had been a depressing example of how far humanity still had to go. The twenty-third century was evidently not as perfect as some wished to believe.

"What's this about?" Sulu asked cautiously, apparently determined not to provoke Chekov again.

Chekov chose his words carefully. "Drake is not . . . commander in chief material," was all he would say.

Sulu's brow knitted in confusion. "What do you know that the Federation Council doesn't?"

But Chekov wouldn't answer. He couldn't.

He feared that despite the years they had spent on the *Enterprise,* a void had opened between himself and Sulu.

Chekov couldn't comment on Drake because Kirk had sworn him to secrecy.

And Chekov's loyalty to Kirk was absolute.

But Sulu was a starship captain now.

He had been willing to risk his friends' lives to follow orders to the letter.

Kirk would never have done that.

To Chekov, that meant Sulu had lost the capacity to think for himself, to question authority.

Which made him just the kind of officer who would blindly follow the orders of criminals like Admiral Drake.

Chekov left the transporter room without saying anything more.

As far as he was concerned, Sulu could no longer be trusted.

NINE

The instant Kirk had coalesced from the transporter beam, he knew he had failed.

Again.

It was not an impression he was used to. He had always fought failure. He drew comfort from the certainty that this aspect of him, at least, would never change.

He shifted his boots in the sunbaked dust. He smelled the heat of the place, heard the silence. Felt its weight. He fought the impulse to grab his communicator and request an immediate beam out.

In the holographic environment simulator, he had found there were no answers for him in the past.

In the safe harbor of Carol Marcus's embrace, he had found there were no answers for him in comfort and distraction.

His Starfleet duties were little more than routine—filling his days with detail that in the end amounted to nothing.

His friends knew him well enough to support him, but never pretended they could give him direction.

So he had come here. To the final port in a fruitless mission.

And again there was nothing for him.

He might as well have stepped onto the sterile soil of a lifeless world.

But he was in Iowa.

On the farm.

Where he had been born. Where so long ago his father had held his hand on summer nights and first shown him the stars where he would find his first, best destiny.

With unsparing insight, Kirk knew he no longer belonged here, either. Hadn't for years.

Nor did he belong to any of the other worlds he had encountered in his travels.

He had no starting point to return to, no final destination that drew him.

He had no home.

Kirk inhaled deeply, sweeping the past from his mind, if not his heart.

He had often thought he could teach Spock a thing or two about controlling emotions.

He opened the front flap on his uniform jacket in a futile gesture against the heat. He walked toward the farmhouse. He tried not to remember how he once ran for it, bare feet kicking up dust, or sometimes mud, depending on the season.

His boots thudded on the worn wood of the porch steps. He tried not to remember how he once raced up them, hands and feet slapping the risers in giddy excitement, his brother Sam charging right behind him, because their father had returned from space.

He put his hand on the quartz screen of the lockplate by the front door. The scanning mechanism was a century old, an anachronistic antique, like most of the fixtures in the house. But it still worked.

The door lock clicked.

Kirk stepped into the front hall.

His bootsteps echoed. The house was empty. All the furniture long gone to cousins. He smiled fleetingly. His mother's three-hundred-year-old Amish rocker was in his nephew Peter's home on Deneva. What would its makers have thought to know the eventual fate of their work, hundreds of light-years from its birthplace?

He looked around the too-quiet house, thinking about the fate of *his* work. His job.

If he left Starfleet, he wouldn't have even that anymore.

The summer sun blazed through the windows. The dusty air was close and oppressive. Again, he turned away from his memories, of so many other summers when this house had been alive with hope and promise.

He went upstairs.

His room was much smaller than he remembered.

The doorframe still bore the marks his older brother had made to measure Kirk's growth.

Kirk ran his fingers over them, remembering how Sam had gouged them into the wood with a penknife.

His parents had protested each new mark Sam had added. But George Kirk had never repaired the damage.

His father had known. Memories were the markers of the journey through life. It was necessary to know where you had come from. Only then could you know where you were going.

Kirk ran his hand along the smooth upper reaches of the doorframe, where his height had never been recorded.

He knew where he was going. All humans did.

But how would he get there?

What would the rest of his journey bring before its inevitable end?

Wood creaked downstairs.

Kirk stopped breathing.

Another, barely perceptible scrape on the bare floor below.

The air in the old farmhouse was subtly different.

There was someone else here.

Kirk came alive.

His hand reached instinctively for his belt and his phaser.

But, of course, there was no weapon there. Weapons were no longer needed on this perfect Earth.

His mind quickly sifted through options and strategies. The intruder—how easily he fell into thinking like a starship captain—was most likely one of the advocates handling his parents' estate. That's why Kirk was here, after all. A final visit before deciding whether or not to sell the place.

But an advocate would have shouted out a greeting by now. An advocate would make more noise, having nothing to hide.

Kirk moved swiftly, silently, to the stairway. He knew the location of every loose floorboard. Each step revealed the depth of his education by experts in the martial arts of the Klingons and the ancient patterns of Vulcan self-defense.

Except for that damned nerve pinch, he had mastered them all.

The hallway was empty. He glided down the stairs, as silent as a Vulcan. Even the dust was not disturbed, so knowing was his step.

He saw a shadow move across the hallway floor, just for an instant blocking the sun. The intruder was in the kitchen.

Kirk was aware of every nerve end. His heart was calm, his breathing steady. But he was ready to uncoil. To be all that he had trained to be. All that he had been born to be.

Like smoke, he moved through the hallway of his home and into the kitchen doorway.

His hands were raised in the Klingon first position, his body tensed for impact.

He was prepared for anything.

Except for what he saw.

TEN

She.

From the reception.

Of the Klingon brow, the Romulan ears.

She wore a black jumpsuit, so formfitting it would forever lay McCoy's concerns to rest. This was no girl, this was a woman—superbly muscled, an athlete by any standard. And though her costume seemed designed only to emphasize her form, there was something about it that might have made Kirk think it was some type of uniform.

If Kirk had been able to think.

But his only reaction to her was visceral, as it had been at the reception.

She exploded into his senses.

"At last," she said. Her voice rich, low, filling the kitchen, focusing Kirk's attention absolutely.

Dimly, he thought he should say something.

"Who . . . ?" But it was no good. His voice cracked, as if unused for years. As if words were not needed.

Her smile was instant. As if he had known her forever. As if this were a reunion and not a first meeting.

She moved toward him until she was so close, he could feel the heat of her.

"Teilani," she said.

Her breath carried flowers and soft winds, erasing the staleness of the empty house.

Kirk's heart thundered. He tried to speak again.

But she placed a hand to his face.

"Shhh," she admonished.

Her touch was incredible, both soft and bitingly electric at the same time.

The kitchen seemed to spin around Kirk.

Her arms moved around him, one hand pressing into his back, one hand forcing his head down, his lips to meet hers.

He was aware of nothing but the weight of her body against his. The yielding softness of her lips against his.

The taste of her. The scent of her.

He kissed her with an urgency he hadn't known in years, crushing her to him, closer and closer, feeling her back arch in response, until his body burned with the anticipation of the only way an embrace this intense could end.

It took that long for him to fully realize what he was doing.

For his consciousness to catch up to his senses.

With the clear thought that he would probably regret his decision for the rest of his life, Kirk pushed her away.

"No," he said.

He felt her surprise. Her dark eyes seemed to glow with the force of her energy. Or the sun from the kitchen windows.

"But, James, at the reception . . . I saw this in your eyes."

"Who are you?" he asked, keeping her away from him with his hands on her shoulders, fighting the need to be overwhelmed again.

"Teilani." She repeated her name as if it alone explained her existence.

"No," Kirk said. *"Who* are you? Where are you from? What are you doing in my parents' home?"

She took a step closer. "Why do you resist what you know your heart wants?"

Kirk did want her. He wasn't fooling himself any more than he was fooling her.

But he had long ago learned that mere appetite could not be allowed to rule his life.

He had not needed Spock to teach him about balance in all things. It was his nature.

He dropped his hands from her shoulders, moved back a step.

"How do you know me?"

She laughed, the sound thrilling, exotic.

"The whole galaxy knows you," she said simply, as if explaining something to a beloved child.

Kirk felt almost dizzy, intoxicated. He forced himself to think about pheromone scents. Subsonic fields that might affect his thought processes. Any one of dozens of possible technological explanations for what had happened to him. For how he *felt.*

McCoy's voice echoed in his ear. The words still possessed their bite. *You're old enough to be her* grand*father.*

"You're not answering my questions," he said.

She regarded him through half-closed eyes. The delicate tip of her tongue played tantalizingly across her lips. Their surface glistened. She moved a hand to the neck of her jumpsuit, to the tiny control switch of the fabric sealer.

"There's time enough for talk, later," she said, leaving no doubt as to what she expected to happen *now.*

She pressed a finger to the control. The fabric of her jumpsuit parted down her neck. She lifted her finger, held it poised, ready to part the fabric even more.

Kirk willed himself to keep his eyes locked on hers.

"There won't be a later," he said. "Unless you answer me now."

With that, everything changed.

Teilani's smile this time was one that encouraged friendship, not desire. She tugged once on her collar, an odd gesture. Her jumpsuit stayed open, though. A casual look. Not necessarily seductive.

Hell, Kirk thought. She's seductive just standing there.

"Ask me whatever you wish to know, James. I can have no

secrets from you." Then she turned her back to him and walked to the window over the kitchen sink.

Kirk's pupils automatically widened as his eyes traced the unbroken line of the jumpsuit along her back, down her legs, each curve undisguised. But he looked away. It was no time for distraction.

He moved to the other side of the kitchen, leaned against the counter. The sunlight shining through the window over the sink caught her hair in a mesmerizing interplay of light and shadow.

A halo, Kirk thought. As if his visitor were some mythic creature descended from the heavens.

"Why were you at the reception?" he asked, mentally shrugging off the vision. The question seemed so prosaic for one so celestial.

"I was invited."

She smiled again and this time he returned it, relaxing a fraction. It was to be a game, he decided with relief. He could deal with that. Enjoy it, even. The rules would give him a badly needed focus.

"And *why* were you invited?"

"To celebrate the selection of Starfleet's new commander in chief."

"That's not what I meant," Kirk said. "Invitations went out to Starfleet personnel, diplomats, industry leaders from the Federation—"

"And to the Klingon Empire," she continued. "The Romulan Star Empire. The First Federation. The unaligned worlds."

"And which are you?"

She looked down for a moment, as if the question were difficult, required thought.

"Unaligned," she said. "For now."

That made no sense to Kirk. The heritage of her brow and ears clearly said she was one of either the Klingon or Romulan empire. "But your . . . parents . . ." Kirk said, unsure as to how blunt he could be. Despite Spock's logic, one of her parents might even have been Vulcan.

Teilani traced a finger along the sweep of one delicately pointed ear. "Once, my home was a colony world." She neglected to say of which empire. "We opted for . . . independence, many years ago."

Kirk's instincts instantly told him her statement was the beginning of a story. Her initial, mind-dazzling approach to him had been some sort of smoke screen. She had something to tell him. Something she wanted from him.

He was pleased he had turned her advances aside, seen through her game before he knew it was even being played.

Good instincts, he decided. At least *they* still worked.

The afternoon was shaping up to be far more rewarding than he had first thought when he had arrived.

"Tell me, *Teilani,"* Kirk began. "Why is it—"

It was then the attack began.

ELEVEN

☆

Kirk saw it like a slow-replay holoprojection.

The kitchen window behind Teilani erupted in a starburst of glittering glassite shards. Each glint and sparkle of sunlight on the shattered fragments etched a pinpoint afterimage of black against his eyes.

A spray of green blood blossomed over her shoulder, expanding like a galaxy in space.

Her scream was low, drawn out, distorted.

Her arc through the air seemed effortless.

Kirk surged forward, trapped in dreamlike slow motion, as if the air had thickened, as if the kitchen expanded to stretch the distance between her and him.

She hit the floor, hair flying. She slid. Moaned. Blood smearing from the angry green gash atop her shoulder, the black jumpsuit torn.

Kirk heard the whistle of another projectile cutting through the air.

The far wall shuddered with a spray of plaster.

But Kirk was not distracted from what he knew he must do. Even as he scooped her into his arms, he assimilated the details of the attack, calculated his response.

Holding her securely, he burst through the kitchen doorway, heading for the stairway.

Teilani's eyes were shut tight with pain, though the bleeding had stopped already.

Kirk halted by the stairway. He heard footsteps running outside. Teilani stayed limp in his arms.

There were at least two attackers, Kirk knew. The angle of the two projectile blasts had told him that—each from a different location of cover. The first blast to hit the wall had come from beside the barn.

Kirk began to see his strategy. Projectile weapons meant the attackers weren't local. Local farmers who kept weapons preferred old-fashioned laser rifles. Times were slow to change in Iowa.

Projectile weapons also gave Kirk a clue to the attackers' motives. He considered it rapidly. If they had wanted to kidnap either Teilani or him, they'd be using phasers to stun them. If they had just wanted to kill Teilani or him, they'd have used more powerful phasers to disintegrate them.

Their use of projectile weapons indicated they wanted to kill someone, *and* have a body left to show for it. To prove that the job had been done, or to teach others a lesson.

Kirk could imagine there would be a few old-guard

Klingons who would want to phaser him out of existence. He knew there were others in the galaxy who'd pay to drag him back to some alien world for a slow and painful death. There were exceptions to every argument, Kirk knew, but he was certain even Spock would conclude that whoever was charging up the porch stairs of his family farmhouse, they weren't after James T. Kirk.

They were after Teilani.

He heard them fumble with the lockplate. They probably had transmitters that could open any lock made in the past fifty years. Kirk thanked his father for his love of antiques.

His glance swept upward. The stairs. The Academy taught that high ground was always preferable. But that meant it was always expected.

Kirk pushed his boot against a section of the wood paneling that ran up the side of the stairway.

A hidden, half-sized door popped open.

The damp smell of the cellar enveloped him.

It had been his playground as a child. He and his brother had fought many valiant last stands there in endless games of Humans and Romulans.

He ducked down, forcing his way through the small door as he heard a projectile blast the front door's ancient lockplate.

He winced as he realized that with his injured shoulder he could barely compensate for Teilani's added weight as he bent over.

He sat down heavily on the top step, still holding Teilani. She stirred and looked up at him.

He shook his head before she could speak, then reached out to find the crosspiece he knew so well on the small door and pulled it shut.

The instant after the cellar door clicked shut, Kirk heard the front door burst open.

The enemy entered his house.

He was surprised at the anger he felt.

Two harsh voices spoke. Their speech was clipped. He couldn't make out the language.

But it wasn't human.

Rapid footsteps rang out above them, past the hidden basement door into the kitchen. Kirk eased Teilani to the step below him. He placed a hand on her shoulder to guide her down the wooden stairs, into the darkness.

She moved silently. As if she was as classically trained as Kirk.

He followed behind her. Twelve steps down to the dirt floor.

The footsteps were slower now, more cautious. They retraced their direction to the hidden doorway. Then stopped.

Kirk nudged Teilani under the staircase.

She didn't resist. She didn't speak. She followed his unspoken orders. Whoever she was, Kirk guessed she wasn't a civilian.

His curiosity about her grew.

Then the footsteps resumed, became fainter. They moved upward, to the higher ground. Kirk was pleased. It meant the attackers had been classically trained, too. It also meant they didn't have anything resembling a tricorder that could scan for life signs.

Kirk smiled. This was going to be easy. He reached for his belt. Brought out his communicator. Held the mute button as he opened it, cutting off its distinctive chirp.

In the pale light of its status indicators, Kirk and Teilani looked at each other. Neither showed fear. There was only intense expectation.

Kirk knew the feeling well. Every time he faced death.

Kirk moved closer to Teilani and put her arm around his waist. He tapped the silent, emergency recall button on the communicator. In seconds, the Starfleet transporter grid would beam him and Teilani to an orbital station.

He braced for the cool wash of the transporter beam.

It didn't come.

Something thudded upstairs. He felt Teilani's arm tighten involuntarily around him. Classically trained for combat, he decided, but not experienced.

He risked opening an audible communications channel to see what had gone wrong.

For an instant, static hissed.

Kirk closed the communicator. Whoever the attackers were, they had a subspace jammer operating nearby. The transporter wasn't going to save the day.

But that suited Kirk.

The two intruders remained upstairs. Chances were they'd been briefed on the type of structure they might find on a human farm. That meant they'd know there was an attic to be searched. Eventually, they'd think about a cellar as well.

But chances also were they hadn't been given a full grounding in human history, and how humans had responded to various threats throughout the centuries.

Kirk moved out from under the stairs, drawing Teilani out with him. In the darkness, he guided her toward where he knew the far wall would be. He lifted his feet only a centimeter from the ground, sliding each forward slowly, just in case any boxes or furniture still remained down here. Without being told, Teilani matched her movements to his, exactly.

Though the farmhouse had been remodeled over the years, and the decades, most of it dated from almost two hundred and fifty years earlier. Good, solid, pre-World War III construction.

The Earth had been a different place then. Dark, paranoid, no one certain if the human race would survive long enough to use the incredible promise of Zefram Cochrane's startling breakthrough of warp propulsion.

So humans had taken measures to insure their survival.

The day that little Jimmy and his brother had found the old bomb shelter under their house had marked one of Kirk's most exciting summers.

Their parents hadn't wanted them playing down there, ten meters beneath the side yard. But Kirk and his brother had scavenged wood and plastic, rescued discarded furniture, made it their secret starbase.

And like all good secret starbases, it had secret entrances. One from the house. And one from the barn.

While the intruders investigated the high ground, Kirk and Teilani would outflank them.

Kirk reached out blindly and touched the cellar wall exactly where he estimated it should be. He slid his fingers along the rough polycrete, dislodging dust and old cobwebs, till he found the edge of the tunnel door. It wasn't disguised. He found the small handle. Twisted it.

The door was stuck.

He let go of Teilani, held one hand open and ready, then tugged on the handle. With a crack of old paint, the door popped open.

Kirk heard Teilani take a sharp breath and hold it.

He listened more carefully.

Nothing.

He had learned there was never any sense in hoping for the best in these conditions. The intruders must have heard the door open. They were just trying to decide from where the sound had come.

Kirk quickly reached into the tunnel and explored the wall's surface. He found the switch. Light channels flickered into subdued life on the ceiling.

Kirk motioned for Teilani to go first. She crouched down to fit under the tunnel's low ceiling and started forward.

Kirk listened one last time for footsteps. They were coming downstairs. Fast.

He crouched. Entered the tunnel. Pulled the door shut behind him. Threw the sliding lock.

"Run," he said. The time for silence was over.

They scrambled along the tunnel, passing through dark sections where the light channels had finally given out. It turned sharply at thirty meters, where the entrance to the bomb shelter was. Kirk felt it was a small victory. At least the enemy couldn't just pull open the door and fire wildly down the tunnel. Now he'd be able to hear them as they approached the turn.

Teilani slowed as she saw the bomb shelter's entrance. But it was not Kirk's destination. If they entered the shelter, it would only be a trap. There would be nothing to prevent one attacker from remaining on guard outside while the other went for a phaser, which could easily burn through the heavy metal door.

So Kirk urged Teilani to keep running. The door to the barn entrance was dead ahead. Once there, she moved to the side to let Kirk pass. He saw her frown, puzzled by the crude attempts at Romulan words Kirk and his brother had written on the tunnel wall in their childhood.

Kirk didn't bother to listen for their pursuers in the tunnel. He shoved open the door, pulled Teilani through, then closed it behind them.

They stood in a sunken stairwell, which was open to the barn. Kirk looked up to the rafters overhead. Enough sunlight filtered in through the old boards that he could see where he was going.

He sprinted up the polycrete stairs, no longer concerned about noise. Teilani followed. At the top of the stairs, Kirk paused, looked around. There were still some old hay bales by the empty horse stalls. He headed for them.

Together, he and Teilani tossed five bales into the stairwell. The attackers would have to dig their way out once they realized they couldn't open the door.

"I don't hear them," Teilani whispered.

For a brief moment, as he looked at her, Kirk couldn't help noticing the incongruous strands of hay in her hair.

"Maybe they haven't found the cellar yet," Kirk whispered back. He reached out to brush away the straw, remembering the romantic adventures he had had in this barn. All the hay he had had brushed from his own hair.

Then he heard the thud of a vehicle door outside.

He crept to a narrow gap between two boards in the barn's high wall. Teilani followed. Shoulder to shoulder they peered out through the slit.

An antigrav car was parked in the yard, halfway between the barn and the farmhouse. It was a late-model, self-drive rental, the kind that could fly off the programmed flight paths.

The attackers wore nondescript civilian clothes that would not attract attention on any world. One, with bare, hard-muscled arms and a long, sleeveless vest, sat in the passenger side, intent on adjusting some piece of equipment on his lap. The other, in a dull gray tunic, stood beside the open door, holding ready a gleaming silver projectile gun, looking anxiously about.

But their clothing, their weapons, and their equipment weren't the important details Kirk focused on.

His attackers' foreheads were furrowed like a Klingon's.

But their ears were pointed.

Just like Teilani. Youths, no older than she was. And in the same superb state of fitness.

"Do you know them?" Kirk whispered. For an instant, he took his eyes off the youth with the gun.

Teilani shook her head.

Kirk wasn't certain if he could believe her.

"But they're your people," he said.

"There are many like I am. I don't know them all."

"But you know who sent them," Kirk persisted. "Tell me why they want you."

Her dark eyes burned into him.

"They don't want *me,* James. They want *you.*"

TWELVE

Kirk didn't believe her.

There was no reason for these youths to pursue him.

He didn't know them. Had never known anyone like them.

"Why?" he asked.

But close beside him, Teilani shook her head, held a finger to her lips. Listened intently.

The youths were talking. Kirk didn't understand a word. Their words were too faint, their language unknown.

But Teilani's ears were apparently as sensitive as Spock's. And she knew their language. "They think we might have transported away," she whispered.

"How could we? They're jamming my communicator."

"That's what they're checking now."

Kirk watched the two Klingon-Romulans in heated conversation. The one in the vehicle slammed shut the cover of the equipment on his lap. Kirk decided that was the subspace jammer. They would have to know it was functioning properly. They'd have to know that he and Teilani were still somewhere near.

Kirk stared at the antigrav car. Suddenly realized what he had missed.

"How did you get here?" he asked her.

"Car," Teilani said. "I parked it down by the gate."

Kirk calculated the odds. The gate was three hundred meters down the drive. Even at Teilani's age he couldn't outrun a projectile over that distance.

The youth in the car got out. Kirk watched the powerful muscles in his arms flex impatiently as he also drew a gleaming projectile gun from inside his vest.

Now both youths stood in the yard, dark eyes sweeping the area, weapons held ready.

"They're going to find us," Kirk said softly.

Teilani looked at him, alarmed. "You're giving up?"

Kirk felt insulted. "No. I'm stating the inevitable. If we're going to take control of the situation, we have to make them find us under *our* terms, not theirs."

Teilani raised an eyebrow in appreciation. Kirk almost smiled at how familiar her expression was.

"Tell me what to do," she said.

Kirk looked around the barn. It was all so familiar. He and Sam had saved the Federation a thousand times here.

He decided the enemy wouldn't have a chance.

It took less than a minute to set the trap. Baiting it would not be any additional trouble. The Klingon-Romulans were already beginning to move toward the barn.

Kirk watched them from his vantage point high in the hayloft. Teilani now crouched by the empty horse stalls. He signaled to her. She ducked down, out of sight. Kirk tossed a small piece of chipped polycrete so that it hit the barn door.

Instantly both Klingon-Romulans fired at the door, splintering its ancient wood. The barn reverberated with the twin explosions.

Then the youth in the gray tunic ran forward and kicked away the remains of two barn boards, creating a new entrance in the closed barn door.

He eased through slowly, gleaming weapon leading the way.

Then he was in the barn, looking all around.

"There is no escape!" the Klingon-Romulan called out, in precise Federation Standard. There was no trace of any accent Kirk could identify. "Accept your fate! Die honorably!"

Kirk held his position, knowing he could not be seen. The

youth's sentiments had more than a touch of Klingon sensibility to them. But Kirk thought it interesting that the hunter had not called out the name of his intended prey—either Kirk or Teilani.

The youth remained in position, unmoving. Kirk understood the strategy. Wait for your opponent to make a mistake.

But mistakes were for the impatient young. Kirk didn't make them anymore.

At least, not in situations like this.

In the end, Kirk's patience, and experience, won out.

The youth in gray said something over his shoulder, moved farther into the barn. His partner edged warily through the splintered door.

Kirk waited till the two Klingon-Romulans stood shoulder to shoulder, each checking a different angle of the barn's interior. Then Kirk tossed his second chip of polycrete.

It landed far back in the barn's depths.

An instant after it bounced against a wooden post, two explosions followed as the Klingon-Romulans fired.

Kirk was impressed by their reflexes.

But the chip hadn't been intended to draw their fire. It was Kirk's second signal to Teilani.

She made her move.

Like a molten shadow she flew from a stall, somersaulting over the half-height door, flipping over, landing precisely on her feet and continuing on.

The barn rang with the sounds of explosions as the attackers' shots traced Teilani's path, always a heartbeat behind.

But Kirk didn't stop to admire her acrobatics. He had no doubt she would end up vaulting onto the hay bales in the sunken stairwell, safely out of range of any more explosive shells. And by then, the enemy would no longer be a threat.

Kirk would see to that.

It was his turn.

Leaping from the hayloft. Rocketing down on the rope

looped around the old hay pulley. Pulling up his legs just *so* to hit each Klingon-Romulan squarely in the back with each boot.

The bare-armed youth just started to turn in time. Just managed to see Kirk's boot as it drove toward him.

The wrenching impact sent shocks of fire along Kirk's legs and up his back. His teeth clacked together, sending sparks of pain flashing through his jaw.

But the pain was easily ignored in the satisfaction of feeling his enemies' bodies become unresisting deadweights as they absorbed his charge.

Kirk released the rope and landed running. He spun around, ready to dive forward.

And he had to dive.

The youth in the gray tunic lay facedown on the barn's polycrete floor. But his bare-armed partner was on his knees, aiming his weapon.

Kirk hit the floor on his shoulder. He gasped in shock as his strained shoulder crunched on impact.

Reflexively he slapped the ground to absorb his momentum and spare further affront to his back and arm. The sudden stop of his forward motion saved his life as an explosive shell ripped out a hole in the polycrete just before him.

The left side of his face stung with a spray of stone chips.

Kirk jumped to his feet, ready to dodge again.

The kneeling youth brought his weapon up.

Teilani charged. Her bloodcurdling Klingon death cry filled the barn. The youth's weapon wavered.

That moment's distraction was all Kirk needed.

He leapt forward.

Teilani hit the floor and rolled at the exact instant a projectile blasted through the air above her.

Kirk hit the youth shoulder to chest.

It was the final indignity to Kirk's challenged muscles. Something tore in his shoulder. Kirk's teeth ground together.

He tasted blood from the cuts on his face. But still he grabbed the bare-armed youth by the front of his vest and drove in hard with a solid head butt.

Stars flashed before Kirk's eyes with the sharp crack of his forehead against the youth's heavy brow ridges.

But green blood flooded from the attacker's nose. His dark eyes lost focus.

Kirk let go of the fabric of the vest.

His adversary fell back with a moan.

Kirk longed to do the same. But he settled for sitting back on the floor, taking inventory of his aching joints and limbs.

He was disgusted to hear himself wheeze as he fought to recover his breath.

Right now, he felt old enough to be Teilani's *great*-grandfather.

She knelt beside him. She held both attackers' weapons. "You're hurt, James."

Kirk laughed at the understatement. The action sent a new wave of agony through his shoulder, forced him to gasp for breath. But he laughed again.

Teilani frowned. "You think this is . . . amusing?"

Kirk shook his head, barely able to speak. "No . . ." he gasped. "I was . . . I was just thinking . . . that I haven't felt . . . this good . . . in years."

He saw the baffled expression in her eyes. He couldn't help it. Laughter welled up in him, uncontrollable.

The pain only made it harder to stop.

THIRTEEN

When he felt he could breathe without setting fire to his shoulder, Kirk stood. He even accepted Teilani's offered hand to help him to his feet.

For a moment, he felt light-headed. He didn't know if it was from oxygen starvation or adrenaline letdown. He didn't particularly care. From experience, he knew the sensation would pass, so the sensation could be ignored.

The first thing to be done was to consolidate his gains. He knelt beside one of the felled Klingon-Romulans, opened his vest, felt inside for an ID packet or set of credit wafers. But only found a clip of microexplosive projectiles.

Then Kirk realized that something wasn't right.

He held his hand to the youth's chest.

It wasn't moving.

He put his fingers to the youth's neck. Felt nothing where a human carotid artery would be. Moved farther back along the jaw to where the Vulcan and Romulan equivalent would be. Then pushed under the jaw for the Klingon pulse point.

The attacker was dead.

"I didn't hit him that hard," Kirk said.

He went to the second youth, still facedown on the floor. He rolled the body over. There was a small pool of coagulating blood from the youth's mouth, a few splattered drops of it on his gray tunic, but no more than would result from a split lip or dislodged tooth.

Yet this second youth was also dead.

"No," Kirk protested. It made no sense.

Teilani tried to comfort him. "But they were trying to kill *you,* James."

"That's not it," Kirk said. These were young men. Fit and strong. They weren't meant to die from a blow to the jaw or a kick to the back.

It was becoming apparent to Kirk that he had seen too much death in his years. More and more it sickened him to play a part in adding to the universe's store of it.

"*Why* were they trying to kill me?" Kirk asked. He felt the need to make their deaths count for something. Anything. He took Teilani by the shoulders again. "You owe me answers."

But she touched his face again, held out a single finger stained with red blood. Kirk's blood.

"There's a medkit in my car," she said.

Kirk looked down at the bodies of the two young Klingon-Romulans. They weren't going anyplace. He nodded wearily. He started for the barn door. Teilani quickly took hold of his hand, as if to steady him. He didn't protest her action. In the back of his mind came the terrible thought that he might stumble without her support.

Outside, Kirk paused before beginning the long walk to the gate and Teilani's car. He drew in a deep breath. The air had become sharper, sweeter, more intense than before.

Kirk knew the reason for the change.

Victory. Triumph. Life.

His life.

Will it always be this way? he wondered. Could he only find purpose in cheating death? And how much longer would his aging body *let* him cheat death? What would happen when his reflexes could no longer achieve what his instincts demanded?

An unwelcome memory surfaced. Captain Christopher Pike in his life-support chair. A starship captain reduced to little more than an inert receptacle for an imprisoned mind.

Kirk never wanted to face that—the day the mind outstripped the body. But as he limped along the dirt driveway to the gate, now with his arm around Teilani's shoulders, he had to admit that his body *was* beginning to succumb to the ravages of time.

"Tell me, Teilani," he said, each word an unexpected effort. "Why did they come here?"

"So you would not be able to help me."

"Help you do what?"

"Bring peace to my world."

She was almost as infuriating as Spock could be, answering only the specific question, never volunteering additional details.

"Where is your world? What's its name?"

Kirk caught Teilani smiling at him, affectionately. "Don't try to change the subject again," he warned. He knew the power over him that that smile unleashed.

"I'm not. It's just that I know you must be in pain, yet you still hunger for knowledge." She gave his hand a firm squeeze that was not necessary for support. "I was right to choose you."

Kirk groaned. She was maddening in many ways. "For *what?*"

They were almost at the gate. Kirk could see a groundcar parked behind it, on the shoulder of the country road. From a nearby stand of chestnut trees, he heard cicadas whine in the heat. Birds sang songs he remembered from childhood summers.

Teilani paused imperceptibly. She seemed to come to some decision. "My world has many designations, James, depending on whose charts it appears. But for those of us who were born there, who live there, we call it *Chal.*"

She looked at him as if testing him for any prior knowledge of what she was about to tell him. But the name of her planet meant nothing to Kirk.

"It began as a colony," she continued. "A joint venture of sorts. I think you can guess who its founders were."

Kirk nodded. "The Klingons, and the Romulans."

"One of many attempts to bring the two empires together." Teilani frowned. "And a failure, like all the others."

They were at the gate. Teilani carefully lifted Kirk's arm from around her shoulders so she could walk ahead and open the latch, swing the gate open. The gate wasn't a security device. Just a simple barricade to keep neighbors' livestock from wandering in.

"You said you opted for independence," Kirk prompted her. He fought to keep his balance without her young body to lean on.

"In the end, neither empire wanted us. So we chose to make our own way."

As Teilani swung the gate open, its old hinges squealed.

Feeling sudden kinship with the antiquated gate, Kirk awkwardly started for the groundcar. He squared his shoulders as best he could, somehow resisting the humiliating temptation to shuffle. He felt embarrassed by his condition. Exhausted. Vulnerable.

"I can't imagine either empire willingly giving up a colony world," he said. "Not if there was a chance the other side would claim it."

They stood before the groundcar—another self-drive rental. It was a touring model with an extended hull, and wide bench seats in the back under a clear viewing dome. Kirk knew it was a favorite of tourists who crossed the light-years to visit the Amish farms nearby.

"As far as either empire knew at the time, my world had nothing of value. Chal was nothing more than a failed experiment from the past. More regrettable than exploitable."

"At the time," Kirk repeated. "Then something has changed?" He stood back as Teilani punched in the operating code on the door. It swung up with a soft hiss of air.

"Yes," she said, and Kirk was surprised to hear in that one word the same weariness he felt. As if Teilani bore a burden far beyond her years. She lifted the door all the way open so

Kirk could enter. As he gripped the side of the car to step inside, he reflected on his new role—the one being protected, not protecting. It was . . . different.

Kirk chose a rear seat. Teilani entered a moment later and took the driver's seat. She punched more controls on the dash. Kirk felt cool air begin to circulate, cutting the heat that had built up beneath the dome.

Teilani pivoted the driver's seat around to face him, then reached below to open a small compartment marked with a red cross. The medkit was required equipment for all cars. An example of the pervasive regulations that made Earth what it was today.

"There's trouble on your world now, isn't there," Kirk said. He slipped easily into the diagnosis of conflict. The habit of too many years. Too much experience. "Two factions, at least. You represent one. Those people who tried to kill us, they represent the other."

Teilani laid out the contents of the medkit like a soldier. She ripped open a sterile swab.

"As you suspect, our world has something of value after all. Something neither empire knew of. Some on Chal want to profit from our past and our world's treasure. Pit both empires against each other and side with whichever promises the richer price." She fixed her lustrous eyes on Kirk. They were mesmerizing in their clarity and unwavering gaze. "But some of us don't want a return to the conflict and the violence of the past. We cannot allow our world to be plundered and exploited. Chal must be preserved for our children, and their children. Not squandered."

The spray hypo she held against his injured shoulder hissed against his skin. A cool sensation of relief eased the shoulder's pain.

Kirk had no doubt which side Teilani was on. He thought it odd that one so young should worry about the future. He hadn't when he had been her age. There had only been the eternal present for him. He tried to keep that same state of mind these days, but it was more difficult with each passing year.

Teilani reached out to wipe his face. But he stopped her.

"How about *your* shoulder?" he asked.

She touched the tear in her jumpsuit, crusted with blood. "It's fine," she said.

Again, Kirk didn't take her word as given. He took the swab from her, remembering the explosion of green that had burst from her.

"We'll look after you first," he said. "I've just got a few scrapes."

She tried to pull back, but he wouldn't let her. He braced her shoulder with one hand, then used his other hand to begin cleansing her wound with the swab.

The dried green blood flaked away.

Kirk stopped.

There *was* no wound.

Only a purplish green bruise and raised yellow welt. With no indication that the skin had ever been broken or blood had ever been spilled.

"I *saw* you get shot," Kirk said.

Teilani held his hand against her shoulder.

"There was blood," Kirk said. "The projectile *exploded. Threw* you across the kitchen. I *know* you were hurt."

Teilani's eyes sought his. Held them.

"I told you my world has a treasure, James."

He pulled on the fabric of her jumpsuit, exposing her shoulder, to be certain he was not mistaken.

Except for the bruise and welt beneath the original tear, her skin was unmarked and flawless.

"How is this possible?" Kirk demanded.

Teilani took his hand and held it to her shoulder. He could feel her pulse.

"This is the treasure of my world, James. The gift it bestows on all who live there."

Kirk felt the heat of her unblemished body warm his hand. But a chill spread through him, too.

"Come home to Chal with me, James. Come home with me and save my world." Her eyes bore into his like phasers set to an infinite power. "Come home, and be young *forever.*"

FOURTEEN

When that impossible day came to an end, Kirk had no clear memory of it.

Too much had happened. Too much had changed.

The bittersweet return to his boyhood home, perhaps for the final time. The disturbing shock of urgent passion triggered by Teilani's unexpected appearance. The fierce but welcome fight to cheat death one more time. The rebirth that followed survival. As it always followed.

And then—Teilani's revelation.

Of Chal and its secret.

A world where youth was eternal. Where death had no dominion.

As Teilani had tended his wounds, she told him more of Chal. Nameless to all but its colonists, poor in resources, a water world with only vegetation and a handful of animal species on its minuscule island landmasses. A distant, worthless world. On the farthest reaches of the two empires' reluctantly shared, often disputed border.

She had slipped off his jacket, his shirt. Her cool hands and skillful fingers had probed the muscles of his shoulder. Kirk had closed his eyes as her hands moved over him, kneading, caressing, somehow taking away the fire and the pain.

And then Teilani's touch had brought a sudden memory of being in a different place, being soothed the same way.

He smelled wood fire. Remembered Miramanee, the tribal priestess on the Preserver planet. Saw her dark hair swaying above him, bound by her headband, all that she wore. She moved her hands across him in an ancient ritual of her people, calling him Kirok, making him hers.

The memory flashed through him in an instant and he was with Teilani again. She told him of the fitful truce between the empires. The selection of her nameless world as a place to strengthen their bonds. In time, the empires had fallen apart again. Trade broke off. The colony world had been abandoned.

Eventually, even the founders left, returning to the more familiar, profitable worlds of their youth. But their children chose to remain behind with what was familiar to them. Hybrids all, Klingon *and* Romulan. With the perversity of youth, they had determined to side with neither empire, to strike off on their own.

And they had. Forging a new home. A new culture. Working for a distant future when they could bequeath an independent, functioning world to their children.

But Chal had changed their future. Even as their own children grew to adulthood, that first generation did not age.

Eventually, all had realized that illness never struck their world. Inevitable accidents, provided they weren't instantly fatal, resulted only in injuries that healed without trace. Almost at once.

Kirk moved his fingers across Teilani's unmarked shoulder.

Less than an hour after being shot, her wound was gone completely.

It was Teilani's turn to close her eyes, to push her shoulder into Kirk's hand, sighing as their flesh again made contact and she guided his hand beneath the fabric of her clothing.

"Chal needs a hero," she breathed into his ear. "*I* need a hero. To show us how to defend ourselves from those who would destroy us."

Her lips brushed his neck. Her hands moved across his back, delicately raking her sharp nails across his skin, awakening nerve endings to a heightened awareness of what it was possible to feel.

Kirk was engulfed by sensations he no longer wanted to question, no longer was able to question.

He moved his face against her shoulder, delighting in the warm scent of her hair, the delicacy of each tiny thread of it feathering the back of her neck.

Another memory claimed him, pulling him from the here and now. He was in his cabin on the *Enterprise,* tangled in the glittering bedspread. His lips trailed across the neck of Marlena Moreau. In another universe, a dark reflection of his own, she had been the captain's woman. *His* woman. In this instant, her scent still clung to him, blending with Teilani's.

Kirk brought himself back to the moment. Brushed his lips across Teilani's. Savored her sweetness. "You could go to the Federation Council," he said softly. "If Chal is unaligned, you could petition for membership, for protectorate status."

He listened to the words he said with a sense of unreality, as if someone else were speaking. One hand slipped to her waist, imprinting the feel and the shape of her into his senses.

The past claimed him again. He felt the smooth skin of Kelinda. The icy beauty of the Kelvan explorer afire with the sensations he brought to her for the first time in her human form.

Kirk knew what it was like to be overwhelmed by unexpected desire, as he had overwhelmed Kelinda. Teilani reawakened those same sensations in him now, as her hands caressed him.

"We cannot go to the Federation," Teilani said, her breath quickening in response to his own caress. Kirk felt as if two strangers conversed in the car while two others communed in an exchange far more primal. "We are too deep in Klingon territory, in Romulan territory, for either to accept a Federation claim."

Her hand captured his. Raised it to her lips. Moved her soft tongue against and between his fingers, taking his breath away.

"We must do this on our own," she whispered, "or not at all."

Her other hand sought the dash behind her, found a control.

Slowly, the viewing dome darkened into total opacity, encasing them in a cocoon of silence and privacy. A universe of their own.

"All or nothing," she said. They were her final words.

All else that followed was beyond language.

Each sound she made, each move, propelled Kirk further from himself, into a realm of inexpressible perception.

He was as overwhelmed as he had been by the tears of the Dohlman. Elaan of Troyius was within his arms again, demanding lips crushing his with a passion he had never encountered before.

But which he now encountered again.

Come home with me and be young forever.

Teilani had reawakened the youth of his past, given purpose to his present, and now she was giving him back his future.

His future.

In the soft lighting of the car, Teilani drew away from Kirk. Once more, she held her finger to the fabric sealer control at her neck, kept it there.

This time, the fabric of her jumpsuit parted completely, fell away from her, nothing hidden, all revealed.

Kirk held his breath at the beauty of her perfection.

She reached out for Kirk.

He did not hesitate.

He flew through the years—

. . . to the ruins of Triskelion and Shahna, the drill thrall, as her mane of auburn hair engulfed them both . . .

. . . to the haunting, empty duplicate of the *Enterprise,* where he was caught in the rapture of Odona's love, as she sought to save the people of Gideon but lost her heart to Kirk instead . . .

. . . to the hyperaccelerated realm of the Scalosians, where Queen Deela's pulse fluttered in time with his own, each second of passion stretched to last an hour . . .

Teilani was one and all women to him.

Each touch was familiar, calling forth cherished memories.

Each kiss was unique, searing new pathways through his senses.

Her hands, her lips, her body kept him trembling on the brink of an ecstasy he had never imagined.

Until all thought was finally driven from his mind.

Until all that could exist was the brilliant clarity of the moment.

A wave of cleansing resurrection.

For the first time in years, he was truly *alive.*

When Teilani adjusted the dome control again, the sky was red with sunset.

Kirk lay back on the bed they had made by folding the rear seats together. He gazed up at the darkening sky.

He knew the *Enterprise* was up there, as he always did. But in the sanctity of this moment, he couldn't hear her call to him.

He was at peace.

Teilani lay beside him, one hand tracing patterns on his chest, radiant with the same peace Kirk felt, glowing with the sheen of their exertions.

"So it's true," she said in a languid voice.

Kirk turned on his side. He ran his fingers through the satin waves of her hair. "What is?"

She raised herself up on one elbow to look at him directly. Her smile became wicked, delightful. "What they say about humans."

She laughed and Kirk felt his cheeks redden.

Suddenly she kissed him again. Deeply. Expertly.

The effect was literally breathtaking.

She rolled over on top of him. Held his face in both her hands. Her nose brushed his as she covered him with kisses, her hair falling forward in an enclosing curtain.

The fragrance of her hair, her breath, swept over him.

"Come back with me?" she asked.

Kirk narrowed his eyes, as if to reduce the influence her loveliness had on him. His finger lightly trailed along her body, traced the swell of her breast where she pressed against him, the curve of her hip. Flawless. Somehow more than perfect. "Why does a planet blessed with people like you, need someone like me?"

A small smile flickered across her face. She pushed herself up and sat back on him, knees tight against his sides. Her hands moved down his chest. "Experience," she said. "I can attest to its value."

And then—

—she *tickled* him, both hands digging into his ribs in a move so sudden and unexpected that Kirk choked in surprise. He couldn't remember the last time that anyone had tried that.

Years. Too many years.

She collapsed in giggles atop him. He had no choice but to burst into laughter as well. He reached up under her arms to give as good as he got.

The car rang with their laughter. Some part of Kirk thought it was as if two children were playing. *And what's wrong with that?* he asked himself.

Out of breath, Teilani stopped her attack, lay upon him. What had been playful one moment became intensely erotic the next.

Kirk felt exhilarated by the quick recovery of his desire.

For one long delicious moment, they stared at each other, each knowing where the next moment would lead.

Then the viewing dome vibrated.

Kirk recognized the sound that caused it. He pushed past Teilani, sat up, stared into the sunset.

Down by his parent's farmhouse, the attackers' antigrav car was taking off.

Teilani held on to his arm, watching with him as the car banked over the barn and sped off toward the north.

"There must have been *three* of them," she said.

Kirk stared after the car. "Then why didn't the third one come after us, too?"

Teilani's voice shook with a burst of anger, with hatred. "Why do they want to destroy my world? Why do they do *anything?*"

She pressed her head against Kirk's chest.

He held her close.

There were no more questions in his mind.

No more uncertainties.

Time was slipping too quickly through his fingers.

He would not let this second chance slip through as well.

FIFTEEN

Leonard McCoy was immune to the Parisian cityscape spread out before him. It was aglow with entire galaxies of lights, drawing the eye unerringly to the floodlights bathing the newly restored Eiffel Tower. But the beauty of the ancient city held no charm for him tonight. He scowled over his mint julep.

"Our ancestors had a descriptive medical term for what you're going through, Jim."

"Did they?" Kirk asked, without enthusiasm. He had just finished telling his two closest friends about his intention to resign from Starfleet and accompany Teilani to Chal. But the evening was not progressing as smoothly as he had hoped. He should have realized. Things seldom did when both Spock and McCoy were involved.

The doctor sourly regarded his drink. "They called it 'middle-aged crazy.'"

By the kitchen alcove, Spock raised an eyebrow. "Indeed. A most fitting description."

Kirk slumped in his chair. An uncomfortable position because it was Vulcan, and most Vulcan chairs were not meant for anything other than ramrod-straight posture. "Spock, not you, too."

"What did you expect?" McCoy's exasperation was evident. It gave his voice an edgy tenseness that flattened the friendly warmth of his Southern drawl. Even to Kirk it was unsettling to hear strong emotions being voiced in the serene sanctuary of Spock's quarters in the Vulcan Embassy.

"I don't know what I expected," Kirk said. "But what I had hoped was that . . . you'd wish me well."

Spock handed Kirk a thimble-sized glass filled with a yellow liquid. Kirk looked at it skeptically. It smelled like licorice. "You keep the makings for McCoy's *mint julep* here, but no scotch?"

"The doctor is a frequent visitor," Spock said. "He maintains his own supply of refreshments."

Kirk looked at his two friends. McCoy was a *frequent* visitor? *Here?* He felt out of touch, as if he had ignored the people closest to him. After a few moment's thought, he realized he had. And regretted it. But it was still time to move on.

"As you must know," Spock continued, "we, of course, do support you in any decision you make and indeed wish you well."

"Even if we also think you're a horse's ass," McCoy grumbled.

Kirk couldn't take it anymore. "Didn't you hear a word I said?" He jumped to his feet, began to pace. "I *love* her, Bones."

McCoy was not impressed. "Didn't you hear a word *I* said? You're crazy!"

Spock stepped between the two men as a mediator. "Captain, if I may, you say you are 'in love.' How are we to expect that this time is different from any of the others?"

Kirk stared at Spock, surprised by the bluntness of his question. "The point is, *I'm* different. Don't you see . . ." Kirk looked around at the plain gray walls of the Vulcan-designed room. They were the same walls that confined his existence, pressing in on him from all sides, restricting movement and freedom and life itself. "Spock, I'm dying here."

McCoy couldn't let that go. "Speaking as your doctor: No, you're not."

Kirk ignored him. "That's not what I mean, and you know it. My time's running out. *Your* time. Spock's time. This past year it's been as if everyone expects me to sit in my rocker and stare at the sunset and wait for night to bring an end to everything. But now, Teilani's showing me . . . a new horizon."

"She's blinding you, is more like it," McCoy said.

Kirk had no argument with that. "Yes, she is. And I love it. I can't stop thinking about her, Bones. I can't stop remembering what it's like to be with her."

"Your hormone levels would probably short out my tricorder."

Kirk grinned. "Exactly. Can you know what it's like to feel that way again? Bones, she's . . . incredible. Beyond incredible. I mean, when she—"

McCoy turned away. "Spare me the details."

But Kirk wouldn't let himself be ignored. He couldn't keep Teilani bottled up inside him. "I feel like I'm twenty again. That thrill, that expectation, it's all come back to me. Each morning. Each day. Each *night.* Everything is new again. Everything, Bones."

"The only thing that's new is the *Enterprise*-B."

That stopped Kirk.

McCoy was visibly working to hold in his anger, now. "Almost finished. Up in spacedock. Going to be launched within the year. And she's already been assigned to Captain Harriman—*not* James T. Kirk."

Kirk angrily rejected the diagnosis. It was too simplistic. He felt his temper spiraling upward to match McCoy's. "You're not listening to me. This is *not* about the *Enterprise.* This is about me. My feelings. My needs." He turned to Spock. "Spock, you know, don't you? We spoke of passion. You said that's what I needed. And Teilani has made me feel that again."

"Of that, I have no doubt, Captain. But that same passion has adversely affected your judgment."

Kirk was astounded by Spock's blanket assessment. "Exactly how has my judgment been affected?"

"Have you stopped to consider what Teilani's motives in this matter may be?"

"Spock, what does it matter?"

McCoy stepped to Spock's side.

"It matters because she's using you, Jim."

Kirk spread his arms wide. "Then let her use me. My God, Bones. Do you know what it means to be useful again? You've got medicine. Spock's got diplomacy. But what do I have? What *did* I have until Teilani came to me and said her world needs me?"

McCoy shot Spock a sideways glance. "Well, I suppose it is a more original line than, 'Come here often, sailor.' "

Kirk didn't know how much more of this he wanted to hear. "Bones, Spock himself confirmed everything Teilani told me. The failed Klingon-Romulan colony. How neither side claimed it. How it declared independence."

"So she read the same handful of paragraphs in a Starfleet almanac that Spock did," McCoy said dismissively. "Ha. No one even knows the exact location of this Chal place."

Spock steepled his fingers in a meditative pose. "To be fair, Captain, the drastic nature of your intentions does not seem to coincide with the apparent threat faced by Chal. I therefore suspect you have not told us everything Teilani has revealed to you about her world and its predicament."

Kirk wore his best poker face, though he knew it had long since stopped working on Spock and McCoy. "I've told you everything that's pertinent. Some things, minor things, she did tell me in confidence. There's no need to repeat them."

He still found it difficult to believe in the amazing medical properties Teilani claimed for her world.

But if he dared tell anyone, even his friends, what Teilani had told him about . . . being young forever, they'd lock him up. The galaxy was littered with false fountains of youth. Not to mention the con artists who fleeced those desperate enough to believe in them. He had no intention of looking more foolish to his friends than he apparently already did.

"In confidence," McCoy sputtered in the midst of a sip. "Pillow talk is more like it."

"Bones, don't."

McCoy slammed down his glass, as if he'd lost his taste for his favorite drink. "And if I don't, who will? Face it, Jim, you've got all the symptoms of someone escaping reality at warp nine. We all know you need something to do. But to go off, you'll excuse the expression, half-cocked with this *child—*"

Kirk faced McCoy as if facing an accuser, shouted back at him, surprising himself as much as his friend. "She's an adult, Bones. She knows what she's doing. Her planet has no defense system, no military history. They need me . . . someone of my experiencc to . . . set up a police force, show them how to defend themselves, secure their world and their future."

"And you think there aren't a thousand consulting companies on a hundred worlds that are better equipped to do that than you? You don't think that the Federation would jump at a chance to set up a joint peacekeeping operation with the Klingons and the Romulans to improve relations?"

"There are other considerations," Kirk insisted.

"I'm sure there are. *Her* considerations!" McCoy held up his fingers as he counted them out. "*Your* reputation. *Your* prestige. *Your* instant access to virtually any level of government and industry in the Federation and almost anyplace else you'd care to mention." McCoy's eyes were wide with indignation. "How long do you think it's going to be before your little playmate snuggles up to you in bed some night and asks if you could set up a teeny-tiny meeting between her and some planetary official? Or some industrialist that she couldn't get to in ten years of negotiations?"

"What's wrong with *any* of that?" Kirk demanded.

McCoy shook his head in pity. "She's a third your age."

"Which is how she makes *me* feel!" Kirk took a deep breath. He hadn't wanted any of this to happen. "Bones, even if everything you say is true, what's *wrong* with it?" Kirk reached out to his friend, anger turning to a plea for understanding. "Teilani and I are *both* adults. We're *both* going into this with our eyes wide open. If I can take five steps with her, and then drop dead on the sixth, at least I will have had those first five."

Kirk turned to Spock. His Vulcan friend revealed no trace of what he was thinking. "Spock, you understand what I'm saying."

"I do," Spock said.

At last Kirk felt hope. Perhaps there was a way back from this emotional precipice after all. "Then help me here. Help Bones see that what I'm doing isn't wrong."

But Spock shook his head. "I cannot. For in this instance, I find myself in the unique position of agreeing with everything Dr. McCoy has said."

Those simple words, spoken so calmly, were more of a shock to Kirk than if McCoy had come right out and punched him.

"Spock . . . no."

"If you have been forthcoming with us, Captain, then I must say your actions involving this woman are uncharacteristic, unsuitable, and ill-serving your past reputation and accomplishments."

Kirk stared at Spock. Mortified. In his own Vulcan way, Spock was shouting at him, too.

"To abandon Starfleet and your career in order to become little more than a mercenary, apparently paid by the sexual favors of a young woman about whom you know little or nothing, is not an act of passion."

"Then just what is it?" Kirk demanded hotly.

"It is an act of desperation. And desperation is also an emotion with which I am familiar."

The silence in the room was physical, like a jungle to be hacked through.

"Spock," Kirk said quietly, "you once asked me if we had grown so old that we had outlived our usefulness. . . ."

"The times have changed, Captain. As have our abilities. Our functions and our goals must change with them. To refuse to accept the inevitable is the first step toward obsolescence, and extinction."

Suddenly, Kirk felt empty. There was no need to control his emotions. He no longer felt anything. "What if I don't want to change?" His voice sounded flat to him. As if it came from a great distance.

"Then that would be . . . unfortunate."

"Unfortunate . . ." Kirk said. Three decades of friendship dissolving in that one spoken word.

That one verdict.

Kirk faced Spock, and then McCoy, and it was as if he looked at strangers. Had they ever known him well? Had he ever understood them so little?

After almost thirty years, Kirk could think of nothing more to say to Spock or McCoy.

"It's late," Kirk said. He stared at them both, fixing them in his memory. In case he might never see them again. "I have to . . . take care of some loose ends."

Spock and McCoy let him go. In silence. As if they, too, could think of nothing more to say to him.

Times had changed.

Kirk continued on his journey.

Alone.

SIXTEEN

With no hint of hyperbole, San Francisco Travelport called itself "The Crossroads of the Galaxy." And rightly so.

The vast central hall of the enormous complex echoed with a symphony of travel and commerce—boarding calls, arrival and departure times, lost-child announcements, commercial messages in all the languages of Earth.

Its very air was an overload of intermingled aromas—from the precise harshness of filtered and reconditioned air, to the exotic spices of food kiosks representing dozens of worlds, and the complex tapestry of scents and perfumes from the milling, passing crush of humanity and other species, in all their varied forms.

When Kirk had first come here as a boy to see his father off, the sights and sounds of this crossroads had overwhelmed him. Became magic to him. Claimed his imagination and his heart forever.

To step beyond any of the departure lounges was to go by suborbital shuttle to anywhere in the world in less than an hour. Or by impulse liner to the Moon in less than a day. The Martian Colonies in less than a week.

Or even by warp to the stars, for however long time itself might last.

But now, for all its romance, the teeming Travelport was little more than a meaningless way station to him. One last stop, one final obstacle to overcome before he could begin what he had to do.

Instead of magic, today—his first day out of Starfleet since enrolling in the Academy forty-four years ago—Kirk saw only aimlessness and confusion.

Cut off from the Starfleet infrastructure and orbital transporter grid he had come to accept as second nature, Kirk almost felt as if Earth had become an alien planet.

He had to think about *how* to do almost everything. Without a Starfleet communicator on his belt, he had to remember his personal transmitter code, how to access the commercial data spectrum, even endure listening to advertising messages as his request was passed through the worldwide computer nets.

It took five times as long to do anything.

Even leaving Earth was going to take hours.

So the Travelport he had once associated with unlimited possibilities had become nothing more than an infuriating bottleneck.

He knew what was beyond each of the departure lounges.

He knew exactly where he wanted to go.

But he couldn't just say "One to beam up" anymore.

James T. Kirk was a civilian.

As a student of anachronistic language constructions might have put it, he thought it sucked.

Finally, the computer screen Kirk stood before in the Travelport's Public Communications Hub changed to show his call had been put through.

Kirk sighed. It was about time. He tensed for what was to come. The conversation he had put off till the very last.

But Carol Marcus wasn't home.

Kirk relaxed.

Carol could never be one of his "loose ends." They had loved each other once. Made a son. Only time and the stars had been able to pull them apart. Only heartbreak and circumstance had been able to bring them back together.

The memory of what had been between them still remained. But it was clear to both of them now that that memory was no longer enough.

Kirk felt certain Teilani had nothing to do with his achieving this insight, except to accelerate his recognition of the inevitable. It was time for Carol and him to continue their own lives. Otherwise, both risked descending into the stultifying abyss of habit and familiarity that had drawn him back to her on his return from Khitomer, and the *Enterprise*'s last voyage.

The computer screen waited for Kirk to indicate whether he wished to leave a message or make a further call.

Kirk hesitated. Carol deserved more than the brief farewells he had recorded for his office staff at the Academy. But he didn't know how much more than that he had to give right now.

In the end, instinct won out. Whenever the urge to hesitate grew too strong in him, Kirk knew it was the signal that he must take action. Only then could he continue to move forward.

He touched the message bar on the screen.

The computer said it was recording.

"Carol . . . I know what I want now." But how could he explain it to her? "I . . . uh, you helped me find it." He felt flustered. It was not like him to struggle for words. But all his skills, all his bravado, evaporated when it came to facing and expressing his own desires. "Thank you for . . . everything you've brought to me, shared with me." He placed his hand on the screen, picturing Carol on the other side, sometime later this day, watching her messages, her fingers joining the phantom images of his own. "I'll always love you," Kirk said. A universe of emotion in that simple promise. Then he disconnected.

Maybe that was always part of the problem, he thought. He loved them all. And always would.

The insight made him stop and stare at the patient computer screen for a few silent moments. There was no question that he knew the finality of his next action. What he was leaving behind. Who he was leaving behind. Forever.

But he *was* moving forward again. Contemplating the risks and the chaos that might accompany the voyage only filled him with anticipation, even excitement.

With a lightness of being he had not felt since his return, Kirk turned away from the computer. He headed toward the central hall of the Travelport.

Teilani waited for him there, under the holographic display that showed the times and dates on Earth, the Moon, and Mars.

Her face lit up as she saw him emerge from the crowd.

Kirk increased his stride, moving with purpose again. He felt himself quicken in return.

He didn't know what would happen next in his life.

But here at the crossroads of the galaxy, he was no longer without direction.

Once again, Teilani surprised him.

Kirk was beginning to think he should come to expect that as normal.

As it turned out, they didn't have to wait hours to book last-minute passage on a shuttle. Teilani had a private yacht. Standing by, already cleared for launch.

Customs and immigration clearance was no more difficult than slipping an ID wafer into a reader and having a retina pattern confirmed.

As Kirk and Teilani were swept along a moving walkway toward a private shuttle pad, she told him that the simplified procedures were part of the diplomatic privileges of her invitation to Admiral Drake's reception the week before.

That detail *had* been troubling Kirk. "If your world is so distant, considered so inconsequential, why did the Federation decide to invite someone from Chal?" he asked.

"We're not unknown to the Federation, James. Over the years we've set up specialized trade relations with various groups. We do have accounts in most of the key interstellar exchanges." She put her hand on his, where he held the moving handrail. "And I *asked* to be invited. I'm sure the Federation Protocol Office didn't have to think twice about complying. It was a large reception, and an invitation to delegates from Chal could be considered a gesture of goodwill. To both the Romulan *and* Klingon empires,"

Kirk turned his hand over to grasp hers in his. They were nearing the pad. He could smell fresh air blowing into the transfer tunnel.

"But you didn't talk to me at the reception," he said, remembering his first glimpse of Teilani. When he had first felt the need to be with her. Like this.

"I wanted to. But you were with your friends. And the admiral." Teilani shrugged.

Kirk relived the moment Teilani had turned away—the moment Androvar Drake had stopped at his table.

"Do you know Admiral Drake?" he asked suddenly. He couldn't be certain, but he thought he recalled seeing a flicker of recognition in her eyes that night. Although those three Romulan ales still cast a pall on a full recollection of the evening.

But Teilani said, "No."

The walkway slowed and they stepped off. Teilani had no luggage. Kirk carried a single, soft-sided bag. Inside were two real books, a few treasured computer wafers with images of friends and family, and a change of clothes. The contents of the bag were all he truly wanted to take with him. A lifetime distilled into less than four kilograms of idiosyncratic, personal belongings. Everything else he had collected over the years was in long-term storage. The prospect of walking away from so much of the accumulated detritus of life added to his sense of liberation.

They emerged from the tunnel, onto the tarmac.

Teilani's sleek yacht was caught in a web of floodlights. Its smooth white hull glowed stark against the night.

Kirk's eyes brightened. Starfleet craft were of necessity designed for multipurpose applications, resulting in solid, utilitarian designs.

But the manufacturers of private spacecraft were under no such restrictions.

Teilani's yacht not only *could* travel at warp one, it *looked* as if it could. An aggressive set of double curves swept around from the flight-deck windows to flow smoothly over the long blisters of the miniaturized warp nacelles tracing the lower edge of each side.

"I like it," he said with understatement. He began to walk around the yacht in the center of the pad, giving it a pilot's traditional preflight visual inspection. Teilani accompanied him. "But I've never flown anything like it."

"Oh, you don't have to fly it, James."

Kirk froze as he passed by the flight deck. Not because of what Teilani said, but because of what he saw.

One of the attackers from the farm.

Alive.

Kirk instantly pushed Teilani behind him.

The youth looked up, startled. He had been doing something inside an open access panel on the yacht's hull.

Kirk rushed forward, pressing the advantage of surprise.

"James, no!" Teilani shouted after him. "He's the *pilot!*"

Kirk's upraised fist paused a split second. Just long enough for Kirk to take in his target's features.

He was one of Teilani's hybrid race—furrowed brow, pointed ears. Young like her. Like the two attackers who had tried to kill them.

But in the brilliant glare of the floodlights, he also saw that Teilani was right.

Kirk had never seen this youth before. Though the pilot

resembled the attackers so strongly that Kirk at once wondered if he might be related to them.

The shaken pilot held out a hand to Kirk. "I am Esys," he said nervously. "It is a great honor to meet you, sir."

Kirk slowly lowered his fist to take the offered hand. "I apologize. Teilani and I had some—"

"The attack, sir," Esys interrupted. "Yes, she told me. The Anarchists are everywhere."

"Anarchists?" Kirk asked.

Teilani took Kirk's arm. "He means the people who are against us. It's as good a word as any. They want to tear apart our culture, yet offer nothing to replace it."

Teilani saw the shadow of a smile cross Kirk's face.

"Does that amuse you?" she asked.

"Different worlds, different ways," Kirk said. "I was just thinking that on Earth, it's more traditional that young people like you are in favor of anarchy."

"On Chal," Teilani said, "we are *all* young." Her eyes met Kirk's and held them. "As you will be."

Kirk's smile faded. He hadn't admitted that part of Teilani's story to Spock and McCoy because he still couldn't accept it himself. Because, if everything he had done since meeting Teilani—abandoning his friends, giving up Starfleet, hurting Carol—was simply the result of a desperate desire to recapture his youth at any cost, then his friends would be proven right.

James T. Kirk would be nothing more than a self-obsessed fool who had selfishly gambled away everything he held dear in a vain attempt to deny and delay the inescapable passage of time.

Kirk refused to so define himself. He *knew* he loved Teilani. He wanted—needed—to be with her for whatever time remained to him.

That was what had driven him to abandon everything for Chal.

Passion. Not desperation.

Love. Not an impossible dream of youth, however appealing, however real.

But Kirk also knew, better than anyone, the greatest fear of a man who had been a starship captain. That, in the end, he was just like everyone else.

Full of hope, rejecting doubt, Kirk held Teilani's hand tightly as they boarded the yacht.

He had made his decision.

He chose the future.

SEVENTEEN

Teilani's yacht shot up through the night as if it had gone to warp.

Kirk was unprepared for the g-forces that slammed him back into the copilot's seat.

"What's wrong with your inertial dampers?" he asked, trying not to sound as if he were gasping for breath.

Esys shot him a glance. "Oh, sorry, sir." He ran his fingers over some controls.

A moment later, all sensation of movement vanished as the inertial dampers absorbed and redirected the momentum of everything within the speeding craft. Kirk shifted in his chair, grateful he could breathe again.

Esys shrugged apologetically. "I sort of keep the dampers tuned down. So I can feel how I'm flying."

Kirk nodded, feeling foolish. He used to do that himself at the Academy. All young pilots did. Half the fun of flying trainers had been to see who could set their dampers the lowest. The resulting g-forces and inertia would wrench the fledgling pilots against their seat harnesses and slam them from side to side in the cramped, one-person flight cabins, ideally without causing blackouts as blood rushed from the bravest pilot's head. How had he forgotten what it was like to bc that young?

Kirk felt Teilani put her hand on his arm, leaning forward from the passenger seat behind him. "Not quite like Starfleet?" she asked.

"Just like Starfleet," Kirk answered.

Through the flight-deck viewport, the last retreating wisps of cloud were visible only because of the ocean of light from San Francisco that dramatically lit them from below.

Ahead, the stars brightened. As the yacht rose and the atmosphere thinned, their twinkling ceased.

Eyes fixed on the stars, Kirk felt an unexpected but familiar sensation of anticipation come over him. He was going back. Where he belonged.

Though the manner in which he was returning was not familiar.

On this voyage, Kirk was a passenger. Teilani had still not shared with him any details of the trip ahead of them. Because she was still finalizing them, she had told him.

Kirk turned in his seat to look at Teilani. "Is your ship as impressive as your yacht?"

She nodded. "Even more, I'm told." She smiled playfully.

Kirk was coming to know her well enough that he recognized her expression. She was deliberately withholding information, making him work to obtain it. Making the conversation a game.

He liked that in her. He remembered doing the same when he was her age—*No!* he warned himself. *Don't start thinking like that.* Once a person was an adult, age should no longer matter.

But the inner voice in his head—perhaps Spock's, perhaps McCoy's—told him he was wrong.

Again, he ignored it.

He saw Teilani watching him carefully, as if she could recognize *his* feelings through *his* expressions. He winked at her, then settled back into his seat, eyes front.

Esys handled the controls smoothly.

The stars were crisp and unwavering.

Kirk was back in space.

With satisfaction, he watched the western seaboard of North America recede on a flight-console viewscreen. He had assumed they were headed for a low orbit to rendezvous with Teilani's ship. But they were still climbing.

Kirk spoke over his shoulder. "Is your ship in free orbit, or docked?"

"Docked," Teilani said.

Kirk patiently folded his hands together. He tried to concentrate on not thinking about how *he* would fly the yacht if he were at the controls. Chal was several weeks away at maximum warp. No doubt Teilani's ship had required servicing for the voyage ahead.

But judging from their continued ascent, Esys was taking them past the orbital plane of most commercial spacedocks.

"Are we going to the Moon?" Kirk asked. There were still shipyards there, though most specialized in manufacturing with lunar materials, rather than providing service and repairs.

He heard Teilani's amusement in her cryptic answer. "No." Whatever was going on, she was enjoying herself.

"Coming up on terminator," Esys announced.

The stars shifted past the viewport as the yacht's orientation changed.

Kirk saw the curve of the Earth below them, a dark hemisphere wrapped in the glowing strands of transport ways. At major hubs and intersections, vaguely defining the shape of the continents they served, cities clumped like sparkling dew on a spider's web.

Above it all, the impossibly thin arc of Earth's atmosphere began to stand out in a pale blue glow. The yacht hurtled toward dawn at thousands of kilometers per hour.

"On docking approach," Esys said. His eyes darted from his controls to the viewport and back again.

Kirk stared dead ahead, but saw nothing.

At this speed, he didn't expect to. That's what sensors were for.

The curve of the atmosphere brightened. Kirk squinted at the hotspot that announced where the sun would appear.

Then the Earth's thin layer of air flashed red, flared blue-white, and the sun was before them.

In the sudden wash of that brilliant dawn, Kirk saw at last his destination.

He gasped. Teilani had struck again.

Kirk *was* back where he belonged.

Teilani's ship was the *Enterprise.*

EIGHTEEN

The mighty starship still bore the damage of her final battle over Khitomer. Angry scorches marred her saucer and her engineering hull. A double hull breach yawned wide on the saucer where General Chang's final photon torpedo had punched through her.

Apart from her battle damage, empty gaps were apparent in

her main sensor array, where industrious Starfleet engineers had reclaimed state-of-the-art equipment not permitted on the civilian market.

Her name was gone, too. Blasted from her hull by particle etching beams, along with her registration numbers and Starfleet colors.

But there was no disguising her identity from Kirk.

In his eyes, she was beautiful still.

Gleaming white in the orbital dawn.

A steed of incomparable heart, rising nobly on a mountaintop, eager to renew the pursuit.

"How . . . ?" Kirk began to ask. But his throat, his chest, his *heart* were so full of emotion, he could say nothing more.

Teilani left her seat and knelt by Kirk's. "My planet negotiated for her, James."

"But . . . she was going to be used in wargames." *A blaze of glory,* Drake had told him.

"A goodwill gesture on the Federation's part. She's to become the first ship in Chal's planetary defense group." Teilani lightly kissed Kirk's cheek as he marveled at the vision she had arranged for him.

But Kirk barely felt Teilani's caress as Esys guided the yacht around the *Enterprise.* Lights burned in some of her decks, though her running lights and sensor array were dark.

"Of course," Teilani continued, "she's not quite the ship you remember. The closest things to weapons she has are navigational deflectors and tractor beams. Sensor capability has been downgraded by fifty percent. The Fleet communications system has been replaced with a civilian model."

What did any of that matter? It was the *Enterprise.*

"But I thought you could live with those changes," Teilani said.

Kirk still had a hard time grasping the reality of what had happened. "You *own* her now?" He turned to her. He had to know.

"She's *yours,* now, James. Free and clear. A gift from my world. To you."

"I . . . don't know what to say."

"It's not what you say—it's what you'll do."

At that moment, Kirk feared he would do anything.

Esys guided the yacht toward the hangar bay.

The *Enterprise* called out to Kirk.

Beyond the clouds. Among the stars.

One last time.

And Kirk, at last, could answer that call.

The turbolift doors parted and Kirk stepped onto the bridge of the *Enterprise* for the first time in months. It was an action he had never expected to take again.

He sensed Teilani and Esys remain behind in the lift, giving him this moment.

Kirk paused on the upper deck, immersing himself in the sensations of his return. The artificial gravity felt right. The air smelled a bit too much like chemical cleansers, but the temperature was set precisely where he preferred it. As if his personal preference file had not been deleted from the ship's computer.

Overall, though, Teilani was right. The *Enterprise* was different.

Most noticeably, her warp generators were offline. He missed the almost subliminal hum of them, vibrating through every rigid part of the ship's superstructure.

The bridge environment was quieter, too. Without the background chatter of department heads and more than four hundred crew working together. Replaced instead by the slow flickering of the status lights on her new, automated control stations.

Uhura's communications board was just an empty hole in the back wall. Her chair remained, but the extensive nerve center of the *Enterprise*'s comm system, linking her with

Starfleet and from there the universe, had been replaced with a few gray boxes of ordinary switches and automated controls.

Similar holes existed in the tactical console, where weapons panels had been removed.

The *Enterprise* had a makeshift, unfinished feel to her.

But Kirk had seen her and her namesake in worse condition. Given the choice—and Kirk always made certain he *was* given the choice—he preferred to think of his starship now as half-built, not half-disassembled.

The greatest change of all, though, was not in the hardware of the vessel. It was in the crew.

They were all Teilani's people.

Young Klingon-Romulans in such robust and dynamic health that Kirk felt another year older for each one he saw.

They took up most of the control positions on the bridge. Impossibly young, unlined faces working efficiently, with total concentration. By now, their ridged Klingon brows almost appeared to Kirk to be a natural match for their sharply angled Romulan ears.

There wasn't a Starfleet uniform in sight, either. They wore a series of variations on what Kirk took to be the clothes of their world—loose-fitting white trousers and tops, some with sleeves, some without, some with splashes of color, some unadorned. Yet the simplicity of the designs did nothing to hide the perfect muscles that sculpted their lithe, lean forms.

The young Chal crew nodded respectfully to Kirk as he went to the center of the bridge. His chair, at least, hadn't been changed or removed. He was glad. It always took too long to get used to a new one.

He sat in it. Put his hands on either arm.

It felt good to be back.

But not right.

He glanced to his right.

Spock's science station was dark.

He idly tapped his finger above the control that would send

his voice to McCoy's sickbay. But he doubted anyone was there to answer.

Except ghosts.

Kirk sighed. Teilani came down to the lower deck to stand by him. He saw concern in her eyes. Esys took the navigator's chair at the helm console.

"Is something wrong?" Teilani asked.

But before Kirk could answer, something changed.

He held up his finger, asking Teilani to stay quiet.

He leaned forward, ears straining.

But it wasn't a sound. It was a vibration.

The matter-antimatter reactor had just started up. The warp engines were online again. As smooth as they had ever been.

The heart of the *Enterprise* had been restored.

Kirk smiled.

Some of his new young crew smiled back, though it was clear they weren't sure what had prompted his reaction.

Kirk studied his crew again.

The oldest Chal he had seen was no more than twenty-five standard years. But a matter-antimatter reactor like the one that powered the *Enterprise* was a hellishly complex device that could take at least that long to master.

How could these *children* have brought this ship back to life? Unless . . . ?

Without looking, Kirk touched the control that opened a line to the engine room.

"Kirk to Engineering."

"Scott, here, Captain."

To Kirk, it was as right to hear the warm Scottish lilt in that greeting as it was to be on the bridge again. And he wasn't surprised to hear it, either. Perhaps because the *Enterprise* and her engineer shared a bond as strong as his own with his ship.

"Mr. Scott, I thought you had retired."

"Aye. So did I."

Kirk grinned. He had long ago learned that Scotty was only happy when he had something to complain about. "Then I trust Starfleet came up with a suitable reward for duty above and beyond."

"Starfleet has nothin' t' do with me being here, Captain."

That *was* surprising.

"'Twas the lass. Teilani. Starfleet put her in touch with me, and she told me what it was she was planning to do with the *Enterprise.* I figured if the time wasn't quite right for the old girl t' retire, then it wasn't quite right for me, either."

Kirk wasn't going to argue with him. When was it ever right to give up doing what you lived to do?

"You've done a magnificent job with her, Scotty."

"Och, if ye could see the shambles the reclamation team left this engine room in, you'd call it a bloody miracle."

"When you're involved, Mr. Scott, I always do. Glad to have you aboard."

Kirk was about to sign off, but Scott wasn't finished.

"Captain, just so you know . . . th' *Enterprise,* sir . . . well, she's . . ."

Kirk knew what Scott was trying to say. The signs were everywhere. "I know. She's been through a lot."

"That's puttin' it mildly, sir." It was Scotty's turn to sigh. "She was never repaired properly after that last go-round with Chang. And the best parts of her, well, Starfleet's taken those back. Left her in a kind of depleted condition, if ye know what I mean."

Kirk knew. "The question is, will she get us to Chal, Mr. Scott?"

"Aye, I'll see to that. But afterward . . . I don't know if she'll be up to much in th' way of planetary defense. Without a complete overhaul, I mean."

"And that's not very likely, is it, Mr. Scott?"

The chief engineer sounded as if he were speaking about the death of a dear friend. "This is an old design, sir. I'd never say it to an admiral's face, but there was good reason for scheduling her to be decommissioned."

"Your secret's safe with me, Mr. Scott."

Scott chuckled. "Aye. We oldsters have to stick t'gether, don't we?"

Kirk winced.

"Warp power is online and ready when ye need it, Captain."

"Thank you, Mr. Scott," Kirk said. "I think."

"Scott out."

Kirk caught Teilani's sly grin. But before he could say anything, she took his hand, kissed it.

"On Chal, none of that will matter anymore. Young, old . . . everyone will be the same."

"Did you tell Scotty what to expect there?"

Teilani shook her head. "He'll find out when we arrive."

"Will he be able to stay?"

"If he wants to."

It struck Kirk that what Teilani said was odd. Who wouldn't want to stay on a planet where there was no aging, and no death?

Unless there was something else she hadn't told him. If there was some price to be paid for what Chal offered.

But he didn't care. There was a price to be paid for everything, and for Teilani's love, no price was too high.

"Are we expecting any more passengers or supplies?" Kirk asked.

Teilani shook her head. "You may give the word anytime, James."

Kirk faced forward. The Earth filled the viewscreen, clouds white, oceans sparkling.

A place he no longer belonged.

"Mr. Su—" he began, then caught himself. "Mr. *Esys,* lay in a course for Chal. Best possible speed."

Esys adjusted the helm controls. "Course laid in, Mr. Kirk."

Kirk shifted uncomfortably in his chair. He hadn't been called "mister" since he had been an ensign.

"Take us out of orbit," Kirk said. "Ahead, warp factor one."

The *Enterprise* hummed to life around him.

The sensor image of Earth shrank in the viewscreen as he left her at the speed of light.

Once again, Kirk went where he had *always* gone before.

Into the unknown.

Even as the *Enterprise* streaked from Earth and the heart of Sector 001, the *Excelsior* returned.

The sleek starship under Hikaru Sulu's command traveled under a total communications blackout.

Kirk's aging starship, rescued from her inglorious fate as an expendable target, hurtled out of Sol system on a flight path duly registered with the sector's traffic-control computers. As commander of a civilian vessel, Kirk was under no obligation to communicate with Starfleet Command.

Within the faster-than-light infinities of warp space, the *Enterprise* and the *Excelsior* passed each other by tens of thousands of kilometers. Each ship registered as nothing more than a nonthreatening sensor blip on the other's navigational-hazard display.

The encounter lasted less than a ten-thousandth of a second.

Then the *Enterprise* accelerated to warp seven and in a heartbeat left the entire system light-hours behind.

At the same time, the *Excelsior* dropped to sublight velocity and put out a priority call to Starfleet Headquarters.

Now traveling away from each other at millions of kilometers per second, the commanders of both vessels had nonetheless committed themselves to a deadly collision course.

NINETEEN

Chekov found Androvar Drake's sprawling house in San Francisco's old Presidio district vaguely unsettling.

It wasn't a home, he decided. It was a military museum.

Of the worst kind.

Everywhere he looked in Drake's study, there was another reminder of humans' ongoing need to subjugate one another. Antique plasma guns. An entire suit of combat armor belonging to a mid-twenty-first century Fourth World Mercenary, complete with a drug-delivery inhaler mounted on its chest. Battle flags from Colonel Green's genocidal campaigns. A set of slowguns from some long-forgotten colonial uprising, ingeniously designed to fire projectiles that would kill people without puncturing environmental domes.

Worst of all, each weapon, each emblem, each uniform, was reverently displayed in elegant cabinets or mounted in spotlit frames on the wood-paneled walls. As if each were a work of art.

Androvar Drake was a product of the past, Chekov decided. Unfortunately, he was now one of the most powerful individuals of the present.

It was not a reassuring juxtaposition.

Then Chekov was startled from his reverie by Admiral Drake himself. "You don't approve of my collection, do you, Commander?"

Unlike his collection, Drake seemed surprisingly warm and welcoming. He had greeted Chekov, Sulu, and Uhura as if they were intimate friends. Prepared tea for them himself. Ushered them from his private transporter pad into his study only after taking them aside for a few moments to admire the spectacular view over the Bay.

"Your 'collection' does seem to concentrate on some of the worst moments of history," Chekov said.

Drake nodded, unperturbed. "Precisely its purpose." He got up from behind his massive mahogany desk and opened a display cabinet near a freestanding bookcase filled with real books. He withdrew a small booklet containing several plastic tickets, and handed it to Chekov.

Chekov read the fine print on the tickets. "A ration book?" he asked.

"From Tarsus IV," Drake confirmed. "Half the colony. Four thousand colonists. Massacred. Because the food supply was destroyed. And Starfleet couldn't provide support in time." He gestured to encompass the room. "Everything here. A reminder of those dark times that have tried human souls and dignity. Since the era of interstellar exploration began."

Chekov studied Drake. The admiral's pale eyes were intense. But Chekov saw no sign of compassion in his words.

"Everything here. A reminder that we must not let any of it happen again. That in my new position, *I* must not let any of it happen again."

Chekov handed back the ration booklet. Of course Drake was good. He had to be. He had convinced the Council to put him in total command of Starfleet.

But he didn't fool Chekov.

Chekov was certain Drake didn't keep that ration book from Tarsus IV as a reminder of Starfleet's obligation to provide for endangered colonies.

James Kirk had been at Tarsus IV. As a young teenager.

Kirk had seen the four thousand colonists massacred before his eyes.

Their deaths haunted the captain to this day. He had told Chekov so.

Chekov was convinced Drake kept that ration book because it was a reminder of something that had hurt Kirk long ago.

"A very admirable goal," Uhura said.

She exchanged a look with Chekov. She wasn't convinced by Drake's act, either.

But Sulu avoided looking at Chekov. Publicly, he was maintaining a more neutral demeanor, as befitting his rank. But this past week on the *Excelsior,* he and Chekov had barely spoken. That suited Chekov.

"Then you understand why we requested this urgent meeting with you," Sulu said, attempting to get Drake back on topic.

"Absolutely," Drake confirmed. "A rogue agent presents an unacceptable risk to Starfleet's integrity. The mere possibility of a Klingon superweapon going on the open market could destabilize a dozen nonaligned systems. To say nothing of what it might do to the ongoing peace process between the Federation and the Empire."

Drake placed the ration book back in its case, then returned to his desk.

Chekov, Uhura, and Sulu sat across from him, each in a separate chair. Drake appeared to be thinking something over. No one disturbed him.

"You all have exemplary records," he said at last.

No one responded. Chekov could sense a big "but" coming. It was clear that Drake was leading up to something.

"Commander Chekov, Commander Uhura, Starfleet recognizes and especially appreciates your valor and self-sacrifice in undertaking a potentially deadly covert assignment to stop the flow of Klingon armaments to the illegal market. Captain Sulu, your exploits on the *Excelsior* are carving a place in history alongside Jim Kirk's himself."

Chekov shot another glance at Uhura. He could see that she also felt Drake was piling it on thick enough to choke a Gorn.

"Which is why I have decided to bring you all on board another, ultrasecret operation, already under way."

Chekov was shocked. Knowing what he did about Drake, he had been expecting Drake to thank them and say good-bye, sweeping their concerns about Jade and the Klingon superweapon into a black hole.

"What kind of operation, sir?" Sulu asked.

Drake's friendly attitude disappeared. He became distant and formal. He pressed a control on the computer screen beside him. Chekov saw a red light on the screen start to blink.

"I am now recording this conversation," Drake announced. "Everything I am about to tell you is classified at the highest level. If you cause to be made known anything of what you learn here today, to any party other than those directly connected to the operation, you will be subject to indefinite solitary confinement in a Starfleet detention center. Before you leave this meeting, you will be required to sign a formal security oath agreeing to these conditions." Drake looked each of them in the eye, beginning with Chekov. "Is that clear? Please reply audibly."

One by one, Chekov, Sulu, and Uhura stated that they understood and agreed to the conditions Drake had set out.

Chekov felt uneasy, not knowing what would follow. He knew Uhura well enough to sense the same reticence in her.

But there was no way to be certain what Sulu thought of this escalation of the meeting.

Drake held his finger over another desk control. "I am now going to ask two other officers to join us. They are also involved in this operation." He pressed the control. "Gentlemen, if you would be so kind."

A side door in the study opened inward.

"Come in," Drake said. A small enigmatic smile flashed across his face for an instant. "I believe you all know each other."

Chekov, Uhura, and Sulu instantly stood.

The two other officers were Spock and McCoy.

At any other time, an impromptu party might have begun as the former *Enterprise* crewmates unexpectedly met again.

But the surreal surroundings and Drake's presence precluded anything like that from even beginning.

The admiral directed Spock and McCoy to take their seats, then began his briefing.

"Bottom line: Admiral Cartwright and his co-conspirators appear to have been the tip of the proverbial iceberg. I regret to inform you that the entire Starfleet command structure might be compromised by a cabal of senior officers. Traitors who will stop at nothing to prevent the Federation from achieving a secure peace agreement with the Klingon Empire."

Chekov was shocked.

But Sulu asked the first and most obvious question. "Does the Council know that?"

Drake didn't appreciate the interruption. "That's why *I* was selected commander in chief, Captain Sulu. Certainly there were other candidates more qualified in areas of diplomacy and exploration. But my background in security was considered essential to what the Fleet needs most under present conditions."

"And because you're drawing us in," Uhura added, "you must think that this rogue agent, Jade, is somehow connected to the renegade command officers."

Spock nodded his head at Uhura. "A logical inference, Commander. And a correct one."

Sulu turned to Spock. "You already know what happened at Dark Range Platform?"

Again Spock nodded. "Admiral Drake shared your report with us just prior to this meeting."

Drake waved an imperious hand to silence them, determined not to allow any further interruptions or exchanges he did not invite.

"Because of the checks and balances in Starfleet Intelligence, it is almost impossible for an agent to go rogue," Drake explained, *"without* some type of support from within Starfleet itself."

"Admiral, I don't understand," Sulu said. "Doesn't a rogue agent, by definition, have to be acting alone?"

But Drake shook his head. "Every computer record pertaining to the agent code-named Jade has been selectively deleted from Starfleet's databanks. We have no identification picture, no fingerprints, no DNA structure. We will be able to reconstruct a great deal of it. But the process will take weeks. That all points to an inside accomplice."

"Sir, are you seriously postulating a connection between a rogue agent, a Klingon superweapon, and a conspiracy within Starfleet?" Sulu asked.

Spock calmly steepled his fingers. "Consider this, Captain Sulu. Fortunately, the diplomats and negotiators for both the Federation and the Klingon Empire are aware of the strong, antireconciliation sentiments within their own camps. They understand that random acts of terrorism undertaken by a handful of detractors do not mean each government is not committed to peace."

Chekov felt himself begin to relax. It was almost soothing to hear Spock lay out a rational explanation for something that had so confused and upset him. He noticed that Drake also seemed pleased by Spock's analysis, because the admiral let Spock continue.

"Consider, however," Spock continued, "what might happen if a Klingon 'doomsday' weapon were used. Not just to destroy a ship or a colony, but to lay waste a planet. Perhaps Earth or Vulcan itself. Consider also the ramifications of an investigation into the use of the weapon. An investigation which finds no evidence of any Klingon conspiracy to employ it."

Sulu understood what Spock's logic had described. "Because the weapon would have been used by a group within Starfleet."

"Precisely," Spock confirmed. "If an official investigation cannot show any evidence of a Klingon conspiracy, then the public conclusion must be that the investigation was conducted in bad faith. That would logically lead to the further conclusion that the weapon was therefore used *with* the support of the Klingon government."

"Damned if you do, damned if you don't," Uhura added. "If the official investigation does find evidence of a *Starfleet* conspiracy to use the weapon, then the public conclusion will be that it was a Klingon plot to shift blame from the Empire."

Spock proceeded to forge the remaining links in the chain of logic. "In the confusion that would follow, the individual worlds of the Federation would have to choose sides. No doubt, some would withdraw. Treaties would be abrogated. Trade agreements canceled. The Council would be in chaos."

McCoy shook his head at Spock. "It's a wonder you can ever sleep at night."

Drake wrapped up the analysis with the ultimate conclusion. "And under those conditions, the Federation would be vulnerable to Klingon attack."

"But surely the Klingons have no motive to attack us anymore," Sulu said.

Drake fixed him with a stern gaze. "The Empire has no motive to attack a *strong* and *secure* Federation. But if they see us begin to fall apart? If they think we would use an attack on the Klingon Empire as a way to reunite our members. Then the Empire will have no choice but to strike first."

"And," Spock added, "knowing that is the likely Klingon action, the conspirators still within Starfleet could convincingly argue that the Federation should therefore launch a preemptive strike."

"Good Lord," Dr. McCoy moaned. "It's World War III all over again. Everyone trying to second guess everyone else."

"Which is why Starfleet needs all of you to help stop that Klingon weapon from falling into the wrong hands," Drake concluded.

Chekov started to ask if anyone had any idea what the weapon code-named Children of Heaven might be. But he stopped. He looked at McCoy and Spock.

He had been so surprised to see them, and so pleased, that he hadn't stopped to wonder *why* they were part of this meeting.

"Excuse me, Keptin Spock, I know vhy the rest of us are here. But vhy are you and Dr. McCoy part of this operation?"

McCoy and Spock looked to Drake.

Drake looked uncomfortable. "This is an extremely difficult situation for me," he said.

"For all of us," McCoy snapped.

Drake continued. "I have been conducting an internal investigation. A very discreet one. Attempting to ascertain the sympathies of various Starfleet officers in sensitive positions. Looking for at least one individual who is unquestionably connected to the conspiracy within Starfleet to start a war with the Klingon Empire."

"And have you found someone?" Uhura asked.

Drake nodded gravely. "I have."

Chekov couldn't stand the suspense.

"Vell, who is it?"

Drake's answer struck Chekov like lightning.

"James T. Kirk," the admiral said.

TWENTY

Chekov was outraged and didn't bother to hide it. "That is *impossible!*"

Drake raised his voice without shouting. His words echoed off the hard-paneled walls of the study. "Don't you think that's what *I* said?"

Silence reigned.

"But then," Drake said in a lowered voice, "I saw proof."

"Pah," Chekov spat. "Vhat proof?"

Slowly, almost reluctantly, Spock stood up.

Drake pressed a control and a section of wall slid away to reveal a display screen. There was a picture on it of a beautiful young Klingon woman in a black jumpsuit. Or *was* she Klingon?

"The young woman's name," Spock said, "is Teilani. She is a hybrid—her parents were Klingon and Romulan."

The picture changed. The young woman was now in a formal gown, her dark hair swept up to reveal her pointed ears. There was a large party of some sort going on behind her. Chekov concluded these were surveillance images, likely taken without the young woman's knowledge.

"As far as Starfleet Intelligence can ascertain, despite her relatively young age, she is a high-ranking official in her planetary government."

"What planet?" Uhura asked.

"A colony world somewhere on the frontier between the Klingon and Romulan empires," Spock said. "Jointly settled by both empires approximately forty years ago, during one of their sporadic periods of truce. The planet's name is Chal." Spock gave Uhura a significant look. "A Klingon term for 'heaven.' "

"The Children of Heaven," Uhura murmured.

Spock continued. "Given what we know about the Crimson Level of the Imperial Forecasters, it is logical to conclude that some of their more extreme weapons were developed on planets far removed from Klingon centers of population. In the event something went wrong."

McCoy muttered in disgust. "Same as testing fusion bombs on Pacific islands in the twentieth century."

"Precisely, Doctor. All evidence to date suggests the joint Romulan-Klingon colony on Chal was the center for the development, construction, and storage of a weapon. The weapon was code-named Children of Heaven. It was intended to be used only in the event of the total defeat of the Klingon Empire."

"But vhat does *any* of this have to do with Keptin Kirk?" Chekov demanded.

The picture changed again.

Kirk and Teilani.

Both in civilian clothes.

Locked in each other's arms. Kissing.

The background of the picture showed more civilians, some carrying luggage. Chekov guessed it had been taken at a travelport somewhere on Earth.

"Three days ago, Jim Kirk resigned from Starfleet," Drake said. "He didn't talk to anyone. He didn't deliver his resignation in person. He simply logged his resignation request onto his personnel file, and left."

Chekov found that difficult to believe. He knew the captain had been scheduled to retire after returning from Khitomer. But Kirk had since taken on so many committee appointments and teaching assignments that Chekov had decided he'd have to stay in the Fleet forever, just to complete them.

"Left?" Sulu asked. "For where?"

"Presumably, Chal," Spock answered. "Twenty hours ago."

Uhura stood up. "I, for one, don't like where this is going."

"Where *do* you see it going, Commander?" Drake asked.

"You're making the captain out to be one of your conspirators. And that's ridiculous. Captain Kirk might have played hard and fast with the rules in his day, but I refuse to believe he's a traitor."

"So do I," Chekov added. He stood to join Uhura.

"As do I," Sulu agreed. He rose to his feet to stand with Uhura and Chekov.

But Drake told them to sit down again. That there was no need for confrontation. "You'll get no argument from me. Jim Kirk is one of the most dedicated officers ever to wear a Starfleet uniform. But the point is, he's not wearing that uniform anymore."

Sulu reacted with exasperation. "A man like the captain does not change his beliefs overnight."

Chekov was gratified by Sulu's support of Kirk. He was also surprised that he was willing to argue with his commander in chief.

"Usually, no," Drake agreed. "But look at that picture, Captain. Jim is sixty-two years old. That woman is what, *maybe* twenty?"

"They are both adults," Chekov said stiffly.

Drake looked at him with a pitying expression. "I'm not going to pretend that Jim and I are close friends. But listen to what Captain Spock has to say."

Spock folded his hands behind his back. "The captain's behavior in the week leading up to his resignation was emotionally erratic."

Uhura batted her eyes at Spock. "Maybe he's in love, Mr. Spock."

"He believes he is," Spock stated.

Sulu shrugged. "For the captain, that could explain a great deal."

"But not treason," Chekov said firmly.

"She is a very attractive young woman," Drake pointed out. "And I regret to say that there sometimes comes a point in a man's life when he begins to wonder if he is still attractive to others. If he still has what it takes to—"

"I am not prepared to believe that Keptin Kirk vould throw avay everything he believed in because of . . . some pretty face!" Chekov interrupted.

"Teilani is only part of the bargain," Drake said.

"Bargain?" Uhura repeated.

"Kirk's new job is coordinator of Chal's planetary defenses. His payment is a unique one. In fact, the only inducement his psych profile suggests might cause him to abandon his most deeply held convictions."

"Believe me," Chekov scoffed, "there is nothing that Keptin Kirk vould vant that badly."

Spock cleared his throat. "Teilani's government has given the captain the *Enterprise.*"

Chekov's jaw dropped open. "Is that . . . possible?"

"She'd been decommissioned," Drake explained. "She was slated to be a target in some field trials we're running. Then one of the resource-management departments received an inquiry about converting her to civilian use. Starfleet has a long-standing commitment to recycling and reusing obsolete equipment for the benefit of colony worlds, so Chal's request was in order."

"That ship was part of him," Uhura said quietly.

Chekov felt as if Drake had somehow engineered all this. He hated the look of false disappointment on the admiral's face. Disappointment in James Kirk.

"I trust you all agree that the gift of it to Kirk does put a different light on his actions," Drake said. He looked directly at Chekov. "Believe *me,* Commander, I'm not for a moment suggesting that Jim has been a willing member of any conspiracy in Starfleet—if such a conspiracy really does exist.

But what I'm afraid the evidence does suggest is that he might be being *used* by the conspirators."

Drake settled back in his chair. "At least you must admit the possibility that Jim might not be questioning this young woman's motives too closely. His career was essentially over. What did he have to look forward to? Suddenly a beautiful young woman comes into his life, gives him a purpose, and hands over the one thing that means more to him than anything else—his ship." Drake looked sternly at Chekov. "Whatever else Jim Kirk has been in his day, he's still human. That means he can make mistakes."

Chekov didn't know what to say.

What Drake said seemed plausible—for anyone except James Kirk.

But Spock was part of this. And McCoy.

Could the captain, in the end, simply be someone who finally made a wrong choice, blinded by the desire to have one last adventure in life?

Could Kirk really be that *ordinary?*

"Admiral, what *are* Teilani's motives?" Sulu asked.

Drake looked at Spock. Spock answered once again.

"It is the admiral's belief that Captain Kirk is being deliberately manipulated as a pawn. Someone is using him in an attempt to turn the *Enterprise* into a delivery system for the Children of Heaven weapon. What that weapon is, where it is intended to be used . . . these are questions which Starfleet has yet to answer."

But Chekov knew Spock well enough to read between the lines of what he said.

"Captain Spock, vhat are *your* beliefs?"

Spock gave Chekov a look of total disinterest. "I am puzzled that you ask that question, Commander Chekov. Surely you know that under these speculative conditions, personal beliefs are not logical."

Chekov was in no mood to take that kind of evasion from

Spock. He was surprised that Spock would even attempt to so deflect him. But before he could press his questioning, he saw something in Spock's eye . . . just what, he couldn't define.

But they had served together for almost thirty years.

Spock was sending him some kind of message, some kind of—

The realization of what was happening in this room suddenly burst through Chekov like a nova.

Spock was lying.

Chekov turned away from Spock and faced Drake. The dynamics of this meeting were suddenly much clearer.

Spock didn't trust Starfleet's new commander in chief either.

McCoy was being unnaturally quiet, so Chekov had to assume that he was in unspoken agreement with Spock as well.

But Drake didn't appear to recognize Spock's distrust of him. Which wasn't surprising. People who didn't know Vulcans well tended to take them at face value. They even believed the old story that Vulcans never lied.

But Chekov had learned that Vulcans were extremely adaptable. Given the right motive, a *logical* motive which did not involve personal gain, few Vulcans would have any reservations about exaggerating or withholding information.

And Chekov had absolute faith in Spock's motives, whatever they might be.

"So," Chekov said, playing Spock's game, "does Starfleet consider Keptin Kirk to be a security risk?"

"I hesitate to characterize the situation in that manner," Drake said disarmingly. As if he were trying to protect Kirk's good name.

Chekov caught Uhura's eye. He saw the doubt she hid there. She had sensed what Spock was doing as well.

Only Sulu remained an enigma. Chekov still had not forgiven his friend for delaying Chekov's and Uhura's rescue from Dark Range Platform. Unquestionably, each Starfleet officer had a duty to follow orders. But on the frontier, days and weeks away from command, Starfleet officers also had a duty to adapt to emerging situations. Sulu's refusal to do anything at Dark Range except follow the letter of his orders unsettled Chekov. He no longer had any idea what Sulu was thinking.

"How *vould* you characterize it, Admiral?" Chekov asked.

Drake looked at the ceiling as if the right words might be written there. "A *potential* security threat." He adopted a rueful expression, as if he were saddened that Kirk's career had come to this. "I know as well as you that Jim would never willfully do anything harmful to Starfleet or the Federation. But the evidence being what it is, we can't rule out any inadvertent action on his part. Just think of the Starfleet secrets he's had access to in his career."

"If he represents such a 'potential' threat," Chekov said bitterly, "then vhy the hell did Starfleet allow him to get the *Enterprise* in the first place?"

Drake looked at Sulu. "That's where you come in, Captain. You people served with Kirk. No one knows him better."

Sulu didn't understand. Neither did Chekov.

Drake spoke as if making a confession. "We don't know where Chal is."

"But Spock told us," Uhura said. "In the Klingon-Romulan frontier."

"Which comprises more than thirty-three hundred stars," Drake said. "Remember: Chal was a product of the Klingons' Crimson Level. Starfleet Intelligence has never come across any reference to it in any computer records it's obtained from Klingon or Romulan sources."

"So Starfleet has made Captain Kirk a pawn as well," Sulu reasoned. "And you want the *Excelsior* to track the *Enterprise* in order to locate Chal."

Drake nodded. "And then return with the Children of Heaven. Whatever it is."

"What about Captain Kirk?" Sulu asked.

"Oh, I want him back, too," Drake said. "Preferably alive."

For the first time in the meeting, Chekov was heartened to see Sulu show an emotional response. "Are you saying Captain Kirk is *expendable?*"

Drake remained seated, his tone, calm. Though the sudden chill in his voice was menacing. "Are *you* suggesting one man is more important than the safety and security of the Federation? If you can't handle your assignment, *Captain,* tell me now so I can put someone else in command of the *Excelsior.*"

Chekov wondered if Sulu still had the fire to question authority. If the drive and desire for seeking the truth of the matter, which had fueled his promotion to starship captain, had survived the burden of command.

But Spock defused any potential confrontation.

"You must excuse Captain Sulu, Admiral. Dr. McCoy and I have had ample opportunity to digest the current state of affairs. But it is still a considerable shock to those who are new to the operation."

Drake's attitude softened. Slightly. "What do you say to that, Captain?"

Sulu took a breath. Stood at attention. "Captain Spock is correct, sir. I apologize. Of course I will follow my orders, track the *Enterprise,* and return to Earth with the Children of Heaven *and* Captain Kirk."

Chekov was disappointed but not surprised by Sulu's ready capitulation.

Drake leaned back in his chair. "Very good. When can you be ready to leave?"

"Four hours."

"Make it two."

"Yes, sir."

Then Drake surveyed the others. "No doubt you will have other technical questions. But before you ask them, Captain Spock will provide you with background files on what we know about Teilani, Chal, and the Imperial Forecasters. *After* you sign your security oaths." Drake held a finger over the record control on his computer screen.

One by one, he looked at everyone else.

No one had anything more to say.

"I believe we're finished for now. Thank you, one and all. And Godspeed." He stopped recording. The side door swung open again. Spock led the way through it.

Chekov was the last to leave. At the doorway, he looked over his shoulder.

Drake was looking at him as if he had expected Chekov to turn around. He waved farewell as if they were friends.

He's good, Chekov thought as he walked through the door and heard it swing shut behind him. But the captain's better.

Then the door clicked and Chekov heard the faint buzz of a security screen.

Drake had locked his study and sealed it with a forcefield.

Chekov stared at the door.

He wondered what secrets Drake was hiding behind it, and from whom.

TWENTY-ONE

The *Excelsior* was Sulu's ship, but at this moment everyone looked to Spock.

He, Chekov, Sulu, Uhura, and McCoy had gathered in a briefing room as soon as they had beamed aboard the starship from Drake's home.

By unspoken agreement, no one had discussed their meeting with Drake. Until they could be sure they were in secure surroundings.

But as soon as the briefing-room doors slid shut, Spock began speaking. He was framed against the room's large display screen. A color schematic of the *Excelsior* filled it.

"As I see it," he said without preamble, "we are faced with three possibilities."

Everyone settled back into his and her high-backed conference chair. They had all come to trust Spock's logic over the years.

"First, it may be that events are exactly as Admiral Drake has described them to us. Captain Kirk, for personal reasons, has become an unwitting pawn in an attempt to discover the secret of a powerful Klingon doomsday weapon. The organizers of this attempt are members of a conspiracy within Starfleet to stop the peace process between the Federation and the Klingon Empire, and one member of that conspiracy is the Starfleet Intelligence agent code-named Jade. When Jade discovered information pertaining to the Children of Heaven, Captain Kirk was put into motion as someone who could act on that information to locate the weapon, without realizing his role."

"But put into motion by whom?" Sulu asked.

"In the first scenario, by the alleged conspirators within Starfleet." Spock explained. "However, the second possibility is that Teilani's people themselves may be responsible for involving the captain. When they learned that Starfleet Intelligence had uncovered the location of the *Chalchaj 'qmey,* they may have decided to seek the help of a protector. Captain Kirk and the *Enterprise* make a most formidable first line of defense."

"And the third possibility?" Uhura asked.

"That nothing Admiral Drake said to us is correct."

"Are you saying the commander in chief of Starfleet lied to us?" McCoy asked. He was the only one at the table who did not appear to be reassured by Spock's analysis.

"That cannot be discounted," Spock admitted. "Which is why I did not offer any of these theories to Admiral Drake in our meeting with him. However, it may simply be that the admiral himself is not aware of the true state of affairs, and passed on incorrect information without intent to mislead us."

McCoy wasn't happy with that answer, either. "But, if what Drake told us is a lie, Spock, what's the truth?"

Spock thought a moment before replying. "I believe the truth is known only to one person involved in these events. Captain Kirk."

"Is that what your damned logic dictates?" McCoy asked.

"Where the captain is concerned, logic seldom applies. However, based on our past experience with him, it seems reasonable that he is in some way driving these events, and not merely an observer of them."

"Captain Spock," Sulu said, "in light of these three possibilities, can you suggest what our course of action should be?" No matter what was discussed in this gathering, on this ship the command decisions were Sulu's to make.

"You should, of course, follow orders," Spock answered. "I am not altogether comfortable with having to question the motives of Starfleet's commander in chief. Making contact with Captain Kirk is likely to help us discover the true state of affairs."

Chekov had reached his breaking point. Despite his promise to Kirk, he had to confide in someone. Who better than those in this room?

"Excuse me, Captain Spock," Chekov said, "but I feel it is wery important that we do question Drake's motives. *Especially* since they somehow involve Captain Kirk."

All eyes turned to Chekov.

"Admiral Drake and the captain have had . . . their differences in the past," he began.

"We know that," McCoy said. "Jim and Drake were in the same class at the Academy. Served on the *Farragut* together."

A frown clouded McCoy's face. Everyone who had served under Kirk on the *Enterprise* knew what had happened on the *Farragut.* The *Enterprise* had almost suffered the same fate when the deadly cloud creature had reappeared and threatened her.

"And after that, they ended up in separate postings," Chekov continued. "They became keptins vithin a month of each other. Each vas assigned von of the first twelve Constitution-class starships."

Sulu nodded appreciatively. The competition for those early command positions had been fierce.

"Each vent out on a five-year mission. They returned vithin six months of each other. Both vere immediately promoted to the admiralty."

McCoy looked at Chekov with suspicion. "It sounds as if you've compiled a dossier on Drake."

Chekov folded his hands together on the table, knowing what he was about to set in motion. "I have."

But Sulu reacted with impatience. He didn't appear to be interested in pursuing what Chekov had to say. "Then it couldn't have amounted to anything. The results of any investigation conducted by Starfleet Intelligence would have been turned over to the Council. If you had turned up anything that might indicate Drake wasn't fit to be C in C, he wouldn't have gotten the job."

"I didn't inwestigate Drake for Starfleet Intelligence," Chekov said. "I inwestigated him for Keptin Kirk."

Spock gave Chekov a curious look. "Commander Chekov, are we to understand that you used the facilities of Starfleet Intelligence for a *personal* inquiry?"

Chekov shrugged. "There is no one in this room who has not bent the rules for the keptin."

Uhura laughed. "Bent the rules? Pavel, we've demolished them."

"And ve have been justified each time."

Spock took a chair at the table, giving the floor to Chekov. "Please continue, Commander," he said.

Chekov addressed everyone. "After their return, for two and a half years Drake and Kirk vere posted to Headquarters. Kirk vas chief of operations. Drake became a deputy chief in Security Services."

McCoy tried to speed along the account. "And after the V'Ger incident, Jim took command of the *Enterprise* again and gave up his career path at headquarters. This is ancient history."

Chekov waved a hand for emphasis. "But Admiral Drake did *not* give up his career path. And, as of ten years ago, he vas in charge of Starfleet's adwanced strategic technology dewelopment programs. Veapons research."

Spock remained noncommittal. "Ten years ago, we could have gone to war with the Klingons at any moment. Starfleet has always had a military responsibility, and does to this day."

"Von of the projects Drake headed vas code-named Rising Star."

Spock shook his head. The name meant nothing to him. Nor to anyone else in the briefing room.

"It vas a feasibility study for deweloping veapons using protomatter."

That meant something to everyone.

Protomatter was one of the most volatile forms of matter known to exist. So hazardous that most ethical scientists had long ago denounced its use in any type of research.

But protomatter *had* been used in at least one notable scientific project in recent memory. And had yielded predictably tragic results.

"Genesis?" McCoy asked.

Chekov nodded. Project Genesis had been an ambitious research program to develop a process by which uninhabitable planets could become life-bearing. It had been directed by

Dr. Carol Marcus, aided by her son—and Kirk's—David Marcus.

Though the initial results had been promising, the process had been abandoned when it was discovered that the only reason Genesis worked was because David Marcus had used protomatter in the initializing matrix. All products of the reaction were thereby rendered dangerously unstable.

Spock seemed concerned by the implications of Chekov's revelation. "I find it most difficult to accept that the Genesis Project was a secret Starfleet weapons research program from the beginning."

"Genesis had nothing to do with Starfleet," Chekov said. "It *vas* a legitimate scientific inwestigation, completely independent of any military application or influence. Carol Marcus vould not have pursued it under any other conditions. But, after the keptin's son vas murdered by the Klingons, *on* the Genesis Planet, Keptin Kirk became . . . obsessed. He vanted to know everything about the project."

"So he asked you to investigate Carol Marcus?" McCoy asked. His skeptical tone said how unlikely he thought that was.

But Chekov said, "No. Only von Genesis scientist acted outside of the project's strict guidelines. The keptin's son." Chekov stared down at his hands on the tabletop. He remembered how distraught Kirk had been over David's death. "The keptin asked me to find out how David had obtained the protomatter he used in his vork."

Spock made the connection at once. "Admiral Drake."

"The admiral vas sharply critical of Starfleet's decision to abandon protomatter veapons research. Yet, vhen it vas abandoned, his department became responsible for storing the protomatter Starfleet had already manufactured, until means for its safe disposal could be deweloped."

McCoy seemed as if he could barely stay seated. "And you're saying Drake deliberately provided some of that protomatter to David Marcus, knowing it would be incorporated into the Genesis Device?"

"Exactly," Chekov said. His voice trembled with indignation. "Just to see vhat vould happen. Veapons research by proxy."

Spock was the only one at the table who remained calm. "Commander Chekov, you have raised a series of most disturbing allegations. If what you say is true, then Admiral Drake could face a court-martial. Indeed, he *should* be court-martialed. Why didn't you and the captain present your findings to Command?"

Chekov had wrestled with that question for almost a decade. The answer was inadequate, but unavoidable. "Because Drake had spent sixteen years at Starfleet Headquarters. He knew how its bureaucracy vorked better than anyone. There vere no records that could be traced. No direct connection between David and Starfleet at any level. I don't believe the keptin's son ever found out vhat the original source of his protomatter vas."

Uhura sat forward. "Pavel, does Captain Kirk believe Drake is responsible for the death of his son?"

"Not exactly," Chekov said. "He accepts that David vas . . . his father's son. He made his own choices. Even if he didn't have the experience to understand vhat might happen because of them. But the keptin also knows that David might not have been *able* to make the choices he did if Admiral Drake had not been there, tempting him with protomatter to begin vith."

"What did you do with your report?" Spock asked.

"I gave it to the keptin."

"What did he do with it?"

"Vhat could be done? There vas no proof of any misconduct on Admiral Drake's part. Shortly after the Genesis Planet self-destructed, Starfleet disposed of its entire supply of protomatter. Vonce that happened, there vas no vay to determine if any of it had gone missing."

"Didn't *Starfleet* try to find out where David had obtained his protomatter?" McCoy asked.

"Of course," Chekov said. "But because Admiral Drake vas able to produce records showing that all of Starfleet's supply vas accounted for before it vas destroyed, the Genesis Investigation Committee didn't pursue that part of their inwestigation. The official werdict vas that David had obtained protomatter from an unknown source outside the Federation. Possibly the Klingons."

McCoy settled back in his chair, suddenly looking older than his years. "Do you have any idea how serious these charges are?"

"Vhich is vhy I cannot believe the Council woted for Drake."

McCoy sighed, looked across the table at Spock. "So what does this do to your logic?"

"It appears to be an unrelated fact," Spock said.

"How can it be?" Chekov demanded.

"Even if everything you have told us is true, Commander, Drake's involvement in the death of David Marcus could be nothing more than a coincidence. If you had uncovered evidence suggesting that Drake had deliberately provided protomatter to David, *knowing* he was Jim's son, then a causal connection to the current situation might be made."

"What 'causal connection'?" McCoy asked.

"That Admiral Drake specifically manipulated events to propel Jim on his journey to Chal, knowing it would place him in great danger."

"It makes sense to me," Chekov said.

"But it is not logical," Spock countered. "A rivalry stemming from Academy days is hardly motive enough for what you are attempting to accuse the admiral of. Without a motive for the admiral's actions, his possible complicity in supplying protomatter to David and Jim's involvement with the Children of Heaven cannot be linked. We are, I regret to say, back where we started from, with no indication Admiral Drake intends to do the captain harm."

Chekov disagreed. "But Sulu's orders say ve're to enlist the keptin's help in taking possession of the Children of Heawen, vhatever it is. And if the keptin does not cooperate, then ve are to use force."

Sulu glanced at Chekov in annoyance. "I am aware of what my orders entail, Commander."

Everyone looked uncomfortable with that exchange. No one at this table could ever conceive of a situation in which they would take arms against Kirk.

But Sulu was a Starfleet officer *and* a starship captain.

Under orders.

Chekov could no longer be sure what Sulu would do when forced to choose between his personal wishes and his sworn duty. Not after Dark Range.

McCoy voiced the frustration Chekov felt. "So, what's the key to all this, Spock?"

"In what way, Doctor?"

"What's the piece of information you need that'll tell you what possibility we're dealing with here?"

Spock looked thoughtful, as if he had never considered the question before.

"At the heart of these events is a single unexplained coincidence," Spock finally said. "On the frontier, on Dark Range Platform, a Starfleet Intelligence agent makes contact with a Klingon who can tell her about the *Chalchaj 'qmey.* That agent immediately goes rogue. At almost the exact same time, a young Klingon-Romulan woman makes contact with Captain Kirk, and invites him to journey to the presumed location of the very same Children of Heaven."

Spock looked around at everyone at the conference table. He had their full attention. "There was ample time for Jade to transmit a coded subspace message from Dark Range to someone here on Earth. The question is: To whom?"

Spock paused. No one spoke.

"I believe if we can find out who the link is between Jade and Teilani, then we will know the truth about Captain Kirk. And Admiral Drake."

"Unfortunately, we have no time to do that," Sulu said. "We're leaving orbit in ninety minutes."

"Then we must accept that we are on our own," Spock concluded. "And finding Captain Kirk is our best strategy."

Sulu stood. The meeting was over.

Chekov could sense the conflict in the room.

If the *Excelsior* found the *Enterprise,* everyone here would have to follow orders and confront Kirk, pitting loyalty to Starfleet against loyalty to the truth.

It was a no-win scenario the equal of the *Kobayashi Maru.*

But at least Chekov knew that comparison would give them the clue they needed to find the proper action to take.

As Captain Kirk had long ago shown them that, when forced to choose between two equally undesirable options, the only thing to do was to change the rules.

All they had to do now was to figure out what game was being played.

As Chekov left the conference room, he thought again of Admiral Drake's study. Of the sealed door.

And of the secrets behind it.

TWENTY-TWO

Even as the door to Drake's study sealed itself behind its forcefield, another door had opened.

An inner door.

Hidden behind the display case that held the uniform of a Fourth World Mercenary.

As Chekov and his crewmates signed their security oaths in an anteroom, a woman had stepped through that hidden door.

She was compact, attractive, with finely drawn features and dark complexion, a strong intelligence in her eyes. But her mouth was not used to smiling.

She still wore the flight suit and tight-fitting hood she had worn on Dark Range Platform.

Drake rose to greet her.

"You heard?" he asked.

The woman pulled off her flight hood, shaking loose her dark hair.

A streak of white blazed through it.

The starkness of the color made the resemblance between Drake and the woman more striking.

Her code name had been Jade. But her real name was Ariadne.

Drake.

Father and daughter.

"I should have disintegrated them in the cargo bay when I

had the chance," Ariadne said. "Or ejected them from the airlock when I got rid of Kort."

Then she kissed her father's cheek.

His eyes kindled with pride. For her and all she had done.

"No," he told her. "You did the right thing. If Chekov and Uhura had disappeared altogether, Intelligence would have launched a full investigation."

Drake's daughter made a playful face. "You're saying they're not going to investigate *my* disappearance from their ranks?"

She went to a small cabinet against the wall, pressed a hidden switch. The cabinet unfolded into a bar.

Drake joined her there, gloating. "No one even knows you've disappeared, my dear. Kirk created such a paranoid group of officers that they actually came to me first, convinced no one else could be trusted. So the situation is contained. Intelligence doesn't know any of you are back on Earth. They think you'rc all still deep under cover, hunting Klingon generals who've gone into business for themselves."

The woman gave her father a snifter of brandy, poured the same for herself, then lifted her glass in a toast to her father's success.

"What if *Kirk* goes into business for himself?" She closed her eyes, savoring the brandy's aroma. "We've been after the *Chalchaj 'qmey* for years. That pathetic Klingon on Dark Range finally gave us the connection to Chal that we needed. But now we're tossing a potential superweapon into Kirk's lap."

Drake sipped his brandy, unconcerned. "Kirk is a man of the moment. He has no vision. So he'll do exactly what we want him to do. Lead us to Chal. And to the Children of Heaven. Then, one way or another, he'll be . . . superseded."

Ariadne drank the contents of her glass in one quick toss. "I still think torturing Teilani would have been simpler."

Drake put down his snifter and rubbed at his face. He'd

been working twenty-hour days since obtaining his new position.

"That wouldn't have been wise. Or profitable. We tried interrogating some of her compatriots right after Khitomer. When the Chal first started inquiring about membership in the Federation. No matter what we did to them, we learned nothing to indicate any of them knew what their world is sitting on. And they have incredible control over their autonomic nervous systems. As soon as they realized there was no escape, they literally willed themselves to death."

Drake poured more brandy into Ariadne's glass, then his own. "It was one thing for a few aides to disappear. Accidents still do happen, even on Earth. But we can't risk Teilani suddenly vanishing. Someone might start asking questions."

Ariadne frowned. "'Willed themselves to death'? They're half Klingon. They should have died trying to escape. How could they commit *suicide?*"

Drake patted her hand with paternal condescension. "Klingons are animals, Ariadne. Never forget that."

Drake stared up at a two-dimensional photoprint framed above the bar. He was in it, much younger. The handsome woman beside him looked out with a face softened by love. Together, they held a small girl on their laps. A streak of white blazed through the child's dark hair.

Drake's face darkened as he looked at the image of his wife. The family he used to have.

"Never forget that," he said again.

"How did you manage to get Teilani to go after Kirk?"

In a lightning change of mood, Drake winked at Ariadne. "I told her to."

Ariadne laughed scornfully "And Kirk doesn't suspect?"

Drake shook his head. "I gave her his complete psych file. Told her how sorry I was that Starfleet couldn't get involved in defending a planet so deep in Klingon-Romulan territory. But suggested—off the record, mind you—that Kirk couldn't refuse the challenge. As far as I can tell from the surveillance we ran on him before they left, she's using everything in his file. Pulling his strings as if he's her personal puppet."

"What if she tells him that recruiting him was your idea?"

"She won't. Kirk's a proud man. I made it clear to her that if he got any hint that he's been manipulated into helping Chal, he'd walk away at once."

Ariadne walked over to an armchair, sat down, hooking one leg over the arm, letting it swing. "How'd anyone that predictable ever last so long in the service? Let alone command a starship?"

Drake grinned, the smile of a predator. "Thirty years ago, he was different. Would have ripped the throat out of a Klingon with his teeth if he had to. But the years have not been kind to Kirk." Drake chuckled. "I've done my best to keep it that way."

Ariadne gave her father a curious look. "Why so personal? What did Kirk ever do to you?"

Drake's eyes flamed with sudden anger. "This isn't personal! Kirk is the epitome of the cancer weakening Starfleet and the Federation. To stay strong, we have to remain intact. Pure. There's no more room for Klingons and aliens. Our borders have to be secure. We have to look to ourselves, not to outsiders. Cartwright knew that. But he wasn't careful."

"At least Cartwright didn't talk about us at his trial," Ariadne said.

"Only because he knows we're the last ones left of his organization. If he ever dares breathe a word about us, he knows he'll never get out of confinement." Drake sat back down behind his desk. "We're Admiral Cartwright's last hope for freedom. And we're the Federation's best hope for security."

"So what's Kirk?" Ariadne asked.

"Debris. To be tossed aside by the waves of history."

"From what I've heard, he doesn't sound the type to let himself be tossed aside."

"He doesn't have a choice anymore," Drake said with venom in his voice. "Kirk's day is over. Starfleet knows it. His friends know it. And *I* know it." He settled back in his chair, hands clasped behind his head. "And I intend to see the expression on Kirk's face when he knows it, too."

"Whatever you've got planned for him," Ariadne said dryly, "I'm glad to know it *isn't* personal."

Drake frowned.

Sometimes children could be such a burden.

TWENTY-THREE

Kirk missed his Starfleet sideburns.

He had had them ever since the Academy. A tradition whose origins were lost in time.

But two days ago, Teilani had carefully shaved them off.

Slowly. With a naked Klingon *SeymoH* blade.

After covering him with hot lather.

Kirk had heard stories of the *SeymoH* blade and how the Klingons employed it. Not for cutting, but for delicate, maddening, and indescribable scraping.

He used to think it would be an experience he would never have. Simply because he would never trust any Klingon to get that close to him with a drawn knife.

But Teilani was something different. Something special.

And smart.

She had told him that his Starfleet sideburns would cause him to stand out where they were going.

Not on Chal. But on Prestor V.

It was a bleak, backwater planet just inside the boundaries of the Klingon Empire, close to the Federation's watchposts.

For generations, Prestor V's only industry had been provided by the Klingon garrison that was stationed there. But with the Empire's recent military cutbacks, the garrison had been recalled.

Prestor V then became the latest in a long list of planets to look elsewhere for support in the new era of peace. So, like many others before it, the colonial government solved its problems by turning to institutionalized piracy and theft.

Prestor V was also to be the *Enterprise*'s first port of call on her voyage to Chal.

For supplies, Teilani had said. And equipment.

She had explained everything to Kirk as she had drawn the edge of the blade across his skin, awakening each nerve ending with a combination of exquisite pressure and the constant danger of serious injury.

Kirk hadn't said much during the discussion. Teilani had proven herself very resourceful in redirecting his attention.

Meanwhile, the *Enterprise* had arrived at Prestor V on schedule.

Now Kirk and Scott sat at a wobbling table in a dingy spaceport bar, on the outskirts of the planet's capital city. They were waiting for Teilani to join them.

Neither had their Starfleet sideburns anymore. Though Scott had had to shave his off himself.

Looking around the bar, Kirk could see that Teilani had been correct in suggesting the sideburns go. It was not a Starfleet-friendly environment.

Like any good Klingon drinking establishment, this one had a number of ears nailed to the wall behind the bartender's station. Most of them human. Kirk wondered if any had fallen to a *SeymoH* blade in the hands of a jealous lover.

Probably not, he decided. If a spurned Klingon lover had a *SeymoH* blade handy, an ear might not be the first trophy taken.

Kirk looked away from the collection of ears and smiled at Scott.

Scott smiled back.

Both smiles were forced.

The silence was awkward.

"We haven't done this for a long time, have we?" Kirk said. "Sit in a bar, wear civilian clothes for a change, have a few drinks."

"No," Scott agreed. "We haven't."

Kirk sipped what passed for this planet's beer. Scott did the same.

More awkward silence.

"After Khitomer, I got very busy," Kirk said. "At headquarters."

"So I understand."

Kirk couldn't stand the tension any longer. He used to like touring alien bars with Mr. Scott.

"Scotty, is there something wrong?"

"Why? Should there be?"

Kirk shrugged. He wasn't sure what he was trying to say. "I don't know. It's just that . . . you and me . . . here in this bar . . . shouldn't we be having . . . *fun?*"

Scotty sighed noisily. The Prestor beer left an attractive little fringe of blue foam on his mustache.

"Captain, we've been traveling on th' *Enterprise* for th' past eight days and you've barely said two words t' me that weren't havin' t' do with th' engines."

Kirk grimaced. What could he say? "Scotty . . . I've been . . . busy."

"Aye, sir, that ye have been." Scott poured a fresh glass of the blue beer from the copper pitcher on the table. Something small and green with too many legs shot out from beneath the pitcher the instant Scott lifted it. "But the point of the matter is, you're always busy."

Kirk heard the recrimination in Scotty's tone. He knew he couldn't make up for anything he might have done, or not done in the past. But at least he could try and change things for the future.

"Mr. Scott, I am not busy now." Kirk raised his glass in a toast. "I am sitting in this fine establishment hoping to have a drink with an old friend."

Scotty didn't look convinced, but he appreciated the effort. He clinked his glass against Kirk's.

"To old times," Scott said.

Kirk disagreed. "To new times."

Scott countered with the one toast neither could argue with. "To th' *Enterprise.* Th' finest ship Starfleet ever saw."

"And to her crew," Kirk added.

At least this time when silence followed, there was some semblance of a connection between the two men.

Kirk couldn't help himself.

"So, how *are* the engines?"

Scott's eyes twinkled. There was a reason most of Kirk's conversations with him revolved around technical matters.

"I've had to rework th' intervalve couplings t' keep th' power groupings online," Scott said. "And with th' new disruptor cannons being installed, I've—"

"Excuse me?" Kirk interrupted. "Disruptors?"

"Aye," Scott said innocently.

Kirk stared at his chief engineer. *"Klingon* disruptor cannons . . . on the *Enterprise?"*

"Captain, we don't have any phasers. Our tractor beams have been downgraded. And all but one photon tube has been welded over with duranium." Scott leaned forward and dropped his voice. "If th' *Enterprise* is t' be part of a planetary defense system, then she needs something t' defend herself with, don't ye think?"

Kirk couldn't argue with that. "But where did we get disruptor cannons?"

Scotty smiled. "Ask me nae questions, I'll tell ye nae lies. Teilani was the one who did the dealing. Right here in this bar I'm told."

"She *bought* them," Kirk said, not quite believing it.

"We're in Klingon territory, sir. And in Klingon territory, currency is still widespread. As are a number of ex-officers who see nothing wrong in selling surplus equipment t' th' highest bidders. Let me add that Teilani is quite th' negotiator, too."

Kirk smiled inwardly at that. He knew from experience that she was skilled at getting her own way.

"Is there anything else being installed on my ship I should know about?"

Scott scratched at his mustache. "A few antimatter pods. Ten photon torpedoes. Twin disruptor cannons. Shield augmenters. Tractor enhancers." Scott looked at Kirk. "That's about the lot."

"That's just about everything Starfleet took out of her when she was decommissioned."

"Aye. I never would have thought it, but with th' new equipment and a few more weeks' work, I should have th' old girl back close t' her original condition."

"Except she'll have Klingon disruptors instead of phasers."

Scott finished off his glass of beer and wiped his mustache free of foam. "The pieces all fit in the holes Starfleet left. So why not? After all, there're not a great many Starfleet officers willin' to sell off parts of their own Fleet."

Don't be so sure, Kirk thought. He looked around the bar. It was still fairly early in the evening and only half the tables were filled. Almost all of the clientele were Klingon. None of them appeared to be paying any attention to the two humans sitting by themselves.

Just the same, Kirk leaned forward and gave Scott a conspiratorial whisper. "Does any of this refitting make sense to you, Scotty?"

The whisper made Scott nervous. He leaned forward to speak in the same hushed tone. "Why not? Ye've got t' want t' have a whole ship to command, don't ye?"

"Chal is deep within the Klingon-Romulan frontier. At

worst, we're going to face a few Orion pirates. As long as our shields are up to strength, a few photon torpedoes are all we need."

"Teilani seems t' know what she wants."

"Don't I know it," Kirk said with a smile.

Scott poured the last of the blue beer from the copper pitcher. Something thick and green plopped out of the pitcher and into his glass. Scott eyed it warily. But it didn't move on its own.

"Could be that Teilani knows more about what t' expect around Chal than we do," he suggested.

"I have no doubt of that," Kirk agreed.

Scott shrugged. "When in Rome." He upended his glass and bravely swallowed the thick green sludge.

Kirk flinched. "Scotty. How could you?"

"Trust me, Captain. There's nothing that could be alive in a brew as foul as this one."

Kirk's first impulse was to thank Scotty for calling him "captain" again. But he decided not to. The title had probably just slipped out without Scott being aware of what he said.

The surly Klingon bartender lumbered over to Kirk's table with another battered copper pitcher of blue beer. She was old and deeply wrinkled with a mane of pure white hair. Her leather apron carried an ominous collection of stains. It looked ready to burst from the pressure it exerted on her massive breasts crammed under her armor chest plate.

Kirk tried to send the pitcher back but the bartender muttered that it was free.

"Free?" Kirk asked.

The bartender said any customer who ate the green sludge got a free pitcher. It was house policy.

"What, exactly, is the green sludge?" Scott asked politely.

The bartender gaped at Scott in admiration. Her deeply ridged brow rippled as her eyes widened. "You didn't know?" she mumbled.

Scott shook his head.

The bartender erupted with a bone-chilling howl of Klingon laughter, whomped Scott on the back, then went back to her bar, still snorting in amazement.

A look of panic crossed Scott's face.

Kirk pushed the copper pitcher closer to the engineer. "Drink up, Scotty. Who knows what you get for doing it twice?"

Before Scott could reply, Kirk suddenly felt familiar hands move across his back and slide around his chest.

He lost his breath as quickly as that.

Teilani whirled him around and kissed him. Innovatively. Thoroughly. But only for a second.

It was her usual dramatic entrance.

"I'm done," she announced as she dragged over a chair and sat at the table.

Her dark jumpsuit clung to her curves. Her exotic face was flushed, vibrant with satisfaction. The energy she radiated was nothing less than blinding. As always.

Kirk felt the pull of her nearness, as if he were a moon trapped in helpless orbit, drawn by irresistible force.

"I didn't know you had anything more to do," he said. He decided he could stare at her for hours. He wondered how he could ever have thought that a Klingon brow was ungainly, or that pointed ears were alien.

Both features looked perfect to him now, especially the way they blended in Teilani.

"The *Enterprise* is a big ship, James." She reached out to pour herself a glass of beer. "She needs a great deal of supplies."

Scott held out a cautioning hand. "Careful of the sludge, lass."

"I know," Teilani told him. "If you accidentally eat any of it, they have to give you a free pitcher to help dredge the worms out of your system."

Kirk was impressed by how quickly the color drained from Scotty's face.

The engineer quickly excused himself.

As soon as he was gone, Teilani reached across the table and squeezed Kirk's hand.

"Happy?" she asked.

"Exhausted," Kirk answered.

For all the time they had been spending in his quarters, sleep had been a low priority for both of them.

Teilani liked his answer. "Ready to start work?"

Kirk was puzzled.

"As coordinator of Chal's planetary defense force," Teilani explained.

"Now?" Kirk asked.

Teilani's face became serious. "We're being followed."

Kirk immediately glanced around the bar. No one was overtly looking at them.

"Not *here,"* Teilani said. "In space."

"Who?"

"The people who went after you on the farm."

"What sort of ship do they have?"

"A Tholian starcruiser. Emerald class."

Kirk knew the vessel well. A crystal-faceted teardrop hull, similar to the ships that had once captured the *Enterprise.* A crew of twenty, maximum cruising factor of seven point five, exceptional shields. But little in the way of firepower.

"We can outrun it," he said. "Or outfight it."

"Good," Teilani said. "Then I think we should outrun it."

"We'll still meet up on Chal, won't we?"

"Not if they don't think we're going there."

Kirk didn't follow her reasoning. "Where else would they think we were going?"

Teilani wasn't taking this as seriously as Kirk thought she should.

"They're going to be able to track us here, to Prestor V, easily. They're also going to find out about all the equipment we've taken on board. So what we have to do is make them think we've gone to another system, looking for spacedock facilities. So we can install everything."

"That means they don't know about Scotty," Kirk said. "He could refit the ship holding his breath, walking her hull in a pair of magnetic boots. No spacedock required."

"But since they won't know Scotty, when we leave Prestor V, I think we should set up a false trail. Just to give us some extra time to . . . prepare for things on Chal."

It was Kirk's turn to be serious. "You still haven't told me what we're going to face on your homeworld."

Teilani bit her lip, hesitating.

"Scotty told me about all the weapons systems you were having installed aboard the *Enterprise.* Is that why you wanted me down here most of the day?"

"James, no. I'm not hiding anything from you."

Kirk believed her, if for no other reason than his heart longed for her. "Then at least tell me who those weapons are intended to be used against. I know it's not just a Tholian starcruiser."

Teilani looked away from him, making up her mind.

"If things work out the way I hope," she said, "they won't have to be used against anyone. Just the fact that we have them should be enough to get the other side to the negotiating table."

"What other side?" Kirk asked.

"The Anarchists, of course. Those among us who want to destroy Chal."

"How?"

"By telling the galaxy what we have to offer."

"If that's all they have to do, then why haven't they done it already?" Kirk asked. "A few broadbeam subspace transmissions and the whole quadrant would know about your world in weeks."

Teilani wrapped both hands around her glass of beer. "They're not that fanatical, James. The Anarchists know Chal could never withstand the billions who would come to it after that kind of announcement. No, what they intend to do is keep its location a secret, so they can sell access to Chal to a select few."

"Teilani, is that so wrong?"

She lifted her chin in determination. "When you see Chal you'll understand why even that level of exploitation is intolerable."

Kirk allowed himself to be completely captivated by her eyes. "What *is* Chal like?"

She eased forward over the table, until her lips brushed against his, full of promise.

"Ten more days," she whispered. "Then you'll see for yourself."

TWENTY-FOUR

Ten days later, the *Enterprise* slipped into standard orbit of Chal.

Kirk almost felt like a boy again.

He remembered the excitement he had felt on his first school trip to Tranquility Base. The first time he had left Earth to set foot on another world.

This was better.

He couldn't explain why.

He stared through the forward viewport of Teilani's yacht as the *Enterprise*'s hangar doors ponderously opened.

A welcoming blue glow—reflected light from the world below—swept into the hangar deck.

Kirk watched as Esys reset the yacht's controls for manual flight. He saw the young Klingon-Romulan adjust the inertial dampers to full strength.

"That's all right," Kirk said. "Leave them at minimum."

Kirk wanted to feel what it was like to *fly* to Chal.

He felt Teilani touch his shoulder from the seat behind him, understanding his excitement.

The sleek yacht rose from the hangar deck, slowly floated toward the open doors under automatic tractor-beam control.

Passing from the hangar to space was like moving from the darkness of a cave to a lustrous summer day.

Chal was a sapphire before him.

Rich deep blue beyond any word Kirk knew in any language.

An ocean world, ninety percent of her pure azure waters, scrolled in elegant curlicues of brilliant white clouds.

The yacht banked away from the *Enterprise,* moving down. Kirk felt the shudder as Esys took control from the tractor beam.

The binary suns of Chal glinted from the world's vast ocean, leaving dark spots in Kirk's vision.

It was as if every summer day on every beach that ever was had been collapsed into one perfect, shimmering blue moment.

"What does 'Chal' mean?" Kirk asked. He had heard so many different names for worlds that he had never thought to ask.

"Heaven," Teilani said.

Kirk understood.

He fell toward paradise.

The yacht shook satisfyingly as it entered Chal's atmosphere.

Kirk grinned along with Esys as the dampers did little to dilute the sheer sensations of speed and descent.

Ahead, on the distant horizon, rapidly losing its curve as

they neared the surface, Kirk saw a string of islands rise from the sea.

They were one of four archipelagoes that daubed the ocean like artist's brushstrokes.

The largest island, in the archipelago closest the equator, was where the colony of Chal had first been founded, where its first and only city remained. It had a population of almost one thousand, Teilani said. Small enough that they had little impact on the world's ecology. That there was food enough for the taking, without requiring anyone to work in agriculture for more than a few weeks in any year.

Neither was there much work required in the way of support services or maintenance. The building materials used and technological infrastructure the colony's founders had installed were robust and capable of self-repair.

By all accounts, to Kirk the colony sounded more like a resort camp than a working community. It was almost as if the Klingons and Romulans who had created the colony had intended that their descendants would never have to work to maintain their blissful existence.

The air of Chal whistled past the yacht as Esys slowed the craft to subsonic velocity.

They flew a few hundred meters above the ocean.

The main island rushed at them like a wave of green, held apart from the ocean by a border of white sand.

"Almost home," Teilani said.

They raced along the shore, twisting and curving with it. Completely inefficient, but unquestionably *fun*.

Kirk watched deep jungle flash by to the side, highlighted by vivid explosions of color from flowers that beggared those of Earth.

He saw a handful of ground vehicles parked on the beach below them. Groupings of Chal looked up from the sand on which they lay and from the water in which they swam.

Sports and games were high among the pursuits enjoyed by the Chal, Teilani had explained. Loosely organized committees arranged the minimal work schedules. A more formal group of volunteers formed the planet's government, such that it was. Teilani was the one responsible for maintaining contact with other worlds.

With no industry and no exports, Kirk was uncertain where Chal's trade credits originally came from. Teilani had no answers either. She had merely taken over her position, inheriting a system set in place from the beginning. Computers provided almost all the suggestions and advice for running the colony. And with only a thousand or so inhabitants to cater to, with food and shelter and recreation abundant for all, actual government involvement in anyone's daily life was rare and inconsequential.

Kirk was surprised that the colony had been provided with such a stable organization from the beginning. Most colonies served as laboratories for creating new forms of social interaction.

The yacht eased to the right, following the curve of the shore. The city was before them.

Nestled in green. Clear, clean stripes of beige and cream and pale pink walls and roofs arranged like scattered seashells, raised on a small outcropping of black volcanic rock, caught in the jungle's edge, overlooking the sweep of a protected harbor and kilometers of wide white beach.

There was a central structure larger than any other building—a covered stadium, Kirk guessed. But all around it, everything was low and simple. Nothing more than two stories. Nothing that could get in the way of the glorious sunlight that bathed the scene.

Esys brought the yacht around, slowing it gradually.

Kirk saw a series of circular landing pads carved into the black rock at the city's edge.

Yellow concentric circles glowed. Numbers written in Romulan script identified them.

Gently, the yacht touched down.

At the same instant, the yacht's hatch sprang open.

Kirk gasped as the rich air of Chal flooded the cabin.

He smelled the ocean, the flowers, the damp green of the jungle.

For a moment, he felt dizzy. His skin tingled. His heart raced.

Esys and Teilani were standing already.

He pushed himself out of his seat.

There was something different about the action.

"What's your gravity here?" Kirk asked.

Teilani smiled at him as she stood in the hatchway. Beyond her, Kirk could see lush jungle fronds sway in the breeze.

"Point nine eight," she said.

Kirk worked it out. That only meant a difference in his weight of about a kilogram and a half. Not enough to account for the ease of movement he felt.

"Oxygen content of the atmosphere?" he asked.

Teilani's smile grew puzzled. "Twenty-one percent."

Again, just slightly off Earth normal. But not enough to account for the undercurrent of energy surging through his body. He felt a rush of exhilaration.

"Are you all right, James?" Teilani asked.

He joined her at the hatchway, swung her off her feet, hugged her, smothered her laughing face with kisses. That was his answer.

Esys laughed as he passed them in the hatchway.

Kirk knew he would hear a lot of laughter on this planet.

He decided he was going to like it here.

Everything was new.

Because of Teilani.

TWENTY-FIVE

☆

The *Excelsior* dropped from warp and smoothly banked on impulse to enter standard orbit of Prestor V.

On the spacious bridge, Chekov looked up from the security officer's station. "Ve have them," he announced.

Sulu swiveled in his center chair to look over at Spock.

Spock had taken over the science station.

Chekov knew some of Sulu's bridge crew hadn't been pleased to relinquish their key positions to what were, after all, interlopers. But the ease with which those of the *Enterprise* had fallen into their old routines was remarkable to witness. It was as if not a day had gone by since their first five-year mission.

Even Lieutenant Janice Rand, once Captain Kirk's yeoman, now Sulu's communications officer, worked perfectly with Uhura at the station they shared.

Spock confirmed Chekov's readings.

"Sensors are picking up impulse ionization readings consistent with the *Enterprise*'s engines. I estimate she was in orbit here, within the past eight to twelve days."

"Any idea how long she stayed?" Sulu asked.

"Judging from the residual ionization trails, multiple orbits. Two to three days at least," Spock said.

Sulu looked ahead at the main viewscreen. Prestor V was a scabrous brown and purple planet below them. "Then that means she did some business here."

He tapped his finger on the side of his chair. Chekov could

see him working out the sequence of orders he was going to give. The expression on his face, the position he assumed in the chair, all reminded Chekov of Kirk.

"Mr. Chekov," Sulu began, "continue an intensive sweep for the *Enterprise*'s warp signature. Just in case they remained in orbit a few days longer and we can still pick up their warp heading. Commander Uhura, contact all orbital docking facilities. Ask if the *Enterprise* has booked space in them in the past two weeks."

"Ask?" Uhura said. "Sir, this is a Klingon borderworld. No one's going to answer any questions a Starfleet ship *asks.*"

Chekov hid his smile as Sulu frowned, the rhythm of his orders lost.

"Very well," Sulu said with a sigh. "Find out what they use for currency here, withdraw it from ship's stores, and assemble landing parties to beam over to the docking platforms and inquire about the *Enterprise* in person."

"You mean, bribe the dockmasters," Uhura said, looking for clarification.

"Whatever it takes," Sulu acknowledged.

He stood up to face the viewscreen. "The *Enterprise* came here for a purpose. I'm going to guess it was to replace some of the equipment Starfleet removed from her. So far there's been no evidence that Captain Kirk has been trying to hide his trail. But once the *Enterprise* was resupplied, he might have changed tactics."

Chekov thought Sulu was stating the obvious. If anything was consistent about Kirk's tactics, it was the frequency with which he changed them.

Spock looked up from his science station. "Captain Sulu, if Captain Kirk wished to replace all the equipment Starfleet removed from the *Enterprise,* then that would include weapons systems."

"Of course," Sulu said.

"Then I submit that he must have dealt in extralegal channels."

"It's a Klingon borderworld," Uhura reminded Spock. "The whole planet is extralegal."

Spock was unperturbed. "There are various levels of extralegal activity, Commander. To replace weapons systems, I suggest Captain Kirk would have made contact with suppliers close to the old Klingon garrison that was stationed on this world. Logically, they would be the ones with access to any military matériel that was left behind."

"Or stolen," Chekov added.

"As I said," Spock agreed, "there are various levels of extralegal activity."

Sulu nodded, surrendering to Spock's logic. "I'll want landing parties to go to the surface, as well. To look into 'extralegal' supply options." He glanced at Spock. "Will that be sufficient?"

"Again, the inhabitants of Prestor V might not be willing to aid Starfleet personnel in their inquiries."

"Undercover, Captain Spock?" Sulu asked.

"That would be the logical approach."

Sulu looked in Chekov's direction. Chekov could see what the captain was thinking.

"Pavel, I believe you're our designated criminal," Sulu said.

Chekov heard Uhura chuckle at her station.

"All right," Chekov said. "But this time, *I* get to carry the money."

TWENTY-SIX

Kirk thundered across the sands of Chal.

He stayed crouched and low in his saddle as his mount pounded along the beach, sending billowing clouds of glittering sand flying with each hoofbeat.

Teilani rode at his side, hair streaming in the wind of their race.

He caught her eye.

The suns of Chal sparkled in her. The passion of their contest. Of their lovemaking only an hour ago. The joy of home. Everything united in that one expression that transformed her face. Making her beauty transcendent.

She snapped her reins and yelled at her steed to spur it on.

The horselike creature, glossy brown and native to a distant Romulan colony world, snorted and took off, its powerful legs driving against the beach.

Kirk urged his own mount on. He gulped down air as if he had been drowning. He had never known breathing to be so elemental an experience.

Even as he closed the gap between them, Kirk wondered what a thorough analysis of Chal's atmosphere would find. He had only been here a single day, but had felt the planet's influence from the moment he first landed.

The treasure of this world, Teilani called it.

Be young forever.

Only a length ahead of him, Teilani guided her mount

around a jagged black rock and hauled back on the reins to bring the race to an end.

Kirk was still getting used to the creatures. They weren't the same as the horses he was familiar with on Earth. He overshot Teilani, had to circle back.

She was waiting for him, resplendent in the simple white clothes she wore. They were decoration more than protection in Chal's benign climate—loose, open, innocently plain yet captivatingly sexy.

Kirk wore a version of the same. As did everyone else he had met on Chal. Everything, even these clothes, was a celebration here, of unfettered life and love.

It seemed as if there was nothing to hide on this world. Nothing to be denied.

Kirk dismounted, went to Teilani. He was out of breath. She teased him for it. Then apologized with a kiss.

They walked to the water's edge.

Gentle waves bordered by translucent foam lapped at the white sand.

Tiny flying creatures chased the water. Some skittered on impossibly tiny feet, leaving delicate tracks in the sand. Others glided gracefully on the soft breeze, skimming the curl of the gentle surf.

On the horizon, brightly colored sails of small boats darted swiftly between air and sea.

This world wasn't a resort. It was a playground.

Everything about it had been designed from the beginning to offer a world without stress, without need.

Kirk slipped his arm around Teilani. She leaned her head on his shoulder.

"Now I know why you want to keep this world a secret," Kirk told her.

"Do you?" Teilani asked.

Chal's binary suns hung like an hourglass in an unbroken blue sky. The primary star was yellow-white, the smaller secondary orange-yellow. From space Kirk had seen the incandescent plasma bridge that joined the two, as the primary stripped off gases from the secondary that spiraled around it.

But the light those suns cast on this alien shore was warm and inviting.

"If people knew what it was like here, you'd be beach-to-beach hotels and travelports inside a year," Kirk said. His words seemed banal to him, in the face of such perfection.

"And that would be the end of everything." She held him closer. "But that's why you're here."

Kirk looked into her eyes. The face of his old enemies—Klingon and Romulan—improbably joined, looked back.

But they were enemies no longer.

In Teilani's arms, he had left the past behind.

"I'm here because of you," Kirk said. He nuzzled her wind-tossed hair. "You told me you needed someone to save your world, remember? And then you brought me to . . . heaven."

She held his hand to the side of her face. Pressed her open lips against his sun-warmed skin. "Were you expecting a war zone?"

"Some sign of imminent danger at least," Kirk said. His fingers traced the ridges of her forehead.

"There is danger all around us, James."

"I thought the *Enterprise* would put an end to that. That just her presence would bring the other side—the Anarchists—to the negotiating table." He moved his fingers down the side of her head, pushed her hair away from her ear, kissed its curves, drinking in the intermingled scent of sun and sand and sea and her.

"But that's just here on Chal," she whispered into his ear.

Her breath was warmer than the sun, melting him.

Kirk ran his hands along her back, the silky fabric of her light tunic no barrier to the softness of her skin. "You have other enemies?" he asked.

Teilani stepped back from him, holding his hands against the sides of her waist.

"You're feeling the effects of Chal, aren't you?" she asked, as if she hadn't heard his question.

"Yes," Kirk admitted. Nothing to hide, nothing denied. "I feel . . . young . . . younger . . . more alive than I have in . . . years."

"What is that worth, James? Not just to you, but to entire planets? Entire empires?" She released his hands. Slowly lifted her own hands to the neck of her tunic. "Youth is the ultimate limited resource. Chal has survived these past years because no one knew of her. But now, with the changes in the Klingon Empire, the old secrets are being revealed."

She unfastened the top closure on her tunic, moved down to the second.

"Chal cannot remain a secret for much longer. But to survive, she must."

The second closure parted.

Her skin was intoxicating.

Her tunic slipped from her shoulders.

She was intoxicating.

Kirk was undone.

His hands encircled her. He brought his lips down to hers.

But he didn't kiss her as she expected.

"Is there something you aren't telling me?" he whispered.

"Make love to me, James."

She drew his own tunic from his shoulders, pushed it away so their skin met as she pressed against him.

"Who is your enemy?"

"James, please."

Her hands stroked his back. Their pressure hypnotic.

But Kirk stepped back. Breaking contact.

They stood, poised on the brink of their desires.

"Teilani, I need to talk," Kirk said.

Teasingly, she reached out for the drawstring of his pants. "But *I* need you," she said.

Kirk surrendered. How could he not?

With Teilani at his side, time had no meaning.

They could talk whenever, love whenever, do whatever their hearts desired, whenever and for as long as they wanted.

Kirk had found his Eden.

Perhaps, he thought, *I have found my home.*

A deep rumble resonated through the air.

Kirk turned to look past the jagged rock, along the beach toward the city.

It was kilometers away, hidden by a curve of jungle.

But from behind that curve, a billowing fireball blossomed, rising into the air on a trail of black smoke.

Teilani's face was white with fear. Or rage. Kirk didn't know.

"They're attacking again!" she said. "They said they would talk but they're attacking *again!*"

"Who's attacking?" Kirk demanded. "The Anarchists?"

"Yes," she said. "The Anarchists. The old ones. Our *parents.*"

TWENTY-SEVEN

Kirk stared at Teilani for a moment, then decided it was not the time or place for more questions.

He sprinted across the sand, back to his mount.

In his saddlebag, he found his communicator.

He flipped it open.

"Kirk to *Enterprise.*"

Scott answered.

Kirk gave his orders.

Everything happened at once.

Within seconds Kirk and Teilani were beamed from the beach to the landing pads by the city. Right beside Teilani's yacht.

Kirk felt the heat from the new fireball that exploded not more than a kilometer away in the jungle.

Smoke wafted through the lush growth toward the simple city buildings. He could hear screams and shouting voices carried on the wind.

A new transporter column sparkled into being.

Kirk ran to it.

He pulled on the jacket that lay atop the equipment Scott had beamed down. He tossed the second one to Teilani. Then he strapped on the equipment belt, adjusted the position of the Klingon disruptor pistol that hung from it.

He flipped open the screen on his tactical scanner.

"Transmit," he said into his communicator.

The screen came alive with moving dots of color.

Teilani watched over his shoulder as she sealed her jacket. "What is it, James?"

"The *Enterprise* is sweeping the area with her sensors. This screen shows the position of the attackers."

There seemed to be twenty of them, moving in from the jungle.

He heard the whistle of a shell screaming through the sky. Instinctively he pulled Teilani to the landing pad, hunched over her.

An explosion rocked the next pad, spraying shattered stones to rattle off the hull of the yacht by Kirk.

"Scotty," Kirk yelled into his communicator. "Can you pick those shells off in flight?"

"Negative, Captain. We don't have the precision aim we used t'."

Kirk dragged Teilani toward the shelter of the yacht. He studied the screen.

"What sort of defense does the city have?" he asked.

Teilani looked helpless. "Hand disruptors. Projectile guns."

"That's it?"

She nodded, an expression of shock distorting her features.

"What are they after?"

Teilani stared blankly at him.

"The Anarchists! What's their objective?"

Teilani was frightened. Kirk filed her reaction. She hadn't behaved this way when they had been under attack at the farm.

"Teilani! I can't help you unless you tell me what they're trying to do!"

"The power station," she said. "In the center of town."

"The large domed building?"

She nodded.

Kirk found the building on the tactical screen. It was the structure he had thought looked like a covered stadium.

The Anarchists were about three kilometers distant from it.

Whatever they were using to launch the explosive shells had more than enough range to reach the station. The fact that they weren't shelling it told Kirk their objective was to get *to* the station, not destroy it.

That made defense easier.

"Scotty—can you lock transporters onto the twenty or so life signs in the jungle to the north of the city?"

That would be the easy way, Kirk knew. Transport all the Anarchists directly to the *Enterprise*'s brig.

"Sorry, sir. The jungle is full of life signs, birds and animals I'm guessing, and we just don't have precise enough control to isolate the attackers. Unless ye could talk them int' carrying communicators."

"How about a low-intensity disruptor burst?"

"Aye," Scott answered. "If ye don't mind knockin' out a few wee beasties, too."

Kirk looked at Teilani. "What are the life-forms here like? Can they stand up to a stun setting?"

"I . . . I think so," Teilani said.

She flinched and shrank as another explosion rocked the landing pads.

Kirk coughed as a gust of fine powder and dirt rushed past him.

"Do it, Scotty."

"Targeting now, Captain. Setting disruptor cannons to lowest power. Ye might want to cover your eyes. . . ."

A section of sky to the north of the city suddenly flared with orange light.

Kirk checked his tactical screen.

The dots that represented the Anarchists were still there, indicating they were still alive.

But they weren't moving.

"Good shooting, Mr. Scott."

"Fish in a barrel, sir."

Kirk told Scott to stand by, then flipped his communicator closed. "It's over," he said to Teilani. The *Enterprise* had worked her magic.

"Only for now," she said. "They aren't the only ones who threaten us."

Kirk stood and brushed the dust from his jacket and pants.

The jacket Teilani wore was too big for her.

For just this moment, it made her look too much like a young girl, frightened and alone.

Kirk hugged her. With compassion this time and for no other reason.

"Vacation's over," he said gently to her. "No more secrets."

He felt her nod against his chest.

"Tell me everything," Kirk said.

Teilani held nothing back.

TWENTY-EIGHT

It was night in Prestor V's main city. A light rain fell, coating the corroded streets with an oily yellow sheen. The air stank of sulfur.

There were public streetlights lining all the thoroughfares in the warehouse district surrounding the spaceport. But none of them worked. The only light came from windows haphazardly shuttered by twisted blast shields.

The Klingon engineers who had built this city fifty years earlier had not intended their temporary structures to last. And they hadn't.

Down one narrow street, a glowing sign sputtered and sparked, creating a pool of flickering red light.

Chekov paused in that light. To check out his "associates" one last time.

He was not filled with optimism.

"Please," Chekov pleaded as he adjusted Dr. McCoy's collar, "look more . . . menacing."

"How am I supposed to do that?" McCoy grumbled.

"Scowl," Chekov said. "Hunch your shoulders. Do *something* to make them think you're a vanted, desperate man."

McCoy snapped the collar of his long dark coat even higher around his neck, shoved his hands deep into his pocket. He glared in an expression of . . . annoyance.

Chekov sighed. He looked at Spock.

Spock hesitated a moment, then snapped up his own collar. "How is this?" he asked.

His neutral expression hadn't changed.

"Perfect," Chekov said without enthusiasm. He hoped Uhura was having better luck with her landing party on the other side of the spaceport. "Come vith me."

He led Spock and McCoy into the bar.

The sulfurous smell from outside had permeated the low-ceilinged room they entered. So had the mist.

Chekov peered through it, counted the ears nailed up behind the bar. He saw Spock and McCoy looking at them as well.

"At least," Chekov whispered, "none of them are pointed."

"There's always a first time for everything," McCoy said cheerfully, looking at Spock.

Chekov walked over to an empty table and sat down, trying to swagger as best he could.

As Spock and McCoy joined him, a nearby table of Klingons made a show of smelling a terrible odor and changed to a table farther away.

The bartender, a craggy old Klingon female with an explosion of thick white hair, approached Chekov's table. Before Chekov could order, she slapped down a copper pitcher filled with something blue and foamy. Three chipped glasses followed.

"Two credits," the bartender wheezed.

Chekov thought, Here goes. He locked eyes with her.

"*Federation* credits? Vhat do you take us for?" Chekov dropped a Klingon colonial coin on the wooden table. "Ve deal only in talons."

The bartender reached under her stained apron and brought out a tiny scanner, no larger than one of McCoy's medical sensors. She held the device over the coin. The scanner glowed orange on one end.

The bartender pocketed the scanner and the coin.

"Anything else?" she growled. Her tone was slightly less belligerent.

Chekov motioned for the bartender to lean closer. "Ve are in need of some . . . equipment."

The bartender grunted. "This is a bar, not a shopping mart."

"Perhaps I misunderstood my friend's adwice," Chekov said.

The bartender eyed him suspiciously. "Who's your friend?"

"Kort," Chekov said. He dropped his voice. "Of the Imperial Forecasters."

Chekov was pleased with the way in which the bartender tried not to let her surprise show. "Kort! How is the old bladder these days?" she asked.

"Not too vell. Life on the Dark Range is getting . . . difficult. His sources of supply are being compromised by Starfleet Intelligence, and the Empire's own internal peace forces."

"And he sent you here?"

Chekov could tell the bartender was intrigued, though still not convinced. He played his final card.

"Vhat is the path of the fourth-rank vatch dragon?" he asked her.

The bartender's mouth sagged open in astonishment as Chekov quoted the death poem of Molor.

Chekov had no idea of the significance of the words. Only that they had had a powerful effect on Kort when Jade had used them in the cargo bay. Judging from the bartender's reaction, they were still useful.

"Vell?" Chekov prompted.

"By Praxis' light, in seasons still to come," the bartender muttered nervously.

"Wery good," Chekov said. He placed five more talon coins on the table and slid them toward the bartender.

The bartender sat down, passed her arm over the coins. They disappeared without so much as a single clink.

Years of practice, Chekov decided.

Then the bartender nodded her head at Spock and McCoy. Strands of white hair fell over her eyes. "Who are they?"

"I am a dealer in kevas and trillium," Spock said. "My name is Sarin and I was born—"

Chekov kicked Spock's boot under the table, interrupting his recitation of the backstory Chekov had created for him.

"My talkative friend is . . . a client," Chekov explained. "They both are."

"A *Vulcan?"* the bartender asked. "For a client?"

Chekov shrugged. "Times are tough. And a customer is a customer."

The bartender leaned closer over the table. She smelled terrible.

"So what do you need, friend of Kort?"

"A starship," McCoy said brightly. Then he cleared his throat, scowled unconvincingly. "A starship," he repeated in a rougher tone.

Chekov felt embarrassed. "Something discreet," he added.

The bartender studied McCoy with a frown. *"Another* dealer in kevas and trillium?"

"That's vhat it says on the cargo manifests," Chekov explained. "You see, for the most part, my clients' dealings vith the authorities are wery cordial. They pay the . . . 'inspection' fees, and the border patrols inspect only the manifests."

The bartender looked at Spock with a glimmer of respect. "Smuggling, eh? An honorable profession."

"Except," Chekov said, "border patrols are not the only parties interested in my clients' shipments."

"Orion pirates?" the bartender asked.

"No vonder Kort likes you," Chekov said approvingly.

The bartender looked pleased. "So . . . you're looking for something to fight them off. A Bird-of-Prey?"

Chekov lowered his voice conspiratorially. "Actually, ve vere thinking of something that might stop a fight before it even began."

The bartender waited.

Chekov also waited.

He looked at McCoy.

McCoy looked startled. He'd forgotten his line.

"Oh," the doctor stumbled, "a starship! A *Starfleet* starship."

The Klingon reared back with a scornful laugh. She didn't bother to keep her voice low. Several patrons looked at her with curious expressions.

"You come to the Klingon Empire to buy a Starfleet vessel? You might as well go to Earth to buy a *QIghpej.*"

Chekov had no idea what a *QIghpej* was and had no desire to find out. He spoke quickly to keep the bartender's interest alive.

"Ve understand there vas a Starfleet wessel here not too long ago."

The bartender's laughter died abruptly. She pushed her long white hair back from her forehead with an indescribably filthy hand. "So what if there were?"

"Ve vould like to . . . obtain it."

"You and which spacefleet?" Her cooperation and respect obviously had limits. Even for a friend of Kort's.

Chekov pulled a small datacase from his jacket and flipped it open like a communicator. There was a credit wafer inside. The denomination on it was astronomical. And it was drawn on a nonaligned repository.

Chekov bared his teeth in what he hoped approximated the Klingon style of smiling. "Kort suggested you might be the person to arrange a boarding party."

The bartender immediately checked to see that no eyes were upon them. Then she reached out to touch the credit wafer. Her eyes widened with avarice. Chekov snapped the small case shut, then slipped it back inside his jacket.

The bartender looked at him intently, obviously calculating her chances on taking the datacase by force.

"Don't do anything you vill regret," Chekov warned.

He waited for Spock to make his move.

The bartender's hairy hands slid back across the table, as if getting ready to pull something else out from behind her apron.

Chekov kicked Spock's boot again.

"I *said.* Don't do anything you vill regret."

Spock hurriedly opened his cloak to show the butt of a phaser II.

The bartender's hands stopped.

"I've shown you ve can pay," Chekov stated. "Now . . . can you deliwer?"

The bartender nodded slowly. "I can field three ships. Twenty soldiers per crew. Fully armed. The Starfleet vessel is undercrewed, improperly armed. We can take it with a minimum of damage. I guarantee it."

Chekov remained calm. He hoped McCoy would remember to do the same.

"Then there *vas* a Starfleet wessel here recently."

"In private hands," the bartender confirmed. She grinned unpleasantly. Her stained teeth were as unpleasant as Kort's had been. "Ripe pickings."

"But only if ve know vhere it is *now.*"

Chekov pulled out another handful of metal *talons.* He held them in his fist in front of the bartender.

"The spacedocks at Delstin VIII," the bartender said slowly, keeping her eyes fixed on Chekov's fist.

"You're certain?" Chekov asked.

The bartender nodded. "Her master came to this very bar." She pointed two tables over. "Sat at that very table with his female and his engineer. Talked about how hard it was going to be to install the equipment they had purchased. How they had to find facilities to refit their ship before they could continue to wherever it was they were going."

Chekov shook his head slowly. "I'd like to believe you. But

people have been known to lie vhen so many talons are at stake."

The bartender bared her ghastly teeth. But it was no smile. "Do you question my honor?"

"That depends," Chekov said, deeply grateful for his six months of experience in undercover negotiations, even if his teacher had been Jade. "Describe the ship's master to me."

Her face wrinkled in distaste. "He was . . . human. Pasty. Pinkish. No fangs to speak of. A disgracefully smooth forehead, with not even a single ridge of a warrior." The bartender shrugged dismissively. "What can I tell you? You all look alike."

"Vhat about the others?" Chekov persisted. "The engineer?"

The bartender smacked her lips together. "Ah, now he was more formidable. A large man, more powerful. True, his forehead also lacked character, but he did wear a warrior's mustache."

"That sounds like Scotty," McCoy said.

The bartender shot a suspicious glance at the doctor. "You know the people on the ship?"

Chekov rubbed his hand over his face, thinking dark thoughts about amateurs.

But at least they had what they needed. Now all that remained was getting out in one piece.

"A lucky guess," Chekov said firmly. He began to stand.

The bartender's hand shot out and grabbed the wrist of Chekov's clenched fist.

"The master of that ship was a Federation lackey," the bartender snarled. "As was the engineer. So what does that make *you?*" She stared at Spock and McCoy. "And your clients?"

"Ve are not looking for trouble," Chekov said evenly. He looked at Spock and nodded.

Spock took an interminably long moment to realize what Chekov intended.

He opened his cloak again to show his phaser.

The bartender did not release Chekov's wrist.

"Now you tell me," she hissed. "What is the path of the *fifth*-rank watch dragon?" she asked.

Chekov didn't have the slightest idea what the rest of the code might be.

The longer he went without speaking, the more twisted the bartender's expression became.

"Answer . . . or die!"

Chekov could do nothing except wait for Spock to use his phaser. *If* he remembered he was *supposed* to use it. Undercover work was turning out not to be among Spock's many areas of expertise.

But it was McCoy who acted first.

"The path of the fifth-rank watch dragon is . . ." he began.

The bartender looked at him. "Yesss?"

"The yellow brick road!" McCoy hollered, and flipped the table into the air.

The copper pitcher smacked the bartender on her forehead, sending forth an explosion of foam that turned her white hair blue.

The coins from Chekov's almost-numb hand clattered against the upended table and scattered across the floor.

All through the bar, chairs fell over and tables squealed as customers leapt to their feet, drawing daggers and pistols and even a few swords.

The bartender still hadn't released Chekov's wrist. So Chekov pulled her forward and chopped at her shoulder.

She shrieked at him, nearly felling him with the foul blast of her breath.

A chair smashed into kindling against the back of her head.

She spun around to confront her attacker.

McCoy stared at the two small useless pieces of chair back he still gripped.

The bartender flung Chekov to the side and leapt at McCoy.

McCoy threw the pieces of chair away as he jumped backward.

Chekov recovered and dove at the bartender's waist, knocking her down before she could reach McCoy.

With an earsplitting screech, she bucked wildly, knocking him off her back.

Chekov landed on another table, flattening it as he crashed to floor.

His lungs emptied of air in an explosive wheeze. He gaped uselessly for a breath like a suffocating fish.

The bartender loomed over him. Both hands plunged beneath her apron and reemerged bearing ornate knife handles.

She flicked the handles and gleaming blades snicked into position.

Spock's hand came down on her shoulder, thumb and forefinger poised for a nerve pinch.

The bartender roared and shook Spock's hand free.

Spock raised an eyebrow.

The bartender elbowed him in the stomach, grabbed his phaser, then tossed it across the room.

Spock doubled over.

She turned back to Chekov, hurled a knife.

It thunked into the shattered tabletop beside his head. His breath returned to him a split second later.

The bartender raised her arm to throw again.

Spock straightened up behind her, reached out, and tore a strip from the top of her apron to expose the leather armor she wore over her shoulder.

The bartender wheeled, her arm descending on an arc toward Spock's neck.

McCoy grabbed at her arm, deflecting her aim, then hung on gamely as she shook him back and forth, screaming.

But McCoy didn't let go, even as he lost his footing.

Then Spock attached himself to her other arm.

Chekov decided if he lived through this night, he'd be able to laugh at the image of the Klingon bartender draped with McCoy and Spock. It looked like the performance of some avant-garde dance troupe.

Then Spock succeeded in snapping the armor off the bartender's shoulder to gently squeeze the bare flesh at the base of her neck.

The bartender hit the floor a second later, landing on top of McCoy.

Chekov struggled to his feet, almost able to breathe normally.

McCoy kicked and twisted to roll the bartender off him.

For the first time since the fight began, Chekov remembered the others in the bar. He realized he should brace for another attack. But all around them, the bar's other customers were busy with their own fights. At least ten were under way that Chekov could see.

No one else cared about them or the bartender.

Klingon death cries rang out in the establishment. Coins changed hands as bets were made. A free-for-all raged on behind the bar, where every drink was now on the house.

Wood splintered. Glass shattered.

Chekov looked back to Spock and McCoy, standing over the bartender's unconscious form.

They were arguing.

Chekov couldn't believe it.

"That's why *you* had the *phaser,* Spock!"

"There were too many innocent bystanders, Doctor."

"She was going to *kill* Chekov!"

"Doctor, please. It was obvious she intended to maim him first. His life was not in immediate danger."

Chekov barreled toward the two officers, hooked his arms through theirs, and dragged them toward the door.

Neither seemed to notice.

"You were going to let her *break* his arm?"

"My nerve pinch stopped her."

"On the *third* try!"

Chekov burst through the door and onto the street.

He inhaled deeply, desperate for fresh air.

But he had forgotten about the sulfurous rain. He started coughing.

Spock supported him. McCoy thumped his back.

"Good thing you had us along, isn't it," McCoy said.

Chekov moaned. He reached for his communicator.

"Chekov to *Excelsior.* Three to beam up."

This part of the mission had succeeded, at least. They knew where Captain Kirk had headed after leaving Prestor V.

Somehow, Chekov hadn't expected that following the captain would be so easy.

Unless, of course, Kirk had arranged things so it only seemed to be easy.

Chekov decided he wouldn't be surprised if that was the truth of the matter.

But what did continue to surprise him was that Spock and McCoy kept up their argument even as the transporter dissolved them.

Some things never change, Chekov thought. But who would want them to?

TWENTY-NINE

Kirk hefted the crate of emergency shelter supplies, pivoted, and threw it to the top of the cargo pallet.

The stacking indentations on the modular crate's bottom meshed with the matching pattern on the crate below it, locking both into place.

The pallet was full.

Kirk wiped his hand across his forehead to clear the sweat away. With so much work being done in the *Enterprise*'s cargo transporter room, the air was getting thick.

But Kirk didn't mind the heat. It wasn't slowing him down.

He rotated his shoulder, raising his arm over his head.

There was no resistance from strained muscles or ligaments. Only ease of motion. Freedom.

He slapped the side of the stack of crates.

"This one's done," he told the transporter tech.

The young Klingon-Romulan at the transporter console activated her controls.

The cargo pallet shimmered, then vanished.

A moment later the youth reported that the base on the planet's surface confirmed transport of supplies.

Kirk clapped his hands together, turned to his work crew—seven of Teilani's people. Their simple clothing, also drenched in sweat, clung to their supple forms.

But none of them looked tired.

In fact, Kirk thought, *they look the way I feel.*

Ready for more.

"Two to go," he told them.

They started eagerly for the doors leading to one of the *Enterprise*'s cargo bays.

Kirk followed, falling in with their energetic stride.

The doors to the corridor opened.

Scott stepped in, scowling.

Kirk hesitated in midstep. "You want to see me?" he asked, already knowing the answer.

Scott frowned. "I *was* lookin' for Bonnie Prince Charlie. But I suppose ye'll have t' do."

Kirk told the others in the cargo crew to continue without him, then went into the corridor to find Mr. Scott.

The engineer was waiting by a Jefferies tube.

Kirk assessed Scott's mood as he approached, tried to make light of it. "Scotty, you look as happy as a Klingon with a tribble in his pants."

The engineer was not amused. "We're not in Starfleet anymore, sir."

"That's right," Kirk agreed cautiously.

"So I feel I'm within my rights to ask ye what in thunderin' blue blazes is goin' on around here."

Kirk felt relieved. He thought Scott was coming to him with a serious problem.

"Scotty, we're saving a world."

"That's what Teilani told me when she offered me this job. But I've nae seen any sign of any world-saving goin' on. All I see is my diagnostics tellin' me th' poor transporter phase coils are overloadin'. Captain, we've got *shuttles* for routine cargo transport. Why not use them till I get th' *Enterprise* back in trim?"

Kirk leaned against the wall by the Jefferies tube. It seemed odd to look down the *Enterprise*'s corridor and not see any Starfleet personnel moving through it. The ship felt deserted with only a few dozen Chal aboard.

"Teilani's city is under siege. The shuttles might be shot at."

"Under siege by who?" Scott asked. "I thought we were supposed to be part of a planetary defense system for a world establishing her independence. I tell ye, I'm not comfortable with turnin' the *Enterprise* into a gunboat just to resolve some local political squabble. It's nae right."

Kirk understood Scott's position, but he felt his temper rise, nonetheless. "First of all, Mr. Scott—the *Enterprise* has never been, and *will* never be, a gunboat. And what Teilani's world is facing is not some 'local political squabble.' They're fighting for their lives down there."

"But *who's* fighting, Captain? I know ye keep wantin' me t' beam down and look around for m'self, but there's so much work t' be done up here . . ."

Kirk could see that Scott was preparing to draw a line.

"Captain, I have t' know that what we're doin' here is on the up-and-up."

"Scotty, you don't trust me?"

The engineer looked pained. "Och, don't put it that way. But the fact of th' matter is, th' way ye've been carrying on with that young lass—"

"She's not that young."

"—I sometimes have t' wonder if ye know what ye're doin'." Scott took a deep breath, as if what he had just said had taken considerable effort. "Ye can see th' predicament I'm in, can't ye?"

Kirk decided there were only a handful of people in this universe who could question him as Scott just did. The engineer could be prickly at times, outright rude at others, but the years they had spent together, fighting on the same side, added up to a friendship between them that was deeper than either would admit.

Kirk put his hand on Scott's shoulder. "I apologize, Scotty. You tried to tell me your concerns in the bar on Prestor V, and I should have done a better job of listening. It's just that you're so good at what you do, that sometimes I think you'd do just as well without me."

"We're part of a team, sir."

Kirk nodded. "And I have taken that for granted. Far too often." He looked around at his beautiful, empty ship. For all the accomplishments he had achieved with her, he was beginning to realize he had missed a great many opportunities as well.

Kirk looked down at his clothes. He needed to change.

"Walk with me, Scotty. I'll tell you everything Teilani's told me."

The captain and the engineer headed down the corridor together. Kirk felt as if he were back in uniform, giving a briefing.

"Chal was originally a joint colony founded by Klingons and Romulans during one of their truces."

"Aye, that much is in th' computers."

"But it has nothing in the way of exploitable resources. So when tensions rose between the empires, both withdrew their support."

"Leaving the original colonists' children behind." Scott seemed impatient. "I did know enough t' ask Teilani about her world."

Kirk and Scott came to a turbolift, waited for a car to arrive and the doors to open.

"They weren't *left* behind," Kirk said. "They *chose* to stay. To their parents, it was a colony world, different from their own. But to the first generation born there . . ."

"Aye, 'twas their home."

The lift doors puffed open. Kirk and Scott entered.

"Deck Five," Kirk said. The turbolift sped up through the ship as Kirk continued. "For forty years, they lived in peace, completely ignored by the rest of the galaxy."

"Because no one knew where they were," Scott said.

The lift slowed, then stopped. The doors opened. Kirk and Scott continued their walk.

"Teilani doesn't know how, but all records of Chal's location were purged from the central surveys of the two empires. Some think it was a final gift from one of the original colonists, to insure their children wouldn't be disturbed."

"Wishful thinkin'," Scott said.

"In any event, time passed Chal by. It became a forgotten paradise."

"With trouble brewin'."

"I'm coming to that," Kirk said.

They had arrived at his quarters. The doors opened. Kirk saw Scott purse his lips disapprovingly at the disarray. But there was nothing Kirk could do about that. He and Teilani had been energetic in their use of the quarters, to say the least.

Scott remained by the open doors while Kirk dug through his closet, searching for fresh clothes.

"As it turns out, Chal does have one resource that is imminently exploitable. What to do about it caused a split among its inhabitants. Along generational lines."

"What kind of resource would that be?" Scott asked. "I've looked at th' sensor results and I haven't seen anything worth comin' all this way for."

"Trust me," Kirk said. "It's there. If word gets out, then both empires will want to restake their claim to it. Chal will be torn apart."

"No secret that powerful can be kept for long," Scott said skeptically.

Kirk found a set of civilian clothes he had brought from Earth. He slipped them on. They felt looser.

"In this case," Kirk said, "even the older generation who wants to exploit the planet knows what would happen if they went public. So they want to keep the secret to themselves, too, and exploit it a little bit at a time. Sell what they have to sell without letting anyone know where it came from."

"But sell what?" Scott asked.

Kirk continued to ignore Scott's questions. "Teilani is part of the younger generation—those who don't want Chal to be exploited at all. They fear that even controlled access to their planet's treasure will eventually result in everyone finding out about it. Leading to the same probability of war between the empires."

"Captain," Scott interrupted. "What *is* this 'treasure'?"

Kirk lifted a hand to restrain the engineer's questions. "For now, Teilani's group is in control of the city and the small spaceport and the subspace transmitting station. As long as they maintain that control, the secret remains contained on Chal. That's where we come in."

"Are ye going t' tell me or not?"

"The older generation who want to exploit Chal have become anarchists. They're trying to tear down Chal's society, cause chaos, so they can steal a spacecraft or take control of the transmitting station. So far, they refuse to negotiate with their children."

Scott's face was nearly purple with frustration. "For pity's sake, what aren't ye telling me, man?"

Kirk adjusted his new shirt, turned on the fabric sealer to close it. "I'll tell you everything if you'll just be patient."

Scott folded his arms with a huff.

"Scotty, the *Enterprise* is here to get the Anarchists to the bargaining table. You saw how easily we stopped the attack this morning. You know very well that even with commercial sensor equipment, the *Enterprise* can track down any group of Anarchists on this planet. With her disruptors, she could destroy them, too."

Scott looked alarmed. "Not while I'm aboard her."

"Relax, Scotty. I wouldn't allow that to happen either. Even Teilani doesn't want that to happen. She simply wants to make certain that the Anarchists stay confined to Chal and eventually realize that they have to work out a compromise. Because as long as the *Enterprise* is here, they can't possibly win by violence."

Scotty stroked his mustache. "So where does th' Prime Directive fit int' all this?"

"It doesn't," Kirk said. "Chal is an independent world with

warp technology. An authorized member of her government, recognized by the Federation, has requested aid. The Prime Directive does not apply."

"So we're here to stop a fight, not start one?"

"Exactly."

Scott threw his hands into the air. "So what's Chal got that's so bloody valuable?"

Kirk tugged on his shirt. "Notice anything different about me, Scotty?"

Scott didn't understand the question. "What? Other than ye've been walkin' around like a schoolboy in a daze over a . . . a schoolgirl."

"Look at me," Kirk said. He swung his arms around in the air.

Scott blinked in total lack of comprehension.

"Two weeks ago, I couldn't have done that," Kirk explained. He rubbed at his shoulder. "My shoulder had been acting up. One too many jars and bumps, I guess. I was stiff, sore."

"Tell me about it," Scott said with sudden empathy. "My knees need replacement and some days my back doesn't loosen up till I've been on the go half the day."

Kirk paused. He hadn't intended this to turn into a comparison of old war stories.

"The point is," he said, "I have full movement in both shoulders now."

Scott looked at Kirk, about to ask a question. But all he could manage was, "So?"

"Look at me, Scotty! I feel wonderful! Charged with energy! Ready for . . . for anything! And I've only been on Chal for three days."

Scott tapped his foot against the carpeted deck. "I think ye'd better spell this one out for me, sir."

"It's the treasure of Chal, Scotty. Restoration. Rejuvenation. *Youth.*"

Scotty looked troubled. "Captain, no. You cannae believe that."

"I don't have to *believe,* Scotty. I've been down there. I know how I feel."

"I wish Dr. McCoy were here to give ye a full medical scan. T' find out what they've been puttin' in your coffee."

Kirk turned to the built-in desk, opened a drawer, pulled out a Starfleet-issue medical tricorder.

"That's what *I* thought. But look at these readings."

Kirk handed the tricorder over to Scott. The engineer scrolled through the display screens.

"Nothing," Kirk said. "No drugs, no chemicals, no stimulants natural or otherwise."

Scott shut off the tricorder, handed it back.

"It's Chal," Kirk said. "Just as Teilani said it would be."

Scott thought for long moments.

"Captain, I'm an engineer, not a doctor. But I cannae see how such a thing could be possible without some terrible price. And I cannae understand how you could fall for such a swindle."

Kirk carefully put the tricorder down. "It's not a swindle. You've seen Teilani. You've seen the others like her. If you'd just beam down and spend a day there yourself, you'd feel it, too."

Scott's eyes seemed to well up with tears. "Captain Kirk, I know we've had our differences in th' past. But I've always respected ye. And it tears me apart to see ye caught up in this."

"Caught up in what?"

"Whatever it is this lass has done t' ye."

"Scotty, Teilani hasn't done anything to me. I love her. I—"

"How can ye?"

Kirk didn't understand Scott's discomfort. "I know enough to leave explanations for love to the poets."

"That's not it. I mean, what do ye know about the lass? Really know about her? Aye, she's young, attractive, I'm nae blind to that. But how can ye think there can ever be anything more than just . . . just this carryin' on like jackrabbits between ye?"

Kirk frowned at Scotty's characterization.

"Seriously," the engineer continued. "I've nothing t' say one way or another about two grown people havin' a fling that's not hurtin' anyone else. But it's not just a fling t' ye. Ye've thrown away your life, your career, your—"

Kirk had had enough. *"Scotty!* I've moved on! I have a new life now. A new mission."

Scott shook his head with a sorrowful expression. "I don't care how ye justify it t' yourself. But I know what I see. She's pullin' your strings like you're her—"

Kirk clenched his jaw, determined not to lose his temper with Scott the way he had with Spock and McCoy. *"Mr.* Scott—you're stepping over the line here."

"Because you're refusin' to. I don't know. Maybe deep inside ye know you're foolin' yourself, not thinkin' things through. I hope so, 'cause it's not a pretty picture seein' ye playin' the fool to her."

Kirk took a deep breath. Thought of Chal's beaches and jungles and piercingly blue skies. Felt calm returning. "Come down with me, Scotty."

But Scott drew back. "I'll not be tormenting myself with impossible dreams. We had our chance at youth. We used it well. We pushed some boundaries, I'll admit. But now our day is almost over. It's the nature of things, sir. We have t' accept that."

"Scotty—think of all the miracles we've seen in our voyages. All the different ways that space and time and living flesh have been changed and altered. What's wrong with continuing to push at those boundaries? *Why* must we accept . . . *anything?"*

Scott gave Kirk a look of abject pity. He spoke slowly, sorrow in his voice. "Because otherwise, sir, we will surely go mad, desperately seekin' that which we cannae have."

Kirk didn't know what to say. The line Scott had drawn had become a wall.

"It appears I'm onboard for th' duration," Scott said stiffly. "And I shall do my best t' keep this fine ship t'gether for ye. But I will nae be a party t' attacks on anyone below. And I will nae be leaving the *Enterprise.* Until ye come t' your senses."

Scott turned to go.

"Now, if you'll excuse me, I'm needed in th' engine room."

The doors slid shut behind him.

Kirk stood alone in his empty quarters.

But Scott's words remained.

Maybe deep inside you know you're fooling yourself, not thinking things through.

Might it be true? Could it be?

Kirk had always been the master of the bluff and the well-crafted lie. How else had he survived for so long? Cheated death so often?

But what if he had taken that characteristic of survival and pushed it that one step too far?

What if he had come all this way, burned so many bridges, because he *was* desperate for something he could never have again?

Could his friends be right?

For all the times he had lied to others to wrest victory from defeat, what if this time he was simply lying to himself?

Kirk had crossed half the sector to solve the mystery of Chal.

But now he feared he had found a mystery more profound.

Himself.

THIRTY

Five light-years from the spacedocks at Delstin VIII, the *Excelsior* dropped out of warp and came to relative stop.

The trail of the *Enterprise* had abruptly disappeared.

On the *Excelsior*'s bridge, Chekov worked with Spock to reconfigure the main sensors.

Sulu waited impatiently in the center chair.

But for all the increased activity on the bridge, no one was surprised by what had happened.

They had all served with Captain Kirk. They had seen him cover his tracks too many times to think following him would be easy.

Chekov finished entering the final adjustments on his tactical board. "Sensors reconfigured," he announced.

"Commencing scan," Spock said from his science station.

All waited while the *Excelsior*'s elaborate system of sensors probed the surrounding vacuum for any trace of the *Enterprise*'s distinct warp signature. Almost imperceptible distortions in subspace sometimes lingered after a starship's passage at faster-than-light velocities, like the wake left by an oceangoing vessel—sometimes for days.

The *Excelsior* had followed just such a wake on a direct course from Prestor V to Delstin VIII, precisely where the Klingon bartender had said Kirk was taking his ship.

Any other commander might have saved time by not bothering to scan continuously for the *Enterprise*'s warp signature along the entire route until arriving at the ship's stated destination.

But Sulu had wisely tracked it all the way, waiting for it to cease abruptly, as he knew it must.

The instant it had, Kirk's crew immediately knew that this was the point at which the *Enterprise* had left warp, changed heading, and then continued on her way.

Any other commander would have missed the end of the trail and arrived at Delstin VIII. There, a day would have been lost to frantic scanning to determine that the *Enterprise* had never arrived. Then the commander would have been forced to backtrack. Slowly. To find the point along the projected route where the *Enterprise* had surreptitiously changed course.

By that time, the *Enterprise*'s warp signature would have faded into the natural background ebb and flow of subspace, undetectable.

But Sulu wasn't any other commander.

"Sensors have made contact," Spock said. "Subspace disturbance at bearing one four four mark twenty."

Chekov confirmed the distortion pattern. "It is the *Enterprise*'s varp signature."

The helmsman, a young human, asked if he should lay in a course to match the new trail.

Chekov saw Sulu smile knowingly. "Negative, Mr. Curtis. If I know Captain Kirk, we should find at least *three* warp trails from this location."

In the end, they found four.

Kirk had looped back three times to muddy the subspace waters, laying false trails.

The most obvious trail to follow was on a bearing that headed toward the Klingon-Romulan frontier, the general location of Chal.

Sulu discounted that one right away as being far too obvious.

Of the other three trails, one headed back to the Federation, one to the Klingon Empire, and one straight out of the galactic ecliptic.

Sulu chose to follow the course heading for the Klingon Empire, because who would ever believe Captain Kirk would willingly return there? No one except his former crew, who knew Kirk could be counted upon to do the unexpected.

Chekov knew that if Sulu had guessed wrong, then within six hours the warp trail would end with a return loop, indicating it had been a false heading. Meanwhile, the *Enterprise*'s real path would have become even more difficult to locate.

But Sulu hadn't guessed wrong.

Five hours later, the *Enterprise*'s trail ended again, but without a return loop, indicating that Kirk had once again dropped from warp to change course.

This time, they found three possible trails.

Chekov was impressed by Captain Kirk's efforts.

But McCoy was puzzled. "Who did he think was following him?" he muttered as he sat by Uhura's communications post. "My ex-wife?"

"Whoever it was," Sulu said, "he couldn't be expecting it to be us. We'll find his pattern."

Spock confirmed the method behind Kirk's evasive maneuvers. "It is a feint he has used in chess many times, to hide the true focus of attack through misdirection."

Chekov looked up from his tactical displays. "It is not like the keptin to repeat himself."

"No, it is not," Spock agreed.

"Unless," McCoy suggested, "he laid down a series of course changes that would throw *everyone* off his trail—*except* for his friends."

"An intriguing speculation," Spock allowed. "But given the captain's somewhat erratic emotional state in his final days on Earth, I find it . . . unlikely."

Everyone looked at Sulu. It was time to choose which of the three warp trails to follow.

"Logically, we should choose the trail that leads away from the obvious choice," Spock suggested.

McCoy stood behind Sulu's chair and objected. "C'mon, Spock. Who the hell would know what the 'obvious' choice was except someone who's spent the past thirty years wrangling with Jim over a chess board? You said it yourself: Where Jim's concerned, logic seldom applies."

McCoy folded his arms and stared at Spock, as if daring him to top his argument.

Sulu glanced back at McCoy, then at Spock again.

Chekov had seen Kirk caught in the same position uncountable times.

Logic versus gut feeling.

Sulu made his decision.

"Commander Spock, if we are seeing a repeat of one of Captain Kirk's chess strategies, which trail is the obvious one?"

Spock gave the bearing.

"Mr. Curtis," Sulu said, "lay in a course on that bearing. Commander Chekov, resume tracing the *Enterprise*'s warp signature."

The bridge crew acknowledged their orders.

"Ahead, maximum warp," Sulu ordered.

The *Excelsior* smoothly stretched into the infinite realms of warp speed.

McCoy beamed at Sulu. "You make a damned fine captain, Sulu. Keep it up."

Chekov knew the real purpose of what McCoy had said. He glanced over at Spock.

Spock betrayed no reaction to McCoy's dig.

But Chekov suspected he was already plotting some form of logical, unemotional revenge. After thirty years, how could he not?

Chekov smiled to himself. It was almost like being back on the *Enterprise*.

Then the *Excelsior* hit a brick wall.

The main viewscreen flared orange white.

Collision alarms sounded.

The bridge lurched as the inertial dampers failed to keep up with the ship's sudden loss of warp drive.

An environmental station shorted out in an explosion of sparks.

Power to the bridge failed, then instantly reset.

"What the hell was that?" Sulu said.

Chekov pulled himself back to his tactical board. His fingers flew over the controls. There was nothing . . . nothing . . .

. . . and then, where there had been nothing—

—there was something.

The viewscreen showed it best.

Three Klingon battle cruisers dropped from warp dead ahead.

"Damage is consistent with photon torpedo impact," Spock announced.

"Captain," Uhura shouted over the alarms, "we are being hailed."

"Onscreen."

Chekov's eyes widened as the viewscreen image changed to show a Klingon bridge.

The Klingon commander was young, eager eyes gleaming viciously.

"Federation starship," he barked. "You have intruded in restricted Klingon space." His yellow teeth grinned through his wispy beard.

"Surrender . . . or *die!*"

THIRTY-ONE

Kirk was one with the night.

He leaned with his back against the rough bark of an alien tree, listening to the sounds of the jungle around him.

Eerie calls from night-feeding birds. The chitter and hissing of unseen insects. The random rustle of leaves and branches as arboreal creatures swung through the jungle's canopy overhead.

But he heard nothing that betrayed the presence of the fifteen Chal who moved through the jungle with him, closing in on the Anarchists' base.

His soldiers.

Kirk wished he could take credit for their training. But, in truth, they had none.

Instead, the Chal's innate abilities to move stealthily, to follow orders, to think in tactical terms, all seemed to stem from their childhood games.

Elaborate games of hunts and chases through the jungle. Intricate strategy and tactics played out with twigs and stones on squares drawn into sand on the beach.

As Teilani had explained those children's pastimes to him, Kirk had first been astounded by the complexity of the military concepts contained within them. But then he had reminded himself that he wasn't dealing with a human culture.

Teilani and her people apparently had had a typical Klingon and Romulan upbringing.

They had learned their lessons well.

In the jungle, a shadow moved toward Kirk. His hand tightened on the grip of the disruptor at his side. Then relaxed as a faint shaft of light from Chal's glimmering moon revealed to him an unmistakable silhouette.

Making not a sound, Teilani crept up beside him.

Like Kirk, she wore the dark jumpsuit that was the uniform of those who fought for Chal. Like Kirk, her face was darkened with camouflage to better hide within the night.

But unlike Kirk, this was the first time she had faced real battle.

With swift but cautious movements, Teilani brought out her combat tricorder and showed its display to Kirk.

Sixteen muted green dots were arranged in a half circle around the target's coordinates.

Each Chal was in position. Each of Kirk's soldiers.

All that remained was for him to give the word.

He hesitated on the brink of action, savoring the anticipation of the moment when his plans would be unleashed.

The people of Chal had been in conflict for years. The city-dwellers had the advantage of a defensible position and hard technology. The Anarchists had the advantage of the jungle and elaborate jamming devices.

Only Mr. Scott's wizardry with the *Enterprise*'s weakened sensors had enabled Kirk to finally locate the Anarchists' stronghold, two hundred kilometers from Chal's main city.

But the stronghold was protected by a complex web of sensor screens, forcefields, and jammers. Its presence ruled out any attempt to stun its fighters by low-power disruptor fire from orbit. Neither could Kirk capture them by transporter or even beam in a sneak attack.

High-powered disruptor beams could punch through the relatively weak forcefields. Two photon torpedoes could decimate the Anarchists' entire compound along with several square kilometers of surrounding jungle.

But that was not the reason Kirk had come to Chal.

Lasting peace and reconciliation were never a question of brute force.

He was here to bring both sides in the conflict together. And the *only* way to accomplish that was by direct, physical confrontation.

Nothing could have pleased Kirk more.

He slipped his disruptor from its holster and checked again that it was at its stun setting.

He looked at Teilani, saw the faint reflection of moonlight in her eyes.

She reached out to touch Kirk's face, a silent gesture of her feelings. Her hand slid down to his neck. She tugged on the collar of his jumpsuit as if adjusting it.

"Now," he whispered.

The Anarchists' first perimeter line was only twenty meters ahead of them.

Teilani cupped a hand to her mouth. She made the sound of a nightfeeder, shrill and piercing. A sound that belonged to the jungles of Chal.

Then she made it again.

The signal had been given.

Kirk pushed away from the alien tree and began moving carefully through the darkness.

Teilani at his side.

In his mind, Kirk saw his strategy played out as if looking down at the levels of a chess board.

Fortunately, Spock was not on the board's other side.

The clearing came up before him.

Because of the moon and the stars, the night sky of Chal was slightly brighter than the stark black shadows of the surrounding trees and the Anarchists' watchtowers. The towers were each five meters tall, roughly constructed of wood and vines. Surveillance had shown that each held two guards, linked to the perimeter sensor web.

They were Kirk's first target.

Teilani silently held her combat tricorder out for Kirk to see.

Its pale screen showed they were a meter from the first sensor alarm threshold.

Kirk nodded.

Teilani repeated the nightfeeder's cry. Three times.

Kirk counted down from five. Then charged forward.

In his mind, he saw his soldiers move in perfect coordination with him.

Instantly the jungle roared to life with disruptor firings as each watchtower was hit by multiple beams.

Cries of surprise followed as the Anarchists behind the defensive perimeters heard the sensor alarms.

Then there were explosions.

Kirk recognized their distinctive sound.

Microexplosive shells from projectile weapons like those used by the attackers at the farm on Earth.

Those weapons had been his chief concern for this attack.

The jumpsuits used by the Chal contained an energy mesh that could dissipate much of the force of a disruptor beam. Even if the Anarchists set their weapons to kill, it would be unlikely if any of Kirk's attacking force would suffer more than a heavy stun.

But the explosive shells could be fatal.

It had been Teilani who told Kirk not to be overly worried about them. The Anarchists were unskilled with weapons, she said. They were unlikely to hit anyone they aimed at.

That contradicted what Kirk had seen at the farm. But he hadn't pressed the matter. If all went according to plan, the Anarchists would have little time to fight back.

Kirk ran past the closest watchtower.

There was no covering fire from it. Its guards had been stunned as planned.

The first stage of the attack was complete.

Ahead of them now was a wooden barricade reinforced

with metal sheets from old shipping containers. Beyond it, Scotty's low-resolution sensor scans had revealed a compound of wooden huts—the Anarchists' camp.

Teilani swung her projectile gun up. Fired a burst of shells set for contact detonation.

A section of the barricade disintegrated in flame. Over the din surrounding them, Kirk could hear simultaneous explosions nearby as the other Chal reached their sections of the wood and metal structure.

Before the smoke had thinned, Kirk had hurled himself toward the opening. The blast-torn edges of wood crackled with flames.

Kirk leapt forward through the smoke and the fire, arms outstretched.

His trajectory carried him low even as he heard the whistle of shells streak over him.

He hit on his shoulder, flipped over, was firing his disruptor even as he came to his feet.

Three Anarchists dropped in the orange glow of the disruptor beam.

Kirk ran on.

His breath came easily. His shoulder felt no different after his fall and tumble.

He exulted in his renewed vigor.

He *was* twenty again.

More explosions shattered the jungle night.

An enormous fireball flared overhead as a munitions crate erupted.

Flickering red light played across the compound. He ran on.

Kirk saw dark figures rushing about in confusion—the Anarchists, completely taken by surprise.

Kirk saw his soldiers—the Chal, efficiently picking off each Anarchist with disruptor stuns.

Kirk paused in the center of the storm he had unleashed. In control. Triumphant.

Teilani rushed to his side, combat tricorder in hand.

"Each team is in!" she shouted in her excitement. "No casualties!"

Kirk flipped open his communicator. His voice strong and clear. "Scotty—beam in the second wave!"

Instantly the warble of transporter beams blended with the cries and explosions of the compound.

In groups of six, three more teams of Chal took form near the breeched barricade.

Each member of the second team carried medical tricorders and multiple sets of prisoner restraints.

As Kirk and his soldiers continued to mop up, his plan dictated that the second wave would locate the stunned Anarchists, then disarm and bind them.

Four days ago, the Chal had made no effort to capture the Anarchists who had attacked the city. As soon as they had recovered from Scott's low-level disruptor stun, they had disappeared back into the jungle. Under his leadership, Kirk would not allow the Chal to make that mistake again.

Both sides *must* be brought together.

Teilani watched the second-wave teams fan out through the compound. "James—it's going perfectly."

"It's not over yet," Kirk cautioned.

"Soon," Teilani said. She ran off to help with the capture of the Anarchists.

Kirk checked the compound. The sounds of combat were diminishing. But he saw four Anarchists run between two huts. There was no sense of panic or confusion to their movements. They knew where they were going, what they were doing.

Kirk recognized the signs of a counterattack in the making. He sprinted toward the huts they had run between, slid to a stop by the corner of one. Carefully peered around the edge.

He heard an antigrav generator come online.

Kirk charged around the corner, swinging his disruptor up.

Ten meters away, a hover truck lifted into the air.

One Anarchist drove it. The other three operated the smart cannon mounted on its cargo bed.

The hover truck's headlight flared into life, blinding Kirk.

He heard its impeller fans whine as it flew straight for him.

Unable to see, he fired his disruptor, then dove to the side, feeling the bulk of the speeding truck closing.

He hit the ground hard.

The scream of the hover truck's engine became the thunderous explosion of a wooden hut.

Kirk looked up, realizing he had managed to stun the driver.

The truck was embedded in the ruins of a hut.

One Anarchist leapt from the truck's cargo bed, saw Kirk. Ran at him.

The disruptor had slipped from Kirk's hand, wrenched out by the impact of his fall.

Kirk saw it, out of reach.

He rolled to the side, leapt to his feet.

The Anarchist trained his projectile gun on him.

He was just like any other Chal.

Though an Anarchist, a member of the world's first generation, he looked no older than Teilani.

But there was murderous rage in his eyes. He aimed his weapon.

Kirk was out of options. He knew a single shell from the gun could tear him in half.

There was only one thing to do.

He charged.

The Anarchist fired twice, point-blank, before Kirk slammed into him.

Kirk didn't even hear the whistle of the shells.

He only felt the impact of his fist on the Anarchist's jaw.

He only tasted the dust of the ground as they rolled against it.

The Anarchist swung his weapon for Kirk's head.

Kirk blocked the blow, punched again.

The Anarchist slumped back. The weapon fell from his hand.

Kirk smelled the acrid odor of the shells' propellant. He looked down at his chest.

The projectiles had missed.

For an instant, Kirk saw Teilani spinning through the air in his parents' barn, a string of projectile explosives missing her by a heartbeat.

Kirk reached up to his collar. Felt a small, curved, metal tube coiled inside the fabric.

Teilani had adjusted it just before the attack began.

He saw her standing by the kitchen window, hand on her collar, an instant before the projectile had hit her shoulder.

Grazed her shoulder.

Kirk's stomach tightened.

What else was before him that he hadn't seen?

In his mind, Spock, McCoy, and Scotty all seemed to answer at once.

And the answer they gave was *Teilani.*

THIRTY-TWO

Kirk glanced around the Anarchists' compound. No other Chal were nearby. The sounds of fighting had ended. The battle had been fought and won.

But Kirk knew a different war on Chal was still in progress. The device hidden in his collar was proof of it.

He hauled the unconscious Anarchist to his feet. Flipped open his communicator.

"Kirk to *Enterprise.*"

"Scott here, Captain."

"I've got a prisoner with me, Scotty. I want you to beam us both directly to the brig."

Scott took so long to answer that Kirk almost added, *Scotty, that's an order.*

"I take it there's more goin' on down there than you've told me, isn't there?" Scott said.

"Please, Mr. Scott." Kirk could hear footsteps approaching from around the corner of the nearest hut.

Scott sighed over the open channel. "Energizin'."

The dark jungle compound dissolved around Kirk, changing into the bright, plain walls of the *Enterprise's* brig.

Kirk's prisoner moaned, coming around. Kirk eased him onto a bench in one of the holding cells, then stepped out and activated the security field. Blue forcefield emitters glowed around the cell's opening.

The Anarchist shook his head, looked around. Saw Kirk.

Stared at him with hatred. Then pushed himself to his feet to face his captor eye to eye.

"Where have you brought me?"

"You're on the *Enterprise,"* Kirk said. "A starship orbiting Chal. My name's Kirk."

The Anarchist blinked in surprise, took another look around. "A *Federation* ship?"

Kirk heard the fear in his prisoner's voice. Wondered why.

"No. It's . . . a private ship. Serving Teilani."

At the mention of Teilani, the Anarchist spit at Kirk's feet. The spittle crackled as it hit the security forcefield and vaporized.

"You're in no danger," Kirk said. "After we've talked, you're free to return to Chal."

That confused the Anarchist. "Talk about what?" He eyed Kirk warily.

"To begin with, what's your name?"

The Anarchist seemed puzzled by the question. "Torl."

"Fine, Torl. How old are you?"

Torl became even more confused. "In your standard years, forty-two."

Kirk studied his prisoner carefully, looking for any sign that he was lying. Saw nothing. Only a youth no older than twenty.

"Then it's true. There's something on Chal—in the air or the water—that keeps people . . . young."

Torl's mouth opened in astonishment. "What?"

Kirk skipped a beat. He hadn't expected that reaction. "You all look about the same age. Your generation, Teilani's generation. Isn't that the result of living on your world?"

Torl smiled with sudden knowledge. Baring his teeth, he looked disconcertingly like a full-blooded Klingon.

"Tell me what Teilani told you, human."

It took Kirk only an instant to make his decision. As long as Torl was locked in that cell, Kirk had nothing to lose by revealing all that he knew. Or thought he knew.

"The colony on Chal was jointly founded by the Klingons and the Romulans," Kirk began.

"Correct."

"It was deemed a failure, and abandoned by both sides."

Torl snorted in derision. "It was an unqualified *success.*"

Kirk didn't see where that fit in. "Then why were you abandoned by both Empires?"

"We weren't abandoned. We were hidden."

"Why?"

Torl stepped closer to the security screen, as if conducting his own examination of Kirk's honesty.

"You really don't know who we are, do you?" Torl asked. "You have no idea *what* we are."

Kirk gestured with open hands, as if grasping for some truth just out of reach.

"You're the children of the original colonists—Klingon *and* Romulan."

"Children of the original colonists?!" Torl laughed. "Only half correct. We are the Children of Heaven."

"The children of . . . Chal?" Kirk asked, trying to reconcile Teilani's revelations with what his prisoner was saying.

Torl's smile disappeared. "The *Chalchaj 'qmey.*"

Kirk recognized the phrase as Klingon, but beyond that, it meant nothing to him.

Kirk's prisoner looked troubled. He held out a hand as if to touch the almost invisible security screen. "Why are you here, human? What business of yours is Chal?"

"I'm trying to help stop thc fighting."

"Why?"

"So this planet will be at peace."

"Why?"

Kirk took control of the conversation again. "Do you *want* to keep fighting?"

"No," Torl said simply. "I want to destroy Teilani and her people. Then the fighting will stop."

"So you can sell the secret of Chal to the rest of the galaxy."

Torl struck out against the security screen in anger, then flew back from the crackling impact.

He collapsed onto the bench, looked up at Kirk, and actually snarled.

"Is that what *she* told you we were trying to do?"

"Yes. That you want to exploit Chal."

"Human, we want to *bury* Chal. To wipe it out of existence."

"Why? It's a paradise."

Torl jumped to his feet in rage. "It is an obscenity!"

Kirk would not accept that. "I've been down there," he argued. "I've felt its influence. It's one of the most beautiful worlds I've ever seen. Filled with bright, healthy people."

Torl's eyes smoldered with repressed fury. "At what cost?"

"You tell me."

Torl thought a moment. "Has she shown you the Armory?"

Kirk shook his head. He had never heard of an armory on Chal.

"The large building. In the center of the city."

"That's an armory? With weapons?"

"If you believe truth is a weapon."

Kirk had had enough. "What *is* the truth?"

Unexpectedly, the prisoner's expression changed once more. To mournful sorrow. "Evil, human. This world is not *chalchaj*. It is *chalwutlh*. The underworld, not heaven." He looked out at Kirk, his anger gone. "I don't know who you are or why you're here, but you must know that peace grows between our kind. The Klingon Empire and the Federation reach out to each other. If their fragile efforts succeed, the Romulans cannot stand against them. They must lay down their arms as well. Do you believe that is a good thing?"

"Yes."

"Then for peace to have its chance, let this world die. And all its secrets with it."

"*What* secrets?" Kirk asked.

Torl seemed to age before Kirk's eyes. His shoulders

slumped. His hands hung loosely at his side. "For what I am going to tell you, please forgive me. Remember that in the decades past our people were manipulated by their rulers to hate you. To consider your species as nothing more than animals."

He sat down on the bench. He leaned back wearily against the wall. He began to weep.

Kirk felt the hairs bristle on his arms. Torl wept as if he was torn apart by monumental anguish. Shame.

"What secrets?" Kirk asked again, almost afraid of the answer he was about to hear.

Then a new voice rang out in the brig.

"Mr. Kirk! Stand back!"

Kirk spun around. Two Chal stood in the doorway leading to the corridor. Each held a disruptor, aimed past Kirk.

Kirk recognized them.

The attackers from the farm.

The attackers who had died.

He read their intent in their eyes.

"No!" Kirk shouted. He stepped in front of Torl, blocking the attackers' line of sight.

One of them twisted the setting stud on his gun.

An instant later, Kirk felt himself fly backward, each nerve on fire with the all-too familiar sting of a disruptor set to stun.

He fell into the security screen.

A new wave of agony erupted against his back as he was thrown forward again, ears ringing with the crackle of the forcefield.

He hit the deck hard, unable to use his arms to break his fall.

His chest was paralyzed. He couldn't breathe.

The attackers walked past him.

Lungs burning with unspeakable pain, Kirk forced himself onto his back.

Just in time to see two disruptor beams hit Torl.

Just in time to see Torl fall back, body glowing with the incandescent light of a heavy stun.

The attackers looked down at Kirk. Reluctantly, they put away their weapons.

Kirk sensed a third person entering the brig.

Teilani.

Her face was still dark with camouflage. She knelt by him, spoke softly.

"It's over, James." He could barely hear her through the ringing in his ears. "They're our prisoners now. All of them."

Kirk was finally able to gasp for air. It tore through his lungs like liquid fire. The deck spun beneath him. He felt himself begin to fall.

"Thanks to you, James," Teilani said. "We won."

As the darkness claimed Kirk, he thought he could still hear Torl weeping.

THIRTY-THREE

"Go to hell," Sulu said to the Klingon commander. To his crew he added, "Go to red alert. Full power to shields. Phasers on standby."

The *Excelsior* prepared for battle.

Chekov read his tactical displays. "All three cruisers have locked veapons on us."

Sulu stood to face the viewscreen. "Klingon commander. I am Captain Sulu of the starship *Excelsior.* We are searching for a Federation vessel under the authority of—"

"You have five seconds to lower your shields and prepare for boarding," the Klingon snarled.

Sulu ignored him. *"Under* the *authority* of Chancellor Azetbur."

The Klingon blinked. "How dare you invoke the name of our chancellor for your foul crimes."

"I say again—the *Excelsior* has full diplomatic clearance to conduct her search in Klingon territory. Contact your central command for verification. Then I'll be more than happy to accept your apology." Sulu turned to Uhura. "Close the channel."

The viewscreen returned to an image of the three Klingon vessels hanging ominously in space.

"Veapons still locked on," Chekov said. He wondered how far Sulu was prepared to push the confrontation. "You know, the *Excelsior* can outrun them," he added, trying to be helpful.

Sulu sat back in his command chair. "I know the speed of my own ship, Pavel. But where could we go? Deeper into Klingon space, there're bound to be other cruisers in position to intercept us. The only direction open to us is back to the Federation. And then we'll have lost any chance of picking up the *Enterprise's* warp trail."

"I thought Admiral Drake personally cleared all this through Azetbur," McCoy said.

"Presumably, we're about to find out," Uhura said. "I'm picking up a flurry of encrypted messages. They're all going out from the Klingon lead ship. They're attempting to contact their central command."

"Can you decode?" Sulu asked.

Janice Rand activated the translator subroutines. "That's odd," she said. "It's an old code. We can crack it. Two minutes, maybe three."

"Any idea how long it will take for them to get a reply?" Sulu asked.

Chekov saw Uhura look to the ceiling as she worked out the

time and distance. "If they have to get a message all the way back to their homeworld, it could take half a day for a reply."

"We can't wait half a day," Sulu said.

McCoy offered his opinion. "Since we *can* outrun them, why not just keep going after the *Enterprise?* While they're chasing us, they might hear back from command and call the whole thing off."

Spock rose from his science station. "Doctor, what if Admiral Drake has *not* obtained the necessary clearance for us?"

McCoy spoke sharply. "What do you mean? He told us himself that Azetbur had okayed the mission."

"Admiral Drake has told us a number of things," Spock said blandly. "That does not make them true."

"It doesn't matter either way," Sulu said. "At the speed we'd have to go to keep ahead of those ships, we wouldn't be able to scan for the *Enterprise*'s wake. If Captain Kirk changed course again, we'd miss the changeover point completely."

The bridge fell silent. It seemed there was nothing they could do.

A damage-control team arrived to begin replacing the modular components of the damaged environmental station.

The battle readiness of the Klingon cruisers remained unchanged.

Lieutenant Rand announced that the computer had decoded the Klingon's message to central command.

"But . . . I don't understand," she said as she read the results onscreen. "It's . . . just random bits."

Sulu checked the screen over her shoulder. "Is it a code within a code?"

"Nothing the computer's seen before," Rand said. "Nothing I've seen either."

"Lieutenant, please transfer the output to my system," Spock said.

Rand did so. Even Spock was puzzled.

"The only logical way this message makes sense is if we assume it is a prearranged signal. That is, it is not the content of the message that is important, merely the fact that this particular pattern has been sent."

"But that would mean the Klingons were expecting to intercept us," Sulu said. "Even though they claim to be unaware of our mission."

"Curiouser and curiouser," Spock agreed.

Finally, ten minutes after the Klingon's message had been sent, Uhura announced that a reply was returning. "There must be a command ship nearby," she said.

"The return message is in the same code," Rand reported.

Sulu returned to his command chair. "On your toes, everyone. What's happening, Uhura?"

Uhura held her earpiece close. "Ship-to-ship communications . . . all encrypted . . . sounds like—" She looked up in alarm. "Sir! They're initiating a countdown!"

Sulu's hand hit the comm controls on his chair. "Engineering! I want—"

Two of the Klingon cruisers disappeared from the viewscreen.

"Damn!" Chekov said as his sensors told him what had happened. "Ve've been englobed."

At warp speed, the two cruisers had positioned themselves 120 degrees from the first and from each other, in a circle around the *Excelsior.* The *Excelsior* could run. But the Klingons had made sure that at least two or three photon torpedoes would impact before she had reached her top speed.

"The Klingon commander is hailing us," Uhura said.

Sulu glowered. "Open a channel."

The Klingon commander reappeared on the viewscreen, sprawled comfortably in his chair, a position of supreme confidence.

"Captain Sulu of the *Starship Excelsior,"* he said with mock deference, "my central command has no record of any diplomatic clearance being given to you or your vessel. Therefore, I give you your choice. Prepare to be boarded. Or prepare to die." The Klingon scratched delicately at his beard. "And by the way, your ten seconds are up. So I would appreciate hearing your answer—*now!*"

"Unfortunately," Sulu said, "I know you're lying. We decoded your message. You didn't ask your central command about—"

"baH cha!" the Klingon shouted, then disappeared from the screen.

"Torpedoes launched!" Chekov warned.

Instantly, the *Excelsior* rocked with multiple impacts.

"Shields at ninety percent!" Chekov reported. "They are firing again!"

Sulu jumped from his command chair and went to the helm. "I'll take over, Mr. Curtis."

The young helmsman left his position as Sulu slid into his chair.

The captain's fingers flew over the controls.

"Engineering, prepare for warp pulse—on my mark!" Sulu said.

The *Excelsior* rocked again. The torpedoes were being concentrated on screen overlaps, where the shields were weakest.

Chekov saw what was coming. The Klingons were going to punch through the weakened areas of overlap with their disruptors.

"Keptin! Ve have to move!"

"So they can send one up our tailpipe?" Sulu muttered as he reset fine controls on the navigation board. "I don't think so."

"Shields at seventy-eight percent!" Chekov shouted. "Ve are experiencing fluctuation feedback!"

"Brace yourselves!" Sulu ordered.

His finger jabbed at his board.

Instantly the single cruiser on the viewscreen expanded as the *Excelsior* accelerated for it at the speed of light.

Chekov held on to his tactical board, bracing for the moment of impact.

But the *Excelsior* swept beneath the cruiser—missing its shields by only the six meters Chekov read wonderingly from his controls. Then the warp pulse ended. The *Excelsior* lurched ninety degrees from her warp heading to bob up behind the cruiser. Again Sulu's ship escaped devastating impact with its shields by less than the length of a shuttle.

For one instant, Chekov had no idea what Sulu was trying to do, other than prove he was a madman.

But then Chekov saw the torpedo traces on his board.

Their targeting computers hadn't been able to make sense of Sulu's maneuvers either. They were locked on to the—

The viewscreen flared white as the *K'tinga*-class cruiser fell victim to the torpedoes launched by its sister ships.

Its shields had been tuned against Starfleet weapons, not Klingon.

Chekov cheered. He glanced at Sulu. "Vhere did you learn to fly like that?"

Sulu looked pleased. "Captain Kirk once told me he had always wanted to try that maneuver."

The bridge angled as Sulu spun his ship around in place.

The *Excelsior*'s shields registered multiple hits from floating debris—the wreckage of the destroyed cruiser.

"Two-to-one odds we can handle easily," Sulu said. "Uhura—open a channel, please."

The cloud of debris was replaced by the astonished face of the Klingon commander.

"I'm not looking for a fight," Sulu said. "All I want you to do is shut down your warp cores."

"So we will be left here defenseless?" the Klingon sneered.

"No," Sulu said patiently. "So I know it will take you at least six hours to power up again before you can follow us."

"I am willing to die!" the commander proclaimed with clenched fist.

"That is also an option," Sulu said. "Now, shut down your warp cores. Or we will shut them down for you."

He nodded at Uhura. She cut the channel.

The viewscreen showed a long view with a Klingon cruiser hanging in opposite corners.

"Damage report?" Sulu asked.

Chekov was unused to a starship's commander being beside him at the helm.

"No damage, Keptin. Shields at eighty-eight percent and climbing."

"Weapons status of the cruisers?"

But before Chekov could report, his long-range sensor display lit up.

"Incoming wessel!" He had to check the readings twice. "At . . . varp factor ten!"

"Reinforcements?" Sulu asked.

"I . . . don't know. It is such a small ship."

"I recognize the configuration," Spock said unexpectedly. "It is a Vulcan warp shuttle."

"A shuttle? This far out?" McCoy asked.

"At varp ten, Doctor, wery few places are far avay." Chekov adjusted his sensors. "Coming into wisual range."

The viewscreen image changed again to show the small, angular craft on approach. Six of them in a row would barely be as long as one of the *Excelsior*'s warp nacelles.

"What kind of *shuttle* can reach warp ten?" McCoy asked.

As the shuttle came closer, Chekov adjusted the sensor image to maximum magnification. The first detail he noticed was a third nacelle in the center of the shuttle's propulsion carriage, accounting for its improbable speed. Then he saw the colors painted on its hull. "Vell, that answers that," he said.

It was a Starfleet vessel.

Uhura looked up from her station, hand to her earpiece. "The shuttle is hailing us, Captain."

"What are the Klingons doing?" Sulu asked.

Chekov scanned them. "Their varp cores are still online. But no veapons are locked."

"Onscreen," Sulu said.

It was Drake.

Chekov could see that the admiral was seated in the shuttle's forward section. Other than the pilot who was off to the side of the screen, there appeared to be no one else on board.

"Captain Sulu," the admiral said, "lower your shields so I can dock."

"Sir, we are involved in a firefight with two Klingon cruisers. I must request that you withdraw to a safe distance."

"Leave the Klingons to me, Captain. I've got a coded message for them from their High Council." Drake adjusted some controls on the console in front of him. "Stand by, *Excelsior.*"

"The shuttle is transmitting to the Klingon ships," Uhura said. "A new type of encryption code."

"What's their response?" Sulu asked.

Chekov watched his board. Conducted a second scan. "They're . . . powering down their veapons. Keptin—they're dropping their shields."

Sulu stood up from his helm position. Mr. Curtis replaced him at once. Chekov guessed the captain of this ship often took control of her himself. Captain's privileges.

"Admiral Drake," Sulu began, "may I ask what you're doing here?"

"I'll come aboard as soon as I dock, Captain. The message I've relayed to the Klingons explains the situation to them, and gives them their orders."

"Their orders, sir?"

Drake grinned. Chekov hated the look of it, so patently calculated. "It seems we've been caught up in the middle of some typical Klingon skulduggery, Captain. The orders Azetbur issued giving you diplomatic clearance were held up by the homeworld's bureaucracy. These ships were just doing their duty. But now they're ordered to escort us as we track the *Enterprise.*"

Sulu looked appalled. "Sir, I don't think the commander is going to want to escort us. We've just destroyed one of his ships."

"So I can see," Drake replied. "But, *c'est la guerre.* Now lower your shields."

Sulu went back to his command chair. "Mr. Curtis," he said to the helmsman. "Bring the ship around to give the admiral a straight path. Commander Chekov, lower the aft shields—but only around the docking bay. Then raise them as soon as the shuttle has docked."

"Thank you, Captain Sulu," Drake acknowledged. The viewscreen returned to an image of the shuttle moving closer, its passenger cabin separating for docking.

Sulu looked over to Spock. "Captain Spock, what would you say the odds were for the commander in chief of Starfleet to come this far into Klingon space without an entire flotilla for security?"

"Incalculable," Spock said.

"What?" McCoy exclaimed. "Did I hear right? You're admitting statistical defeat?"

"Without all the facts at my disposal, Doctor, I cannot begin to assess any of the reasons why Admiral Drake has undertaken such a dangerous and apparently foolhardy mission in what can be considered enemy territory."

"The shuttle has docked," Chekov said. "Shields are up. Still no response from the Klingons."

Sulu stood. "Captain Spock, Doctor McCoy, Commanders Uhura and Chekov—I'd appreciate it if you would accompany me to greet the admiral. Mr. Curtis, you have the conn."

The young helmsman took the center chair. The four officers went with Sulu to the turbolift. Chekov understood that Sulu was hoping Drake was going to offer them another briefing on their mission to find Captain Kirk.

But Chekov wondered what good it would do. Drake's presence had unquestionably changed the nature of their original mission.

The *Excelsior* and her crew were no longing tracking Kirk for Starfleet and the good of the Federation.

As far as Chekov could tell, they were hunting him for Admiral Androvar Drake.

THIRTY-FOUR

Drake's shuttle thudded gently against the *Excelsior's* aft airlock. The computer confirmed a solid docking.

In the pilot's chair, Ariadne shut down the maneuvering thrusters. She turned to her father.

But he cut her off before she could begin again. "Don't worry about it."

"But they destroyed one of our cruisers. How are the mercenaries going to react to that?"

Drake got out of his passenger seat. "They've already agreed to betray their empire. Besides, the loss of a third of them means their payment isn't split as many ways. And we *can* finish the mission with only two cruisers. Remember, the *Excelsior* is on our side."

"I wouldn't trust Sulu."

"He's a Starfleet officer and I'm his commander in chief."

"But he served with Kirk." Ariadne left her seat as well.

"Chekov and Uhura, the whole time we were undercover on Dark Range, Kirk was all they talked about. I don't think you understand the loyalty they have to him."

"They're all good officers," Drake said. "Starfleet's finest. The loyalty they have is to the chain of command."

Drake took his daughter by her shoulders, smiled at her warmly, no hint of calculation.

"This is why I've worked so hard to get to this position. If I have to, I *can* replace Sulu as commander of the *Excelsior.* I can have his entire command crew thrown into the brig. I *am* Starfleet."

"That's what Cartwright and Colonel West thought."

Drake's smile faded. "Every war has casualties."

"The assassination at Khitomer was exposed because Cartwright underestimated Kirk."

Drake looked aft as he heard the *Excelsior's* airlock hiss open. He hugged his daughter.

"Ariadne, ever since Kirk killed your mother, he has always underestimated *me."*

Ariadne stepped back from Drake. "Father, the *Klingons* killed Mother."

Drake's face hardened. "And Kirk let them get away with it." He lifted his kit bag from its storage alcove behind the passenger seat. "But once we have control of the *Chalchaj 'qmey,* once I can dangle that before our friends on the Federation Council, war will be inevitable. The Klingon Empire will be crushed. And Kirk and all his bleeding-heart sympathizers with it."

Drake handed Ariadne her flight helmet. "Keep that on, and make certain all the comm imagers are offline. I'll say my pilot has to stay on alert status in the shuttle in case of emergency evacuation."

Ariadne pulled on her helmet, stuffed her hair into place beneath it.

Drake gave his daughter's hand a squeeze.

"I'm doing this for you," he said. "For the future."

But even as he said that, Ariadne feared her father might become a casualty of the past, fighting a war that had ended years ago.

THIRTY-FIVE

In his dream, Kirk held his child in his arms.

David. Three months old. So fragile. So full of life and promise.

The baby's tiny, perfect fist held Kirk's finger, squeezing mightily.

"Look at that grip," Kirk said. "Definitely going to be a starship captain. I should probably reserve a space in the Academy right now."

But Carol Marcus didn't return Kirk's smile.

She slipped her arm beneath David's thick blankets, lifted him from Kirk's embrace.

"When are you shipping out?" she asked.

Kirk knew what was coming. He was prepared for it. "I don't have to ship out, Carol."

He could tell she didn't believe him.

He tried to convince her. "Pike's ship, the *Enterprise,* she's coming back. She's going to be in spacedock for more than a year. They need an exec to handle the refit."

"And then what?" Carol asked.

Kirk didn't understand the question. "More than a year, Carol. I can live here, on Earth. With you and David. Help look after him. And you."

Carol's lower lip trembled. She fought back tears. "And *then* what? When the refit is over? Are you going to ship out on the *Enterprise?"*

Kirk didn't speak because she wouldn't like what he had to say. If things went the way he planned, he'd be the *Enterprise's* next captain.

But speaking wasn't necessary. Carol read his answer in his eyes. "I thought so."

Kirk caressed his son's delicate scalp, silken with tiny blond curls. "A year, Carol. Maybe two. With you and the baby."

"It's not enough, Jim." She couldn't hold back the tears. "He needs more than that. *I* need more than that."

"Carol . . . I love you."

She shook her head sadly. The baby stared up at her. Fascinated by her tear-filled eyes. "That's not enough, either."

This time Kirk didn't speak because he could think of nothing to say. This couldn't be happening. Not to him.

"I don't want you helping me," Carol said. "Or David."

"I'm his father."

"You fathered him. There's a difference."

"Carol . . . don't."

"I know what's right for my child, Jim. I don't want you involved."

"Carol, don't push me away."

She looked at him with such pity that Kirk felt shocked. "Jim, I don't have to push you away. Sooner or later, you'll go away yourself. Don't you see that? Don't you know what that does to me? What it will do to David?" Her voice rose in distress.

The baby began to cry.

Kirk reached out for him but Carol hugged their baby closer, gently rocking his small, bundled form.

"I won't have my son raised by a ghost a thousand light-years from home. I won't have him celebrate his birthdays with month-old subspace messages." She closed her eyes, wrapped herself around her child. "I won't have him look up at the stars and know his father died among them. I won't have that."

Kirk felt his heart torn from his chest. Every particle of him cried out for him to fight. To reject this banishment.

But he did love Carol. He knew she loved their child. And because he wasn't certain what to do, he offered no resistance.

Like a tumbling asteroid spinning away in space, he watched as Carol and David fell from him and his life.

The hole they left was never filled, but the pain it caused strengthened him.

That was the last time he ever let anyone take control from him without a fight. That was the last time he let anyone make his decisions for him.

From that day, he had strived to do nothing that would leave him with any regrets.

Each day became his best day. Each goal achieved or he knew the reason why.

Two years later, he was the new captain of the *Enterprise,* setting out on a five-year mission.

Against incredible odds, he brought his ship home.

And every time he faced defeat, every time he faced death, he remembered the feel of his small son in his arms, so fragile, so full of life and promise.

Nothing can take that from me, he told himself. Life is too precious. The promise of the future too vital.

From the day that Carol had asked him to leave, each fight had been for the children. Not just for his child, but for all children. For the future, for everyone. There was nothing more important.

All he had to do was remember his baby in his arms.

It was what Kirk remembered now.

In his dream.

Feeling a cool cloth press against his forehead.

Smelling the rich jungle scents of Chal.

His eyes fluttered open.

A face hovered close to his.

"Carol?" he asked uncertainly.

The face came into focus.

"Teilani," she said softly.

As quickly as that, Kirk was alert.

He had lost a battle. But the war continued.

He rolled off the bed, pushing his way through the filmy gauze that hung around it.

He was in Teilani's house.

Two walls were open to a sunlit courtyard surrounded by dense green vegetation.

The exotic birdlike creatures of Chal serenaded them from nearby trees.

He stood naked on the cool tiled floors. He moved his arms and shoulders. No trace of any injury from the disruptor stun or his fall against the security screen.

Teilani slipped off the bed, wearing only a wrap of fabric as transparent as the gauze around the bed.

But her beauty had no effect on him.

Kirk escalated the stakes, changed the rules.

His heart ached more than he could bear, but Teilani was the enemy now.

"Where are my clothes?" he demanded.

She smiled playfully, oblivious to his mood. "Come to bed, James. I want to see if you've fully recovered."

She reached out for him.

But Kirk turned from her and went to a wooden chest. Inside were his civilian clothes from Earth. He began to put them on. He wished they were his Starfleet uniform.

"James, what's wrong?"

"The attackers at the farm—they were *your* people, not Anarchists."

Teilani moved closer to Kirk, slipped her arms around him. "How could they be? They tried to kill you."

He twisted away from her. "That game's over."

He looked around the spacious room. He saw his jumpsuit lying with hers on a chair. Stormed over to it.

"They *couldn't* kill me," he said. He tore at the collar of the jumpsuit. Ripped out the silver coil of metal hidden in it. He pressed the activation switch on one end, saw a small ready light glow.

"Some sort of forcefield emitter, isn't it?" he said as he threw it at her. "Diverts the projectiles. That's why you told me not to worry about the projectile guns last night. That's why you tugged on my collar just before we attacked—to turn it on. And that's why I could be shot point-blank and not get touched."

Teilani stood her ground. "But, James, at the farm, you saw me get shot."

Kirk grabbed his shirt and yanked it over his head. "I saw you tug on your collar just as you turned your back to the window in the kitchen. A second later, the shot *grazed* your shoulder. Wouldn't surprise me if you could dial the emitter up and down like inertial dampers. Make the projectiles swerve around you—or just nick you to make it look good."

"You don't have to do this, James. The Anarchists' threat has ended."

Kirk pulled on his jacket, looked for his boots.

Scott had been right. Deep inside, perhaps he had always questioned Teilani and her motives. But he had been so caught up in the adventure of being with her that he had refused to question himself and his motives.

"The Anarchist in the brig was shot by the same two Chal who were at the farm. You must have some innate Vulcan abilities on your Romulan side. Meditative control of the autonomic system? Is that it? Make your heart stop for a few minutes to fool the human into helping out?"

Teilani still held to her injured innocence. "I haven't tried to fool you."

Kirk sat on the edge of the bed as he pulled on his boots. He knew the anger he felt was at his own stupidity. But he directed it at her. "You've lied to me from the beginning, haven't you? From that first meeting on the farm."

"You fell in love with me that day."

"We made love," Kirk said. "There's a difference."

"I won't believe you don't care for me."

Kirk reached out to touch her face. "I can see now how well you played me. First, you threw yourself at me. But I said no. So a minute later we're running for our lives, fighting side by side . . . and then . . ."

Teilani held his hand in place, kissed it. "And then you felt what I felt."

Kirk took his hand away. "You offered me a challenge when I didn't have one. You offered me a chance to save a world. That's my job, Teilani. It's what I do. Who I am. I couldn't refuse you and you knew it."

Teilani remained indignant. "Tell me you never loved me. That you don't love me still."

Kirk just felt embarrassed. "It made perfect sense to me that something connected to the Romulans and Klingons was something Starfleet couldn't get involved with. It made perfect sense that there was something I could do as a civilian."

Teilani raised her voice. "I want to hear you say you don't love me."

Kirk didn't take his eyes from hers. "I love my work."

Teilani slapped him. Her Klingon nails raked his cheek.

Kirk felt the scrapes she had left. Looked at the dabs of blood on his fingers.

"I can still help you," he said quietly. "There is a secret on this world that I think even you don't know about."

Teilani's face twisted in anger. "What lies did the Anarchist tell you?"

"Have you ever been in the Armory?" Kirk asked.

He saw her flinch.

"How you blinded me. How I let myself be blinded. That first attack should have made me suspect it wasn't your power station. If the Anarchists had really wanted to bring chaos to your society, they would have concentrated their shelling on it, to destroy it. But they wanted to *get* to it. They wanted to get inside. Why?"

Teilani's jaw tightened. She looked ready to explode.

"What's in there, Teilani?"

She turned away from him. "I don't know."

Kirk was surprised to sense that she was telling the truth.

He went to her. Put his hands on her shoulders. "Then go there with me."

He felt her shiver.

"Why won't you just accept that you've done what you were supposed to do?" she said. "We've won! Chal is safe! You can stay here and be young with me forever."

Kirk turned her around to face him, looked down into her eyes.

"You don't know how much I want to do exactly that," Kirk said gently. "But from what the Anarchist said, there might be more to that secret of Chal, too."

She leaned against him. Her head beneath his chin. "I know you love me." He felt her tremble.

"That's not enough," Kirk said.

His communicator chirped.

Kirk pulled it from his jacket, opened it, acknowledged the call.

"Scott here, Captain. I'm picking up vessels approaching at high warp. At least two of them are Klingon."

"Civilian?"

"From their power curves, I'd have t' say they were battle cruisers."

"How soon till they're here, Scotty?"

"Only six minutes. These sensors just aren't th' same as the old ones."

Teilani held a hand over the communicator. "You didn't stop the Anarchists in time, after all."

"In time for what?" Kirk asked.

"What we feared. If they couldn't destroy us, then it was

just a matter of time before they approached someone who could. Just as I approached someone I thought would be able to save us."

"Are those Klingon ships coming here to destroy Chal?"

"That's why we wanted you to have a starship, fully armed and shielded."

"The truth would have been more useful than a starship," Kirk said. "The Federation is at peace with the Klingons. At least we're trying to be."

He pulled the communicator away from her.

"Scotty, beam me directly to the bridge."

"Will that be one to beam up?" Scott asked.

Kirk stepped back from Teilani. "One, Mr. Scott."

But as soon as he said those words, Kirk knew Teilani would take them as a challenge.

The beam dissolved him just as she fell into his arms.

THIRTY-SIX

"Put your eyes back in your head, Mr. Scott. I want you on tactical."

The engineer blinked in embarrassment as Teilani stepped away from Kirk on the bridge of the *Enterprise*. Her transparent wrap offered little more than the suggestion of clothes.

Kirk took the center chair.

Esys was at the helm. Scott left the engineering substation for tactical beside him. Two other Chal held positions at communications and the science station. About twenty others were scattered through the ship, in Engineering, the disruptor banks, and the remaining photon-torpedo launch tube. Automated controls handled the rest of the ship.

"Can you put the ships onscreen?" Kirk asked.

Teilani came to stand by his chair.

"Still beyond visual range," Scott said. "But two of them are definitely Klingon battle cruisers."

"Full power to shields, Mr. Scott. Any idea what the third one is?"

"'Tis not in th' database that came with th' sensors," Scott said. "I'll try a manual scan."

"Um, Mr. Kirk?"

Kirk turned to the Chal at communications.

"I, uh, believe we're being hailed, sir."

Kirk remained calm. "The third switch on the left. The green one. That's it. Press it."

The young Chal hit the right switch. Kirk now had control of ship-to-ship communications from his chair.

Kirk opened the channel and turned back to the viewscreen.

And nearly jumped from his chair.

It was Sulu.

"Captain Kirk," his former helmsman said. "Good to see you again."

Kirk saw Sulu react to Teilani's almost clothed presence.

"Sulu—are you traveling with Klingons?"

"We're being 'escorted,' sir."

Kirk heard the qualification Sulu put on the word. "I see. Is this a social visit?" he asked lightly.

Sulu was about to answer, but his attention was caught by something to the side, offscreen. Instead, he sat back as someone else moved into view.

Kirk gripped the arms of his chair so tightly the frame creaked.

Drake.

"Hello, Jim."

"Admiral."

Kirk watched Drake's eyes move, obviously taking in Teilani on the *Excelsior*'s viewscreen. "I see you're enjoying yourself. As usual."

"Th' ships have dropped from warp," Scotty announced. "They're moving to match our orbit."

Kirk shifted in his chair. More than anything, he wanted to take Teilani aside for any information she could provide explaining how Chal had come to be caught up between the Klingon Empire and the Federation. But Kirk knew better than to turn his back on Drake for an instant.

"You're a long way from home, Admiral. Anything I should know about?"

Drake adopted a serious expression. Kirk visualized his fist driving into the middle of it.

"Sorry, Jim. This is Starfleet business."

"Depending on whose charts you believe, this is either Klingon or Romulan space."

Drake's serious expression became stern. "I'm here under the combined authority of Starfleet and the Klingon High Council."

"Authority to do what?" Kirk asked.

"That's classified, Jim."

Kirk tapped his fingers on the side of his chair. He could wait.

Drake remained silent for a few moments longer, then spoke over his shoulder to Sulu.

"Captain, send down the security details to secure the city."

Kirk had no idea what Drake was up to, but for the simple reason that it was something Drake wanted to do, Kirk was going to stop him.

"Mr. Scott, I want a level-seven photon discharge into the ionosphere over the city."

Scott didn't question the order. "Aye, sir." The bridge rumbled with the launching of three photon torpedoes, one after the other.

Kirk received his third surprise of the day when he heard Spock's voice come from the *Excelsior*'s bridge.

"Admiral Drake, the *Enterprise* has created an area of high ionization over the Chal city. We will be unable to beam anyone down for at least twenty minutes."

"Spock, is that you?"

Spock stepped onscreen behind Sulu. "Greetings, Captain."

Then McCoy stepped on from the other side. "Fancy meeting you here." McCoy's eyes widened more than Scott's as he saw Teilani.

Kirk sat back in his chair, feeling that the odds might have shifted back in his favor.

But Drake cut in. "This isn't a reunion, Jim. This is a Starfleet matter. I am ordering you to withdraw."

"I am not a Starfleet officer. This is not a Starfleet vessel. You are not in Federation space. Do I have to make it more clear than that?"

"Commander Krult," Drake said. *"Cha yIghus!"*

Scott spun around from his tactical board. "Captain, the Klingons are bringing their weapons online."

Drake grinned coldly. "Do I have to make it more clear to *you,* Jim?" He stepped forward. "I am now advising you that you are operating an illegally armed vessel in a restricted area of Klingon space. Your actions here could set back the new era of detente between the Federation and the Klingon Empire. For that reason, I am *suggesting* you withdraw from this system." He smiled in challenge. "Or face the consequences."

Kirk had had enough. "Sulu, what is that pompous ass going on about?"

Drake raised his hand as if to give an order to fire. But Sulu stepped down from his chair.

"Admiral, if I could have a moment?" Sulu asked.

Drake nodded curtly.

"Captain Kirk," Sulu began. "I know this is an awkward position for all of us to be in. But Starfleet *is* in possession of classified information suggesting that Chal could pose a threat to the peace process between the Federation and the Empire."

Kirk knew his former crew well. Sulu wasn't lying. He was incapable of lying.

"What are your intentions?" Kirk asked.

Sulu took a breath, clearly more uncomfortable than Kirk. "My *orders* are to dispatch security teams to the planet's surface and secure any war matériel we find. We do have the authority from the Empire, sir."

That information made several pieces fall together to form a pattern. Drake wanted war matériel. The central structure in the city was an armory. The Anarchist Kirk had questioned in the *Enterprise*'s brig seemed to think that the secrets contained in that armory were worth destroying a planet for peace to have a chance.

"Just so I'm sure I understand, Sulu. You say you are to *secure* whatever war matériel you find?"

"Yes, sir."

Kirk watched Drake carefully. The Anarchist had wanted to destroy something. Drake wanted to obtain it.

"Would this have anything to do with the *Chalchaj 'qmey?"* Kirk asked.

Teilani grabbed Kirk's arm at the same instant he saw Drake's eyes darken.

Sulu reacted as well.

Kirk realized that while everyone else recognized what the Klingon phrase meant, he himself was apparently not expected to.

"What do you know about the *Chalchaj 'qmey?"* Drake said coldly.

"Enough to know that I'm not letting you get near it," Kirk bluffed. "Captain Sulu, you are in violation of Chal orbital space. I ask you to withdraw."

Sulu bit his lip and looked at Drake.

"Captain Sulu," Drake ordered. "The *Enterprise* is a threat to this mission. I am ordering you to neutralize that threat."

Kirk ignored Drake. "Spock, talk some sense into the admiral. The Federation recognizes Chal as an independent world. Starfleet has no authority here."

Spock displayed no sign of conflict. "Unfortunately, Captain, the Empire does *not* recognize Chal's independence. However, the planet's cooperation in this matter might move the High Council to change its view."

"Spock, listen to me. If you proceed with what Drake is planning, you'll be following orders, but you will not be doing the right thing."

Spock drew himself up, held his hands behind his back. "Captain, with respect, sir. Can you be sure *you* are doing the right thing?"

McCoy turned to Spock. "Spock! Are you out of your mind?"

Spock kept his eyes locked on the hidden imager on the *Excelsior*'s bridge, so it was as if he stared directly at Kirk. "Doctor, I merely point out that since none of us know exactly what the *Chalchaj 'qmey* is, it hardly seems logical to fight over it."

Thank you, Spock, Kirk thought. Drake was on a fishing expedition.

On the *Excelsior*'s bridge, Drake realized that Spock was giving away secrets, too. "That's enough, Captain Spock." He stared at Sulu. "Captain—you have your orders."

For a moment, Sulu appeared torn by indecision. But starship captains could not be indecisive. "Weapons officer," he said. "Target the *Enterprise*'s impulse thrusters."

"Sulu," Kirk warned. "Withdraw or be fired upon."

McCoy threw up his hands in disgust. "Is everybody crazy?"

Sulu shook his head. "Captain Kirk, I'm sorry."

Kirk knew Sulu had no choice. He was doing what he thought was a reasonable compromise—disabling the *Enterprise* until the mystery could be solved. Any attempt on his part to delay acting on Drake's orders would be mutiny. Knowing Drake's excesses, it might even be treason.

Kirk closed the channel to the *Excelsior* and brought a tactical display up on the viewscreen. "Mr. Esys—set course bearing eighty-five, mark zero."

Esys started to turn in his chair. "But, that'll put us right in—"

"Do it, lad!" Scotty barked. "Th' captain knows what he's doin'."

"Full impulse, Mr. Scott. *Now!*"

The *Enterprise* shuddered as she blazed toward Chal.

Teilani held on to Kirk's chair as the bridge bucked and a new sound rarely heard on a starship thundered through the bulkheads—the scream of air being ripped asunder as the ship descended through atmosphere.

"Entering the zone of ionization," Scott confirmed.

"How long can we stay in it, Scotty?"

Scott had to shout to be heard over the howling wind. "Thirty seconds!"

"James! What are you doing?"

Kirk reached out for Teilani's hand, trying to reassure her. "Disappearing," he said. "They won't be able to lock on to us through the ionized area we made."

"But for less than a minute?" Teilani said. "What good is that?"

"A few seconds will be long enough. Prepare for warp, Mr. Scott."

Kirk didn't hear Scott's reply. He thought it was just as well.

But Esys, who was not Starfleet-trained, questioned Kirk again. "You can't go to warp in the atmosphere!"

"Who would you rather believe, Mr. Esys—someone who's done it, or the textbooks?" Kirk smiled at the young Chal. "Set course bearing two four five, mark one eighty."

Kirk saw Scott shake his head in despair.

"She'll hold, Scotty!" Kirk shouted.

"Aye," Scott called back. "But will I?"

"Warp one . . . *now!"* Kirk commanded.

The *Enterprise* groaned as she was suddenly torn from the atmosphere of Chal at the speed of light, traveling back on a reverse course that would put her only a few kilometers behind the *Excelsior* and her Klingon escorts.

"On standard orbit!" Scott shouted, still caught up in the moment though the roar of rushing air had instantly stopped.

"Take out those Klingons," Kirk said. "Photon torpedoes —full spread."

That was too much for Scott. Even he had to question Kirk's plan now. "Sir, th' disruptors would have more of a chance!"

"No disruptors!" Kirk ordered. "Fire torpedoes!"

Scott muttered again but four more torpedoes launched sequentially, overloading the Klingons' aft shields.

"They never saw us comin'!" the engineer exclaimed. Then his tone changed abruptly as he added, "The *Excelsior* is comin' about."

"Put the Klingons between her and us, Mr. Esys."

The *Enterprise* shuddered as Esys overcompensated and almost collided with a battlecruiser.

It swerved away, forcing the second cruiser to change course.

Kirk watched the chain reaction spread on the tactical display. Now the careening Klingon ships were forcing the *Excelsior* to pull back.

But the first Klingon cruiser executed a roll to slide past the second and began firing.

The *Enterprise* absorbed the first shots easily.

"Do I return fire?" Scott asked urgently.

"Wait for the second cruiser to come about," Kirk said.

"The *Excelsior* is locking phasers!"

"Wait for the second cruiser, Mr. Scott. . . ."

"They're getting ready to fire!" Scott warned.

Teilani's nails dug into Kirk's arm.

The *Enterprise* shuddered as the second cruiser finally fired along with the first.

"Fire full disruptors!" Kirk shouted.

The orange beams blasted forth from the *Enterprise*'s saucer.

They passed through the first battle cruiser's shields as if they weren't even there.

Its bridge erupted into a tiny nova as the main hull began to spiral away, passing into the beams hitting the second cruiser.

Caught in those beams, the first cruiser's main hull blew apart in a string of small explosions as her antimatter containment bottles failed.

But by absorbing the second set of beams, she let the second cruiser escape.

"What happened?" Teilani asked.

"They assumed we had phasers," Kirk said, "and set their shields accordingly." He sighed. "I always wanted to try that."

He reopened a channel to the *Excelsior.*

Drake was in the command chair. His expression was the same as it been on Tycho IV when he had told Kirk of Faith Morgan's death.

"Excelsior," Kirk said. "Once again I ask you to withdraw."

Drake's reply was emotionless. "You're dead, Kirk. Do you hear me?"

"Put Captain Sulu on," Kirk said. "I want to talk with someone who's responsible."

"Weapons officer," Drake ordered. "Retarget the *Enterprise.* All phasers on the bridge."

"We took a beatin' in the atmosphere," Scott whispered. "Shields won't hold more than a minute under all that."

But with any luck, Kirk knew, the *Enterprise* wouldn't have to face that fire. By changing his orders, Drake had just given Sulu and his crew an opportunity to withdraw. Provided they saw the situation the way Kirk did.

"Admiral Drake," Kirk said, "am I to understand that you have just given orders to destroy a ship belonging to a sovereign world because it has tried to preserve its territorial integrity?"

"Your atoms will orbit Chal until its sun goes nova," Drake promised.

"Mr. Spock—isn't Admiral Drake's order a violation of Starfleet general policy?"

Spock stepped up beside Drake. He raised an eyebrow. "Starfleet does specify that in matters of self-defense, Starfleet vessels will respond to force with equal force, and no more."

Good, Kirk thought. *Spock knows where I'm going.*

"He attacked us," Drake told Spock.

"No," Kirk corrected. "I attacked the Klingons. Mr. Spock, has this vessel directed any fire toward the *Excelsior,* or any other Starfleet vessel?"

"No, sir, she has not."

"So, in your opinion, is Admiral Drake justified in ordering the *Enterprise*'s destruction?"

Spock nodded his head a fraction of a centimeter, letting Kirk know he had found a way out.

"Technically, a case could be made that the admiral's orders are in violation of Starfleet command directives," Spock acknowledged.

"Now, I know I'm no longer part of Starfleet," Kirk said as he saw Drake smolder, "but in my day, such violations were grounds for a general inquiry."

"As they are today, sir," Spock agreed.

"Fire!" Drake ordered.

Kirk braced for impact.

Nothing.

"Fire, damn you!" Drake said as he sprang to his feet. "Fire or you'll all be charged with mutiny!"

Sulu returned to the viewscreen. "Admiral Drake, with respect, sir. You are in violation of Starfleet command directives. I must request that you relinquish command of this vessel in order that we may convene a general inquiry."

"This won't work and you know it," Drake said. "We're in battle."

"Shut down the disruptors," Kirk ordered Scott.

Sulu looked offscreen. "Commander Chekov, is the *Excelsior* in danger of attack by the *Enterprise?"*

Chekov's there, too, Kirk thought. No wonder the *Excelsior* didn't fire on Drake's command.

"No, sir," Kirk heard Chekov reply. "The *Enterprise*'s disruptors are powered down."

"Admiral, please," Sulu insisted. "I don't wish to invoke General Order One-oh-four, Section C."

Drake stared at Sulu. "You wouldn't dare."

"He doesn't have to dare," McCoy said as he joined the line of officers standing up to Drake. "I'm senior ship's surgeon and I'd love to give you a medical exam to establish your frame of mind."

Chekov stepped onscreen. "I am villing to testify about the improper orders he gave me."

Even Uhura was there. She joined Chekov. "I have placed all bridge recordings on a message buoy, Captain Sulu, for transmission to Starfleet Command."

Kirk watched as Drake looked at each of the former *Enterprise* officers assembled before him.

Without any trace of emotion, he stepped down.

"You will hold the inquiry *now,"* he said to Sulu.

"After we have withdrawn from this system." Sulu took over his chair. "Captain Kirk, this could take several hours. But I suspect we will be returning after that."

"Understood, Captain Sulu," Kirk acknowledged. "Thank you."

"Thank *you,* sir. I didn't see how we could get out of that one. Sulu out."

The viewscreen flashed back to an image of Chal.

The *Excelsior* streaked away into warp.

There was no trace of the second Klingon cruiser, only debris from the first.

Scott spun around in his chair. His forehead dripped with sweat. "I swear ye have the luck o' th' d'vil."

"Wrong afterworld, Mr. Scott," Kirk said. "This is heaven, remember?"

Kirk got up and went to Teilani.

He tried to be gentle. "You know the lies have to end now, don't you. Whatever you've been keeping from me, the Federation knows about it. And the Klingons. How soon before the Romulans get here? Who knows how many others?"

Teilani couldn't meet his eyes.

"Teilani, your Anarchists had nothing to do with what just happened here. The one I talked to yesterday was ready to die rather than let anyone know what's in the Armory. Whatever secrets you're trying to hide, you're no longer in control of them. And that makes them dangerous."

"I don't know what to do, James."

He tilted her head up, to make her look at him, to see there was no anger in his eyes.

"I understand why you brought me here, now. To take care of a problem you felt you couldn't. But it is Chal's problem. Your problem. Not mine."

Panic flashed through her eyes. "You're leaving?"

"No," Kirk said. "But I can only *help* you. I can't take responsibility for you. You have to do that for yourself."

"How?" she asked.

With that plaintive question, Kirk saw she was a child in so many ways.

But she could not remain a child forever.

No one could.

"What is the *Chalchaj 'qmey?"* Kirk asked.

Teilani took a deep breath. "I . . . don't know, James. It's . . . it's whatever is in the Armory."

"And you've never been there?"

She shook her head.

"I'm afraid, James."

"That's part of growing up," he said. "And that's what you have to do, now. It's what all your people have to do."

She held his hand, not to distract him, but for support.

"Are you ever afraid?" she asked.

Kirk smiled at her. He leaned down to whisper his secret into her ear. "All the time."

She looked at him in wonder.

"I just don't let it get in the way."

A new look came to Teilani's eyes. Kirk guessed it was disillusionment. But there was nothing wrong with that. Generally, that was what inspired people to make a change.

Teilani looked down at her transparent wrap. "I suppose I should get some clothes on," she said.

"And then we'll go down to the armory?" Kirk asked.

"Together," she said.

Kirk took her hand.

The future waited. This time, for both of them.

THIRTY-SEVEN

When the *Excelsior* had withdrawn a light-year from Chal's territorial space, the ship's main briefing room was set up for a formal inquiry.

The large display screen no longer showed the starship's schematic. Instead, a series of still frames from the bridge recorders filled the screen. They showed the sequence of events leading up to Sulu's requesting that Drake step down from command. Time codes ran under each image. Uhura had been busy.

Like the others gathered in the room, Chekov had not yet taken his seat. Admiral Drake had still to arrive. Everyone was too tense to pretend that what would happen next was merely a formality.

"So what are the odds this time, Spock?" McCoy asked.

Uhura, Sulu, and Chekov ceased their own conversation, waiting for Spock's reply.

"For what, Doctor?"

"For us getting away with this."

Spock thought a moment. "If we analyze our present situation according to regulations, we have done nothing wrong. Therefore, there is nothing to 'get away with,' as you put it."

"And if we don't go by regulations?" McCoy prodded.

"Anything is possible," Spock said.

McCoy rolled his eyes. "Thank you for those reassuring words."

"They were not meant to reassure."

"No kidding."

"Doctor, even to you it should come as no surprise that we are in a precarious position."

"Well," McCoy said, "you were going to leave Starfleet anyway, so what's a discharge a few months early going to matter?"

"I do not refer to our position within Starfleet. That is covered by regulation and we were justified in pointing out to Admiral Drake that his orders were inappropriate."

"Then what do you mean by precarious?"

"The admiral does not appear to be engaged in a Starfleet mission."

That got everyone's attention.

Sulu sat down on the corner of the conference table. He

knew how Spock's mind worked. "What did we miss, Captain Spock?"

"When the admiral was confronting Captain Kirk, he ordered our Klingon escorts to prepare to fire their torpedoes," Spock said. "No matter how far along the peace process is with the Empire, it is highly improbable that any Klingon commander would place his ship in a position where it would be expected to take orders from a Starfleet officer."

Chekov remembered the readings on his tactical display. "But Keptin Spock, as soon as the admiral gave that order, the Klingon wessels did arm their torpedoes."

"Precisely, Commander," Spock agreed. "Which I take as evidence that the Klingon ships may be other than Klingon armed forces."

"Mercenaries," Uhura said. "In battle cruisers."

"That has some significance to you?" Spock asked.

"They vere our mission objectives," Chekov answered. "When ve vere undercover."

"Fascinating," Spock said.

McCoy looked back and forth from Spock to Chekov and Uhura, missing something. "The commander in chief of *Starfleet* is commanding Klingon mercenary ships? How in blazes does that happen?"

"The answer to your question lies in the sequence of events, Doctor. Following the events at Khitomer and the arrest of Admiral Cartwright, Starfleet Intelligence began an intensive effort to halt the sale of Klingon armaments on the illegal markets. That effort was specifically directed at obtaining the type of vessels now apparently under Admiral Drake's command." Spock looked at Chekov and Uhura. "During your mission, were you successful in negotiating the sale of Klingon battle cruisers?"

"At least five attempts led to arrests," Uhura said.

"Do you know the disposition of those vessels?"

Chekov shrugged. "Ve vere used to initiate the deals. Jade

vould take over for the money negotiations, and then other agents vould make the arrests."

Spock nodded. "And because you were out of direct contact with Starfleet, you had no way of knowing the end results of your efforts."

Uhura frowned. "Only what Jade told us."

"So," Spock concluded, "the Klingon vessels accompanying the admiral may have been obtained as a result of coopting the efforts of Starfleet Intelligence."

Sulu interrupted. "Captain Spock, with respect, sir, this is all circumstantial."

"What is?" Spock asked.

"This case you seem to be building that Admiral Drake is connected to Jade's efforts to get the Children of Heaven."

"He is here," Spock said patiently. "If obtaining the Children of Heaven were a Starfleet objective, there are many other commanders to whom the task could have been delegated. The fact that Drake is personally involved, backed by Klingon mercenary ships, suggests this is not a Starfleet operation."

"You're forgetting, Captain Spock," Sulu said. "The admiral is also backed up by the *Excelsior.*"

"Vhat has *happened* to you?!" Chekov exploded. "Starfleet gives you command of this ship and you lose your common sense?"

Sulu did not respond to Chekov's anger. "I worked hard for this ship, Pavel. I respect the chain of command that gave it to me."

"It sounds more like you vorship them."

Sulu got to his feet and jabbed a finger at Chekov. "Don't push our friendship. *Or* your luck. I can understand the pressure you've been under. But this isn't Dark Range anymore. We're professionals who have a job to do."

Uhura crossed her arms and stood shoulder to shoulder with Chekov. "Then do it."

Sulu seemed surprised that a confrontation was developing. "I am."

McCoy put himself between Sulu on one side and Chekov and Uhura on the other. "I don't think that's what she means, Captain."

For the first time, a glimmer of anger broke through Sulu's professional detachment. "There is nothing going on here that is not covered by regulations, Doctor. I am—we are *all* compelled to follow our orders until such time as conditions warrant otherwise."

Chekov took a step forward. As far as he was concerned, Sulu might need another punch in the nose to get his thinking in gear. "You're vorking for Drake, aren't you?"

Sulu started forward, only to be restrained by McCoy. "I'm working for Starfleet! The way you should be!"

Chekov wasn't prepared to push past the doctor. He turned to Spock. "Are you going to let him get avay vith this?"

Without hesitation, Spock took up a position beside Sulu. Chekov was shocked.

"Commander Chekov," Spock said, "I assure you Captain Sulu's actions are logical, legal, and proper."

"But are they right?" Chekov asked.

"As he has pointed out," Spock explained, "all we have are suspicions. Nothing concrete."

McCoy kept his position in the middle. "What's it going to take to convince you one way or the other, Spock?"

"That will depend on Admiral Drake's next action. If it is reasonable, then—"

"Vhy must ve wait for *him?* Vhy can't ve take the next action?" Chekov interrupted.

McCoy flashed a strained smile at Chekov, trying to defuse the tension. "Commander, perhaps you've been undercover too long."

"So now you're on *his* side?"

"We're all on the same side. All that's going on here is a disagreement over tactics."

"There is no 'disagreement,'" Sulu said sternly. "This is my ship. I'm in command."

That was Chekov's breaking point. "And you're putting Captain Kirk in danger!" He pushed forward, forcing McCoy out of the way.

Uhura grabbed at Chekov's uniform jacket.

Sulu turned sideways, ready to defend himself.

Spock pulled Sulu back, positioning himself before Chekov.

One more second, and the first blow would be struck.

The briefing room doors slid open.

Everyone froze as Admiral Drake stepped in.

For a moment, his eyes widened as he realized what he had just interrupted.

Then he brought his wide, insincere grin into play. "Normally, I'd say 'As you were.' But in this case, I think I'll just ask everyone to take a seat."

Chekov and Sulu exchanged an angry glance. Chekov tugged on his jacket.

He and Uhura sat at one end of the briefing table. Sulu and Spock sat at the other. McCoy chose the middle.

Drake walked over to the display screen, studying the images. Then he turned to face his audience.

"Those records won't be necessary," he said. "Captain Sulu . . . all of you . . . I am prepared to acknowledge that you were performing your duty when you . . . 'reminded' me of Starfleet regulations."

Instantly, Chekov knew Drake was setting them up for something. His opening statement could only be a distraction.

"However," Drake continued, "to perform my duty, I must point out to you that there are certain diplomatic concerns at stake here. Which I cannot reveal to you." Drake's eyes narrowed as his smile vanished. "And, if I choose to, those concerns are more than enough to authorize me to place all of you in the brig pending court-martial."

He looked them all in the eye again, then turned the smile back on.

"But I, for one, understand the mitigating circumstances of the intense, personal loyalty you feel to your old captain. And I salute you for it."

Chekov was confused. Everything he had come to know about Drake had led him to expect some form of censure, if not punishment.

McCoy voiced the confusion Chekov felt. "So what's the purpose of this damned inquiry, Admiral?"

Drake gestured magnanimously. "There is no inquiry. Simple as that. Because this is a delicate situation, I will make a full report to the Federation president and Chancellor Azetbur, asking for their explicit direction. I will make their responses known to you, so that you will understand the reasoning behind your orders. Since that process will take at least two days, in the meantime I will direct the *Excelsior* to monitor the *Enterprise*'s location. As long as the *Enterprise* remains within the Chal system, we will stand by."

"What if the *Enterprise* leaves?" Sulu asked.

"Then we will follow. At a distance. Until we receive further instructions. Is that acceptable, Captain Sulu?"

The commander in chief of Starfleet had just asked a captain if his orders were suitable. Chekov was glad to see Sulu look uncomfortable.

"It seems to fall within regulations," Sulu answered.

"Vhat about the Klingons?" Chekov asked.

Drake nodded, as if that were a question Chekov was within his rights to ask. "They will stand by with us."

No one said anything else.

"Thank you for your . . . indulgence," Drake said, "in what is a difficult situation." He headed for the doors. "That is all."

In a moment, he was gone.

The silence he had left behind was brittle.

"Well?" McCoy asked Spock. "Was that reasonable enough?"

"Too reasonable," Spock said.

McCoy sighed. "How can you be *too* reasonable?"

"We challenged the admiral's authority and he has accepted and excused it without a formal inquiry. That can only mean he has something to hide."

"Or," Uhura said, "he's in a hurry to do something else."

"But what?" Sulu asked. "Think about what you're suggesting. I mean, how can a traitor possibly be chosen by the Federation Council to be Starfleet's commander in chief? Starfleet Intelligence would have to be . . ." Sulu hesitated. He looked at Chekov, then glanced away.

"It all comes back to Starfleet Intelligence, doesn't it?" Chekov said darkly.

"But how could Drake compromise the entire division so quickly?" Sulu continued, speaking to himself as much as to anyone else at the table. "He's only been C in C for a handful of days."

"Perhaps Admiral Drake is part of a larger process," Spock suggested. "I for one would be most interested in knowing his relationship with Admiral Cartwright."

Sulu looked pained. "That first time we met with Drake. He told us he suspected Starfleet Command had been infiltrated by a cabal of senior officers. That Cartwright was just the tip."

"Perhaps," Spock suggested, "that was one of the few times when the admiral was telling us the truth. He only neglected to mention that he himself was part of that cabal."

"So vhat do ve do now?" Chekov asked.

All eyes turned to Sulu.

The *Excelsior* was his ship.

The next move was up to him.

Chekov wondered if he had the strength to make the right one.

THIRTY-EIGHT

Kirk and Teilani took their positions on the transporter pads in the *Enterprise.* Kirk still wore his civilian clothes, though he was outfitted with a disruptor pistol, communicator, and combat tricorder. Teilani wore her jumpsuit, similarly equipped.

In Kirk's eyes, the outfit added to her years. She looked ready for a fight in a way she hadn't before the jungle assault.

Innocence lost, Kirk thought.

Scott adjusted his controls at the operator's console. "Locked on t' the Armory's coordinates." He made a soft whistle. "That's a large installation."

"It's the biggest structure on Chal," Kirk said.

"More than that, sir. It extends underground through almost the entire city."

Kirk looked at Teilani but saw no comprehension in her eyes. "As far as we've ever been told, the Armory's our power station," she said.

"What about it, Scotty? Any sign of power generators?"

"Aye. But they only make up about a fraction of what's down there."

"Any idea what *is* down there?"

Scott looked puzzled. "Not with these sensors. Lots of equipment. Most of it dormant." His puzzlement turned to a frown. "That's a sly little trick."

"What is?" Kirk asked.

"They've got a transporter shield over the place. Hidden in

th' power generator fields so it would disperse any beam that struck it before an operator could recover the signal."

Kirk attention sharpened. The sensor maps of the Armory's exterior had revealed no entrances. Teilani had confirmed that the Chal were aware of no way in.

"Someone's gone t' a lot of trouble to keep visitors out," Scott said. His fingers tapped over the controls. "But the modulation routines are fairly old-fashioned."

"Forty years?" Kirk asked. That was when the colony had been founded.

"That would be about right," Scotty said absently. Then he smiled. "We're through!"

"No chance we'll be scattered?" Kirk asked.

"None at all," Scott said proudly.

"In that case, keep a lock on us the whole time we're down there, and energize."

The transporter chime grew as the surrounding room seemed to break apart into glowing bits of energy.

"Of course," Kirk heard Scotty's warbling voice say, "when I say 'none,' I mean very little. . . ."

Before Kirk could respond, a new location formed around him.

He saw it only in the glow from the transporter effect.

When he felt solid, he was in utter darkness.

"James?" Teilani asked from beside him.

"I'm right here," Kirk said. "Don't move. We'll ask Mr. Scott to beam down some lights and then . . ."

Lights flickered overhead.

Far overhead. Two hundred meters at least, Kirk estimated.

A geodesic pattern of glowing light channels took form. There was something odd about it, though. Their pattern was precisely regular, but they only covered half the enormous ceiling.

Then they brightened enough that Kirk could see there was something hanging above him, directly overhead, blocking almost half the ceiling from his view.

The light channels continued to intensify until the enclosure Kirk and Teilani had transported to was as bright as day.

The object above them was a Romulan Bird-of-Prey. An old one.

Kirk had seen one just like it, almost thirty years earlier, when the first cloaked Romulan vessel had tested Federation resolve at the Neutral Zone.

Teilani stared up at it. "James, what is it?"

"An old Romulan starship. But it can't possibly be here. It must be a holoprojection of some sort."

Kirk used his combat tricorder.

The ship was real.

"Why would they *bury* a starship?" Kirk asked.

"James, look over there."

One hundred meters away, new lights were coming on. They seemed to originate from within a series of transparent display cases which ringed the wide plaza on which Kirk and Teilani now stood. Directly behind and on top of the display cases, Kirk recognized Romulan data conduits. The flickering status lights that lit the dull gray tubes indicated the presence of a major computer complex.

"There must be some type of life-form sensor operating," Kirk said. "When our presence was detected, the installation was switched on." Kirk aimed his tricorder at the lit display cases.

"But why?" Teilani asked.

Kirk's tricorder registered no energy sources other than the light fixtures and the computer pathways. No explosives. No booby traps.

"Time to find out," he said.

The floor they crossed was polished black stone. Kirk recognized the patterns in it as the same in the rock around Chal's city. Whatever the purpose of the structure they were in, it had apparently been carved from solid rock.

By the time Kirk saw what was in the first display case, though, the Armory's purpose was becoming clearer.

"It's a museum," Kirk told Teilani.

The display before them contained a mannequin outfitted in a Romulan warrior's uniform, again forty years old in style.

Mounted beside it, a series of hand weapons were also on exhibit, power cells removed.

There was a white floor panel before the display case. Kirk's tricorder identified a pressure mechanism under it. Teilani tapped her foot against the panel.

A voice spoke to them from a grille above the display case. At the same time, a spotlight shone on the first weapon—a small hand disruptor.

"Is the voice Romulan?" Kirk asked.

Teilani nodded. "It's explaining how to use the weapon."

"I suppose your colony's founders didn't want you to lose your heritage."

The voice paused as the spotlight dimmed. Then a second weapon was illuminated and the voice began again.

"Unusual," Teilani said.

"What?"

"The last thing the recording said." She looked up at Kirk. "There are ten thousand of those hand disruptors stored here."

"The Armory," Kirk murmured. The name suddenly made perfect sense. "It's not a museum, it's a munitions dump."

"For what purpose?"

Kirk shrugged. What other purpose could there be. "War."

"With whom?"

Kirk tapped his chest. "With me. The Federation."

He glanced down the curving wall of display cases. Many held other mannequins. Some in environmental suits. Some in camouflage.

"Forty years ago, the Romulans and the Klingons must have been preparing for an all-out war with the Federation. So they founded Chal to be a secret supply base. In case the Federation overwhelmed either or both empires, Chal could supply a surviving force with the weapons they needed to continue the fight."

Teilani stared in at the Romulan weapons.

Kirk watched her reflection in the clear panel.

He could see what she was thinking.

That she and her kind were one of those weapons.

Teilani began walking along the curve of the cases.

Each pressure panel she stepped on began an informational sequence.

Dozens of recorded Romulan voices whispered in the Armory. Spotlights flared and dimmed on hand weapons, medical equipment, computer consoles, ration containers, navigation and communication devices, protective clothing, tactical bombs, enough supplies for an army.

Kirk stared up at the Bird-of-Prey. He could see the pylons holding it in position. One of the display cases would no doubt contain the information for opening the roof of the Armory and flying the spacecraft skyward.

He wouldn't be surprised to find a Klingon battle cruiser down here, as well. Perhaps an entire section filled with Klingon display cases.

Teilani had moved ahead of him as he had studied the starship.

He saw her in front of the first display case in the series.

Her hands were pressed against its clear viewing panel.

He went to her side.

It was the proof of her suspicions.

What Kirk had expected.

The mannequins were more lifelike in this display.

A Romulan male and a Klingon female held a baby.

The baby had a furrowed brow. Pointed ears.

A holographic projection came to life. DNA molecules spun within it. Separated, moved together in combination.

Parts of the twisted molecule were trimmed by quick flashes of atomically precise particle beams.

Another display showed egg cells being mechanically opened by microscalpels, so their dark nucleii could be replaced with new ones.

"We were *made,"* Teilani said. She looked at her hands. "Genetically engineered."

Kirk put his hand on her shoulder. Remembered how quickly it had healed. Understood the reason why.

"There is no shame in that, Teilani."

She shrugged loose from his touch. Turned around the corner.

He gave her her privacy.

He thought about the marks Sam had carved into the frame of his bedroom door, charting his growth.

He remembered his father's wisdom.

It was necessary to know where you had come from. Only then could you know where you were going.

This was the beginning for Teilani.

He heard her gasp.

Kirk sped around the corner.

Another curve of display cases ran there, also backed by enormous data conduits. Teilani leaned against the tenth case along, her fist against the clear panel. Her cheek pressed against it.

Kirk glanced into the cases as he passed.

Holographic images flashed before him.

Federation starships laying waste to planets.

Romulan and Klingon cities in ruins.

Kirk recognized them as scenarios for battles feared but never fought.

In another case, another display.

Klingon and Romulan bodies among the ruins.

It was as if Kirk looked through a window he had never known. Is this what had driven the two empires? This fear of annihilation? Not knowing that the Federation would never have pursued such destruction. That their fears were groundless.

Among the holographically constructed ruins, Chal emerged.

Male and female Chal, combining the heritage of their creators.

Images flashed.

The Chal worked among the ruins. Lived among the ruins. Children played around them as the ruins were re-formed. As a devastated world was rebuilt.

As the holographic images of the Chal grew old.

Kirk stopped a few meters from Teilani. "Don't you see," he said. "You're not genetically engineered to *fight.* You're genetically engineered to *thrive* in environments polluted by energy radiation, biological warfare agents. You're survivors."

Spock had said it that night at the reception in Starfleet's Great Hall. *Hybrids generally take on the most positive attributes of their parents, becoming exceptional specimens.*

But when Teilani looked at him, tears streaked her young face.

"Teilani, no," Kirk said gently. He reached out to brush the tears and the sorrow from her. "The people who founded this colony loved you. You were their hope for the future. Even if their civilization crumbled in a war that could never happen, you, your brothers and sisters, would carry on to the future. You are their children."

Kirk understood the Klingon phrase now. *Chalchaj 'qmey.* "The Children of Heaven," he said. "All that is good."

But Teilani slowly shook her head. Turned back to the display case. As if mesmerized by its contents.

Kirk moved to her side. Placed an arm around her shoulders.

Looked in.

Saw the holographic displays that so held her.

Felt his stomach tighten.

For what I am going to tell you, please forgive me, Torl had said while captive in the *Enterprise*'s brig. *Remember that in the decades past our people were manipulated by their rulers to hate you. To consider your species as nothing more than animals.*

Genetic engineering was only part of what made the Chal so fit, so strong, so impervious to injury.

There had also been operations.

Transplants. Of tissues and organs.

From *humans.*

This case didn't project holographic simulations.

They were actual real-time images of men and women, some in forty-year-old Starfleet uniforms.

Butchered. By alien surgeons. For the organic material necessary to create each Child of Heaven.

Teilani threw herself into Kirk's rigid arms.

"Forgive me," she cried, racked with sobs.

Torl had called this world an *obscenity.*

For peace to have its chance, let this world die. And all its)secrets with it, he had pleaded.

Kirk understood why now.

So did Teilani.

"The Anarchists are right," she wept. "Chal must be destroyed."

Kirk turned his eyes from the atrocities before him.

The origin of Chal could not be forgotten.

Could never be forgotten.

But the innocent could not be punished with the guilty.

"No," Kirk told Teilani.

She looked up at him in shock. Kirk went on, realizing that each word he said to her was a word he should say to himself.

"Teilani, we're not responsible for the world we're born into. Only for the world we leave when we die. So we have to accept what's gone before us in the past, and work to change the only thing we can—the future."

Teilani's fingers pressed against the display case. "How can I change *this?*"

"You can't."

"Then what's the point of anything?"

Kirk remembered the words Scott had said. *Because otherwise, we will surely go mad, desperately seeking that which we cannae have.* He remembered what Spock had said. *To refuse to accept the inevitable is the first step toward obsolescence, and extinction.*

Kirk wondered how he could have ignored his friends for so long. To not see the treasures that were already part of his life.

"The point is to change what we can. To leave this universe so that others can make it even better. And not to turn away from the challenges it gives us."

McCoy's words came back to him. *The only thing that's new is the* Enterprise-*B.*

For an instant, he saw the new ship's command chair.

And in that instant, he knew he could ignore its siren call.

That chair would be Harriman's challenge.

Kirk knew there would be others for himself.

Not distractions. Not escapes.

But work.

His work.

"Show me how, James. Show me how to not turn away."

Kirk drew Teilani to him and held her close. Without the passion of the past. But with love.

"You already know how," he said gently. "Just by coming down here, you showed you know how."

And Kirk knew how, too.

He had crossed the light-years to discover what he had always known, but never understood.

Life was for living.

No more. No less.

And to wait for it to end, as it must, was to waste it.

His horizon was near.

But for the first time in his life, he felt ready to meet it.

As he felt ready to meet all the challenges of his life.

On his own terms.

"I don't know if the Chal can live with their secret," Teilani said. She forced a smile through her tears. "But I can help them try."

Kirk hugged Teilani.

It was like holding a child in his arms.

A child of the future.

A future he had helped to survive.

"Thank you, James. For being the hero we needed. That I needed."

He kissed her forehead. Her warrior's brow.

"I should thank you," he said. "I suppose we both should—"

"Drop your weapons and raise your hands," a stranger said.

Kirk and Teilani spun around to face a human woman whose drawn phaser was leveled at them.

Kirk had no idea how long she might have been in the Armory with them.

"Who the hell are you?" Kirk asked.

"What a fitting choice of words," the woman said. "I'm Ariadne Drake. And that's where you're headed."

THIRTY-NINE

As soon as she voiced her name, Kirk saw the resemblance, knew who she must be.

"Can't your father fight his own battles?" Kirk asked.

Ariadne flashed a smile, as cold and unfeeling as Kirk remembered Androvar Drake's to be.

"You aren't a battle, Kirk. You're a mopping-up exercise."

She motioned with her phaser. Kirk recognized it as Starfleet-issue.

"Move away from the display case," Ariadne said.

Teilani looked to Kirk. He shook his head.

Teilani stood her ground.

"Isn't that touching," Ariadne said. "You're willing to die for him."

"For my world," Teilani said defiantly.

"What world? Chal is a test tube. And you're just a medical experiment."

Kirk knew he could never draw his disruptor fast enough to drop Ariadne before she fired. So he calculated how many steps it would take to reach her. When she could be expected to fire, how he might roll to avoid it.

But if she didn't track him, she'd be able to hit Teilani.

He wasn't willing to risk that. Not at these odds.

"I won't say it again—move away from the case."

Kirk held his place. The only reason he could see for why Ariadne didn't shoot right away was because she was worried about damaging whatever was in the case. He thought he could use that against her. "You'll never learn what's in it," he said.

"I already know what's there," Ariadne told him. She held up a tricorder. More Starfleet equipment. "I've been watching you and recording since you got here and activated the displays. You see, they aren't triggered by human life signs. Only by animals like her."

"The Chal are not animals," Kirk said.

Ariadne cool glance chilled him. "You've seen how they were bred, how they were *manufactured.* If you can still believe they're human, then my father was right about you. You've lost whatever fire you had."

"At least I haven't lost my mind," Kirk said.

"But you've lost your honor."

Kirk thought that was an odd thing to say. But Teilani reacted more strongly.

Of course, Kirk thought. Her Klingon upbringing. A charge of lost honor was the ultimate insult.

Ariadne was trying to break the bond they shared. Divide and conquer.

"That's a lie," Teilani warned.

"It's the truth," Ariadne said. "He even lied to you about why he came here."

Involuntarily, Teilani glanced at Kirk. She had no experience in confrontations such as this.

"She's just trying to provoke you," Kirk said.

"Go ahead," Ariadne taunted, "ask him why he's here with you."

"He came because he loves me," Teilani said.

Ariadne laughed. She gestured at Kirk with her phaser. "Fool. He's been at war with the Klingon Empire—*and* the Romulans—since before you were born."

"That war's over and done with," Kirk said. He looked at Ariadne. "Put down your phaser. There's nothing here for you."

"Oh, yes there is. I want what *you* came for. Eternal youth."

"There is no youth here," Kirk said. And with that he finally accepted the truth for himself. In a world undamaged by war, Teilani and her people would stay young for decades. It was in their genetic structure. But there was nothing on Chal that he had not brought himself.

Love. Excitement. Challenge.

Passion.

Spock had been right.

Teilani looked at Kirk, confused. "But James, you said you felt younger. You are younger."

Kirk couldn't help smiling, in spite of Ariadne's phaser. "You didn't give me any choice. Keeping up with you is like training for a marathon."

"He's lying to you," Ariadne sneered. "He's known all about the Children of Heaven project from the beginning. What it could mean to him."

"It can mean *nothing* to me," Kirk said. "The Chal have been genetically engineered for health and youth. Their bodies' systems have been augmented by transplants."

"Human transplants," Ariadne said with a terrible smile. "And that works both ways."

Kirk saw instantly what Ariadne meant.

But Teilani didn't.

"Eternal youth—from the combination of Klingon and Romulan genetics, and human tissue," Ariadne explained. "For the process to work on the Chal, their creators used transplants from human donors of tissues that could not be cloned. But humans already have those tissues. So for the process to work on us, all we will need will be transplants from the Chal."

Teilani grabbed Kirk's arm. "James, is that true?"

Kirk's expression confirmed her fears.

"See?" Ariadne gloated. "That's all you are to Kirk. That's all any of the Chal are to humans. Cattle. Bred as a source of transplant tissues."

Teilani looked at Kirk with an expression of betrayal. *"Did you know about us?"*

"No," Kirk said.

"Ask him if he wanted youth," Ariadne said.

Kirk didn't wait to be asked. "I came here because of you, Teilani."

"But who brought you to the Armory?" Ariadne asked. "Kirk did. Because of the library computer. He knows it has all the medical files he needs to understand the process that created you. So he can be young forever."

Teilani had no defenses against the poison Ariadne spewed.

But Kirk did. And Kirk had heard the one piece of information he had been missing.

The library computer. Ariadne said he wanted the files in it. Which meant *she* wanted the files.

That was why she hadn't killed them where they stood. Phaser emissions might disrupt the energy flow in the data conduits that ringed the display cases.

"For the last time," Ariadne said. "Move away."

Kirk took Teilani into his arms. She fought against him but he hissed a question into her ear.

"How long can you stop your heart?"

The question stopped her.

"Step away from her!" Ariadne warned.

"How long?" Kirk repeated.

"Three minutes, maybe four," Teilani said.

"If you want to know the truth, do it," Kirk whispered.

"Now!" Ariadne shouted.

Kirk stepped back from Teilani. "I had to say good-bye."

Ariadne aimed her phaser.

Kirk began to move to the side, away from the case.

"You, too," Ariadne told Teilani.

Teilani's eyes rolled up to show her whites.

With a moan, she slumped to the floor.

The attackers at the farm had used the same trick of autonomic self-control to make Kirk think he had killed them. So he would leave their bodies and allow them to escape.

"I'm not falling for that," Ariadne said. "If you—"

In the absence of Klingon-Romulan life signs, the lights of the Armory cut out.

Instantly, Kirk was enveloped in absolute darkness.

He heard Ariadne swear. Heard her phaser beep as she adjusted its power settings.

But by then his disruptor was in his hand and he fired.

Full power.

In the strobelike flashes of the weapon's discharge, the display case exploded.

Kirk dropped to the floor, skidded to the side as Ariadne fired a stun burst where he had been standing.

He fired again, into the data conduits.

A chain reaction sped along the gray panels behind the row of cases.

Ariadne's voice rose with rage.

Kirk changed position again.

But this time Ariadne didn't fire.

He heard her boots charge across the stone floor even as a series of explosions blossomed at connecting points along the data conduits.

The lights in the Armory began to power up again.

Kirk ran to Teilani as she returned to consciousness.

She looked around in confusion, silently asking what happened.

"I destroyed the computer."

Teilani stared at him intently, seeking truth. Seeking honor.

"Then you've destroyed the secret that could have made you young forever."

Kirk thought of Torl's words.

"But at what cost?"

Kirk heard Ariadne curse.

He left Teilani, ran to the woman.

She had broken the transparent panel of a different display

case, stepped into it. There was a library computer console inside. She was frantically trying to pull datachips from it.

But flames flickered at its side. The metal was blistering hot.

Ariadne's fingers were streaked with blood.

Kirk reached through the shattered panel and pulled her out.

She kicked and struggled in his grip.

"You fool! You don't know what you've done!"

"Yes, I do," Kirk told her.

He grabbed Ariadne's phaser from her belt. It was set to kill. But before he could adjust it, he heard a transporter cascade begin.

Five meters away, four columns of light took form.

Orange columns, not blue.

Klingons.

And Androvar Drake was with them.

FORTY

Kirk held the phaser to Ariadne's head.

But the three Klingons aimed their disruptors at Kirk as if Ariadne weren't present.

The commander in chief of Starfleet simply smiled.

"Go ahead, Jimbo. Press the firing stud."

"At this range," Kirk warned, "even stun can be fatal."

"C'est la guerre," the admiral said. "Isn't that right, Commander Drake?"

Ariadne didn't struggle against Kirk's chokehold. "I'm ready to die for what I believe in."

Admiral Drake folded his hands behind his back. "Like father like daughter, eh, Jimbo?" He took a step forward.

Kirk felt the heat from the flames in the shattered display case behind him. Teilani ran to his side.

One Klingon tracked her with his disruptor as if he were computer-guided.

"What's keeping you, Jimbo?" Drake taunted. "Oh, that's right, I forgot. You're the fraud in Starfleet. The famous starship captain who chokes when it counts."

Kirk shoved the emitter node of the phaser against Ariadne's temple, making her gasp with surprise. "I'm not in Starfleet anymore. I've got nothing to lose."

"Except your nerve. Isn't that right, Jimbo?" Drake advanced another step. "Like when you hesitated on Tycho IV? You think Captain Garrovick would believe you now? Do you think he'd believe you might actually *do* something?"

"I did the right thing on Tycho IV, Drake. More than you know."

"What excuse have you got for the war, Jimbo?"

Kirk didn't follow Drake's reasoning. He glanced at the Klingons. One was making hand gestures to the other. A battle code, Kirk knew. But he couldn't decipher it.

"What war?"

"*The* war," Drake said. "The great war that never happened. Because of you. And you don't even remember, do you?"

Kirk shook his head. The Klingons began to spread out, keeping Kirk, Ariadne, and Teilani in their crossfire.

Admiral Drake looked up at the distant ceiling, admiring the Bird-of-Prey.

"Twenty-seven, twenty-eight years ago. Stardate 3198.4. Doesn't ring a bell? I was in the Kalinora Sector. Two Klingon battle cruisers had picked off a Starfleet hospital ship. Said it was on a spying mission." Drake looked back at Kirk. Something had changed in him. His eyes were even colder, emptier.

"A spying mission, Jimbo. Women and children were on that ship. *My wife* was on that ship."

Kirk stepped back, closer to the flames. Teilani followed. Ariadne didn't fight him. The curve of the display cases meant the Klingons couldn't flank him. But Kirk knew that if Drake really did believe his daughter was expendable, they could drop Kirk at any moment.

"The galaxy was different back then," Kirk said. "We were on the brink of war."

"Oh, we weren't on the brink of war, Jimbo. We were *at* war. I chased those Klingon ships." Drake ran a finger along his scar. "Got this blowing the first one out of space. Told Starfleet what had happened. The Code One signal went out. We *were* at war."

Kirk remembered that. Not the date, but Starfleet's declaration of war. It seemed fitting to Kirk that that low point in Federation history had somehow been precipitated by Drake.

Kirk tightened his grip around Ariadne's shoulders and neck. It was clear that the Klingons were going to try and stun him from different angles at once, hoping he wouldn't be able to discharge the phaser in time. It was a risky strategy. A disruptor stun made muscles contract. Even in the face of a heavy disruptor fire, Kirk would be able to fire the phaser. "That war never went anywhere," Kirk said.

"Because of you," Drake shot back. A vein pulsed in his neck. "You brought the Organians into the war. And the Organians stopped it before it could begin. Before I could punish the Klingons who had killed my wife."

"If your Klingons fire now, you'll be killing your own daughter."

"But I'll be able to take revenge on the one responsible, won't I?"

For just an instant, Kirk wondered what it would be like to tighten his arm against Ariadne's throat. To feel her struggle. Go limp. Die by his hand. "You already have," he said quietly.

Drake cocked his head, as if not quite understanding what Kirk meant.

Then Drake smiled.

Genuinely.

"Ah, you found out about David. The young man eager to make a name for himself. Hungry for protomatter."

An explosion echoed through the vast chamber. The Klingons turned their heads to see a ball of flame roll along the data conduit opposite Kirk's position. Whatever chain reaction Kirk had set off inside the library computer, it was spreading.

But Drake was not distracted. His complete attention focused on Kirk. As it had been since they'd first met at the Academy.

"You should be proud of your son," Drake said. "Thanks to his pioneering work and great sacrifices, Starfleet will be resuming protomatter research. Under my direction. In fact, when we test the first protobomb, you can be sure I'll give David the public honor he's due."

"He was a child!" Kirk said. "He didn't know the risks!"

"Neither do you, Jimbo." Drake shook his head in scorn. "Now, either kill my daughter or drop your weapon. For once in your life, do something!"

Kirk thought of David. He increased the pressure on the firing stud.

He wanted to see Drake broken.

Defeated by the greatest loss a parent could know.

As Kirk had been defeated on the Genesis Planet.

And it would be so easy now.

But at what cost?

Kirk dropped the phaser, kicked it away. Released Ariadne.

She hesitated a moment, then rushed to her father's side.

Drake smirked at him. "I always knew you were a coward, Kirk."

Teilani stayed with Kirk. Held his arm. Protected. Not protecting.

"I know what it's like to lose a child," Kirk said. "I won't be a party to that. Even to stop you."

Drake walked over to retrieve Ariadne's phaser. "I'm so very deeply touched. As will be my associates in Starfleet Command." Drake changed the setting on the phaser. Pointed it at Kirk. "There're are seven of us left. Not even Cartwright knew us all. Safer that way."

"Who are they?" Kirk asked.

"All you need to know is that they're patriots, dedicated to keeping the Federation free of alien influences. We've had too much of that recently." Drake waved the phaser at Teilani. "That's all right, Teilani. The charade is over. You can come back to me, now."

Kirk knew Drake had said that only to hurt him. But then he felt Teilani shrink closer to him.

"That's right," Drake said with amusement. "She's been working for me all along."

Kirk looked into Teilani's eyes. The flames from the display case and the data conduits flashed madly in them. Along with the truth.

"I'm sorry, James."

It explained so much Kirk wasn't even surprised.

"That's why you didn't approach me at the reception, isn't it? Because Drake was with me. And you knew him."

"He told me you wouldn't understand."

"But I do."

"My people needed help to survive the Anarchists' attacks. My aides said the admiral was going to be the new commander of Starfleet. That I should go to him. But Drake said the Federation couldn't get involved in a Klingon-Romulan matter. He said you were retiring. That you'd accept the challenge."

"I gave her your psych file," Drake snickered. "You were an open book."

Kirk wouldn't give Drake the satisfaction of seeing how he really felt.

"You did what you had to do," he told Teilani. An innocent pawn in a game between Kirk and an old enemy.

She squeezed his hand. "But I did fall in love with you. You must believe that."

Kirk raised her hand to his lips and kissed it. "I do."

Then Kirk turned to face Drake. "I think I can put the rest together. How you needed someone not involved in Starfleet to locate Chal."

Drake nodded imperiously.

"I'm curious. What were you going to do with the Children of Heaven process?" Kirk asked. "Bribe Federation officials with eternal youth? Get them to overturn treaties? Stop the peace talks?"

"Everyone has a price, Jimbo. Yours has always been your vanity."

"I think you're underestimating the people we have in Starfleet," Kirk said. "They won't accept such outright manipulation."

Drake's phaser never wavered. "Think again, Jimbo. Cartwright *almost* succeeded. Throw in a few assassinations, a border incident or two, and the paranoia so recently buried in humanity will come back in force. I guarantee it. I've made an exhaustive study of it. Under my guidance, my vision, the Federation will become stronger than ever before. It's the only way it can survive."

Kirk slipped his arm around Teilani, holding her closely to him.

"Study your history, Drake. If threats of war, bribery, and murder are the only way the Federation can survive, then it doesn't deserve to."

Drake smiled. He handed his phaser to his daughter. "That kind of attitude only proves your cowardice, Jimbo. You know what your problem is? You just can't see the future. Never have. Never will."

Kirk's grip on Teilani was like duranium. "I can see the future well enough." As if adjusting his collar, he tugged on the lapel of his jacket. Drake didn't even blink at the tiny movement. "That's why I didn't even think of coming here without knowing how to get back."

Drake frowned uneasily. He turned to his daughter.

Then Kirk gave an order he had never given before.

"Beam me up, Scotty."

As the Armory dissolved into energy around him, Kirk had the fleeting impression of a phaser beam crackling through the space he had occupied a heartbeat before.

But it had no effect on him or Teilani.

Drake had lost his battle.

Now it was time to make certain he lost the war.

FORTY-ONE

Kirk stepped down from the transporter platform the instant the beam released him.

"Scotty—tell whoever's on communications to raise the *Excelsior*. We have to get a message to Starfleet Command *now.*"

Scott grinned from behind the transporter console. "I think ye'd better talk to communications yerself, sir."

Kirk wasn't in the mood for games. He hit the transmit control on the console. "Kirk to bridge."

"Spock here, Captain."

"Spock?" Kirk slowly realized that he was standing with his mouth open. "What are you doing here?"

"It appears I am waiting for your orders."

Kirk looked at Scott.

Scott shrugged. "Captain Spock and the others thought ye might need a wee bit o' help."

"The others?"

"Aye. It's like old home week, if ye ask me."

Kirk told Teilani to follow him. He ran out the doors toward the closest turbolift. He was on the bridge in less than a minute.

Spock was in the center chair, vacating it the instant Kirk stepped from the turbolift.

Uhura was at what was left of communications.

Chekov was at tactical.

And McCoy was trying to stay out of the way at the engineering station. Which is exactly where Scott headed, sending the doctor grumbling over to environmental.

Kirk had to pause for a moment to take it all in.

He was back.

They were *all* back. Except for Sulu.

"I . . . I don't know what to say," Kirk stammered.

The *Enterprise* suddenly rocked with the impact of a direct disruptor hit.

"'Go to Red Alert' might be appropriate," Spock suggested.

Kirk jumped into his chair. "Red alert! Full shields! Chekov—report!"

"Drake has transported back to the Klingon wessel, Keptin! He is attacking!"

Kirk gripped the arms of his chair as the *Enterprise* rocked again. "Mr. Esys, bring us about. Chekov, lock phase—*disruptors* on Drake's ship. Spock—what happened after you withdrew?"

"Admiral Drake did not pursue our insubordination with a formal inquiry."

"Disruptors locked on, sir!"

"See what they've got, Mr. Chekov. Fire!"

On the main viewscreen, the Klingon battle cruiser shuddered as its shields flared in a sphere of glowing orange light.

"Their shields are tuned to disruptor fire," Chekov reported with disappointment.

"Photon torpedoes, Mr. Chekov. Target their port nacelle."

Kirk turned back to Spock. "Didn't hold an inquiry? So you immediately knew he had something to hide."

"Precisely," Spock said.

McCoy stepped down behind Kirk's chair. Kirk twisted around. "Teilani, may I introduce Dr. Leonard McCoy. Dr. McCoy—Teilani."

Teilani raised an amused eyebrow at Kirk as McCoy kissed the back of her hand.

"Charmed, m'dear," McCoy said with his best Southern drawl.

"James has told me a great deal about you, Doctor."

"Very little of it is true, I can assure you."

"Torpedoes loaded!" Chekov announced.

"Fire at will."

The inductance twang of the torpedo launcher echoed twice in the bridge.

Two explosions flared off the Klingon's shields.

"Their shields are at ninety percent," Spock said. "As are ours."

"So we're evenly matched?" Kirk asked. He was surprised at how good it felt to be back in the midst of action. Even battle.

"Not exactly," Spock said. "We do have the *Excelsior* standing by."

"Uhura, hail Captain Sulu."

"Aye, Captain."

An instant later, Sulu was on the main viewscreen. He looked contrite.

"Captain Kirk, I believe I owe you an apology."

But Kirk would not accept it. "None needed, Captain Sulu. I'm well aware of the chain of command. You handled a difficult situation with—"

Bridge lights flashed as a Klingon torpedo hit the *Enterprise*'s shields.

"No damage," Spock said.

"Return fire, Mr. Chekov," Kirk ordered. Then he turned his attention back to Sulu. "As I was saying, I'm well aware of how awkward it is to be caught in the middle like that."

Sulu looked relieved. "Thank you, sir. With Admiral Drake on one side—"

"Oh, I didn't mean Drake," Kirk interrupted. "I meant Spock and McCoy."

Sulu laughed.

"You did what you had to do," Kirk continued, suddenly serious. "As a starship captain, you had no other choice."

"Our disruptors aren't making any dent in her shields," Chekov said. He looked at Kirk. Then at Sulu on the viewscreen. For all they had been through, there were no hard feelings between them.

Chekov sighed. It seemed he still had a great deal to learn about starship captains.

"Captain Sulu, stand ready to make your presence known," Kirk said. "Uhura, hail the Klingon vessel."

Sulu flickered off the viewscreen to be replaced by Drake, calmly sitting in the Klingon ship's center chair.

"Do you want to hear my terms for your surrender, Jimbo?" Drake asked.

"That won't be necessary, Drake. Captain Sulu, take out the Klingon's nacelles, please."

Drake gripped the sides of his chair as the Klingon bridge twisted under the *Excelsior*'s phaser barrage.

Drake barked out commands in Klingon.

Kirk heard photon torpedoes being launched over the Klingon audio pickup.

"The *Excelsior* is evading fire," Spock announced.

"Very good," Kirk told the admiral. "But you can't keep up firepower like that forever."

"I don't have to," Drake said. "As far as I'm concerned, you lost this fight the day you arrived."

The viewscreen cut back to an image of near space in Chal orbit. Drake's battle cruiser began to bank.

"His warp engines are powering up," Chekov said.

Kirk was puzzled. It wasn't like Drake to run from a fight.

Then the Klingon ship stretched into a rainbow streak and was gone.

"Heading, Mr. Chekov?"

"Out of the system, sir. No obvious destination."

Teilani grabbed Kirk and kissed him. Kirk saw McCoy and Uhura's surprised reactions.

But he didn't care.

"James! You beat him!"

"Not yet," Kirk said. He glanced over at Spock. "We have to keep Drake from contacting any of his co-conspirators in Starfleet Command. Start tracking him, Mr. Esys."

Then Sulu came back onscreen. "Captain Kirk, are you analyzing Drake's course?"

Kirk looked down at Chekov. "Mr. Chekov?"

Chekov shook his head. "These sensors can't track him at high varp speed."

"Is there a problem, Sulu?"

Sulu looked as if there were. "I'm transmitting our sensor readings to your science station."

A few moments later, Spock looked up from his viewers. After thirty years of friendship, Kirk could read the signs of alarm in Spock's placid expression.

"The admiral is moving into a slingshot trajectory."

"No," McCoy said in shock.

"What does that mean, James?"

Kirk pounded his fist against the arm of his chair. "He's attempting to go back through time. Probably to ambush us a week ago, before I had a chance to destroy the library computer in the Armory. That's what he meant when he said I had lost the day I had arrived here."

"Can he really go back to the past?"

"Unfortunately." Kirk turned back to Sulu. "Captain Sulu, has any ship of the *Excelsior*'s design ever undergone a temporal slingshot maneuver?"

Grimly, Sulu shook his head.

"The *Enterprise* has," Kirk said.

"But not in its present configuration," Spock cautioned.

"Close enough, Spock." Kirk held out his hand to Sulu. "What do you say, Captain? One last time around the block?"

Sulu grinned. "I always seem to say that. Stand by, *Enterprise.*"

The viewscreen jumped back to show Chal.

"James, I don't understand."

"Sulu has navigated us through the slingshot maneuver several times," Kirk said. "Better drop shields, Mr. Chekov."

A moment after Chekov's acknowledgment, a transporter beam formed before the viewscreen.

Sulu stepped from it.

"Request permission to come aboard," he said. Then he went straight to the navigator's station.

Mr. Esys slipped out of his chair.

"Captain Sulu," Kirk said. "Lay in an intercept course and proceed."

Sulu manipulated the helm controls like a concert pianist. Chal fell away from the viewscreen and the stars began to smear as the *Enterprise* jumped to warp.

Scott leaned down by Kirk. "I dinna know if this is th' time t' be tellin' ye, but I dinna think th' *Enterprise* can withstand a temporal jump."

Kirk felt like laughing. He was back in a life-or-death chase on the bridge of the *Enterprise,* with his full command crew at his side.

All of them. Even Sulu.

No matter what the future held, he knew he could not lose today.

"With any luck, Mr. Scott, we'll intercept Drake before he snaps around the sun."

The bridge rumbled with the whine of the warp engines. But the stars moved faster. The *Enterprise* still accelerated.

"We're going to hit some gravimetric turbulence," Sulu warned. "That's a binary sun."

"The Klingon ship's not built for this kind of action," Kirk said. "Just get us within disruptor range so we can spoil his trajectory. Uhura, keep us in touch with the *Excelsior.* We'll want her in position when Drake comes around the primary star."

Then Kirk kept his eyes fixed on the viewscreen. Chal's binary suns began to fill it. Drake's vessel was a slender streak of silver light heading between them.

"Drake is close to temporal dislocation," Spock said.

"Faster, Captain Sulu."

The bridge began to vibrate.

Scott's eyes widened nervously.

Kirk winked at him. "She'll hold," he mouthed silently. He could feel it.

"Coming up on disruptor range," Chekov said.

"Twenty seconds from temporal dislocation," Spock announced.

"Lock disruptors," Kirk ordered.

The viewscreen blazed with the yellow primary and orange secondary sun. The plasma bridge between them writhed like a living creature.

"Fifteen seconds," Spock said.

"Disruptors locked—but she's still out of range, Keptin."

Kirk felt Teilani's hand tighten on his arm. "James, what happens if Drake gets away?"

"Don't worry, if he *had* escaped, we wouldn't be here to chase him," Kirk said. "Right, Spock?"

"Actually, Captain, no. This could just be an alternate timeline in which the quantum probability waves—"

Kirk held up his hand to stop his science officer. "You know time travel gives me a headache, Spock."

"Ten seconds," Spock said.

"Entering the plasma bridge," Sulu shouted.

On the viewscreen, the yellow primary rushed to one side as the orange secondary rushed past the other.

Now the screen was filled with twisting tendrils of superheated plasma—the surface of the smaller star being peeled away by the awesome gravitational forces of the larger star.

Slicing through those tendrils, Drake's ship was a dark dagger.

A warning chime sounded.

"Shields at seventy-three percent and falling," Scott said. "She canna take these temperatures for long."

"Five . . ." Spock counted down. "Four . . . three . . ."

"In range!"

"Fire!"

The viewscreen flared with flickering disruptor feedback.

The *Enterprise* screamed as her frame twisted from her passage through the plasma bridge and the opposing gravitational fields of the stars.

"Got her!" Chekov shouted.

"Drake's ship has dropped from warp," Spock said. "He did not achieve temporal dislocation."

"Full magnification!"

On the viewscreen, Drake's ship cartwheeled slowly through the plasma streams, disappearing into a wall of seething light.

"Stay with her, Sulu." In the time it had taken Kirk to give that order, the *Enterprise* had overshot Drake's crippled ship by tens of thousands of kilometers. But Sulu brought the ship around and dropped her to impulse speeds as well, returning her to the point of last contact.

Kirk scanned the glowing patterns of braided light on the viewscreen. "Where is he?" Kirk asked.

"There is no sign of the Klingon ship, Captain. But our sensor capabilities are degrading." There was unexpected tension in Spock's voice. "We cannot scan more than a few hundred kilometers in any direction."

"Any sign of debris?" Kirk asked.

"The exterior temperature is in excess of thirty thousand degrees Kelvin. If Drake's shields have failed, physical debris would exist for only a few seconds at most."

"Any sign that's what happened?"

"No, sir," Spock said. "And no indication of an operative impulse drive either."

"Then we have to assume that he's in here with us. Either lying in wait or needing rescue." Kirk shifted in his chair. He wiped at the sweat on his forehead. It wasn't a good sign. The bridge felt a good ten degrees warmer than usual. "How are we doing, Scotty?"

The engineer answered from his station behind Kirk. "Not too well, sir. Our radiation shields can only take another twenty minutes o' this punishment. So we'll have t' pull out in ten."

Kirk didn't understand. "Scotty, at full impulse we can be out of the plasma in under thirty seconds."

But Scott shook his head. "We canna go t' full impulse in this kind of environment, sir. We canna afford to reduce our shields even a tiny bit to vent our impulse exhaust, so we're limited to no more than ten percent."

Kirk knew better than to argue with Scott about absolutes. "Did you hear that, Captain Sulu?" Kirk said. "We have ten minutes to find Drake."

McCoy moved around to where Kirk could see him. "Jim, is that a good idea? What if he's already out of here? He could be trying another slingshot run right now."

"Unlikely, Doctor," Spock said from his science station. "Drake knows the *Excelsior* is still on patrol. He will no longer have the element of surprise on his side, and so cannot reasonably expect to succeed in another attempt to slingshot."

"So what are you saying, Spock? He's hanging around in this garden spot looking for us?"

"If his ship was not too badly damaged by our disruptor blast, his shields and sensors will be up to full military strength. He will, therefore, be in a position of strength in this environment."

McCoy frowned at Kirk. "If you need a translation, Jim, I think that means we should get out of here."

Kirk listened carefully to each word Spock and McCoy said. But he didn't take his eyes off the viewscreen.

The plasma threads were hypnotic.

They flowed past the *Enterprise* like glowing currents of luminous water.

Kirk thought of Chal. The way the waves rippled up on the beach.

The planet had been one type of paradise.

But this ship was another.

The one that counted.

"Picking up something," Chekov said tentatively.

Spock studied his readouts. "It could be a ship," he said.

"But which one?" Kirk asked. "Drake's or the *Excelsior?*"

"We should know in a moment. . . . We're getting a stronger—"

Then the viewscreen flared brilliant white and even as Kirk flew from his chair, he knew his ship had been hit by a photon torpedo.

FORTY-TWO

Ariadne turned around from her weapons station on the bridge of the Klingon cruiser.

"Direct hit!"

Drake leaned forward in his command chair. His eyes drank in the scintillating whorls and eddies of the plasma bridge between the stars.

And *there*—one dark spinning spot dead ahead—was the *Enterprise.*

With James T. Kirk trapped helplessly inside her.

All that Drake hated. And feared.

Small enough to be blotted out with his thumb.

"QIH poj!" Drake commanded.

The Klingon science officer analyzed his readings. "Damage as follows . . . no impulse engines . . . shields at thirty-three percent . . . failure estimated within five minutes."

Drake sat back in his chair, overcome with contentment. "Navigator, take us in. I want a clear view."

The navigator hesitated only long enough that Drake knew something was wrong. But the cruiser slipped forward, gently buffeted by the jets of starstuff.

"Admiral," the science officer said uncertainly, "may I remind you that *our* shields are only at forty-two percent. We cannot last much longer than the Federation vessel."

"But we *can* last longer," Drake said. "Which means we can last forever, compared with Kirk."

Drake stepped down from his chair and stood behind his

daughter. Placed his hand on her shoulder. Felt her take his hand in hers.

"Now that you've met him," Drake said, "you understand, don't you?"

"Why you hate him?" Ariadne asked.

Drake nodded.

She shrugged. "To tell thc truth, he reminded me of you."

Drake's hand closed tighter and tighter on his daughter's hand until she pulled it away from him. "Except for one thing," he told her. "I am better than Kirk and always have been. This day proves that. Finally."

The *Enterprise* floated in the center of the screen, slowly turning in the pressure of the raging plasma currents.

"No inertial control," Drake said. "That means they're putting all their power into shields."

"Tuned to radiation only," the science officer confirmed. "Sensors show artificial gravity is also off."

"Ahh," Drake sighed happily. "Desperation." He looked over his shoulder at the science officer. "What's the internal temperature?"

"In the bridge, thirty-seven degrees. Climbing rapidly."

Drake smiled fiercely, not noticing the perspiration running down his own face.

"Admiral, *our* interior temperature is thirty-three degrees. Also climbing rapidly."

"Yes," Drake agreed. "But we have impulse power. We can leave at any time."

"Why don't we finish him off?" Ariadne asked. "Another torpedo will overload his shields. Then we can leave with a margin of safety."

Drake nodded. He had raised his daughter properly. "Very well. Stand by on torpedo. But hail Kirk for me. I want him to know who's responsible. I want to be the last thing he sees."

"The *Enterprise* is not responding."

For an instant, disappointment flashed across Drake's face. Then he brightened.

"So, he stayed a coward to the end."

"Her shields are fluctuating."

The *Enterprise* seemed to shimmer.

"She's gone into overload," Ariadne said. Her tone was even and colorless.

Drake leaned forward, face now dripping with sweat, fists clenched in expectation.

"Yesss," he breathed. "You know I'm out here, Kirk . . . doing this to you . . ."

Plasma sparks jumped along the *Enterprise's* nacelles.

Drake licked his lips.

Ariadne kept up her calm commentary. "There go her generators. Emergency batteries coming online. They'll only be good for a few seconds."

The port nacelle strut began to twist.

"Structural integrity field is overcompensating."

The nacelles flared, one after the other.

"Hull breach!"

The engineering hull blossomed into a tiny sun.

"Antimatter release!"

The saucer buckled.

For a breathless moment, the bridge dome rose out of the saucer's center as the outer rim shattered like ice.

"Superheated overpressure . . ."

And then the saucer tore itself apart like a starship made of sand, crushed by an unstoppable wave.

In seconds, all that remained of the *Enterprise* was a river of sparkling, incandescent wreckage, flaring as the plasma reduced it to glowing, disassociated ions.

Drake was exhausted.

He stumbled back to his chair. His uniform was drenched.

It was over.

Kirk was defeated.

Even running the Federation was going to be a letdown after that.

"Navigator," Drake said, "plot a course to take us out of here."

"Uh, Admiral," the science officer said, "we are being hailed."

Drake shrugged. He had been expecting this. "The *Excelsior?"* he asked. Sulu was an annoyance, but he could be dealt with.

"No, sir. It's . . . uh . . . it's Kirk."

Ariadne paled as her father screamed.

His anger was a match for the torrent of plasma they rode.

FORTY-THREE

☆

Kirk stepped forward as Androvar Drake appeared on the *Excelsior*'s main viewscreen.

It was the first time he had ever seen Drake overwhelmed by emotion.

"I saw you die!" Drake said.

"No one died," Kirk told him. His command crew was at his side, along with Teilani. They had been safely transported from the *Enterprise* with her skeleton crew of Chal, minutes before her shields failed, leaving her as a decoy to draw Drake closer. "You only saw the *Enterprise* go out in a blaze of glory. Just the way you wanted."

Someone spoke to Drake on the Klingon bridge. But he stared straight ahead, his eyes feverish. Fixed on Kirk as if nothing else existed for him in the universe.

"Admiral," Kirk said. "I want you to tune your shields to

reflect radiation only. We're going to have to beam you and your crew to the *Excelsior.*"

"You couldn't fool a midshipman with that tactic, Jimbo."

"It's not a tactic. We're monitoring your shield status. They won't last long enough to let you leave the plasma bridge. You wanted to watch me die so much that you hesitated, Drake. The same sin you accused me of. But in your case, it wasn't the right thing to do." Kirk allowed himself the luxury of a smile. *"C'est la guerre."*

Drake sat at rigid attention in his chair. A Klingon chair.

"Every time we've gone head-to-head, I've beaten you, Jimbo. Now it's come down to whose vision of the Federation is going to survive."

Spock stepped up beside Kirk. "He has less than five minutes of shields remaining."

"Drake," Kirk said, "let's continue the debate over here."

"You're the past, I'm the future. Always have been."

Drake imperiously pointed his finger at someone offscreen. Ariadne moved into view, said something into his ear.

Chekov and Uhura both reacted with surprise. "That's Jade," Uhura said.

"The rogue agent," Chekov added.

"She's Drake's daughter," Kirk said, so much becoming clear. "Admiral, please—if not for yourself, then for your crew. For your daughter."

"Set a course for the rendezvous point," Drake said to Ariadne. "We'll deal with the *Excelsior* when we've been reinforced. Full impulse till we're out of the plasma. Then maximum warp."

"Admiral—you can't do that. Full impulse will overload your shields in here."

On the viewscreen, Ariadne turned to look out at Kirk. It was impossible to tell what she was thinking.

Kirk turned to his science officer. "Tell her, Spock. Tell her what readings to look for."

"Check the radiation pressure on your aft shields," Spock

said. "You will see it is out of balance and will not withstand impulse venting."

Ariadne looked at her father.

He shook his head.

"Get us out of here," he said.

Ariadne moved offscreen.

Kirk remembered her words in the Armory. *I'm ready to die for what I believe in.*

"Check the readings, Drake. Let me get you out of there."

"So you can win?"

Kirk knew Drake wasn't going to allow himself to be saved.

"So your daughter—your child—won't die."

A terrible smile twisted across Drake's sweat-covered face. Kirk remembered it from Tycho IV. When they had been surrounded by death. When Drake had believed they would not survive because he had no faith in Captain Garrovick.

"See you in hell, Jimbo." Drake pointed forward. His voice was hoarse but sure. "Take us out."

There was nothing more Kirk could do. He had no choice but to accept the inevitable.

Drake looked directly into the viewscreen. Kirk knew he would be the last thing Drake would see. "Full im—"

The image from the Klingon bridge winked out.

The viewscreen showed the Klingon battle cruiser flare as its shields failed.

It seemed to expand in all directions at once, dissolving in a shower of sparks.

One of them was Drake.

One of them was Drake's child.

Teilani took Kirk's hand. "He believed you, James. About the shields. I saw it in his eyes."

"I know," Kirk said.

"So why could he not accept your offer to save him?"

Kirk stared at the coils and jets of the plasma stream.

There was no trace of Drake's ship.

No trace of the *Enterprise.*

"Once, he was a starship captain," Kirk said. "And starship captains think they're invincible."

"Why, James?"

Kirk smiled. Sadly. Proudly. He had always known the answer to that question, but at this moment, in this place, it meant more to him than it ever had before.

Because it was *the* answer.

"They have to be," he said. "It's their job."

Trailing streamers of fire, the *Excelsior* came about.

She flew for Chal.

FORTY-FOUR

As Chekov stepped onto the *Excelsior's* bridge, Chal was a jewel on the main viewscreen, so brilliant she cast blue light over the station-keeping crew.

Mr. Scott was debating some fine point about warp balance with the engineer.

Uhura and Janice Rand were whispering together, laughing.

Sulu was in his command chair, sipping tea.

He glanced up at Chekov as Chekov stood beside him, hands behind his back.

"Have you been down there?" Sulu asked.

Chekov shook his head. "Another time, perhaps." The *Excelsior* had to be under way within the hour. A full session of the Federation Council had been called to investigate Drake's actions. Kirk was to be a key witness.

"I hear it's a paradise," Sulu said.

"Eden," Chekov agreed.

They stared at the screen in silence.

Chekov wondered what it was about humans that they spent their lives looking for Edens, knowing it was the one place they could never remain.

After a few long moments, he cleared his throat. "I heard you apologize to the keptin."

Sulu put down his tea cup. So gently it didn't make a sound against its saucer.

"His view of the situation was correct," Sulu said. "I didn't know it at the time. I should have." Sulu grinned for a moment. "He *is* Captain Kirk, after all."

"I vould like to apologize," Chekov said abruptly. "To you."

Sulu looked at Chekov, perplexed.

"For punching you," Chekov quickly explained. "Vhen you saved us from Dark Range. And for arguing with you. Doubting your command decisions. Trying to fight you again vhen—"

Sulu nodded, motioned for Chekov to stop. "I don't need a list, Pavel."

Chekov grimaced. Stopped talking. Rocked back on his heels. "Vell, anyvay. I apologize."

Sulu smiled as if to say the apology wasn't necessary. "I think we all got on each other's nerves this time out."

Chekov glanced back. Mr. Scott and Uhura were coming over, apparently interested to know what Sulu and Chekov were discussing.

"You think by now ve'd be used to each other."

Sulu stared across at the viewscreen. Chekov saw the way he gripped the arms of his chair. The same way Captain Kirk did.

Chekov had tried it once. Knew why Kirk and Sulu did it.

So they could feel their ships. Sense the vibrations of the engines. Feel a part of them.

Sulu was born to sit in that chair.

The captain of the *Excelsior* looked around to see his friends gathered at his side. "Maybe when we're all together, we need the captain to keep us from each other's throats," he said.

But Chekov shook his head. "No. I think maybe, ve're just a family. Ve have had our good days. Ve have had our bad ones."

Chekov held out his hand in friendship.

Sulu took it. "But mostly, we've had good ones, haven't we?" he said.

Scott and Uhura agreed.

So did Chekov. "To tell the truth, looking back, they've all been good. And the days ahead vill be even better."

Sulu gave Chekov a skeptical look. "You think we'll all be together again?" He looked out at the viewscreen, past Chal, to the stars. "Out there?"

The stars filled Chekov's eyes and he smiled. "A man can dream, can't he?"

FORTY-FIVE

☆

The suns of Chal were setting.

They cast long shadows on the beach.

Kirk found Teilani there.

She was sitting on a smooth, sea-polished log that was half-buried in the sand. She wore the loose white tunic of Chal, her legs drawn up, arms wrapped around them. Staring out at the deepening red of the sky.

He sat beside her. Wordlessly gave her his gift.

She unwrapped the cloth he had bundled around the thin, rectangular object.

It was a metal plaque.

The plaque.

Kirk had pulled it from the bulkhead by the turbolift, just before he had left the *Enterprise* for the final time.

Just before he had consigned her to the flames and the stars and all eternity.

Teilani ran her fingers across the raised letters.

"U.S.S. Enterprise," she read.

Kirk heard the question in her voice. She didn't know what the plaque meant. He wondered if anyone could truly know, except for those who had served aboard her.

She read the last line on the plaque aloud. "'To boldly go where no man has gone before.'"

"They're going to change that," Kirk said. "On the next one."

Half-built in spacedock. Assigned to Captain Harriman, not Kirk.

The way it should be.

Teilani held the plaque to her heart. He could barely hear her when she spoke. "I'm going to miss you."

"The price we pay," Kirk said gently. "For loving what we cannot keep forever."

Teilani's eyes shone with unshed tears. "Do you love me?"

Kirk kissed her cheek. "Yes," he said.

"Then don't leave."

Kirk held her. He had always known this moment would come. Even when his heart had dared dream of eternal youth, his mind had known that nothing truly lasted forever.

The knowledge of death was the price to be paid for the knowledge of being alive.

"Chal needs you," Kirk said. "There'll be a Federation task force here within the month. They'll work with you. Advise you. Help you do all that you must to make this world your own."

"Where do you belong, James?"

He tapped his finger on the plaque.

"A long time ago, Drake told me to keep this for my grandchildren. A piece of the *Enterprise* to hang over the fireplace."

Kirk stood. He still had far to go.

He touched her hair again. Shining waves. Remembered their silk cascading around him.

"When you have children," he said, "tell them about the *Enterprise.* And her crew. To keep us alive here. Forever young."

She could hold her tears no longer.

They ran from her face to the plaque she held to her heart.

"I promise," she said.

Kirk gave her hand a final squeeze, a final sensation, a final memory to keep in his heart.

And then Kirk let go the dream, turned away, continued his journey.

Alone.

Teilani watched Kirk as he walked away from her. From her life. From her world.

The long shadows of the setting suns made his footsteps in the sand deep and dark, unmistakable.

The stars above began to flicker in the twilight, as if guiding his way.

Teilani watched as Kirk dissolved into glittering light, reclaimed by those stars, until only his footsteps remained.

Though she knew she would never recapture what she had lost this day, she felt the change Kirk had wrought within her. So her tears were tempered with happiness, for she knew a part of him would always be with her on Chal.

As she left the beach, returning to her home, Teilani knew exactly where she would hang the plaque.

And in the years to come, she knew she would sit by the fire, beneath that plaque, to tell the story of the ship called *Enterprise.*

And her crew.

And her captain.

Who would live in her heart, forever.

FORTY-SIX

From his stateroom on the *Excelsior,* Kirk watched the stars streak past him. He never tired of the sight.

Spock and McCoy stood beside him.

He watched their reflections in the viewport.

As always, they were as entranced as he was.

"After the investigations are completed, Starfleet will require a new commander in chief," Spock said.

Kirk couldn't help himself. He laughed.

"I do not think laughter is an appropriate response. You are a logical choice."

Kirk turned to his friends. "Spock, I don't want you even suggesting it."

McCoy pursed his lips. "And why's that? Because it's a job for a younger man?"

"No, Bones—because it's a job for a different man." Kirk patted McCoy's shoulder. "Who knows? Maybe I'll take up with another 'inappropriate' companion and head off to Andromeda."

McCoy frowned, looked at Spock. "Do you suppose he's ever going to let us forget that fight?"

"It was not a fight, Doctor. It was a difference of opinion.

We have had them in the past and will undoubtedly have them in the future."

Kirk raised a cautionary finger. "Ah, but it was a *legitimate* difference of opinion."

Spock raised a skeptical eyebrow. "Hardly, Captain. As Dr. McCoy and I had surmised, your relationship with the young woman did not last."

"Spock, *nothing* lasts. That's what makes everything . . . so precious."

McCoy looked bemused. "I might know an exception to that nothing lasting forever business."

Kirk and Spock waited expectantly.

"Did you know some hotshots at the Academy have programmed your missions into their holographic simulators?"

Kirk didn't react. "I, uh, might have heard something about that. What's your point, Doctor?"

"My point? Dear Lord, Jim—you've been digitized, rerecorded, and holographically enhanced. Cadets will probably be watching you and your adventures for the next hundred years."

Kirk looked back to the stars. "You know, a month ago, before Chal and Teilani, when I didn't know where I was going in what remains of my life, I think I would have resented that kind of attention."

"And now?" Spock asked.

"Now," Kirk said, "I only hope they enjoy those adventures as much as I did."

McCoy nodded sagely. Spock looked confused.

All was as it should be.

Kirk smiled at the sight of the three of them standing together, reflected against the stars. Bound by a friendship that surpassed all the years and all the adventures. Still boldly going long after they had all thought their mission had ended.

No one could have predicted the adventures that had

brought them to this point. No one could predict the adventures that still awaited them.

But whatever the universe had in store for him next, for however long his own journey continued, Kirk knew at last he was ready to face it.

Forever young.

EPILOGUE

Night had fallen, and the stars encompassed all the sky of Veridian III.

Some among them had watched over a child named Kirk, on a farm in Iowa on Earth. Others had watched over a child named Spock, on a mountain villa near the Plains of Gol on Vulcan. Together, they watched over Veridian III tonight.

Spock spoke softly to those stars now.

"I am now, and will always be, your friend."

There was no logic to saying those words aloud.

But it felt *right.*

"Good-bye, Jim."

An era had ended.

It was time for Spock to move on with his own journey.

He glanced down the slope. The honor guard still stood by Kirk's grave, almost imperceptible in the moonless night.

Then Spock's ears heard the faint chirp of a communicator badge. Riker spoke, his words indistinct on the night air.

The starship that was to transport Kirk's remains was overdue. No doubt, Spock concluded, Riker was receiving an update.

Spock's communicator vibrated silently against his wrist.

"Spock here."

It was Riker. His voice betrayed his emotions. "Ambassador, there appears to be some trouble at the salvage site. I'm going to have to ask you to remain here while we beam back to check the situation."

"Of course, Commander," Spock agreed. "What is the nature of the trouble?"

"I'm not sure," Riker replied. "It almost sounds as if they're . . . under attack."

The area around Kirk's grave lit up as Riker and the honor guard were beamed away.

Spock was intrigued.

He glanced up at the stars, calculating the likely position of ships in standard orbits.

A few stars in that ecliptic moved. Streaks of multicolored energy discharged between them.

Starships in orbital battle.

"Fascinating," Spock said.

But except for the moving lights in the sky, the night remained silent and still.

Spock found a place to sit on a nearby rock, the better to preserve his strength. He rearranged his robes, the better to conserve his body heat.

The battle in space still raged above him.

As his eyes adapted to the distant discharges, he could identify the distinctive blue signature of Starfleet phasers.

But the return fire was unidentifiable. He had never seen its like before.

The situation presented an interesting set of problems. In his mind, Spock began to deconstruct them as a series of logical arguments, attempting to identify likely attackers, their motives, tactics, and probable odds of success.

But he was interrupted in his calculations.

The night air thrummed. Something large was approaching through the sky.

Spock rose to his feet. He scanned the dark horizon, trying to identify any occultation of stars that would indicate the presence of a flying craft operating without running lights.

The thrumming increased.

He could see nothing, but his robes began to swirl around him, blown about by some kind of backwash.

Spock raised his hand to shield his eyes from a rising whirlwind of dust.

Directly above him, the stars wavered, and then were blacked out by a silhouette of something he couldn't identify.

A sudden light danced at the edge of his vision.

He looked down the slope toward Kirk's grave.

Amber rays spiked out from between the rocks of the simple cairn.

Above the thrumming and the wind, Spock heard an oddly musical chime.

The light emanating from Kirk's grave brightened, then began to fade. Spock clearly heard the sounds of rocks falling against themselves.

The logic of this situation was inescapable, yet made no sense.

Among the stars, the signs of a space battle had ended.

Above Spock, the watching stars returned and the thrumming backwash vanished as suddenly as if a ship had gone to warp.

Spock drew an emergency light from his belt and made his way down the slope to Kirk's grave.

He played the light across the cairn.

The rocks had *fallen in.*

The grave was empty.

Spock looked to the stars.

"Jim . . .?" he said.

It was not at all logical, but for a moment, a most improbable thought came to him—

Perhaps some journeys were never meant to end.

There were always *possibilities. . . .*

STAR TREK®

THE RETURN

I have another life having nothing to do with acting, directing or writing. It involves my universe of horses, those beauteous creatures whose form and function fill me with delight.

So to that world of horses, to the people who train and care for my four-footed friends, to the driven, excuse the pun, fellow competitors who try to take the blue ribbon away from me, but most especially to my pals, the horses, I dedicate this book.

ACKNOWLEDGMENTS

My thanks to . . .

Gar and Judy Reeves-Stevens, whose creative skills made the book possible.

Kevin Ryan, who as they say in the biz, "put the package together."

Carmen LaVia, who did his thing.

PROLOGUE

He fell. . . .

Alone.

Twisting through the air of Veridian III. The shriek of the metal bridge echoing in his ears. Spinning. The sun flashing into his eyes. The shadows engulfing him. One following the other, over and over as he fell. Light. Shadow. Light. Shadow. Like the beating of wings. Like all the days of his life. Intersecting . . .

In an Iowa cornfield—he sees the stars. A boy of five in his father's arms. I have to go there, he says. And you will, Jimmy, his father answers. You will . . .

In Carol's arms, in their bed—even as he knows he must leave her, the son they had created quickening within her . . .

In Starfleet headquarters—Admiral Nogura reaching out to shake his hand: Congratulations, Captain, the Enterprise *is yours. . . .*

In Spacedock—Captain Pike beginning the introduction: Your science officer, Lieutenant-Commander Spock . . .

On the streets of old Earth—squealing brakes, Edith, haloed in the headlights of her death . . .

Through all these days and more, alone he fell, hearing the whispers of the past. . . .

I am, and always will be, your friend. . . . Dammit it, Jim– I'm a doctor not a bricklayer. . . . Let me help. . . .

I've always known I'll die alone. . . .

Then one shadow blocked the light. Broke his fall. Ended the kaleidoscope of days. He turned his head, looked up, saw a face he recognized, not from the past, not from the present.

From the future.

"Did we do it?" the falling man asked. "Did we make a difference?"

The other, in his odd uniform, but with the familiar touchstone of Starfleet on his chest, knelt by his side.

"Oh, yes. We made a difference. Thank you."

Somewhere within him, the falling man was aware of pain, deep and incurable. Somewhere within him, he became aware he couldn't feel his legs, his arms, as if he and all existence were evaporating together.

The edges of his vision blurred, darkened, joined one final shadow deep enough to swallow whatever else remained.

But the other, this stranger, this . . . Picard, had offered his friendship. In another lifetime, perhaps it might have been so. So much might have been. So many possibilities.

"Least I could do," the falling man said, ignoring the final shadow for the sake of his friend, "for the captain of the Enterprise*."*

Voices called to him from the darkness then, their summons more than whispers.

Through the latticework of the twisted metal above him, he glimpsed the edge of something moving, coming closer.

He closed his eyes.

What was it he had said to Picard when they had met? When Picard had challenged him to return for one last mission?

He remembered. His eyes opened.

"It was . . . fun," he told Picard. He tried to smile. To spare this friend.

What lay beyond the bridge swept closer, chasing him as it had always chased him.

Through the mangled steel the shape was clearer now. Closer. Known.

He gazed up at it, amazed Picard did not see, did not know.

He tried to warn Picard. To help him escape what he no longer could.

But the momentum of his days had crested. The dark well of his vision swirled inward. Too quickly. And the face of that which chased him, caught him, claimed him.

The final wisps of existence lifted from him in a feathered haze of light, revealing all that lay beyond, still to come.

"Oh my," he whispered.

As he saw.

As he knew.

And then he fell again.

Alone . . .

ONE

James T. Kirk was dead. . . .

As Commander William Riker resolved from the transporter beam beside the grave of that Starfleet legend, he was surprised by the sudden thought that had come to him. Of all that had happened on this desolate world of Veridian III only a month ago, inexplicably, the fate of James T. Kirk weighed most heavily on his mind.

Half a planet away, the shattered hulk of the *U.S.S. Enterprise* lay in ruins, slowly being carved into transporter loads of recyclable scrap by a team of Starfleet engineers. Though the ship was beyond salvage, in accordance with the Prime Directive no trace of it could remain on this world. A primitive civilization existed on Veridian IV, the next planet out from the Veridian sun. If someday voyagers from that world landed here, they must find no trace of advanced technology which might affect the natural development of their science.

Riker had expected that the full emotional consequence of the great ship's loss would have consumed him by now. She had gone before her time, and in his dreams he had always hoped to one day sit in her captain's chair.

But in the days that had passed since the *Enterprise* had blazed through the atmosphere of this world to her first and final landing, Riker's thoughts still kept turning to the fate of the captain of an earlier *Enterprise.* The first *Enterprise* . . .

"Sir, is that . . . *him?*"

Riker turned to Lieutenant Baru. The seam ridge that bisected the young Bolian officer's deep blue face pulled taut as her eye ridges widened. She looked into the distance, past the grave.

Riker nodded, smiling inwardly at her reaction, recognizing the earnestness of youth. The *Farragut's* chief of security had personally recommended Baru, and the three other officers accompanying Riker, to be part of the honor guard to escort Kirk's remains to Earth. Riker knew what she saw. What they all saw now.

A lone sentinel on a distant outcropping. The dry desert wind shifting the elegant black robes he wore. The reddening sun reflected from the silver script embroidered in their folds.

He had come.

From Romulus.

Against all logic.

"Spock," Baru said. With awe.

Riker understood.

He knew the Vulcan ambassador—had worked with him—as a living, breathing individual. Yet Spock was as much a legend as Kirk.

As much a legend as the friendship that had bound those two on the first *Starship Enterprise.*

The officers of the honor guard stood at ease, respectfully refraining from staring at the distinguished visitor. Instead, they faced the simple cairn of rocks Jean-Luc Picard had built for Kirk's remains. The setting sun drew long shadows from it and caught an old-fashioned Starfleet insignia pin with a gleam of dying light.

Riker breathed the still, dry air of the Veridian desert. He glanced upward to the darkening sky, as if he might see the

Farragut sliding into orbit far overhead, come to claim Starfleet's honored dead, to bear Kirk home.

From his sentinel's position, Spock remained as motionless as the time-smoothed stones of this place.

What could it be like, Riker wondered, *to lose your closest friend, then seventy-eight years later, to lose him again?*

A hint of the power of that answer existed in the extraordinary circumstances that had brought Spock here. In fewer than four days after the crew of Riker's *Enterprise* had been rescued, Starfleet Intelligence had mounted an emergency extraction mission to bring Spock from the homeworld of the Romulan Star Empire to Veridian III, so he might accompany his friend on his final voyage.

The extraction was not an operation to be undertaken lightly. Relations between the Romulans and the Federation had been strained for centuries. Spock had become instrumental in the efforts to reduce those tensions by decades of secret negotiations intended to reconcile the Romulans with the Vulcans and, hence, the Federation.

Though the Romulans were an offshoot of the Vulcan race, they had rejected the logic which had saved their Vulcan ancestors from succumbing to their primitive, passionate, blood-drenched beginnings. So who better than Spock—a child of emotional humans and logical Vulcans—to understand both sides and work for unification?

Riker had spent many long evenings discussing Spock with Captain Picard. Both understood that the process Spock was involved with was simply the playing out on a larger scale of the struggle he had faced in his own divided heart.

But whatever extraordinary actions Starfleet had taken to bring the ambassador to this world at this time, Riker knew that none of them would have been questioned, even given the Federation's need to officially remain ignorant of Spock's activities.

Starfleet, the Federation, the galaxy itself, owed Spock too much to deny him anything.

Just as they owed too much to Kirk.

On the horizon, the last radiant spike of the dying sun flared, then vanished behind a distant peak.

Overhead, stars emerged from the deepening twilight.

Far away, Riker saw Spock bow his head, as if lost in memory.

What would it be like? Riker wondered.

A warm breeze stirred the small branches and dried leaves of the lone bush that shared the outcropping.

Lieutenant Baru caught Riker's eye.

"Yes, Lieutenant?" Riker realized he had whispered his inquiry. In the fading of the day, this forsaken plot of alien rock had become a solemn place.

"Sir, shouldn't we have heard from the *Farragut* by now?"

Riker tapped his communicator badge. "Riker to *Farragut.* The honor guard is in position."

No response.

"We arrived ahead of schedule," Riker told the lieutenant. The *Farragut* had been the workhorse of the rescue and recovery mission on Veridian III. Riker was not surprised the overburdened starship might be running late. "We'll give Captain Wells a few more minutes before we sound general alarm." He smiled at her.

Lieutenant Baru was too new to her rank to return the smile. She nodded once in silent acknowledgment, then returned her gaze to the cairn.

Silent minutes passed.

The night grew darker.

His communicator chirped.

Riker smiled again at Baru as he tapped it. She was too tense. He'd have to talk to her about that. Not every day in Starfleet brought life-or-death decisions.

"Riker. Go ahead."

But his smile faded as he realized the garbled, static-filled call did not come from the *Farragut.*

"Commander Riker! This is Kilbourne! We're—" An explosion of static washed out the rest of the transmission.

Riker held his fingers against his communicator, forcing an override. Kilbourne was the chief engineer at the salvage site. The honor guard stepped closer, on alert.

"Kilbourne, this is Riker. Say again."

Static whistled. Riker didn't understand the cause of it. There was nothing in this planetary system that could cause subspace interference.

Then, for a heartbeat, the static cleared and Kilbourne's distraught voice cut through the Veridian night.

"—can't tell where they're coming from! Two shuttles gone! We need—"

Then nothing.

Not even static.

Riker's communicator chirped uselessly as he tried to reestablish a link.

Riker looked at the four officers gathered around him. Their Starfleet training came to the fore. There was nothing youthful about the intent expressions they wore.

"This will have to wait," Riker said. He tapped his badge again. "Riker to Ambassador Spock."

A moment passed. Then the deep, familiar voice answered.

"Spock here."

"Ambassador, there appears to be some trouble at the salvage site. I'm going to have to ask you to remain here while we beam back to check the situation."

"Of course, Commander," Spock agreed calmly. "What is the nature of the trouble?"

"I'm not sure," Riker replied. He looked through the darkness that now blanketed Kirk's burial mound to where he knew Spock waited. But in his black robes, the ambassador was invisible. "It almost sounds as if they're . . . under attack."

Spock did not respond. Logically, Riker knew, he required no response.

"Riker to transporter control—five to beam to salvage site."

With Kirk's honor guard beside him, Riker tensed with anticipation as the computer-controlled satellite transport system reacted at once. "Energizing. . . ."

In the cool tingle of the transporter effect, the gravesite shimmered. There was an unsettling moment of quantum transition. . . .

And then Will Riker beamed into Hell.

TWO

Driving rain sprayed through the ragged hole in the canopy of the portable transporter platform, drenching Riker the instant the transporter's exclusion field shut down.

The platform shuddered in the concussion of a nearby flash and bone-jarring thud.

There had been thunderstorms at the salvage site for days now.

But the flash hadn't been lightning.

The concussion hadn't been thunder.

"Move! Move! Move!" Riker shouted over the storm and the nonstop roar of explosions. The platform shuddered again. Sparks flew from one of the pads. Riker shoved the honor guard ahead of him, toward the steps that led to the duraplast walkways linking the buildings of the salvage camp spread out before him.

When the guards were clear, he charged after them into the storm.

It was night in this region of Veridian III, and Riker had been prepared for partial darkness. But the emergency lights weren't operating, and the bombarded camp had become a collection of looming shadows, black against black, hidden by night and rain.

Except when the sky blazed with alien fire.

Riker caught up with Baru. She leaned over the walkway railing, staring to the east where a sputtering ball of plasma flared against the duranium skin of the *Enterprise*'s lifeless saucer. The starship's primary hull rose from the raw mud like a cliff of glacial ice, two hundred meters distant. All around the ship, energy beams and the flash of chemical explosions played like crazed lightning over the towering cranes, personnel barracks, and hastily constructed shuttle landing pads to the west of her.

"What's happening, sir?" Baru shouted, her voice almost lost in the deafening barrage.

Riker angrily pushed his rain-flattened hair from his eyes. "We're under attack!" he yelled back. A sudden wind caught him and spun him off balance—the wake of a low-flying craft, he knew. Released from its grip, he grasped the railing to steady himself, then looked up. But he saw nothing except low storm clouds, flickering with their own lightning and the explosions that bloomed beneath them in the camp. Baru still clung to the handrail, mesmerized by the infernal spectacle before them.

A wave of heat blasted him from the side as a barracks building detonated in a rocketing fountain of blinding plasma fire. Flaming debris arced downward, its flame untouched by the rain. Riker rapidly calculated that they were within range of the downfall. He grabbed Baru's arm, yanking her off the walkway, into the mud. "Let's go!"

Riker jabbed at his communicator as they ran, their boots

caking with thick mud each labored step. *"Riker to Kilbourne!"*

An enormous thunderclap reached out and scooped them up from behind, tossing them into the rain. Baru's arm flew away from his grasp.

Riker twisted as he fell through the hiss of crisscrossing shrapnel, in time to see the transporter platform engulfed by plasma. As he struck ground, columns of steam shot up all around him where molten metal hit cold mud.

Riker lay face-down in the mud, lungs aching with the need to breathe. His ears rang with the thunder of whatever had hit the transporter platform.

A double pulse of wind shocked him into action. As he fought to lift his arms from the mud, he heard the sound of air being sliced by fast-moving vehicles.

He wrenched his back as he rolled free and struggled to his feet. His uniform clung to him, with ten extra kilos of thick clay that not even the stinging rain could dislodge.

Riker brushed his hair again without thinking. Mud stuck to his forehead.

"Lieutenant Baru!" he called.

A thick shaft of green energy stabbed through the night and the storm, piercing the *Enterprise*'s hull. The impact point was close to a wedge already removed by the engineers. Riker saw the inner decks lit up with the discharge of whatever type of weapon was being used. He saw no trace of Baru or the other members of the honor guard.

The beam sliced through the *Enterprise,* pivoting from its origin point, fired by a flying craft.

A chain reaction of explosions started deep within the hull of the *Enterprise.* Instinctively, Riker knew that some of the ship's self-destruct charges must have been triggered. They had been deactivated by the engineers, but not all of them had been removed.

"Commander!"

Riker wheeled to see Baru struggling toward him. She was

layered in mud, its dark wetness shimmering fitfully in the strobing flares of the attack. She limped, one hand wrapped tightly over her shoulder. Her other arm hung uselessly.

An enormous gout of flame flared from the *Enterprise*'s hull. A second later, another gout blasted out through the saucer's side. Even through the wind and the rain, Riker could feel the heat.

"Who's doing this?" Baru cried as she reached his side.

Riker shrugged. He had no idea, nor even suspicions.

"We have to get to a shuttle," he said.

There was nothing they could do down here. But some of the engineering shuttles were armed. He had to go up. To fight back.

Baru's gaze swept the camp. The mud around them glistened in firelight, lightning, and plasma bursts, as if they stood in a sea of flames. "There won't be any shuttles!" she said.

Riker took hold of her good arm. "We won't know till we look. This way."

Bodies lay scattered around the debris of the burning communications center. More explosions shook the saucer hull. Riker's jaw tightened as he heard screams blend with the roar of the unseen craft, the hum of their weapons, the roar of the flames.

But there was no way to know from where the screams came. No time to search for whoever made them.

Never enough time . . .

They skirted the burning mound of wreckage that had been a storage warehouse. Beyond it, Riker could see the smoking pits that were all that remained of the shuttle pads.

Two *Tesla*-class shuttles lay in pieces nearby, split open like used packing crates. A third shuttle was intact, though its frame was out of alignment where it angled into the mud, hurled there by an explosion not quite near enough to destroy it. Ragged figures milled about it. Riker and Baru fought the mud as they staggered closer.

Kilbourne was there. Four engineers worked with him. Two still in their sleeping robes. The attack had been that sudden.

"Who are they?" Riker asked as he leaned gratefully against the shuttle's hull, leaving a muddy handprint to be washed away by the pounding rain.

Hunched over his tricorder, Kilbourne looked up at him with shadowed eyes. "I don't know. They . . . they took out the *Farragut.*"

Riker felt acid course through his stomach. The only other Starfleet vessels in the Veridian system were a handful of transport freighters and engineering support cruisers. Without the *Farragut,* the survivors of the salvage camp—and Deanna Troi—were at the mercy of its attackers.

Kilbourne returned his attention to the small screen of his tricorder. Riker touched Kilbourne's shoulder. "Then what are they after?" Both of them glanced over at the looming mass of the *Enterprise*'s saucer. The open ground between it and the camp was a nightmarish field of destruction. The saucer itself still crackled with energy discharges, long bolts of plasma sparking out as if in combat with the lightning.

"I don't know," Kilbourne repeated wildly. "There's nothing important left in her. All the tactical computer cores were pulled on the first day. Phasers . . . shields . . . everything classified has already been taken out."

The ground shook as a blinding flash of light exploded from the saucer's interior with a booming echo.

Kilbourne held out his tricorder. Riker recognized the traces on its display.

"Whoever they are—they're flooding us with sensor scans. They know where each one of us is." Kilbourne stared up at Riker. His haggard face was streaked by blood and rain and mud. "We've got to retreat, Commander. Into the forest."

Baru stiffened at Riker's side. Riker looked at the engineering shuttle. It couldn't fly. But that wasn't all it was good for.

"Does this shuttle still have demolition charges?" Riker demanded. They were low-yield photon torpedoes designed for clearing orbital wreckage. The shuttle would normally carry four and be capable of firing two at a time.

But Kilbourne looked at him as if Riker were mad.

"You can't be serious."

Riker grabbed the chief engineer by his shirtfront, twisting the sodden fabric in his fist. He ignored the startled protests of Kilbourne's staff as they gathered around him. "Starfleet doesn't run," Riker spat at him.

He grabbed Kilbourne's tricorder and thrust it at Baru. "I want both torpedoes prepped for atmospheric detonation. Do it manually so they don't show up on the enemy's sensors."

Kilbourne's agitated voice shook. "The second you turn on the shuttle's targeting system, whatever's attacking is going to incinerate us!"

Riker smiled grimly. "Probably." Then he turned his back on Kilbourne and told Baru how to use the tricorder to open the shuttle's torpedo bays.

It took less than two minutes to prepare the torpedoes for simultaneous activation, target lock, and launch. Throughout that time, the unknown assailants' attack never lessened. The *Enterprise*'s saucer crumpled in on itself in three sectors. Fires blazed inside every open level.

One of Kilbourne's junior staff huddled against the side of the shuttle, hands pressed tight to his ears, eyes clenched shut, rocking, trying to shut out the assault on his senses.

Baru handed the tricorder back to Riker. Her expression was unflinching. "That's all we can do with the tricorder, sir. If you want to launch those things, we're going to have to do it from inside."

Riker met her gaze. He nodded his understanding.

The torpedoes could be launched only by the controls on the shuttle's flight deck. But the instant they were brought online, the enemy's sensors would detect them, target them, and direct fire at them.

And at whoever was on the flight deck.

"Get your people out of here," Riker ordered Kilbourne.

Riker felt Baru's hand on his arm.

"Sir . . . you can't do this alone."

Riker watched as Kilbourne and his engineers fled into the rain. The ground shuddered in a series of explosions. Riker wondered what was left to explode in the camp.

"Don't worry," Riker said. "I plan to live forever."

He punched a command sequence into the tricorder. Then he hefted the tricorder in his hand, paused for a moment, and threw it into the storm. It landed fifty meters away, disappearing into the mud.

Riker answered Baru's unspoken question. "In thirty seconds, that tricorder's going to put out a signal that makes it look like a phaser bank coming online."

"A distraction," Baru said. She smiled. Riker had no time to smile back.

He jerked his head to the side. "Follow Kilbourne. Take cover in the forest." Then Riker pulled himself through the off-angle door of the shuttle, out of the rain.

Inside the shuttle, the flight deck was at a twenty-degree slope. Riker braced himself on the copilot's chair as his mud-coated boots slipped on the traction carpet. He forced himself to finish counting out the thirty seconds in his head. He counted out an additional five to give the enemy time to react. Then he activated the shuttle's torpedo substation.

Swiftly, he set the torpedoes to target any moving object one hundred meters in altitude or above. As soon as the panel confirmed his input, he hurried back through the shuttle's cargo hold to the airlock door.

The instant he appeared in the doorway, a green bolt of energy hit the mud fifty meters in front of him, vaporizing the tricorder in a spray of steam. Riker felt the rush of relief. The distraction had worked.

But the beam did not shut off. It pushed on through the mud, rending it like water before the prow of a ship, closing on the second weapons signal—the shuttle.

Riker gripped the sides of the door and pushed to leap free.

His boots slipped.

He fell, chest slamming into the raised ridge of the airlock seal.

He felt a rib crack, lost his breath, looked up to see the inexorable green bolt crackling toward him, ten meters away, wreathed in steam.

He pulled himself up even as he knew he wouldn't make it.

Never enough time . . .

"Deanna," he gasped, willing his final word to her, his final emotion. *Imzadi . . .*

He thought of Kirk.

Falling . . .

The beam reached out for him.

A hand grabbed his wrist.

"Commander!"

She hadn't left him.

Riker's eyes met Baru's as she hauled him out of the shuttle with desperate strength.

He saw what she saw. Knew what she knew. All in that one terrible moment as he was hurled away from her to safety.

And heard her cry . . .

Heard the hiss of vaporized flesh . . .

Heard the hum of torpedoes launching . . .

The shuttle sliced in two . . .

The taste of Veridian mud for a second time as the shuttle erupted.

Too late for Baru.

But not too late for the torpedoes.

Riker rolled onto his back in time to see two ionized streaks of plasma exhaust bank into the storm clouds as the torpedoes sought their targets.

The clouds lit up like dawn.

A heartbeat later, the concussion of the torpedo detonations shook Riker deeper into the mud.

For a silent moment after, even the rain stopped.

When it began again, it felt gentle. Warm. Slow as tears.

Riker carefully, painfully, drew himself up into a sitting position. He strained to breathe. He choked on mud.

He saw Baru's hand, reaching for him, out of the mud. In relief, he gripped it. Pulled.

And the hand and forearm and nothing else of the young Bolian slipped from the mud.

Riker dropped the hand in horror.

In the awful silence, he heard it hit the mud.

He sat alone in the night. Hellish fires from the camp and the saucer still lit the low roiling clouds. But there were no more explosions. No more screams of low-flying craft. The warm rain bathed his eyes.

The attack was over.

Then Kilbourne was beside him. One of his engineers, still in a sleep robe, held a medikit. They helped Riker to his feet.

"Why?" Riker asked. Though he expected no answer. Certainly not from Kilbourne.

"I . . . don't . . . know," Kilbourne said grimly as he broke open a hypospray. "There was nothing here to steal. No secrets left. No . . . nothing. If you hadn't launched those torpedoes. . . ."

But Riker knew that part wasn't true. "They didn't stop the attack because of two demolition torpedoes."

"Why else would they?" Kilbourne jammed the hypo against Riker's neck. Its cool tip hissed as it delivered its healing agents.

"For the same reason all successful attacks end," Riker said, rocking as the painkillers flooded his body, as he finally surrendered to the overwhelming exhaustion he had held at bay. "They accomplished their objective."

"What objective?" Kilbourne raged. "Name one thing on this stinking planet worth dying for!"

For that question, Riker had no answer.

But somewhere, someone did.

And Riker knew he couldn't rest until he had found those responsible, and answered that question for himself.

THREE

Alone in the darkness by the gravesite, Spock had found a rock to sit on, the better to preserve his strength. Once settled, he had rearranged his robes, the better to conserve his body heat.

He was 143 standard years old. Advanced middle age for a Vulcan in good health. But whatever encounter Riker and his officers had beamed into, those days of action were behind him.

Quite illogically, he found he missed them.

For almost half an hour, he maintained his position, observing moving points of light against the stars, and the streaks of multicolored light that were exchanged between them.

Starships in orbital battle.

"Fascinating," Spock murmured.

As his eyes adapted to the distant discharges, he recognized the distinctive blue signature of Starfleet phasers.

But the return fire was unidentifiable. He had never seen its like before.

The situation presented an interesting set of problems. In his mind, Spock began to analyze them as a series of logical arguments, attempting to identify likely attackers, their motives, tactics, and probable odds of success.

But he was interrupted in his calculations.

The night air thrummed. Something large was approaching through the sky.

Spock rose slowly to his feet. He scanned the dark horizon, searching for any occultation of stars that would indicate the presence of a flying craft operating without running lights.

The thrumming increased.

He could see nothing, but his robes began to swirl around him, blown about by some kind of backwash.

Spock raised his hand to shield his eyes from a rising whirlwind of dust.

Directly above him, the stars wavered and then disappeared, blacked out by a silhouette of something he couldn't identify. A sudden light danced at the edge of his vision.

Spock looked down the slope toward Kirk's grave.

Amber rays spiked out from between the rocks of the simple cairn.

Above the thrumming and the wind, Spock heard an oddly musical chime.

The light emanating from Kirk's grave brightened, then began to fade. Spock clearly heard the sounds of rocks falling against themselves.

The logic of this situation was inescapable, yet made no sense.

Among the stars, the signs of a space battle ended. Above Spock, the watching stars returned and the thrumming backwash ceased as suddenly as if a ship had gone to warp.

Spock drew an emergency light from his belt. He began to descend the slope to Kirk's grave.

He played the light against the cairn.

The rocks *had* fallen in.

The grave was empty.

Spock looked to the stars.

It was not at all logical, but for a moment, a most improbable thought came to him—

Perhaps some journeys were never meant to end.

"Jim . . . ?" he said.

There were *always* possibilities. . . .

FOUR

High above Veridian III, flashing in sunlight, a thirty-meter-wide slab of curved duranium hull metal slowly spun in the silence of space. The black letters etched into its surface read *U.S.S. Faragut* NCC-60597.

It was the largest piece of debris that remained of the starship. The rest was a cloud of dazzling shards, slowly dispersing.

Aboard the *Avatar of Tomed,* the Romulan commander, Salatrel, watched the hull metal impassively on the main viewscreen of her bridge. Beside her, she could sense her subcommander's elation.

"A great victory, Commander," Tran said.

Salatrel turned in her command chair. One upswept eyebrow arched, disappearing beneath the dark bangs that framed her aristocratic features, pointed ears, and full lips.

"This was no victory," she said. "They had no reason to

expect us. They had no warning. It was an operational procedure. Nothing more."

But the young Romulan officer held her eye in a way he would not dare if this ship had still been a part of the Empire's fleet. With an insincere inflection of servility, he said, "They were expecting *something,* Commander. We lost two attack craft to torpedoes at the secondary target site. We are at war."

"I have not yet given that command," Salatrel replied sharply. "Don't make me remind you again."

An instant too slowly, Subcommander Tran dropped his gaze in response to the icy threat in his superior's tone. The most common language of the Romulan homeworld conveyed precise meaning by word and by inflection, and the weapons officer knew how close he had come to insubordination.

The communications officer's voice rang out, across the expansive bridge. "Commander, the second wing has confirmed transport at the primary target site."

Salatrel rose from her command chair. How long had she waited for this moment?

"Kirk?" she asked. The harsh and hated human name felt odd in her throat. Alien.

Her science officer answered from the engineering console where transporter displays flashed. "DNA analysis confirms identity of the remains, Commander. When the attack craft dock, the remains will be beamed directly into the stasis unit."

For the first time since this mission had begun, Salatrel permitted herself a small smile. She sat back in triumph.

"Decloak," she commanded her crew, "and prepare to receive incoming craft."

She glanced up at Tran, who remained standing beside her. "You'll have your war soon enough, Subcommander."

Tran's eyes narrowed with predatory anticipation. "War, and victory," he said.

On the viewscreen, the frozen cloud that was the *Farragut* sparkled in its death throes.

Closer in, amongst the spinning, twisting wreckage of the *Farragut,* a handful of shapes moved of their own accord.

Some of the starship's crew had managed to don environmental suits as their ship was torn apart around them in the unexpected attack.

Now they moved toward each other in the maelstrom of debris, homing in on each other's rescue beacons. Circuit panels, bulkhead sections, chairs, blankets, and frozen bodies sailed lazily past them, glittering with ice crystals.

Some larger pieces, intact equipment operating on self-contained power sources, still sparked.

The survivors avoided them. Using their maneuvering thrusters, they each eased out from the slowly tumbling ruins until they could see Veridian unobstructed.

From the voices on the emergency channels, six had survived. From a crew of six hundred forty.

Gradually, they floated free and toward each other, linking hands, exchanging information, until they formed a single six-spoked star.

But as they linked their communicators and broadcast their position to whatever fleet vessels had survived the attack, their view of Veridian III once again became obstructed.

By a wavering green mass that shimmered like a mirage, until it solidified into the double-hulled, raptor-prowed form of a *D'deridex*-class Romulan Warbird.

The *Avatar of Tomed.*

The veterans among the survivors knew they only had seconds remaining to them.

The Romulans were not known for taking prisoners.

As the monstrous starship—almost twice the length of Starfleet's *Galaxy*-class vessels—smoothly changed its orientation, the twin hangar bay doors in its lower hull slid open.

Like flashes of verdant light, seven sleek attack craft, no

larger than transport shuttles, returned, slipping easily through the forcescreens that held the Warbird's internal atmosphere.

The hangar doors slid shut again.

For a long heartbeat, the first visual discontinuities of the Romulan cloaking field began to warp the edges of the Warbird's silhouette.

And then, almost as an afterthought, a particle beam spun out through space and vaporized the six survivors.

By the time their incandescent atoms had dispersed in the vacuum to join the remains of their crew and their ship, the *Avatar of Tomed* had vanished as simply and as swiftly as it had appeared.

The hull metal fragment spun slowly in the silence of space.

The name of the *Farragut* faded into darkness.

Phase One was complete.

FIVE

Most Starfleet vessels were duranium white, proudly bearing the Federation's colors, boldly lit by running lights and identification beacons so all would recognize them on their missions of exploration.

But not all Starfleet missions involved exploration.

And some Starfleet vessels were as dark as the void between the stars, intentionally coated in microdiffracted carbon to absorb all visible radiation that fell upon them.

The *U.S.S. Monitor* was one such vessel, the latest in the

Defiant-class, space black, on silent running, closing in on a dying, ancient world deep in the Core Frontier. Its destination: New Titan.

The ship was little more than an armored command saucer with integral warp nacelles. Over-powered, densely shielded, excessively armed, carrying more weaponry than three *Galaxy*-class starships. She was the result of Starfleet's fevered preparations to fight a war against the Borg. A war that had yet to come to pass.

But there were always possibilities. . . .

The *Monitor* eased into a nonstandard polar orbit over New Titan. The only sign of its presence was the winking out, then reappearance, of the stars it passed.

Its double-sealed hangar door opened.

A small personnel shuttle emerged, propelled by low-gain tractor beams, undetectable past ten kilometers.

The shuttle was aerodynamic, designed for unpowered atmospheric gliding. Like its base ship, it carried no markings, no operational running lights.

Its mission was not exploration, either.

The shuttle swiftly twisted through three axes at once, setting its course. Its impulse engines glowed faintly, tuned to emit in the almost invisible ultraviolet instead of the visible blue spectrum. Much less efficient, but far less noticeable.

It moved away from the *Monitor,* dropping for New Titan like a falling lance. In less than three minutes, hidden within the coruscating aurora of the planet's north pole, the shuttle met atmosphere and began to leave its blazing trail.

Inside, the craft shuddered heavily. Artificial gravity and inertial dampening had been turned off to reduce the risk of stray radiation being detected on the planet's surface.

The pilot, tightly strapped into her seat, maintained her calm expression and kept her hands steady on the controls. Behind her, her five passengers hung tight to the bench seats running along both sides of the shuttle's hold.

Their expressions were unknown, for each wore a carbon-black combat helmet with an opaque blast shield in place, capable of deflecting a full force beam from a type-3 phaser. The rest of their black uniforms were as heavily armored.

Their seat webs creaked as the shuttle slowed, increasingly buffeted by the thickening density of the air. Equipment swung from straps, metal clips creaking.

Three of the passengers braced themselves with phaser rifles, wedging the stocks against the shuttle's deck. The only identifying insignia they wore was the Starfleet delta slashed by a bolt of red lightning—the unit crest of Starfleet's newest intelligence division. That, and their nametags: WEINLEIN, BEYER, KRUL.

The other two passengers also wore carbon-black commando armor, though not the lightning-bolt insignia. Instead of weapons, their equipment harnesses carried sealed carryall pods.

But they also wore nametags: CRUSHER, PICARD.

Jean-Luc Picard felt himself shift as the shuttle slowly banked. The hum of its engines shut off, making the hold eerily free of sound. Picard knew that he and his team were in glide mode now, covertly traveling where a transporter beam couldn't be risked.

Through the heavily filtered blast shield he wore, he saw the subdued overhead lighting switch from full-spectrum to red.

It was almost time.

He opened his helmet.

Across from him, Weinlein lifted her own blast shield, and yanked open her helmet's visor. She was mostly human, though there was a hint of alien heritage in the assured gaze of her dark eyes. Picard regretted there had been no time to train with her directly. But then, events had moved too quickly for even Starfleet to be completely prepared.

With a black-gloved fist, Weinlein tapped the helmet of Beyer beside her. He opened his helmet as well. Fully human.

And surprisingly young to wear the intelligence section's delta, Picard thought. Though the very idea of Starfleet forming a unit of this nature had been an even greater surprise.

But he knew it shouldn't be. Starfleet had given Commander Elizabeth Shelby a free hand to develop whatever systems and technologies she felt were necessary to fight the Borg. Both the *Defiant* class of starship and this unit were the results of that mandate.

Beyer tapped the helmet of the third commando.

Krul lifted his shield, opened his visor, and grunted, sweat gleaming from the ridges of his crested forehead.

Years of working with Worf on the *Enterprise* were responsible, Picard knew, for the sense of confidence he felt now in the presence of a Klingon on a mission such as this.

Weinlein looked past Beyer at Krul, responding to his growls with a grin. "Are you still complaining?"

Krul bared his teeth at her. Unlike Worf, he wasn't Starfleet. He was an exchange officer from the Klingon Defense Force, just as Shelby had drawn the other members of the unit from independent planetary defense forces throughout the Federation. "Human battle gear," Krul snarled. "Too much protection. Not enough weaponry."

Picard hid a smile as Weinlein and Beyer exchanged a puzzled look. Each commando carried the equivalent of two kilotons of explosive force. In addition, Krul carried extra Klingon munitions. Just in case, he had said.

Weinlein unfastened her seat web, stood up, holding one hand against the shuttle's low ceiling as she leaned over to tap Beverly's helmet.

The doctor fumbled with her shield and visor, and looked up at Weinlein grimly. Mutely.

Picard could see the unasked question in Beverly's eyes. "How much longer?" he asked for her.

"You in a hurry?" Beyer asked.

"Stow it, Jerry," Weinlein ordered. She checked the readout on her wrist-mounted tricorder. Picard recognized it as a heavy-duty model, specially hardened for use in non-Class-M environments. "We'll be over the drop zone in three hundred seconds." She strapped herself back in her seat web.

Beyer held up his fist. Beside him, Krul reached up to meet it with his own. The salute of warriors ready to face death.

Picard and Beverly looked at each other past the confines of their battle helmets, uncertain of how to respond to the bravado of their support team. "This isn't a side of Starfleet we see very often," Beverly whispered.

Picard caught sight of the equipment pod strapped to her waist, marked with the Starfleet caduceus. It was the interface, he knew. He had thought of little else since Shelby had first proposed this mission to him. . . . . He forced himself to smile. "It's a big galaxy, doctor."

But Beverly frowned as she followed his gaze to see what he looked at.

Awkward in her battle armor, she reached out to put her hand on his. "It will be all right, Jean-Luc. We won't have to use it."

It was Picard's turn to recognize the lie in Beverly's smile.

Their team leader unfastened her seat web again. "Thirty seconds," Weinlein announced. She stood up, then moved to the rear of the shuttle and pulled down three times on a side-mounted, manual release lever.

With a sudden roar of wind, the rear decking of the cargo hold dropped open onto darkness.

Exactly as they had trained, Picard and Beverly sealed their helmets and got to their feet.

Weinlein watched the readout on her tricorder. She raised a finger, paused, brought it down, pointing to Krul.

Without hesitation, the Klingon stepped over the open deck and dropped through it.

Weinlein was already pointing at Beyer. The human followed Krul two seconds later.

Picard approvingly noted the precision of Weinlein's command of her troops. Perhaps her combative approach was necessary, given the nature of the personnel she led. He would remember that when they reached their objective and command authority switched to him.

Then Weinlein pointed at Picard, and as he had done a dozen times in the *Monitor's* holosuite, he stepped out into nothingness. Trying not to dwell on the fact that he had never done this before, in realtime.

For the first few seconds, Picard had no sense of movement or direction until he felt the abrupt tug of the antigravs pulling on his equipment harness.

He flipped over, dangling feet first, with still no sensation of falling, though he knew from the training simulations that the surface of New Titan was rushing up at him at ninety kilometers per hour.

He looked up and saw the densely packed stars of the galactic core, blazing in the cloudless night sky, brighter than the Earth's full moon. A dark object moved against them, then slowed, becoming the silhouette of Beverly, he decided. Or Weinlein.

He felt a gentle tugging to one side and wheeled slowly as he descended. Weinlein had told them she'd be using discontinuous sensor sweeps to monitor their position and rate of fall. The antigravs would step up their displacement effect fifteen meters off the ground, so that the actual landing would be no more jarring than stepping off a curb.

At least, that's what the holosuite technician had told Picard during the simulations.

He recalled the technician's grin as he had said it.

Picard rocked in his harness as the antigravs on his back began to work harder, changing his angle of fall and rate of descent. He tried not to speculate if it had felt like this on the *Enterprise,* as she had fallen through the atmosphere of Veridian III.

Tradition held that the captain must go down with his ship. But Picard had been on the surface with Kirk.

He still awoke at night, these past weeks, anguished, sweating, wondering if he might have made a difference had he stayed aboard, in command, as every regulation in Starfleet had stated he should.

But then, he and Kirk would not have had their chance to make a difference on the planet's surface, as they indeed had done.

So many possibilities, Picard thought. And never enough time to explore them all.

The harness dug into Picard with a sudden, sharp snap. His simulated training paid off as he reflexively swung his legs together and bent his knees.

Then he slammed into dirt as if he had stepped off a three-meter wall, not a curb.

But he rolled as he had been trained, absorbing the impact along the side of his body.

A moment later, Beverly hit and rolled an arm's length away. He was about to reach out to her when Weinlein landed between them, coming to rest on her feet with no sign she had done anything more than step forward.

Before Picard could speak, he felt Krul and Beyer behind him, soundlessly detaching his antigrav units from the back of his harness. Weinlein unhooked Beverly before reaching around to deftly disconnect her own antigravs.

Picard watched, silent. This was a part of the mission the commandos controlled. And they did their jobs well.

Krul and Beyer piled the antigravs together, preparing them for phaser immolation. Picard used the moment to pull down his visor and touch a forearm control on his armor.

Instantly, small projectors on the inside of his helmet cast a green-tinged, three-dimensional image of the people and terrain around him, created by low-level, discontinuous sensor scans. Because of the sensor emanations it produced, night-vision gear had not been safe to operate in the air. But close to the ground, there was less chance of signal scatter.

Above all else, Picard knew, they must remain undetected.

A phaser hummed. The antigravs expanded in a cocoon of light, then faded into nothingness.

Beyer was the first to break the silence. "They tracked us . . ." he hissed, pointing ahead where a Starfleet-blue phaser beam cut through the night from the horizon and found an unseen target that flared in a silent explosion.

Picard recognized the glimmer of an antimatter reaction.

"Was that our shuttle?" Beverly asked.

Weinlein nodded. "She had to activate the engines to climb out of the atmosphere. Which means the sensor fields they're using are more sensitive than we thought." She looked at Krul as the Klingon held out a small Klingon tricorder. "Give me a reading, Krul. Starfleet phaser cannon?"

Krul growled in acknowledgment.

Weinlein glanced at Picard. "That's a good sign. It means whoever's there is making do with the equipment at hand. They haven't brought in anything new."

Picard was struck by Weinlein's apparent complacency. Had she simply dismissed what had just happened so easily? "Our pilot just died. How can that be a good sign?"

"We all knew the risks," Weinlein said briskly. She pointed ahead. "Two kilometers, double time. Krul on point."

The Klingon jogged off into the darkness, distinguishable only by the green trace he left on Picard's visor.

Weinlein turned to Picard. Her features were ghostly in the soft glow of the galactic core, overlaid by her night-vision silhouette. "Not to put too fine a point on it, Captain Picard, but move it."

Startled again by her directness, Picard started after Krul, keeping the Klingon's sensor shadow centered in his visor. He could hear Beverly just behind him. Weinlein and Beyer ran behind Beverly.

The terrain of this region of New Titan was rough, strewn with boulders. It reminded Picard of the nature preserves on Mars. But the air was different here. The terraformed craters of Mars were sharp with the tang of oxide-rich soil and lush vegetation. New Titan smelled acrid and lifeless. Whatever ecosystem had spawned the oxygen in this world's atmosphere had long since fallen into extinction.

Extinction.

As they ran, Picard's attention kept flicking ahead to their destination, to what Starfleet Intelligence projected they might find there. And how, of all the possibilities they faced, extinction was, he feared, one of the most likely.

Fifteen minutes and two kilometers later, Krul waved them to a stop at the base of a low hill. Thankful for the respite, Picard bent over, hands on his knees, gasping for breath. This short run was nothing compared to the marathons he competed in on the holodeck. But to run across broken terrain at night, carrying thirty kilos of equipment, armor, and supplies—that wasn't part of his job description.

Beside him, Beverly breathed deeply but evenly, as if she were used to this kind of exertion. Picard wondered if he should take up dancing.

Their team leader stood before them, commanding their attention. "This is it. All systems power down. Stay low."

Her hands hit the controls on her forearm padd. The green glow of her night-vision display faded from her helmet. Picard did the same and blinked as his eyes adjusted to the starglow.

He followed Weinlein up the hill, dropping to his belly a few meters from the top as she did.

Then they looked over the rise, and Picard's throat suddenly felt as dry as the rocks he lay across. In a barren arroyo, where half a kilometer away a plasteel perimeter barrier glowed in the glare of fusion-powered spotlights, lay their first objective—Starbase 804.

To the side Picard saw an equally brightly lit landing pad,

safely away from the low buildings within the perimeter. There were no shuttles on it.

Studying the base, Picard could identify all the familiar structures without having to read their markings—subspace relay, clinic, recycling processor.

By the manuals, what lay before them was a type-seven, forward reconnaissance starbase, standard issue on Class-M planets when atmospheric domes were not required.

But this starbase was no longer standard issue.

Weinlein pointed straight ahead. "Captain, do you confirm what I see?"

Picard swallowed hard. The reports from Starfleet Intelligence were correct. How could he not confirm it when the jarring truth rose before him from the very center of Starbase 804?

Floodlights sprayed up its sides, bringing every centimeter of chaotic detail into hideous relief—pipes and conduits, duranium sheets, prefab housing sections, even parts of the shuttles that should be on the pad. There were traces of everything used in the construction of a starbase, now taken apart and reassembled into one of the most basic shapes of technology.

A cube.

"I . . . confirm. . . ." Picard said. His gut, his chest, his body felt packed in ice.

Weinlein brought her forearm up to her helmet and tapped a single control. Picard knew her words would be recorded, compressed, then transmitted in a theoretically undetectable microburst to the *Monitor,* far above them in polar orbit.

But her words would also be forever burned into his mind.

"Archangel, this is red leader. We have positive confirmation. Repeat, positive confirmation."

Picard kept his attention riveted on the cube in the center of the starbase. He thought of the equipment Beverly carried. Of her assurance that it would not have to be used.

But all that had changed.

Beside him, Weinlein completed her report.

"Starbase 804 has been assimilated by the Borg."

Within their armored gloves, Picard squeezed his hands into fists.

He was running out of possibilities.

SIX

Over the centuries, the Dante Field had been mapped, explored, and abandoned by every spacegoing culture in the sector. Drifting in interstellar space, dozens of light-years from the nearest star, it was simply a collection of asteroidal debris, the castoffs of some unknown system's Kuiper Belt, perhaps even the remnants of a solar system which had never formed.

Whatever its origin, each of the thousands of asteroids in the field was worthless and without interest. Devoid of minerals, too far from the trade routes to even qualify as a hazard to navigation.

But being worthless had become, to some, its greatest value.

The *Avatar of Tomed* decloaked as she dropped from warp on the outskirts of the Field.

Moving with deceptive grace, the giant Warbird effortlessly banked through the cloud of frozen rocks, avoiding the larger bodies, scattering the smaller ones with her shields and tractor beams.

But her course was not intended to avoid *all* the asteroids. Near the field's center, one asteroid remained in the *Tomed's* heading. It was more than three kilometers long, a slowly spinning shard of rock, scarred by millennia of impact craters.

The Warbird closed on it, without slowing, until a new impact was inevitable.

But then one small part of the asteroid's surface rippled with holographical distortion as the Warbird made contact and—

—passed safely through.

Inside the hollow body, beyond the holographic camouflage, the rough interior was studded with directional grids of docking lights.

Eight other Warbirds were docked within the main cavern, with twenty-seven Romulan Birds-of-Prey, more than a hundred scoutships, and uncounted other, smaller vessels.

The *Tomed* followed the line of pulsing lights that guided it to its bay. It expertly slipped between two other Warbirds and made precise contact with the docking conduits that would hold it in place.

On the *Tomed's* hangar deck, Commander Salatrel stood with her senior officers as the artificial gravity fields of her ship and the asteroid base were brought into phase. Then, with a rumbling hiss of air, the hangar doors opened into the main conduit leading to the station corridors. A sudden wind rushed past her as the atmospheric pressure of the *Tomed* equalized by expanding into the endless tunnels of the base. The folds of her uniform were disturbed, and her dark hair fluttered for just that instant of equilibrium being sought.

Before the sudden wind had died, service technicians on wheeled cargo haulers rumbled in, bringing new armaments and supplies for the smaller craft parked on the *Tomed's* deck. Shouted commands echoed back and forth. Mechanics' tools whined. Induction motors roared. Metal clanked against metal as the hangar filled with the smells of ozone, lubrication sprays, and carbon.

Salatrel took a moment to contemplate the sudden onslaught of activity, then walked through the maelstrom, an eye of calm.

She had not yet given the order, but there was no mistaking the swell of anticipation and excitement that flooded the station in her wake.

Without doubt, Dante Base was now on a war footing.

Deep within the hollowed-out asteroid now designated Dante Base, Salatrel ignored the tunnels that led to her private quarters. There would be time enough for rest when the mission was under way. Or when she was dead.

Instead, she headed through two sets of blast doors to arrive at the ultrasecure secondary docking cavern.

Where the other ship waited.

What the other ship's ultimate configuration had been, Salatrel could not be certain, for its forward hull covered the observation ports beside the main airlock portals, obscuring everything beyond.

Even its method of docking had been unorthodox. Instead of the clean seal between adaptable docking rings, the other ship appeared to have grown into the metal and rock of Dante. Tendrils of cable and connecting conduits spread out of the portal like connective tissue, anchoring the ship to the asteroid not in one place, but in hundreds.

Salatrel walked from the corridors of the asteroid to those of the ship without ever seeing a clear line of demarcation between one and the other.

But once she was without doubt within the ship, Salatrel followed the Romulan markings that had been affixed to the bulkheads, to lead her to the security doors protecting the cavern's central chamber.

As the doors unfolded, grinding on their metal hinges,

Salatrel stood for a moment in the entrance, scenting the slightly fetid liquid that pulsed through the twisted pipes lining the chamber. Overhead, where the arching dome of the chamber's ceiling swept into shadow, there was nothing to see. But ahead and to the sides, an overlay of technology, both alien and Romulan, defined the chamber's circumference and its roughly textured walls.

Directly ahead, sunken into a central, circular deck, was the control pit, where Romulan computers had been installed. The shafts of light from their screens and operational surfaces spiked up through the haze that filled the chamber, mercifully hiding those who worked among them.

Her eyes traced the myriad light channels that snaked along the curved walls, angling in through the empty air to converge like a web on the immense machine at the heart of the chamber. Here and there along the machine's alien outline, she could see, Romulan devices had been attached to its ancient golden metal. The haphazard patches were based on incomplete knowledge, she was certain. Still less than a quarter of the machine's inner workings were understood to any degree.

But those were merely details.

Her scientists had assured her that as far as results were concerned, the restored machine would perform as promised.

"Commander Salatrel?"

Salatrel turned to acknowledge Tracius, her centurion. She accepted his salute with sincere warmth.

The elder Romulan was taken aback, as always, by Salatrel's familiarity. His family and hers were joined by centuries of common purpose, but he was old fashioned enough to still believe that their familial association and affection should not be part of their professional relationship.

"I understand you have had great success," Tracius said stiffly.

Salatrel smiled at his predictability. "That remains to be

seen." Then she noted the diplomatic padd he carried—a small computer device programmed with the stolen codes of the Star Empire's diplomatic corps. "You have news?" she asked.

Tracius held up the padd. Its compact screen glowed with Romulan script. "Spock is no longer on Romulus."

Salatrel stared at the padd, intrigued. "Dead?" Though she knew that was too much to hope for.

"Extracted. Starfleet Intelligence mounted a most extraordinary operation. Beamed him out of the capital."

Now Salatrel was more than intrigued. "How is that possible?" The government maintained strict control over all transporter activity in Dartha.

"Apparently, Starfleet has developed methods of circumventing our security precautions."

"And they risked exposing those methods to recover one aging ambassador who does not even have official status?"

Tracius offered Salatrel the padd. "Spock is gone. More than that is supposition, my commander." His bearing was rigid with disapproval. As if she were still a child and he still her tutor.

Salatrel graciously declined Tracius's unspoken offer to check his conclusions.

"Perhaps I should have asked: What is your interpretation?"

The centurion paused—a delaying tactic, Salatrel knew, which allowed him to gather his thoughts. In that moment, she studied Tracius pityingly. His white hair, cut short in the old style, looked dingy and limp in the dull amber light of the chamber. He deserved better than this. At his age, he should be writing his memoirs in a country estate, revered at court for his hand in guiding the history of his people.

But history had not unfolded as it should.

Because of one man.

One human.

"I believe it is connected to Kirk," Tracius said.

Salatrel waited for more.

"They were friends."

"A long time ago, Tracius."

Tracius's eyes didn't waver from her own. It was not a challenge of insubordination, as Subcommander Tran had proferred so daringly. It was a reminder of an unpleasant lesson taught long ago.

"What is time between friends, Commander? Is that not why we are here today? Because of the past?"

Salatrel drew herself up and smoothed the silver mesh of her command tunic. The lesson this time would be for Tracius to learn. And he would learn it from her. "We are here only for the future."

She turned from him, then, and was surprised to feel his hand on her arm.

It was not proper behavior for a centurion. But it was for a friend.

"Spock, with his insane dream of unification, is more dangerous than you know. And what you're planning can only serve to involve him in our plans. And for what?" He waved his hand to the murky outlines of the waiting machine. "This . . . abomination? It is without honor, Commander. This *new* plan of yours—so hastily conceived of—once put in motion, can end in only one of two ways."

"No," Salatrel said. "It shall end in only one way." She lifted Tracius's hand from her arm. Defeat was not an option.

Only victory.

This time when she turned, Tracius did not stop her.

Unaccompanied, Salatrel approached the ark. That was the name her scientists had given to the alien machine's central component—an elongated container, three meters along its widest axis, made from bulging, asymmetrical panels of a transparent mineral, bound by gilded struts of tarnished metal, like some grotesque inner organ trussed in gold wire.

Salatrel studied the curves and swellings of the machine that cradled the ark—the forms of flesh and technology combined as one. It was no wonder her scientists could not fully comprehend its workings. Even those who had supplied it said it was tens of thousands of years old, removed from the ruins of a race so obscure they had no name, as if fate had wiped them from the memory of the universe.

She glanced into the shadows of the control pit facing the ark. The Technicians worked among their Romulan computers there in the dark center of the chamber, precisely moving silhouettes, pinpointed by red dots of coherent light shining from their various arrays.

A scientist's voice echoed from hidden speakers. "Transporter systems are online."

Another replied, "Locking on to stasis unit. Commander, it is time for Phase Two."

Without knowing it before, Salatrel now realized she had waited all her adult life for this moment, never expecting it would be so perfect, so personal. Yet it had come and gone in less than a heartbeat. "Proceed," she said. As simply as that, the shape of the galaxy would now change.

Responding instantly, the alien machine began to vibrate. Thick conduits, formed of fleshlike plastics, not metal, swelled as their internal pressure increased. A rhythmic thudding began to shake the scarred metal deck.

"Backup buffer initialized," an unseen scientist announced.

The deeper, duller voice of a technician intoned, "Phase transition coils are online. Temporal translator is phase matched."

An electrical hum spread thrillingly through the moist air of the chamber. Mist spilled out of the control pit where the Romulan computer consoles had been installed to operate the device, bypassing the original alien controls that appeared to require direct implantation into a living nervous system.

Salatrel's chest tightened. Despite her bravado before Tracius and the station crew, she knew she had gone into battle feeling less tense than she felt now. She had led a mutiny against her own admiral and hijacked her warbird with less fear and less doubt than she felt now.

Ever faster, the broadcast voices of the scientists and the technicians rattled through the rest of the systems check until the phase transition coils were synchronized with the pattern buffer and the temporal isolation conduits.

Salatrel fought to compose herself by picturing the subspace pathways now linking her warbird with this device, and the unimaginable pathways through sidestepped spacetime that reached back into the past. She forced herself to focus on the one final command that remained to be given.

The deadened voice of Vox, the warrior who once had been her lover, reached out to her through the sounds of machinery and power, gushing liquid and hissing steam. "Commander . . . ?"

Salatrel stared fixedly at the ark, now suffused with a blue-white glow.

"Energize," she ordered.

It all happened at once.

A soaring exhalation filled the chamber, disconcertingly like the cry of a living thing. It came from the machine.

The slow wave of light within the liquid-filled ark quickened rhythmically with an orange gleam that fractured into stabbing golden flickers.

The conduits labored, pulsing erratically.

A harsh, warning alarm sounded sharply on a Romulan console.

"Primary matter stream confirmed."

"We have initiated temporal lock."

A second warning alarm sounded.

"Switching to backup emitter."

"Secondary matter stream confirmed."

An energy discharge crackled off a resonating coil a hundred meters away, lighting the vast chamber with the uncontained fury of a storm.

"Matter streams blending. Temporal consolidation is confirmed."

Salatrel realized she was digging her thumbnail into her palm.

Retrieval had been the easy part.

The light in the ark began to fade. A shadowy mass now became visible in the dense, murky liquid.

Desiccated, corrupted, monstrous remnants of the hated past, floating before her.

Awaiting invasion.

"Now confirming nanite transmission," a Technician stated.

Salatrel glanced up. Above two of the consoles in the control pit, holographic images of DNA helices spun through the air faster than she could read their base pairs.

Three alarms shrieked at once. A siren warbled, filling the chamber with its desperate song.

The projected DNA models lost focus and cohesion.

"Vox?" Salatrel called out to the darkness.

A sudden flash and explosion from the machine's flank sent sparks cascading through the chamber. The machine had rejected one of its Romulan devices.

"*Vox!*" Salatrel shouted, poised to run to the control pit where the silhouettes of the Technicians still moved at the same plodding, deliberate pace.

"Medical team to the ark," Vox calmly announced.

Three Romulan scientists charged out of the darkness toward the small scaffold platform built around the transparent container. Salatrel ran to get there first.

She ducked as a nearby conduit burst, spewing thick green liquid through the air that splashed noisily on the rocky floor. The Second Complex now reeked with the unlikely stench of chlorophyll.

Salatrel reached the scaffold first. The ark was two meters above her. She stared up into its darkened heart, saw the shape within.

Saw that shape *move.*

She leapt for the ladder, two of her scientists close behind her.

"Opcn it!" she commanded as they reached the top of the ark.

The two scientists attached a polyphasic grappler to unlatch the metal clamp holding the topmost panel in position.

The shape within the ark struggled, arms flailing.

"No!" Salatrel shouted. She grabbed the tool from the startled scientists' hands, spun it around and smashed it handle first on the transparent panel.

The panel cracked.

She swung again.

A gout of liquid sprayed into her face. She lost the grappler in the depths of ark.

She clawed at the edges of the shattered panel with her hands.

The shards of it slashed her palms. The dark liquid streaked with the green of her blood. But the pain could not stop her.

Salatrel tugged at the metal band between the broken panel and the next. Her scientists saw what she was doing and pulled on the opposite side.

The few remaining Romulan controls and devices exploded spectacularly in the pit and on the machine. Salatrel and her scientists held fast to the scaffolding.

Salatrel's face was smeared with the ark's nutrient fluid. Rivulets ran into her mouth. It tasted bitter, salty, like an ocean choked with life.

"Get him out! Get him—"

She gasped as a hand shot up from the ark, grabbed her arm.

She felt something sharp slice along her arm, into her shoulder, as the unexpected power of that hand drew her against the ragged edges of the panels, toward the suffocating depths of the ark.

But to die now, here, with him, was not why she had risked her life, her name, her world.

With the strength of primal rage, Salatrel pulled back, bracing herself against the ark itself, feeling it bend and buckle until the terrible hand slipped off her arm and she stumbled back, free. Except . . .

The hand was gone, swallowed again.

The dark shape settled in the fluid, no longer moving.

The scaffolding gave way in one corner, sending the two scientists tumbling to the deck below. But Salatrel did not fall.

"No," Salatrel choked.

Flashing lights and sirens blended with the spraying mist of chaos and the roaring liquid from the dying ark.

"No," Salatrel shouted.

Dark liquid erupted from the ark.

"Live!" Salatrel screamed, daring to command even him.

Then above it all rose the soul-shattering wail of pain, of confusion, of . . .

. . . *life.*

For a moment, Salatrel stopped breathing.

And then she felt the hand return.

This time grabbing her neck.

Pressing, squeezing, crushing.

Salatrel gripped the muscled forearm with her own torn hands. And saw—

Kirk.

Eyes alive with a madness she could not comprehend.

The flesh of his shoulders and neck twisted and shimmered as its contours changed, reformed and realigned by the microscopic nanite devices that still worked within him, restoring him, rebuilding him.

His mouth gaped open as he heaved with deep, desperate gasps for air.

But Salatrel could hear only the pounding of her own blood, thundering in her ears as her creation increased the pressure.

His mad eyes bore into her. His mouth moved, awkwardly, trying to form a word.

. . . why . . .

Salatrel's vision flared with searing silver dots. She felt herself spinning into darkness, saw the shadowy shape of her grandfather reaching out to welcome her as this monster's next victim, as—

A different hand joined hers in the struggle.

She saw that hand squeeze and twist on the iron-muscled forearm that held her, and suddenly the pressure was gone.

Salatrel pawed at her neck, felt the acid pain of air rushing into her ravaged throat.

Vox had saved her.

He stood before her, in profile, his noble Romulan brow high and defiant, his ear fiercely pointed, his eye dark and piercing. He held Kirk in place without effort.

Salatrel shook her head as her vision cleared.

For a moment, she was confused. Her beloved was before her.

She touched his shoulder, about to say his name.

His real name.

And then he turned to her and the nightmare returned.

Half his face was gone.

Obscenely replaced by black circuitry patches, laser sights, tubes and coils of bioneuronic implants—the inescapable hallmarks of assimilation.

His old name was no longer a part of him, along with everything else he had been.

He was Vox, now.

Romulan speaker for the Borg collective.

The alien machine stirred, rumbling ominously.

"We must leave the chamber," Vox said impassively.

Salatrel nodded, unable to speak.

Kirk's body was frozen in a contorted posture, his strength no match for the implanted manipulator that had replaced Vox's right arm.

The other technicians came then. Their proud Romulan features also torn apart by the machinery that had claimed them.

The technicians were Romulan no longer.

They, too, were Borg.

Like Vox.

But for now, they served Salatrel.

"We will take him to the medical facilities in Dante Base," Vox said.

Manipulator arms swung up. Drill bits and cutting blades spun. What remained of the ark was disassembled in seconds.

"We should save these components," Salatrel said distractedly. The ark's transparent mineral still hadn't been identified by her scientists or the Borg technicians. It seemed to have a dilithium-like fourth-dimensional molecular branch. Her scientists had told her it helped the reanimation machine focus the necessary temporal transference. Without the temporal capture of Kirk's final pattern of brainwaves from the moment of his death, this machine would have produced nothing more than a mindless, biological reproduction of the original.

But Vox stared blankly at Salatrel, not answering.

"So we can use it again," she explained.

"This device cannot be used again," Vox said. "It will be assimilated."

Salatrel sighed, but she knew resistance was futile.

With Vox beside her, she watched as her attacker, her monster, her creation was taken away, staggering, unable to speak. Kirk's ancient uniform hung in tatters, destroyed by the energies that had coursed through him once his body had been transported into the ark. He walked stiffly, like an *auroto*—the living dead of Romulan myth. Salatrel found that fitting.

"Amazing," Salatrel whispered. She felt herself begin to tremble as the enormity of what she had done began to filter into her consciousness. "In ten days, that creature will cause the Federation itself to fall before me."

"You are wrong," Vox said.

Startled, Salatrel forced herself to look into her former lover's left eye, trying to ignore the hideous visual sensor that had replaced his right one.

"We have made an agreement," Vox said. "The Federation will fall before *us*."

Salatrel nodded, relieved that Vox had meant nothing more than what she had already accepted.

Romulans and Borg working together.

It was the price she had paid to restore the hated James T. Kirk to life.

In ten days, she would know if it had been worth the bargain.

SEVEN

Come back, Jean-Luc. . . .

Picard ignored the distant whisper deep within his mind and walked among the Borg alone.

His heart raced. He felt sweat trickle beneath the combat armor he wore. His hesitant breaths thundered in his helmet behind his closed visor.

But the Borg ignored him.

All around Picard, they went about their task of assimilating Starbase 804. Teams of them worked as little more than ants or termites, using their biomechanical implants and augmentations to carve up the prefab buildings, remove the Starfleet equipment, and process everything for the greater good of the collective.

Picard tried his best to ignore them in return.

To his left, where the infirmary had been, a heavy construction Borg—a configuration Picard had never seen before, with four arms and thick, double-kneed legs—fired microbursts from an implanted energy weapon into a diagnostic bed that was balanced precariously on a pile of rubble.

To his right, a severed human leg was draped across half of a transport cart.

Two dogs—sleek Dobermans, pets of the personnel who had been assigned here, no doubt—trotted past. But they did not stop to investigate. Bioneuronic implants studded their skulls. Biomechanical tubes were grafted to their chests.

One dog turned to look at Picard as it passed. One eye clear though expressionless, so unlike the breed. The other eye had been replaced by a laser sensor.

But Picard was alone, and the Borg were not concerned with individuals. The dogs trotted on, into the smoke that still clung to the ruins of the starbase, echoing with the sounds of machinery.

With the same icy control which had let him face the unknown for decades on the bridge of a starship, Picard grimly kept one foot moving after the other, as if he were no more than a machine himself.

It was his greatest fear. But one he would have to face—if not for his own sake, then for that of Starfleet. Or even the Federation.

After Veridian III and his encounter with the Nexus, by the time he had been evacuated to a Starfleet facility with his crew, Picard had been sure he would draw at least a year behind a desk.

A *Galaxy*-class starship had been lost on his watch. The

flagship of the Fleet. The boards of inquiry alone would take months.

But Starfleet was nothing if not responsive, and realistic. True, the *Enterprise* had been lost, but three other of her sister ships had also experienced catastrophic failure in less than a decade since the *Galaxy* class had first flown. Clearly, there were matters of design and technology implementation to be addressed by Starfleet's Engineering sections.

Picard felt fortunate that the *Enterprise*'s flight recorders had been recovered intact. His bridge crew had given their reports to investigation teams staffed with Betazoids, to whom no lie could be told. And acting on depositions given by Guinan, other El-Aurian survivors of the *Lakul* disaster had been located and interviewed. Thus the power and the nature of the Nexus had been confirmed by the El-Aurians, if not fully comprehended by Starfleet.

And neither Starfleet nor the Federation Council could forget the millions of innocent lives which had been spared on Veridian IV by the actions of Picard, his crew, and, most notably, James T. Kirk, in keeping with the highest and most noble ideals upon which the Federation had been founded.

By the time Picard was asked to testify before the formal hearing on Starbase 324, Starfleet already had all the information it needed to begin an overhaul of starship defensive-shield systems. Antique scows like an almost century-old Klingon Bird-of-Prey would no longer threaten the Fleet's most advanced, state-of-the-art vessels.

Given all the ground that had been covered behind the scenes, Picard's testimony had taken less than half a day.

He was still reeling from the speed of the inquiry and its conclusion as he and Will Riker had left the hearing room.

And only when Picard saw Commander Elizabeth Shelby waiting for him did he understand that Starfleet had its own reasons for dealing with the *Enterprise* hearings so quickly.

The young commander had been as brusque and efficient in that hallway as when she had been temporarily assigned to

Picard's *Enterprise* after the destruction of the colony at Jouret IV. She waved Picard into an empty office and bluntly stated the facts.

Starfleet Intelligence had reason to believe that a series of distant outposts on the Core Frontier was being raided by the Borg.

"But the Borg are defeated," Picard had protested. He had seen it himself. Hundreds of the once-mindless creatures had been awakened to their own individuality. The threat of the collective had been removed.

But Shelby had looked on Picard with an expression almost of pity. For a moment, Picard had felt as if he were withering into doddering antiquity, faced with the clear-eyed judgment of youth.

"Captain, it is Starfleet's belief that what you contacted, what you and your crew defeated, was only *one* branch of the collective. A single tentacle, if you will, of a monster that's spreading through the galaxy." She had clasped her hands together and leaned closer over the office's bare conference table. "Think of what you've seen of the Borg's activities, Captain. Starting eight years ago with the missing outposts on the Neutral Zone. Go back eighty years to the El-Aurian dispersion. Truly contemplate the unstoppable power and technology of the Borg, and their mission to destroy life."

Picard had felt the sweat break out on his forehead.

"Do you honestly think you have *changed* that by changing just the handful of Borg with which you've had . . . personal contact?"

Picard had found it hard to breathe in the cramped office. Elizabeth Shelby had taken his lack of response as an invitation to continue.

"We're not saying we believe that facing the Borg is a hopeless proposition. You *were* able to neutralize one branch. To us, that clearly implies the other, yet-to-be engaged branches can also be defeated."

At that Picard had disagreed, vehemently. "But whatever

strategy we use on one branch, the next branch instantly knows what to defend itself from."

Shelby had only smiled at his passion. Picard still remembered that smile. Predatory, focused, and intense. How had one so young become so cold? Almost as if there were something of the Borg in her as well.

"We're not just going after the branches, Captain," she had said, making a fist for emphasis. "We're going after the head."

Picard's lack of comprehension had been obvious.

"The source," Shelby had explained. "Somewhere out there is the central point from which all the branches emanate. We shall find that source, and we shall destroy it. And when we do, each branch of the Borg will wither and die without any further action from us. Or any other civilization unlucky enough to encounter them."

The young commander's argument had been persuasive, Picard allowed. There was even a kind of logic to what she had told him.

But then she had given him his new orders, direct from Admiral Stewart, Hanson's replacement at Starbase 324.

Picard was to join the tactical team to be based at Starbase 804, the closest fleet facility to the threatened region on the Core Frontier. Once there, when suspected Borg activity was detected, Picard was to be deployed with Starfleet's new, anti-Borg intelligence unit, to investigate and, if necessary, infiltrate the area of enemy action. His task would then become to carry out the mission objective—the capture and return of a Borg vessel. Shelby gave him to understand that even if the *Enterprise* had still been intact, he would have been temporarily reassigned for this mission.

Picard had known the reason why as well as Shelby did.

Four years ago, Jean-Luc Picard himself had been assimilated—made part of the Borg collective and its irresistible groupmind.

As Locutus of Borg, he had actually led the collective against Starfleet in the devastating Battle of Wolf 359, giving the Borg full access to every Starfleet secret locked in his mind.

And though every trace of Borg technology had been surgically removed from his body . . .

. . . in his mind, the tendrils of the collective remained. And Starfleet knew that, too.

Shelby had put the pieces of the interface on the table then.

The latest from Starfleet R & D—special branch. The branch Shelby headed at Starbase 324 in preparing the Federation for all-out war with the Borg. The ungainly, overpowered *Defiant*-class starships had come from that effort.

Along with the innocuous-looking pieces of microcircuitry and inert silicon that lay on the table before Picard.

Pieces which he recognized.

And which filled him with dread.

One part was simply an insulated cable, containing a microprocessor on one input jack and a slender transformer on the other.

The other was a sleek power cell, coupled with a short-range subspace transmitter, small enough to be carried unseen in a hand.

But the third piece was an asymmetrical plate of silicon, curved to fit the contours of the human face and skull.

In this case, Picard's face and skull.

Together they formed a Borg-derived neural interface. Just like the one that had been implanted in Picard's flesh, and into his mind.

"You will be accompanied by Dr. Beverly Crusher," Commander Shelby told him. "She's already been briefed."

"What about Will?" Picard had asked. For what Starfleet was asking of him, he wanted to be fully prepared—to go into action with his own command crew, the best crew in the Fleet.

But the commander had only replied, "Riker has other duties." Picard had had no trouble hearing the dismissal in her young voice as she said his name. That, too, was left over from the events of four years ago. Will Riker's refusal of a captaincy in order to remain Picard's first officer on the *Enterprise* had prevented the ambitious Elizabeth Shelby from taking his place.

At the end of their meeting, Shelby had ushered Picard out a back door, where two security officers had met him and taken him under armed guard to the private quarters that had been put aside for his use.

The guards, Shelby had assured him without irony, were not because he was a prisoner. But because he had become an invaluable resource.

After all, if the Borg were indeed massing on the Federation's frontier, and if, as had been long suspected, all-out war with the Borg was inevitable, then Jean-Luc Picard had become the most important living being in the Federation. And Shelby would see to it that he would be treated as such.

Except for Beverly, Picard had had no contact with his crew since that day.

"We require your power pack."

The flat, emotionless voice startled Picard from his reverie into the past.

A Borg barred his path.

Once it had been human, female. Starfleet.

Beneath the cybernetic augmentations fused to its chest and rib cage, he could see the remnants of a Starfleet duty uniform. The fabric had been cut away over its left shoulder, heartlessly exposing a ravaged section of blue-white flesh. But its communicator was still in position. Borg wires extended from it and entered that abused skin in a seemingly random series of small puckers. A thicker red cable ran up from the communicator and into its temple.

Whatever it had been, it was a Borg now, manipulator arm extended, a cutting blade whirring.

"Are you defective?" the Borg asked.

If Picard didn't answer, he knew his remaining life span could be measured in seconds.

"I will give you my power pack," he said.

Everyone on the team had been ordered not to argue with any Borg they might contact unless hostilities had begun. Picard didn't need to be ordered. He still remembered the parameters by which individual Borg operated: Achieve the collective's goals through the expenditure of the least amount of energy and resources.

It was the same natural law which had arisen from the principles of self-organization to govern everything in the universe, from simple chemical reactions to the evolution of reproductive strategies among living creatures.

Thus, Borg were likely to first *ask* their victims to cooperate before exerting any physical effort in assimilating them. Each major Borg offensive invariably began with the selection and assimilation of a leading individual from the target population who could function as Speaker—bridging the gap between the collective and its new component.

So far, that cautious, though logical, husbanding of resources was the only quirk of Borg behavior that gave Starfleet any hope of victory.

But even as Picard hurriedly slipped his suit's power generator and battery coils from his back, he knew that, eventually, one of the many branches of the Borg collective that Starfleet suspected had spread throughout the galaxy would, sheerly by chance, discover the survival advantage of overwhelming its technologically advanced victims *without* negotiation. When that happened, when the Borg ceased being socialized ants and became blindly guided sharks, intelligent biological life was doomed.

Picard handed his power pack to the Borg.

The Borg did not take its eye or its sensor off Picard.

"We require the protective device encasing your sensory stump."

Picard blinked, taking precious seconds to realize the Borg meant his helmet.

The Borg responded by going back into its secondary programming loop.

"Are you defective?"

"I will give you my protective device," Picard said quickly, steeling himself for the result.

The mission to Starbase 804 was dependent on Picard removing his helmet and revealing himself to the Borg only at a key point in the operation. But that point hadn't been reached. Picard knew that Weinlein and her commandos had not yet determined an access path into the Borg vessel at the center of the starbase. But he also knew that if he did not remove his helmet now, the mission would be over before it had begun.

The Borg held out its living hand.

Picard surrendered his helmet, keeping his head downcast, eyes averted. He became strongly aware of the oily smoke of burning flesh, mingled with the acrid fumes of scorched plastic and synthetics from the devastated starbase.

The Borg did not step away.

"You will direct your visual sensors upward," the Borg said.

Picard took a deep breath.

What if he met the Borg's gaze?

What if he stared into that eye and . . .

"Locutus?"

The name carried such weight and importance within the collective that recognition of Picard's face had somehow triggered a deeply buried emotional response of surprise—a relic of the biological being this Borg had once been.

Picard himself was not surprised.

Starfleet had counted on him being recognized in just this way, exactly as he had been recognized by the Borg known as Hugh, years ago.

Hugh had been a young Borg, lost to the collective when his scoutship had crashed in the Argolis Sector. Picard's *Enterprise* had rescued him. Picard's crew had nurtured the nascent individuality in Hugh, and those newly formed threads of lone personality had eventually led to the total subversion of one of the Borg collective's many branches.

But the Borg who stood before Picard now was not from Hugh's branch. It looked troubled.

Picard understood the programming conflict it must be going through.

Hugh had been cut off from the collective. Because of that loss of communication, when he had first met Picard aboard the *Enterprise,* he had not been troubled by his inability to detect Locutus within the groupmind. But this human Borg was still a functioning unit of whatever branch of the collective was assimilating Starbase 804. And clearly, from its confusion, the collective was troubled because Locutus was physically here, yet not present among their joint thoughts.

The Borg trained its manipulator arm on Picard. The whirring blade stopped and folded into an inner compartment, even as Picard heard the click of another compartment opening.

The thin blue rod of an X-ray welding unit glowed along the mechanical arm. Picard knew the welder could torch through duranium as easily as through human flesh.

The collective had long ago evolved the response of treating anomalous phenomena as threatening, and therefore subject to immediate destruction.

At this moment, Picard was obviously a threat.

But he also knew how the Borg functioned.

"Are you defective?" he asked.

Whatever the Borg had been about to do, its primary behavior was now circumvented by a diagnostic subroutine. A verbal order from Locutus had been enough to trigger it.

Picard looked around quickly. A work crew of augmented Borg carried pieces of a shuttle in a single file, like cutter ants carrying carved sections of leaves. Why the Borg had not simply scooped this base up with one of their tractor beams, Picard didn't know. The Borg ship that had landed in the base's center was smaller than most of the cubeships Starfleet had catalogued. Perhaps it was not powerful enough to assimilate whole installations at once, as the colony on Jouret IV had been assimilated. There the Borg ship and crew had left only a smooth-sided crater behind.

Picard could see no sign of the rest of Weinlein's commando team. Each had planned to enter the base separately, to avoid attracting the collective's attention. They were to rendezvous by the ruins of the communications building in two more hours to brief each other on what they had seen. But until then, they were to remain alone.

"No defects detected," the Borg announced. It raised its manipulator arm again.

"You will continue your work with the power packs," Picard ordered. It was a shock to discover how easily the harsh tone of Locutus returned to him.

The Borg angled its head. Communing, Picard knew. He remembered the feeling well. The sense of support. The release of abandoning power to—

"Locutus is missing," the Borg stated. "You are defective." It stepped toward Picard. Its manipulator arm rose with the hum of its internal actuators. The X-ray welder began to glow, began to whine as its quantum capacitor built its charge.

"No," Picard said, thinking fast. "You—"

Picard stumbled back as the female Borg suddenly shimmered in a blaze of phased energy, then vanished. He looked around. Saw Sue Weinlein three meters away. The stock of her phaser rifle was braced on her hip as she scanned the immediate area, paying careful attention to the long line of workers carrying the shuttle parts.

"Don't look at me," Weinlein said. Even as a group of only two, they couldn't appear to be interacting, otherwise they might become a target for assimilation.

"Have you been following me?" Picard asked. The afterimage of the phaser burst still floated across his vision.

"My job's to get you to that cubeship," Weinlein said. "Keep walking."

Picard marched forward.

"Picard!"

He turned.

Weinlein tossed him his helmet. "Save it for showtime."

Picard pulled the helmet on, closed the visor.

He wished he were somehow locking Locutus back into his deep and hidden cell, somewhere in his core.

But he knew it was too late.

All around him, he heard the whisper of the collective. Though whether it sprang from the Borg or his own subconscious, he could not be certain.

Come back, Jean-Luc . . . .

Picard marched deeper into the starbase.

Deeper into enemy territory.

And for the first time, despair took hold of his soul.

Because he knew he would no longer be alone.

Come back. . . .

EIGHT

The hull of the *Starship Enterprise* had been built to withstand asteroidal impact, Iopene antimatter streams, and the distortional stresses of warp speed.

But here, on Veridian III, echoing with the soft drumbeat of a summer rainstorm, the once-mighty ship leaked like a molecular sieve.

Riker moved carefully through the tilted corridor on deck eight. He had learned his lesson and wore engineer's grip boots, to keep from slipping on the waterlogged carpet. Beside him, Deanna Troi moved just as carefully.

The saucer creaked.

Riker's hand found Deanna's, and for a timeless moment, they held their breaths.

Then they looked at each other in the soft light of Riker's handheld torch and laughed.

"That sounded just like an atmospheric containment breach," Deanna said.

Riker nodded. "I know."

But planetbound, sliced to pieces, and half-disassembled, the *Enterprise* no longer had to be atmospherically sealed. Their sudden apprehension had been the result of training, not fact.

"Settling?" Deanna asked.

Riker nodded again. The settling of a body decaying in death.

A third of the saucer had already been removed before last night's attack on the salvage camp. With so many support beams missing, and with no structural integrity force field to keep the immense structure in alignment, the saucer was in no shape to even support its own mass. And no additional salvage operation would begin until a Starfleet support team answered the distress calls Riker had put out after the attack.

"We'd better hurry," Riker said. He had survived the crash of this grand ship. He had no desire to die in her collapse, weeks later.

Deanna held her tricorder ahead of them. She had been trapped in her barracks during the attack, spared the onslaught of energy weapons by a well-placed locker which had struck her from behind. The locker threw her forward between two bunks, where she had been sheltered by their mattresses.

The rescue crews had found her unhurt an hour after the last explosion had rocked the camp. Riker had sat by her side until she had awakened with the dawn.

He remembered the look that had appeared on her face as she sensed his emotions at seeing her safe. She hadn't been prepared for the intensity of them.

Neither had Riker.

Wisely, at least for now, both had tacitly agreed not to mention it. The events of the past few weeks had been confusing enough without adding the extra complication of a return to the emotions of years gone by.

Riker read Deanna's tricorder's display, then looked along the corridor, past a shifting curtain of water that trickled down from the outside rainstorm, into impenetrable darkness. The emergency lighting circuits had long since expended their power. The once-familiar ship might as well have been an ancient network of tunnels and caves.

"That way," Deanna said. "One of the classrooms."

They moved carefully down the corridor, following Riker's torchlight, sliding their feet so as not to lose their footing.

Deanna paused at an intersection, squeezed Riker's hand tightly. "I know," she said. "I feel it, too."

Sadness, Riker thought. For all the ship had been through, to end like this, in a meaningless crash that had accomplished nothing.

He thought of the other *Enterprise*s which had been lost in service to Starfleet. Kirk's original, whose sacrifice had bought an unexpected victory over the Klingons at the Genesis Planet. Rachel Garrett's *Enterprise-C,* whose valiantly hopeless efforts at Narendra III had cemented the peace between the Federation and the Klingon Empire. And joining them now, the *Enterprise-D,* a random victim of a lucky shot.

Riker felt Deanna's eyes on him. "Don't start," she said.

"Sometimes, things happen for no reason at all. This was one of them. Accept it, and move on."

At the end of the next corridor, near an inoperative turbolift station, Riker and Deanna found the door to classroom twelve jammed open with a fire-blackened chair. A light shone over the chair from the classroom.

"In there," Deanna said.

The corridor floor shifted suddenly. Riker almost lost his footing again. "If anyone would know better than to be in this death trap . . ." he muttered.

Then Riker and Deanna stepped over the chair and into the classroom.

"Commander Riker, Counsellor Troi. I shall be able to converse with you in a moment."

Spock was lit by the glow shining up at him from the computer display inset on the small desk top at which he sat. A handheld torch rested on the edge of the study corral.

"I'm surprised you could find a terminal in working condition, Ambassador," Riker said. Riker had no idea from where Spock had been able to draw power. But the ambassador's prowess with starship systems was legendary.

"It was not working when I found it," Spock acknowledged.

Riker and Deanna glanced at each other, not quite certain how to proceed. It was not as if either felt they could order the ambassador to do anything. But they certainly could not allow him to remain here. Whole decks had given way in the saucer. This section of Deck 8 was already unsupported at too many critical points.

Riker watched the ambassador change the configuration of his input panel from the simple controls of a child's educational datapal to that of a full-functional library retrieval terminal. He wanted to know what Spock was doing, what had compelled him to risk entering the ship, but couldn't bring himself to ask. He felt he had no right. It was the legacy of living in a chain of command.

"The children's educational computers were not tied in to the tactical cores which Starfleet engineers have already removed," Spock said. "It was a simple matter to use this terminal to access the noncritical memory cores still remaining in the ship's main system."

"We have computers in the salvage camp," Deanna said. "Whatever work you need to do can be done there. In safer surroundings."

Spock did not bother to look up. "Thank you, Counsellor, but I find I am in need of Starfleet personnel records extending back quite some time. They would not be part of the salvage system."

"Personnel records?" Riker asked. "Anyone in particular?"

Spock hesitated. But he kept his attention focused on the screen. "James T. Kirk . . . I never really accepted the fact . . . never really *believed* . . . that he was dead."

Riker saw how stiffly, almost formally, the ambassador sat in the child-sized chair. It had been a difficult admission for him to make.

"You were not the only one," Deanna Troi said softly.

Spock turned to regard the counsellor with an upraised eyebrow. "Indeed."

Deanna smiled. Riker felt bathed in her warmth, though it was directed at Spock and not him. "Montgomery Scott said the same thing," she told the ambassador. "Believed as you believed."

Riker remembered his conversations with the feisty old Scotsman. Scott had been the chief engineer on the original *Enterprise,* where Kirk and Spock had first served together. After Kirk's first recorded death, on the maiden flight of the *Enterprise-B,* Scott had led an intensive search of the sector in which that ship had been damaged by the mysterious energy ribbon known as the Nexus.

Decades later, when the chief engineer had been rescued from transporter storage and had come aboard the

Enterprise-D, he had explained the details of his search, how he had used experimental sensors sensitive enough to detect individual molecules, let alone the body of his captain.

In his personal quest, Scott had found the remains of other victims of the force of the Nexus—shattered bodies blown clear of the ruptured El-Aurian ships. But he had not found *all* of the recorded El-Aurian dead. And, more importantly to him, he had been unable to find any trace whatsoever of a human body.

"In fact, the first thing Mr. Scott said when he was recovered from transporter storage," Deanna explained to Spock, "was that he half expected to hear that it was Kirk who had rescued him, taking the first *Enterprise* out of mothballs just to come after his old friend."

"Hardly logical," Spock replied. "The *Enterprise-A* was destroyed at Chal, long before Mr. Scott's unfortunate crash."

Deanna wasn't willing to let the conversation go. "It was what he *hoped,* Ambassador. Not what he knew."

Riker sat back against another small desktop. It had been decorated with crude, cut out crayon drawings of some unfortunate adult with a Starfleet uniform and no hair. Riker decided Picard would not be amused. "What about your inability to accept Kirk's death, Ambassador? Is that logical?"

Spock's expression was unreadable. "Yes," he said. "I have mind-melded with the captain. That process typically creates a trace impression in the minds of the participants—a fleeting sense that they still remain in contact with one another, even after the meld has dissolved, as long as both remain alive."

Deanna glanced at Riker. Her expression he could read. Spock was not being forthcoming, and she knew it. Vulcans controlled their emotions, but they still had them. And Deanna's Betazoid heritage allowed her to detect each repressed nuance.

"In all the years that have elapsed since his disappearance, I have never felt him die," Spock said. The Vulcan ambassador spoke as if to himself, as if Riker and Deanna weren't present.

Deanna leaned forward, fascinated. "Is his death something you would expect to feel?"

Vulcan and Betazoid, Riker thought, looking at the two of them. Thought without emotion, and the sensing of emotion without thought. He remembered the underpinnings of the Vulcan philosophy of IDIC—infinite diversity in infinite combination. He was looking at a strong example of it now. By such was the Federation made strong.

The computer terminal chimed. Spock turned to it without answering Deanna's question.

At least, Riker concluded, he had not answered it in words.

A multicolored image of a tropical fish darted across the display screen. Riker recognized it as something for the children.

"Program completed," the computer announced.

Riker stepped forward to look over Spock's shoulder. On the display, he saw a picture of Kirk he recognized from history tapes. In it, Kirk was a young man, wearing a century-old Starfleet uniform. It felt odd to see the same delta insignia on Kirk's chest that Riker wore as a communicator. Most images of Starfleet personnel from that era showed them with a variety of different symbols on their uniforms. At the time, each ship and starbase had had its own distinctive symbol—a historical echo from the first, primitive days of space exploration when each separate flight had been awarded its own unique mission crest.

But over time, for all it had come to mean to the Federation, the *Enterprise* delta had been adopted by all of Starfleet, so today it could be seen throughout the known galaxy. But to see it on the uniform of someone from another century reinforced in Riker the sense that when he looked at images of the original *Enterprise's* crew, he was looking at how it had all begun.

Text flowed up the screen beside Kirk's image. Riker swiftly scanned it and recognized it. It was Kirk's service record. The key events were required reading in the academy, and Riker was once again reminded just how much of the man's career had been key events.

"Even given what you feel, is there a reason you've called up Kirk's personnel file?" Deanna asked.

Spock kept his eyes locked on the screen. He adjusted a control so the scroll rate of the text increased. Riker was impressed by how quickly the ambassador was assimilating the information. Even for a Vulcan.

"The captain was not known to exist in our present era," Spock said, still reading. "Yet, within two weeks of his unanticipated return to . . . life, a well-planned and -equipped military operation was carried out to retrieve his remains from Veridian III."

Deanna folded her arms in thought.

"Are you suggesting that someone *expected* Kirk to appear in this time period?" she asked.

Riker could see that Spock was flagging certain entries in Kirk's record, as if marking them for further consideration. But consideration for what?

"That would not be logical," Spock answered. The sound of dripping intensified in the hallway. Riker could hear water beginning to flow like a stream. But there was no sense of distraction in Spock's voice as he continued to scan the rapidly moving text. "It would imply a cross-temporal knowledge of events. If someone from the future, having learned of the captain's return on this planet, decided to travel into the past to retrieve him, then why would that observer not return to the moment *before* his death, instead of so many days after it?"

The text on the display froze in place for an instant. Spock glanced up at Deanna who now stood beside him. "Therefore, the answer to the mystery with which we are faced will not be found in the present or the future, but in the past. Specifically, Captain Kirk's past." He turned back to the screen.

The deck shifted suddenly. Riker grabbed the corral wall, without comment, trusting to the legendary Vulcan's assessment of the odds.

"But how could anyone from the past know Kirk would end up on Veridian III?" Riker asked. "I don't understand . . . the logic of it."

"Perhaps because there is no logic to what has happened," Spock said. "What this salvage camp has been subjected to was an act of unrestrained emotion. A deeply felt, indeed, uncontrollable need to wreak some sort of vengeance on the captain."

Riker was surprised by the emotion he heard in Spock's voice. "Forgive me, Ambassador, but now it sounds as if you're applying logic to emotion."

Spock lowered his head for a moment. "Believe me, Commander Riker, at the most fundamental level, they are one and the same." The ambassador imperceptibly sighed then, and Riker was reminded he was speaking with a being who had lived for almost a century and half.

"So you came here to look for the captain's enemies?" Deanna asked.

"That is correct," Spock said.

"But how many of them are likely to have survived into this time?" Riker asked.

"All it takes is one," Spock replied.

Riker watched as Spock swiftly sorted the flagged entries on the display screen. He saw an image of a human wearing what seemed to be formal wear from Earth's seventeenth century, complete with ruffled shirt front and collar. Beside him, an image formed of the twentieth-century madman, Khan Noonien Singh. Then a large humanoid with a silvery robe. And then the infamous Tholian Grand Admiral Loskene—Riker was startled that Kirk might have had dealings with that brilliant Tholian leader, who still vexed the Federation today.

After a few more unrecognizable aliens joined the collection, another human in a extravagant outfit appeared—this one a man with a large moustache and a plumed hat. Then Riker saw a Klingon commander in a uniform as old as the one on Kirk.

"Your friend seems to have made more than his share of enemies," Riker noted.

"His was a forceful and direct personality," Spock said. "Such people are loved, or they are hated. By their natures, they allow no middle ground."

"Are all these beings alive today?" Deanna asked.

More images sorted themselves on the screen. A female Romulan commander appeared in an equally antique costume. Riker remembered her face but not her name from his academy studies. She had been involved in Starfleet's first retrieval of a Romulan cloaking device. The details of that operation were still classified, but Riker decided it would make sense that Kirk had been involved. Was there nothing the man hadn't done in his lifetime?

"I do not know how many of them survive," Spock said. "These are merely the ones with the motive to hate the captain beyond ordinary reason, and the native ability or technological opportunity to have cheated the years between their time and this."

Another Klingon appeared. And another. Klingons had clearly had no love for Kirk, nor he for them.

Spock entered more commands on the control panel. Several of the images vanished from the screen as the computer apparently cross-referenced other sources and discovered who was dead.

In the end, Spock was left with four possibilities. As the

program came to an end, Riker pointed at the screen, trying to be helpful.

"Khan Noonien Singh is dead," he said.

Spock turned to look at Riker. Riker could almost swear he saw the flicker of a smile form on the ambassador's lips. "I know."

The dark classroom creaked as if it were on a seagoing vessel, moored in rough waters.

Riker glanced at Deanna. Time was rapidly running out for this shell of a starship.

Spock stared at the four faces on the display screen. Four ghosts from the past: Khan, the humanoid in seventeenth-century clothing, the human with the plumed hat, and an insectoid creature whom Riker thought resembled one of the Kraal, long since vanished from Federation space.

Deanna broke the silence.

"Ambassador, please excuse my directness. But do you honestly believe that one of those four beings is responsible for attacking this base and stealing Kirk's remains?"

Spock put a hand on the screen, as if trying to blank out his past.

"They were not his remains," he said softly.

"I beg your pardon?" Riker said.

Spock rose from his chair and tugged on his cloak to straighten its folds. The formal aspect which Riker had first noticed had returned to the venerable Vulcan.

Spock looked Riker in the eye, hiding nothing.

"I remind you that I still have not felt James Kirk die," he said.

Before Riker could respond, Spock held up a hand to silence him. "As illogical as it sounds, Commander, I still *feel* his presence. As the counsellor can confirm."

Deanna nodded at Riker. She sensed he was telling the truth.

"A mind-meld echo?" Riker asked.

But Spock slowly shook his head, almost with an expression of sorrow.

"He is out there, Commander. In some way I cannot yet fathom, James Kirk still survives." Spock held his hand to his temple, terribly fatigued. "And he is calling to me. . . ."

NINE

Spock!

Kirk ran, calling for help, something chasing him.

His movements were slowed by liquid. Something thick.

The deck below him seemed to shift with the characteristic lag of artificial gravity. Voices called out to him.

This is the El-Aurian transport ship Lakul . . . *we're caught in some . . . energy distortion. . . .*

Someone was in trouble. Kirk had to run faster. Always had to run faster.

Their hulls are starting to buckle under the stress. . . .

Faster. Never enough time.

The young captain looked at him.

You have the bridge. . . .

Kirk took the chair. The center chair. When had he wanted anything else? Anything more?

But this time, it wasn't right.

He turned his back. Left the bridge.

Keep things together until I get back. . . .

I always do. . . .

Into the bowels of the ship.

Running. Always running.

Reconnecting the circuits. Making the deflector arrays do what they were never supposed to do.

Changing the rules.

The way he always had.

That's it! Let's go!

The command from the bridge, the young captain: *Activate main deflector. . . .*

And then . . .

And then . . .

And then what?

Nothing made sense.

Horses. Antonia. The stars in space. Making the jump. Burning the eggs in the kitchen. The man in the strange uniform. Starfleet uniform.

Make a difference. . . .

The man from the future.

Picard?

Jumping through space. Through time.

You don't appreciate the gravity of your situation, Captain. . . .

Falling.

Yosemite.

The ground swirling up and the sudden pressure on his ankle as . . .

Spock!

He hadn't been alone at Yosemite, climbing the mountain.

But this time, he was.

Until he felt the pressure of a cold cloth on his forehead.

Kirk's eyes flew open as the shifting gravity stopped its wild movement.

The only darkness he saw was caused by the cloth.

He reached for it. Needed to take it away. To get away. Something was gaining. He had to keep running.

"Shhh."

He moved the cloth and saw . . .

He didn't know her.

"Do you know where you are?" the woman asked.

At some level, he understood she was beautiful. Dark hair. Haunting eyes. Sensuous, upswept, pointed ears. The word "Romulan" came to him, though he didn't know what it meant.

"My ship?" he asked. Somehow, he was always onboard his ship.

Wherever that was.

But the woman shook her head. So serious.

He felt she needed help. He wanted to help her. It was one way to stop running.

"Do you know who you are?" she asked.

Of course he did. He smiled. Opened his mouth.

Nothing came out.

Panic.

"It's all right," the woman said.

She soothed his forehead, his temples, with the cool cloth.

"I know who did this to you."

"Did this?" Kirk said.

"You were very brave."

Kirk felt relief. People counted on him. All four hundred thirty aboard the . . . the *Enterprise.*

He frowned.

"The *Enterprise* . . . what is it?"

"Can you sit up?" the woman asked.

Kirk did. His head swam but he hid his symptoms. It wasn't right to show weakness. Not when so many needed him. Looked to him for strength, for guidance.

He looked around.

He was on a bed. A medical gurney, he knew.

But the room he was in wasn't familiar. A black cube of a room, marked with yellow grid lines.

"Where am I?" he asked. He felt he had nothing to hide from this woman.

"You were injured," she said. "In battle."

Battle. His next question was reflexive. "The ship?"

"*Your* ship . . . it's out of danger."

Kirk sighed. Nothing else mattered.

"For now," the woman concluded.

"I have to get back to the bridge," Kirk said. He wasn't clear as to what the bridge was, or what he needed to do there. But if he could set foot on it. Sit in that center chair one more time. He knew everything would be fine.

"In time," the woman said.

She shifted her position where she sat on the edge of the gurney. Kirk was aware of a cool breeze across his chest. He looked down, expecting to see a uniform of some sort. But what kind of uniform? He saw nothing.

Nothing . . .

He gasped.

Who was he?

The woman looked at him in concern. "Are you all right?"

Again, Kirk refused to admit weakness. "You said I was injured. In battle?"

"Against the enemy."

Kirk was at a loss. "Who is the enemy?"

The woman picked up a small padd, pressed a control. A far corner of the stark room faded away, opening up into the immensity of space. Kirk braced himself for the wail of the loss-of-pressure alarms. But the air remained still.

"This is the enemy," the woman said.

The viewpoint in space shifted. A vessel came into view. Kirk felt a tugging in his heart. The vessel was magnificent.

Her forward saucer was connected by a short neck to a small, tapered engineering hull. From both sides of that lower hull, bold pylons thrust out on dynamic angles, ending in flattened warp-propulsion nacelles.

Kirk gazed at the ship, knowing every centimeter of her but not certain if he had ever seen her before.

"The *Enterprise,*" the woman said, spitting out the name. "The enemy."

Kirk was surprised. This ship didn't *feel* like the enemy. He was missing something.

The woman looked at him. "Say it. The *Enterprise.* The enemy."

The woman adjusted another control on her padd.

Kirk gasped with sudden pain.

"Say it," she said.

"The *Enterprise,*" Kirk gasped. "The enemy."

The woman smiled her approval. Instantly Kirk felt the pain end, a wave of pleasure sweeping through him.

"Who are you?" he asked.

She caressed his face. "The monsters who did this to you will not survive," she said.

Kirk took her hand, the question still in his eyes.

"Salatrel," she said.

Then she leaned forward and kissed him.

Kirk responded, surprised by the sudden explosion of emotion he felt. He heard her fingers on the padd. More waves of pleasure pulsed through him.

He looked into her dark eyes. "Are we . . . ?"

"Yes," she whispered.

She held him close. "I thought I had lost you," she said.

The thought of losing her was unbearable to Kirk. He crushed her to his chest, determined never to let her go.

He made his confession.

"I . . . I don't know who I am. . . ."

Her eyes blazed into his. Twin novae.

"They will not go unpunished."

"Who?"

"The enemy."

Kirk looked past her at the *Enterprise.* It was a holographic model, he finally realized. A wave of fear swept through him as he gazed upon it. Revulsion.

"The Federation," he said as the word floated to his consciousness.

"Starfleet," the woman said.

Instantly, Kirk felt a stab of incredible pain slice through his bowels.

"Starfleet," he gasped. The word was foul. Loathsome.

"Look what they did," the woman said, her hand busy on the padd she carried. Kirk's heart began to race with apprehension.

The image of the hated ship faded away, replaced by another—dynamic, birdlike, with a double hull and raptor-prowed bridge.

The *Enterprise* streaked at it, weapons blazing.

The raptor ship erupted in plasma, in death.

"A colony vessel," Salatrel said. "Women and children. Farming supplies."

Kirk's breath quickened. Sweat beaded on his forehead.

Another image rippled into view. A fleet of raptor-prowed ships.

"A mercy mission," Salatrel said. "Defenseless."

The fleet was consumed by the fire of the *Enterprise,* one ship after another.

"And this," she said.

A planet spun through space. The holographic viewpoint spiraled in like a reentering spacecraft. Below Kirk stretched farming fields in checkerboard perfection, rolling with the gentle curves of the world. Until over a rise, a city appeared. Fresh, bold, new. A colonial capital.

Then the tractor beam struck. Scooping up the city like a handful of dirt. Within the immense tractor beam, the delicate spires of the city's temples crumbled. Kirk could hear the distant cries of hundreds, thousands.

The city ascended into the clouds, dropping huge clumps of soil. Only a gaping, scooped-out crater remained.

"Why?" Kirk asked.

"Butchers," Salatrel answered. "Remember," she said.

Another ship appeared. Kirk recognized it. Knew it was old. A foreshortened saucer with small nacelles close to its body. Its underside painted with a bird of prey.

And inside, the bridge.

"I've seen this before," he told Salatrel.

His stomach tightened. He knew how this ended.

"Was I there?" he asked.

"Yes," she said.

Kirk saw the bridge of the vessel. Other Romulans. The commander in his silver mesh and cloak of command came forward. Green blood ran from his mouth. Kirk stared at the image intently. He *had* been there. He had witnessed this himself.

The commander spoke. "I regret that we meet in this way," he said. "You and I are of a kind. In a different reality, I could have called you friend."

"Yes," Kirk said. He remembered the words. Understood the kinship he had shared with this commander. They had been the same. Yet now, the commander was dead and Kirk lived. Why?

The bridge collapsed, blew apart. The transmission ended.

"He didn't have to die," Kirk said.

Regret overwhelmed him. A regret he had harbored for years.

"A noble house fell with him," Salatrel said bitterly. "Chironsala. One of the oldest on Romulus. And all the generations that followed were cursed."

Kirk turned to Salatrel. He reached out to her face, to her ears, traced their tips.

Then touched his own.

"Am I . . . ?" he began to ask.

"No," she said. "Human. A patriot. Dedicated to peace. To noninterference."

"Noninterference," Kirk repeated. Of course. It was as if the words were engraved on his mind.

"Dedicated to the destruction of the enemy," Salatrel added.

"The *Enterprise,*" Kirk said. "The Federation. Starfleet."

In the wave of hate he experienced with each word, the regret and the pain retreated from his body. Warmth returned. Understanding.

"What do you want to do?" Salatrel prompted.

"Help," Kirk said. "Let me help." The words felt perfect. As if he had always longed to say them.

Salatrel smiled. She touched the padd she held at her side.

Her smile was like the sun of a summer day in Iowa. Kirk wanted to fall into it. Find his answers there.

"How?" she asked.

Kirk thought a moment. He replayed the sickening scenes she had shared with him. The senseless brutality. The pain he felt as he recalled them was physical, as if his nerve ends were actually being fired.

"Stop them," he said. The pain lessened. Momentarily.

"Destroy them?" Salatrel asked. The pain increased.

"Destroy them," Kirk said. This time, the pain did not just fade. Pleasure took its place.

"Kill them," he sighed. Nothing sounded better. Felt better.

Salatrel moved her hand across his chest. He drew a deep breath. Every sensation felt new.

"They almost killed me, didn't they?" Kirk asked.

Salatrel studied him. "Almost," she agreed.

Slowly, she drew away the thin sheet that covered him. "But I wouldn't let them take you away from me."

The coolness of the air was like water washing over Kirk. He dimly understood that his mind was full of questions. How had he been hurt? How long had he been in this place? How long had he known this exquisite woman? The very thought of her filled him with longing and anticipation.

But he was unable to focus on any of those questions. He could only respond to the here and the now.

The pressure of her nails across his shoulders. The cinnamon scent of her dark hair as it brushed his face.

"Are you glad you're back?" Salatrel whispered in his ear. The heat of her breath pulsed into him, making his lungs falter, forcing him to inhale through his mouth.

"Yes," Kirk said. He nuzzled his face against her neck. Hungrily kissed the fine hairs that covered her nape.

"Are you ready to help again?" she asked. Her hands moved over his shoulders, squeezing the muscles there, digging in, releasing, making a promise.

"Anything," Kirk said.

"The enemy?"

"Destroy him. Kill him."

Her lips moved over his, the tip of her tongue electric against him.

"Who is the enemy?" she asked.

Kirk struggled to concentrate. He needed Salatrel. He had to feel her in his arms. It was almost as if he had never held anyone ever before. But he didn't have the answer she wanted. It was one of those elusive questions floating in the shadows. The questions he couldn't answer. Couldn't yet focus on.

"Show me?" he asked.

"Is that what you want?"

"Show me," he pleaded.

Anything to answer the question. To give her the answer. To quell the pain that rose within him again.

"Watch," Salatrel said.

She aimed her padd at the holographically blurred corner, pressed a control.

An image appeared there. Life size. A humanoid.

Kirk gasped as the figure resolved.

Kirk recognized him.

"The enemy," Salatrel hissed. "He must be destroyed. He must be killed."

"Killed," Kirk agreed. It was the only way. The only way to find peace. The only way to find himself.

The figure reached for him from the holographic haze, gloating, fueled by the thousand atrocities committed by the Federation and Starfleet against the Romulan race.

"Kill," Salatrel urged.

Kirk nodded. He spoke the name of the enemy.

"Jean-Luc Picard."

His body arched. There could be no escape from the agony.

Until Salatrel came to him and held him, and the agony became ecstasy so incredible that nothing else mattered.

Except the single thought . . . his single purpose . . .

Jean-Luc Picard must die.

TEN

☆

Worf, son of Mogh, groaned with pleasure as the fangs of the *krencha* lanced into his shoulder.

The Klingon shifted his mass to the side, going with the impact of the ravenous beast instead of fighting it. He slammed into the hard solid dirt of the forest path, felt the rough bite of the ragged stones pierce his flesh, even as the *krencha,* taken by surprise, flipped forward, losing the purchase its fangs had given it.

Worf continued his sideways roll, kicking his legs into the

air to build momentum, then pushed with one arm to leap onto his feet.

The *krencha* was already waiting for him. Its four running legs scuffed the soft soil of the ground off the path. Its two killing legs thrust forward. Its tongue slithered out from its reptilian lips, scenting the air, to detect its prey's fear.

But there was no fear in Worf.

He reveled in his long-delayed vacation to the Almron Preserve—the boundless tract of pristine nature encircling the First City of the Klingon Homeworld, Qo'noS.

Slowly, he bared his fangs at the three-meter-long creature before him, drawing his lips back in a fierce grimace of victory as he shook his head from side to side. His tightly bound warrior's queue of hair thrashed his shoulders and spattered the blood that flowed from his wounds. The blood dripped down his bare chest to the simple belt and loincloth he wore.

In the face of death, Worf was aware of each subtle movement of life all around him—here the errant stirring of a breeze among the leaves, there the passage of an insect. He heard each crack of a twig. Each creak of a branch. And every silver-purple leaf was distinct in his peripheral vision. Even the stench of the predator before him cut into his nostrils like the exhilarating bouquet of that nectar of the gods—prune juice.

Worf was *alive.*

As he had not been since the saucer of the *Enterprise* began its long fall, since life and death were separated only by the space between two heartbeats.

Here, in Almron, Klingons could live as Klingons had always been meant to live—always in that space between heartbeats, between death and life, defeat and victory.

The *krencha* sprang.

Worf ducked forward, presenting his uninjured shoulder, again to absorb the energy of the attack and turn it back against the beast.

But the creature was not fooled a second time. Its thick, stubby tail lashed out to the right, altering its trajectory so that Worf came in too low.

As Worf stumbled, the *krencha* slashed downward with its killing legs. Its razor-sharp claws slashed at Worf's unprotected back.

The sudden shock of pain stopped him from slapping his arms to the ground to break his fall. He was out of control. Sent sprawling. Tasting dirt as the rich soil of Qo'noS filled his open, gasping mouth.

Behind him, the *krencha* shrieked in anticipation.

The forest erupted with a cacophony of *blas rika* calls—the flying scavengers of Qo'noS. *Krencha* could be counted on not to finish their kills all at once. There would be offal remaining for the leather-winged creatures of the night.

But Worf had not lost yet.

The *krencha* bent forward so that all six legs came in contact with the forest path for greater speed.

It charged forward, shrieking, rippling toward its fallen prey.

Worf was still down. Defenseless.

And he wouldn't have it any other way.

For only in this instant, this sacred still moment from one heartbeat to the next, could he step into the perfection of *K'ajii*—the warrior's path.

Worf took that first step and time seemed to slow.

He saw the creature's square-pupiled, yellow eyes lock onto him like sensors. He saw the spittle stream from its razor fangs with each jarring thump of its forward legs.

Its dense fur rippled in the wind of its passage.

Its powerful, thick tail curved up behind it, ready to change direction in a moment.

But with the way of the *K'ajii* silent and still within him, Worf chose that moment with exquisite precision.

The curled toes of his bare foot came up under the

krencha's primary tracheae when its fangs were only a meter from his throat.

The explosion of acrid breath from the creature enveloped Worf with the stench of rotted meat as the *krencha* sailed past him, missing its target.

Then, even before his adversary had landed, Worf spun around and leapt forward, landing on the creature's midsection before it could right itself.

Its scream made Worf's ears vibrate.

Its killing legs lashed out to embrace Worf in a deadly corkscrew hold, a last attempt to crush the life force from him.

But this was no mere fight to the death. For a Klingon, no fight ever was so meaningless.

It was a fight for honor.

For if a Klingon did not have mastery over nature, then how could he expect to protect and preserve it?

Worf risked freeing one arm from around the *krencha's* right front killing leg and slapped his hand forward to grab the creature's snout. At once, it collapsed its neck, trying in turn to loosen his grip so it could snap off his offending fingers.

There was a graft and cloning first-aid station at the entrance to the nature preserve, but Worf had never had to use its services. Since he had been a teenager, at least. And he had no intention of starting again now.

Then, the *krencha* paused. It was tiring. Like most predators, it had evolved for the sudden sprint and quick attack. Prolonged battle was a waste of resources.

Worf swung his other hand up and grabbed the creature's lower jaw.

The *krencha* wailed as if it knew the battle had been lost.

It had.

Worf wrapped his legs around the creature's elongated chest, locked his heel against his instep, and began to squeeze. The creature's struggles were lessening.

Then Worf pulled the creature's jaws apart.

He shimmied along the beast, bringing his face perilously close to the gleaming fangs.

His fingers pressed into either side of the *krencha's* dark gums. The sticky saliva threatened to make him lose his grip, but the knowledge that he would also lose his fingers help him focus, maintaining *K'ajii*.

Worf's arms quivered with exhaustion as he brought the creature's head around to face him. He locked eyes with the beast. Saw its soul.

And with the last erg of strength he possessed, Worf pulled the creature's jaws apart and snapped one hand forward and one hand back, pivoting its neck to hear the telltale snap.

At once, the *krencha* went slack beneath him.

Worf trembled as he pulled open the creature's jaws and inhaled deeply of its dying breath, infusing its spirit and its strength into his own body, honoring the beast as Klingon hunters had for millennia.

Then he stood respectfully beside his fallen foe. He drew his fingers through the bite wound on his shoulder and traced the blood around the *krencha's* lips, giving his valiant opponent its final reward.

Then Worf knelt and said the words of the hunter's bargain.

If Worf had lost this battle, then he would have fed the creature. But Worf had won, so he graciously accepted the creature's matching offer to feed him.

Worf took his *d'k tahg* knife from his belt, and held it over the first of the creature's two hearts.

"*jIyajbe'*. Isn't that overkill?"

Though strained and exhausted by his battle, Worf leapt to his feet, instantly adopting the warrior's first position, *d'k tahg* held ready as its secondary blades clicked into place.

The voice had spoken in the Warrior's Tongue of Qo'noS. It had been natural, not broadcast over a communicator. But Worf had heard no one approach, no transporter harmonic.

How could it be possible for someone to sneak up on him here, with all his senses so refined for the hunt? He cursed himself for his lack of preparation that had made him so vulnerable.

"Show yourself," Worf called out in challenge.

He whipped his head around as branches moved behind him. Too late he realized they had moved because a rock had been thrown into them. When he turned back, his visitor was facing him, showing no sign of having just moved, as if he had always been there.

Worf slowly took his measure of the being who had outmaneuvered him so easily. His first impression was that the visitor was a holy man. He wore the ceremonial robes and mask of a *k'hartagh*—one who sought peace in maintaining the balance of predator and prey. They were common enough in Klingon nature preserves. The ceremonial combat Worf had just undertaken was based in part on a belief system of endless cycles in which the hunter and the hunted traded places. The *k'hartaghan* offered themselves up to nature as prey in order to return as predators. Provided a predator could be found which could defeat them.

Though Worf carried a knife, he would not have used it against the *krencha,* as that would be a violation of the balance. But what had the *k'hartagh* meant about overkill? That was a military term, out of place in the forest.

"Who are you?" Worf demanded, keeping his confusion hidden.

The *k'hartagh* made no move. His intent was impossible to read through the silvery purple and brown camouflage robes he wore. Even his eyes were shielded from view by the carved wood slit eyeshields he wore, and the cloth mask that hung from them.

"That is not important," the *k'hartagh* said in the Warrior's Tongue. "You are Worf, son of Mogh."

Worf's eyes widened with surprise. He growled softly. His

retreat to this preserve had been confidential. He had a career in Starfleet to consider. And some of the more ancient Klingon ceremonies were not ones of which Starfleet might approve.

"Do not make me repeat myself," Worf warned.

The *k'hartagh*'s hands moved behind his robes, drawing something from his back. Then in one fluid movement, sliding one foot forward while throwing his robe aside, the *k'hartagh* took a stylized pose which Worf recognized as the position of Heaven's Centered Balance, First Level. And in his hands, the *k'hartagh* held a gleaming *bat'telh.*

Worf blinked despite himself. He slowly realized that the *k'hartagh*'s move and pose were part of the *raLk'jo bat'telh* discipline—an ancient school of martial combat that had not been practiced in the Klingon Empire for almost a century. The *k'hartagh*'s age notwithstanding, Worf did recognize that the difficult First-Level move had been perfectly executed.

Faced with such an ancient, stylized form of battle with the distinctive, crescent-shaped weapon, whose name meant "blade of honor," Worf dismissed the possibility that the *k'hartagh* intended the display as a provocative gesture. From his study of history, Worf knew that warriors of the *raLk'jo* discipline viewed the *bat'telh* largely as a ceremonial weapon.

Worf lowered his knife and assumed a nonconfrontational stance. "I have never met a master of the *raLk'jo* discipline," he said respectfully.

"Is that why you face me with a coward's posture?" the *k'hartagh* said with an inflection of disdain.

Worf felt his grip tighten on his knife. "Do you wield the *bat'telh* in other than a ceremonial demonstration of your discipline?" Worf asked.

"If I have to, I will kill you with it," the *k'hartagh* calmly replied.

Worf instinctively bared his teeth, appalled by the *k'hartagh*'s lack of respect for an ancient school of combat.

"Control yourself," the *k'hartagh* said in response to Worf's expression. "I'm not interested in butchering you where you stand."

His arm shifted again behind his robe. Then Worf marvelled as, one-handed, he brought out a second *bat'telh,* flipped it around, and threw it to stick into the ground a meter in front of Worf.

"Does that ease the sting of my insults?" the *k'hartagh* asked.

Worf straightened and slid his *d'k tahg* back into its scabbard. The *bat'telh* was not a plaything. The *k'hartagh* was insane.

"I will not fight you," Worf said. "It is clear you do not know what you are doing."

Again, the *k'hartagh* slipped his hand inside his robe. When it withdrew, he held a disruptor. "I need answers," he said. "And how can I be sure you're telling me the truth, if I haven't beaten you in combat?"

Worf snorted at the *k'hartagh*'s audacity. Was that what this was about? He expected to *defeat* a Klingon in combat so that he would answer questions truthfully?

"Go away," Worf said. In the surrounding forest, he could hear the wingbeats of scavengers approaching. It would be dishonorable if he did not dress the *krencha* before sunset and take measures to preserve its meat. And the shadows were already lengthening.

The *k'hartagh* extended his arm, aiming the disruptor at Worf. It was a new model, Worf saw. Government-issue. He found it curious that such an advanced energy weapon was in the possession of one trained in such an old way of combat.

"Fight me," the *k'hartagh* said, "or die without honor."

"There is no honor in fighting the insane," Worf growled.

The disruptor's golden beam punched a hole in the ground five centimeters in front of Worf's feet, sending a billow of dust and smoke into the Klingon's eyes.

"There is no honor in dying without combat," the *k'hartagh* replied.

Worf's eyes narrowed. "Very well. But when I defeat you, you must answer *my* questions."

The *k'hartagh* stepped back as Worf approached the *bat'telh* imbedded in the ground. "*If* you defeat me," the *k'hartagh* said.

Worf drew the *bat'telh* and hefted it in both hands. The balance was good, though he sensed it was a mass-produced model. Something of offworld manufacture, for no Klingon would dream of owning a *bat'telh* that was not handcrafted and thus imbued with its maker's spirit. Worf's own, which he had pulled from the ruins of the *Enterprise,* had been in his family for ten generations.

The *k'hartagh* stepped sideways, presenting his weapon in the ancient pose called the Dragon's Passage from Thought to Action, Third Level. As Worf understood the ancient discipline, it was meant to be a conservative opening, showing respect for his opponent. . . . It was not what Worf would have expected from an insane holy man.

Remembering his history tapes, Worf countered the *k'hartagh's* presentation with the Position of Unwavering Determination, Third Level. In the symbolism of this specific *bat'telh* discipline, Worf thus signified he would not give in to idle threats.

The *k'hartagh* stepped forward, now facing Worf directly, angling his *bat'telh* gracefully through the arc of the Gentle Cut, to end in the Repose of the Dragon's Teeth, First Level. Worf was again surprised.

The underlying philosophy of the *raLk'jo* discipline required that no presentation could be made unless the warrior had perfected that move in combat. If the *k'hartagh* had indeed mastered the Repose of the Dragon's Teeth, then Worf realized he was in trouble. The Dragon's Teeth was an especially savage attack, and Worf was not certain if his own defenses were adequate to deflect the attack without fatal injury to the *k'hartagh.*

Knowing he had waited a heartbeat too long, Worf countered with the point-forward pose of the Mountain's Scorn, Fourth Level. In that way, he told the *k'hartagh* he did not believe the holy man's expertise matched the boldness of his posturing. And making the presentation with his hands in the *raLk'jo's* simple, Fourth Level alignment implied that Worf believed the *k'hartagh* could be beaten at that juvenile level—a grievous insult.

But though it was impossible to read the *k'hartagh*'s expression through his cloth and wooden mask, Worf did see the amused nod his opponent made. Since there was nothing amusing about the insult Worf had made, for the first time he had the sudden suspicion that the insane *k'hartagh* wasn't even Klingon.

And then the *k'hartagh* attacked.

Even as the crescent blade of the *k'hartagh*'s *bat'telh* sliced through the air, Worf recognized that it was not a killing blow. Perhaps the holy man had been telling the truth when he said he merely wanted Worf to answer questions.

Rather than deflect the blow, Worf sidestepped with a modern evasive step, moving his own weapon out of the other's path, thus avoiding any chance the *k'hartagh* could turn his own movement against him.

But the *k'hartagh* had anticipated him.

His blade dipped to the side, then followed Worf in a move so swift it had begun before Worf had even made his own decision to act.

The *k'hartagh*'s *bat'telh* caught Worf's and slid along its upper length in a spray of sparks, almost succeeding in wrenching it out of Worf's startled grip when the two curved tips met and momentarily locked.

Worf reacted instinctively, pulling his weapon in close to his chest. He pivoted in place, extending the blade in midspin to bring it into slashing position, fully expecting to meet the *k'hartagh*'s blade in a defensive block.

But when Worf had spun completely around, his blade

slipped through empty air. Once again the *k'hartagh* had anticipated him and had ducked, rising the instant Worf's blade had passed, swinging his own point first against Worf's arm.

Worf cried out, more in surprise than in pain as the slick blade sliced through his triceps as if his flesh offered no more resistance than a cloud.

He wrenched his *bat'telh* back into a forward defensive pose, with no attempt at fighting within the bounds of the *k'hartagh*'s discipline, expecting a savage follow-up and preparing to block.

But the *k'hartagh* had stepped back, breaking the rhythm of his attack. He held his *bat'telh* straight forward in the Whelpling's Lunge, Tenth Level. In the *raLk'jo,* it was one of the first poses taught to children. Thus, in a battle such as this, there was no deadlier insult.

"Will you yield?" the *k'hartagh* asked.

Worf bellowed a Klingon death cry and lunged forward, *bat'telh* whistling through the air.

The *k'hartagh* had not been ready for the ferocity of Worf's attack. Still, he skillfully sidestepped, leaving his weapon in place to deflect Worf's blow. But Worf again did the unthinkable by releasing one hand from his weapon and striking out at the *k'hartagh.* Worf's nails raked his attacker's throat and chin, attempting to grab the ceremonial mask and rip it off.

But the *k'hartagh*'s leg came up in a completely unexpected Vulcan defensive strike, adding to Worf's momentum and making him slam into the ground.

As Worf pushed himself to his knees, he was momentarily shocked when he looked to the side and saw that the approaching *k'hartagh* wore trousers and boots beneath his robes. But then, he also carried a disruptor. Clearly, the *k'hartagh* was not what he appeared to be.

And then Worf had no more time for observations as he felt the *k'hartagh*'s *bat'telh* smash him on the back of his skull.

Worf wondered if it were just his head that fell forward as the forest floor flew up at him. No *bat'telh* master could have missed such a simple decapitation blow when his enemy's back was turned.

Worf's last thought flew to the *Enterprise* slicing through the atmosphere of Veridian III. And then, like the noble Klingon warrior he was, Worf, son of Mogh, embraced his death as *K'ajii* demanded and fell unrepentant into darkness.

ELEVEN

Thirty minutes later, Worf awoke with a hideous headache.

His arms and legs were bound by rope, tying him securely to the rough purple trunk of an *arhksamm* tree.

Worf shook his head. It was a bad idea. But the sudden increase in pain made him even more alert. And even angrier. From the lump on the back of his head he could tell he had been hit with the *flat* of his attacker's *bat'telh!* It was the ultimate act of mockery. What a teacher did when instructing a novice.

Then he smelled something burning. Wood. And . . . *krencha* meat.

Worf turned his head. The *k'hartagh* was crouched by a fire. On a purple branch, he had skewered the *krencha's* gizzard. A delicacy. Worf's mouth watered despite his outrage.

The *k'hartagh* glanced over at Worf. Saw he was awake. Got to his feet and walked over to him.

Worf glowered at him.

The *k'hartagh,* still in robes and mask, tore a strip from the gizzard and offered it to Worf. Juices flowed down from the punctured organ, dripping onto the forest floor. The scent made Worf ravenous. The cooking had restored it to body temperature—it would be the same as eating right after the kill.

But Worf turned his head. "You did not kill me," he complained.

"That wasn't the point," the *k'hartagh* said. "I need you to answer my questions. Truthfully."

Worf stared back at his attacker.

His attacker waved the strip of gizzard before his face. Then he sighed. "Are you going to deny the *krencha* its reward by wasting its death? What about the hunter's bargain?"

Worf clenched his jaw. The alien *k'hartagh* was right. The flesh of the beast he had killed must be eaten, or else the death had been wasted. But the way the *k'hartagh* explained himself . . . something was wrong.

"You are not Klingon," Worf said accusingly.

"Eat," his attacker replied. He held the gizzard strip close to Worf, quickly snapping his fingers back as Worf bit into the meat.

It was delicious. Worf could feel the power of the *krencha* surge into his body. For an instant, the *arhksamm* tree to which he was tied was nothing more than a twig. The ropes that held him, mere threads.

"We can be finished in a few minutes," the *k'hartagh* said.

Worf frowned at his use of "minutes." That was an Earth term.

The *k'hartagh* studied Worf in silence for a few moments, as if giving Worf a chance to say something. When it was clear that Worf wouldn't, he began.

"Where is Jean-Luc Picard?"

Worf hid his surprise. He replied by asking, "Where did a human learn *bat'telh* of the *raLk'jo* discipline?"

The *k'hartagh* rocked back on his heels and held up a cautionary finger, hidden in gloves. "Know your enemy," he said.

Worf frowned. What was that supposed to mean? "Klingons and humans are not enemies."

The *k'hartagh* angled his head as if surprised. Worf didn't know what to make of it.

"Since when?" the *k'hartagh* asked.

For Worf, the interrogation was taking on a surreal aspect. He momentarily forgot his shame and discomfort. "Who are you?" he demanded.

Again, the *k'hartagh* seemed to hesitate.

"Jean-Luc Picard. Where is he?"

Worf took a deep breath. "I am a Starfleet officer. I will not—"

"What?"

Worf blinked at the *k'hartagh.*

The *k'hartagh* held a hand to the side of his head, as if he felt the same pain there that Worf did.

"If you are in trouble," Worf said warily. "Perhaps I can help you."

But when the *k'hartagh* spoke again, his voice was harsher, withdrawn. "Where is Jean-Luc Picard?"

"Why do you want to know?" Worf asked, now genuinely puzzled by the entire situation. His thoughts of honor and death receded as he studied the stranger. His Starfleet training claimed him in their place.

The *k'hartagh*'s hand shot out and grabbed Worf by the neck. "I have to kill him!"

That was all Worf had to hear.

In a sudden flush of rage—his immediate reaction to a threat against his commanding officer—Worf pushed against the ropes that bound him to the tree.

The tree trunk creaked.

The *k'hartagh*'s hand tightened on Worf's throat.

Worf's blood-smeared and bared chest swelled as he drew a mighty breath to roar.

But the *k'hartagh*'s hand unerringly found both sets of carotid arteries. He squeezed, blocking the flow of blood so that Worf's voice was effectively silenced.

Worf saw dark stars flicker at the edges of his vision. Knew he had only seconds of consciousness remaining. Felt his wounded arm burst through the rope and fly ahead of him to smash the *k'hartagh* across his face.

The *k'hartagh* flew backward.

Worf struggled against the remainder of his ropes. The ones tied across his chest were unbroken. He clawed at them, only then noticing he had the *k'hartagh*'s ceremonial mask tangled in his fingers.

He looked across at the *k'hartagh* as he rose from the ground.

Worf felt his mouth drop open, all elements of *K'ajii* driven from his mind, so great was his shock.

He *recognized* his attacker.

Even with the bloody streaks that Worf's raking nails had left, his face was a perfect match for that on the history tapes Worf had scanned after hearing of Picard's encounter on Veridian III, when the *Enterprise* met her death.

"What are you staring at?" his attacker snapped.

Worf couldn't think what to say.

His attacker was a dead man. A dead man twice over.

And a hero from the past. Starfleet's past.

James T. Kirk.

"Where is Picard?" Kirk demanded.

In his confusion, Worf's voice was uneven. "I . . . don't know." All he could do was stare at Kirk. At the impossibility of Kirk.

Kirk stared at the Klingon, as if searching for something in his eyes.

Then Worf began thinking like a warrior again and tugged at the ropes across his chest.

Kirk pulled out his disruptor, adjusted its setting.

But Worf refused to go quietly. He strained against his ropes. One snapped. A second. He snarled as he gathered his strength. To stand. To lunge forward and—

—the disruptor beam took the Klingon in midleap.

Kirk did not step back as the Klingon's body crumpled to the forest floor at his feet.

Despite the pain that had burned into him as he had made the decision, Kirk had set the disruptor to stun, not to disintegrate.

Kirk knelt by the motionless body. Turned the face upright to face him.

"You recognized me."

The Klingon remained silent, eyes closed, his breathing rough and erratic.

Kirk released the Klingon's massive head, letting it fall back into the dirt.

A part of him wanted to kill this alien monster. To crush the life from it. Kirk knew such an act would bring him intense pleasure.

But for a reason he could not articulate, he resisted.

Instead, he stood, reached to his belt for a communicator, flipped it.

Then stared at it as nothing happened.

He tried again to flip open its top. Then he remembered. The device wasn't meant to open. He pressed the activation control.

"Go ahead," a disembodied voice said.

"I'm finished down here."

"Did the Klingon know anything?"

"No."

"Is he dead?"

Kirk stared at the Klingon's body, lying helpless before

him. He winced as he felt a sharp stab. He longed for Salatrel's caress. For her to take these troubled thoughts from his mind and make everything better.

But still he wondered why he needed to have those thoughts taken away by someone else. Shouldn't that be his responsibility? When had he relinquished it?

But the disruptor was heavy on his belt, so easy to use.

To destroy the enemy.

Starfleet.

The Federation.

Klingons were the enemy, too. He knew that without Salatrel's having to tell him.

But then, why did he find it so hard to understand why a Klingon would be part of Starfleet? If both were enemies, why did that strike him as so wrong?

He shook his head to clear it of confusion.

"Is the Klingon dead?" the voice persisted.

Kirk put his hand on his disruptor. Drew it. Set it to full disruption.

Aimed it.

It was the easy way to get rid of the confusion. The pain. Simply press the stud and it would go away, dissolving like the flesh of the Klingon at his feet.

What could be easier?

Kirk made his decision.

He pressed the stud.

The tree behind the Klingon bloomed with a wavery light, then vanished into quantum mist.

"He's dead," Kirk said.

Sharp pain still attacked him as he voiced the lie. But somehow, it hurt less than he had expected. Perhaps the pain could be controlled, at least in part, without Salatrel's touch.

And if so, what other secrets had she hidden from him? What other lies had she told?

"Stand by for beam-out," the voice said.

Kirk stared down at the Klingon lying silent at his feet.

The Klingon opened his eyes.

"Who am I?" Kirk asked.

But before the answer could reach him, the transporter beam found him and beamed him away.

TWELVE

Starbase 804 was gone.

Through the low-lying haze that blanketed the devastated site, the broken ridges of injected foundations traced out the plan of the buildings and the walkways that had once existed. Tattered clothing and fabric fluttered across the stripped ground like dying animals, snagging on snapped-off pipes and power conduits. Here and there, crumbled bricks of silicon and twisted sheets of duraplast formed random accumulations of debris. Apparently neither substance was of much use to the Borg.

Picard gazed over those ruins. Seventy-eight people had been stationed here—humans, Vulcans, a family of Klingon archaeologists, children, pets, dreams.

All gone.

Absorbed into the monstrous cube that had arisen in the center of the base, towering thirty meters above them, ominous and all-devouring. The alien graveyard of the raw materials assimilated from the starbase.

In only three days.

"This makes no sense," Beverly said. Her voice betrayed the stunning sense of loss they both felt.

She stood beside Picard in the twilight, both still in the black commando armor they had worn since their arrival. Weinlein and the rest of her team had determined that the Borg here did not view two humans together as a group worthy of assimilation, provided they kept one hundred meters distant from any other member of the team.

The long, red rays of New Titan's sun hit the starbase dedication marker lying half-buried in the ground at Picard's feet. The Starfleet delta brought back to Picard the image of the insignia on the cairn of rocks he had built for James T. Kirk.

The sun had set on a legend of Starfleet the day Picard had buried Kirk. Now he felt as if the extinction of Starbase 804 marked the end for the Federation as well. Because the Borg that had been at work here were unlike any Starfleet had faced before: Starfleet's greatest fear had become real.

There *were* indeed other branches of the Borg collective active in the galaxy. And Picard knew all too well that whatever defenses worked against one branch would not necessarily work against another.

"It *must* make sense," Picard said, though in his heart he did not feel any conviction. "They are machines. Ruled by logic. What they are doing *has* to fit their programmed purpose to survive."

He felt Beverly look at him. With the professional gaze of a physician. For three days, he and Beverly, and Weinlein's team of specialists, had had to watch as Starbase 804 melted before them. For three days, Picard had had to fight the overwhelming pull of the groupmind, never really knowing if it were truly there, or simply a manifestation of the secret doubts he harbored.

For the same three days, he had been unable to carry out his mission.

Because there was no Borg vessel here to recover.

Picard felt the vibration of the communicator in his armor. The modified versions developed for the commandos were designed to be silent in the field, and experiments on the second day had confirmed the Borg were not interested in the commandos' ground communicator signals. Weinlein, however, still used untraceable microbursts to report to the *Monitor* in polar orbit.

Picard touched the contact surface at his neck. "Picard here."

It was Weinlein. She was on the other side of the Borg structure, a kilometer away. The other two commandos were hidden somewhere else among what few ruins remained.

Weinlein began speaking rapidly, wasting neither time nor words. "Krul and Beyer have completed the scan of the cube. Absolutely no indication of a propulsion system. No field coils. No warp core. Not even any propellant."

"That proves my point. They *are* waiting to be retrieved," Picard said. That had been Krul's theory as well.

But Weinlein still didn't agree. "By what? Anything that could pick up that cube by tractor or by transporter could have lifted the starbase out of here in minutes. Just like Jouret IV. Why send down an assimilation crew if they've got a vessel that could do the same work in a thousandth of the time?"

Picard frowned and glanced at Beverly. She tightened her lips in silent commiseration. They both knew Weinlein was committed to her conclusion that they had made contact with a group of Borg who had somehow been separated from whatever branch of the collective they were part of. The team leader had reasoned that however this orphan branch of Borg had come to New Titan, their actions against Starbase 804 were only their blind response to their programming. Like all Borg, they were compelled to assimilate raw material and life-forms to serve the collective. And when they had reached the limit of what the starbase had been able to offer, they had simply retreated to their cube and entered their sleep mode.

The commando leader compared the Borg to worker ants in an ant farm, who would continue to build their network of tunnels, even if they had no queen to serve. Thus, in her opinion, the primary objective of this mission could not be achieved. Without a real Borg vessel to capture, Weinlein maintained there was nothing Starfleet could learn here.

But Picard felt just the opposite. He knew, as no one else did, that if any Borg were cut off from their branch of the collective, their nature absolutely dictated they make every effort to rejoin it.

The material at Starbase 804 had included two runabouts and six shuttles. But their propulsion systems hadn't been incorporated intact into the cube.

Because the cube didn't need to go anywhere.

Because something was coming to retrieve it.

"You and I have been through this before," Picard said.

"And I was willing to wait to see what the Borg would do. To give you the benefit of the doubt, Captain. But I have no more doubt. All the Borg in that cube have been in sleep mode for more than three hours. There are no further signs of construction or modification. Therefore, in accordance with our orders, we will proceed with our secondary mission."

Picard had known it would come to this. He was ready, if not enthusiastic. "Understood," he said, without further argument.

"Rendezvous in fifteen minutes, behind the barracks wall. Weinlein out."

Picard took a last look at the sun on the horizon.

Beverly tried to reassure him. "This will be easier, Jean-Luc. We won't need the interface. Only you."

But Picard didn't believe that either. "They are waiting for retrieval. And when their vessel comes and finds its assimilation crew is gone, captured by Starfleet, the result could be . . . most calamitous."

"But the *Monitor* is still here. And it was designed to fight the Borg." For an instant, despite her words, Beverly's voice wavered.

Picard knew why. He looked into her eyes. But all he saw was the flames of war. Of destruction. "At Wolf 359, Starfleet lost thirty-nine starships. Eleven thousand beings perished. *That* is what it means to fight the Borg. Whatever Commander Shelby's intentions are—one lone starship, no matter how well designed, will not even slow them down."

Beverly met his gaze directly, but Picard could see she did not want to say what she was going to say next.

"At Wolf 359, the Borg knew each weakness in our ships and shields. They knew our tactics and our weapons' capabilities and limitations. It was as if they could read our minds."

"They could," Picard said. He would not hide from the truth, no matter how harsh. "Mine."

Beverly took hold of both of Picard's arms, to make him understand.

"You were *not* responsible, Jean-Luc! The Borg sought you out to be their Speaker. Their liaison. You couldn't resist them. No one could."

Picard felt his jaw clench. Felt emotions he had buried far too long rush up in him like magma, seeking the violence of release. "I *tried* to resist them, but . . ." Then the next words froze in his throat. Words he had never dared speak before. But words he could no longer hold back.

"What if I didn't resist them *enough?"*

Beverly's mouth curved down in confusion. "What?" She released her hold on him.

How long had he held this secret? Picard didn't know. It had been four years since the Borg assault on Earth. But his terrible knowledge of what he believed to be his own personal failure seemed to have been with him all his life. Poisoning all his memories.

"When I was . . . taken . . ." Picard felt what was almost a wave of relief pass through him as he finally felt himself begin to say the words that might expose him for what he feared he was, what he had been. Not even his Starfleet debriefers had heard everything that had happened to him at the hands of the Borg. Counsellor Troi had known he was hiding something. Had tried to get him to talk about it over the years. But he had always resisted. Until now. When the possibility of failure rose up before him again.

And there had never been room for failure in his life. He would not allow it.

"When I was taken, the Borg . . . they put me in . . . an assimilator. A chair. A frame. Something that . . . grew from the wall of their ship. There were straps, or metal bands. Something held me there, physically.

"I fought them the whole time. I tried to get out. To get up. But they were all around me. Simply staring at me. And then . . . before . . . the process began . . . and I gave up. . . ." Picard kept his eyes fixed on the horizon, almost invisible now. "Do you understand, Beverly? Before they assimilated me, I stopped fighting."

Beverly stared at him as she struggled to comprehend what Picard was confessing.

". . . you were in their ship. We know they have drugs. Sonic and visual brainwave inducers. They wouldn't *let* you fight. It was no longer your decision to make."

But Picard shook his head. "There were no drugs. No inducers. There were just Borg. Watching. Waiting. Letting me sense the . . . presence of the collective."

Picard stared into the darkness enveloping the desolate ruins before him. Like a web of shadows, spun by the monster at its center. The cube. The Borg. Enveloping everything.

"Jean-Luc, the Borg collective is a machine-based, subspace communications system. How could you possibly sense it before they had put implants in you?"

"How does Deanna sense emotions?" he asked the darkness. "In their ship, in the face of so many of them, I knew. I felt. It—them—their overwhelming . . . presence. And I somehow watched *with* them, through them, at myself, remaining in that frame, as the machinery descended." He closed his eyes, seeing it all anew. "The blades. The needles. I felt them cut into me!" He couldn't breathe. "And I didn't *fight* them. Because . . . I *wanted* to belong. . . . I wanted so much to belong. . . ."

Picard felt Beverly's arms draw him close to her. His cheek brushed the hard surface of her armor, her soft fragrant hair. Her hand moved from his armored back to stroke his neck, the back of his head.

"It's all right," she said. "None of it was real. The Borg manipulated your mind, made you one of them, so you could do nothing *except* want to be part of the collective."

He recoiled from her support, forced his breathing to become normal, squared his shoulders, and shook his head once. "No."

Beverly's voice sharpened. "If you insist on having this argument, let me tell you that I *am* going to win it. Because you're too close to what happened to understand it." She held up her hand to stop Picard before he could protest. "But right now, we have a mission. And we will perform that mission. And we will beam back to the *Monitor* with our prisoners. And then I'm going to take you into the holosuite and . . . well, never mind what I'm going to do. But you're going to feel a great deal better."

She was so intent, so like the Beverly of old, that Picard almost smiled.

"I'm sure I will," he said. "I do already."

This time, Beverly shook her head. "You never could lie to me, Jean-Luc. But the point is, you were not responsible for your actions as Locutus. Any more than you'd be responsible if I gave you . . . ten milliliters of cordrazine."

Picard tugged on the waist of his armor in a futile attempt

to straighten his cumbersome chestplate. He tried to lighten the moment. "If I have to live in this outfit much longer, I might take you up on that, Doctor."

Beverly smiled at him as if the real Jean-Luc were back. But Picard knew even her relief was a charade. The only thing that had returned was his self-control. As long as he didn't have to use the interface, surely self-control would be more than sufficient to capture ten Borg and return to the *Monitor.*

"Time to play soldier?" Beverly asked.

Picard appreciated her more in that moment than he ever had. For trying to set right what she never could.

"Thank you," he said.

Beverly regarded him seriously. "Save it for the holosuite."

Picard nodded, not even daring to think that far ahead.

Once again, it was time to engage the Borg.

THIRTEEN

☆

Kirk held his dying wife in his arms. Over the evacuation alarms, he heard his children screaming, caught behind the sealed doors of his quarters.

"Help them," Kalinara sobbed. Half her face was ripped away by the cluster explosives that had been transported throughout the *Talon of Peace.* Her green blood smeared Kirk's hands and arms, bubbled at the corner of her torn lips. But still she thought only of the children. *Their* children.

"I can't leave you," he choked.

"For our children," Kalinara murmured, fading quickly. "For our future . . ."

He felt her grip loosen on his hand. Heard the terrible rasp of her last breath as it escaped her seared lungs.

The ship shuddered all around him. The cowardly attack continued. One thousand colonists aboard Kirk's ship faced death.

"Father!" screamed the piteously young voice behind the door. *"He's here! He's go—"*

Kirk staggered to his feet as his child's voice stopped midword. He stumbled to the sealed door as the deck in his quarters lurched beneath his feet.

The artificial gravity generators couldn't last much longer. And after they went, the structural integrity field would fail.

He could picture his double-hulled ship collapsing in space. Its quantum core spiraling out of containment. The explosion that would result, one dying star among so many.

Everything would be lost.

But it wasn't lost yet.

Kirk joined his hands together and swung them down against on the door, trying to jar the backup battery circuit. It had to open. It *had* to release his children. There might be time to reach an escape pod. He could carry Kalinara. The medics could stabilize her. It might not be too late. It couldn't be. He wouldn't let it be.

His fists bled as he pounded on the unmoving door.

"Lora!" he shouted. *"Tranalak!"* Tears streamed down his face. He smelled smoke. Somewhere belowdecks he heard a rumbling explosion. The sirens wailed in unison.

His wife had just died. His children were dying. And all because of—

The door trembled beneath his blows.

He drew back. Hope soared within him. There was a chance.

But then the door ground open.

He was here.

The monster. With Kirk's children.

Five-year-old Tranalak lay sprawled at his feet, dark eyes staring up, lifeless. Eight-year-old Lora was held aloft in the his grip, her tiny feet kicking and flailing as she struggled to free herself.

The monster grinned at Kirk as his hand flew across the child's throat with a glint of Federation steel.

Then he discarded her small body, letting it fall awkwardly to the deck—

Kirk flung himself at the monster before him.

Kirk flung himself at Picard.

His hands were talons as they sought Picard's throat.

But the monster threw back his head, laughing, laughing—

—even as Kirk's hands grasped in vain at his fading body.

Even as Kirk fell alone to the floor. No longer a deck.

The shuddering stopped.

The sirens faded.

Kirk lay gasping on the black floor, marked with its grid of yellow lines.

Alone with his hate. His rage. His pain.

"Do you remember now?" Salatrel asked.

Kirk pushed himself up, still trembling. He stared at his hands, unbloodied, unmarked.

"Your wife?" Salatrel said. "Your children?"

Kirk stood up, body aching, out of breath.

He looked past Salatrel at the entry arch behind her. At the controls to the side. The closed door in the center.

"What is this place?" he gasped.

The Romulan woman frowned. She aimed a tricorder at him.

Kirk knew it was a tricorder, though it seemed too small.

"A holodeck," she said as she adjusted controls on her device. "One of the few useful contributions the Federation has made to the galaxy."

Kirk struggled to make sense of it. Some terms seemed so familiar. But the context was so wrong.

"But this is a . . . Romulan ship?" he asked.

Salatrel stepped closer. He could sense her annoyance.

"I have nothing to hide from you," she said. "You are on the *Avatar of Tomed.* It is a *D'deridex*-class starship. Just as was your own *Talon of Peace.*"

"Starship . . . ?" Kirk said, grasping at the familiar word. "I had a starship, didn't I?"

Salatrel's frown eased. "You *are* remembering."

"And my wife and children?"

"Killed. Five years ago. When Picard led his cowardly attack under color of truce."

"Picard," Kirk repeated, hearing the sound of it in his own mind. He was certain he knew that name. It was from his past. But then, why didn't the context fit?

Salatrel glanced up from her tricorder. Her eyes narrowed. "Do you doubt me?" she asked.

"Why would I?" Kirk replied. "You saved my life."

Salatrel stepped closer, put a hand to his face. "Just as you saved mine," she said.

Kirk felt his heartrate slow as he gazed into Salatrel's eyes. "Will I remember that, too?"

"The doctors say you will eventually recover all your memories." Salatrel replaced her tricorder on her belt. She removed her padd. "You will be restored."

Kirk nodded. He was impatient for that to happen.

Salatrel brushed her lips against his. He felt the electricity of her contact even as he heard her fingers tap on her padd.

"Tell me about the Klingon," she said.

"Klingon bastard!" Kirk spat. "You killed my son!" He gasped and stepped back, trying to lose the distraction of Salatrel's presence. Where had that thought come from? Those words?

"No," Salatrel corrected him, sharply. "*Picard* killed your son. *And* your wife and daughter. The Klingon was his chief of security."

Kirk thought back to the forest. To the Klingon. Klingons were the enemy. At least, he thought, they had been. Once. And he *had* had a son. Who had died. Because of . . .

A wave of sudden pain and anxiety shot through him.

"The Klingon," Salatrel repeated. "Tell me."

"But I already have," Kirk said. He forced the pain from his body. He knew what battle injuries felt like. But this ache throughout his entire body was different. He didn't know where it came from.

"I need to hear it again. What did he tell you?"

The pain increased.

"Nothing," Kirk said, wincing.

Not in words, he thought.

Salatrel grabbed his chin. Forced him to look at her. "You can't hide anything from me," she said.

"Why would I?" Kirk answered. The words felt programmed into him. He said them, but he resisted them, trying to find the web that connected all the turmoil in his mind.

He knew Picard.

He knew Klingons and Romulans. Starfleet and the hated Federation.

He knew the torment of the death of his son.

But Salatrel? And holodecks? And a wife dying when a colony fleet was destroyed by the *Enterprise?*

Where were the connections?

He held Salatrel's gaze.

Where was the truth?

The only thing he was certain of was that he did not see it in Salatrel's eyes.

But he had seen it in the Klingon's.

There was a pattern here, maddeningly out of reach.

If only he could speak with . . .

An image came to him. A tall man, strong features. Pointed

ears. But not a Romulan. A Vulcan. And at his side. An older man. Hands behind his back. An easy smile. A human from . . .

"What is it? Tell me," Salatrel demanded.

Kirk frowned. If he was a Romulan patriot, a human dedicated to Romulan peace, had married a Romulan woman, had two children with her, had become a hero of the revolution against the evil domination of the Federation . . .

Why did he remember a Vulcan and a human as his . . . friends?

Where was his wife in his memories? And where was Salatrel, this woman who had been his lover for the past three years, fighting at his side?

Salatrel studied the padd she held. "You must tell me what you're thinking. You know I've always been here for you."

"I know," Kirk said. And even as the words formed on his lips, he knew they were false.

But Salatrel did not seem to recognize that. As if, despite all she had said, he did have some secrets that could be hidden from her.

"Would you like to know how we met?" she asked.

Kirk nodded.

Salatrel stepped away from him, back to the arch in the wall. Kirk followed. Watched as she tapped in commands on the controls. It seemed like a simple enough system.

"Computer," she said. "Run program Salatrel four." She turned to Kirk. "We arrive at Trilex in six hours," she said. She held up her padd. "Keep trying to remember . . . me."

Kirk held out his hand to touch her but she vanished from view, even as she touched another padd control.

He heard birds singing. Felt a warm breeze. Smelled the rich growth of a forest all around him.

He turned to see an Iowa vista. Gentle hills. Old trees towering into the summer sky, dappling the ground with the interplay of leaf shadow and sunbeams.

Kirk knew this place. It fit perfectly into the gaps, the cracks of his memories. His eyes widened at the wonder of it. The security of it.

Then he heard hoofbeats.

He wheeled, truly remembering the moment.

She rode for him, on a glorious mare, its coat gleaming in the sun and mane alive in the breeze.

He looked up at her, to see her smile. Antonia's smile as she . . .

No. Not Antonia.

Salatrel smiled back at him as she rode closer.

An automatic wave of pleasure coursed through him.

Even as he knew something was wrong.

Salatrel slipped from the horse's side, smiled at him, held out her hand.

"I'm with the peace mission," she said. "Salatrel, of Romulus."

"I don't remember this," Kirk said.

Salatrel moved into his arms, pressed herself against his body, held him tightly in the sunlight and the forest.

"It's all right," she said. "I do."

Then she kissed him.

For a moment, Kirk hesitated. Some of what he was experiencing was merely unknown. Some, he felt certain, was false. But somewhere at the core of this experience, he sensed elements of the truth.

All he had to do was sort one from the other.

But for now, the desire he felt as he held Salatrel in his arms again made rational thought almost impossible.

So he returned her kiss.

And surrendered—if not to her, then to the heat of the Iowa sunshine.

FOURTEEN

In the deepening twilight, Picard and Beverly crept across the broken ground toward the barracks wall.

The wall was a landmark in the ruined starbase, because, apart from the Borg cube a hundred meters distant, it was the largest structure remaining—a fractured plane of extruded silicon, less than two meters high at its tallest, running no more than ten meters side to side.

On the far side of the wall, closer to the cube, barracks beds and lockers were fused together, melted by whatever tool the Borg had used to extract the optical data network circuitry from the recreational computer system. The body of a young ensign in a duty uniform was half-buried in the rubble of another wall which had fallen completely.

From the pattern of damage the commando team had catalogued, Weinlein had concluded that the Borg had struck at night, spent at least four days "convincing" base personnel to willingly join the collective, and then had forcibly assimilated any who remained at large.

Picard tried not to think of what those four days had been like for the personnel of Starbase 804. He and Beverly had already been in transit, expecting to be stationed here during Starfleet's investigation of the outpost raids in this part of the frontier. What if they had arrived a week earlier? Or if the Borg had arrived a week later? It could all have been over by now, and he would have been back among—

"Get down!" Weinlein ordered.

Picard and Beverly dropped to the ground behind the wall. Weinlein, Krul, and Beyer were already crouched in position. Krul and Beyer looked as if they had just returned from Wrigley's Pleasure Planet, rested and calm. Weinlein was her usual, crisp self. Picard was irritated at his own frayed state. After three days of field rations and sleeping in armor, he felt anything but at his peak.

Weinlein jerked a finger at the tricorder mounted on her forearm. "Still no movement." She gave Picard a cold grin. "Fish in a barrel."

"You know my objections." Picard's tone matched Weinlein's own.

"Noted and logged," she confirmed. "But even if they're expecting some kind of mother ship to come for them, what are the odds that will happen in the next twenty minutes?"

"Why twenty minutes?" Picard asked. The idea of a timetable after all these days of waiting was unexpected. . . .

Weinlein pulled on her battle helmet. "Because that's how long this is going to take."

Beside her, Krul and Beyer snapped fresh power supplies into their phaser rifles.

"How many Borg are in there?" Beverly asked. As if it mattered.

"Forty-two humanoids," Weinlein said as she sealed the rim of her helmet to her armor. "Three of the multilimbed construction units. One scuttler."

"And two canines," Krul added. His smile looked almost feral.

"We only need ten of the humanoids," Weinlein went on, ignoring Krul. "Shelby's people say that's double the minimum required to maintain a groupmind when they're cut off from their branch of the collective."

"I know the theory," Picard said. He pulled his own helmet from his back harness. "But what does Shelby say the rest of the Borg will do as we . . . make off with their fellows?"

"The commander says that once they see you, they'll be trying to make contact with Locutus. That's why you'll be front and center. You'll be verbally activating all their internal diagnostic subroutines, while we collect our ten."

Picard shrugged away from Beverly's touch. Concern again flared in him that Weinlein's tactics might prove too simplistic. "You saw what happened when I attempted that with the unfortunate woman who stopped me on our first day here. I only delayed her for a few minutes at best."

Weinlein ignored his protest as she checked her tricorder. "The *Monitor* will be overhead in seven minutes, thirty seconds." She held up an emergency transporter beacon armband. "While you delay the Borg response, my people and I will slap these on our ten targets, then the *Monitor* beams us all out. The Borg will stay in stasis till we hit Starbase 324 and Commander Shelby takes them off our hands."

Picard tugged his helmet on. He looked forward to taking action at last, though he knew he also was reaching the point of invoking the authority Starfleet had given him to take control over the mission. "You obviously don't think the Borg will activate their shields."

Weinlein put her gloved hand on her visor. "Not if Locutus tells them not to." She snapped the opaque visor down and her face disappeared. Now she and Krul and Beyer were little more than machines themselves.

"We start forward in one minute," Weinlein said. This time Picard heard her on the speaker in his helmet. "Krul and Beyer go first and take up position by the main airlock. Then Picard and I sweep in."

"What about me?" Beverly asked. She tugged her own helmet into position, sealing it to her armor.

"After all four of us are inside, you take up position immediately outside the airlock. If all goes well, you just sit tight till the *Monitor* locks on."

"And if all doesn't go well?" Beverly asked.

"Whatever else happens, Picard has to come out."

Beverly snapped her own visor down.

Picard stared at the four dark apparitions before him. One lone starship to stand up against a Borg vessel? Three commandos to go after more than forty Borg? What was Starfleet thinking? What was *Shelby* thinking?

Or was it not thought on Starfleet's part, but desperation?

Picard put his hand on his own visor. It was dark enough now that he would need night vision to make the run to the Borg cube. "Permit me one last word of caution," he said. "Once we're inside, no fast movements until we're certain the Borg have identified us as a threat."

Weinlein's helmet angled in amusement. "Captain, if we move fast enough, they won't have *time* to identify us. Fifteen seconds." She held her finger over a forearm control. "Microburst signal to the *Monitor* in three . . . two . . . one . . . mark!"

She pressed the control, sending an untraceable coded message to the starship, setting it in motion to be in position for the emergency beam-out.

"Stand by, Captain. We go in eight . . . seven . . ."

Picard began to pull down his visor.

A double flash of blue light flickered at his side.

"Resistance is futile," said the Borg.

Picard pulled Beverly away, behind him, as he turned to face the two Borg that had materialized two meters away with all the suddenness the Borg transporter was known for.

Both cybernetic creatures had arms that ended in the glowing discharge nodes of antimatter streamers. At fine focus, the devices were good for careful dissection of scrap and salvage. At wide beam, they were more destructive than phasers.

The nodes swung to Krul and Beyer, whose phaser rifles were already trained on the Borg.

And even as Weinlein yelled at Picard to take off his

helmet, Picard stepped forward to confront the enemy, helmet in hand. "No!" he commanded.

The Borg instantly looked at him, instantly froze.

Their red sensor lasers converged on his face.

"Locutus?" one said.

Then both Borg dissolved in a slow pulse of quantum mist.

"Frequency one used," Beyer barked over the comm circuit.

"Engaging random frequency selection," Krul responded.

The individual force fields that protected combat-ready Borg constantly adapted to whatever weaponry was trained against them. No one phaser frequency could be used more than once, because the force fields around every other Borg in the collective would immediately change to repel that frequency.

Weinlein grabbed Picard's arm. "Let's move it! We need those prisoners!"

But Picard pulled back. "They know we're here."

Weinlein snapped up her visor. Picard could just make out her lean features in the soft glow of the status lights on her in-helmet display screen. "They'll be confused. We still have time!"

"No!" Picard said forcefully. This time he had to make Weinlein understand. "They've always known we were here! Think! They didn't beam to get us until we sent the microburst to bring the *Monitor* out of hiding."

Picard felt the adrenaline of battle sharpen, then slow his senses to a hyperacute state. The mission would succeed or fail in the next few seconds.

"You're saying this is a trap?" Weinlein asked incredulously.

"What else would it be?"

"Then where are the rest of them?" Weinlein demanded. "Why aren't they coming after us?"

Picard felt an incongruous bubble of laughter rise up in

him. It was so obvious. "They don't want *us.* They don't care about *us.* They want the *Monitor.*"

Weinlein stared over the wall at the dark cube towering over the devastated starbase. "But they have no weaponry installed in that thing. No propulsion systems."

"Because they're the *bait!"* Picard said. "That's all they are!" It was perfectly clear now. "That's why they didn't assimilate the base in seconds. They needed to draw out the process, to draw us in."

Weinlein muttered in an ancient Vulcan dialect. She reset controls on her forearm padd, then jabbed the communicator contact at her neck.

"Archangel! This is red leader! Override alpha alpha one alpha! You are heading into an ambush! Confirm!"

Picard heard all the confirmation he needed.

Subspace static.

A glance at his own tricorder told him all communications channels were being jammed. The source was the cube.

Beverly looked up from her own tricorder. "We are now within a Borg force field," she announced softly. "No beam-out possible."

Weinlein looked stricken. Beside her, Krul and Beyer kept their phaser rifles in firing position, constantly scanning the immediate area.

Picard recognized the expression in Weinlein's eyes, dark and shadowed as they were.

The look of a commander who has run out of options.

In contrast, Picard felt his own control increase. "Lieutenant Weinlein, we are trapped in enemy territory, out of contact with command. As Captain, Starfleet, I am countermanding all of Commander Shelby's orders." He reached forward and pulled Weinlein's duty phaser, type-5, from her harness. "I am now in command of this mission."

In that moment, Picard saw Krul and Beyer swing their phaser rifles onto him. Beverly stepped into their line of fire, but Picard gently pushed her back.

"I'm not the enemy," Picard said. He pointed over the wall toward the cube. "That is."

Weinlein hesitated, as Picard knew she must. But in the end, she waved to her soldiers. "Stand down. The captain's in command."

The rifles lowered slowly. But they were lowered.

Picard didn't stop to acknowledge his victory. "Listen carefully. There is a working transporter in that cube, as well as a force-field generator and whatever equipment they're using to jam subspace. Our objective is to take control of all three systems."

Weinlein frowned. "If you don't want us to take prisoners, why not just blow it up?"

"Because somewhere up there is a Borg ship waiting for the *Monitor. That* is our target. The mission's primary objective is once again within our reach."

"But there's only one way you can take control," Weinlein said.

"I know," Picard answered, aware that somehow he had moved beyond fear, beyond anxiety. As if, somehow, this moment had always been waiting for him and he could no longer avoid its arrival.

He reached out to Beverly, handed her the phaser, and pulled the small carryall pod from her belt.

The interface.

He ran his hand around his armor's neck seal, then pulled his helmet off.

"We go back to the original plan," he said as he popped the carryall's seal.

Even in the near darkness he could see the alien, convex shape of the neuromolecular attachment plate inside.

It was cold to the touch as he pulled it out. A thick cable came out with it, designed to be plugged into the plate and the power cell already in place beneath his armor.

Momentarily, he was surprised by how little he was affected

by the sight of it—its same outward size, shape, and appearance the same as the one the Borg had attached to his skull.

And then he understood why.

Above him, a starship was in danger.

Around him, Starfleet personnel looked to him for leadership.

And on the thousand worlds of the Federation, an interstellar civilization unmatched in history teetered on the brink of extinction, to be saved or destroyed by what a single individual would accomplish in the next few minutes and hours.

In the middle of action, there was no room for doubt. He could not afford it or allow it.

He was a starship captain.

It was time to make a difference.

FIFTEEN

The steady pulse of the *Tomed's* singularity generators throbbed in the corridors of the ship. To Salatrel, the comforting sound was as much a part of her life as her own heartbeat. Even now, with her mind focused on the next stage of her plan, she was aware of the power of the ship which she commanded, and she took strength from it.

She stood in the corridor outside the Starfleet holodeck which the Borg had helpfully assimilated from one of the Starfleet vessels they had defeated since arriving in this quadrant. She had not been lying when she had told Kirk it was one of the few useful contributions the Federation had made to the galaxy—and to this mission.

Romulan holographic simulators would never have been able to re-create an Earth environment with as much convincing detail as this unit could. And judging from the way Kirk was reacting to meeting her holographic duplicate in a re-creation of his home region of Iowa, the illusion was perfect.

Salatrel watched, as emotionless as her distant Vulcan cousins, as Kirk embraced her own duplicate on the observation screen. Vox stood beside her. To her left, his cranial implants and sensor eye were what she saw. She preferred it that way. There was no chance then of confusing him with what he once was. And could never be again.

"Kirk is lying," Vox stated.

Salatrel folded her arms. "The collective's thinking is too binary. My medical scans show he is merely confused. That is to be expected at this stage of his conditioning."

"Our analysis of the regeneration device indicated that his memories should have returned intact."

On screen, Salatrel's duplicate and Kirk took a red and black patterned blanket, and some type of food container made of stiff, woven plant tendrils, from the storage units on the sides of the equinoid's rider's seat. Once again, Salatrel congratulated herself on her decision to make use of the Starfleet holodeck. No Romulan programmer could have dreamed of such an unlikely combination of artifacts and creatures. "Obviously, the regeneration device was flawed. It self-destructed before the process was completed. There is nothing sinister in that."

Vox turned to her. She glanced up at him and again suffered and banished the automatic pang of anguish. Anger was clearly, and familiarly, expressed on the half of her former lover's face that still remained Romulan.

"At your request, the collective provided the technology

you required to return Kirk to functional status. He is not functional. This project should be terminated."

"You still don't understand the elegance of this," Salatrel said sharply.

"Elegance is not a useful quality. Efficiency is useful. Reduction of effort leading to increase in resources is the ideal. Life is improved when all contribute to the good of the whole."

"That is what we are doing here," Salatrel said in a more conciliatory tone. "Consider. Who is the greatest villain ever to subvert the will of the Romulan people?"

Salatrel watched as Vox's stern expression seemed to soften, as if that part of him which was still Romulan were being released from that which was Borg. "The Butcher of Icarus IV," he said by rote. "James Tiberius Kirk."

"Exactly," Salatrel said. "Just as our people were prepared to throw off the yoke of the Federation, to stand against the injustices forced upon us by the Treaty of Algeron, James Tiberius Kirk murdered the patriots who were to lead the first wave of our redemption."

The tragic story of the Battle of Icarus IV was known to every Romulan child: How the first cloaked Romulan vessel had set out to probe the Earth outposts belligerently arrayed at the boundaries of the Neutral Zone. And how, after her successful mission, but before her triumphant return, Kirk and his ship had defeated her commander by dishonorable tactics—feigning helplessness near the tail of the Icarus comet to lure the Romulan vessel to her destruction.

To Romulans, if Kirk had fired upon women and children who had raised their arms in surrender, it could be no greater crime.

But Borg severity had already returned to Vox. He no longer seemed touched by the story.

"James Tiberius Kirk was a soldier. He did his duty to defend his territory. We could expect no less."

"He defended a monstrous violation of our sovereignty *and* our dignity. His butchery set back our people's aspirations for generations, as the appeasers held on to power." Salatrel's voice rose in its intensity.

Vox gazed at Salatrel as if he didn't care what she said or thought. But Salatrel could read another expression on Vox's face, as well. The one that came with assimilation. It was the way the Borg had of reducing everything, and everyone, to raw material. As if they constantly calculated the return they could expect against the exertion of instantly consuming what they saw.

"These are the facts," Vox stated, and Salatrel waited for what he would say next. It was what Vox always said when they had this argument. "Your grandfather was the commander of the first Neutral Zone penetration mission to test the Cloaking Device. James Tiberius Kirk killed your grandfather. Therefore, your involvement in this procedure is suspect."

"Kirk's name is reviled throughout the Star Empire," Salatrel retorted automatically, as she always did. "My involvement in this procedure is fortunate."

Vox brought their argument back to the present. "Where is the elegance in chance?"

Salatrel turned away as if to study the display screen, no longer trusting herself to retain self-control if she continued looking at Vox's disfigured face, with all that its ruin represented.

In the holodeck simulation, Kirk and her duplicate sat on the patterned blanket in a sheltered area beneath a tree. Despite her assurances to Vox, Salatrel frowned. It was unusual that Kirk was still involved in conversation. According to her psychographic projections, he should have initiated lovemaking by now. But an analysis of that anomaly would have to wait. She marshaled her energy to defeat Vox, if only in words.

"In regard to the assimilation of the Federation, who is the greatest threat to the will of the collective?" Salatrel asked, still watching the screen and Kirk's atypical behavior.

"Jean-Luc Picard," Vox answered.

"Once again," Salatrel said, "exactly. You sucked all the information you needed about the Federation and Starfleet from his mind when he was assimilated. And the other half of that equation is that all the information Starfleet needs to defeat you a second time is buried somewhere in Picard's mind. Can't you see the . . . logic of the situation? You and I will turn our two greatest enemies against each other. The Romulan people at last will have their revenge against Kirk, while the Borg will be able to remove the last barrier to their successful assimilation of the Federation."

"Only if Kirk accomplishes his mission in the seven days remaining to him," Vox said.

"We are working on a way to remove the nanites. He might last longer."

"No," Vox said. "The neuronic implant will kill him long before the nanites fatally reconfigure his body."

Salatrel whirled to face Vox. *"What?"*

"To construct these holographic simulations, to create a cover story he would accept and believe, we required information beyond that which was contained in available files." Vox continued as if oblivious to her stunned reaction. To understand Kirk's personality in the time we have available, it was necessary to install a neuronic interface in order to make his thoughts available to us. It was not necessary to inform you of our action."

Salatrel's body was rigid with fury and fear. What else might Vox have done without her knowledge? Her plan depended on Kirk acting as he had in the past, not slowed down by a subspace interface with a Borg hive of unimaginative drones. "You made Kirk a Borg?"

"No," Vox said. "At this stage, that would be counterproductive to the task he must perform. He must function as a human in order to move among others of his kind. The collective is not in contact with him."

Salatrel forced herself to relax. Kirk was still hers to command. But Vox was not finished with his surprising revelations.

"Elements of his emotional makeup were downloaded for analysis." A small smile appeared on Vox's taciturn features. "He is not as easy to control as you imagine. That is why I say he is lying."

Salatrel weighed her position. As she had told her centurion, Tracius, the only possible result of her actions was victory. Any other would result in her not being alive to witness it.

And victory depended on *her* retaining control, not the Borg.

She decided to call Vox's bluff.

The collective's bluff.

"Then why don't you assimilate him? Why don't you assimilate all of us?" Her hand dramatically swept the corridor, her ship, the entire fleet of dissidents that fought at her side.

Whatever Vox thought was not apparent in his expression. "We have a treaty," he answered calmly. "The Borg and the Romulan dissidents. You assist the collective in assimilating the Federation, and we allow the Star Empire to exist unassimilated. As a . . . curiosity. Long-term study of an unassimilated culture will allow us to be more proficient in welcoming other cultures to the collective. It is an efficient use of our resources."

Salatrel searched Vox's Romulan eye for the truth. "Do you honestly expect me to believe that?"

Vox's expression remained unchanged. "If you wish to survive, you have no choice. Resistance is futile."

Salatrel's pulse quickened at the Speaker's last statement.

Her dissidents had not resisted the Borg. The Romulan Warbird crew who were assimilated at the time Vox became Speaker for the Borg retained enough of their Romulan dignity and fervor to actually suggest the treaty to the collective. And why would the Borg waste resources on the relatively small Empire when the Federation hung behind the Neutral Zone, ready for plucking?

Resistance had never been an option, or even a strategy.

So why had Vox mentioned it?

Unless it had been a signal.

From somewhere deep inside the Romulan Vox used to be.

Unsettled, Salatrel checked the display screen again. On it, Kirk gently removed her duplicate's hand from his leg. What was wrong with him? That wasn't typical of Kirk, either.

"Why is he doing that?" she asked crossly. "Resisting her seduction?"

Vox studied the screen. "He knows she is an illusion."

"Indistinguishable from reality."

"He is a man of the moment," Vox said. "Steeped in reality. He does not belong in that device, any more than he belongs in this time." Vox turned to Salatrel. For a moment, it seemed to her that his Romulan voice spoke to her. "You do not understand what you have unleashed."

For the sake of her plan, Salatrel would not, could not accept that verdict. Not from the collective. And not from Vox. Too much depended on it, and on her.

"Watch," she said to the Speaker. "I'll show you what I understand. Kirk is only a puppet to be manipulated. And I am his master."

Salatrel strode to the arched entrance to the holodeck.

"What do you intend to do?" Vox asked. Against reason, Salatrel hoped his question betrayed an interest in any answer she might make.

"Take my duplicate's place," she said. "Remove the illusion."

If she could, she would torture whatever remained of her lover in Vox.

"And I want you to observe every moment."

The Speaker looked at her blankly. But Salatrel was sure that some part of him was alive to pain. She longed for that surety.

"That is not an efficient use of my time," Vox said.

"What if Kirk and I will be plotting revenge against the collective?" Salatrel said. "If he was wired into the collective the way Picard was, then wasn't there the same sort of exchange of data? Doesn't he have the same secrets locked in his mind? Isn't he just as big a threat to you as Picard?"

"Kirk will be dead in seven days. Picard is missing. Perhaps Starfleet has imprisoned him for losing his ship at Veridian."

"The Federation is not the Star Empire," Salatrel persisted. "Those cowards probably patted him on the hand and apologized for giving him a substandard vessel. He's out there, Vox. Ready to work against you. Unless Kirk stops him." She turned the knife. "And you know it. Otherwise, you never would have expended the resources you already have."

For once, Vox had no response.

Salatrel put her hand on the entrance control.

"Observe carefully," she said. "We'll see if I can bring back any more memories for James Tiberius Kirk. Or for you."

Then the door slipped open with a gentle hiss of machinery, and Salatrel stepped through.

Vox watched the observation screen impassively, the holographic duplicate fading as the real Salatrel stepped up to Kirk.

Embraced by the welcoming comfort of the groupmind, Vox noted that Kirk did not react with surprise to the duplicate's disappearance. The reconstructed human was more in control than Salatrel imagined.

Vox's consciousness floated among the thousands of eyes and hands engaged in the work of the collective in this sector, sharing all that he thought and felt with so many others that a blanketing numbness was its end result. At some level, no more important than that of one small processor in a massively parallel neural network, Vox watched Kirk as Salatrel switched off the closure on her tunic, allowing it to fall from her shoulders, so she stood before Kirk, naked.

And Vox continued to watch as Kirk embraced the woman who had been his lover. But whatever discomfort the tiny spark of individual volition still left within him felt, it was insignificant compared to the bliss of the collective.

In seven days, Kirk would be dead.

Shortly after, the Federation would fall.

And then, despite their bargain, the Romulan Star Empire would also become fulfilled as it, too, received the gift of bliss.

The Borg had recently learned that lying was an excellent way to preserve resources. And this branch of the collective especially had become quite practiced at it.

Certain in his knowledge that Salatrel would join him again, Vox observed what happened on the black and red patterned blanket beneath the tree.

His sensor eye was unwavering in its concentration.

His organic eye was bathed in a distorting veil of moisture.

Emotions were futile.

The collective was all.

SIXTEEN

The Borg cube loomed in the darkness, surrounded by the glow from its blue and red power conduits, illuminating the broken ground around it.

It was implacable, impenetrable.

But Picard didn't care.

He had committed himself to action without doubt.

Others depended on him.

He ran for the cube, leading his team.

In a flash of blue radiation, two Borg materialized ten meters before him, weapons already trained on him. But before they could fire, they were already shimmering in quantum disintegration.

"Random frequency selection engaged!" Beyer called out.

Beverly was at Picard's side. Beyer and Krul behind them. Weinlein covered their flank, between the team and the cube's secondary airlock.

Twenty meters from the main airlock, Picard knew the only reason the Borg hadn't already attacked was that the collective's groupmind was analyzing the loss of its first two teams of soldiers. The next response would be overwhelming, but it was still several seconds off.

Picard yanked out a handtorch from his harness and put his thumb on its activator. He didn't want to depend on the red and blue glow of the power conduits. He had to be ready.

He was ten meters from the main airlock. It was sealed, but

the phaser rifles still had fourteen more frequencies to cycle through. Enough to get his team through the door.

A blinding blue flash came from the side opposite Weinlein's approach. Picard faltered, momentarily startled by what he saw. The Borg response *was* overwhelming. A configuration unlike any Borg Picard had ever encountered.

It was bipedal, but three meters tall, with piston-like legs and thick crushing disks for footpads, digging into the soil. Propellant gases hissed from its leg joints as it began to stalk forward. Two pairs of arms swung forward, searchingly, manipulators opening and closing with molecularly sharp carbon cutters and whirling blades. Their target: raw materials.

Phaser beams streaked past Picard and flared in a blinding halo around the Borg giant. The beams resolved into facets like a jewel carved out of energy. Disconcertingly, the sudden light revealed a small, impassive, humanoid head centered protectively in the Borg's immense shoulder plates. It was the only biological component visible. Picard saw Beverly recoil at the sight.

The phaser beams cut out. The Borg colossus advanced. Untouched.

"They've adapted to the base phaser pattern!" Beyer shouted.

"Discard phasers!" Weinlein commanded. "Krul, you're go!"

The powerful Klingon lunged past Picard.

The Borg's arms swung down on him, intent on dismembering its attacker.

But Krul fired a Klingon thrustergun first.

An antique, Picard knew, hand-tooled with intricate engravings of Kahless battling Molor. He had examined it when they had shared a meal two nights ago. It fired simple projectiles of explosive-packed metal, propelled by a centuries-old chemical-reaction technology.

The Borg's forcefield had been set for phaser harmonics.

Undetected, the metal projectile traversed the force field's perimeter and punched into the creature's implanted breastplate before the collective could reconfigure its defenses.

Sparks arced from the Borg's immense chest, along with a spray of dark liquid. One arm snapped back, flailing out of control.

Picard saw the shock on the face so cruelly embedded in the appalling construction.

Four more projectiles pockmarked the Borg's armored body. The last one caused a defensive force-field flare, but the collective had not been fast enough to save this unit.

It began to topple.

From Krul's throat rose a Klingon victory cry, as he drove his fists into the air.

Just as an antimatter stream spurted from the glowing node of one falling Borg arm.

The incandescent beam sliced neatly through Krul's legs, mid-thigh.

The Klingon fell.

Then the massive Borg construct struck the ground before him, thrown onto its back as its one good arm still sprayed a continuous stream of antiprotons so that the arc of the beam hit the side of the Borg cube.

Picard staggered back with the force of the explosion.

A particle cannon turret instantly swung out from the cube's side and returned fire at the fallen Borg giant.

Its chest exploded and its arm fell back, useless and impotent.

Then the cannon turret swung sharply, toward Picard and his team.

Picard charged forward and threw a smart grenade, catching a glimpse of it spiraling around the cannon turret, heading for the contact point where the cannon joined the cube.

And just as he dove for cover in the dirt, he felt himself lifted up, thrown back, hitting the dirt on his back, lungs without air.

Another explosion flared above him.

His ears rang. His chest heaved.

Then Beverly was at his side, pulling on his arm.

He was aware of smoke rising from his chestplate.

He gasped, coughed. "Was I hit?" he asked. But he felt so detached, it was as if her answer were unimportant.

"Your armor was hit," Beverly said. "Good thing they went for your chest, not your head."

Picard felt stabbing pain in his lungs as he drew a breath to respond.

Beverly frowned at her medical tricorder.

Something else exploded nearby. The air was dense with sound and smoke.

"Three cracked ribs," she told him. "Here."

A hypospray tingled against his neck.

The pain melted.

Another explosion.

"Can you stand?" Beverly asked urgently.

Picard knew he had no choice. He got to his feet. His chest was numb.

"Krul?" he asked.

"His armor's life-support will cut off the bleeding and deliver stimulants," Beverly promised. "He can hold on till it's safe to get him." Then she pulled Picard's arm over her shoulder and guided him forward, into a pit carved by an earlier explosion.

Weinlein was there, setting up a photon mortar with sure, practiced movements. She glanced at him. "Are you ready?"

Picard felt around for his torch. He had dropped it. Weinlein saw what he was doing, then tossed him hers.

"Yes," he said.

"We've got one more cannon to take out, then you can get to the main airlock."

"What about you?"

Weinlein nodded into the distance.

Picard looked.

Krul scrabbled in the dirt next to the body of the Borg construct. He was roaring threats in Klingon. Battle cries. No sense of giving up.

Another explosion went off at the side of the cube. Picard heard thudding, then Beyer leapt down into the pit.

"That's the last cannon," he said roughly. "I'm going for Krul."

Picard pulled himself up and switched on his handtorch. "And I'm going for the airlock."

"Jean-Luc!" Beverly said behind him.

He glanced back for an instant. Read the worry in her face, and the faith, and knew what she was about to say. He nodded.

"I will," he told her.

Beyer took off toward Krul. Picard sprinted for the airlock. He held the torch under his face, making his features distinct.

The cube looked badly damaged. The antimatter stream from the giant Borg had cut a large hole through its side.

Large enough that Picard changed his strategy and ran for it instead of the airlock. It was the better entrance.

Behind him, Beyer shouted a warning.

Picard spun, then stumbled as he saw—

—the thorax of the fallen Borg construct opening like a metal flower.

Next to the construct, Krul still screamed out his challenges, unaware. Beyer struggled to wrap his arm around Krul's writhing form while he aimed a hand disruptor at the opening in the construct.

But the beam dissipated against the Borg force field. Behind it, eight gleaming metal spider legs unfurled from the thorax, as if testing the air.

Then the legs braced themselves on the fallen construct and slowly straightened to lift up the central, disk-shaped body slung between them.

A Borg scuttler had emerged.

Picard and the commandos had seen it darting through the ruined Starbase at speeds no human or Klingon could match and suspected it was a wholly mechanical device. But now that it was still, Picard could see a single organic shape resting in the center of its body—the braincasing of whatever once-living organic being had been built into the unthinkable device.

Beyer yelled at Picard to keep running as the cybernetic insect raised four of its legs, then angled down toward Beyer, metal legs flashing, as it picked up speed.

Picard groaned as Beyer dropped his disruptor and unloaded a full charge from his Vulcan pulse wand. But this branch of the collective must have faced that weapon before, and the battle was over instantly.

A green nimbus flared around the scuttler as it launched itself into the air, drew its forward legs together, and sank into Beyer like a living javelin.

Beyer flew backward, with the creature now a part of his chest.

The scuttler used its rear legs to brace itself against the fallen, limp body, then yanked its forelegs from Beyer's bloodied chest.

Picard saw Beyer's legs spasm once, then fall still.

The scuttler turned in a blur to Krul.

Krul bellowed at the creature—the machine—as it stood over him.

Picard could see the Klingon's fists strike out to pummel the scuttler's cybernetic shell. Heard the clang of armored fists on metal. The dull thud of armored fists against whatever ghastly remnant of the creature was organic.

But the scuttler was not preparing to impale Krul as it had Beyer. Two metal legs had folded up against his body and moved inside an access panel.

There was a chance for Krul.

Picard took it.

He started to run toward Krul.

"No!" Weinlein shouted. She struck him from behind, hit his legs. Dragged him down.

An instant later, the ground erupted in front of him.

Together, they rolled behind a mound of earth and silicon bricks. Beverly ran to join them.

"There's another cannon," Weinlein gasped. "The mortar can't get past the new shields they've thrown up."

Picard pushed her away. He knew the debris they hid behind wouldn't protect them for long. And Krul needed his help. He crawled to the edge of the mound to peer into the blue and red landscape.

A Klingon shriek of defiance cut the night.

Beverly moved up beside Picard. The scuttler still crouched obscenely over Krul. Two of its legs seemed to be attached to the Klingon's helmet.

"What's it doing?" Beverly asked.

Weinlein joined them, with an ancient Romulan curse. She slammed down her visor, activating her telescopic sensors. Another curse. "It's attaching an implant."

Picard froze. "They'll know our plans."

Then he grimaced as a sharp feedback whine cut through the open communicator circuit.

"Red leader one, this is Archangel—"

The *Monitor* had arrived and her more powerful equipment had managed to punch through the Borg jamming. But because her commander was breaking the communications blackout, it could only mean one thing.

"—a cubeship has just dropped from transwarp. It is closing in to engage." Picard could picture Captain Lewinski of the *Monitor* secure in his command chair, ready to fulfill his duty, as well as to test the design specifications of his ship.

But Starfleet couldn't take the chance.

Picard slammed his fist against his communicator contact.

"Negative, Captain. Do not engage the Borg! Repeat—do not engage the Borg! They are ready for you!"

Static and feedback whine warbled over the circuit. Borg countermeasures. Krul shrieked defiance again. And again. A particle blast hit the ground nearby, scattering some of the cover shielding Picard and his depleted team.

Lewinski's voice came back online. "Say again, Picard."

"You must withdraw, Captain! Pull back at maximum warp. Allow the cubeship time to recover their assimilation crew down here." Picard gambled that the Borg had not yet broken the constant cycling of Starfleet encryption schemes. "It will be the only chance we have to get aboard."

Picard heard the disappointment in Lewinski's voice, tempered by imperceptible relief. "Acknowledged, Captain. Godspeed."

"Aboard?" Weinlein said.

Picard turned to her. "The collective will not abandon this team. They will not abandon—" Another particle blast sprayed them with dirt and stinging silicon fragments. The sensor ghosts constantly transmitted by their armor were still confusing the Borg's scanners, but the Borg were getting closer each minute.

"They will not abandon these resources," Picard continued fiercely. "Especially if they think there are secrets to be gained from the Starfleet computers that were here."

Weinlein lifted her visor. Her eyes bore into Picard's. "If that scuttler implants Krul, the Borg won't come near this place." She broke the seal on her helmet and tugged it off. It was the first time Picard had seen her out of her full battle gear. Her ears were pointed. Half-human, half. . . .

Weinlein reached inside her armor and pulled out a small medallion. She pressed it into Picard's hand.

It was a Vulcan IDIC. The triangle receding into the whole and expanding from it at one and the same time. Infinite diversity in infinite combinations.

"For my parents," she said. "My mother's Vulcan. They'll need to take it to Mount Selaya."

Krul's voice rose once more. This time it was weak.

Weinlein squeezed the IDIC in Picard's palm. "Live long and prosper, Captain Picard. Now get the hell into that cube!"

Then she jumped up and swung her helmet arcing into the air behind her. The instant it left her hand, she charged forward, shouting Krul's name.

Picard knew exactly what she was doing. Exactly why she was doing it. He wanted there to be another way but there was no time. He and Beverly ran, too—straight for the Borg cube.

To one side, particle blasts chewed up the ground as the cannon closed in on Weinlein's helmet, the source of the sensor ghosts.

To the other side, Weinlein attacked the scuttler even as its legs trembled over Krul's exposed skull, as if weaving a metallic cocoon for its prey.

Picard and Beverly reached the shattered opening into the cube. There were no Borg to meet them.

"No," Beverly whispered.

Picard looked back. Saw what she saw.

The scuttler with three legs raised.

Weinlein dodged, but not quickly enough.

Picard heard her cry of protest, as powerful as Krul's defiance had been.

But as it lifted two more legs to try to impale her again, Weinlein struck it and it toppled from Krul's body, its wires still connected to the Klingon's skull.

Another particle blast lit the night. The cannon was still aimed at Weinlein's helmet.

As the rumble of the explosion died down, Picard heard the telltale whine of an overload building in a phaser prefire cell. Picard could see Weinlein. The commando leader stood tall. Her arms were not raised to deflect the scuttler's next blow.

Picard knew why. She was holding her phaser.

The scuttler brought its second pair of legs down, and this time it didn't miss.

Weinlein's legs buckled, but she did not release her grip on the phaser.

It was the only way.

"Don't look," Picard said as the overload whine reached its crescendo.

He held Beverly's face against his chest. But he watched until it was over.

White light blazed into the depths of the Borg cube stretching before them, followed by the crack of the explosion.

Picard blinked.

Only a smoking crater remained.

Weinlein and Krul were gone. The scuttler was gone. But Picard's chance to fulfill the mission still remained. Because of Weinlein's sacrifice. Beyer's and Krul's sacrifice. Picard stepped into the cube. Beverly followed him.

"You will be assimilated."

Picard turned, ready to face the Borg standing beside him, weapon held ready.

"Resistance is futile," the Borg said.

Automatically, Picard accepted the challenge. It was his turn to act now.

"Are you defective?" Picard began. He shoved Beverly behind him.

The Borg stepped forward. "You are not qualified to assess my operational status."

Picard held the torch to his face. "Are you certain?"

"Locutus?" the Borg said.

It lowered its weapon.

"Are you defective?" Picard repeated.

The Borg's sensor eye flashed as it was compelled into a diagnostic subroutine. Picard motioned urgently to Beverly.

She approached the Borg, placed a hypospray against a

small patch of exposed flesh at the base of its jaw, then pulled its cerebral cables free as it collapsed to the deck.

Beverly smiled shakily at Picard. "What do you know? It worked." She reset her hypospray, began to place it back on her harness, then thought better of it. She kept it in her hand. "What now?"

Picard looked for a way deeper into the cube. There was no way to know which—

As if a bomb concussion had moved past him, he lurched forward, slamming into a bulkhead made of mismatched pipes and metal patches.

Beverly staggered back at the same instant.

"What was that?" she asked.

All around them, the cube creaked and groaned.

Picard felt the deck angle beneath him.

He glanced back outside, past the jagged opening.

The smoking crater beside the fallen Borg construct was still there. But beyond, about fifty meters distant, there was a sharp dark line, like a horizon on an asteroid.

Picard leaned forward, looked outside the creaking cube. Beverly was beside him. Her breath drew in sharply.

The ground in a fifty-meter circle around the cube was moving skyward. In the light of the concentrated stars of the New Titan sky, Picard could see the rest of the planet's surface rush away.

They were in the grip of a Borg tractor beam.

And Picard knew it was drawing them up to the waiting cubeship, which had anticipated their every move.

"We're being retrieved," Picard said.

SEVENTEEN

The stripped-down, single-level bridge of the *Monitor* was cramped, but only because of the extra shielding that surrounded it.

Captain John Lewinski liked that about his ship. As far as her specs were concerned, she was virtually indestructible.

"Any more signals from the surface?" he asked his communications officer.

Ardev turned from his station, blue hearing stalks twisting to remain pointed at the speakers in his control console. "The Borg have completely jammed all frequencies," he whispered in his Andorian rasp.

Lewinski angled his chair toward his science officer. "Sensors?"

Science Officer T'per remained serene, as always. "The Borg are generating a sensor blanket, sir. At the time it was initiated, full life signs came from Picard, Crusher, and Weinlein. Krul's battle suit had activated emergency medical life-support routines. There were no readings from Beyer."

Lewinski chewed his lip, thinking the situation through. Two casualties before the main Borg vessel had arrived. That was not a good sign.

"What is the cubeship up to, Mr. Land?"

The navigator didn't take his eyes off the main viewscreen. The *Monitor* was operating with sensors at their lowest power setting to avoid Borg detection, resulting in a low-resolution image. Though Lewinski had followed Picard's suggestion to withdraw at maximum warp, he had taken the *Monitor* behind the New Titan system's gas giant, cloaked, and returned to a geostationary orbit above whatever was left of Starbase 804.

The Borg cubeship was also holding a geostationary position, though only five hundred kilometers from the planet's surface. The power expenditure for such a maneuver must have been stupendous, though so far sensors could not pick up any sign of what kind of system the Borg were using.

"Hard to tell, Captain," Land replied. The ship's navigator had a clipped, Anglo accent. Though fully half the *Monitor*'s crew was human, apart from Lewinski, Land was the only native of Earth aboard. The Federation had become that diverse. "The ship is bleeding sensor ghosts on every frequency. I am picking up strong indications of a tractor beam, though."

Lewinski glanced over at T'Per. The young Vulcan met his gaze without expression. "T'Per, which option provides the least risk? Increasing sensor gain from this position, or moving closer and maintaining low power?"

T'Per raised an eyebrow in thought. "For the least risk, we should withdraw."

Lewinski smiled at her, but drew no response. "That wasn't an option."

"Then you should have stated which option provided the lesser risk," T'Per noted, unsmiling.

Vulcans, Lewinski thought. *Couldn't live with them. Couldn't live without them.*

"The lesser risk, Mr. T'Per."

"Moving closer, but only by a factor of less than one half."

Lewinski turned his chair to face the screen. "Take us in, Mr. Land. I want to look up their tailpipe."

"Wherever that is," Land muttered. The *Monitor* surged forward at quarter impulse and was in visual contact with the Borg cubeship within seconds.

"Definitely a tractor beam," Lewinski said softly, fingering his goatee.

The increased-resolution image of the main screen showed a telltale purple beam emanating from the surface of the cubeship closest to the planet. It stretched down to the surface of New Titan.

Lewinski quickly polled his crew for power levels, sensor readings, and any indication that the Borg had sensed their cloaked presence.

But the cloaking device was working perfectly. Lewinski thought the Romulan science team at Starbase 324 would be pleased to hear that. That is, after they had gotten over their outrage that Starfleet had operated the device aboard a *Defiant*-class ship without a Romulan observer.

Land adjusted the viewscreen's image, angling it away from the Borg cubeship, toward New Titan. There was an object at the base of the tractor beam, increasing in size as it drew nearer. "We've got a mass coming up from the surface, Captain."

"It's got to be the starbase," Lewinski said. If Picard had been right in his transmission, then they were watching the Borg retrieve the bait.

"Life signs on the tractored mass," T'Per announced. "Forty-two Borg . . . no . . . forty Borg, two assimilated animals . . . small . . ."

Lewinski scratched his fingers through his beard. "Bottom line, Mister. Any of the red team on that?"

T'Per's fingers flew skillfully over her science panel. "Medical telemetry from armor belonging to . . . Picard and . . . Crusher, sir. No injuries."

Lewinski exhaled slowly. Some of his crew joined him. . . .

If none of the red team had made it to the cubeship, the *Monitor* had orders to attack. But now, all he could do was observe.

"Intriguing," T'Per said beside him.

Before them, a half hemisphere of soil, one hundred meters across, fifty meters deep, and topped by a thirty-meter-tall Borg cube, was rising up beneath the cubeship.

Lewinski got the specs from the screen on the arm of his chair. On the screen, the tractored chunk of planet was nothing more than a dark smear against the bulk of the Borg vessel.

"Contact," Land announced when the tractored soil vanished inside the ship.

"Any idea what they're using for a power source?" Lewinski asked anyone.

"No change in energy consumption," T'Per said.

Lewinski shook his head. He was glad he wasn't attacking.

On the screen, the Borg ship began to rotate.

"Keep your eye on weapons sensors," Lewinski cautioned. He leaned forward in his chair.

T'Per's voice was clear and strong. "I am definitely detecting a power surge, Captain."

"Stand by on shields, Mr. Land."

"Captain," T'Per said, "may I remind you that if we do raise our shields, the Borg will detect us."

Lewinski kept his eyes on the screen. "What if they've detected us already, and they're powering up their weapons?"

"Logically," T'Per said, "we would have been scanned."

"Those aren't logical Vulcans, Mr. T'Per. They're Borg."

T'Per's voice cooled noticeably. "There were Vulcans stationed at the starbase, Captain. Therefore, there could be some Vulcans now aboard the recovered cube, contributing their intellect, and logic, to the collective."

"I for one," Lewinski said, still keeping his concentration locked on the screen, "do not even want to contemplate what a Borg Vulcan might be like."

Land glanced over his shoulder with a grin. "There'd be a difference?"

"At ease, Mr. Land," the captain warned.

"Shields on full standby," Land confirmed.

On the screen, the Borg ship had rotated until it had changed its orientation to New Titan by one hundred eighty degrees.

"I'd like an explanation for what we're seeing," Lewinski said to his bridge crew.

"They're getting ready to do something, Captain," Land volunteered. "But I just don't know—what?"

On the screen, the Borg ship disappeared in a flash of light.

"Sensors!" Lewinski demanded.

"The Borg vessel generated and then entered a transwarp conduit," T'Per reported.

Lewinski sat back in his chair, amazed. "That quickly?" He hadn't even seen the multi-dimensional opening form. Only a flash of light.

"Playing it back at slow speed," Land said.

On the screen, the disappearance of the Borg cubeship played out again, this time slowed by a factor of one hundred. Sure enough, a transwarp conduit opened. The Borg ship didn't vanish; it appeared to dissolve into a spray of light, then was lost as the conduit opening collapsed around it.

In Starfleet's first encounter with Borg transwarp conduits, the crew of the *U.S.S. Enterprise* had determined that the secret to entering them had been the transmission of an encoded, high-energy tachyon pulse. However, once the *Enterprise* had used that technique several times, the conduits no longer responded to it. As if the transwarp network, like the Borg themselves, had adapted.

Lewinski rubbed his hands over his face. He had had four hours sleep in the past three days. "Go to full power sensors and stand down from cloaked running," he said. "Lieutenant Ardev, contact Commander Shelby at Starbase 324. Tell her Picard and Crusher are aboard a Borg vessel. But that vessel is now in transwarp, and we are unable to pursue."

Land twisted around in his chair to look at his captain. "Can't we *try* to search for them, sir? We have a heading from the sensor logs."

Lewinski sighed, deeply grateful he wasn't Picard. "The way those conduits move through other-dimensional space, Mr. Land, their heading at entry wouldn't tell us anything. I'm afraid that Captain Picard and Dr. Crusher have just gone . . . where no one has gone before."

Lewinski suddenly felt the full weight of deferred exhaustion. T'Per stepped up to the side of his chair, hands behind her back.

"Then it is most unlikely they will ever be able to determine a way to return," the science officer said.

Lewinski stretched back in his chair, thinking dark thoughts of Vulcans and logic.

EIGHTEEN

"Shit," Data said. "Damn, hell, . . . *sal'tasnon!*"

La Forge sighed, and the visor of his helmet fogged up. The local temperature on Trilex was hovering around fifty Kelvin, and despite the heating elements built into his well-insulated environmental suit, he felt the chill. It didn't put him in the mood to waste time.

"Data," La Forge said, feeling the vibrations from his helmet's exterior speaker, "exactly who taught you how to curse like that?"

"Counselor Troi," Data answered. The android looked

across the small excavation site from where he knelt in the ice, and smiled. Behind him in the dim red light of Trilex Prime, the eerie, corroded spires of the frozen city could be seen emerging from the ice field like fingers from a grave. "She has told me that I must feel free to express my emotions." Data's innocent grin grew larger. "Damn, damn, damn."

La Forge decided it was time for a break. The ruins of the Trilex civilization had been frozen for hundreds of thousands of years, ever since the planet's sun had gone nova. A few more minutes' delay in this library structure wouldn't make any difference. He stepped cautiously over the grid of red string that defined the excavation area to see what Data was up to. "So what's wrong this time?" he asked, though he dreaded the answer.

Data, who did not need an environmental suit to withstand the cold of the planet, wore his standard duty uniform. He brushed ice crystals from his knees as he stood up, holding out an environmentally sealed tricorder. "This *patak* piece of *flax* is no damn good," he explained.

Then he angled his head as he studied La Forge's expression inside the engineer's helmet. "In case you are not fluent in the Klingon vernacular, I was stating that this tricorder, due to bad design, was no longer functioning."

La Forge took the tricorder from Data's hand. "I get the picture, Data. But why didn't you just say that in the first place?"

Data looked confused. "I did." Then he smiled. Mercurial changes in his mood and expression were the norm these days, La Forge knew.

"Ah," Data said, "I see from where your confusion might originate. My original statement was infused with an emotional content indicating my annoyance with the tricorder's malfunction. Perhaps you have not yet become used to me as an emotional being."

La Forge took a deep breath, then flipped open the transparent covering that protected the tricorder's surface from extreme conditions. "Data, I admit, ever since you installed that emotion chip, you have . . . taken some getting used to."

"Do I disappoint you, Geordi?"

La Forge rolled his eyes. "You're my friend, Data. You can't disappoint me. But it would be nice if we could go back to having a conversation without you sounding like your mouth's a sewer."

Data looked off to the side, an indication that he was accessing his deepest databanks. He frowned, even appeared to shudder. "That is a most unpleasant image, Geordi. But I do not know what you intend by it."

La Forge scraped the tip of his gloved thumb along the inside of the tricorder's container. "Just stop cursing, Data."

"But would that not mean I was denying my emotions?" Now Data looked troubled. "Geordi, from my sessions with Counselor Troi, which I have enjoyed very much, I have learned that such a course of action could endanger my emotional health."

La Forge snapped shut the tricorder's case. He grabbed Data's hand, then slapped the tricorder into it. "You had an ice buildup inside the cover that was interfering with the control surfaces. If you had stopped cursing for a second to examine the problem, you wouldn't have had to waste our time here."

Data narrowed his eyes as he squinted at the tricorder. He pressed a few controls and smiled happily as he read the results. "Geordi, you're a *kreldanni* genius!"

"Data!"

"Geordi, do you believe I am not expressing my emotions appropriately?"

"Not all the time, Data. But . . . sometimes, yeah."

Data's mouth twisted down in a horrible grimace. "I feel so . . . so bad."

La Forge suddenly saw what was going to happen. And he didn't want to deal with it. "No, Data. Don't say that!"

"B-but I do," the android sobbed. "I've hurt your feelings."

"No, Data! No, you haven't! I feel great! I feel happy!" La Forge grabbed Data by the shoulders. "Data, whatever you do—*don't cry!*"

But he was too late.

The emotional mimetic systems designed into Data's android body were both subtle and robust. Data was still discovering all the complex ways in which they could interact. Tears were one of their many functions.

But not at fifty degrees Kelvin.

Puffs of water vapor billowed from Data's eyes as molecular micropumps excreted saline solution through Data's tearducts. Unfortunately, the liquid promptly sublimated in the intensely cold and thin atmosphere of Trilex.

La Forge groaned as Data reached out blindly with his hands. Two patches of ice crystals glittered on his face, one beneath each eyebrow.

"Geordi," the android said plaintively. "I have frozen my eyelids together."

"Oh, Data," La Forge sighed. "Not *again*."

Data stumbled over to an equipment locker and sat down as if his artificial muscles had buckled. "I am such a failure," he said.

La Forge shook his head and glanced down at his in-helmet status displays. He still had oxygen for four more hours. The *Bozeman* would be back overhead in less than two. He had no excuse for not indulging his friend.

"It's okay, Data," La Forge said as he sat down beside the android. It was an awkward maneuver in his suit, but he managed to put a supportive arm around Data's shoulders.

Data slumped, going into one of his depressions. He seemed to have them at least every other day by La Forge's reckoning. The only positive thing about them was that they seldom lasted more than a few minutes. Data might have emotions now, but his internal processor's clock still ran a thousand times faster than the human brain.

"No, it is not, Geordi. We must face the facts that my emotional skills do not measure up to the rest of my abilities." Data turned his face to La Forge. His eyes were still frozen over. "I am an emotional cripple. And my eyes are still frozen over." Then he slumped forward again, and sobbed.

La Forge had had enough.

"Data, so help me, if you don't pull yourself together, I'll . . . I'll turn you off until we're back on the *Bozeman*."

Data instantly sat up again. "You would do that? Really?"

La Forge made no effort to hold back his own feelings.

"Data, I gave up my leave time to come here with you. Between us, we used up every favor anybody in Starfleet ever owed us to get passage here and permission to dig. And after all that effort, *and* sacrifice, you're costing us the chance of doing any work at all by constantly having these emotional breakdowns. If you don't stop, I'll turn you off in a Klingon minute."

Ignoring the ice crystals glittering on his face, Data took on an expression of stoic resignation. "I understand, Geordi. You hate me."

"That's it!" La Forge stood up and began reaching around for Data's hidden function switch. "You're going to take a nap."

Data was up and backing away at once. "But I am not tired."

La Forge moved slowly to avoid slipping on the slick frozen surface of the ice. "You're an android. You never get tired. But I do!"

Data stopped trying to get away. "Geordi. Now that I have emotions, I can understand them better in others. I can *hear* the anger in your voice. It's directed at *me*."

"I *am* angry, Data. But not at you. I'm . . . angry at how . . . self-indulgent you've become. Emotions aren't helping you develop your humanity. You're so caught up in yourself, you're driving everyone else away."

Again Data's mood changed. His expression became one of

delight. "In other words, I am behaving like an adolescent. Geordi, I am happy now."

La Forge sighed again. He'd pay good credits to see how Deanna Troi would handle the emotional gravity whip Data was riding. La Forge could barely keep up. But he had to try. "Why's that, Data?"

"Plotting my emotional growth against a timeline extending from the moment I installed the emotion chip, if I have now reached the adolescent stage, marked by mood swings and intense, antisocial, emotional self-involvement, then I can extrapolate that, in approximately fourteen days, I shall have reached full adult emotional maturity."

"Do me a favor?" La Forge asked.

"It shall be my pleasure," Data said grandly.

"See if you can make it through the next fourteen days without a single curse word?"

Data shrugged. "Why the hell not?"

La Forge sighed again. Heavily.

"I heard that," Data said.

"Well, hear this then. I'm going back to work." La Forge returned to his corner of the excavation. So far he had melted through eight squares of ice, going down a meter to the floor of the ancient structure. It was easier than the digging he had once done with Captain Picard, when the captain had eagerly tried to introduce the engineer to his hobby. At least in conducting a dig on an ice planet, there was no dirt to shovel away. A type-1 phaser on low power simply melted the years away.

"It is very nice of you to help me like this," Data said.

"I'm not being nice," La Forge said as he checked the power level on his phaser. "I'm interested in finding out what happened here, too."

He glanced up as Data aimed his own excavation phaser at his face. Ever since the emotion chip, going anywhere with Data was like being with a five-year-old. Disaster loomed at every moment.

"Tell me you're not going to do something stupid," La Forge said.

"I may be an emotional cripple, Geordi, but I have ensured the phaser is set to its lowest power level. I am not crazy."

Data fired a weak beam at his face and the clumps of ice covering his eyes vaporized. He blinked rapidly.

"So far," La Forge muttered. Then he located a new square to melt away and positioned himself over it.

As the millennia-old ice vaporized away from the secrets it covered, Data walked over to stand close by La Forge's side.

"Be careful you do not let the beam touch the keys themselves," Data said.

La Forge kept his temper. "I know, Data." The tricorder had shown that the floor of the structure was littered with hundreds of cylindrical pieces of metal which other archaeologists had identified as data keys, designed to be placed into Trilex computer stations. Unfortunately, when Trilex Prime had gone nova, apparently without warning, all the computer systems on the planet had been wiped clean. Since the Trilex civilization had been pervasively computer-based, with artificially intelligent machines even achieving equality under the planet's laws, much of its culture had been lost beyond hope of recovery.

But the data keys had encoded information in a different way, which left them unaffected by the radiation surge of the nova. Though each held little information, Data had hoped that recovering enough of them might make it possible to place them together like a jigsaw puzzle to obtain a fuller picture of the Trilex culture.

That was important to Data, and to La Forge, because most archaeologists, including Captain Picard, had concluded that when its sun had gone nova, Trilex had been embroiled in a war between its organic inhabitants and its artificial, machine-based life-forms.

Some scholars had taken that to mean that organic life and synthetic life could never live in peace.

Since La Forge had first met Data, the android had always had an interest in the "Trilex Question," as it was known. But upon receiving his emotion chip, it had become an obsession with him.

La Forge could understand that.

To be really human, as Data desired, meant more than just having the capacity to feel. It meant having the capacity to stare up at the stars and ask the hardest questions of them all: Who am I? What is my purpose here?

La Forge knew those questions were in Data. And if they were to have meaningful answers for him, it was important for Data to know that he was more than just a mechanical oddity built by an eccentric scientist. It was important to know that he had a place in this universe. And for him to truly know that, it was critical that whatever had happened on Trilex had had nothing to do with the impossibility of organic and synthetic life-forms coexisting.

Finding emotions had only been the first step in Data's long voyage of self-discovery. Now he had to do what every other human must—find himself, and define himself, in his own terms.

Thus La Forge had been happy to help his friend. Especially since they had been ordered to take their accumulated leave while waiting for reassignment. To a new *Enterprise,* La Forge hoped.

"I think you have almost reached them," Data said.

"I know, Data," La Forge answered, keeping his beam moving slowly over the opening he had melted in the ice, now half a meter deep. "I've done this before, remember."

"It is just that it is very important that I know if organic life and synthetic life can coexist in peace."

La Forge spoke through clenched teeth. "Not if synthetic life keeps making a pest of itself."

La Forge stopped firing the phaser. Billows of water vapor filled the area, coalescing into clouds of sparkling ice crystals.

It was almost like a slow-motion replay of the transporter effect.

He checked his tricorder to see if the data keys had been exposed. He had to scrape his helmet visor to get rid of the frost that had formed there.

"Pretty good," he said to Data. "Looks like we've got another eleven keys down there to add to the collection. Do you want to pick them out while I—"

La Forge stopped talking as he saw a sudden energy spike on his tricorder's display.

"What the hell was that?"

"Geordi, I do not believe it is fair that you require me not to curse, while you continue to do so."

"Not now, Data." La Forge changed the settings on the tricorder. "That almost looked like a beam-in nearby. But the *Bozeman* is hours away."

"Geordi—"

"Not *now,* Data. I'm trying to concentrate."

"You do not have to. It was a beam-in. Look."

La Forge slowly raised his helmet.

Data was pointing straight ahead, across the excavation site, to where the spires of the city rose from the ice, against the dying sun of Trilex.

But for now, the ancient ruins were hidden by the swirling billows of ice crystals. Slowly settling. Not to reveal the ruins. But to reveal the shape of a stranger in an environmental suit that was not Starfleet-issue.

"Can I help you?" La Forge said.

He carefully placed his tricorder back on his belt and began to move his hand to his phaser.

Trilex was a protected historical site, administered by the Vulcan Science Academy.

If there had been any other expeditions to this world planned when Starfleet had submitted their proposal for a dig, he and Data would have been informed.

"First, move your hand away from your phaser," the stranger said.

La Forge noted that his universal translator had not switched on. The stranger spoke English.

"This is a restricted site," La Forge said.

He peered through the thinning ice cloud as the stranger stepped forward. There were two large devices clipped to his belt. One was a hand weapon. La Forge took as a good sign that it had not yet been drawn.

"I won't be here long," the stranger said. "I just want to ask a question."

"Are you an archaeologist?" Data asked.

La Forge waited for the answer. As far as he could tell, the stranger was humanoid, but his features were obscured by the reflective visor on his helmet.

"No," the stranger said. Then his hand went for his belt.

La Forge was ready to draw against him. But the stranger removed a flattened green cylinder about half a meter long, not his weapon.

"Who are you?" La Forge asked.

"I said *I* had the question," the stranger answered. Then he aimed the cylinder at La Forge and Data.

Instantly La Forge drew his phaser, reflexively resetting its power level to stun.

"Whatever that is, put it down," La Forge commanded.

But the stranger did not move the cylinder. "Where is Jean-Luc Picard?" he asked.

Of all the reasons La Forge had been prepared to hear to explain the stranger's presence, that was the least likely.

"That is a question more suited for Starfleet Command," Data volunteered. "Because of the chain of command we operate under, it is not appropriate to ask us."

The stranger's helmet angled until the visor was pointed directly at Data. "I'm surprised your ears aren't pointed," he said. Then he began to raise the cylinder.

La Forge pressed the firing stud on his phaser.

The blue beam shot out to the stranger.

Then evaporated in a blue nimbus around him.

La Forge felt his mouth open in astonishment. The stranger had a personal force field. But where was its power generator? Not even Starfleet had perfected such a device.

"Now it's my turn," the stranger said.

A puff of vapor blew out of the end of the cylinder. La Forge shoved Data aside as he sensed more than saw a dark streak rush past him.

For a moment, nothing happened. Then La Forge glanced behind him, expecting to see the impact of whatever the stranger had shot at him.

Instead, he saw a smart projectile hovering two meters beyond.

Then it was gone and La Forge felt a giant's hand crush his chest.

He fell back into the excavation grid, tangled up in the red grid string as he tried to right himself.

But he couldn't breathe, let alone move.

Data spoke with a voice of rage. "I will not let you hurt my friend!"

"Then answer my question. Where is Jean-Luc Picard?"

Through a red haze of pain, La Forge saw Data step past him. La Forge gasped as he felt the sudden bite of intense cold. He realized his suit must have been punctured. Though he could see only what was directly in front of his visor—nothing but the icy cliffs of the ruins they worked in, looming up all around him—La Forge could still hear Data and the stranger on his helmet speaker.

"Your weapon will not work on me," Data said. "I have no need of an environmental suit. Also, my strength and reflexes are many times greater than any organic being's. You will not succeed in fighting me." It was Data's idea of a threat, La Forge supposed bleakly.

"I have no intention of fighting you," the stranger said.

La Forge heard an electric crackle.

Heard Data moan.

Then saw Data fall beside him, his limbs rigid in the stance he had taken to face the stranger.

The stranger came to stand over the fallen friends. La Forge began to shiver uncontrollably as the stranger knelt beside them. He glanced down at La Forge's suit.

"I estimate you'll freeze to death in less than fifteen minutes," the stranger said.

"Th-the *Bozeman* will b-be here b-before that," La Forge bluffed.

The stranger didn't bother to reply. Instead he removed a series of cables from a pod on the side of his belt. Each ended in a universal induction sensor. "These are dataprobes," he said. "I can use them to download the contents of the robot's processors."

"H-he's an android," La Forge said.

"But if I download the contents of his processors, he will be wiped clean." The stranger gestured to include all of Trilex. "He'll be like these computers. Empty. Dead. Just like you."

La Forge saw the power overload light flashing on his in-helmet display. He didn't expect to last even fifteen minutes.

"So," the stranger continued, "tell me what I want to know, and I'll seal your suit and leave the robot—the android—intact. Your choice."

"G-go t-to Hell," La Forge said through shivering lips.

The stranger pulled his hand weapon from his belt, aimed it at La Forge.

"Didn't anyone ever tell you you shouldn't curse?" the stranger said.

Then La Forge saw a blinding blue light flash from the emitter node of the stranger's weapon.

His last thought was of all that was left when a star explodes . . .

Cold. And darkness. And death.

NINETEEN

Shit, Data thought.

Whatever the stranger had fired at him from his flattened cylindrical weapon, he felt each of his muscles and joints freeze in place. Not from the temperature of Trilex. But from an interruption in his movement subroutines.

As Data fell backward beside Geordi's prone body, he formulated a hypothesis to account for the effect the stranger's weapon had had on him. The most likely explanation was that he had been hit with a precisely focused subspace-radiation pulse. The pulse that had been created by Trilex's exploding sun had been strong enough to wipe all local computer circuitry clean of information. But the stranger's pulse had obviously been specifically modulated to interrupt only those subroutines in Data that governed physical functions.

After creating and comparing several equations which could be applied to constructing the stranger's device, Data decided it had most likely been developed as a covert device to access secured computer networks. He felt it was extremely improbable that the device had been constructed just to immobilize him. Though, he concluded, it was certainly effective in that regard.

By the time Data had hit the ice beside Geordi, his positronic brain had had enough processing time to review the contents of the last four standard years of the journal, *Subspace Multiphysics B,* and the Cochrane Institute's abstract index from 2355 to the present. As the stranger spoke to Geordi and prepared his dataprobes, Data had correlated enough information to hazard a guess as to the origin of the device.

But then Data had seen the flash of a disruptor discharge and was filled with the certain knowledge that Geordi had been killed.

For long nanoseconds, Data waited for the emotional response to that knowledge to flood through his positronic pathways.

But nothing happened.

He felt . . . empty.

He began formulating another theory to account for the lack of connection between his movement subroutines and his emotions. Could it be that true emotions were possible only when the intellect was contained within a functioning body, subjected to the stresses of daily survival? He found that a fascinating proposition. And though he did not feel sad about Geordi's death, he did regret he would not be able to discuss his new theory with his dead friend.

"What about you?" the stranger asked. The dataprobes dangled on their cables from his hand. His weapon was back on his belt.

"What about me?" Data replied. Once again he was impressed with the selectivity of the weapon. His facial muscle analogs were still able to function, permitting speech.

"Are you going to tell me where Picard is?" He held out the probes. "Or do I wipe your mind clean of everything?"

"There is no need to do that," Data said promptly. "I am in possession of no information regarding the whereabouts of Captain Picard. Furthermore, if I did, I am fully capable of erasing that information from my own datastorage so that it would be unretrievable by you."

The stranger began examining Data's head. "You won't mind if I don't take your word for it?"

"I do not mind in the sense that you mean," Data said as he heard one of his cranial access panels swing open. "Though I do regret that your nature is such that you will effectively be ending my existence for no reason."

The stranger stopped his investigation of Data's head and moved so that his visor was looking down at Data's face like a baleful cyclopean eye. "What do you know about my nature?" he asked.

Data studied his own reflection in the stranger's visor. It might be the last thing that he saw. But still, he felt nothing.

"I do not 'know' anything about your nature, as I do not know who you are. However, based on my analysis of scientific papers published over the past decade in the area of subspace multiphysics on which your weapon appears to be based, I have concluded that you are a Romulan. And I know how thorough and precise the Romulans are in their investigative work."

The stranger put his hand to his visor and pressed a control. The reflectivity faded away, leaving a clear covering in its place.

Data blinked several times to ensure his optical sensors were working properly, especially since the unfortunate freezing incident might have damaged his lenses.

"Do you still think I'm a Romulan?" the stranger asked.

"No," Data said. "But I do not believe you are who you appear to be, either."

The stranger's brow furrowed in his helmet. "And who do I appear to be?"

Data studied the stranger's pupils for the telltale contraction that might indicate he was lying. But there was no sign of it. Neither had the stress levels in his voice changed.

"Do you not know who you appear to be?" Data asked.

The stranger hesitated. Data could see that he seemed to be having an argument within himself. Something emotional. But Data no longer had access to his emotions. Whatever the stranger was feeling, it was a mystery to them both.

"Tell me," the stranger said.

"No," Data answered.

"Why not?"

"If I am to answer your question, you must do something for me."

The stranger tried, but could not restrain a small smile. "I'm supposed to negotiate with a robot?"

"An android," Data corrected.

"An android. What do you want?"

"Is Geordi still alive?"

"If you mean the human beside you, no. I killed him. And I will kill you, too."

Data heard the stress levels go up. Saw the pupils dilate.

"There is a strong probability that you are lying," Data said. "I can tell from your physiological reactions."

The stranger's face clouded.

"Where is Jean-Luc Picard?"

"You are under stress," Data said calmly. "Let me help."

The stranger's eyes lost focus, as if staring kilometers away. "Let me help . . ." he whispered.

"An old starship which has been assigned to scientific support duty will be returning to this location in one hour, thirty-seven minutes," Data said helpfully. "There is a medical officer on board who could—" Data stopped talking as the stranger suddenly slammed a dataprobe lead against his open cranial circuits. "That is neither necessary nor useful," he reminded the stranger.

"I don't have time for this," the stranger said.

"Strange, you are very much like Geordi," Data observed. Then he heard a high-pitched buzzing in his auditory recognition circuits. The stranger's face and everything around him broke up into coarse pixels that swirled like a closing wormhole, collapsing into a starless void from which there could be no return.

TWENTY

Against the void, a single blazing point of blue luminescence shone forth. Hyperdimensional flares suddenly bloomed from it, their elevenfold symmetries scintillating in dynamic protest as they were forced to conform to the rigid confines of normal, four-dimensional space-time. Then the quantum-gravitational pressure between the two realities could no longer be contained and space itself was torn apart, twisting open like the mouth of a mythical sea monster.

From the center of that majestic explosion of forces which humans still could not measure, control, nor define, a single *Galaxy*-class starship flew, for all its might as fragile as a windblown seed before the awesome power of the passageway it had just traversed between the stars.

Once again, the Celestial Temple of the Prophets had allowed its mysteries to be glimpsed, and the Bajoran wormhole had been opened.

The starship, *Challenger,* banked gracefully in the solar wind, then made its way to the strange, intriguing object that glittered like a dark jewel before it.

The Cardassian mining station once called *Terek Nor*. Now known throughout the Federation as Deep Space 9.

"And that's it?" Riker asked.

Data stepped around the frozen holographic recreations of his body, Geordi's, and the stranger's, as he joined Riker and Troi by the opening to the library structure. Except for the temperature, they were in an exact simulation of conditions on Trilex.

"Yes," Data said. "That is the extent of my memory of the incident. Obviously, the stranger connected his dataprobes at that point, canceling out my higher brain functions as he attempted to extract information from me."

Riker scratched at his beard, staring hard at the holographic stranger. "Attempted?"

"My mind was not erased as he had threatened, and my emotional routines have returned to operational status, so I must assume he was not successful in his efforts."

But Troi shook her head, unconvinced. "No, Data. Geordi's environmental suit was patched when the away team from the *Bozeman* found you. You didn't do it. Geordi couldn't do it. Therefore, the stranger must have. And since he took action to prevent Geordi from dying, it's fair to conclude that the stranger took similar action not to harm you, as well."

Spock's voice echoed around them. "A most logical evaluation, Counselor."

Troi smiled. "Thank you, Ambassador."

Riker sighed. "End program."

Data watched as the simulation of the Trilex archaeological dig faded away around him. It was remarkable how detailed the illusion had been, considering it had been created within a relatively cramped holosuite installed over the Quark's bar in DS9's Promenade, and not in a full holodeck.

Ambassador Spock stepped from the corner of the suite,

hands behind his back. "However, I believe it is time we accept the facts as they have been presented and stop referring to the assailant as 'the stranger.'"

Riker regarded Spock with polite forbearance. "Ambassador, with all due respect, the assailant *cannot* be James Kirk."

Spock continued, appearing not to hear the commander. "Computer, re-create the visitor to the Trilex site."

A three-dimensional projection of the stranger appeared in the center of the room, complete with environmental suit, equipment, and helmet.

"Now access the visual records downloaded from Lieutenant-Commander Data's memory banks, and remove the visitor's helmet to show us his face."

The helmet faded out, revealing a three-dimensional image of what was, in Data's judgment at least, a striking reproduction of the stranger's face as he had directly observed it. His features were most sharply defined in the area that had been visible through the helmet's visor, then eerily melted into lower-resolution detail toward the sides, ending in a basic, polygonal wire-frame extrapolation of the back of his head.

"Computer," Spock continued, "access the personal memory archives which I uploaded to the library system from my quarters. Run from code sequence 294-07."

A holographic viewscreen formed beside the reconstruction of the visitor. On the screen, Data recognized old update footage—a recording of an actual event instead of a mere holographic simulation.

"How does is feel to be back on the *Enterprise* bridge?" a disembodied voice asked. On the screen, the subject of the question blinked in the glare of the old-fashioned spotlights that had been trained on him.

"Freeze image," Spock said.

The Vulcan ambassador walked up between the holoscreen and the reconstruction. He gestured to the screen. "This is update footage of Captain Kirk, taken hours before he . . .

disappeared on the maiden flight of the *Enterprise-B.* Computer, isolate Captain Kirk's face from the update image, dimensionally enhance, and overlay onto the reconstruction."

Data observed with interest as everything on the holoscreen, except for Kirk's face, faded out. A moment later, the two-dimensional image expanded as it was enhanced to become a semitransparent, three-dimensional portrait of the famous and infamous captain. The portrait moved past Spock and settled like a ghostly cloud over the head of the reconstructed figure of the stranger.

Then the two images merged. Detail came to the low-resolution areas at the side of the head. Detail came to the unresolved areas at the back of the head. But in the face, nothing changed.

The images were a perfect match.

"Computer, quantify degree of fractal correlation," Spock asked.

"Ninety-nine, point nine nine nine nine—"

"That's enough," Riker interrupted. He gestured imploringly at Spock. "Mr. Ambassador, I have never denied that the assailant *looks* like James Kirk. Nor have I questioned Worf's account that the same individual is responsible for the attack on him. But . . . sir, James Kirk is dead. He gave his life to save Captain Picard, the crew of the *Enterprise,* and millions of beings on Veridian IV." Riker moved closer to the implacable Vulcan. "I'm very familiar with your . . . early exploits and adventures with your captain and your equally illustrious crew. But the fact remains, Picard buried your friend himself."

Spock's expression didn't change. "And those remains were then transported away by a group unknown."

"Remains, sir. Not a body in frozen stasis. Or transporter storage. A lifeless shell." Data saw that Riker was uncomfortable with being so blunt with the ambassador. "I'm sorry. But surely you of all people can understand that the dead cannot return to life."

Spock raised an eyebrow at Riker. "There appear to be some of my 'exploits and adventures' with which you are not familiar."

Riker looked confused. Spock did not deign to enlighten him.

Then Data heard footsteps in the corridor outside. A moment later, everyone else turned to the door as the entrance chime sounded.

"Enter," Riker said.

The door slipped open to reveal DS9's head of medicine, Dr. Julian Bashir. Ducking and bobbing behind him, trying to peer past the slender human into the holosuite, was the eponymous Ferengi who owned the establishment, Quark.

Bashir held up a medical padd as he entered. "Mr. Ambassador, I have the results of the tests you requested. I thought you'd want to see them personally."

But Spock declined the offer. "Thank you, doctor, but I already know what the results are. I believe Commander Riker would be more interested in reviewing them."

Bashir didn't question Spock's direction. He handed the padd to Riker. "Commander."

Meanwhile, Quark was studying the reconstructed figure in the center of the holosuite.

"So what's the story on this hew-man?" he asked.

"Nothing you need to worry about," Riker said.

Quark looked around with an expression of wide-eyed interest. "I understand. Is there a reward?"

Riker didn't bother looking up as he adjusted the padd's controls. "Quark, not now."

"I just don't get it," the Ferengi complained. "Starfleet commandeers my finest holosuite—"

Troi crossed her arms. "Every OHD panel was dirty, Quark. We had to wipe them off ourselves to get a clear simulation."

Quark looked mortally offended. "Did you bother to ask me for cleaning services? For a very small, additional fee, I could have—"

"Quiet, Quark," Riker said as he studied the padd.

The Ferengi sidled closer to Riker, peering indignantly up at him. "You'd better not be using that thing to copy my holosuite programs."

Riker looked over at Data. "Data, could you do something about him?"

Data went to Quark and put his hand on the Ferengi's shoulder. "Quark, we have paid for a full hour of use in this holosuite. That time is not yet up."

Data tried to steer the Ferengi toward the door, but Quark didn't want to go. "And that's another thing. It was Commander Riker and the Betazoid who booked the holosuite." Quark's burgundy-rimmed eyes narrowed in what even Data could see was a lascivious leer. His voice dropped to match his expression. "So I gave them the honeymoon special rate, if you know what I mean."

Data began to push the Ferengi toward the door more forcefully, gathering a fistful of Quark's lurid jacket for a better grip.

"But now," Quark went on more quickly, talking back over his shoulder as he was propelled forward, "now that I see you've turned my most sacred honeymoon program—the Mists of the Poconos—into a common orgy for four . . . for *five* of you—" Data firmly pushed Quark outside the door. The Ferengi spun around and fussily straightened his crooked lapel. "Well, I'm going to have to charge you extra!"

Data put his finger on the Cardassian door control. "If you recall, we provided our own program."

"I know," Quark muttered. "I've never seen copy protection like it."

Data pressed the control. The door began to slide shut.

"Not that I tried to copy it, you under—"

The door closed and sealed. Data was the only one in the holosuite whose ears could continue to hear what the Ferengi was saying, and he was impressed. It would add to his rapidly increasing store of curse words. When Geordi allowed him to use them again.

Data turned back to the others, just as Riker returned the medical padd to Bashir.

"I will confess," the commander said, "that some of this is beyond me."

"Well," Bashir replied, "for your purposes, the conclusions are all you need to be concerned with."

"And your conclusions are . . . ?" Riker prompted.

"They're not *my* conclusions, Commander. DNA is DNA."

"And DNA can be cloned."

"Oh, without question. It can be cloned. It can be engineered. It can even be reproduced by transporter duplication. But each of those techniques leaves a telltale signature on the reproduced DNA helices. With cloning, even a single generation will result in measurable replicative fading. Genetic engineering shows unmistakable traces of amino acid padding at cojoined sequences. And transporter duplication always results in a slight quantum mass imbalance. A bit more tricky to detect, but the samples obtained from Worf's fingernails were large enough to yield unquestionable results."

Riker's frown deepened.

Bashir looked even more contrite.

"Commander Riker, I have cross-checked my results with the tissue profile I obtained from Starfleet Medical Archives. The person who attacked Worf on Qo'noS was, without question, James Tiberius Kirk."

TWENTY-ONE

There were long moments of silence in the holosuite, broken only by the muted confirmation tones coming from Bashir's medical padd. Data watched as the doctor brought up a small display to show to Riker.

"It's all right here, Commander," Bashir said. "An absolute match to Kirk, James T. Born, Earth, 2233. Not a clone. Not a reconstruction. And not a transporter duplicate."

"Therefore," Spock added, "logic demands that the assailant on Trilex is also the captain." He looked at Riker, as if challenging the commander to argue with him.

Riker was up to the task. "No, Mr. Ambassador. Logic demands that Dr. Bashir made an error in his tests. Logic demands that . . . whoever stole Kirk's remains controls a cloning or replication technology unknown to Federation science. Logic demands that we exhaust every possible alternate explanation before we accept the . . . absurdity that James Kirk has come back to life and for some reason is searching for Captain Picard."

Spock remained unmoved by Riker's outburst, but said nothing, until Troi approached him, studying the holographic image of Kirk.

"Mr. Ambassador," she began, "is it possible that your logic is perhaps being influenced by . . . other considerations?"

"By my emotions, you mean?"

Troi paused, obviously hesitant to be speaking about emotions with a Vulcan.

"Do not be embarrassed, Counselor. I am aware that you have the ability to sense emotions. I have no doubt that you are sensing mine now. Which is why you have raised your concerns."

"Well, yes, sir."

Spock thought the matter over for a few moments. "I can see the irony in the situation. It does appear that because of my lifelong emotional connection to the captain, I am the only one present who can readily accept the apparently illogical premise that he is still alive."

"Then you admit it is an illogical premise?" Riker asked.

"Upon cursory examination," Spock answered. "But consider this, Commander. If some technologically advanced group did seek to create a duplicate of Captain Kirk, then why create a duplicate with no knowledge of his identity?"

"The duplication procedure was flawed," Riker suggested.

Spock gave Riker a pitying glance. "Enough is published about the captain's life to enable the most rudimentary of psychological programmers to create a convincing personality simulation. Through a combination of drugs, pain and pleasure stimuli, and exposure to holographic simulations of false memories, it is possible to make almost anyone falsely believe he is another person for a given period of time. Only the strongest personalities would be able to resist contemporary techniques."

Spock steepled his hands, as if announcing an unshakeable conclusion.

"Therefore, I submit that Captain Kirk's body has been reanimated by a technology unknown to us. I submit that what would be called, in a Vulcan, his *katra* has been retrieved by means of a temporal displacement, created by a technology unknown to us. I stand before you as a living example that the successful refusion of mind and body is possible. This much is known and must be accepted. Our only question is: Why has this been undertaken?"

Riker still wasn't convinced. "*My* question is: *Who* would undertake this . . . deception?"

Spock betrayed a slight, Vulcan hint of surprise. "Whoever they are, they are undoubtedly connected to the Romulan Star Empire."

Data was amused as Troi, Riker, and Bashir each said at the same time, "Romulans?"

Spock turned to the reproduction of Kirk as he had appeared on Trilex. "I apologize. I had thought it was obvious." He pointed to the flattened green cylinder hanging from Kirk's belt. "This is a device of Romulan design and manufacture. Developed by the intelligence service to overcome computer security systems by transmission of precisely timed micropulses of subspace radiation."

Data felt a moment of exhilaration. "Ambassador, that was exactly my conclusion."

"Indeed."

Data began talking faster. "Yes. When he used it against me, I cross-correlated ten years of scientific research papers and detected a noticeable Romulan absence in the field, implying they had made significant advances which they wished to keep secret."

"Very enterprising, Mr. Data."

Data nodded. "I cannot tell you how . . . happy this makes me feel. That my logic yielded the same conclusion as yours."

"Actually, Mr. Data, logic had little to do with my identification of the device. I have seen it before." Spock turned back to contemplate Kirk's image.

"Oh," Data said.

"On Romulus," Spock continued, almost as an afterthought, "it is a popular item in demand by illegal arms dealers. But I do commend you on your efforts."

Riker broke in testily. "So it's a Romulan device. That still doesn't explain why the Romulans would be behind this."

"If I may," Dr. Bashir interrupted. "We are working with Romulans here at DS9. They've provided a cloaking device for the *Defiant,* and the ship has actually operated with a Romulan observer on the bridge."

Riker stared silently at the doctor.

Bashir looked confused for a few moments, then alarmed. "Oh, yes," he added, "I suppose I should mention that what I just said is, uh, classified."

He gazed down at the yellow grid pattern on the dark floor.

"I believe that all of these events should be considered classified," Spock agreed, returning his attention to the discussion at hand.

"Classified or not," Riker said, "you still haven't explained a Romulan connection to these events."

Because his emotion chip now allowed him to see beneath the surface of most people's reactions, Data could tell Spock was untroubled by Riker's continued resistance.

"No doubt," Spock explained, "in regard to Captain Kirk's involvement, there is a personal connection linked to something in his past. As for Captain Picard's connection, I am not able to provide a hypothesis without knowing where Captain Picard is."

Data noted how quickly Riker tensed. He restrained his sudden impulse to add additional processing power to his visual and auditory senses in order to examine Riker's next words for signs of dishonesty. He had long ago decided that it was best never to do so with his friends and coworkers, unless there was a compelling reason.

"Are you now asking the same question this Kirk-clone was asking?" Riker said.

Data saw Spock tense as well, though the subtle signs of a Vulcan were far harder to discern. Some type of confrontation was building between the two, as each sought to somehow protect his own captain. But from what, Data didn't know.

"To be sure," Spock said, "this matter might be solved

more quickly if all pertinent information were made available."

Riker obviously heard something in Spock's words which Data had been unable to decode.

"I'm afraid I can't tell you what you want to know, Ambassador."

"Cannot?" Spock asked. "Or will not?"

Troi stepped between them. "Gentlemen, I can sense where this is going. It might be a good time to remind ourselves that we're all on the same side."

Data saw Riker adopt the same expression he did when playing poker. "Mr. Ambassador, is it possible the people who stole Kirk's remains on Veridian III were Romulans?"

"It is likely," Spock confirmed.

"And this Kirk-clone looking for Captain Picard, he's using a Romulan weapon?"

"You are identifying the pattern I have seen," Spock agreed.

"And exactly how many years have you spent working with Romulans, sir?"

Troi looked at Riker with alarm. "Will! That is out of line."

Spock's eyes narrowed. To Data, it was a most disconcertingly human expression. "Are you suggesting that I am somehow involved in these attacks against former members of Captain Picard's crew?"

Riker smiled coldly. "You have pointed out a Romulan connection. You, yourself, are connected to the Romulans. And you *were* by Kirk's grave when the remains were stolen."

Spock drew himself up with an almost regal air. "Commander, though I am a Vulcan, it would be wrong of you to believe that what you have suggested does not cause me considerable offense."

"I'm just trying to do my job, sir. You have been out of Starfleet for many years. Perhaps you've forgotten that part of it."

Data watched Spock's fingers tightly grip the edge of his

robe as he pulled it tightly closed, as if he were trying to hide his visceral response to Riker's challenge.

"Are you blind to the real pattern being developed here?" Spock asked. "Worf, Data, La Forge. You could be next, Commander."

"Is that a threat, Mr. Ambassador?"

Julian Bashir's mouth dropped open at the belligerence in Riker's tone.

Troi looked away from Riker in dismay.

Data watched with utter fascination.

Commander Riker had actually managed to enrage Ambassador Spock. Data could tell by the slight twitch at the corner of the ambassador's mouth. And Data could not help but feel that Riker had done this deliberately.

The ambassador spoke in slow and measured tones. "Vulcans never *threaten,* Commander. We only state our intentions. Good day."

Spock swept past Riker toward the door. He faltered when it did not open before him until he had pressed the control.

Then he was gone.

Troi was incensed. "I can't believe you did that, Will."

Riker looked shaken himself. "Neither can I."

"But why?" Bashir asked. He gazed at the closed door. "That man . . . he's . . . he's a legend."

Riker looked apologetically at Bashir. "I'm sorry, doctor. I'm going to have to ask you to leave. And to not talk about this with anyone. Understand?"

Bashir looked pained, as if he were given those orders every day. "I understand, Commander," he said formally. Then he left as well.

Troi folded her arms and looked at Riker. "You know, you were moving back and forth so quickly between truth and lies, I couldn't keep up."

"It was a most distressing conversation," Data added. "For all concerned."

But Riker remained silent, at a loss for words.

"You know what this is about, don't you?" Troi said.

"No," Riker answered, "I do not have the slightest idea what this is about."

Data put it together, his emotion chip at work again. "If I may be permitted an emotional insight, I believe it is apparent that you do, however, know the whereabouts of Captain Picard."

"This is not a conversation we should be having," Riker said stiffly.

Troi reached out to touch Riker's arm. "Will, *is* the captain all right? Are we in danger?"

"There are steps we can take, and will take," Riker said. "But we shouldn't discuss them here."

"You mean, where Ambassador Spock might overhear us?" Data asked.

For the first time, a smile came to Riker's face. "I mean, where Quark might hear us. If I know him, he's close to getting computer access to everything we're doing in here."

Troi gave Riker a questioning look. "Even if *you* don't know what we're doing."

But Riker did not respond to Troi's attempt at lightening the situation.

"Deanna, *I* know what I'm doing here. It's Spock's involvement I don't understand."

"Will, Kirk was his friend. They served together for decades. What we're seeing is nothing more than loyalty. The same loyalty you would show to Captain Picard in the same situation."

But Riker disagreed. "If Captain Picard has taught me anything, it's the need for teamwork. The strength of the whole crew acting together. If I were in the same situation Spock is in, you can bet I wouldn't be trying to run the investigation on my own. I'd listen to the experts at my disposal. I'd . . ." Riker shook his head, too upset to continue.

Troi remained calm. "Perhaps they did things differently back then."

"That's not my concern. Spock's involvement is. There's something . . . not right about it."

"Do you mean the Romulan connection?" Data asked.

Riker shrugged. "Spock has spent more time working for Vulcan-Romulan unification than he ever did serving with Kirk. But it's more than that." Riker looked at Troi. "The way he was acting on Veridian. Going back into the *Enterprise* to call up Kirk's service record. Always so caught up in the past."

Troi looked as if she couldn't believe the conversation were taking place. "His friend died. It's a natural time to become introspective and look to the past."

"Unfortunately, Deanna, there's nothing natural about this at all."

Not even Data's emotion chip could help him gain additional insight into whatever information Riker was refusing to share. But Data decided that under the circumstances, that was to be expected. After all, he reminded himself, as an android, he was not natural himself.

TWENTY-TWO

☆

The *Avatar of Tomed* blazed among the stars, leaving no wake of rainbow light, nor any other sign of her passing.

She was fully cloaked.

In Federation space.

Which could be construed by some as an act of war.

Which it was.

Though declaration of that war was still five days away.

On the starboard hangar deck, Kirk circled the battered shuttle parked in the forward service bay. He ran his fingers along its duranium hull, feeling the micropits and grooves of years of interstellar erosion and outgassing.

"I don't recognize it," he said at last.

Beside him, Salatrel consulted her padd. "You shouldn't expect to. It's an old *Montreal*-class shuttle. You've never flown one."

Kirk considered the shuttle's ungainly lines. Asymmetrical landing legs balanced the craft over its single warp engine, which extended behind the flight deck and cargo cabin as if it were a last-minute minute addition of a handle.

"I've never flown one," Kirk agreed. "And I've never seen one." Shuttles should be blocky and solid in appearance, though he couldn't recall why he knew that.

"The controls have been altered," Salatrel said. "But you'll know how to fly it."

Kirk turned to her. The outfit he was wearing bothered him. It felt awkward. Improper. The quartermaster had explained it was a civilian outfit, popular with humans. Kirk was haunted by the feeling that he should be wearing a uniform of some kind. Salatrel, however, had been adamant that he had never worn one, because he had never been an official part of the Romulan forces. Only a volunteer, a freedom fighter against the Federation's injustices.

"So flying a shuttle is another of my forgotten skills."

Salatrel nodded.

"I seem to have quite a number of them." Kirk was still intrigued that he had been able to fight the Klingon with such confidence and skill. Where had he learned such moves? And why?

And meeting with the human and the robot—*android,* he

corrected himself—on Trilex. He had felt comfortable in the environmental suit. Why? He had known how to operate the weapons Salatrel had given him, except for the subspace device he had used against the android. How?

"Are you all right?" Salatrel asked.

She looked at him, but kept glancing back at the padd she held.

"Isn't that what that thing is for?" Kirk asked in return.

Salatrel didn't answer.

"What does it do?" Kirk persisted. "Show you my vital signs? Let you know if I'm about to remember something?"

"It *is* a medical monitor," Salatrel said.

Kirk studied her, knew she was keeping something from him.

"What's my name again?" he asked, testing her.

Salatrel held up the padd. "This tells me you already know the answer."

"Yar," Kirk said. "A fine and honorable human name." That's what Salatrel had told him.

"Yar," Salatrel repeated. As if the alien name held meaning and honor for her.

Kirk smiled, not convinced that it held meaning for him. "It's growing on me."

Salatrel checked the padd. Kirk saw she wasn't convinced either. He could understand why she might want to keep a medical monitor on him. But why did she find it necessary to use it as a lie detector?

"Perhaps we should go back to the holodeck," Salatrel said, frowning at the padd.

"No," Kirk said. He didn't need any more treatments. Salatrel kept showing him scenes from his past, trying to provoke a return of his memories. Some he had seen often enough that they were becoming familiar.

His Romulan wife, Kalinara.

His children with her, Lora and Tranalak.

The colony ship they'd been on, the *Talon of Peace.*

He was beginning to get a sense of himself in that life. Or was he?

Had he really commanded a colony ship?

Been an explorer on the deck of a starship. Lost his wife to a brutal raid? Witnessed a child—his child—butchered by a Klingon bastard who—

Kirk gasped and pressed his hand against his temple.

No, not "child"—*children.* And it hadn't been a Klingon, it had been that monster Picard who had slaughtered them.

Hadn't it?

"I will find him," he said.

Salatrel looked at him with concern, but she had already put the medical padd away.

Kirk stretched out a hand, to lightly trace the smooth skin on her neck. "Did you know my wife? Kalinara?"

"Yes."

"And would she approve?"

"Of what?"

Kirk drew her to him. Kissed her. Felt her stiffen just for an instant like an actor caught without lines, then melt against him, kissing back.

"Yes," she said against his cheek. "I think so."

Kirk released her then and stepped back. "So do I."

Salatrel's communicator chimed. Her bridge informed her they were nearing the launch area.

Kirk picked up the small civilian bag the quartermaster had packed for him and headed toward the shuttle's open hatch.

He put his hand on the frame, about to pull himself up. Then he stopped, turned back to Salatrel.

"What happens after?" he asked her.

She blinked at him, not understanding. "After what?"

"After I kill Picard."

Kirk suddenly knew that whatever she would say next would be a lie.

Salatrel smiled without any hesitation and reached up to caress his face.

"Life begins again," she said.

Kirk kept his face absolutely still, suppressing his true reaction. Another forgotten skill he vaguely remembered having been taught by . . . The name and face wouldn't come to him. "Won't the Federation want revenge? Won't someone have to come after me?"

"I'll protect you," she said. She gave his hand a squeeze of farewell.

Kirk did not question her further, letting her take his silence as acquiescence.

He entered the shuttle. He turned and held her gaze until the hatch slid shut.

Then he performed as he knew he was expected to—waiting for the *Tomed* to drop from warp. Allowing a tractor beam to position his shuttle outside her cloaking field. Remaining adrift as the *Tomed* departed without communication, undetectable by Federation sensors.

Only when Salatrel and her ship were light-years away, did Kirk permit himself to consider her final words to him.

He knew he could not have any locator beacons or micro-communicators implanted in him. The risks would be far too great that signals from any communications device could be detected. Perhaps not on a remote planet such as Trilex. But certainly on the Klingon homeworld, and where Kirk was traveling next.

Thus he could be confident that however his thoughts affected his physical life signs, Salatrel would be unable to monitor him unless standing beside him with her medical padd.

Kirk watched the stars slowly pass the viewport of his drifting shuttle. At last reflecting on her final words.

Life begins again, she had lied.

Kirk felt certain that when he killed Picard, as he knew he

must and would, his usefulness to Salatrel would end. From her actions and her tone, it was obvious she did not expect him to survive beyond the successful completion of his mission.

And how would his end come?

I'll protect you, she had lied again.

Kirk also felt certain that Salatrel saw herself as the agent of his death.

But what of now? What of his life?

His name was not Yar. Yet he had lost a wife, children . . . a child, at least, a family, absolutely.

But to what? To an enemy? To fate? Or by his own choice?

Kirk looked at his hands on the shuttle controls. They had fought a Klingon. Outdrawn a young man with a phaser. Rewired leads into a positronic brain. And he knew they could move over this shuttle's controls with equally practiced skill.

So what kind of life had he led before his memories had been taken from him, that he could do these things?

And what kind of man had he been, that here—adrift in space, set into motion on a plan of which he had no understanding, knowing he faced impossible odds that brought death from all sides, he felt so . . .

. . . *alive.*

A time display flashed on the control surface. Kirk's right hand moved automatically to activate the shuttle's warp engine. With his left, he fired the attitude thrusters to place the small ship on its proper heading.

The action comforted him.

Perhaps he would never be able to answer all the questions that faced him in this new life.

But as long as he could still take action, he knew he could survive.

The engines came online. Kirk set his course.

For a place called Deep Space 9 and a man named Will Riker.

TWENTY-THREE

Romulus was a gray world. Ravaged by the constant tectonic stress of orbiting a double sun.

But to the first pilgrims who had landed here, refugees from the Vulcan Reformation, this bleak world had become home. And as the generations had passed, they were Vulcans no longer, but Romulans—reveling in the raw passions that had marked their ancestral race so early in its history. Using that instinctual fury to conquer this planet, instead of controlling it and themselves within the cooler paths of logic.

Spock understood what it was that had drawn those first Romulans to this world. The need to give vent to emotions too powerful to be suppressed, just as the world's fiery core released its terrifying pressures in displays of blazing, molten rock.

Sometimes Spock felt he was the only Vulcan who *could* understand the Romulan psyche. Which is why he had been trying to unify the two peoples for nearly eighty years.

But that very part of his unique nature that propelled him to such a pivotal role in galactic history was the same which now compelled him to risk all that he had worked for since he had retired from Starfleet and had last seen James Kirk.

His action was not logical.

But Spock had long ago come to terms with logic.

It was a valuable tool. Perhaps *the* most valuable tool.

But it was not the only one.

Spock had returned to Romulus because it was the human thing to do.

For his captain, for his friend, he could do no less.

"What does a Vulcan want with Romulan weapons?" Tiral asked with a sneer.

Spock glanced around the *dinglh,* a small Romulan eating establishment with a partial view of the Firefalls of Gath Gal'thong. Most of the other customers were gathered at the small tables near the grimy windows that overlooked the continually erupting fields of fire. Spock and his guests were well isolated in a shadowed corner, free to conduct their business, bothered only by the constant tremors that rumbled deep beneath the floor.

Spock leaned forward conspiratorially and lowered his voice, forcing Tiral and her companion to listen more closely. "Technically, the micropulsers are not weapons," Spock said. "They are military devices."

Tiral snorted, letting him know she recognized an attempt to change the subject and that she had no intention of accepting it.

But Spock merely steepled his fingers and waited. In any prolonged negotiation, victory invariably came to those who could afford to act last. And he knew he had elevated patience to an art form of meditative beauty. Even for a Vulcan.

An ancient, grizzled server with a limp approached their corner with three glass tankards of *greel.* Sloppily, he thumped down a tankard before each person at the table. Their server wore a veteran's ribbon over his heart, on the far right of his chest.

Spock lifted his tankard and made a show of holding the pale yellow liquid to the light. When he replaced the tankard on the table, he took care his fingers did not smear the surface of the glass. He was determined to make this easy for everyone involved.

"I prefer water," Spock informed the old Romulan. Then

he directed his gaze toward the windows and the great spouts of lava that glowed on the horizon. The server and Tiral had proven so inept at their wordless communication that Spock wanted them to be free to signal each other without fearing he could see them.

When Spock returned his attention to the table, his tankard was gone. He calculated he had three minutes, fifteen seconds before the server would be able to confirm the fingerprints and DNA residue he had left on the tankard. He had the same amount of time to present to Tiral the pertinent information she would need to devise an appropriate plan once she learned his identity.

As Spock watched, the young Romulan woman took a swift swallow from her tankard of *greel.* The yellow foam clung to the corner of her mouth, alarmingly bright against the black lipcoating she wore.

Spock enjoyed the silence and studied her calmly. In appearance, she was intriguingly unlike the others of her race he had dealt with. Except for a wild tuft of hair springing from her left temple, her scalp was shaved, the faint bristles giving the effect of a pale blue cap. In the bar's hazy green light, a metal disk gleamed silver against her right temple. The lewd pictogram on it identified it as a limbic transducer to which various devices could be attached to heighten sexual pleasure. It was a common enough device on Romulus, and on hundreds of other worlds. But for the young woman to wear it so brazenly in public signaled her desire to shock her elders.

Spock could understand that desire.

In his own way, he supposed, he had been just as rebellious as a youth. Though he doubted this child of Romulus would see the similarity between her choice of dress and his decision to enter Starfleet Academy against his father's wishes.

Tiral wiped the foam from her mouth, then wiped her hand on the *erx*-skin leggings she wore. The yellow foam was just as bright against their shiny black surface as against her lips.

Then she turned to Snell, her accomplice. He was a heavyset Romulan, at least ten years older than Tiral, in a wrinkled business suit. The stiff, upright brown collar he wore was a style that had gone out of fashion years ago, and Spock noted the almost invisible gleam of a limbic transducer beneath his black hair as well.

Even before Spock had sat down at this table, he had concluded Tiral and Snell were both transducer addicts—precisely the type of petty criminal he had sought. In any negotiation, knowing what the other side truly needed was an invaluable bargaining chip.

"So what do you think?" Tiral asked.

Snell sucked on his teeth. He rubbed his thumb and index finger together lightly, but constantly. Spock understood the significance. Snell needed to be transduced. It would be a short negotiation.

"Why?" Snell asked Spock.

With complete equanimity, Spock gave him the explanation he had chosen. "I wish to use the micropulsers to lay waste to the central hall of records, and, in the resulting social upheaval, establish myself as a dominant crime figure in the Romulan Star Empire."

Both Tiral and Snell gasped.

"You're joking," Snell sputtered.

"I am a Vulcan," Spock replied.

Tiral rubbed at her cheek, then extended her hand, moving it up and down as if trying to pull words from the air.

"Why tell us this?" she finally said.

"You asked me."

Tiral regarded Spock for a few tense moments, then leaned back in her chair, and threw an arm over its back.

Spock was pleased. Her posture told him she had accepted his story and judged him insane. She no longer saw him as a threat.

"So you want *ten* subspace micropulsers?" she said.

"To start," Spock said.

"How . . . how will you pay for them?" Snell asked.

"How do you wish to be paid? Federation credits? Starfleet requisition chits? Gold-pressed latinum? Interstellar letters of credit? Merchandise?" Spock watched the look of amazement that spread over both their faces.

He was having the required effect. To two transduction addicts such as they, a wealthy, delusional Vulcan would be a dream come true. As far as they knew, Spock was merely an aide to one of the ceremonial cultural exchange missions that periodically traveled between Romulus and Vulcan. But that would change, Spock knew. In less than ninety seconds. And then he would become even more valuable to them.

"My organization is quite well funded," Spock added needlessly.

"You know we could get a reward for turning you in to the security forces," Snell said, as if trying out the possibility of a threat.

"Undoubtedly," Spock agreed. "However, the reward would not be as great as the profit you could make by selling me the micropulsers. Additionally, the security forces would torture me to learn why I had approached you in the first place. This would place knowledge of your criminal activities in government hands. And in the event you escaped execution by Romulan security forces, my well-funded business associates would be compelled to hunt you down and kill you in a most objectionable manner as a lesson to others who might want to betray us."

"Latinum," Tiral said. She narrowed her eyes. "Five hundred bars . . . for each micropulser."

Spock pretended to think it over. It was an atrociously exorbitant price. To make his ruse look good, he would have to barter. Spock doubted that Tiral and Snell would be familiar with Vulcan customs concerning barter—all based in logic, of course.

"Thank you for your time," Spock said. He stood up from the table.

"Wait!" Tiral said. She reached out, about to touch Spock's arm.

Spock stopped her with a withering gaze.

A primary rule of interstellar etiquette was that Vulcans must never be touched without invitation. Their low-level psi powers made direct physical contact uncomfortable and unwanted. There were few races in the Federation unfamiliar with this rule. Tiral's action had been deliberate. She wished to unsettle him.

But it appeared she had judged that the threat of her touch made enough of a point. She drew her hand back, as if not wishing to cause further offense.

"That was just our opening offer. It's customary for the buyer to make a counteroffer."

Spock straightened his robe. He adopted his most logical-appearing attitude. "That is a most inefficient method of transacting business. I know how much you must pay for the stolen micropulsers. I know the risks you face in procuring them. I know the time it will take you to do so. Factoring in cost, risk, and time, in addition to a profit within the traditional range of illegal operations on Romulus, leads me to a price, converted into latinum, of eighty-three bars per micropulser."

Tiral and Snell tried not to look at each other. Spock did not need to mind-meld with them to know their reaction. He had quoted a price at least twenty-five percent higher than what they would have settled for. Right now, they would be gleefully anticipating telling their friends how they had managed to outbargain a Vulcan.

But Snell couldn't let well enough alone. Even as Tiral opened her mouth to accept Spock's inflated offer, Snell raised the price.

"You've miscalculated, friend. We need another five bars per micropulser, or there's simply no profit in it."

Tiral shifted unhappily in her seat. Spock knew she did not want to lose this incredible opportunity to her associate's greed.

Spock waited a few moments, to build their tension. "My apologies." Snell and Tiral held their breaths. "I have miscalculated. My new offer is *eighty* bars. Would you care to have me check my figures an additional time?"

Snell quickly stuck out his hand as if to shake Spock's. "Eighty bars each—sold."

His hand waited in empty space until Tiral kicked him beneath the table.

Snell clumsily changed his offer to shake hands into a gesture to sit.

Spock sat down again at the table with the two Romulans.

"I think this calls for a drink," Tiral said grandly.

"I am still waiting for my water," Spock reminded them.

Tiral waved over the server.

The server brought three more tankards of *greel* and a large access padd. Spock saw it was not the menu padd which the server had first carried, but the old veteran offered it to Tiral as if it were.

Three minutes, eight seconds, Spock thought. He had been off by seven seconds. An acceptable margin considering whose actions he had predicted.

As Tiral read the padd's display, Spock saw by her crudely controlled expression of elation that she now knew the Vulcan sitting across from her was not a second-level cultural attaché.

The server limped off.

Tiral looked up at Spock. Her grin was that of a predator.

Spock relaxed. Everything was unfolding as it should.

"So, tell us," Tiral said with a tone of condescension. "How long have you been working for the cultural exchange commission . . . Ambassador *Spock*?"

Spock made both eyebrows rise to be sure even Snell could detect his feigned reaction of surprise.

Snell's reaction was even more excessive. He spit out a mouthful of *greel* as he sputtered Spock's name.

Tiral kicked him again and slid the padd over to him.

Then she reached under her tunic and brought out a battered palm disruptor. Judging from its condition, Spock calculated the odds of it exploding rather than firing at fifty-fifty.

"What does your famed Vulcan logic tell you now, Spock? Who's going to pay the most to get you back in one piece? The Federation? Vulcan? Or our own security forces?"

"That is not a judgment I am qualified to make," Spock said. "All three entities would likely be interested in relieving you of me. However, it could be that at my age, the Federation and Vulcan would rather disavow me than risk an interplanetary incident by negotiating with Romulan street criminals. Then again, any contact you had with your own security forces could . . . put you at a disadvantage."

Spock calmly folded his hands on the table. Tiral and Snell stared at him, transfixed by their situation. It became obvious to Spock that the pair was incapable of concluding what their next step should be. It was clear to Spock he was going to have to help with his own kidnapping and ransom even more than he had anticipated.

"Speaking as an interested participant," Spock said gently, "might I suggest that the logical approach at this juncture would be to contact your superiors for further instructions."

Snell spat on the table. "We have no superiors."

Spock shifted his attention to Tiral. Evidently her transducer addiction had not yet resulted in permanent brain damage.

"From whom were you going to acquire the micropulsers?" Spock went on smoothly. No hint of tension in his voice revealed that the answer to his question was the point of this tedious exercise. Kirk had used a micropulser against Data on Trilex. If Spock could identify the source of the micropulser, he would be one step closer to whoever had retrieved Kirk's remains and had somehow brought him back from death. "Would not *they* be considered your superiors in this matter?"

Tiral kept her palm disruptor aimed at Spock as she sought reaction from Snell. "He makes sense to me."

"He's a Vulcan." Snell glared at Spock. "Why should we trust him? How do we know he's not just setting us up?" He restlessly scratched the skin at the edges of his transducer implant.

Tiral fixed her eyes on Spock's. "What about it, Vulcan? Are you setting us up?"

Inwardly, Spock sighed. "Tiral, what possible logical reason could I have to deliberately deliver myself into your hands?"

Tiral chewed the inside of her cheek. Then she shrugged and turned to Snell. "I say we pass him on to Tr'akul and let his organization handle the negotiations for turning him over to . . . whoever pays the most."

Snell stared at Spock. "Spock, how much are you worth, anyway? Factoring in risk, effort, profit . . ."

"I will endeavor to calculate a fair ransom," Spock said helpfully. He glanced over to the main entrance. Uniformed security officers were entering, most likely for a meal, though they could check identity papers at any time. "In the meantime, if you do wish to continue with this kidnapping, I suggest we leave the *dinglh* at once." He nodded at the uniformed officers.

Tiral stood and motioned to Snell to do the same. "Okay—but don't try anything. Otherwise, you're going back to Vulcan as a smudge on the floorboards."

Spock looked at Tiral's disruptor, still trained in his direction. How could these two even walk the streets?

"Please be careful with that," Spock said. "Your finger is covering the emitter node. If you fire, you will lose your hand."

Tiral moved her finger into a safe position.

Snell frowned with sudden suspicion. "If I didn't know better, I'd say you wanted us to kidnap you."

"Such a desire would be so illogical, I believe only a human could think of it."

Tiral and Snell both snickered. Romulans had no respect for humans, either.

"Humans," Snell sneered. "They're even worse than Vulcans. At least you're not one of them."

"Indeed," Spock said.

Then he suggested taking the back way out of the *dinglh* and allowed his two kidnappers to lead him to it, thinking that the sooner Romulus established ties with Vulcan, the better. If Tiral and her like were their culture's brave new generation, Spock calculated the Romulan Star Empire wouldn't last another century.

TWENTY-FOUR

After only two days, they no longer thought of themselves as stowaways, but as parasites in a living body.

Because there was no other way to think of the Borg ship.

For all the machinery it was composed of, for all the pipes and conduits, the power mesh and waveguides, there was another component buried beneath the duranium and the plasteel. . . .

Flesh.

Engineered and transfigured.

Ripped from whatever worlds and forms that had first

given it life. Now woven into the mechanistic nightmare of Borg technology.

The stink of it was everywhere. Fetid fluids dripping on the metallic decks. Soft shapes glistening and pulsing at the end of darkened corridors or twisting overhead as they propelled whatever moved inside them, all to serve the collective.

Beverly Crusher had never seen a ship like it. Had never been briefed about any Borg ship like it.

But each fresh atrocity that Picard saw, each wave of revulsion that sickened his heart—each was accompanied by what he imagined was the whisper of the collective, deep in his mind, telling him that this was right, that this was good, that this was the way all should be and would be.

The ultimate union of flesh and machine.

The destiny of all forms.

To join the oneness in which all could merge.

To return to the oneness which called to them all.

Including Jean-Luc Picard.

Near the end of their first day aboard the Borg vessel, they discovered a blind corridor that Picard had concluded served no purpose. Thus, they could rest there without fear of Borg work crews disturbing them.

"Why would the Borg create something with no purpose?" Beverly had asked.

Picard didn't know. The blind corridor ran to an exterior bulkhead. Perhaps it was some sort of airlock mechanism that would have a purpose if the ship ever docked. But for now, it was simply empty space, ignored by the collective, so it was safe. As far as that word had any meaning on a Borg vessel.

The end wall also had a viewport.

But they kept their backs to it.

Less than a minute of staring into the infinite ripples of the transwarp dimension was enough to induce nausea.

Beverly rationalized that they were looking at distortions in more than three dimensions—phenomena the human eye had not evolved to see, and thus a vista of which they could make no sense. Picard dared look into his memories of the collective, but it was clear his mind had not evolved to hold the mysteries of transwarp, either. Nothing he remembered on the subject made sense. And as he and Beverly rested, all he could think of was withdrawing. From everything.

But Beverly remained strong. For him.

Now, two days after they had come aboard, Beverly checked a readout on her wrist-mounted tricorder. They still wore their armor. The solid dark coverings helped them blend into their surroundings. At a distance, they might be Borg themselves. Picard quickly banished that image. It felt closer to the truth than he liked.

"We're coming up on seventy hours, Jean-Luc."

Picard nodded. He knew what she meant. They had already discussed it.

Given what Starfleet knew about the transwarp conduits the Borg used, seventy hours of travel would take them far enough away from Federation space that they could not expect to return in their lifetimes.

Picard was ready to take over the Borg vessel. He and Starfleet felt he did have a chance at taking control by using the neural interface. But Starfleet had specifically warned him not to attempt such a takeover during transwarp travel. They had doubted if he could maintain the proper functioning of a ship that moved according to physics which the Federation's greatest minds had yet to comprehend. And a ship that dropped out of transwarp uncontrolled might find itself stretched into a single-dimensional string of degenerate matter more than a light-year long.

That type of takeover had not seemed worth the risk. Not to Starfleet. And not to Picard.

At least, not near Federation space.

But at the distance Beverly and Picard had traveled now,

death was already assured. All they had to do was choose the method.

Picard held the neural interface in his hand.

Nothing more to lose.

Beverly didn't even question his decision.

Picard rose to his feet. He stood with his back to the bulkhead and the viewport as Beverly unfolded the cranial inducer from Picard's kit. It had been fabricated by Shelby's R & D team to look identical to the implant plate the Borg had given him when he had been transformed into Locutus. Shelby hoped the similarity of its appearance would aid in confusing the Borg.

But unlike the actual Borg plate, only the center connector, just above Picard's right ear, contained working components. That was where the neural interface would be inserted, drawing power and broadcast signals from the energy cell and subspace transmitter Picard wore beneath his armor.

Picard ran his fingers along the cranial plate.

"It doesn't feel the same," he said.

"It's not supposed to," Beverly said. "The one the Borg grafted to you connected to your facial nerves, to increase the bandwidth of the signals your brain could transmit and receive." Beverly held up the slender connector of the interface. "This is designed only for limited transmission through the skin and skull. It's not even a direct connection."

That was the saving grace of the plan, Commander Shelby had explained to Picard. Over such a limited channel, he would be able to communicate directly with the Borg, but he could not be drawn fully into the collective.

At least, in theory.

Beverly plugged the power-cell end of the interface into the socket on Picard's armor. For a moment she paused, holding the other end free, still disconnected.

Picard looked at it. In the dull light of the Borg ship, it was indistinguishable from a snake, dark and glistening. He looked up and saw an organic tube pulse slowly overhead.

The ultimate fate of flesh and machine. Beverly had done enough. He had to face the next step on his own.

"I'll do it," Picard said.

He took the interface from Beverly and rotated the metal tip in his fingers, feeling for the guide slots. All he had to do was slip it into place. Then he would hear the thoughts of the collective.

And the collective would hear his.

Picard straightened his shoulders, preparing himself. This was his duty and nothing could be more important than that. There was no turning back.

He began to lift the interface to his cranial plate.

Beverly took his hand.

"Jean-Luc . . . I . . ."

Everything she had to say was already in her eyes.

"Yes," Picard said and gently took her hand from his.

Beverly looked away. He moved the connector to its socket. Beverly held her hand to her mouth. Picard wanted to reassure her again. Reached out for her. But saw she was looking at something behind him.

He turned.

And slowly lowered the interface because of what he saw.

"We're docking," Beverly whispered.

"But we're still in transwarp," Picard said.

Together, they moved to the viewport.

Their ship was moving toward what could only be a station of some sort. A Borg station.

But it was in transwarp, unmoving against the multidimensional folds that rippled behind it.

"How is that possible?" Beverly marvelled.

Picard didn't know if she referred to the impossible reality that the Borg had constructed an unmoving station in another dimension, which no stretch of Federation science had ever predicted. Or the impossible shape of the station itself.

If Picard closed his eyes, he could see an image of a central

Borg cube to which six other cubes were attached, one to each face. That is the sense his brain tried to make out of what lay before them. With open eyes, if Picard concentrated on just one cube, it remained unremarkable, each surface ornate with typical Borg texture. However, he could conceive of no explanation for the source of the light that played over the station in a realm where photons could not exist because they moved too slowly.

But if Picard let his eyes drift from one cube section to another, the entire station seemed to balloon in a disorienting way that blurred his vision. Taken as a whole, each cube appeared to be connected to the next not by a single face, but by five. Yet every angle still appeared to be ninety degrees. At least, when he tried to focus on each angle.

Picard rubbed his eyes. For an instant, the cubes appeared to be hollow and he was gazing inside them. Then they rushed at him, constantly whiplashing back and forth as his senses struggled to deal with—

"It's a hypercube," Picard exclaimed, at last understanding. "A shape that can only exist in five-dimensional spacetime."

"But . . . how could the Borg build such a thing?"

"More to the point, Beverly, how can they keep it at rest here?"

The writhing form of the hypercube station slowly rotated before them. The backdrop of transwarp discontinuities shifted as well, making Picard guess that it was actually their ship that moved, if indeed such relativistic concepts had any currency here.

"Jean-Luc—over there!"

Picard felt himself begin to spiral as if he were in microgravity. But he fought the vertigo to look where Beverly pointed.

On the outermost face of the nearest cube, the even texture of power conduits was broken by an irregular collection of shapes. By force of will alone, Picard willed his eyes to perceive the face as a solid, unmoving object, stopping its wild oscillation.

"They're ships . . ." he whispered in shock.

He identified the white saucer of a *Miranda*-class Starfleet vessel, docked in line with an old Klingon cruiser, a dozen other vessels he couldn't recognize, and off to the outer edge, where the forced illusion of stability melted into the distortions of other dimensions, ten *D'deridex*-class Romulan Warbirds.

Beverly shook her head and looked away from the viewport, bracing herself against its raised ledge. Picard did the same. He felt bile rise in his throat.

"Could this be where the Borg originate?" Beverly asked weakly.

"I . . . don't think so," Picard said. "It doesn't seem large enough. And the Borg are three-dimensional beings like ourselves."

Picard closed his eyes to try and stop the corridor from spinning around him. Locating the Borg homeworld, the putative central node of the collective, had become Starfleet's top priority. But after years of analyzing all reports of the Borg's patterns of attack and every scavenged scrap of Borg debris, Starfleet knew only that the Borg homeworld—if there *were* a homeworld—was somewhere in the Delta Quadrant. Given current warp technology, that region of the galaxy was more than seventy years away at top speed. Completely inaccessible.

When Picard felt his equilibrium return, he opened his eyes again and risked another glance out the viewport. Their ship was closing in on that single face of the nearest cube. It appeared to bulge toward them like a huge dome, but the transformation of a two-dimensional shape into a three-dimensional shape was one with which Picard's senses could cope.

Beverly joined him again at the viewport.

"That's where we'll dock," he said.

Beverly touched the interface in his hand.

"There could be a great many Borg on that station," she told him. "We have no way of knowing how strong the influence of the collective mind might be in these conditions."

Picard understood doctor's orders when he heard them.

"Perhaps we should explore the station first," he said.

Beverly reached up and disconnected the power-cell plug from his armor. "That would be wise."

The snap of the connector triggered a wave of relief in Picard.

Still, he took the interface from Beverly and slipped it into a storage pouch on his own armor. "But we'll keep this near." He touched the cranial plate still in position on the right side of his face and head. "And I'll keep this on."

Beverly nodded.

Together they looked out the viewport again.

They were close enough that the vista of Borg machinery looked almost normal. They were coming in near the collection of captured starships.

Picard studied the *Miranda*-class vessel. The *U.S.S. Hoagland* had been a *Miranda*-class vessel lost at the Battle of Wolf 359, with no wreckage ever found. Was it possible that the Borg had somehow assimilated it even as the battle raged, transferring it through a transwarp corridor to this improbable station?

Picard concentrated on the distant white disk, trying to pick out the vessel's name or registration. But as they drew nearer, he could see that the ship had been partially disassembled, with dark conduits and braces connecting it to the surface of the Borg cube like filaments of mold. The Klingon vessel beside it was little more than a collection of Borg pipes and panels arranged in the shape of a battle cruiser. It appeared he was looking at some type of spare-parts repository.

Their ship now travelled over the hulks, moving in toward a circular docking pad. Picard wondered how the Warbirds were faring. If he could get a sense of the state of their disassembly, he might be able to estimate how long they had been captured. He glanced off to the side, looking for the Romulan craft.

But Beverly found them first.

"Jean-Luc . . . those Warbirds. They're intact."

As their ship rotated to line up with the docking ring, Picard had a few seconds to confirm Beverly's sighting.

Ten double-hulled ships, each almost twice the length of a *Galaxy*-class vessel, were connected to the Borg station only by standard docking tunnels and mooring clamps. Each still had operational running lights. Almost all of them had the characteristic green glow between their hulls that signified their singularity drives were operational.

"They must have just been captured," Picard said as the Borg ship's rotation carried them out of sight of the Warbirds. He focused on fixing the Warbirds' location in his memory. "That means there could be thousands of Romulans held captive here."

Beverly's voice tightened. "Being assimilated."

"Not all at once," Picard said. "The process takes time. It could mean there are thousands of able-bodied Romulan prisoners here ready to fight back against the Borg."

Beverly actually laughed. For the first time in weeks. "You mean, you and I could lead a revolt, here in a Borg station?"

"I have always thought the Romulans could be a valuable resource in a galactic civilization," he said with a smile. "An alliance with the Romulans, however formed, could be a very positive development indeed."

No longer laughing, Beverly fixed Picard with a curious expression.

"You've always thought that?" she asked.

Picard nodded, not seeing her point.

"Well, let's just hope you didn't give the collective any ideas."

The Borg ship echoed with the dull clang of docking rings joining.

Picard's stomach tightened with more than vertigo.

But there was no turning back.

TWENTY-FIVE

Riker downed a shot of replicator whiskey, grimaced, then followed it with a swig of synthale.

It didn't help.

As a round of groans broke out around Quark's Dabo table, Riker turned back to Morn beside him at the bar and repeated the punch line, "Change is the ultimate solution?"

The bulky alien, with a chinless, wrinkled face that looked as if he had been partially melted, nodded. And waited. Expectantly.

Riker considered his options. He had just spent ten minutes listening to a rambling monologue which Morn had assured him was the funniest joke in the universe. But Riker didn't get it. Option one was to tell Morn this, and possibly endure another twenty minutes of explanation. Riker chose option two.

He roared with laughter.

Morn blinked at him questioningly, but then joined in, clapping Riker jarringly on the shoulder before sliding off the barstool and wandering off to the waste-extraction facilities.

Quark stepped up behind the bar and deftly removed Riker's almost empty glasses.

"I never get tired of hearing that one," the Ferengi said.

Riker stared at Quark until the Ferengi shrugged.

"All right," Quark admitted in low tones, "I wish I could figure out some way to shut him up. He just never stops." Quark leaned closer. "Has he ever told you about his seventeen brothers?"

Riker shuddered at the thought of it. Then he noticed that Quark had set up another synthale and whiskey.

"I didn't order those," Riker said.

Quark smiled winningly with a mouthful of teeth, each tooth determined to grow in its own unique direction. "I'll put it on your tab."

"No, you won't," Riker said, returning the smile. "I don't have a tab. You're the one who owes *me,* remember?"

Quark put on a face of genuine surprise. "I thought I paid that back to you long ago."

Riker didn't say a word.

Quark couldn't handle the silence.

"You know, my brother, Rom, handles the accounts. I'll have him look into it."

"You do that," Riker said. He stood up.

"Commander—you're not going already?" Quark asked. "The night is young!" He dropped his voice again, giving Riker a lascivious wink. "And the Dabo girls are oh, so pretty."

"If you're suggesting what I think you're suggesting, I'm sure Odo's looking for a good excuse to have Commander Sisko cancel your permit." Riker returned the wink.

The Ferengi sighed. "I've missed you," he said, making sure each undertone of insincerity remained unhidden.

"I'm sure you have." Riker straightened his tunic. "Deduct the first round from what you owe me. You can upload the rest to my account with the purser on the *Challenger.*"

Quark's eyes widened. "You mean the ship that just came back through the wormhole?"

Riker waited for Quark to continue.

"But you came here on the *Alex Raymond,*" Quark said. His eyes narrowed again. "Is the *Challenger* your new posting?"

"What possible business is that of yours?"

Quark shrugged. "What can I say?" Quark tapped the lobe of one of his ears, each the size of a fully spread hand. "I like to keep my ears open."

Riker grinned. "Do you have a choice?"

Before Quark could reply, Riker stepped away from the bar and made his way to the Promenade entrance.

Quark had been right. The night, according to DS9's duty clock, was young, and Quark's Place was crowded. Riker counted at least twenty crew members from the *Challenger,* one of the newest *Galaxy*-class starships to be commissioned by Starfleet.

It would be a fine posting. And many of his former crewmates from the *Enterprise* would undoubtedly find their way to it. Especially after news of its recent exploits in the Gamma Quadrant began to circulate.

But Riker's stars did not follow a ship. They followed his captain. And it was for her captain's sake that he walked slowly along the Promenade, gazing in the shop windows, sampling a *jumja* stick, taking his time as he made his way to the turbolift.

A Cardassian, the only one Riker had seen aboard the station, stood outside a tailor shop, hands behind his back. He gave Riker a friendly smile. Riker nodded, but kept walking, avoiding the temptation to glance behind.

He already knew what he would see.

There had been a Bajoran monk studying the Promenade directory when Riker had entered Quark's, face shrouded by a large hood. The same monk had stepped up to study the same directory when Riker had left the bar a half hour later.

Riker didn't have to look back to know he was being followed.

The turbolift provided a swift, if rough, ride to the habitat ring. Riker stepped into the claustrophobic corridor and wondered once again what the Cardassian designers of the station had been thinking of when they had built it. With the support beams running across the floors as well as the ceilings, it was almost as if they had gone out of their way to make movement through the station difficult.

But then, the Cardassians excelled at overcoming their difficulties, so perhaps their culture encouraged erecting barriers as much as human cultures encouraged removing them. Riker looked forward to discussing that insight with Commander Sisko. Any officer who had lasted as long as Sisko had, caught in the middle of the still-simmering Bajoran-Cardassian conflict, had to understand both sides.

Riker heard the turbolift hum behind him. Another car was arriving. He hesitated at his intersection until he heard the doors just start to open, then he turned the corner and waited.

But after ten seconds, he still was unable to hear footsteps in the corridor. Had the monk missed him?

Riker decided to act as if he had forgotten something. He walked back around the corner, head down at first, heading back to the turbolift.

After a few steps, he looked up, ready to nod in acknowledgment of the monk he knew was in the corridor.

But the corridor was empty.

Riker paused. There were no other intersections between him and the turbolift.

He decided he had been mistaken. Perhaps the monk had been a monk after all. He started to turn back the way he had come.

Then DS9 exploded around him as the monk's fist hit his jaw.

Riker had no recollection of falling. All he knew was that he was lying on his back, staring up into the shadowed hood of the Bajoran holy man who had just decked him.

"What the devil do you think you're doing?" Riker demanded, giving the monk his opening.

But the monk folded his arms, making his hands disappear into his wide sleeves. He stepped back, giving Riker room to get to his feet.

Riker did, moving his jaw back and forth beneath his fingers. "Helluva right cross for a holy man," Riker said, frowning.

The monk remained still.

Riker feinted to the left.

The monk didn't move, his posture rigid as that of a statue.

Riker smiled. He enjoyed a challenge. But the effort of smiling hurt his jaw, and he frowned again.

"There are two way we can do this," Riker began.

"No," the monk said. "There is only *one*."

The monk leapt at him, robes billowing, giving Riker no clear target beneath them.

He felt stiff fingers expertly jab in beneath his ribs, knocking the air from his lungs, even as he partially deflected the hand aimed at his throat.

Riker fell back again as the monk flipped over him.

When Riker regained his footing, their positions were reversed. Now the monk had his back to the turbolift.

Riker spun around and raced off.

This time, he could hear the clanging of the monk's boots on the metal floor of the corridor.

Riker charged past the next two intersections, then hit the long corridor that led along one of the station's outer spokes to a docking pylon on the outer ring.

He glanced behind him.

The monk's fluttering robes made him look like an attacking sea creature—no sign of any structure beneath the dark shape pursuing him, only the embodied action of pursuit.

For an instant, Riker wondered if there such things as ghosts.

He picked up his pace.

By the time he reached the next intersection, the station's habitat sections had been left behind. Now he was in the industrial areas of the docking ring—machine shops, cargo holds, thruster control rooms.

He ran to the right, heading for one of the cargo bays assigned to Starfleet.

The monk followed in close pursuit.

Finally Riker stumbled to a stop by cargo-bay doors marked by the Starfleet delta. He bent over, hands on his knees, urgently drawing breath. He heard the monk closing in. Riker looked around, as if searching for a way out, then slapped the Cardassian wall pad and squeezed through the cargo-bay doors before they had finished opening.

Riker stepped back between two stacks of hexagonal packing modules and kept his eyes riveted on the open door.

He was relieved when the monk appeared and cast a long shadow into the bay.

Whatever the monk was, he was physical. Though Riker once again checked his jaw, thinking that should have been proof enough.

"There's nowhere to run on this station," the monk called out. He paused as if he expected an answer.

Riker said nothing.

The advantage of this section of DS9 was that it was completely under Starfleet control. The security monitors could be turned off at their source, so that any events that transpired here would not be recorded in Odo's office or tapped into by Quark.

The monk stepped through the cargo-bay doors. The instant he was clear, they slid shut behind him.

The monk didn't even bother to examine them.

"Come out, Commander Riker."

Riker stepped into a pool of light in the clear, central section of the cargo bay.

The monk moved toward him.

"You still haven't told me what you want," Riker said.

"I think you know."

"Try me."

The monk stopped in front of Riker. "All right . . . have you ever heard of—"

The monk's hand flew out for Riker's neck.

This time Riker was ready for him.

He parried the hand, then kicked up, caught the monk in the chest, then whirled around and with his other leg threw him off balance.

The monk hit the decking on his back as Riker completed his spin. But before Riker could recover his balance, the monk kicked out, catching Riker's legs.

Riker fell to the deck.

The monk dove for him, driving his elbow into the side of Riker's head with bone-jarring impact. Gasping in pain, Riker instinctively used the monk's momentum to roll him over, flipping on top of him. The monk's legs pushed up, sending Riker rolling over his head.

When the fighters leapt to their feet, both rocked, their exertions catching up with them. Riker shook his head. Tasted blood in his mouth.

"Why don't you ask me what you came here to ask me?" Riker wheezed.

The monk's hands reached into his robes.

Riker froze. The Promenade had weapons detectors. He had counted on the monk being unarmed.

So had Riker's backup.

The cargo bay flooded with light. Riker winced.

"Do not move," Data's voice announced. "Two phasers are trained on your position."

The monk slowly straightened up. "That's a roundabout way of saying you've got me covered," he said.

Data stepped out from behind one stack of crates. To the other side of Riker, La Forge appeared. Both held phasers.

"I want to see hands," La Forge said.

Riker was startled as the monk suddenly pulled down on his robe and the fabric tore away from him.

Though Riker had been expecting what he would find since he set up this ambush, actually standing face to face with someone who looked so much like James T. Kirk was like taking a direct hit.

Again.

Picard had described to Riker his reaction to having met Kirk in the Nexus. The visceral impact of seeing someone in the flesh who up to that moment had only ever been an image on a viewscreen.

Riker knew the man before him was a fraud, a creation of an unknown science. Still, for just a moment, a sense of fleeting wonder touched him as he dared think that the person he saw, the legend he saw, might be real.

The impostor glanced at Data and La Forge, betraying no surprise at seeing either of them. Then he turned his full attention to Riker.

"You recognize me, too, don't you?" the impostor said.

Riker stared intently at the false James Kirk. "Let's just say I recognize who you're *supposed* to be."

There was a strong attitude of competence and control in the impostor's bearing, exactly what Riker would have expected from the historical Kirk. But just for a moment, something else flashed behind those eyes. An unexpressed sense of pain . . . of loss . . . Riker wished Deanna were here now. Though she would have her chance with this . . . whatever he was, soon enough.

"Tell me," the impostor said. "Who am I . . . supposed to be?"

"You really do not know?" Data asked.

The impostor turned to the android, smiling ruefully. "Do you think I'd let myself step into this trap if I didn't have a good reason?"

Riker started. He had seen that smile before, heard that tone of voice in so many captain's log recordings that it was as if he recognized the voice of someone in his own family. It was one thing to duplicate a biological body . . . but to reproduce so exactly the tone and nature of a personality?

"What about the other question?" Riker said sharply. "What you asked La Forge, and Data, and Worf. Why do you want to find Captain Picard?"

As if a live wire had been touched to the impostor, Riker saw the false Kirk's body stiffen as a hate-filled grimace took over his face.

"Picard," the impostor spat. "He must die! *I have to kill him!*"

Then with an enraged snarl, the impostor threw himself at Riker, hands like claws, in response to some elemental fury Riker could never hope to understand.

Data's reflexes were faster than La Forge's, and it was the android's phaser that dropped the impostor.

His hands tightened reflexively on Riker's tunic, but his eyes rolled up and he began to slump, whispering one final word before Riker caught him and gently, almost respectfully, lowered him to the floor.

The three officers stood over their remarkable prisoner for a moment, one unspoken question shared among them.

Riker touched his communicator.

"Riker to Ops . . . four to beam to the infirmary."

And even as the transporter locked onto them, the whispered word still hung in the silence.

The last word the impostor had gasped as the phaser had claimed him . . .

A word, a plea, that only James T. Kirk would use . . .

. . . *Spock* . . .

Riker felt a chill move through him.

And it wasn't the transporter.

TWENTY-SIX

The truck came to a stop approximately fifty-two kilometers southwest of Dartha, the capital city of Romulus. Normally, Spock would have been more precise in his estimate, but Tiral and Snell had placed a cloth bag over his head, forcing him to rely on physical sensations of speed and heading changes alone.

Fortunately, the truck was a wheeled variety, less expensive to operate than an antigrav floater in the loose shale of the southern regions around Dartha. For Tiral and Snell, the cost of energy was of utmost importance, second only to their episodes of transduction.

Spock had already endured many such episodes during his short captivity. Typically, Tiral and Snell would confine him someplace, once even in the cargo compartment of the truck, and then retire to a location where his acute ears couldn't avoid relaying every detail of their addiction.

He concluded his kidnappers were energetic, if not overly imaginative. The seven-year cycle of *Pon farr* gave Vulcan's greatest minds ample opportunity to anticipate and then experience their pleasures, and the detailed records of that anticipation and experience were still banned on more than half the worlds of the Federation. No doubt when full relations were established between Vulcan and Romulus, entire Vulcan libraries would become available throughout the Star Empire, and Spock anticipated the shock waves that would result when Romulans experienced the exquisite discoveries of suppression and discipline.

But for the last hour, Tiral and Snell had remained silent and celibate, directing the truck on a circuitous route which Spock guessed was intended to avoid security checkpoints as well as to confuse him.

At least they had been successful in their first intent.

Spock braced himself against the door of the passenger cabin as the truck swerved to a stop. They had driven off the main transport route fifteen minutes earlier, and the thunder of rocks and gravel against the underside of the vehicle had been continuous since then.

Spock felt the door beside him swing up on its hydraulic hinges. He tensed, waiting for Snell's hand to grab his arm and drag him from the truck's cabin. But instead he scented Tiral's perfume. She, at least, was cultured enough to continue to avoid touching him.

Spock had felt a sense of missed potential as he had contemplated Tiral during his captivity. However she had come to this life of petty criminal pursuits, he knew she had not been born to it. What tragedies there had been in her past he did not know. Given the hardening her present life promoted, it was quite likely he never would.

"Ambassador," Tiral said formally, "if you would step out please."

Spock swung his legs around and made certain his feet had solid purchase before he attempted to stand. His hands were tied behind his back. The shale made finding one's balance a precarious proposition.

He felt his head brush Tiral's hand as he stood. She was protecting him from hitting his head on the overhead door.

"How old are you?" Spock asked.

"Step away from the door," Tiral said.

Spock tested the ground ahead with his boot, found a secure footing, and stepped forward. He could smell the night air through the cloth over his face. There was a tang of sulfur to it. A water reclamation plant must be nearby. A billion years of almost constant volcanic eruptions had made fresh water on Romulus rarer than dilithium.

"Have you ever considered leaving your . . . line of work?" Spock asked.

He sensed a change in Tiral's movements that indicated he had caught her attention. And even her gruff tone of bravado could not hide the bitterness that underlay her words. "Who'd have me, Ambassador?"

"There are those on Romulus who study Vulcan history. They require secrecy and stealth in their pursuits, and it could be you would have skills to offer them." But then, before Tiral could even begin to reply to him, Spock relaxed his muscles and began to fall forward.

By the time Snell's foot made contact with the back of his knees, Spock was already twisting to more efficiently absorb the impact of his fall.

"What did you do that for?" Tiral shouted at Snell.

"The last thing I need is you turning into a Vulcan on me!"

Spock heard more scrabbling against the rock, a grunt of surprise and exertion from Tiral, the sound of a body falling.

Then the sharp slap of flesh on flesh. A shrill cry. A guttural torrent of Romulan epithets.

And then . . . something else. Far off. Coming closer.

Spock felt Snell's hands grab his arms roughly as he was pulled to his feet. Spock slipped, almost fell again, caught himself.

He felt his head forced back by pressure on the bag over his face.

"Careful," Tiral said faintly. Her voice was thick with liquid. Blood, Spock knew. Snell's blows had hurt her.

"Why?" Snell challenged.

"Cause he's not worth anything to us dead!"

Snell's hand struck the side of Spock's head. Next, Spock felt the cloth slide up and off his face. It was night, but he blinked under an onslaught of sudden light, so bright his inner eyelid slid shut to ward off blindness.

The air trembled around him. A craft was approaching. Blazing its way with powerful searchlights which spread across the bleak landscape, as if looking for any others who might be hidden nearby.

Spock stared upward, eyes slits as the beam played across him.

He saw it pick out Tiral and Snell. In the harsh blue cast of it, the green blood on Tiral's face was dark, almost black.

A wind picked up. Small stinging bits of stone danced through the night, stirred up by the craft's backwash.

It was some kind of civilian runabout, Spock noted, aerodynamically sleek for atmospheric travel, large enough for four or five passengers. But even his heightened eyesight could not penetrate the glare of its searchlights to identify the actual model.

It set down twenty meters away. The shale crunched beneath it. Its pilot kept its engine operating on standby. Then the access hatch opened and a set of steps folded down.

Spock's hair streamed in the wind. Tiral and Snell stood to either side, equally mesmerized by the searchlight beam that targeted them.

The shadows of the three people from the craft rippled in that light as they approached, as dark as wraiths, as ill-defined as smoke.

But Spock did not need to see the features of those who approached to know that one was Tr'akul, one of the most notorious smugglers in the Romulan Empire, with few peers in many other crimes.

As two of the figures hung back, one alone approached. He pulled back the hood of his black robe, and Spock saw a Romulan with a cadaverously lean face, accentuated by a scar that ran from cheekbone to chin, dimpling the bone beneath it.

"Greetings, Tr'akul," Spock said.

The Romulan crime lord glanced at him as if he were only a commodity. He reached out, took Spock's jaw, and pushed the Vulcan's head back and forth as if inspecting livestock. As with Snell, Spock set aside Tr'akul's casual, violating touch.

Tr'akul smiled as he flicked his hand like a sleight-of-hand magician and a knife materialized in it. Spock remained silent as the knife scored his cheek.

The hot green blood that trickled from his wound cooled rapidly in the rising wind.

Tr'akul, still smiling, gestured again and the knife was gone. In its place, a small medical sensor. With a flourish, he touched it to Spock's cheek, to Spock's blood.

After a few seconds, the sensor chimed.

Another flick of Tr'akul's hand and the sensor was gone.

Without looking back at his companions, Tr'akul raised his hand and snapped his fingers twice. Then he stepped back.

One companion, also concealed in a fluttering black robe, approached Tiral. He handed her a small case. Opened it for her. Still nothing was said.

Spock shifted his gaze to see what his price had been.

A limbic accelerator.

He mourned Tiral's death, even more so because she could not see its approach.

Tiral fumbled eagerly with the accelerator. Its contact point reflected the light of the searchlight so powerfully that it was like looking at a chemical flare.

Snell took it from her as she struggled to unfasten the second contact. Tiral wrested it back from him.

Spock watched with fascinated despair.

What had Romulus become to give birth to people who had so little sense of history, so little hope?

Tiral looked at Spock. She held the accelerator tightly against her chest.

"Tiral, don't," Spock said quickly. "It will—"

Snell hit him so quickly and so hard in his solar plexus that he saw flashes of light in the corner of his vision.

Felled by primal shock, Spock dropped to his knees, unable to keep his face from falling forward and slamming into the shale.

A small gasp escaped him before he achieved the state of *n'kolinahra* and banished the pain of the assault.

He lifted his head and peered up through the blowing dust and dirt in time to see Tiral and Snell both connected to the accelerator through their transducer implants.

"Just a taste," Tiral warned Snell. "We've got a long drive back."

Spock tried to speak, but there was no air in his lungs.

I grieve for thee, he thought. It was all he could do. A century ago, he could have slipped from his bonds, dropped Tr'akul and his thugs, saved Tiral and Snell, and still learned what he needed to know. And at Kirk's side, there would have been nothing that could have stopped them from going on to . . .

Snell switched on the accelerator. Tiral and Snell embraced.

For the briefest of instants, pure joy lit their faces.

Then they clawed frantically at the transducer contacts on their scalps. Their mouths yawned open without sound.

Green blood exploded from their noses and lips.

Their limbs trembled in a terrible rictus of agony, then went limp as Tiral and Snell slid to the shale, still bound together.

The background whine of the waiting craft swallowed whatever death rattles escaped them. The ending of their lives no more than a troublesome detail, easily dealt with by Spock's buyers.

Spock forced himself to his feet before anyone could touch him again.

He stood before Tr'akul, tasting the copper of the blood that ran from his own nose across his lips.

Tr'akul brought the knife to his hand again, reached around Spock as if to embrace him, and cut the ropes that bound his wrists.

And just before he stepped away, Spock felt the Romulan whisper in his ear—the first words he'd spoken.

"T'raylya ohm t'air ras."

Spock fought to maintain his neutral expression.

The words were a form of Ancient Vulcan, a spoken tongue unknown to all but scholars. From a lament that dated thousands of years before the teachings of Surak.

Forgive me, my brother. . . .

Tr'akul stared deep into Spock's eyes, then dropped his gaze.

Tr'akul's cryptic phrase told Spock that the notorious smuggler was no longer in charge of what would happen next. He was not even in favor of it.

For the first time since developing this plan, Spock conceded to himself that he might have miscalculated.

Spock had expected to find himself ransomed by Tiral and Snell, and he had been. To a logical choice, Tr'akul. But Spock had expected that whichever party bought him would be the same that had supplied the micropulser to Kirk. And that whoever bought him, in turn, from the supplier would be the group that had restored Kirk.

So if not Tr'akul, then who was in control?

Tr'akul gestured to the third member of his party still silhouetted by the searchlight's concealing glare.

The third figure walked forward.

And he drew a disruptor and fired it in one fluid motion so

seamless that Spock barely had time to register it before the orange beam crackled through the night and reduced the person who had carried the transducer to a cloud of disrupted radiation.

The disruptor turned toward Spock.

Spock had no concern for his own safety. There would be no logic in killing him in this way at this time.

But the third figure swung his arm out with the precision of a machine and fired again.

"T'air ras!" Spock shouted, *"bral!"*

But before Tr'akul could run, orange fire flickered over the shale and the smuggler was consumed.

The third figure put the disruptor away.

"You will come with us," the figure said to Spock.

Spock calculated the odds of his surviving a trip with the figure. They were not in his favor.

In a heartbeat, he brought his hand to the base of the figure's neck, positioned his fingers, and pinched the nerves beneath them.

The figure did not react or try to defend himself. And the nerve pinch did nothing.

To test his hypothesis, Spock pinched again.

Still nothing.

Spock raised an eyebrow. "Fascinating," he said. He removed his hand.

The figure moved, pulling back his hood to reveal the cranial implant plates that cruelly puckered the flesh of his Romulan features.

Spock recognized their origin.

"Resistance is futile," Vox said.

"Indeed."

TWENTY-SEVEN

In Deep Space 9's infirmary, Dr. Julian Bashir folded his arms and waited impatiently, as if everyone in the infirmary could interpret the Cardassian medical display as easily as he could.

But Riker wasn't interested in the doctor or the display. His attention remained fixed on the patient on the diagnostic bed, kept asleep by means of the small somnetic inducer on his forehead.

Deanna touched Riker's arm. "You believe now, don't you?"

As unhappy as it made Riker feel, he couldn't argue with Deanna.

"Yes," he said.

Dr. Bashir shrugged. "That *is* what I've been telling you, Commander."

Riker rubbed at his sore jaw. For a dead man, Captain James T. Kirk still packed one hell of a wallop.

"Is this some aftereffect of being in the Nexus?" Riker asked. Kirk had been swallowed by the energy-ribbon phenomenon when he had vanished seventy-eight years ago on the maiden voyage of the *Enterprise-B*. Somehow, Kirk had continued to exist in a dream state until Picard had also entered its realm. Picard had been successful in convincing Kirk to reenter the physical world, to help him stop a madman from destroying the Veridian sun.

Their joint effort had been successful, but fatal for Kirk.

Yet here he was. Again.

Surely the only explanation possible involved some kind of alien metaphysics.

But Bashir had said, "No." Politely. Riker had first met the young doctor three years earlier, when Starfleet had taken over the administration of Deep Space 9. At the time, he had thought Julian Bashir one of the most annoyingly arrogant youngsters he had ever met. But life on the frontier had obviously had a positive effect. Bashir was maturing well.

"I tracked down the El-Aurian who used to run the recreational facilities on the *Enterprise,*" Bashir now explained. He leaned back against one of the infirmary consoles, a disarmingly informal posture. But Riker had learned that Bashir's casual mien hid a keen and disciplined mind worthy of Starfleet's best officer material.

"Guinan," Riker said.

"Exactly. She experienced the Nexus at the time of the *Lakul* disaster, and she is quite adamant that if Kirk left the Nexus of his own volition, unlike her and the others who were forcibly removed, there can be no . . . echo of him left within it. He came out as he went in, flesh and blood and all it is heir to."

"Then how . . . ?" Riker said.

Bashir crossed over to a second display above Kirk's diagnostic bed. He touched the imcomprehensible Cardassian controls and the screen changed to display a quantum-phase interior view of Kirk's skull and brain.

"Two possibilities," Bashir said, "both of them unusual. This. . . ." The display zoomed in to show a dense structure the size of a pen snaking around Kirk's medulla. It branched into a fractal network of smaller structures, absolutely impenetrable to the medical sensors. "And these . . . ," Bashir concluded. The screen shifted to what Riker recognized as an interior view of an artery. Mixed in with the blood cells that surged rhythmically by, there were smaller objects, no larger than single pixel dots compared to the relatively huge blood cells.

"Those dots?" Riker asked.

"Computer, enlarge current view by two factors."

Now Riker recognized the dots, but he still didn't understand. "Nanites?"

"Of a type," Bashir confirmed. "I've never seen this precise configuration before, but they are clearly nanotechnology intended for medical treatment. In this case, repairing the extensive damage to the patient's tissue."

Riker fixed Bashir with a skeptical look. "With respect, Doctor. The patient wasn't 'extensively damaged.' The patient was dead. I would think that what has happened to Kirk is a bit more complicated than a medical treatment."

Bashir grinned. "Perhaps that was an understatement. But take another look at the device in his brain stem."

The display over Kirk returned to the image of his skull and the object within it.

"What is it?"

"According to the scans I can make, perhaps the most sophisticated neural implant known to medical science."

Riker's senses went on alert. He saw Deanna give him a quizzical look, responding to the sudden change in his emotional state.

"What's its purpose?" Riker asked. It was too much of a coincidence that just as one Starfleet captain disappeared on a mission with a neural interface, another from the past came looking for him. Also with an interface.

Bashir frowned. "All I know for certain is that it's killing him." The doctor moved his finger over the outer fractal tendrils of the device. "These contact points are being modified by the nanites to extend further into the patient's cortex. It's like a cancerous tumor. At the rate it's growing, I give him no more than a week."

Riker gave the doctor a sharp look. Most cancers were as easy to treat as contact dermatitis. "Remove it."

"*I* can't, Commander. What's required is far beyond my skill as a surgeon."

"Can't you use the transporter to filter out the extraneous material?" Deanna asked.

"That is a valid treatment, Counselor. But to carry it out, we'd have to create a complete cellular map of the patient's nervous system in order to ensure he would be correctly reassembled. And that, I'm afraid, would take months. Which we don't have."

Riker went back to what the doctor had stated earlier. "You said *you* couldn't remove the device by surgical means. Does that mean someone else could?"

Bashir nodded. "Possibly. I've made another enquiry into Starfleet's medical archives." He grinned again. "They're getting to know me there after everything I put them through just to get Kirk's old records. But there are a handful of devices as complex as this that have been encountered before . . . and have been successfully removed by Starfleet doctors."

"Are any of those doctors available to us?"

"Only one is on active duty," Bashir said. "Beverly Crusher."

Riker understood at once. "She removed the Borg implants from Captain Picard."

Bashir nodded.

Riker's chest tightened. "Are you saying the device in Kirk is a Borg device?"

"I can't even venture an opinion on that, Commander. All neural interfaces share similar design features simply because of what they're designed to do. Does this device resemble a Borg implant? Certainly. Is it identical to Captain Picard's implants as recorded in Starfleet's archives? No. Could it therefore be of Borg manufacture? Perhaps."

Riker thought over his options. "This is an obvious question, but does Kirk know where the implant came from?"

"I only spoke with him briefly, but he has no idea who he is.

And any questions I ask him about his activities in the past few days, or his reported compulsion to kill your Captain Picard, simply trigger a violent response. That's why I'm keeping him under the somnetic inducer. It's preferable to modifying his aberrant behavior through drugs, until we know what's causing his behavior."

Deanna made the connection. "Has he been programmed?"

"Conditioned," Bashir said. "Yes."

"The implant?" Riker asked.

Bashir was emphatic. "Yes. Of that, at least, I *am* certain."

"So the only way we're going to get past whatever blocks have been put on Kirk's memories is by removing that implant. And unless that implant is removed within a week, at most, Kirk will die."

Bashir's next question was what Riker had been waiting for. "Commander, where *is* Dr. Crusher? According to Medical, she's on extended leave. But no one will tell me where."

There was no more time to waste. If Picard had taught him anything, Riker thought, it was that not only must a good leader make correct decisions, he must make fast decisions.

He drew himself up, understanding that there would be no stepping back from what he was about to do. Shelby be damned.

"Dr. Bashir, Counselor Troi, under Starfleet General Order Three, I am now invoking the official secrets regulations of stardate 7500, as amended, stardate 42799."

"But . . . those orders have to do with . . . invasion," Bashir said hesitantly.

Riker pressed on. He was speaking for the record now. "Starfleet has reason to believe the Federation is facing imminent attack. Captain Picard and Dr. Crusher are on special assignment to prevent that attack. It is my opinion that James T. Kirk is in some way involved with these events, and I am taking it upon myself to transfer him to the last known location of Dr. Crusher. I am taking this action in order to facilitate the removal of the implant which is preventing me from questioning him."

"You are both hereby seconded to my command aboard the *U.S.S. Challenger* and ordered to prepare for immediate departure to Starbase 804."

Deanna headed for the infirmary door without a single question. Riker had expected no less from her. But Bashir was another matter.

"Commander Riker, this ultrasecret business is all very interesting, but since everything we say from now on *is* ultrasecret, may I ask just who Starfleet thinks is about to invade us?"

Riker had no time for junior officers who questioned orders in a crisis, no matter how personable. But just this once, he would make an exception. If only to see the color drain from the young doctor's face.

"The Borg," he said.

Bashir's expression was worth the exception.

TWENTY-EIGHT

The *Starship Challenger* eased back from the upper docking pylon which had been its berth at Deep Space 9.

Her Vulcan captain, Simm, a twenty-year veteran of Starfleet command, exchanged polite farewells with the station's traffic controller, then had the helm bank the ship away, setting course for Starbase 804.

As the *Challenger* came about, the Bajoran wormhole irised open again to admit a Klingon mining survey vessel. In the flood of exotic radiation that the wormhole itself emitted, a single directed pulse of tetryons was easily and understandably overlooked.

The faster-than-light particles could exist only in subspace and were an expected, if not regular, phenomenon of any wormhole.

But in this case, the directed beam did not come from the Celestial Temple itself, but from a point four light-years distant from Deep Space 9.

Aboard the *Avatar of Tomed,* Salatrel leaned to the side in her command chair, nervously stroking its arm.

"We're receiving a passive return from the tetryon pulse," Subcommander Tran reported. He turned from his helm board to face her. "He is being moved."

"On the station?" Salatrel asked.

"On the *Challenger,"* Tran answered, smiling coldly.

Salatrel wouldn't give the upstart the satisfaction of seeing her fear. She had not been able to risk outfitting Kirk with a transmitter or a locator beacon, for fear his signal would be detected. But so close to a wormhole with its constant fluxes of broad-spectrum radiation, it had been a simple matter to realign her Warbird's sensors to use tetryons to search for and detect Kirk's implant each time the wormhole opened.

"Heading?" Salatrel asked.

Tran checked his board. "The only port of call that makes sense is Starbase 804."

Salatrel turned in her chair to face her white-haired centurion, Tracius.

"Is Starbase 804 of any particular significance?"

The grim-faced Romulan looked up at the ceiling of the bridge, accessing memories he was too old and too stubborn to commit to a computer. "Another bastion of the Federation's intent to plant her flag and fascist rule on free space. A small frontier outpost. A Klingon contingent of scientists." He returned his attention to her. "It is of no special value or importance."

"Then why is Kirk going there?"

Subcommander Tran rose to his feet. "I submit Kirk is being *taken* there. Unless you wish us to believe he has successfully taken over a *Galaxy*-class starship."

Salatrel bit her lip. If anyone could, Kirk could. "Regardless of whether he's in control or a captive, the question remains, Tracius. Why take him there?"

The centurion's brow furrowed as he put all his years of experience and knowledge about the hated Federation to use. "If they have identified Kirk's implant as a Borg device, they would be taking him to Starbase 324 for study, as they do all Borg technology. If they have executed him, they either would not be taking him anywhere—they'd disintegrate his body and eject the molecular dust into space—*or,* they'd be continuing with their plans to return him to his home planet for burial."

Salatrel struggled to be patient with the old soldier. "I need a third possibility, my friend."

"He is going to meet with Picard."

Salatrel sat up on alert.

Tran took a step toward the centurion. "Impossible!"

Tracius held his hands behind his back. Salatrel recognized the pose. It was an unconscious affectation from his days of study of Vulcan, in an effort to understand the enemy of the Romulan people. In such a pose, the centurion would not be moved.

"These are the facts," he reminded Tran. "Picard's whereabouts has disappeared from all available Starfleet computer networks. Our spies cannot find reference to him anywhere. It is proper to assume that he is in some manner connected to Starfleet's efforts to build defenses against the Borg." Tracius looked meaningfully at Salatrel. "And where better to hide an ongoing and, perhaps, illegal weapons research program than at a remote starbase of no particular importance?"

Tran would not be moved, either. "Starbase 324 is where Borg defenses are being developed."

The centurion stood his ground. "With the cooperation of the Klingons *and* a Romulan team of cloaking specialists. From the Federation's viewpoint, it cannot be a secure location. Especially when some of the weapons they wish to develop could be used against the Star Empire."

Tran and Tracius both turned to Salatrel.

Her decision was swift. "Lay in a course to Starbase 804. Remain cloaked, but stay in the *Challenger's* sensor shadow."

Tran made no move to return to the helm. "I believe Vox should be informed of . . . our new course of action."

Salatrel held his gaze, daring him to defy her leadership. "Vox has other matters to attend to. I will send word back to the Dante Base."

"Other matters!" Tran protested. "You don't even know where he is. You don't even know what he's doing. You're as much a puppet as Kirk is."

Salatrel leapt to her feet. Tran didn't back away. So in full view of her bridge crew, she struck him with the back of her hand, crashing him back to the deck.

Then she placed a boot on his chest and ground its toe into his throat.

"If this were a Klingon ship, you would be food for the captain's *targ*. If this were a Federation ship, they would be performing medical experiments on you before you were dragged off the bridge. But this is *my* ship. And we are Romulans. The only way we will crush our enemies is if we learn to do it together." She pressed harder on Tran's larynx to be sure she had his attention, as well as her crew's. "Do you understand, Subcommander?!"

Tran grunted. Salatrel took that for a yes.

She lifted her boot from his chest and returned to stand beside her chair.

Tran stumbled back to the helm and laid in a course to pursue the *Challenger.*

Tracius leaned close to Salatrel as she sat back in her chair.

"To keep your crew and ship, you will have to provide a clear example of the cost of defying you," her centurion said. "And soon."

Salatrel knew Tracius was right, but for now, all she cared about was tracking Kirk.

She had no idea why he was being taken—or taking others—to Starbase 804.

But if the history of the Federation held any lessons, it was that where Kirk was concerned, things were never as they seemed.

After working so long with the Borg, she almost found that lack of clarity . . . enticing.

TWENTY-NINE

Picard ducked low behind a sharply angled cube of mechanical components that jutted upward from the deck of the Borg corridor, like a forgotten protrusion from some long-ago collision. Beside him, Beverly set her medical tricorder for distance.

The dark corridor in the hypercube station echoed with the monotonous clanking of the Borg work crew marching past. They were a species Picard had never seen. A meter and a half tall, gray-skinned, one enormous and almond-shaped dark eye set below a swollen cranium. If the other eye matched, Picard didn't know. Borg implants obscured the other half of each creature's face.

Beverly passed him her tricorder. The readings told Picard that not only did he not recognize the creatures, Starfleet's xenobiology records didn't either. But the Borg were clearly established and taking victims in sectors other than those known to the Federation.

When the work crew filed by, Picard once again resumed moving along the corridor, Beverly at his side.

Far ahead, the hallway seemed to twist off into a corkscrew, but Beverly and he had already determined that the illusion of distance aboard the Borg station was just that—an illusion caused by whatever dimension the hypercube station existed within. For the most part, they were trying to keep their eyes focused only on what was nearby.

They came to an intersection. Passageways curved off like the vanes of a pinwheel in six different directions. Picard studied his tricorder. The section of the hypercube station under the Romulan ships they had seen prior to docking was to the right.

They hurried on. And the closer they came to the sector that Picard believed held the captive crews of the Romulan ships, the worse the cloying scent of rotting flesh became.

Another intersection brought them to an enormous railed walkway that skirted the edges of an open reservoir, at least a kilometer across.

Picard looked over the railing and immediately swayed back in horror.

The reservoir was a lake of what appeared to be writhing entrails. The squelching, sucking sounds that rose from it were enough to make Picard gag.

Beverly scanned the hellish scene with her tricorder. Her voice was low and unsteady. "It's a recycling tank, Jean-Luc.

The atmosphere is being cleansed, and waste products are being removed from the water."

Picard understood the concept. But most colonies relied on plant-based systems to recycle air and water. It was most unnerving to see the same process undertaken by reclaimed animal flesh.

They moved on, carefully following the path laid out by their tricorder, ignoring all else, hiding from the work crews, breathing through their mouths to escape the ubiquitous stench.

Until they rounded a corner and halted as they saw a ten-meter-long section of burnished green metal corridor which could only have been lifted intact from a Romulan ship.

Picard ran his fingers over that wall. Even though it was Romulan, the fact that it was smoothly finished and recognizable made it a welcome relief from the nightmare of flesh-enrobed rods and pipes and conduits they had come through.

Beverly rapidly scanned the area. "I'm getting a strong life-sign reading in that direction. In excess of a thousand. Most likely Romulan." She pointed down the corridor.

They started forward again. But Picard stopped suddenly, when they encountered the Romulan bulkhead.

"Jean-Luc?" Beverly said anxiously, turning back to join him as soon as she realized she had gone on alone.

Picard stood in front of a Romulan display screen. Beneath it was a control board. Its virtual configuration of command keys glowed, indicating the board was still active.

"The Borg are very efficient in their assimilation process," Picard murmured, staring at the screen.

"You think that computer terminal is operational?" Beverly whispered.

"We won't know until we try." Picard pulled off his armored gloves and tucked them up under one arm. Then he took a moment to reacquaint himself with the fat squiggles of Romulan script and pressed the activate control.

The screen came to life above the board. Picard mouthed the script written across it, which identified the ship whose computer network this terminal had once accessed.

"This is from the ship named *Claw That Rends Our Enemies' Flesh,"* Picard told Beverly.

"Sounds like a Warbird to me." Beverly tried to smile, but failed.

Picard knew he had to avoid any request which might prompt the system to ask for his crew member I.D. or password. He thought for a moment, then began by asking for a display of the day's general orders. On the *Enterprise,* that type of inquiry would have generated a menu providing access to the day's shift assignments, entertainment and education options, and notable events—birthdays, special meetings, and all the other milestones of a community of one thousand individuals.

Picard had no idea what the request would turn up on a Romulan vessel, but it was a reasonable first choice.

He began to read the menu that appeared on the screen.

And he gasped.

"Beverly . . . this terminal isn't connected to the Romulan ship's system . . . it's connected to the *station's* system!"

Beverly pushed closer to look over his shoulder. "But why?"

Picard lifted an armored panel from his forearm sleeves and, on his tricorder, quickly called up a programming screen for his universal translator.

"My best guess is that when the Borg incorporated this deck unit into the station, they connected the air-supply conduits to their own air-supply conduits, the power cables to their own power cables, and the computer's ODN network to . . . whatever computer system they use."

He could hear the real smile in Beverly's voice. And the relief. "How efficient of them."

Picard set his tricorder for field transmit, then held his

breath. If the Romulan computer system had an intelligence file that contained standard translation protocols . . .

It did.

The virtual keyboard shimmered and was replaced by a Starfleet standard configuration. The onscreen Romulan text melted into Federation Standard.

"Jean-Luc," Beverly said in awe. "It's like . . . opening a window into the Borg collective."

But Picard shook his head. "The collective isn't computer based. It's a shared neural network that's distributed among the Borg's organic components. But *this* is the mechanical heart of it."

Adrenaline surged within him. He typed in a request for the current docking schedule.

The Borg system did not request an identifier code. After all, who else but a Borg could access it?

Then Picard smiled grimly as the station's docking schedule began to scroll across the screen. At least half the lines were composed of square bracketed tags reading [TRANSLATION UNAVAILABLE]. Traffic from systems as yet unknown to the Federation, Picard guessed.

But here and there, he saw names he could recognize. From their belligerent tone, Romulan Warbirds. Picard could barely contain his excitement.

"Beverly, this is astounding. Those Warbirds we saw . . . they've all docked here within the past thirty hours."

"The Borg captured ten intact Warbirds in less than two days?"

Even Picard knew that couldn't be right.

Fingers shaking, he typed in a request to ask for the status of the crews. The screen shifted to a visual display.

Of barracks.

Picard pored over the images intently. He recognized the Romulan style of asymmetrical bunks. He saw food replicators, entertainment screens, exercise simulators. The crews of the Romulan vessels hadn't been removed to the hypercube station; they were still onboard their vessels.

"They aren't prisoners, are they?" Beverly said slowly.

Picard shook his head. He pursed his lips.

He asked for the flight plans of the Warbirds.

They were to depart in one hundred hours, towed through the [TRANSLATION UNAVAILABLE] conduit to Sector 3-0.

"Sector 3-0?" Beverly said. "Isn't that near the Romulan Neutral Zone?"

Picard nodded. "It's also the location of the Borg's first attacks in our region of space."

Beverly looked at Picard. "The Neutral Zone isn't well defended these days, is it?"

"No," Picard said, seeing the first broad strokes of the Borg strategy. At the moment, he knew, there was a slowly building rapprochement with the Romulan Empire. Starfleet had welcomed the opportunity to demilitarize the Neutral Zone. Such action meant Starfleet vessels were freed for duty near the Cardassian sectors that were threatened by the Gamma Quadrant's Dominion. So what better place from which to launch an invasion than the poorly defended Neutral Zone?

Still, ten Warbirds, however formidable, weren't enough to invade the entire Federation.

Picard asked the computer to list any other vessels that would be departing at the same time as the Warbirds.

The screen scrolled with a seemingly endless row of:

[TRANSLATION UNAVAILABLE]

"Ships that have no name," Beverly said.

Picard knew what she meant. "Borg ships."

"Then Starfleet was right," Beverly said. "The Borg are going to invade."

"But not by themselves. They've somehow . . . allied themselves with the Romulans. They're going to come at us from the Neutral Zone, where we have no defenses, and where the Romulan outposts won't lift a finger to help us."

"But how can the Borg . . . *cooperate* with an unassimilated race? That isn't possible. Is it?"

Picard contemplated the unthinkable. "Perhaps the Borg decided it was the only way to defeat the Federation."

His own words suddenly came back to him, hideous in their new context.

Or perhaps they thought the Romulans could be a valuable resource in a galactic civilization.

Picard felt cold. "Beverly, is it possible that the Borg did get the idea from me, when I was part of the collective?"

Beverly immediately sought out Picard's hand. "No, Jean-Luc. If they had, they would have acted faster."

But Beverly sounded no more convinced that Picard felt.

He held his fingers over the keyboard, poised to enter another request.

"I have to know," he said. "I'm going to ask it to show me the unit responsible for this plan."

Beverly nodded, making no move to dissuade him.

Picard typed in his request. He prepared himself to see an image of himself as Locutus.

But when the screen cleared again, it displayed a different visual.

"Dear God," Beverly said. Her face mirrored the shock that both of them felt.

Picard could say nothing.

In response to his enquiry, the screen showed two individuals, walking in a corridor somewhere in the hypercube station.

One was a Borg-Romulan of no particular importance.

The second was Ambassador Spock.

THIRTY

Spock paused at the intersection of four passageways leading from the Borg docking chamber which had just received him. All about him, the maintenance crew of the Warbird which had conveyed him here strode off into the depths of the hypercube station, as confidently as if they were on shore leave on their homeworld.

It was a disturbing scene, given all it implied about the state of affairs between the Borg and the Romulans.

But not unexpected.

Spock had already accepted that nothing he could see would match the shock he had felt, though not expressed, when he had realized his investigation into what he had thought was a criminal enterprise had delivered him into the hands of the Borg.

In retrospect, the logic of it was irrefutable.

It required no heroic leaps of faith to accept that Borg technology had reanimated James T. Kirk.

And the purpose of that reanimation was elementary. Kirk had stated it himself.

His mission was to kill Jean-Luc Picard.

Most likely, Spock concluded, to keep Starfleet from accessing some Borg secret still contained in Picard's mind. Some secret, thus far unsuspected, that could lead to the Borg's eventual defeat.

The only question remaining unanswered was why, of all

the hunters who might have been set into motion against Picard, had Kirk been chosen?

Since there was no logical answer, Spock felt certain that emotions would provide a key. The captain had had many run-ins with Romulans during his career. Somewhere in the web of circumstance that had brought Kirk back again was the one Romulan who hated Kirk enough to create the irony of one great hero of Starfleet pitted against another.

A Vulcan would have simply dispatched a trained assassin to eliminate Picard. But then, a Vulcan would never have knowingly allied himself with the Borg. Which is, Spock decided, exactly what logic dictated was under way at this hypercube station.

A Borg-Romulan alliance.

"You will continue walking," Vox stated.

Before responding as ordered, Spock took a final moment to analyze the curves of the passageways stretching into the distance. Once more matching Vox's pace, he continued to organize his thoughts about the Borg-Romulan alliance, while at the same time his mind pursued the more concrete challenge of the station's existence.

"This station is constructed in a Thorne subset of eleven-dimensional transpace, is it not?" Spock asked.

Vox did not look at him as they moved along the corridor. "That is correct," the Borg-Romulan said.

"The power requirement for entering such a subset is generally calculated to be greater than infinity," Spock observed.

"The general calculations are wrong."

Spock thought that over for a few steps. He had made some of those calculations himself, when he had still been an active worker in scientific pursuits. He regretted he would not have time to review his earlier work to look for his mistakes.

But on their voyage here from Romulus, Vox had made it clear what Spock's fate would be, and it would not leave room for pure research.

Just as Vox was Speaker for the Borg in the collective's relationship with the Romulan Star Empire, Spock was to be assimilated to become Speaker to the worlds of Vulcan.

Spock was without question prepared to fight assimilation. He was prepared to die to prevent the collective from accessing the secrets contained in his mind. But he much preferred the option of escaping. And he had not yet come to the moment at which he believed escape was no longer possible.

Another intersection loomed, and Vox stepped to the side to let a work crew pass.

Spock was intrigued by the work crew. What he had thought was a single-file line of humanoids was in fact a single organism somewhat like a terrestrial centipede. Each bipedal segment was linked by its thorax to the one ahead and behind. Each segment's head was little more than a vestigial knob of flesh. Only the more developed segment at the head of the creature appeared to have multiple functioning eyes and sensory inputs, though most of them now were covered by implant plates.

Since there was no logical advantage for such an inefficient shape to have arisen by self-organization or natural selection, Spock deduced that the life-form had been engineered.

"What is the purpose of that entity?" Spock asked.

"It feeds the tubes," Vox said.

Spock chose not to ask for clarification. He had other things to consider.

"When will I be assimilated?" Spock asked.

"By standard Federation units, within eight minutes."

They had come to an open turbolift. Spock recognized its awkward design as having originated on a Pakled vessel. Vox and Spock stepped into it. Vox spoke his command to it, and the turbolift dropped.

Spock decided it was time to see how robust Borg programming was. He began his first line of defense.

"I do not wish to be assimilated."

"That will be corrected."

Spock tried another tack, looking for any logical opening. "Do you enjoy being assimilated?"

"That is irrelevant."

"Why is the crew of the Warbird not being assimilated?"

"It is not yet their time."

Spock found that interesting. Everything he had read about the Borg indicated they had voracious appetites. In the material he had reviewed, there had never been any such idea as "later." Yet the idea of an alliance implied that the Romulans expected some benefit from their relationship with the Borg, other than assimilation.

Spock had read Jean-Luc Picard's reports on being part of the collective. Supposedly, there were no secrets among them. Thus Spock determined it was likely that, this close to his own impending assimilation, Vox would consider him as almost a Borg himself, and be just as candid as he would be to one of his own.

"Do the Romulan crew members know they are to be assimilated?" Spock asked.

The steadily descending turbolift afforded Spock a view of an endless series of metal panels encrusted with tortured mazes of pipes and conduits. None hinted at what lay beyond the levels they shielded, yet Spock knew that whatever the activities, they would all share in one purpose: advancement of the collective.

"No," Vox answered. "They are an experiment. They are not to be assimilated until they aid us in assimilating the Federation. Many resources have been expended on correcting the misunderstandings the Federation has of the collective.

"It appears you wish to take advantage of the Romulans' emotional dislike of the Federation."

"Precisely," Vox agreed.

"Do you not find it a contradiction to acknowledge that emotions confer an advantage?"

Vox didn't hesitate. "That is irrelevant."

"You argue like a physician I once knew," Spock said. "You discount all data except those which support your thesis. It is most illogical."

"Logic is irrelevant."

Spock abandoned that approach.

"What will happen to your alliance with the Romulans once the Federation has been assimilated?"

"The Romulan Star Empire will be assimilated as well."

Even without knowing who was involved, Spock instantly understood how this alliance had come about, and he had no doubt that the Romulan government was fully ignorant of what was being promulgated in the Empire's name.

"In other words," Spock said, "you will betray the Romulans when your goals have been accomplished."

"We will not betray them," Vox said. "We will correct their misperception of the collective."

"I do not believe they will find that reassuring."

"Their beliefs are irrelevant."

The turbolift stopped and its safety gate swung open onto yet another Borg passageway.

"Vox, in that part of you which is still Romulan, do you at least understand the concept of betrayal?"

Vox hesitated. He did not step out of the turbolift. For once, he appeared to be thinking about his response to Spock's questions.

"Yes," Vox finally said. "That is my function as Speaker to the Borg. To bridge between that which is known and that which is unknown. Between the collective and the Romulan people."

"Do you also understand that the Romulan people will feel you have betrayed them?"

Spock was fascinated to see a muscle tremble at the corner

of Vox's mouth. He recalled that Picard's reports had indicated that assimilation did not lead to the total extinction of personality. Perhaps there was a spark within Vox which could still be reached.

"They will feel betrayed," Vox agreed. "But that will pass." Surprisingly, Vox still made no move to leave the turbolift. Spock quickly continued his attack. . . .

"But if they *suspect* you will betray them, what will be their response?"

Vox cocked his head as if caught by Spock's argument. He turned to Spock, who ignored the Borg laser scanner and concentrated on the dark, living, Romulan eye. The only window to what was left of Vox's true self. "The Romulans will attempt to betray the collective," he said.

Spock struck another blow. "Then, since the Romulan government would never agree to such a joint undertaking, logic dictates the Borg have entered into an alliance with a group of disaffected officers. Knowing Romulans as I do, these renegade officers will have developed two plans, both leading to a different victory. If your Borg-Romulan alliance defeats the Federation, the Romulan Armada will attack you without mercy, while the Borg forces are still weakened by the conflict. In turn, if the Federation once again defeats the Borg, the victorious but badly weakened Starfleet forces will be set upon by the Romulan Armada."

Vox seemed unimpressed. "That is an illogical scenario."

Spock lifted an eyebrow. "Explain."

"The Federation cannot win. The Borg fleet will not be weakened."

The flaw, to Spock, was obvious. How could the Borg fleet win a conflict with the Federation without sustaining heavy damage? The Federation, after all, had already gathered considerable information about the Borg.

"The Federation will not fall in battle. It will be betrayed," Vox said. "By a highly placed member of Starfleet."

Spock was startled.

"Who is that individual?" he asked, although he suspected the question was futile.

Vox stepped out of the turbolift and gestured to the side. "You will be assimilated now."

Spock decided that dying here was no longer a useful alternative course of action. He must return to the Federation with his knowledge of a highly placed traitor. But how?

Spock chose the obvious. "Turbolift," he said firmly, "return to the hangar level."

The safety gates began to close.

But just as quickly, the floor of the turbolift car lurched and Spock stumbled against the wall.

"The collective is in control of all functions on this station," Vox said. "Resistance is futile." The Speaker for the Romulans had not moved from his position outside the turbolift.

"You have stated that before," Spock pointed out.

Vox lifted his arm graft and a blue spark leapt out to encase Spock in a halo of radiant energy. Spock collapsed to the floor without sensation below his neck. Yet he remained conscious.

Vox's weapon had been some type of neural blocker. The effects were likely to be short-term, otherwise interference with his breathing, heart function, and endocrine system could be expected.

But even in the short term, Spock realized, his potential range of actions had been severely limited.

Four Borg stepped up to him and lifted him, one Borg for each of his limbs. They carried him along the corridor and into a nearby chamber.

Spock heard another spark discharge, and at once sensation returned to him.

The Borg released him, and he stood by himself.

"Sit down," Vox said.

Spock glanced behind himself. He saw an unusual chair

frame that appeared to be fused with a medical examination table. He looked up. Surgical equipment hung from the ceiling.

"That would not be a wise decision for me to make," Spock said.

"Sit," Vox said and fired his neural blocker.

Helplessly paralyzed, Spock fell back into the assimilation frame, as the other Borg adjusted his position. Above him, the surgical equipment whirred into life.

An incision arm snaked down, exposing a circular blade and three laser cauterization tubes.

Neural waveguides sprang forth from a cranial drill, like silver threads held apart by a static charge.

Excavation scoops connected to suction tubes dropped in incremental jerks until they were poised millimeters above Spock's chest.

A head brace clamped down and tightened around his skull, leaving his temples exposed. He heard multiple drills moving in from either side. A pool of bright light surrounded him.

Though he felt no fear, he allowed himself regret.

There was still so much he had wanted to do.

For Romulus.

For Vulcan.

And for Kirk.

As Vox watched impassively, Spock heard the hum of a surveillance lens as it zoomed out at him from the far wall.

Spock had one last strategy to try.

It had little chance of success. But he long ago had learned that desperation had a logic of its own.

"Starfleet knows about Kirk," Spock said.

Vox's hand rose into the air and the machinery of assimilation stopped.

"What do they know?" Vox asked.

Spock pushed his bluff to the next level. He knew both his

father and Kirk would say this was not the ideal time to bluff. But Spock had nothing more with which to wager. Except his wits.

"Kirk is the highly placed member of Starfleet who will betray the Federation. His murder of Picard will deprive Starfleet of the knowledge which can save it. Because Starfleet is aware of this, they will anticipate any action Kirk might make. Therefore, Starfleet will protect Picard and be able to fight the Borg-Romulan attack. You must withdraw, or be defeated. All else is an inefficient expenditure of resources."

Vox studied Spock for long moments. "What you say is relevant."

Spock allowed himself to experience a moment of hope.

Then Vox continued. "When your implants have been attached, we will know if you are telling the truth."

He lowered his hand.

The equipment began moving, whining, racheting closer.

Spock composed himself, waiting.

Not just for death, but for something worse.

The conscious annihilation of his identity and his volition.

Logically, he knew he should accept defeat and prepare himself for the loss of his existence.

But in a final act of will, he refused. Even as the first slender waveguides punched through his skin and the drills sang as they readied to pierce him.

Jim Kirk had never accepted defeat.

And for his sake, neither would Spock.

THIRTY-ONE

Picard and Beverly jogged endlessly through the dimensionally distorted passageways of the Borg station. The Romulan computer terminal had shown them Spock's location, but the layout of the corridors did not match the map it had displayed, as if the station were in a constant state of growth and change.

"Jean-Luc, stop!" Beverly panted beside him. "We're going in circles."

Together, they halted to rest against a wall of metal mesh. Its complex weave of optical wire flashed with intermittent light signals. Beverly checked her tricorder, reset it, checked it again. Shook her head with a sigh.

"The deeper we go into the station, the less sense these readings make."

"Spock was being assimilated," Picard said. The frustration he felt, the maddening helplessness, made him tremble with rage.

It was one thing to have experienced such a violation on his own. But to see it about to happen to another, especially someone whom Picard knew and respected.

He had to do something.

He had to save Spock.

"According to the map on the Romulan screen, the assimilation chamber should be right here," Beverly said. "But everything's twisted up."

Picard heard the clang of heavy boots on the Borg deck. He didn't have to think about what to do. He touched the side of his face to make certain his neural plate was still in place, then stepped out into the middle of the corridor before Beverly could protest.

The Borg who was approaching stopped.

His laser sensor scanned Picard's face.

"Locutus," the Borg said, "you are malfunctioning. We cannot detect you within the collective."

Picard felt himself slip into his alternate persona far too readily. But there was no time to consider what that meant.

"There is no malfunction. Some units are being suppressed in order to avoid detection by Federation forces when the attack begins."

The Borg remained motionless, giving no clue to whether or not it accepted Picard's lie.

"Where is the closest assimilation chamber?"

The Borg's mechanical arm shifted in its socket. "That information is available in the collective. You are wasting time by asking meaningless questions. You are wasting resources."

The Borg glanced down at Picard. The laser played over Picard's right arm.

"You have been modified," the Borg said. "That is why you are malfunctioning." His arm swung up. "You must be repaired."

"That assessment is correct," Picard said quickly. "You will escort me to the nearest assimilation chamber for repair."

The Borg's arm lowered, and it changed direction as if it were on a turntable.

"You will follow us."

The Borg began marching down the corridor. Picard matched its stride. He heard Beverly's light footsteps behind him as she hurried to catch up.

The Borg heard them as well. It stopped and faced Beverly.

"What is this?" the Borg asked Picard as it scanned her. The Borg's arm began to rise.

"This is a prisoner with information about the Federation. It will be assimilated after repairs have been made."

The Borg lowered its arm, satisfied by the answer. "That is relevant."

Picard felt Beverly's hand brush his as they marched. He glanced down. She carried a photon grenade.

He nodded his understanding. If he had placed them into a no-win situation, they would not allow themselves to be assimilated. It was that simple.

The Borg turned a corner in the passageway and appeared to begin walking up a steep slope without leaning forward. Following directly behind, Picard tensed, expecting to feel the stomach-wrenching sensation of stepping between two different artificial gravity fields. But he felt nothing. The gravitational gradient itself was curved.

Picard marvelled at and cursed the Borg's ingenuity. How could the Federation ever hope to withstand beings with control of such technology?

Through knowledge, he answered himself. The knowledge that he and Beverly could bring back. And the knowledge Spock might have.

If he could be rescued in time.

The Borg turned sharply into yet another corridor. The walls appeared to stretch into infinity.

"The assimilation chamber is ahead," the Borg announced. He continued walking purposely forward.

Picard walked past an open turbolift which he recognized as a characteristically ungainly Pakled design.

The lift platform was rising, and a familiar figure was on it.

Picard's pace faltered and Beverly stumbled into him from behind.

The figure looked their way. For the moment before the

platform disappeared into the next higher level their eyes made direct connection.

Spock.

But his flesh was unmarked.

His skull bore no neural plates.

All his limbs were intact.

Beverly plucked at his arm. "Did you see him?" she asked urgently.

Picard's silence was answer enough.

"Jean-Luc . . . he wasn't assimilated."

The Borg ahead of them stopped. He gestured to an opening in the corridor wall.

"The repairs will be done here," it said.

Picard stood in the entrance to the chamber. He saw the assimilation frame. Beside him, Beverly shuddered.

Picard's heart raced. He had to get away. He had to go after Spock. But if they ran from this Borg, he knew an alert would flash through the collective. Every Borg on the station would be searching for them.

He decided to go to the source.

"This assimilation chamber has malfunctioned," Picard said.

The Borg took on the faraway gaze that indicated it was communing with the collective.

"This assimilation chamber is operational," the Borg replied. "You are in need of repair."

"No," Picard said, daring to argue although the Borg never did. "A Vulcan was here. He was placed in the frame. He was not assimilated. Explain."

For the moment it took the Borg to access the collective, Picard stood on the brink of an exceptional discovery. Perhaps Spock had found some way of defeating the assimilation process. Perhaps some trick of Vulcan mind control could—

"The Vulcan was not assimilated because the effort would have been a waste of resources," the Borg said unexpectedly.

The Borg's statement was mystifying. "Explain," Picard said again.

"The neural waveguides identified the presence of the collective in the Vulcan's mind. Conclusion: The Vulcan is already part of the collective. To assimilate him would be redundant."

Beverly gasped. Picard felt as if he had stepped into free fall.

Spock was *already* a Borg?

And then the awful, hidden pattern instantly became clear to both of them.

A Borg-Romulan alliance.

Spock spending eighty years working with Romulans.

A new era of peace dawning between Romulus and the Federation, leading to a reduction of the forces defending the Neutral Zone.

Making the Neutral Zone the perfect place from which to launch an invasion.

Could it be possible?

With all the new behaviors the Borg had learned, had one of their branches discovered a new way to assimilate an individual's mind? Without the telltale neural plates and bioneuronic implants that made Borg so instantly identifiable?

Or was Spock's incredible treachery the result of some perverse application of Vulcan logic, by which Romulans and Vulcans would be spared the ravages of assimilation by betraying the Federation?

Either way, the answer was the same.

It was why the Borg computer had shown him Spock when he had asked who was responsible for the Borg-Romulan alliance.

"He's one of them," Picard said softly, overwhelmed by the enormity of that knowledge. Starfleet would have to be warned.

"It just can't be true," Beverly said.

"Delay is a waste of resources," the Borg said ominously.

"We certainly don't want to do that," Picard replied as the anger built in him. Then he lunged out and snapped the Borg's interface cable free.

The Borg arced in a spasmodic dance of misfiring muscles. Sparks sputtered from its neural implant plate and the power connections on his chest and shoulder.

Its high-pitched scream was piercing. Agonized, inconsolable, appalling. Because it was alone.

With instant pity, Picard swung the unresisting creature by its shoulders and pushed it into the assimilation frame beyond.

The Borg thrashed and struggled there, without control. Its laser scanner pulsed erratically.

Above the frame, the surgical arms began to descend.

The multiple drills and blades spun and flashed in the light.

With one swift motion, Picard took the photon grenade from Beverly, twisted the activator, and threw it at the keening Borg.

Then he grabbed Beverly's hand and he ran.

The explosion erupted into the corridor behind them like a solar flare. The searing heat was intense.

Three more Borg appeared in the corridor.

"There's been a malfunction!" Picard told them. "The collective is in danger. Communications are breaking down!"

The Borg pushed past them to the burning assimilation chamber. They ignored Picard.

Picard sprinted ahead of Beverly to the Pakled turbolift, hit the wall command-panel to call a new platform. From somewhere below, he heard a platform whine to life.

"Where to now?" Beverly asked gamely.

Picard felt flushed with purpose.

"Spock," Picard said. At last, he had a clear direction to

follow. "If we want to save the Federation, we have to stop him."

Beverly regarded him with incomprehension. "How?"

Picard drew his phaser.

"By whatever means possible."

THIRTY-TWO

As Spock waited for the Pakled turbolift to stop, he dabbed a corner of his robe against the pinpricks of green blood on his temple. Despite the fact that the Borg were a life-form dedicated to efficiency and logic, he had rarely been subjected to more unanticipated developments in any of his journeys.

If he were merely human, he might say he was astounded, astonished, *and* bewildered.

If he were merely human.

But as a human and a Vulcan, he would admit only to a mild sense of unease.

The worst of it had begun with the withdrawal of the Borg's neural waveguides from his flesh.

He had read Picard's reports.

He knew what assimilation by the Borg entailed.

Yet, none of it had happened.

The wires had entered his skin. He had felt them press through the layers of his temporal fascia to make contact with his skull.

And then . . .

Nothing.

After less than a minute, the surgical devices had returned to their storage positions on the ceiling. His restraints had opened. And Vox and the other Borg attendants had left.

As Spock slowly sat up from the frame, he had wanted to ask questions of Vox. But with logic having little to do with his situation, he decided not to draw attention to himself.

If the Borg collective had for some reason forgotten him, or lost interest in him, he was not inclined to encourage it to change its groupmind.

Still the problem remained.

Why had he not been assimilated?

And what was Picard doing in the heart of the collective?

Or more accurately, why was Locutus back among the Borg?

When Spock had seen Locutus from the Pakled turbolift, in the company of another Borg, so much of the mystery he had been faced with had suddenly been revealed.

Picard's current situation did much to explain why Commander Riker had been so uncommunicative on Deep Space 9. The commander must have been aware that Picard was missing. Perhaps he had known that his captain had returned to the Borg.

Spock accepted that the Borg had continued to advance their knowledge in the time that had passed since their first encounters with the Federation. It was quite probable they had perfected a new means by which to assimilate an individual's mind. Without the use of neural plates or other bioneuronic implants.

It was also possible that Starfleet by now might be riddled with such assimilated individuals.

Indeed, if, according to Vox, an act of treason was going to set the stage for the Borg-Romulan attack on the Federation, who better than Picard to be that individual?

Spock reflected on the consequences of this line of reasoning. If Picard had remained assimilated since his first encounter with the Borg, then everything Starfleet had accomplished since that time, each new defensive tactic and each new weapon, had been passed on to the Borg.

In the face of a Borg-Romulan attack, the Federation would not stand a chance of surviving.

The Pakled turbolift stopped on the hangar bay level. Spock paused. Locutus was somewhere below in the station. Logically, Spock understood it made no sense to try to go after him. All that Picard knew would already be part of the collective, so killing him would serve no purpose. Also, assuming that Spock could even find Locutus again, he doubted he would survive for long after attacking him.

Thus, Spock could see only one logical course of action available to him.

He must return to Federation space and warn Starfleet of Picard's treason.

Spock stepped off the lift platform and began walking toward the hangar bay. The immediate problem he faced was to find a way to return to the Federation.

The Warbirds docked with the Borg hypercube station might be useful. Somehow, they had traversed a transwarp conduit to arrive here. Logically, there must be some way to reverse their course.

Spock paused at the entrance to the hangar. Unassimilated Romulans worked side by side with Borg-Romulans, as well as Borg of other races and configurations.

With less than a moment of serious consideration, Spock ruled out a physical confrontation. Even a century ago, such a proposition would have been foolhardy.

Thus, the only weapon remaining to Spock was logic.

He felt his was up to the task.

Spock assumed the efficient attitude of the Borg. It was not difficult for a Vulcan. Then he chose a single Borg attending to a repair in a floor access panel. The Borg had been a humanoid once, but its race was now impossible to identify.

Spock stepped up to it. The Borg looked up at him, no expression in its one organic eye.

"Are your optical sensors intact?" Spock asked. He knew the risk he was taking, but there had to be some reason why he had not been assimilated. This was the perfect time to find out

The Borg withdrew its manipulator arm from the floor opening. A welding tube glowed on the tip of it.

"Yes," it replied.

"Can you identify me?" Spock asked.

"You are Borg," the Borg answered. "Are you in need of repair?"

For a moment, Spock wondered if he had uncovered a joke of cosmic proportions. Could it be possible that to the Borg, the emotionless, disciplined, and logical mind of the Vulcan was indistinguishable from their own? But he quickly dismissed the idea. The Borg groupmind was based as much in technological implants as in brain matter. If the Borg had misidentified him as one of them, it must be for another reason.

"I am not in need of repair," Spock said. "I am in need of transportation."

The Borg stood up. "Where do you need to go?"

Spock thought for a moment. Could it really be this straightforward?

"Locutus is aboard this station," Spock said.

"That is correct," the Borg answered. "He cannot be found in the collective because . . ." The Borg hesitated, taking on a distant look, as if listening to voices only it could hear. "Because some units are being suppressed in order to avoid detection by Federation forces when the attack begins."

With this confirmation of what he had already concluded, Spock felt a new urgency to his mission. He had to trace Picard's—*Locutus's*—treachery to the source. Starfleet had to know if there were others like him.

"I require transportation to the point at which Locutus

began his journey to this station," Spock said. "Speed is of the essence."

"Resources must not be wasted."

Spock's counterargument was prompt.

"The Federation might be tracing the route Locutus has taken. We must inspect that route at once if the invasion is to succeed."

He sensed the hesitation in the Borg.

He spoke to it in its own language.

"Resistance is futile."

The Borg cocked its head, then turned like a soldier on parade.

"A scoutship is available," the Borg said. He began to march away.

Spock looked around, saw that his exchange had not attracted any attention, and followed the Borg.

Logic appeared to have won the day. However, he couldn't help wondering if the same rigid logic which had made the Borg so easy to manipulate could, in the same way, someday bring ruin to Vulcan.

Perhaps Vulcan had been fortunate to meet the emotional humans. Each race tempered the other with the quality most needed, both becoming stronger.

Spock decided he shouldn't be surprised by that.

Somehow, his need to answer Kirk's call and his subsequent search for his lost captain had led to the discovery of an imminent Borg invasion of the Federation, made possible by Locutus.

What connection any of this had to Kirk's as yet unexplained return was beyond even Spock's ability to surmise.

But he did know that a connection existed. And when he discovered it, knowing all that he knew of Jim Kirk's remarkable life, he knew it would have its own logic. Sometimes, beyond reason. But successful in spite of that.

From his captain and his friend, Spock would expect no less.

THIRTY-THREE

Captain Lewinski tapped the arm of his chair as he regarded the static backdrop of stars that filled the *Monitor's* viewscreen.

His ship was among the fastest and most powerful in Starfleet. Being forced to remain in orbit of New Titan for the past three days, doing absolutely nothing, had been his most difficult duty assignment in years. As far as he was concerned, there was nothing he disliked more than waiting. But then, he shared that dislike with most other starship captains. It was probably what made them starship captains in the first place.

Land's Earth-born accent cut abruptly through the background hum of the bridge. "Here she comes, Captain. And is she fast!"

The viewscreen image shifted, making the stars swim past, until a rainbow thread of light shimmered in the upper corner. And as quickly as that, the *U.S.S. Challenger* appeared dead ahead, smoothly dropping from warp no more than five hundred kilometers away.

The massive vessel banked as it came about, adjusting its orbit, its gleaming white hull glowing in the combined radiance of the clustered core stars.

"And she's beautiful," Lewinski said. Then, because he couldn't resist engaging his Vulcan science officer in a teasing debate, he added: "Wouldn't you agree, Mr. T'Per?"

But T'Per did not respond with a comment about the illogic of applying a relative term like "beauty" to an artificial device whose shape was derived from the mathematical realities of warp velocities. Instead, she said: "Captain, we should run a full diagnostic on our cloaking device."

Without prompting, Ardev opened hailing frequencies to the *Challenger.*

"You've had three days to do that," the captain complained to T'Per. "Why now?"

T'Per was unperturbed. "When the *Challenger* dropped from warp, I recorded a tachyon surge. Our cloaking field might have reacted to the *Challenger's* subspace backwash. If so, it must be recalibrated in order to remain functional at warp speeds."

Lewinski sighed. "Any other source possible for a tachyon surge out here?"

T'Per considered the question for a moment. "Only if the *Challenger* were operating a cloaking device. Other than that, we're the only source."

"Do it," Lewinski said, then turned back to face the main screen and Captain Simm of the *Challenger.*

Except that the old Vulcan wasn't on the screen.

It was Will Riker.

"Will, it's good to see you again."

"I wish it were under other circumstances, Captain. And I don't mean to be so abrupt. But we are now operating under General Order Three. Commander Shelby will have provided you with encrypted orders to open at this time. Please do so, then report to the *Challenger* with your science officer in thirty minutes. Riker out."

Riker disappeared from the screen, replaced again by the *Challenger* poised against unchanging stars.

Mr. Land turned around from his helm position. "What was all that about?"

Lewinski stood up and stretched, as if Will Riker's request

were unremarkable. "I guess we're about to find out. Take us in to match orbits, drop the cloak, and . . . I'll be in my quarters reviewing our orders."

Lewinski left the bridge, feeling the eyes of his crew upon him. General Order Three or not, it was a strange experience to have a captain being told what to do by a commander.

But then, this entire mission had been strange. And whatever was to happen next, it had to be better than just waiting.

High above New Titan, the space-black disk of the *Monitor* rippled out of nothingness, less than half the size of the *Challenger*'s command saucer alone. It appeared against the larger vessel's full-spectrum gleam like the featureless shadow of a moon passing over its planet.

Together, these two sides of Starfleet—exploration and defense—kept station over the desolate world beneath them.

And they did not go unnoticed.

On the bridge of the *Avatar of Tomed,* Tran turned to Salatrel in surprise.

"Commander, a vessel has decloaked beside the *Challenger!*"

"Onscreen." Salatrel left her command chair and went to the helm to confirm the readings herself.

The blocky Starfleet vessel they had followed from Deep Space 9 fluttered into focus on the main viewscreen. It was no match for a Bird-of-Prey, let alone a Warbird, and Salatrel felt no concern about facing it in battle.

But the ship that had appeared beside the *Challenger* was a different matter.

Salatrel recognized it at once as a *Defiant*-class vessel, specifically designed, built, and equipped to fight the Borg. From the intercepted data which had been transmitted from the spies among the Romulan cloaking team working with Starfleet on that class of vessel, it was well suited for its task.

"Identification?" Salatrel asked Tran.

Tran's screens flickered with Starfleet ship identity charts, but the main window remained blank.

"It has not been encountered before," Tran said. He paused. "And it does possess a functioning cloaking device."

Salatrel was well aware of the dilemma that placed her in. Starfleet had clearly gone beyond the limits of the Treaty of Algeron and was deploying cloaking technology on its warships.

Fortunately, the Borg had not determined the weaknesses of the latest generation of Romulan cloaking devices. They had yet to assimilate a Romulan with that knowledge. But unfortunately, that meant a fleet of cloaked *Defiant*-class vessels could be an effective force against Borg ships.

It would be simple enough to provide the Borg with the specific tachyon patterns to scan for, which would reveal the presence of cloaked Starfleet vessels. But then, when the Star Empire moved against the Borg, as was inevitable, the greatest advantage of the Romulan fleet would have been negated.

Salatrel turned to her centurion, who had remained at his post behind her chair. "Tracius, can you offer any explanation for that ship's presence?"

She was surprised by the tone of contempt in the centurion's voice. "Look at the scans of the planet's surface."

Salatrel called them up on Tran's board. The radiation signature of a Borg tractor beam flared brilliant white at the coordinates of Starbase 804.

Salatrel's temper flared just as brilliantly. "The Borg took the starbase!" She whirled to face Tracius. "Why?"

His face was clouded with anger. "How can you be surprised that the collective doesn't tell us everything?"

"Because they need us to conquer the Federation!"

Tracius shook his head, shifting from contempt to sorrow in that moment. "Have you learned nothing from me? Before you can defeat your enemy, you must understand your enemy."

"I understand the Federation," Salatrel hissed. The old centurion was presuming on the ties between their families and would continue to do so at his own risk.

"And what of the Borg?"

"What is to understand?" Salatrel flung the words at him. "They are consumers. Single-minded accumulators of technology and living flesh. Ferengi without subtlety. Vulcans without remorse."

Tracius looked tired, as if all the years of living on the run with his former student, the child of lifelong friends, had caught up with him in the seven days since Kirk's return.

"You understand nothing about the Borg," he said. "If they were that direct, then they would not deal with us at all. They would be a school of *trasanara* come to strip our flesh from our bones. And when was the last time a single *trasanarit* emerged from the water and tried to negotiate with its victim?"

Salatrel felt the mood of her bridge change. This was not the Imperial Armada. There were no misconduct tribunals. A breach of the chain of command could be dealt with as quickly as the time it took to fire a disruptor. She could not allow Tracius's challenge to go unmet.

"If you have a point, make it quickly, old one," she warned, trying to undercut any authority Tracius might have among her bridge crew.

Tracius lapsed into the singsong cadence of a tutor. "Why do the Borg prepare a Speaker for each race they contact?"

Salatrel said nothing. She knew from experience that once in teaching mode her centurion would answer his own question.

"To make the assimilation process easier. More efficient. Less wasteful." He raised a weathered hand of sinew and bone to point an accusing finger at her. "And what could be more efficient than becoming our ally, then striking at our heart when our guard is down?"

Is that all? Salatrel thought, feeling relieved.

"Of course I expect the Borg to try and betray us," she said.

"Not *try!"* Tracius insisted. "Do you think they are standing still, waiting for the war with the Federation to conclude? Salatrel, they are betraying us already! This assimilation of the starbase, it's just *one* action that they've taken without informing us. How many others do you suppose there to be?"

"None," Salatrel said. "Vox told me—"

"Vox is one of *them!"*

Salatrel tightened her fists at her side. "Vox *told* me—"

"Your lover told you only what you wanted to hear!"

Without thought, Salatrel drew her disruptor and aimed it at Tracius.

But it was as if her former mentor didn't notice. As if he were sitting on the porch of her father's estate, debating the duty of the individual to the state versus the duty of the state to the individual.

"Can't you see what you've done?" Tracius argued. "The entire movement to overthrow the cowardly appeasers on Romulus has been set aside in order for you to pursue your revenge against one human. The Borg have never truly been committed to our joint venture—to attacking the Federation with such devastating force that the Empire would have no choice but to join in the war. If they had been, do you think Vox would have permitted you to subvert the entire plan?"

Salatrel's hand tightened on her weapon. "The Borg brought us the device which returned Kirk to life!"

"To distract you from everything else they do!"

Salatrel's teeth clenched. "The Borg want Picard dead. Kirk can do that."

"Are there no other assassins in our movement who could have done the same?"

"It would not be the same thing!"

"For history—of course it would be the same. Only for you would it be different."

Some of the bridge crew had stood up from their posts. Salatrel glanced at them. Saw their expressions. She had seen their like before, on the crew of this same Warbird when she had killed the admiral in command and joined the movement to restore pride and purpose to the Star Empire.

"Leave the bridge, Centurion."

But Tracius pointed to the screen, instead. "The Borg are playing their own game against you, moves within moves, intrigue on top of intrigue. And what better diversion to throw you than one you chose yourself?"

"Tracius . . . leave the bridge now."

The old centurion returned his hand to the edge of his cloak and stood proudly, like an orator in Dartha's court.

"You have abandoned the movement, Salatrel. You have become exactly what our Vulcan cousins accuse us of being—emotional, headstrong, swimming in blood, trapped in the past, and unable to grasp the future."

Salatrel closed her eyes. Heard the whine of her disruptor.

Felt the heat of its discharge as Tracius fell.

When she opened her eyes again, a single spike of green light flickered by her chair, then faded, and was gone.

She looked around her bridge again.

All crew members, even Tran, were back at their posts.

Order had been maintained.

She couldn't stop to think about the price.

Salatrel returned to her chair. "Is the *Challenger* in standard orbit?" she asked.

"Affirmative, Commander."

Salatrel hadn't heard that respectful tone in Tran's voice for months. Ironically, Tracius's death had restored discipline to her ship.

"Very good," she said. "Each time it crosses the terminator and comes into line of sight with the local sun, send a tetryon pulse to confirm the location of Kirk."

Tran did not look up from his board. She saw his hands hesitate on the controls. "Commander, they will be able to detect that pulse. We have no wormhole to hide it."

"They'll worry about it until they see it happens each time

they come out of New Titan's shadow. Then they'll catalogue it for later study." She smiled tightly. "Know your enemy, Tran."

"Yes, Commander."

Salatrel settled back in her chair. She realized she still had her disruptor drawn and in her hand. The barrel of it was warm where it lay across her leg.

Her old friend had defied her, she told herself. He deserved to go quickly. As did anyone and anything else that would dare deny her her revenge.

And that included the collective.

THIRTY-FOUR

Everywhere he went on the *Challenger,* Riker faced the ghost of the *Enterprise.* There were subtle differences in the wall coverings between his old ship and this newest one. The computer systems had been updated to incorporate the latest neural gel pack circuitry, replacing the supposedly antiquated isolinear chips of the past. The bridge module was yet another generation beyond that to which the *Enterprise* had been upgraded, prior to its mission to Veridian. And the recreational facility called Ten-Forward on the *Enterprise* was here known as Shuttlebay Four, probably because most *Galaxy*-class ships had only three.

But sickbay was virtually unchanged. And as Riker entered, he half expected Beverly Crusher to step out of her office.

But instead he saw Julian Bashir at Kirk's bedside. And

that scene once again viscerally reminded him that the past was gone and irretrievable.

Bashir looked up from a complex medical scanner as Riker approached.

Kirk was still in induced sleep. En route to New Titan, Bashir had confirmed that reducing the reanimated patient's metabolic rate slowed the nanites as well. Each hour Kirk remained unconscious was an hour longer he would live.

But he still had no more than a handful of days left.

"I'm due in a briefing in ten minutes," Riker said. In present circumstances, there was no time for pleasantries, and fortunately Bashir didn't take offense. "What couldn't you tell me over the comm system?"

Bashir frowned. "Under General Order Three, I can't tell you anything over the comm system. Enemy interception and all that."

Riker sighed. "I'm here. Tell me."

Bashir pointed to the scanner. Riker recognized some of the technical schematics on its display—Starfleet's reverse engineering of the Borg implants that had been recovered from Captain Picard.

"I've been going through the classified files you provided," Bashir explained. "They have far more detail than the papers that were published in—"

"Doctor, I've got a missing starbase I have to deal with. The Borg could return at any second. And I just don't have the time for lengthy explanations."

Bashir gestured with open hands, indicating his helplessness. "Bottom line, Commander—the implant in the patient's brain *is* a Borg device."

Riker put out a hand to the scanner to steady himself. "Why would the Borg reanimate James T. Kirk?"

"I don't know if it *was* the Borg who did this."

Riker blinked at Bashir. "You said it was a Borg implant."

"But the nanites aren't. And the nanites are what restored

him . . . physically, at least. Whatever brought his . . ." Bashir looked uncomfortable as he pronounced the Vulcan term. "Whatever brought his *katra* back to his body is beyond any science I know. And not within the realm of what either the implant or the nanites could have accomplished."

"Any idea where the nanites came from?" Riker asked.

Bashir looked weary. "It took some time, but I've been able to isolate and disassemble some of them. If anything, I'd say they're based on an original model designed by the Daystrom Institute, then modified for a different manufacturing process."

Riker forced a smile. "So someone stole a design and figured out a different way to build them?"

"Essentially."

"Are they of Borg manufacture?"

"That's just it," Bashir said. "According to these classified files, all Borg computer circuits encountered up to now universally contain traces of a distinctive tridithalifane doping agent in their subprocessors. The implant has it, but the subprocessors in these nanites do not."

Riker felt a sudden wave of apprehension. Even if the Borg had assimilated the technology behind the nanites intact, the modifications arising from assimilation would have laced them with tridithalifane. The fact that the tridithalifane wasn't present could mean only one thing. "Do I understand what you're saying here? *Two* different technologies are present in Kirk?"

Bashir nodded glumly. Riker could see the doctor had reached the same conclusion he just had.

"Someone's working *with* the Borg."

"It would appear so," Bashir said.

Riker felt as if the *Challenger's* artificial gravity was fluctuating. The only characteristic of the Borg which gave Starfleet any hope of defeating them was that at a certain base level, the collective was absolutely predictable.

That was why Picard had been chosen for his mission.

Starfleet already knew how the Borg reacted to Locutus. Everything Picard hoped to accomplish was predicated on the Borg reacting exactly the same way again.

But what if the Borg were no longer operating on their own? If, in some unfathomable fashion, the Borg had learned the behavior of cooperation, then a most unwelcome unpredictability had just been added to the equation.

"Doctor, with the additional information in the classified files, do you feel it is possible for you to remove the implant from Kirk?"

"What about Dr. Crusher?"

"Dr. Crusher is missing. We have no idea where she is, or when she might return."

Bashir looked at his patient.

But Riker didn't have time for thoughtful consideration.

"Dr. Bashir—if the Borg have allied themselves with another race, then all of Starfleet's efforts to develop adequate defenses are at risk. It is imperative that we release Kirk from his programming, so we will be able to interrogate him about who did this to him, and why." Riker held Bashir's gaze with an intent stare. "Now, I ask you again. Can *you* remove the implant?"

Bashir lowered his voice, as if afraid his patient could hear him.

"There is no question that I can remove it, Commander. I just don't know if the patient will survive the attempt."

Riker closed his eyes for a moment. There was no time to weigh pros and cons. No time to calculate the odds.

He looked at Bashir, daring the doctor to question him. "Do it."

"You're asking me to perform a procedure which might kill him."

"You may consider it an order, doctor."

Bashir hit the main control on the scanner, shutting it off.

"With respect, I feel compelled to file a formal protest with Starfleet Medical."

"By all means," Riker said. "*After* the procedure."

Riker saw the moment of decision in Bashir's eyes. He would do it, against his better judgment.

"I'll need an hour to familiarize myself with Dr. Crusher's notes and to have the necessary instruments replicated."

"The full facilities of the *Challenger* are yours."

"You'll pardon me if I'm not thrilled at the prospect."

Riker left without replying. It was surprising how much he liked the doctor. Lots of attitude, but he could follow orders.

He decided young Dr. Bashir would go far in Starfleet.

Provided Starfleet survived.

THIRTY-FIVE

Data had participated in many medical procedures in the past, though they had usually involved emergency care. The extraction of the Borg implant from James T. Kirk was one of the few times he had actually assisted in a surgical bay, and part of him looked forward to the experience. He found it brought anticipation of enjoyment.

However, another part of him recognized the seriousness of the procedure, because the outcome could have a direct bearing on the survival of the Federation. That brought anticipation of a different type.

Data decided that having emotions was indeed making it

easier for him to understand why humans so often seemed confused. The experience of both wanting and dreading something at the same time was akin to contemplating the wave and particle nature of light. Unfortunately, there existed no quantum equations to describe the duality of conflicting emotions.

Yet, Data thought.

But then he wondered if that question had ever been addressed on Trilex. And whether the answer had somehow contributed to that society's destruction.

"Mr. Data," Bashir said, interrupting his musings, "if you would please inspect the primary branch of the implant's main core."

Data immediately concentrated on the task at hand.

Dr. Bashir had requested Data's assistance in this procedure because of the android's ability to remain in direct contact with the *Challenger*'s computers. Thus, all Starfleet's information about the Borg, as well as Beverly Crusher's analysis of the implants she had removed from Captain Picard, would be instantly available.

Data did regret that even though he had the medical knowledge to guide Bashir's surgery, he did not have the motor skills to perform it himself. After observing Bashir once, Data would, of course, always be able to re-create the identical operation, in the same way he could re-create great musical performances, note for note. But since human bodies were so varied, inside and out, the ability to exactly reproduce certain movements would not guarantee the next patient to receive the exact same operation would survive Data's ministrations. A successful surgeon's fluid skill depended on being able to adapt to constantly changing conditions—and bodies.

However, Data could still contribute to Bashir's success, and he began his work.

Before him, in the glow of the sterilization field surrounding the surgical table, Dr. Bashir had reflected a flap of Kirk's scalp to expose the occipital bone at the base of the skull. A small, rectangular opening, two centimeters by three centimeters, now punctured the skull. The excised bone fragment was floating in a nutrient bath, to be replaced at the procedure's end.

Within the opening, the dull yellow dura mater had been peeled back to expose the occipital gyrus of the cerebrum, sitting atop the cerebellum. A computer display screen was suspended from the ceiling, over the patient's head. On it was displayed an enlarged, three-dimensional sensor model of the skull's interior, in which the main branch of the Borg implant could be seen at the boundary between the two components of the brain.

Bashir had threaded eight molecular wires through the brain tissue and made contact with the implant at eight key points. The wires would draw off any power-discharge the implant might make in response to being disassembled.

Data verified that the placement of the molecular wires matched that described by Dr. Crusher as those least likely to cause harm to the patient. "The implant's power source has been correctly isolated," Data said.

"Thank you," Bashir replied. He rubbed the back of his gloved hand against the red cap he wore, then held the small cylinder of a number two tractor scalpel near the exposed brain tissue. With deft movements of his fingers, he began to use the miniature force field projected by the scalpel to gently ease apart a path through the brain tissue along the wires.

Data and Bashir both watched the progress of the pathway on the sensor screen. Neurons were being disconnected with each pulse of the scalpel. But the disruption was so minor, no permanent damage would result. At least, if the patient survived.

As Bashir continued with the procedure, Data multitasked his observations among the display screen, Kirk's skull, and

Dr. Bashir, while constantly reviewing Crusher's notes, confirming each step Bashir took, and suggesting refinements when Bashir requested.

Data was constantly impressed by Bashir's calm and proficiency. However, one hour into the procedure, he began to wonder when the young human would realize he was facing a hopeless task.

An hour and a half into the procedure, Data took it upon himself to inform the doctor of his conclusions.

"Dr. Bashir, it is clear by now that what you are attempting to do is hopeless."

Bashir responded by glaring at him. "What is the condition of the implant?" he demanded.

"Eighty percent of the implant has been separated from the brain tissue," Data confirmed. "Bleeding is minimal. The patient's vitals are stable."

"Then that means only twenty percent to go," Bashir said.

Data was puzzled by the challenge in the doctor's voice. Data was not questioning his expertise, only commenting on the inescapable facts.

"Dr. Bashir, the remaining twenty percent of the implant cannot be removed by the procedures Dr. Crusher used on Captain Picard. Please recall that many of the Borg implants in the captain were connected to secondary nerves located outside of the brain. In those instances, Dr. Crusher was able to sever and remove nerve sections for later replacement and regrowth. That is not possible with the brain. That is, if you are hoping to retain the integrity of the personality currently inhabiting it."

"Is there anything you can tell me in ten words or less?" Bashir snapped.

"If you continue using the tractor scalpel on the remaining sections of the implant, you will also cause irreparable harm to the patient's cerebellum. You have reached the point where the implant's fractal tendrils are too tightly entwined to remove from either the blood supply or the brain matter itself."

"That wasn't ten words or less."

Data was prepared to go on for an hour, citing all the pertinent passages in Dr. Crusher's notes. But given Bashir's mood, he simply said: "If you continue, Kirk will be dead in twenty minutes. Ten words cxactly." Data wondered if he had been understood correctly. "Except for those words at the end. And these words."

"That will be enough, Mr. Data."

Bashir looked down at the exposed brain of his patient. Data used a sterile pad to draw away the blood that collected in it.

"I've gone too far," Bashir said. Data sensed Bashir wasn't directing his words to anyone. He was thinking aloud. "A partially functioning implant will completely paralyze his brain-wave activity. He'll never wake up."

"My cursory examination of the *Challenger*'s medical library suggests that other techniques are available," Data volunteered.

Bashir looked up at him with hope. "Well . . .?"

Data felt contrite. "Unfortunately, they would require extensive study and experimentation before they could be applied in this case."

Data saw Bashir's shoulders sag beneath his surgical gown. "Then I have no choice, do I?"

"You could place the patient in stasis," Data suggested.

"Check the literature," Bashir said with a sigh. "Stasis won't slow down the type of nanite he's filled with."

Data gazed down at the bleeding opening into the patient's body. He was suddenly struck by the terrible certainty that he was going to witness a human being die. And there was nothing he could do about it.

He looked at Bashir, wondering if the doctor had reached the same realization.

But Bashir kept his eyes on the patient. He picked up a more powerful tractor scalpel.

Data supposed that was the difference between them.

Bashir still thought there was something he could do.

Data did not look forward to the next twenty minutes.

After drawing a deep breath, Bashir held the tractor scalpel close to the opening. Data saw the gentle pressure he used to activate the force field. Despite the urgency the doctor felt, he was still proceeding methodically.

Until the *Challenger's* collision alarm sounded.

Data's subsystems accelerated to critical speed as he anticipated a spray of blood erupting from the opening. No human he knew could have suppressed a reflexive response to the sirens that warbled throughout the ship, and Data fully expected the scalpel force field to have torn a hole through the patient's brain. Death wouldn't take twenty minutes. It would take twenty seconds.

But against all of Data's expectations, the opening did not disappear in a spray of blood.

Data looked across at Bashir. The doctor's eyes were clenched shut.

Data felt astonishment.

The doctor had actually held his hand steady. His skill and self-awareness had been that great.

"Bashir to bridge," the doctor growled, barely containing his fury. "What the *hell* was that?!"

"Sorry, doctor," Riker's voice replied from the overhead speakers. "We just had a ship drop out of warp nine point nine five, two kilometers off our bow. The computer responded on automatic."

Bashir slowly drew his hand away from the patient's head. "I don't care what it was," he said in low and angry tones. "If you don't want me to decapitate my patient, shut off all alarm systems to sickbay *now*!"

In the silence that followed, Data couldn't help himself. He was designed to acquire knowledge. "Commander Riker, what kind of vessel can travel at that speed? Are we being attacked by the Borg?"

But the tension of battle wasn't detectable in Riker's voice. "It's an experimental Starfleet transport, Data. Two big warp nacelles and not much else. From Earth."

Bashir gazed up in exasperation at the sickbay ceiling and the speakers there. "Does any of this have a point, Commander?"

From his tone of voice, Data could almost picture Riker smiling. "It seems you were premature in concluding there was only one doctor in Starfleet who could deal with Kirk's neural implant."

Data saw the immense confusion on Bashir's face.

"That wasn't *my* conclusion, Commander. Starfleet Medical said Beverly Crusher was the only physician on active duty with experience in—"

Bashir and Data both turned to look into the center of sickbay as they heard a transporter harmonic begin.

"We're beaming a consulting physician directly to sickbay, doctor. He's been fully briefed. And should be able to help."

Data watched as the transporter cloud took on the shape of a squat pyramid. For a moment, he thought a Medusan might have been beamed on board, though that ephemeral race was hardly known for its physical skills.

But then he saw the cloud resolve into a humanoid sitting in a mobility chair.

Data felt his emotion chip accelerate as he realized he recognized the figure.

The mobility chair spun around on its treads and then bounced slightly as it headed for the surgical table, motor humming.

The figure it carried was thin and stooped, his hair a dull gray, his admiral's uniform so loose it appeared to be two sizes too large. Deep creases crosshatched his face, except where a sparse white beard mottled his cheeks and chin.

But there was an intelligence and a quickness in his eyes that belied the age that hung around him like a cloud. Whatever shape his body was in, a much younger person dwelt within it.

"Admiral McCoy?" Data asked.

"*Leonard H. McCoy*?" Bashir croaked.

The admiral ignored Data to squint in disdain at the young doctor. "Who were you expecting? Dancing girls?"

Data was surprised to see Bashir actually tremble and blush. The young doctor had held his scalpel steady when the collision alarm had sounded, but this visitation by the greatest doctor to have served Starfleet had apparently triggered a loss of control.

Data saw the admiral look over at him. "You I know," McCoy said. His voice was low and hoarse. "Bet you're not surprised, are you?"

"Actually, I am, sir."

McCoy narrowed his eyes. "Thought you were an android."

"I now have an emotion chip, sir."

McCoy rolled his eyes. "What they won't build these days. Mind you, I could've put one of those chips to good use in an old friend way back when. . . ." McCoy turned his attention back to Bashir. "Correct me if I'm mistaken, doctor, but don't you have a patient on that table?"

Bashir nodded, quickly checking Kirk's vital signs on the display screen.

McCoy rolled up beside Bashir at the head of the surgical table. "Well, pull back the sheet. Let me see."

Bashir understood what McCoy meant. He lifted the sheet covering Kirk's face.

Instantly McCoy's eyes filled with tears. Data saw his jaw wobble. "Ah, Jim," he sighed, almost inaudibly. "Scotty was right after all."

Then McCoy abruptly sat up straight in his chair, all sign of emotion dropping from his face. He looked up at Bashir.

"Julian Bashir?"

Bashir nodded.

"You're the one who's been pestering Starfleet Medical for all the old records on Jim Kirk?"

"Yes, sir."

"Anyone think of calling his personal physician?"

Bashir's eyes were wide. "Uh, sir, to be honest . . . we thought . . . well, I thought you were dead. . . ."

"Well, I'm not!" McCoy barked. He thumped his chest. "One hundred and forty-four next month. On my third heart, if you can believe it. Grow a new set of lungs every year. And I've got ten new meters of cloned intestines writhing in my guts. And you know why?"

Bashir shook his head.

"Neither do I, son." He slapped the arms of his mobility chair. Then his hand went to a small box at his waist. Data heard microservos whine, and the ancient admiral rose easily from his chair and stepped forward with the characteristic deliberate motion of someone wearing an exoskeleton.

McCoy braced himself on the edge of the surgical table, studying the display screen. "Neural implant. Fractal tendril growth. You've isolated the power supply, but that's not enough. Too entwined in the vascular supply, artificial dendrite entanglement—"

"Artificial dendrites? Is that what it is?" Bashir asked excitedly.

"I've seen it before," McCoy said. "Sigma Draconis VI. Or was it VII? Anyway, had to disconnect a complete cerebellum by pass and then *re*connect an entire brain. Had some help, mind you. But the details aren't important. Don't remember them anyway. This new Borg rubbish, it's just a variation. Lot simpler, too."

Bashir held out his scalpel.

McCoy looked at him and, from somewhere in those craggy features, found a warm smile.

"Why, thank you, son. But those days are long gone." He held up his hands. Once they had worked miracles, Data knew, but now they were skeletal and shaking.

McCoy tapped one thin finger against his temple. "But I've still got it up here. You listen to what I tell you, and we're going to do just fine."

Data could see the wonder in Bashir's eyes. But the young doctor stared at McCoy just a moment too long.

"Well . . .," the admiral said with annoyance, "get a move on. You're a doctor, not a Horta."

Bashir nodded and brought his tractor scalpel back to Kirk's skull.

But McCoy laid a gentle hand on the young doctor's arm. "Tell you what, son. First you want to trade that scalpel in for a number eight. We're going to forget about Jim's gray matter for a bit, concentrate on shunting some of his arteries, then we're going to use a laser . . . an honest-to-God laser beam like we were some kind of witch doctors. And once we get in there, we're going to section a path on the other side of the implant."

As McCoy began explaining the techniques they would use, Data stepped back from the surgical table, knowing that his assistance was no longer required. He was content to watch the effortless blending of raw talent and seasoned experience that unfolded before him.

Riker and Deanna Troi arrived a few minutes after the doctors began working together. La Forge and Worf followed shortly after. Together they watched as the hands of Starfleet's youngest generation, guided by the wisdom of Starfleet's oldest, worked a new miracle that neither could have performed without the other.

As the final section of the implant was removed, and Bashir quickly closed the wound, pronouncing the procedure a success, Data watched as a teardrop escaped McCoy's glittering eyes.

A teardrop of happiness, Data knew.

And he wondered who, in eighty years, might cry for him.

THIRTY-SIX

Kirk heard the metallic shriek of the bridge hit the rocks of Veridian III, and he opened his eyes.

He smelled dust. Felt the heat of the Veridian sun. Heard the twisted struts creak as they settled.

As something groaned and moved within them.

Kirk stepped closer. His boots crunched on small rocks and gravel, each sound crisp and pure. He peered into the tangle of twisted metal. There was someone trapped inside.

Oh, yes, Kirk thought, *I'm there.*

The duality of his existence in this place did not trouble him. It seemed the way things should be.

The desert wind picked up, and he felt it like the hot breath of a pursuing predator.

"It is getting closer," a voice told him, confirming what he felt.

Kirk turned away from the sight of himself feebly struggling in the wreckage of the bridge.

Someone else was approaching, the sun behind him.

Kirk held his hand up to protect his eyes from the glare of the light. Dimly he realized that the sun was in a different part of the sky and that he had no idea what was shining so brightly behind this . . .

. . . Vulcan?

Kirk recognized the jewels and script on the robes.

The Vulcan raised his hand, exposing his palm, separating his fingers in a gesture of both greeting and farewell. Duality again.

From somewhere on top of the rocks towering over him, something exploded. A band of energy rippled through the sky, sparking and crackling. And then it was gone.

But the Vulcan remained.

"Spock?" Kirk asked.

"He is not among us," the Vulcan explained. Then he stepped closer.

Kirk smiled as he recognized him.

"Ambassador Sarek!"

Spock's father inclined his head, as if he had not heard his name spoken for a long time.

Kirk felt he had to make some apology for the condition he was in. If not for himself, then for his other self, lying in the wreckage.

Dying, Kirk thought.

"I'm afraid things are . . . a bit of a mess," Kirk said.

The ambassador studied him, as if he were about to speak. To impart great wisdom. He did. "There is no need to concern yourself, Captain."

Kirk knew, then. The reason that both he and Sarek must meet like this. He heard scrabbling on the rocks. Someone else was climbing down. Sarek waited, the breeze stirring his robes.

"You're dead and I'm dying, aren't I?" Kirk asked.

Sarek looked up at the sky, staring at something Kirk couldn't see. "Have you had this dream before?"

Kirk looked down at his hands. Flexed them. Watched the muscles and sinews move beneath his skin. Everything was in exquisite focus. Each movement perfect. Far too real. "*Is* this a dream?"

Sarek turned back to him. "That is not the question. Logically, you should ask yourself: Is this *the* dream?"

"You mean, the dream where I die."

"You have had it all your life, have you not?"

"When we melded minds," Kirk said with sudden understanding. "When you came to me so long ago, looking for your son. . . . You saw my dreams?"

"It is the way of things."

"Is that why you're here now?"

"What do you think?"

Kirk smiled. "Ah, then this *is* my dream. And I'm the one who makes the rules."

Sarek looked at Kirk with a skeptical expression that only a Vulcan could make. "I do not believe rules are what you are noted for."

Kirk stepped aside as Picard rushed past him, hurrying to the other Kirk, beneath the wreckage.

"He thinks I'm dying. The other captain of the *Enterprise*."

"I have melded minds with him as well."

Kirk was intrigued. "Is that what brought you here? Because there's something we've all shared?"

"Or will share," Sarek replied.

Kirk was growing impatient with this dream. "I don't like riddles."

"There are none here."

Kirk watched as Picard lowered his head in sorrow.

"That's wrong, isn't it? Picard thinking I've died. Because . . . " Kirk held out his hand, struggling to complete his thought, trying to remember something he knew he should know. "I didn't die here."

Sarek folded his robes closer to him. Kirk was surprised by how frail the elder Vulcan suddenly seemed.

"Ask yourself this question, Captain. You have always

known how you will die." Sarek's eyes seemed to burn into him like phasers. "Is this *the* dream?"

Kirk didn't even have to think about the answer. "No. You know that."

Sarek nodded once. "As do you."

Then a light shone out from behind the Vulcan once again. He turned toward it, robe fluttering, as if the light blew against him like wind.

"Sarek, wait!"

The Vulcan hesitated.

"If not here . . . then where? When?"

To Kirk, it seemed as if Sarek's eyes were as bright as the light which engulfed them both.

"You know, Captain. You have always known."

"Then the dream I've always had is real?"

Sarek smiled then, the first time Kirk had ever seen his face express anything other than a stern stoicism.

"You taught my son a song once, Captain." The years melted from Sarek. He was young, strong, and his smile was dazzling. "Life is but a dream. . . ."

Kirk held his hand up to block the brilliance that came for Sarek. All of Veridian dissolved around him. His voice, their voices, became something else, as they became something else. What they had always been.

Live long and prosper, Captain. . . .

But for how long . . .?

Look to the stars, James T. Kirk . . . second on the right . . . straight on till morning. . . .

Kirk squinted at the blinding light that shone past his hand and clenched eyes. He tried to turn his head but felt a sudden pain, as if someone had punched a hole clear through it.

"Turn it off," he said. His throat hurt. He coughed.

The light vanished. He watched the silhouette of a lamp on the end of a folded armature move away.

There was someone leaning over him.

"Sarek . . . ?"

"Seventy-eight damn years floating around in God knows where. Then you come back from the dead, and the first thing you do is insult me."

Kirk's eyes opened wide.

"Bones? *Bones!*"

He ignored the pain and sat up, grabbing his friend's arm. But it felt so thin and . . .

Kirk saw McCoy's face.

"What happened? You look . . . so old."

McCoy grimaced. "Good to see you, too, Captain."

Kirk looked around. He was in some kind of sickbay. Different from what he was used to. Larger area. Smaller equipment.

There were other people by his diagnostic bed.

He recognized them.

And why not? He had tried to kill some of them.

Geordi La Forge. The android, Data. Worf, the Klingon who was no longer an enemy. A woman he didn't recognize, with solid black pupils. And . . .

Kirk stared at the tall man with the dark beard. "Commander Will Riker?"

Riker stepped forward. Held out his hand.

Kirk shook it.

"Captain Kirk. It is a pleasure, sir."

Kirk took a breath, hardly knowing where to begin. "My first impression is that I've been dreaming. But . . . I haven't been, have I?"

Riker smiled. "No, sir."

"This *is* the twenty-fourth century?"

Riker nodded. "Then you do remember what happened on Veridian?"

Kirk rubbed the back of his head. Felt something covering his skin there. It was where the pain came from. "Is that where I was? Someone was going to launch a missile, I recall. We stopped him."

"Yes, sir. You and Captain Picard."

Kirk stiffened as he heard that name.

"Are you all right, Captain?"

McCoy clanked around by Kirk. Kirk didn't know what made the noise. It sounded as if McCoy had something mechanical strapped to his legs, beneath his clothes.

"Of course, he's all right," McCoy muttered. "He's just had his head opened up and his brain cut into. Why wouldn't he be all right? It's not as if he's ever used it."

Kirk looked at McCoy with narrowed eyes. "Bones . . . how old *are* you?"

"Don't start with me. I'm still your doctor."

"Captain Kirk," Riker began. "I'm going to leave you with Admiral McCoy to get you caught up on . . . present conditions. But, I have to know, sir. Do you remember what happened to you *after* you assisted Captain Picard on Veridian?"

Kirk felt every muscle in his body tense at the second mention of that name. And he suddenly knew what he had to do. "I remember falling," he said. "Someone spoke to me . . . and then I woke up here."

Riker nodded glumly. "I see. Well, if anything comes back to you, it's of critical importance for us to know how you came to be here."

"Believe me, Commander. I've got some questions I'd like answered, myself." He turned to McCoy. Stared at him in disbelief. "*Admiral* McCoy?"

McCoy waved a frail hand. "It's a long story."

Kirk didn't smile. "How about . . . Spock?"

McCoy sighed. "Let's start at the beginning." He leaned forward. "With the wake Scotty threw for you."

"A wake?"

McCoy grinned. "You should have been there, Jim. We had ourselves a time."

Kirk glanced at Riker and shrugged. Then he settled back in his diagnostic bed and let his history lesson begin.

* * *

Once the sickbay doors had closed behind them, Riker stopped in the corridor. He had to know.

"You heard what he said," he told Deanna. "He remembered Veridian, then waking up here. And nothing in between."

"Yet he knew your name, Commander," Data said.

"He's very confused," Deanna offered. "His feelings are in great turmoil. Especially in his reaction to seeing Admiral McCoy. Kirk remembers him as a much younger man."

"But is he lying about not remembering anything?" Riker asked.

"Yes," Deanna said. "I believe so."

"You believe so. But you're not sure?"

"Will, he's suddenly jumped almost eighty years into his future. We should expect his feelings to be erratic."

"Erratic. In what way?"

Deanna looked embarrassed. "Both times when you mentioned Captain Picard's name . . . I felt such . . . hatred coming from Kirk."

Riker polled Data, La Forge, and Worf to see if they had any similar observations to offer. "Is it possible Kirk blames Picard for his death on Veridian?"

"It wasn't a focused impression, Will." Deanna thought for a moment. "It was similar to the impressions I get from Bajorans when they think about the Cardassian occupation of their world. How they feel when they think about the atrocities the Cardassians committed. That was Kirk's reaction to Captain Picard."

"There's no reason why Kirk should feel that way."

"Unless," Deanna said, "he is still under the influence of whatever programming he was subjected to."

"Even with the Borg implant removed?"

Deanna nodded.

Riker turned to Worf. "Mr. Worf, I want Kirk under

constant surveillance. But don't let him know. He's not familiar with our techniques. If he doesn't know he's being observed, maybe he'll slip up."

"Sir," Worf said, "since my encounter with Kirk on Qo'noS, I have studied his historical record quite extensively. He does not seem the type of individual to 'slip up.'"

"We had better hope someone does," Riker said. "Because if we don't find out who's working with the Borg soon, we're all going to be programmed. Just like Kirk."

The rest of his crewmates remained silent as Riker looked back at the doors to sickbay.

The man behind that door had once been one of Starfleet's greatest heroes.

Now he might be its greatest enemy.

And to save the Federation, Riker knew that if the moment came, he could and would deliver Kirk to his final death, without a moment's hesitation.

He saw Deanna sense those dark thoughts within him and turn away.

Riker felt the sting of isolation.

He wondered how Kirk felt.

THIRTY-SEVEN

In an instant, blazing like a sudden sun, the *Challenger* moved from the shadow of New Titan, into the light.

A tetryon pulse accompanied the moment of transition, as it had for every orbit the great ship had made of this planet.

In the *Challenger's* astrophysics and astronomy labs, the anomalous radiation spike was noted, commented upon, but set aside in deference to other, more pressing concerns. Specifically, the analysis of the transwarp conduit opening which had been recorded by the *Monitor's* sensors.

Thus the tetryon pulse came and a small part of it returned to its source, after interacting with and reflecting from the tridithalifane in what was left of Kirk's implant.

On the bridge of the *Tomed,* cloaked one hundred thousand kilometers from New Titan and the *Challenger* and her companion ship, Tran read the sensor return on the tetryon pulse he had sent. It wasn't good news.

"Commander," he said, not daring to look up. "The implant has been removed from Kirk." He prepared to die, anticipating the first shock of the disruptor beam that would disassemble him.

Instead, he became aware of Salatrel standing behind him, studying his screens over his shoulder.

"I was told that would be impossible," she said.

There was a flat tone in her voice. It had been there since

she had killed her centurion. To Tran, it reminded him of Vox.

"Do you want me to send a finer pulse, Commander?"

"Would it be detected?"

"I believe so," Tran said.

"And if it were detected, how long before the Starfleet vessels would suspect that a cloaked ship was nearby?"

Tran knew there was no answer he could give which would please her.

"Starfleet has more experience with cloaking devices than we suspected, Commander. I believe they would detect our presence within minutes."

Salatrel walked forward until she was a shadow against the main viewscreen. She held her hands behind her back. Tran saw she still carried her disruptor. She had not reholstered it since she had fired it last.

"I was told the implant would be impossible to remove," she repeated. Speaking to herself, Tran knew. "I was told that even if it malfunctioned, Kirk's programming would hold." Salatrel turned to face Tran and the rest of her bridge crew. "It appears I was lied to, does it not?"

No one said anything.

"There is only one chance we have to succeed," Salatrel said. She paced back and forth in front of the image of the *Challenger* and the smaller, dark ship at its side. "And that is for Kirk to kill Picard. Only then can honor be restored to my family. Does anyone disagree?"

No one did. No one even breathed.

"Picard must die. The Borg and Federation must destroy themselves. And then the wings of the Romulan Empire will embrace all the stars of all the galaxy."

Salatrel turned to face the *Challenger.*

"Take us in, Subcommander. Full impulse. Flood both ships with high-resolution sensors, then take an evasive course behind the sun." She glanced back over her shoulder. "They'll look for us. But they won't find us."

Tran braced himself for what he must do. "With respect, Commander. What shall I set the sensors for? What, exactly, are we looking for?"

"I want to know Kirk's position and location. Other than that, I want to know if any other Borg are on that ship."

"Borg?" Tran said. "On a Federation vessel?"

"The Borg have lied to us, Subcommander, by claiming to be our allies. What if they've played the same game with the Federation? What if another Speaker is there on that ship, helping to prepare Starfleet for a sneak attack on our Empire?"

Tran was appalled by the possibility. By working with the Borg, the Romulan dissidents had revealed almost all the military secrets of the Star Empire to the collective. If the Borg did decide to move against the Empire with the combined might of the Federation. . . . "We would have no defense," Tran said. "We would have . . . nothing."

"Except honor," Salatrel replied. "Tracius and I agreed on that lesson, at least. Honor is the one possession which no enemy can take from you, unless you allow it to be taken." Her eyes grew dark. "And I will not allow mine to be taken. No matter what the price."

Tran thought over his commander's words.

Perhaps she was right.

Even if all the dreams of the dissidents were lost, even if the appeasers in power had led the Empire to its doom, at least Tran could still claim an honorable death.

Or, he thought pragmatically, he could assassinate Salatrel and take command of the *Tomed* himself.

He set a flyby course to intercept the *Challenger.* The war against the Federation wasn't scheduled to begin for another two days.

There was still time to make a decision.

Tran was certain it would be the right one.

His honor depended upon it.

THIRTY-EIGHT

Kirk stood in front of a mirror in an alcove of sickbay, examining himself in his uniform—white sweater, burgundy jacket, black trousers with their pinstripe. He turned around once, then looked back in the mirror. After a moment, he saw his reflection turn, on a three-second delay. The uniform was a perfect fit. All that was missing was his Starfleet insignia.

He looked again at the tiny badge he had been given instead to pin onto his jacket—the Starfleet delta set on an angled rectangle. Supposedly, it functioned as a communicator, as well as allowing the ship's computer to track his every move. Kirk decided he missed the old handheld model. Getting set in his ways, he supposed.

He slipped out of the patient alcove and found McCoy back in his mobility chair, nodding off in front of a desktop computer terminal. The chair was a considerable improvement over the one Chris Pike had been confined to. But McCoy was in better shape than Pike had been. And the exoskeleton support frame he wore beneath his clothes gave him the ability to move around as if he were still under his own power.

The old doctor jerked awake as Kirk came near. It was still a shock for Kirk to see his friend in such frail condition. But then, his own condition wasn't much better. Before the selective painkillers Dr. Bashir had given him, the pains in his joints from the nanites had been almost unbearable.

"Bones . . . you say they . . . 'replicated' this uniform?"

McCoy blinked at him, as he were still unused to seeing Kirk. "Fancy new name for synthesizers, far as I can tell."

Kirk gently probed the incision on the back of his head. McCoy said that with the latest advancements in medical science, the bone and skin would heal scarfree in less than five days.

But Kirk didn't have five days.

"You give any more thought to what I said?" McCoy asked.

"You think they'd go for it?"

McCoy smiled. "Don't ask me how it happened, but you're a hero to these people. Hell, all of us fossils from the *Enterprise* are."

Kirk shrugged. "We were just doing our jobs."

"The point is, Jim, these people would do anything in their power if they thought it would help you."

Kirk thought it over. McCoy wanted him to take a modified shuttle, switch off all the artificial gravity and inertial dampening, then accelerate up to near light-speed and let relativity take its course. Einsteinian time dilation wasn't a factor in faster-than-light warp travel, but it still existed at slower-than-light velocities. And McCoy believed that if Kirk went off on a one-week flight, in the three years that would pass during his absence, Starfleet Medical might have developed a way of removing the nanites from his body.

"The point is, Bones, you have no guarantee I'll even live a week with these nanites inside me."

"It's worth taking the risk, isn't it?"

Kirk shrugged. "There has to be an end to it sometime, Bones."

"I didn't get to be one hundred and forty-four with a defeatist attitude like that."

"What's the record?" Kirk asked.

McCoy grinned. "You're looking at it. *And* I've got my one hundred-and-fiftieth birthday party all planned."

Kirk looked around the sickbay again. So much to digest.

Almost eighty years of history had passed him by. This ship, what he could see of it, looked like it would put both his own *Enterprises* to shame. And the new friends, the new enemies.

Especially the Borg.

Though he couldn't remember much of what McCoy had told him about the Borg. Almost as if he wasn't supposed to remember . . .

"What happened to everyone, Bones? You still get together for reunions. Curse the old captain?"

McCoy managed to smile and look sad at the same time. "Sit down, Jim," he said.

Kirk sat on the edge of the table as McCoy once again slipped into his memories.

And what memories they were.

Admiral Pavel Chekov, commander in chief of Starfleet. The books he had written after his retirement, detailing his adventures on the *Enterprise,* the *Potemkin,* and the *Cydonia,* had made household names of all his crewmates.

Hikaru Sulu, president of the Federation Council for an unprecedented three terms. Kirk had known his helmsman had always had a fondness for politics, and it pleased him to think of Sulu continuing his work, steering the ship of state.

And Dr. Uhura, two-time winner of the Nobel and Zee-Magnees Peace Prize. After her retirement, she had devoted herself to recruiting the best and the brightest for the Academy, tirelessly traveling the worlds of the Federation to make sure the promise of the stars and the challenge of humanity's adventure would be available to all.

And Scotty, who had been trapped in a machine—which seemed all too fitting a fate for him—so that he, too, had survived to meet this next generation of bold explorers and was somewhere out among the stars, still doing what he loved. Flying between the stars, too busy to ever think of actually retiring as he had so often threatened.

Then there were Rand and Chapel, Kyle, M'Benga, Carol

Marcus, and Ruth. On his journey here, McCoy had even called up the old computer records of Kirk's nephews, his admirals, his lost loves, friends, distant relations.

All passed before Kirk like the tail of a comet, bright and sparkling one moment, a memory the next.

"It is quite a lot to take in in one sitting," McCoy said.

"All those lives," Kirk said. "I was part of them . . . but sometimes it feels like I didn't know them at all."

"You won't get an argument from me."

Kirk smiled. "That's a first." Then he looked at McCoy to let the doctor know he couldn't avoid what he had been trying to avoid since the moment Kirk awoke here.

"Spock," Kirk said.

"Still alive and kicking," McCoy answered. "And . . . could be he's part of the problem that's got everyone so worked up."

"I'm listening," Kirk said.

But before McCoy could say anything more, red alert sounded, and Riker's voice reverberated from the speakers ordering all crew to battle stations.

THIRTY-NINE

Riker sat beside Captain Simm on the bridge of the *Challenger*. Every sensor display was lit up, flashing its warnings.

Simm sat with steepled hands. He was a black Vulcan from his world's Regar district. The severe features of his face remained placid amidst the noise and appearance of confusion. Nothing surprised him. But whether that was because he was a Vulcan, or because he had spent twenty years as a starship captain, no one could be certain.

"Report," Simm said. And though his voice was neither raised nor strained, it cut through the cacophony of alerts and warning chimes as if he had spoken in the ear of every member of the bridge crew. And some of those crew members were very familiar to Riker. He had taken great pleasure in reassembling them to share his duty on the *Challenger*.

Worf's voice thundered from his security station at the rear of the bridge. "We have been subjected to a full sensor sweep, Captain."

Data reported from his ops board. "I am recording an anomalous tachyon surge, consistent with a cloaking device."

"Is it from the *Monitor*?" Simm asked calmly.

"Negative, sir," Data replied.

Simm turned to Riker. "Your analysis, Commander."

"Flyby of a cloaked vessel, sir."

"That much is obvious," the Vulcan said. "What was its purpose?"

"It was . . . looking for something," Riker guessed.

"And that would be . . . ?"

Riker hated the Socratic method. "I have no idea, sir."

Simm stood up, acknowledging that the lesson was over. "Three possibilities, Commander. In arriving at them, we must assume that we have been under passive observation for a given period of time, since the probability that a cloaked ship encountered us and decided to scan us at the same instant is remote." Simm folded his hands behind his back. "We must also assume that the decision by the commander of the cloaked ship to scan us was triggered by a precipitating action, and not a random event." Simm glanced back at Riker. "A precipitating action implies that conditions have changed from those which did not require a scan, to those which did. What conditions have changed upon this vessel in the past thirty minutes?"

Riker thought frantically. The Vulcan captain was making him feel like a first-year Academy student. He had no answer.

"James T. Kirk became conscious."

Riker wasn't convinced. "How could anyone know that, sir?"

"Precisely," Simm said. "Hence, in increasing order of probability, we have been under observation by a cloaked ship operating with a telepathic crew. *Or* we have a spy on board, who has reported on Kirk's condition to the cloaked ship. *Or* the cloaked ship's actions were not triggered by the act of Kirk becoming conscious, but by another, related act."

Now Riker understood. "The removal of the implant."

"Very good, Commander." Simm looked up at Worf. "Mr. Worf, earlier there were reports of tetryon pulses accompanying our emergence from the terminator. Was a pulse recorded on our most recent orbit?"

Worf accessed his security displays. "Yes, sir."

Simm wheeled around to face Data. "Mr. Data, Kirk's implant was of Borg manufacture. Therefore, it contained traces of tridithalifane. Will tridithalifane reflect a properly tuned tetryon beam?"

Data angled his head as he accessed the *Challenger*'s main computers. "Yes, sir. It appears possible."

Simm turned back to Riker and raised a finger. "Hence, logic dictates we have been under surveillance by a cloaked ship that knows Kirk is aboard, knows Kirk has an implant of Borg manufacture, and knows that the implant has been removed. That ship is our enemy. Its commander has information that is valuable to the Federation. Hence . . . Commander?"

Riker could feel himself getting caught up in the intellectual game Simm had made out of the encounter. "Hence, we should try to capture that vessel."

"But before we capture it, we must find it." Simm angled

an eyebrow as he studied Riker. "As commander of the cloaked vessel, where would you go after scanning us?"

"If I had seen the *Monitor* decloak, I would assume the *Challenger* had the capabilities of detecting the tachyon surge common to cloaking devices. I would set a course at maximum warp leading out of the system, then angle back and come in from another direction on impulse."

"You're forgetting the enemy has been influenced by the Borg. That maneuver would be a waste of resources." Simm turned back to the viewscreen. "The enemy is hiding on the other side of the sun, out of sensor range. Mr. Worf, hail the *Monitor.*"

Riker and Worf exchanged a look of grudging appreciation for Simm's analysis as the captain of the *Challenger* ordered Lewinski to cloak the *Monitor,* leave the system, then double back to the other side of the sun.

If possible, he was to identify the ship which Simm had concluded was lying in wait there, then return. If necessary, he was to engage it.

"Any idea what kind of ship it is?" Lewinski asked.

"A Romulan Warbird, *D'deridex* class or better." Simm glanced back at Riker. "Its commander knew we would detect the scan, but proceeded anyway. Romulan cloaking devices are the best, hence the ship is Romulan. And only the commander of a *D'deridex* Warbird would feel confident enough to risk exposing his ship to an encounter with the *Challenger.*"

Riker remained sitting in his place on the command bench—unlike the *Enterprise,* the *Challenger* did not have individual seats for its senior bridge officers. With Simm as her captain, he wondered, why had Starfleet even bothered to install computers on the ship?

Lewinski signed off and the port scanners showed the peculiar sight of the *Monitor* rippling like liquid, then vanishing from view.

"*Monitor* away," Data reported.

Simm sat back in the center section of the command bench. "I believe you should now check on the condition of Kirk. We cannot rule out the possibility of two-way communication with the cloaked vessel."

Riker stood up. The captain was correct. But the captain also read the hesitation in him.

"You have a question, Commander?"

"Sir, we came here to bring Kirk close to Dr. Crusher, if Dr. Crusher had returned in time to help him. But now, with the implant removed, it might be better to take Kirk back to Starbase 324 for study."

Simm looked amused, in his limited Vulcan way. "Are you asking me, or ordering me, Commander?"

Riker remained silent.

"Under General Order Three," Simm continued, "Shelby's orders do give you authority over this ship in regard to any action involving the Borg."

"It is a suggestion, sir. We are not yet in contact with the Borg."

Another alarm chimed on the bridge. Riker and Simm both looked up at Worf.

"Sir," the Klingon announced, "a transwarp conduit has just opened before us and a Borg scoutship has emerged." He looked up, eyes wide with surprise. "And sir, it is requesting clearance to land. . . ."

Simm turned to Riker. "You were saying, Commander?"

Riker checked the power setting on his phaser for the tenth time. Worf noticed. In the cold air of the *Challenger*'s main shuttlebay, Riker could see the Klingon's breath cloud with vapor as he whispered, "The shuttlebay is sealed, Commander. Nothing will happen."

Riker knew Worf was correct. But he checked the power setting one last time. It wasn't every day that Starfleet invited a Borg vessel to board one of its starships.

Riker, Worf, La Forge, Deanna, and Data waited by the

cleared landing platform as the main bay doors opened onto empty space. The ship's atmosphere was contained by the annular force field that remained in place. Riker could see the curve of New Titan to the side. Then he saw the dark smudge that was the Borg scoutship, heading closer.

Deanna broke the silence. "Do you realize that there is not one person on this deck who feels this is the right thing to do?"

Riker smiled at her. "Captain Simm is standing by to decompress the bay if anything goes wrong."

"I feel so reassured," Deanna said. Then grimly added, "We should be talking to them with at least a light-year between us."

Worf cleared his throat. "I was able to communicate with the scoutship only through Linguacode," he explained. "It is not equipped with audio or visual communications channels."

Riker realized that made sense. Why *would* a groupmind based on a subspace link require any other type of communications device?

The scoutship glided in between the *Challenger*'s nacelles, then slipped through the atmospheric force field.

Instantly, the hard walls and deck of the shuttlebay reverberated with the hum of the scoutship's engines, and Riker felt the blast of heat from its exhaust ports. Then the scoutship became silent as it switched over to antigrav maneuvering units and floated to a perfect touchdown in the center of the platform.

Riker led the others to the hatch opening in the patched-together ship.

A Borg stepped out and methodically scanned them with his laser as a second figure came out behind him.

"Should I be surprised?" Riker muttered to Deanna as he recognized the second figure. Then he stepped forward. "Ambassador Spock. Welcome to the *Challenger*."

Spock raised his hand and gave the traditional salute. "Peace and long life, Commander. May I introduce my pilot"—Spock gestured to the Borg beside him—"Six of Twelve."

"You will be assimilated," the Borg said by way of greeting. "Resistance is futile."

Spock stepped in front of the Borg. "You will guard the scoutship. I will make arrangements for the efficient assimilation of this ship and her crew."

The Borg lowered its manipulator arm. "That is relevant." He returned to the scoutship and the hatch hissed shut behind him.

Spock joined his surprised welcoming committee. "Six of Twelve is an extremely literal-minded entity, and I doubt he will have any independent thoughts while I am away from him. However, in the best interests of everyone, I suggest you commence jamming all communications channels to prevent him from signaling his presence to any other members of the collective who may be in this region of space."

But no one facing Spock moved to act on his suggestion. Spock studied them all, then pursed his lips.

"Is there a problem, Commander?"

"The last I heard, you had returned to Romulus."

"I did. While there, I attempted to infiltrate a criminal organization which I believed would lead me to whoever supplied James Kirk with his micropulser weapon. Instead, I uncovered a Borg-Romulus alliance which intends to attack the Federation from the Neutral Zone, following an act of treachery by a high-ranking member of Starfleet."

Riker felt momentarily overwhelmed. "And that would be?"

"Jean-Luc Picard."

Riker smiled coldly. "Nice try. But Captain Picard and Beverly Crusher are on special assignment to *fight* the Borg."

"Then I regret to inform you that they have lost their fight.

I encountered Captain Picard on a Borg transwarp station. He is Picard no longer. He is Locutus. Indeed, it is possible that he has always been Locutus."

"No . . . " Riker said.

"Six of Twelve was in full contact with the collective until we left the Borg station," Spock said. "He will confirm all that I have told you."

Riker glanced at Deanna. She gave him an apologetic look. As far as she could tell, Spock was telling the truth. But whether it was the actual truth, or simply a story that had been programmed into his consciousness by the Borg, Riker knew that not even a Betazoid could tell.

"If your story can be confirmed, what do you propose we do?" Riker asked.

"I am not a tactician, Commander. And as you pointed out earlier, I have been away from Starfleet for many decades. However, I would surmise that the first step would be to mass a defensive fleet at the Neutral Zone."

"I'm sure the Romulans would enjoy seeing that," Riker said.

"And," Worf added, "it would leave the entire frontier undefended."

"So that's our dilemma, Ambassador. Are you telling the truth, or are you diverting our attention from the real attack?"

"I am telling the truth," Spock said. "But I do appreciate your position. Unfortunately, since you must suspect that I have been the victim of Borg programming, I am not aware of any procedure which can be used to prove my veracity to you."

Data stepped forward. "Ambassador, if I may, how did you manage to escape from the Borg station where you say you saw Captain Picard?"

As he heard Spock's answer, Riker was surprised that the ambassador could keep a straight face.

"I asked Six of Twelve to transport me to the place from which Locutus had arrived."

"And he brought you here? As simply as that?"

Spock looked pained. "Commander, I cannot explain why, but the Borg somehow believe that I am already one of them. They took me to the station with the intent of assimilating me and making me Speaker to the worlds of Vulcan. But in the midst of the assimilation process . . . they stopped."

"Stopped?"

"As I have said, I have no explanation."

Riker turned to Worf. "Mr. Worf, escort Ambassador Spock to sickbay. I'll want Dr. Bashir to scan him for implants and nanites. And I want you to be in attendance the entire time."

Deanna interrupted. "Will, what about Captain Kirk?"

Spock instantly turned to her, the façade of his Vulcan reserve momentarily disturbed.

Riker watched Spock carefully. "Ambassador, you should know. Kirk is here. In sickbay. With another old friend—Admiral McCoy."

For an instant, Riker could have sworn that he saw Spock smile.

"I must see them at once," Spock said. "Please, make whatever medical tests you feel appropriate."

Worf stepped to Spock's side. "If you will follow me, Ambassador."

"What is Kirk's condition?" Spock asked.

"Not well," Deanna said. "He is infested with nanites that are reconfiguring his body at a molecular level. We have no way of stopping the process in time to save him."

"How much time?" Spock asked.

"A few days," Deanna said. "I'm sorry."

Spock nodded, then turned his attention to Worf. "I am ready, Mr. Worf. Please—"

Riker's commbadge chirped. Riker tapped it. "Riker here."

It was Simm. "Commander, I thought you would be interested to know that another Borg scoutship has emerged from a conduit and requested permission to dock."

Everyone looked at Spock. Spock lifted an eyebrow. "It is possible I was followed, but I have no knowledge of it."

Riker touched his commbadge again. "Captain Simm, I want a constant update sent to Starbase 324, starting now. I want the *Challenger* brought up to full standby on maximum warp, and I want the *Monitor* standing by to come to our assistance."

"You are expecting another Borg vessel to emerge from a conduit?" Simm's disembodied voice asked.

"Put it this way," Riker said as he looked over at Spock's unreadable expression. "Given what's happening here, I'm expecting the worst."

FORTY

Captain John Lewinski tapped out the rhythm to an old blues tune on the side of his command chair. If there was anything better than two-hundred-year-old Andorian blues, he had yet to hear it. Unfortunately, his crew had taken a poll, and he had been asked to no longer pipe it onto the bridge.

"How are we doing, Mr. Land?"

The navigator studied his controls. "Still no sign of anything, Captain. No tachyon surge, no massless sources of heat, no intercepted communications."

Lewinski sighed. He was back to waiting.

Ahead of him, on the main screen, the New Titan sun pulsed, a roiling sphere of superheated gases. Somewhere within a tenth of an AU of its surface, a cloaked vessel was hiding.

But it wasn't doing anything to make finding it any easier.

Ardev spoke up in his Andorian rasp. Even he thought the captain's choice in music was hopelessly out of date. "Sir, we're receiving a microburst transmission from the *Challenger.* We're to go to battle stations and prepare to render immediate assistance to the *Challenger* when called."

Lewinski sat forward. "Is she under attack?"

Ardev's blue hearing stalks twisted forward, disturbing his perfect cap of shiny white hair. "Not yet, sir." He frowned. "Though apparently two Borg scoutships have landed in her shuttlebay."

Lewinski smiled and smoothed his goatee. "Good. Maybe they'll cause some excitement. What are our immediate orders?"

"To continue our search for the cloaked ship, while maintaining our own cloaked status."

Lewinski's smile faded. "In other words, keep waiting."

"Yes, sir," Ardev replied, then turned back to his communications board.

Lewinski leaned back in his chair, tapped out another few bars of "Aladevto's Infirmary." "Anyone feel like some music?" he asked.

As if they had rehearsed, the answering chorus came back without a moment's delay. "No, sir."

Lewinski frowned. He hated waiting. But with the Borg nearby, he doubted he would have to wait for long.

The scoutship in which Spock had arrived had been hidden from view by several pallets of modular crates, a common-enough sight on a busy shuttlebay deck.

In addition to the defensive precaution of standing by to explosively decompress the shuttlebay, Worf had arranged for a Type-6 personnel shuttle to be locked down, with its attitude thrusters rigged to fire at the landing platform cleared for the second scoutship's landing. In addition, transporter control was keeping a real-time coordinate update on every commbadge, ready for an emergency beam-out at any second, should any of the extraordinary defenses be required.

The Borg were not known for asking for anything, and Riker felt he was now prepared for the moment they decided to start taking what they wanted.

Once again, a Borg scoutship, slightly different in configuration from the first, eased in through the shuttlebay door force field. Once again, it switched over from thrusters to antigravs and touched down perfectly.

Once again, Riker kept his hand on his phaser as he, Deanna, Data, and La Forge waited for the hatch to open.

For a moment, Riker didn't recognize the configurations of the two Borg who tumbled out of the craft. They seemed exhausted, hurt. The third Borg, which remained in the hatchway, stoically watching the others leave, was more typical.

But Data ran forward at once. "Captain Picard! Dr. Crusher!"

"Data!" Riker shouted. "Get back here!"

Data turned, halfway to his captain. "But they require help."

"They'll get it," Riker said. "When it's safe."

Data reluctantly turned back to join the others. "I was just happy to see them, that is all."

La Forge clapped him on the back. "It'll be okay, Data."

Picard and Crusher approached Riker cautiously, as though both were attuned to the tension in the air. They wore space-black battle armor. Riker recognized the gear as belonging to the intelligence units established by Shelby.

"Will," Picard said. "Geordi, Data, it's so good to see you again!"

Riker noted that Data had been right. The captain did sound exhausted.

Perhaps the neural implant plate attached to his face and head had something to do with it.

Picard faltered, realizing where Riker had focused his attention. Then he dug his fingers beneath the edge of the plate and began to pull.

On the *Monitor,* Lewinski jumped to his feet as he heard the sensor chime.

"What do we have, Mr. Land?"

"Tachyon surge at search coordinates alpha mary bravo."

The image on the viewscreen expanded to show a section of the New Titan sun. The surface seemed pebbled and pitted with dark granules—each large enough to swallow the Earth, Lewinski knew.

"Mark it, Mr. Land."

An overlay grid flashed onto the screen at the point from which the tachyon surge had originated.

Science Officer T'Per spoke from her station. "I have isolated an anomalous heat reading, Captain. There is a cloaked object at those coordinates."

Lewinski leaned over Land's board, looking past him at the screen. "Is it on the move?"

"Negative, sir. It's in a standard near-solar orbit. I think we caught an engine purge that streamed outside the cloaking field." Land grinned up at the captain. "They weren't expecting us."

Lewinski felt all his senses heighten. The hunt had finally begun. "Take us in, easy, Mr. Land. If *you* need to purge the engines, do it now. I want to get close enough to clean their windshields."

Land's fingers danced over his board as he lay in the

Monitor's new course. Then he looked back at the captain. "Is a windshield anything like a tailpipe, sir?"

"Eyes ahead, Mr. Land."

The *Monitor* eased forward, closing in on its enemy.

In the *Challenger's* main shuttlebay, Riker went on alert, half-expecting to see raw flesh laced with a filigree of neural implant wires, as Picard ripped the plate from his face.

But instead he saw innocuous threads of surgical glue and unmarked skin.

The Borg plate was the duplicate which had been made by Shelby's researchers.

Riker lowered his phaser.

Picard gave him a questioning look. "Will, did you think . . . I had been assimilated again?"

It was Spock's voice which answered. "Not again, Captain Picard."

Everyone turned to see Spock emerge from behind a pallet of modular crates, Worf at his side with a phaser drawn.

"Very good," Picard said. "You've apprehended the traitor responsible for the Borg-Romulan alliance. Ambassador Spock."

Spock and Picard faced each other, almost within reach of each other.

"Captain Picard is the traitor who has betrayed the Federation," Spock said.

Crusher broke the impasse. "Will, we were on a Borg station in transwarp. We saw Spock put into an assimilation frame. But he wasn't assimilated because he is *already* part of the collective!"

Spock turned to Riker. "As I told you, Commander, I was not assimilated. And though I do not have an explanation for the Borg's failure to act, I assure you I am not one of them."

"Neither am I," Picard said.

Riker turned to Deanna. Her face was a mask of confusion. "They're all telling the truth."

"Or they've all been programmed," Riker said angrily.

Picard stepped toward Riker. "Will, I understand your predicament. But surely you can't believe after all we've been through together since . . . since that first time, that I'm still part of them."

Spock also stepped toward Riker. "But there is no logic in what you're suggesting is my contact with the collective, Commander. The Borg and the Romulans are within days, if not hours, of attacking the Federation."

Spock and Picard turned to face each other at the same time. Both spoke at the same time. Their words were identical. "And *he* is the one responsible."

On the bridge of the *Tomed,* Salatrel leapt to her feet as she heard the communications chime.

"Commander," Tran called out. "We are receiving a coded signal!"

"What's the message?"

Tran turned to his commander with a smile of disbelief. "Picard is on the *Challenger."*

Salatrel felt a thrill of hope run through her. "What is the signal's source?" Could it be possible that Vox had returned? That Vox had told the truth?

But this truth was even better.

"The signal is coming from the *Challenger* herself," Tran said. "Commander Salatrel . . . it's a signal from Kirk!"

"Yes!" Salatrel exclaimed. Without thinking, she holstered her disruptor. "Battle stations!" she cried out. "For the glory of the Empire and the House of Chironsala—*battle stations!"*

"She's powering up her engines!" Land called out.

T'Per added, "Picking up Bell discontinuities in subspace, sir. She's got an artificial singularity."

Lewinski pounded his fist into his hand. "She's a Romulan! Distance, Mr. Land?"

"Five thousand kilometers, sir!"

"Lock on all passive target systems. We're going to keep a low profile till—"

"She's moving out!"

"Then so are we. . . ."

With only an almost-imperceptible flickering in the charged plasma flares that leapt from the surface of the dying star to show its path, the *Avatar of Tomed* slipped from orbit and banked away in a course that would return it to New Titan

But she was not the swift and silent raptor of vengeance her commander believed her to be.

The *Monitor* moved through space behind her, not even disturbing the light of the stars it crossed, as it came about to match its course to the Romulan's.

Braced for battle, both ships flew for the *Challenger.*

Riker tightened his grip on his phaser. "You're both going to sickbay for analysis. Captain Picard, what's the status of the Borg on your scoutship?"

"He thinks I'm Locutus. He piloted the scoutship here."

Spock gazed indignantly at Picard. "How is it possible for a Borg to think you are Locutus unless your mind is among the collective?"

Riker gestured with his phaser. "Ambassador, as I recall, a Borg piloted your scoutship here as well. Is your mind among the collective?"

Spock glanced away. "The Borg appear to think so."

A tremor rumbled through the deck. Warning lights flashed as the shuttlebay doors began to slide shut.

Then the red alert sirens warbled and warning lights flashed.

"Will, what's happening?" Picard asked.

"We seem to be in the middle of a Borg expressway," Riker said. He hit his commbadge. "Riker to bridge. Is there another Borg ship in transit?"

Captain Simm answered. "Negative, Commander. The *Monitor* has just informed us we are about to be attacked by a Romulan vessel."

Riker frowned at Spock. "Friends of yours, Ambassador?"

"Commander Riker, it is evident your emotions are being heightened by the danger we are in," Spock answered. "It would be wise for you to consider all your actions in a more dispassionate manner to avoid saying anything which you might later regret."

"Tell it to Kirk in sickbay," Riker said.

Then he saw Picard's shocked expression.

"What did you say?"

Riker didn't know where to begin. "It's Captain Kirk, sir. He . . . didn't die."

Picard seemed stunned. "Will, I buried him."

"He was . . . brought back somehow. By the Borg."

Picard faced Spock. "Is *that* why you have done this? Betrayed the Federation so the Borg would give you back your captain?"

Spock's arm moved back. If Spock had been human, Riker would have expected him to make a fist.

But then Spock relaxed again.

"Do you know *nothing* about me?" Spock said, with absolutely no pretense of hiding his emotions, as if he let loose a lifetime of buried resentment. "We have melded minds, Captain. Has my work, my life, meant so little to you that you can you even consider that I would be capable of such an act?"

Even Picard was taken aback by the cold fury in Spock's tone.

Beverly Crusher put her hand on Picard's shoulder. "That didn't sound like a Borg speaking, did it?"

A profound silence lasted until Riker asked Worf to have the Borg in the scoutships beamed to the brig, making sure to deactivate any built-in weapons systems they might have.

"And for the rest of you," Riker said, "sickbay." He turned to the personnel airlock leading back into the ship.

A shadow moved there, as if the airlock had already been opened. Even though Captain Simm had ordered it sealed until any potential Borg threat had been dealt with.

Riker was momentarily confused. Then his confusion became action as he saw the glowing tip of a phaser node swing out from the edge of the airlock.

"Deanna!" he shouted as the blue wave seared his vision.

But there was no time to know if she had heard his warning. Riker didn't even have time to feel the hard metal plates that rushed up to meet him as he fell.

FORTY-ONE

Picard heard Riker shout, "Deanna!" and then he felt a sudden wave of heat and static charge pass around him.

He shook his head to clear it, then looked around in amazement. Beverly and Data were still standing beside him, but they were surrounded by unmoving bodies that littered the hangar bay deck.

"Have we been hit?" Beverly asked.

"I believe we have been shot with a wide-beam phaser discharge set to stun," Data said. "Your armor appears to have protected you."

Picard touched Data's shoulder. "What about you, Data?"

"I require a higher power setting to be immobilized," Data answered.

"Thanks," a voice said from the airlock behind them. "That's good to know."

Picard's hand jerked back, burning, as an orange beam blasted Data from his grasp. The android skidded across the deck like a broken doll.

Picard and Beverly turned to face their attacker as he emerged from the shelter of the airlock frame.

"Kirk . . .?" Picard said.

The captain of the first *Enterprise* smiled. "What did I tell you on Veridian? Call me Jim." Then he raised his phaser again and fired.

The phaser beam struck Beverly, and she crumpled, moaning, to the deck.

"Beverly!" Picard exclaimed.

"As long as she stays there, she'll be fine," Kirk said. "And you step back from her." He pointed the phaser at Picard and adjusted the power setting. Picard could see his finger work the firing stud.

Picard clenched his fists in frustrated rage. "You're not Kirk!" Picard said. "You're a monster!"

The shuttlebay deck suddenly lurched as the *Challenger*'s impulse engines came online. The shuttlebay rang with the discharge of photon torpedoes.

"Perhaps I am," Kirk said. He glanced down at the phaser he held, adjusted its setting again. "I keep setting this to kill," he complained, "but then I can't fire it. Why is that?"

Picard eyed Kirk incredulously. "The ship's security field prevents unauthorized personnel from discharging phasers onboard."

Kirk glanced at the bodies that littered the hangar deck. "Then how was I able to shoot them?"

"The field must have been modified in here, in case there were trouble with the Borg." Picard felt dizzy. The scene and discussion were surreal. Kirk was *dead.*

"The Borg were the ones who brought me back," Kirk said, almost conversationally. "So I'm told."

Picard looked at the monster before him. At Kirk. He knew that if he had faced this moment a year ago, he would never have accepted that a dead man could return to life. But since then, he had met a dead man in the Nexus, fought at his side on Veridian. He knew he could no longer doubt the evidence of his own eyes, nor his knowledge of the Borg.

"Do you have any idea why they brought you back?" Picard asked. His only option was to keep Kirk talking, not acting, until he had help.

The *Challenger's* deck heaved as the great ship shuddered beneath her wildly fluctuating defensive shields. Picard's ears were perfectly attuned to each specific sound a *Galaxy*-class ship could make. He tried not to imagine what sort of maneuvers the *Challenger* was being forced to perform to account for what he heard now.

"As a matter of fact, I do," Kirk said.

"You see," he said, each word a greater struggle than the one before, "if I'm to have any peace . . . I . . . must . . . kill you."

"Captain, you know that's not right. The Borg have somehow *made* you believe that. But—"

The inertial dampeners roared as everything not locked down was suddenly thrust to starboard. Picard and Kirk stumbled, but kept their footing.

Kirk threw his phaser aside. "Nobody *makes* me do *anything*!" he shouted.

Kirk looked at him wildly, as a series of conflicting expressions washed over his face—frustration, rage, anguish, finally sorrow.

Picard regarded him with the sympathy that could only come from shared pain and memories.

"The Borg can. I know. They've made me do terrible things, too." Those images would never leave his own mind. The Battle of Wolf 359. Eleven thousand deaths. Because of him.

What would *Kirk* do to be free of that pain?

Picard held out his hand to his fellow captain.

"I can help," he said.

"I know," Kirk answered. "By *dying*!"

Then Kirk leapt at Picard and smashed him to the deck, striking out with unthinking rage and hate and . . .

The *Challenger* twisted, engines screaming. Light channels exploded with flares of sparks from an uncontrolled power surge.

Picard and Kirk rolled across the shifting deck, knees digging, fists pummelling, two bodies locked together in the strobing lights and shadows. Picard heard the screech of duranium against duranium as unsecured shuttles began to slide free along the deck.

He looked up just as Kirk was about to land one last, telling blow. He swung up his armored forearm and heard the solid thunk of Kirk's fist against it. Heard Kirk's cry.

The *Challenger* bucked. Kirk flew forward, jarred by the impact. The shuttlebay went dark.

Picard scrambled to his feet as the emergency lights flickered on, but Kirk had already vanished in the shadows.

Picard paused, looked at his crew, still lying helpless on the deck. If he went to them, Kirk would have him and the useless fight would begin again.

He needed assistance. But his armor's communicator was not functioning, overloaded by the phaser hit he had taken. He sprinted to the airlock. Hit the commpanel there.

"Picard to bridge!" He heard only static. "Picard to Security!" The communications system was out. "Picard to Emergency Transporter Control!"

The whistle of a polysonic crowbar sang in his ears as it swung toward him and he ducked. The commpanel erupted in sparks, torn apart by the impact of the tool Kirk had swung.

Picard pivoted on his left foot and rammed his elbow into

Kirk's chest as, with the face of a madman, Kirk raised the polybar to strike again.

The polybar spun from Kirk's hands as he stumbled backward.

Picard had no choice. He charged through the airlock, turned to the left, and ran toward the shadows beyond the flickering corridor lights, hesitating just long enough to be certain Kirk followed.

And Kirk did, face distorted by rage.

Picard rushed on into the darkness, enticing his attacker to pursue him. Setting his trap in place.

High above New Titan, the *Challenger* hung dead in space.

"It is a trick," Tran said. "They are lying in wait for us to attack again."

Salatrel bit her knuckle, considering her strategy as she paced in front of her command chair. "The captain is a Vulcan," she pointed out. "And Vulcans don't bluff."

"Our victory was too easy," Tran persisted.

"It was a sneak attack," Salatrel said, monitoring her bridge crew's reaction to her subcommander's opposition. "Remember the *Farragut* at Veridian." She knew she would have to quickly determine if Tran was arguing with her because he was a coward, afraid of death, or because he really did have some valuable insight to share with her.

Tran pointed to his sensor boards. "Look at the damage pattern!" he urged. "There! There! And there!"

Salatrel checked each point he indicated on the *Challenger* schematic he had called up.

"There is no structural damage to account for her loss of propulsion," Tran said. "No environmental overload to account for the crew death figures we're reading. Commander, I don't believe we've caused a single casualty. I submit the captain knew we were coming and has been transmitting false sensor returns."

Salatrel looked at the main screen. The *Challenger* spun slowly, off-axis. Its propulsion lights were out. Only a few running lights still flashed.

"Then how do you explain that?" She regarded the other ship with scorn. "Only a fool would leave his ship in such a vulnerable condition."

"I say the captain of that ship has taken every hit we've thrown at his screens, and he's diverted the power into his generators to create the power surges we detected. The real damage is meaningless. He can have his primary generators repaired in an hour."

"Look at the shields, Tran." Salatrel gestured at the power readouts on the screen. "They're at less than thirty percent. Two more good hits, and the ship is ours."

Tran stood up to face her. "I promise you he has more power offline than our sensors can pick up. Commander, he is baiting us. Remember the Battle of Icarus IV. It has been a Starfleet tactic for a century."

The reminder of Icarus IV drove rational thought from Salatrel. She made her decision. "Then we will see him power up his weapons when we make our approach, and you will be able to break off our attack in time."

"It is not *his* weapons we must be concerned about."

Salatrel snarled a warning at Tran. Nothing would stop her from achieving her goal this close to victory. "The other ship is gone, Subcommander." She returned to her command chair.

"The other ship is cloaked."

Salatrel stiffened. She could feel her bridge crew tense, wondering if Tran would follow Tracius. "Can you detect its tachyon signature?"

Tran regarded her steadily. "No. Which could mean Starfleet has modified it."

Salatrel had had enough talk. She was ready for action. "Think, Tran! If the other ship is here, cloaked, watching us, what is its purpose? Any commander would have come in behind us on our first run when the *Challenger* fired her torpedoes back at us. The other ship is *not here.*"

Tran sat back at his board, jaw set. "Then, for the glory of the Empire," he said in the formal tongue of obedience, "I embrace my death."

Salatrel smiled. Tran would live for the battle. He wasn't a coward. Only impetuous.

"Prepare for final approach," she said. "Target the support pylons to break her apart. Set sensors to scan for life-support suits and escape pods." She leaned forward in her chair. "No survivors. No prisoners. Proceed."

Tran turned back to her, one last question for his leader. "Commander . . . what if the other ship held back because they do not wish to destroy us? What if they wish to capture us?"

"Starfleet takes no prisoners, Tran. They are murderers, plain and simple."

Tran turned back to his controls. The *Avatar of Tomed* began her final run.

"We've got her!" Lewinski said.

The mood on his bridge was electric.

Captain Simm of the *Challenger* had played his ship like the magnificent instrument it was. Absorbing incredible energies by diverting the Warbird's power to the areas where it would do the least damage.

And the commander of the Romulan ship had fallen for it.

"Put us on intercept," Lewinski said. The time for waiting was finally over.

But T'Per stepped up beside him. "If I may, Captain, the Romulan vessel clearly has capabilities we have not seen before. Her disruptors for one. They are not standard."

Lewinski gave T'Per a long-suffering look. "If that thing were a standard Romulan vessel, do you think it would be attacking a Starfleet ship?"

T'per returned to her station in silence.

Lewinski beat out a drum solo on the arm of his chair.

"All I want you to do is fuse its disruptor cannons, tear apart its torpedo tubes, then target its exhaust ports," he said.

"I thought you wanted us to do something hard," Land replied.

"Decloak at your discretion, Mr. Land. As my noble ancestors once said—*Yee-hah*!"

The *Avatar of Tomed* dropped her cloak in preparation for firing, her Borg disruptors powered and locked on each key structural component of the *Challenger.*

Simm sat patiently on his command bench. Captain Lewinski was a brilliant tactician. The *Challenger* would not absorb another erg of Romulan energy.

The Warbird rippled against the stars, taking on its solid, visible, threatening form.

But just before Salatrel could give the command to fire, an all-too-familiar sensor disturbance obscured her forward scanners as she heard a savage, alien battle cry flooding subspace on all frequencies.

Her shields flared with a sudden overload, allowing Starfleet phasers from the decloaked ship to pierce her defenses and fuse her weapons ports.

Then, before Tran could alter course, the decloaked vessel—the vessel Salatrel had sworn had abandoned the *Challenger*—performed a spinning loop over the top of the Warbird to target her exhaust ports.

The bridge of the *Tomed* echoed with the warning sirens that filled it.

Tran gave her a running commentary on what had happened.

Thirty seconds more, Salatrel knew, and her ship would be dead.

And Kirk would survive her.

This was no longer a battle she could win by herself.

"Engage transwarp," she ordered.

"In front of the enemy?" Tran's shock was apparent.

"The knowledge of our capabilities will give them no advantage," Salatrel said. The real war was that close to beginning.

"Take us out of here, Subcommander."

Salatrel's fingers closed over the handle of her disruptor.

"Transwarp engaged," Tran confirmed.

On the main screen, the *Challenger* diminished, until it was no more than a single point of light, no larger than a star.

Salatrel held up her thumb and blotted that light out.

She would return for Kirk.

And when she did, the full force of the collective would be with her.

Lewinski's mouth dropped open as the Warbird dissolved into light before him, outlined by the faint glow of what he now recognized as a microdurational transwarp conduit, which put the ship completely beyond pursuit.

"Whew . . . how long have the Romulans had that?" he asked.

"I do not believe it is part of the Empire's traditional armada," T'Per said. "Coupled with its nonstandard weaponry, it is logical to assume that the Warbird has been extensively retrofitted by the Borg."

Lewinski thought about the ramifications of that, then dismissed them. "Just tell me they didn't know we were here until we dropped out of cloak," he said.

Mr. Land confirmed it. "The cloak modifications worked, sir. They had no idea we were here at all. Otherwise, they wouldn't have fallen for Captain Simm's ambush."

Lewinski patted the side of his chair. "Then there's still hope for the Federation, after all. Right, Mr. T'Per?"

T'Per remained silent.

FORTY-TWO

Kirk paid no attention to the starship that appeared to be tearing itself apart around him.

All he saw was his prey, farther along up the corridor, almost within his grasp.

Nothing else mattered.

Except killing Picard.

He tried not to think why that was so. He tried not to think at all. Locking McCoy in a stateroom, disconnecting the controls to his exoskeleton, taking away his old friend's communicator pin . . . it all felt wrong. Wrong but still necessary.

Manipulating McCoy's communicator to send out the coded alert signal, though—*that* he had almost enjoyed, because of the technical challenge it had given him. And he had correctly deduced the workings of his own communicator pin. First by using it to listen in on the ship's internal security channels to learn that Picard had arrived in the shuttlebay, then by simply leaving it behind in sickbay so that the ship's computer would not be able to keep track of his movements throughout this vast ship.

And just as Kirk had anticipated, no one person and no automated system had detected his presence in the shuttlebay as he had arrived to take care of Picard. It appeared the twenty-fourth century held no especially great challenges for him.

Except for the phaser-suppression system.

One quick burst could have taken care of Picard once and for all. It had been a disappointment to learn that this future Starfleet had taken safeguards against such actions. Kirk realized that as long as Picard remained on this starship, he would have to deal with his target by hand. Which was fine. He'd always preferred the personal touch.

Up ahead, Kirk saw Picard pause near a large entryway that looked like an airlock. Kirk wondered if the ship had more than one shuttlebay, if Picard were thinking of escaping.

But Picard couldn't escape. Kirk knew that. As certainly as if it had been engraved on his waking mind.

Picard must die. Picard *would* die.

Picard ducked through the large door.

Kirk chased after him.

But when he reached the entranceway, he stopped, suspecting the worse. The door was still open. Sloppy on Picard's part? Or a deliberate prelude to a trap?

Beyond lay another corridor. Except its traction carpet was a different color, and it did not exhibit any of the signs of battle damage that Kirk had seen in the darkened corridors he had just been through.

Picard appeared for an instant at the end of the new corridor. His presence was enough to spur Kirk on, again without thought.

He ran along the new corridor until he came to the intersection where he had seen Picard. No sign of him now.

Kirk looked behind him. Turned, stopped. There was no sign of the large doorway through which he had entered, either.

He leaned against the corridor wall, head throbbing. He touched the sterile covering at the back of his head. Felt it thick and sticky with blood. The surgery, he remembered. But what had it been for? And what was it McCoy had said? Only days remaining? Why was he spending them this way? Why did he want . . . *need* to kill—

The mere thought of Picard's name spurred him to action again. But the corridors he was in were unfamiliar. He needed a plan. He needed to know where to run.

Kirk looked around. Saw a computer access panel. Remembered seeing Picard try to use a communicator in the armored suit he wore. Would the new captain of the *Enterprise* be foolish enough to let the computer know where he was at all times while he was being hunted?

Kirk went to the computer panel.

"Computer, tell me the location of Captain Picard."

"Captain Picard is on the bridge."

The computer spoke to him in almost the same voice he remembered from his first *Enterprise.* Once again, Kirk felt unsettled that with all that had changed in this future, some things remained the same.

"Where is the bridge?" he asked the voice from his past.

"Follow the light path on the wall panels to the turbolift," the computer explained.

A dark panel along the corridor wall suddenly came to life with a pulsing pattern of light. The twenty-fourth century was making it all too easy.

Kirk ran to the turbolift. The light speeded up to keep just ahead of him.

The turbolift had no controls.

"Bridge," Kirk said, then rocked gently as the lift car moved sideways, then up.

When the turbolift doors slipped open again, Kirk stepped forward into an alcove, then paused as he swiftly took in the sweep of this new bridge.

There were no steps. The outer support-station ring sloped up from the ops level to a raised area at the back, marked by a dramatically curved railing of what appeared to be real wood.

Superficially, the design remained the same as those bridges with which Kirk was familiar—the circular arrangement, the forward screen.

But he noted that instead of one captain's chair, raised in

the center, there were three seats, five if he counted the smaller, backless seats to either side. Kirk was puzzled by what that implied. Could it be the captain wasn't as important to a ship in this time?

Kirk stepped out of the turbolift alcove, scanning the bridge for any sign of his enemy.

But it was deserted. Odd. Especially since the ship had just been under attack. What if there were an emergency bridge elsewhere in the ship? He decided he should have asked the computer to distinguish between the two.

As he looked for a computer access panel, Kirk saw a dedication panel to his right. He recognized a faint familiarity in the silhouette of the vessel depicted on it.

Then he read the name on the plaque.

U.S.S. Enterprise.

He stopped. He read the next line, the smaller type.

Galaxy Class. Starfleet Registry NCC-1701-D.

But this ship was dead. McCoy had told him. It had been destroyed above Veridian as he and Picard had—

Waves of agony pulsed through Kirk. Picard must die. Kirk gasped for breath. Was this another dream? Was there any other way to explain his presence on a ghost ship?

Another set of doors opened. Picard stepped out and to the wooden rail. "We have to talk," he said.

As quickly as that, Kirk's conflict was gone again. Instantly, he decided on his strategy. "I know. You're right." He sagged against the wall. Touched his wound again. Held out his blood-coated fingers. "I need . . . help."

Picard came down the slope of the bridge. Trusting.

"Captain Simm appears to have his hands full," Picard said. "All secondary services are offline. But perhaps I can do something about that."

He went to a padded drawer-front on the wall. Opened it. Withdrew an oddly shaped case marked with the Starfleet caduceus.

First aid, Kirk thought. *Perfect . . .*

"Come over here," Picard said. He opened the medikit on one of the chairs in front of a ridiculously small operations console. "Let me see if I can stop the bleeding."

Kirk smiled, nodded, got within arm's length of Picard. Began to stumble, as if trying to brace himself against the chair.

And when Picard reached out to steady him, Kirk rammed his forehead against Picard's face, amazed that a captain of the *Enterprise* would fall for such a trap.

Picard fell backward, catching himself on the other chair.

He straightened up, straightened the chest piece of his armor, raised his hands as if to surrender.

"Captain Kirk, I think there's something you should know before you carry this any further."

Kirk rubbed his face, as his compulsion to simply jump on Picard and begin swinging became unbearable.

"I believe we can reach a consensus here," Picard said. He glanced up at another set of doors on the bridge. Kirk followed his gaze, recognizing Picard's trap in the same instant Picard leapt forward, fist swinging, catching Kirk on the jaw to flip him over the console.

By the time Kirk pushed himself to his feet, Picard had already run into the turbolift.

Kirk followed and stopped by the closed doors. He had no doubt he could defeat his enemy, but the trick was going to be finding him. And how could he find a captain on his own ship? A ship that Kirk knew nothing about, other than it had crashed in . . . Kirk gasped.

This ship couldn't be Picard's *Enterprise.* Which meant, there was only one thing that it could be. Kirk smiled.

He turned to face the empty bridge.

"Arch," he said.

A standard Starfleet holodeck control arch appeared before the command chairs.

Kirk rushed to it, now clearly understanding Picard's strategy.

He hadn't wanted to let Kirk remain loose on the *Challenger.* So he had lured his attacker into a holodeck in order to keep him occupied until the real ship returned to normal operations. And what better maze to place Kirk in than that of a state-of-the-art, twenty-fourth-century vessel of which he had no knowledge?

"Very clever," Kirk said, as he accessed the arch controls. They were exactly like those he had seen Salatrel use on her ship. He was pleased he had paid such close attention.

"Computer, prepare to change simulation programs."

"Holodeck systems, standing by," the familiar voice confirmed.

Kirk grinned with anticipation.

Captain Picard had been good enough to show him the future.

Now it was Captain Kirk's turn to show him the past.

FORTY-THREE

Picard burst out of the turbolift and skidded to a stop.

He had been heading to his *Enterprise*'s battle bridge. It could be completely sealed off from the rest of the ship—even in this holodeck simulation. Kirk would be free to roam the endless corridors until Picard could once again make contact with the *Challenger*'s bridge and have Simm beam Kirk to a detention cell.

Except . . . this wasn't the battle bridge.

Picard looked around, breathing hard in his armor, until he suddenly realized that somehow Kirk had succeeded in changing the rules. Somehow, the legendary captain had worked out how to alter the holodeck's program.

Picard was on the bridge of a hundred-year-old relic—a *Constitution*-class starship, one of the greatest series ever built.

Knowing what he would find there, Picard turned to the dedication plaque by the turbolift. He smiled in spite of what the inscription meant to his odds of survival.

U.S.S. Enterprise.

Starship class.

San Francisco, Calif.

Kirk had gone home, and he had brought Picard with him.

But that was all the time Picard had for sentimentality.

"Computer," he announced.

"Working." The familiar voice was somehow cooler, more mechanistic. Not quite the response Picard had been expecting.

"Arch," Picard ordered.

"Unable to comply," the computer answered.

Picard sighed.

"Computer, identify your make and model."

"This unit is a D-6 duotronic computer comprising—"

"That's enough," Picard said. Kirk had even called up a simulation of the original *Enterprise*'s limited computer, effectively blocking access to the *Challenger*'s system and the holodeck controls. How had he had time to become so proficient?

"Do you like it?" Kirk asked.

Picard turned around slowly as Kirk rose from a chair at some kind of operational station with an antique holographic imager. One that actually required the user to peer in through a narrow blue slot, rather than seeing results on a screen.

"I remember seeing one in a museum," Picard said.

He placed his hand on the red railing and began to ease backward, even as Kirk approached.

"This is the way exploration was meant to be," Kirk said as he looked around the recreation of his first bridge.

"No carpet. No replicators. None of the comforts of home." Kirk stepped down to the center deck, rapped his fist against the back of the command chair. "This was a *machine,"* he said, almost as if Picard weren't present. "You felt it back then. That you were actually going somewhere. The way the deck pitched when the inertial dampeners couldn't keep up."

"They still can't," Picard said dryly.

His mind raced, trying to remember whatever he could about the safety features in these antique bridges. They must have had fire-suppression systems. Emergency egress panels. But all he could see was the single pair of turbolift doors he had entered through. How many bridge crews had been trapped because that single access route had been blocked?

"I'm going to die in your time," Kirk said as he stood in front of the command chair. "So I thought it only fitting that you die in mine. Or at least, a simulation of mine."

"I'm sure you're aware twenty-fourth-century medical science has made fantastic strides," Picard said.

Kirk looked off to the side with a frown. "Twenty-fourth-century medical science is what brought me here." Then he stepped away from the command chair. Picard calculated how many seconds it would take Kirk to circle the combined ops and navigational console in the center of the bridge. He wondered how long it would be before Simm realized that Picard and Kirk were both missing. With Worf unconscious on the shuttlebay deck, Picard worried that it might take too long.

"Kirk," Picard began, "you don't know what you're doing."

Kirk shrugged, almost in resignation. "I used to think that every day of my first five-year mission. Each crew member who died. Each opportunity missed. I'd ask myself, why? Who was I to make those decisions?"

"Those were the risks of the job," Picard said, knowing what the other captain meant all too well. "They still are."

"You mean the twenty-fourth-century isn't perfect?"

"No age is. It's our hope for the future that drives us on, inspired by the accomplishments of the past."

Kirk walked slowly around the console, idly running his hand over one of the two chairs there. "But this is my future."

"You're seeing it through distorted eyes."

"Am I?" Kirk asked. He looked around his bridge again. "Who's the observer here? Who's the visitor out of time?" He glanced back at the turbolift. "If I step through those doors, who's to say I won't find Spock in the recreation room, waiting by a chessboard? Or McCoy, complaining that I haven't been in for my checkup?"

"Is that what you *want* to find? The past?"

Kirk stared at Picard. Shook his head. "A tempting offer. But the past is the past, never to be lived again. I don't belong there." He glanced behind at the waiting command chair. "No one who sits in that chair does."

Picard had the sudden, heartfelt realization that despite the years between them, he was looking into a mirror.

"Then join us in the future. Fight what they've done to you," Picard said.

Kirk swallowed hard. "I've tried. I can't."

"You've come so far, accomplished so much. Don't let it end here."

Kirk took a step forward.

"It has to end sometime." He spread his arms to encompass the bridge. "Why not here . . . where it all began?"

Picard prepared himself for Kirk's attack. He frowned. "Captain . . . if I have to, I will kill you. . . ."

Kirk grinned. "You can try. . . ." And then he attacked.

He ducked under the railing, grabbing Picard's legs and pulling them forward, sending Picard down on his back.

Before Picard could roll to his side, Kirk pulled him off the raised platform and swung him into the console.

Picard kicked to flip Kirk away before he could lunge again.

He pulled himself to his feet.

Saw Kirk crouching, ready to—

Picard ducked to take the force of Kirk's attack on his shoulder.

Kirk brought both elbows down on Picard's back.

The armor saved Picard from the worst of the impact, then Kirk brought his knee up to hit Picard's jaw. However, before Kirk's knee could connect, Picard threw himself back, to roll over the console, landing on his feet.

His movements must have activated some control, because an old-fashioned targeting sight unfolded from the console surface.

He could see that Kirk had now gone beyond reasoning. Blood trickled from the corner of his mouth. His breath came like the panting of a lion on the hunt.

Picard felt the same. Tasted blood in his own mouth. Brought his hands up, ready to gouge, to tear, to defeat this enemy.

With a roar, Kirk attacked again.

This time Picard did not attempt to deflect him.

The captains met head on.

The impact of their collision carried them back to the command chair. They struggled against each other, neither giving thought to defense. Their hands found each other's throats. Their eyes were mere centimeters from each other.

Picard heard the pounding of his heart. His vision was narrowing, dark stars flickering in from the sides. But he would not let go. He saw the same loss of focus coming to Kirk's eyes.

Bound forever in a death grip to Kirk, neither captain willing nor able to yield, Picard was astounded to feel the old bridge swirl away from him. Together with Kirk, he was plunged into an endless black hole from which there could be no escape, trapped in a titanic struggle that would last through all time.

And then the command chair disappeared beneath them and both captains dropped to the floor of the holodeck, gasping with surprise.

FORTY-FOUR

"That is *enough!*" Riker said.

He pushed past Dr. Bashir and kept his phaser aimed at the impossible sight of Kirk and Picard locked in mortal combat.

The two captains looked up at him, then looked around in a daze, as if they had forgotten they had been in a holodeck. Slowly, almost reluctantly, their hands fell away from each other's throats.

"The next one who moves gets a force three stun," Riker said.

But Ambassador Spock stepped forward, into Riker's line of fire. "I do not believe that will be necessary."

"Ambassador, believe me, it goes for you, too."

"Oh, calm down," McCoy grumbled.

Riker heard the whine of the old admiral's exoskeleton as he rose from his mobility chair and walked forward, one sure step after another, until he stood at Spock's side. "No one's shooting anyone," he said.

Riker was tempted to stun *everyone*, but Deanna put a hand on his arm and shook her head in silence.

Riker lowered his phaser so it was aimed at the deck. Deanna was right. Something beyond what they could see was at work here. He could almost sense it himself. Behind him, even La Forge, Worf, Data, and Dr. Crusher maintained a respectful silence. All had recovered from Kirk's attack in the shuttlebay. But Riker had no impression that any of them desired revenge. They only seemed spellbound by the scene before them.

Kirk and Picard stood side by side, spent, breathless. But where Picard silently acknowledged the presence of his old command crew, Riker noted that Kirk's attention was absolutely riveted on Spock and McCoy.

"Spock . . .?" Kirk said, his voice a low and raspy whisper.

"I am . . . most pleased to see you again, Captain," Spock formally replied.

McCoy shook his head in disgust. "Oh, for crying out loud, Spock. It's been eighty years!"

"Seventy eight point four years, Doctor."

"Can you help me?" Kirk asked.

"Yes," Spock said.

Riker saw the look of relief on Kirk's face. Then Kirk glanced at Picard beside him. "Good. Because I don't think I can kill him by myself." Riker raised his phaser again and aimed it at Kirk.

Spock moved quickly to stand between Kirk and Picard. "That is not what I meant, Captain."

Kirk lifted his hands to push Spock aside. "But, Spock . . . I have to . . ."

"No," Spock said, glancing back at Riker. "You are under the influence of Borg programming. The implant responsible has been removed, but the patterns it laid down are still affecting your thoughts and your actions."

Spock raised his own hand, but not in the traditional Vulcan salute.

"A mind-meld?" Kirk asked.

Spock nodded. "You will be able to draw strength from me, until the Borg patterns have faded."

But Picard protested. "Will—you can't allow this. If they're both under Borg control, this could be a way to cover their tracks."

Spock turned to look back at Riker.

"There is another way," he said. There was silence in the holodeck after Spock's explanation. Even Data had nothing to say.

Riker had no idea what to think, it was so audacious.

"Has it ever been done before?" he asked Spock.

"Not to my knowledge," Spock said.

Riker saw Kirk look past Spock to Picard. He saw the raw need in Kirk's eyes, the desire to attack Picard once more. The pressure he was fighting to retain some self-control.

"Remember what it says on the plaque?" Kirk asked Picard, hoarsely, even trying to smile.

Picard nodded, the same tired expression coming to his face. "To boldly go . . ." he said.

And Kirk finished the thought, with the words that had defined both their lives. ". . . where no man has gone before. . . ."

Spock took a moment to compose himself, then reached out to Kirk. The fingers of his right hand sought the *katra* points of Kirk's face, establishing the connection that would allow their minds to merge.

Kirk stared at his friend, wide-eyed. His struggle to clear his mind for Spock to enter safely obvious to all who witnessed it.

"My mind to yours, Captain Kirk," Spock said.

Then Spock turned to Picard.

With his left hand, Spock sought the same connection with the second captain.

Riker caught his breath.

"My mind to yours, Captain Picard."

* * *

And with that, the two generations joined. Mixed and merged in the one mind that knew both, could contain both. The only mind that could bring them together.

Spock's mind reached deep into the experiences and emotions of both captains, seeking the commonality of their drive, their dreams, their experiences.

He absorbed the urgency of Kirk's run through the *Enterprise-B* . . . the shock of his being claimed by the Nexus and the bliss of its embrace . . . and the stirring promise of Picard's arrival to free him from the stagnation of eternal perfection within it.

He absorbed Picard's agony of assimilation as the biochips of the Borg grew into his tissues . . . the detached horror of instructing a fleet of machines to destroy all that he believed in, in a war against the Federation . . . the guilt for those deaths. . . .

He shuddered as in both minds he experienced that same sterile, absolute joy . . . and the revulsion and strength of will that had enabled both to resist it.

And still he went deeper. . . .

To Veridian III . . .

To the death of Kirk through his own eyes and Picard's.

Picard's fear as Shelby laid out the interface.

Kirk's fear as he rose, unprepared, from the liquid of the alien ark.

Then the torture of Kirk's programming . . . the lies Salatrel wove to entrap him . . . twisting the truth of his grief for his murdered son and lost loves . . . to create an automaton with but one, perverted purpose. . . .

Spock touched the deadening, frightful power of the Borg in both minds. Took its measure. Met its challenge.

He reached out to them both.

Giving each his strength . . .

His wisdom . . .

His logic. . . .

Three minds joined. No barriers among them.

Until a dark shadow rose from the depths of their exchange.

A shadow of the Borg, not from Kirk nor from Picard . . .

But from Spock. . . .

He gasped in pain as the impact of that lost memory seared his conscious mind.

Overwhelmed, he sank to his knees and Kirk and Picard knelt with him. They held his hands to their faces, maintaining connection. As one, they reached out to Spock, to heal and save him, as he had healed and saved them.

"I have seen them. . . ." Spock whispered. "I have . . . walked with them. . . ." His body shuddered with the impact of the truth revealed as his voice lowered and took on the eerie harmonics of the collective.

"We are Borg," Spock intoned.

"We are . . . *V'Ger!*"

FORTY-FIVE

Except for the almost subliminal hum of the air circulators, Captain Simm's austere ready room was silent. Kirk was already there when Picard stepped in. He held his hands behind his back, gazing out an observation window at the stars.

Picard hesitated, not wanting to disturb him. But Kirk turned, his serious expression fading in a welcoming grin.

"It's all right, Captain," Kirk said. "I don't want to kill you anymore."

Picard smiled and went to Kirk, to shake his outstretched hand. They each had been examined and treated separately by their respective physicians after Spock had been taken to sickbay. This was their first chance to talk alone. And the opportunity would remain for only a few minutes more before the briefing session began.

"I cannot even begin to imagine what you must be thinking," Picard said.

Picard saw a flicker pass through Kirk's expression and knew he was masking the pain the nanites must still cause. Dr. Bashir had told Picard that he had reached the limit of what neural blockers could do without degrading Kirk's awareness. And Kirk had steadfastly refused to go to that next step.

Kirk narrowed his eyes for a moment. "Do you ever ask yourself why you're out here?"

Picard hesitated. It was unusual for him to feel so comfortable with someone he really barely knew. But what secrets could there be between them? What had one done that the other had not? "Sometimes," Picard admitted. "When I think of other paths I might have taken. Or those I've left behind."

"Family?" Kirk asked.

But Picard did not have to answer. He could see that Kirk sensed the loss he endured. Of his nephew and his brother in the fire that had claimed them.

Kirk looked at the stars again. "All the worlds we've seen, all the beings we've known, and it still comes down to that," he said. "Being alone." He glanced back at Picard. "When you lost your ship, Captain, how'd that make you feel?"

Picard wasn't sure how to answer.

A flicker of mischief played in Kirk's eyes, as if he shared a scandalous secret no one else could ever know. "Not as badly as you thought you should. Right?"

Picard waited for Kirk to continue, as he knew the other captain would.

"When I lost my first ship," Kirk said, "I was numb. I kept waiting for some uncontrollable sense of loss to . . . overwhelm me. It never came. You know why?"

Picard felt as if a burden had been taken from him. Kirk *knew.* He had gone through the exact same experience. "Because, in the end, it's not the ship that matters."

Kirk nodded. "It's the mission."

Picard looked out at the same stars, for the first time allowing himself to ask a question he had never voiced aloud.

"Has it been worth it for you?" Picard heard Kirk sigh, as if it were a question he had often confronted, yet never voiced. "The lack of roots. Of family."

"When I was . . . hunting you," Kirk said, "I thought that if I could just find you, I could . . . find myself."

"You mean, you could find yourself by completing the mission."

The two captains turned from the stars to face each other.

"But the mission never ends, does it," Picard said.

"This one will," Kirk said. And whatever was in his eyes now, even Picard could not decipher.

Two minutes later, James Kirk stood at the head of the conference table, in the observation lounge off the *Challenger's* bridge.

Behind him, on the viewscreen, was an image he had hoped never to see again.

"V'Ger," he said. "A corruption of *Voyager,* the name given a space probe launched from Earth at the end of the 1900's. Earth lost contact with the probe a few years after it passed outside the boundaries of the solar system."

Kirk nodded at Data, who sat in the first seat on the right, yellow hands folded on the tabletop. "According to Mr. Data, later findings indicated the probe had been trapped by what was believed to have been a black hole. Though Data says the phenomenon could very well have been a transwarp conduit."

The image on the screen changed and Kirk took a moment to admire the sleek lines of his refit *Enterprise.* It was hard to believe such a magnificent ship could be considered an antique in this time. "Nearly three hundred years later, the space probe *Voyager* returned to Earth—searching for, it said, its creator."

Riker interrupted. He sat at the back of the table, between Julian Bashir and Deanna Troi. "*It* said? I didn't think twentieth-century science could construct a self-aware machine."

"It couldn't," Kirk replied. "Somehow, the *Voyager* probe encountered . . . something which attempted to repair it. Those repairs gave it self-awareness."

McCoy's gravelly voice spoke up. His mobility chair didn't fit beneath the conference table, so he sat to the side, behind Dr. Crusher. "And you're guessing that 'something' was the Borg? That's a helluva theory, Jim."

Kirk didn't have to defend his theory. Spock did. He sat beside Picard, subdued, recovered from his ordeal in the holodeck. For a moment, Kirk could almost believe he and Spock were back on his old ship, as if time had stood still.

Spock's voice sounded as dry as it always had when he had tangled with McCoy. "There is no guesswork involved, Doctor. I mind-melded with V'Ger. I saw where it had been, a planet filled with living machines. At the time, I had no context for that knowledge, and it was so alien it faded from my mind. But when I joined with Captain Kirk and Captain Picard, whose minds both held strong and recent impressions of the Borg, the connection between V'Ger and the Borg became clear and self-evident to me."

"Looks like you're rewriting history here, Ambassador," La Forge said. "Our *Enterprise* wasn't the first to contact the Borg—yours was."

But Spock shook his head. "V'Ger was reconfigured by the Borg, or more correctly, by a different branch of the collective—that assimilated by direct conversion to patterned energy. The Borg we know in this time assimilate by physical means. But V'Ger clearly possessed the same Borg root-command structure that derived from whatever original groupmind that linked them all."

Kirk looked around the room. "What Spock's trying to say is that V'Ger was part of the collective."

Spock looked at Riker. "And because I mind-melded with V'Ger, the tendrils of that collective remained within me."

Picard took over. "Which explains why the Borg would not assimilate Spock on the hypercube station." Picard paused. "I don't know how I can apologize to you, Ambassador. . . ." He looked up at Kirk. "Or to you, Captain."

Kirk waved the apology aside. "No need, Captain. We were each put in play by a different aspect of the Borg." There was a stir in the room. Kirk knew he had their attention now. "Though Mr. Spock . . ." Kirk stopped to correct himself. He must remain up to date. "*Ambassador* Spock could put it more eloquently: What better way to defeat the Federation than by internal dissension? What better way to save it than by the sharing of knowledge? And what better way to defeat the Borg?"

Riker was the first to bite. "Excuse me, Captain Kirk. Are you saying the Borg *can* be defeated?"

Kirk grinned. "Never underestimate the power of a Vulcan. Each of us had a piece of the greatest puzzle facing Starfleet. My contact gave me background data on transwarp conduits and the hypercube station that somehow maintains them. Captain Picard had all the technical information about their ships—which was necessary for him to lead them into battle. And Ambassador Spock has seen their homeworld."

The room filled with excited and confused conversation. Kirk turned back to the viewscreen as the final image appeared. A starchart, with one star marked in red. Kirk pointed to it.

"This, gentlemen, is the Central Node of the Borg group-mind. Destroy it, and each branch of the collective will be cut off and alone."

La Forge voiced an objection. "Captain Kirk . . . that's a chart of the Delta Quadrant. To get that far would take more than a century at maximum warp."

Kirk walked over to Picard and put a hand on his shoulder. "Fortunately, while we were all playing cat and mouse, Captain Picard and Dr. Crusher were performing their duty. In the shuttlebay of this ship are two Borg scoutships with functioning transwarp engines."

Captain Lewinski stepped away from the rear wall of the conference room to complete Kirk's explanation.

"And the *Defiant*-class ships were specifically designed to accept transwarp drives, should any ever be recovered or developed."

Captain Picard stood up beside Captain Kirk, poised on the brink of the Starfleet's greatest mission. "In ten hours, the conversion of the *Monitor* into a transwarp vessel will be complete. And then . . ." Picard smiled at Kirk.

"And then," Kirk said, "we're going to kick the Borg clear into the next galaxy."

As one, every individual in the conference room, even McCoy, immediately stood to ask to be part of that mission.

"Look at them," Kirk said to Picard. "When it comes to people, nothing's changed between our times."

"The best things never do," Picard said.

FORTY-SIX

The four captains stood on the bridge of the *Challenger* as the viewscreen showed the *Monitor* coming about—Kirk, Picard, Simm, and Lewinski.

Lewinski observed his ship with a pang of regret. Because it was his ship no longer. Shelby had sent his new orders by subspace. The second transwarp engine had to be transported to Starbase 324 at once. He was in charge of that operation. In his absence, by order of Starfleet Command, the *Monitor* would be turned over to Picard.

But Lewinski wasn't one to hold grudges.

He touched his commbadge.

"Lewinski to *Monitor.* Come in, Mr. Land."

Land acknowledged and Lewinski told him to angle the *Monitor* seventeen degrees off the *Challenger's* horizontal axis. "We want to get some glare from the sun," Lewinski explained.

Kirk and Picard looked at Lewinski without understanding what he meant. But after a few seconds, Captain Simm said, "Of course."

Lewinski gestured to the screen as the black disk of the *Monitor* slowly eased forward to fill it, angling gently so that a dull band of reflected sunlight moved over her upper hull, revealing the details of her duranium skin.

"In an operation such as this," Lewinski explained, "when

a ship receives a substantial refit and is sent on such a noteworthy mission, it's not unheard of for it to receive a new code designation for the duration."

He saw the band of sunlight hit the first of the new pattern that he had had his refit crew etch into the ship's black microcoating. He turned his attention to Kirk and Picard beside him.

"It'll never turn up in the record books that way, gentlemen," Lewinski said. "But I wanted to give you both a good send-off."

Both captains' gazes were fixed on the viewscreen as they saw what Lewinski had done.

The fabled name flashed across the hull of the starship, as ephemeral as a ghost, but never to be erased from the minds and hearts of those who saw it.

U.S.S. Enterprise.

"Least I could do," Lewinski said.

FORTY-SEVEN

Spock turned from the new *Enterprise*'s science station as he heard the bridge doors slide open behind him.

Without hesitation, he stood as Captains Kirk and Picard stepped onto the bridge.

He noted that Worf, Riker, Troi, and Data did the same.

It seemed the appropriate thing to do.

As Kirk and Picard surveyed their new bridge, Spock's acute hearing picked up Picard's whispered words to Kirk.

"Captain, once again, you mustn't feel you have to do this. Julian Bashir is a fine—" Picard was cut off by Kirk.

"You're still asking me if I want to spend what might be the last few days of my life in a diagnostic bed? Waiting for a miracle that might not happen, instead of being out here, doing something useful?"

"Or foolish," Picard said.

"Captain Picard, I've done a great many foolish things in my day already. What would you do?"

Picard smiled. "Welcome aboard, Captain."

Spock looked ahead at the viewscreen as Commander Data moved the *Enterprise* away from New Titan and the *Challenger.* The android turned in his chair. "We are ready for transwarp injection at . . ." Spock saw a look of consternation cross the android's face. "Uh . . . at the captain's discretion."

Everyone on the small bridge looked to Kirk and Picard.

Kirk and Picard looked at each other.

They stood on either side of the starship's command chair.

Its empty command chair.

Spock raised an eyebrow. Knowing what he did about both captains, he expected the next few moments to be fascinating.

Kirk was the first to offer Picard the chair.

"Captain, please."

But Picard shook his head graciously, returning the gesture with a flourish.

"No, Captain, I insist."

"Really, Starfleet turned over this mission to you."

"But you were the first to defeat a branch of the collective. The mission is yours."

For an instant, both captains were frozen in place. Then Spock saw the surreptitious movement both made as each began to slip into the chair, stopping at once when they realized the other was about to do the same.

"How long do you two intend to keep this up?" Riker asked.

Picard and Kirk both looked embarrassed, but just as neither was going to be the first to sit in the chair, neither was going to be the first to step away.

Then Kirk saw Spock watching him.

He smiled.

"*Mr.* Spock!" He patted the back of the command chair. "I believe your seat is over here."

Spock was startled. "Captain, I am no longer in Starfleet."

"Retirees are always subject to call-up in time of war." He patted the seat again.

"Sir, I have never sought command."

"Then who better to lead?" Picard said, seeing the same end to the impasse.

Riker looked meaningfully at Spock. "Someone had better get us on our way."

Spock rose reluctantly, smoothing his robes.

"I shall have to rely on you both for guidance," he said diplomatically.

Picard angled the chair around to meet him. "That's what we're here for. Please, Ambassador, take command."

With great reluctance, Spock took the chair, Kirk on his right, Picard on his left.

Only Data looked relieved.

"Captain?" the android said. "We are ready for injection."

The response sounded like a confused choral reading as everyone replied at once.

"Take us out," Kirk said.

"Proceed," Spock ordered.

"Make it so," Picard pronounced.

"Yes . . . sirs," Data said.

Then he turned back to face the viewscreen, and Spock watched with interest as he saw a ripple shimmer among the stars, making it appear as if the depths of space had been painted on a canvas that was suddenly split apart and folded back.

Inside, a pool of multicolored light expanded, as Spock felt himself rocked back in his seat with a kick of acceleration even the battle-hardened systems of this new *Enterprise* could not compensate for.

"We have achieved transwarp," Data announced.

"Decrease the resolution of the forward viewscreen," Spock said. "The effects of observing the transwarp dimension can be disturbing for those who have not experienced it before."

The viewscreen abruptly changed to a undulating wire-frame model of energy densities.

"Speed, Mr. Data?" Spock asked.

"We have exceeded the speed of subspace radio and are continuing to accelerate."

Spock looked to the ceiling. "Bridge to engineering. What is the status of the Borg engine?"

La Forge answered in a voice tinged with awe. "Sir, I couldn't begin to tell you how this thing's working, but it's drawing less power than one-quarter impulse."

"Is there any indication of an operational limit being met, Mr. La Forge?"

"No, sir," the engineer replied. "Diagnostics show we're running at twenty percent of capacity."

"Bridge out," Spock said. "Mr. Data, assuming we continue to accelerate through this medium until the Borg engine reaches eighty percent of its capacity, what is our estimated arrival at the Borg homeworld?"

"Six point two hours, sir."

Spock stood up and faced Kirk and Picard. "Gentlemen, I will be in my cabin. I suggest you take this opportunity to rest."

"Very well done, Ambassador," Picard said.

"Taught him everything he knows," Kirk said with a grin.

Spock left the bridge, wondering if he had done the right thing by healing the rift between Kirk and Picard.

One starship captain was still quite enough as far as he was concerned.

FORTY-EIGHT

The Borg world orbited a sun long dead, a white dwarf star little more than a core of degenerate matter, spinning rapidly, accomplishing nothing except serving as the center of gravity for a paltry system of three planets.

Untold ages ago there had been more.

But some of those planets had been consumed.

One that remained in the dark and sunless system was the Borg world. Whether it was the world on which the Borg had first arisen, or whether it was simply a planet they had chosen near the beginning of their march across the galaxy, no one would ever know.

All that mattered was that, here and now, it was the center. The node to which all branches reported. The wellspring from which all branches emerged.

There were no natural life-forms left on it. No free water. No stones or soil. Everything was engineered—the results of millennia of work and reconfiguration. Each molecule now had a function, each shape a purpose. So that now even the world itself was living, if only in the sense that Borg themselves were alive.

The surface of the solitary planet was banded by rings of light, flickering with the thought processes of a computer that encompassed a sphere larger than the Earth. What thoughts it held were unfathomable except to others who might share its size and structure.

But whether others like it existed was unknown even to its great mind. And so it sent out its children to remake the galaxy, to remake the universe itself if need be.

Anything to escape being alone.

In standard orbit above that world, the *Avatar of Tomed* coasted in space one hundred thousand light-years from home. If not for the Borg-built transwarp engine tied into her warp drive, it would take her almost three and a half centuries to return to Romulus, instead of a mere ten hours. But that great distance was what made this Borg system the perfect staging arena for the invasion that was within hours of beginning.

Spread out before Salatrel, secure from attack, was a vast Romulan armada—not the Empire's, but *hers.*

Eighteen *D'deriderex* Warbirds were among it, their whereabouts a constant embarrassment to the Empire, which publicly declared them as missing on voyages of exploration, while privately acknowledging that never before had they faced such numerous incidents of mutiny.

Forty additional single-hulled Warbirds of older classes hovered at their sides. Five classes of Bird-of-Prey. One hundred seven vessels in all, all outfitted with Borg transwarp capability and self-modulating Borg disruptors, all their controls and functions tied together in the Borg collective.

And assembling with them, joining the spread-wing formation of Romulan victory, was the key to absolute victory—eleven Borg cubeships.

Soon to be more.

Because even as Salatrel watched her fleet assemble in the viewscreen of her bridge, swift Borg scoutships converged on the assembly coordinates, showing the reason why the cube was the Borg's most common shape of choice.

Salatrel changed the focus of the viewscreen to watch as four scoutships met, docking inner face to inner face until a single larger cube was formed, the generalized control mechanisms of each scoutship now combining so that the task of controlling of the entire larger cube would be distributed among four accumulation points.

Then those four scoutships moved as one to join another combination of four, and two more.

The new cubeship comprised sixteen vessels.

And they would combine again.

And again.

Until another single, mammoth cubeship had emerged to serve the collective.

The first time Salatrel had seen the impressive, but so simple, assembly of the Borg vessels, she had instantly understood why they were so difficult to destroy. It was like scratching a holographic plate. Since every element on the hologram was encoded with the whole image, a single point of damage could not do any harm. On a cubeship that had experienced minor damage, every other undamaged part contained information enough to continue every function.

That was the power of the collective.

Groupmind.

Group function.

Destined to conquer all.

Except the Romulan people.

"Victory," Salatrel pledged as she watched the mighty cubeships slip in to join the spread-wing formation.

"Perhaps," Vox said beside her.

"How can *you* doubt the triumph of the collective?" Salatrel asked.

"We do not," Vox said. "We doubt the victory of the Romulan Armada. Picard and Spock escaped from the transwarp station. You were unable to detect the new class of Starfleet vessel. You were unable to destroy Picard. You are weak."

"I took a chance," Salatrel said.

"Chance implies risk. There is no risk. There is only success."

Salatrel felt a chill. Hadn't she said the same to Tracius? The day Kirk had been reborn?

"There will be success."

She felt Vox turn to her, and she forced herself to look up at him.

Surprisingly, his scanner eye was dim. He looked at her only with his real eye. The one she was certain still connected somehow to his Romulan heart.

"Run," he whispered.

"I'm sorry?"

"Nothing can stop them."

"Vox?"

The Borg-Romulan reached out to her with his organic hand, took hers, squeezed. Gently. Just as he had before.

"Leave while you can," he said.

Salatrel stared at her former lover. She had no understanding of how he might be able to defeat the influence of the collective for the length of time it had taken for him to say those words, in the unaltered voice of the warrior she had loved.

"Tell me what I must do," she asked quickly.

But the scanner eye rekindled and painted her with its inquisitive red beam.

"Do not fight us," Vox said, with the harmonic of the collective once again underscoring his words. "Resistance is futile."

Salatrel turned away from him, assailed by old doubts about her future and the future of her people. But her course had been set long ago, when James T. Kirk had entered into the tail of the comet Icarus IV and murdered her grandfather. Everything that had happened since was the responsibility of the Butcher of Icarus. Even the Borg-Romulan invasion of his brutal Federation.

A warning chime sounded. Tran looked away from his board.

"Commander—a transwarp conduit is opening."

Salatrel leaned forward, puzzled. "Aren't all ships accounted for?"

"Yes, Commander."

"Then what is it?"

"That's just it, Commander. The transwarp conduit opened, then it closed. But sensors didn't show that anything came through it."

"That is not possible," Vox stated.

"Did you scan for a cloak?" Salatrel asked as she rose to her feet.

"Yes, Commander . . . but I found nothing."

Salatrel turned to Vox. "It must be an anomaly."

Vox stared at her coldly. "Or James T. Kirk."

On the bridge of the new *Enterprise,* McCoy was the first to speak as they emerged from transwarp. Kirk thought it was typical. McCoy was always the first to react to a situation. Spock was always the first to think a situation through. And Kirk was always the first to put the two extremes together and come up with the winning plan.

Or, at least, *a* plan.

He still hadn't figured out Picard's crew, other than that they worked as a team—and as a team, they seemed unbeatable.

"One ship . . ." McCoy sputtered. "Against all of *them*?! You've got to be kidding, Spock."

"May I remind you I did not request your presence on this journey, Dr. McCoy."

"You needed ballast. And these days I'm the next best thing." McCoy looked up from his mobility chair at Kirk. "What do you think, Jim?"

Kirk shrugged. He had spent the past six hours digesting the specs on this ship. From his twenty-third century perspective, its capabilities were mindboggling. He smiled at McCoy. "I've read what this ship can do, Bones. That fleet out there doesn't have a chance."

McCoy frowned, never one to appreciate Kirk's hyperbole.

"Is there any sign we have been detected?" Spock asked. He was back in the center chair, behaving as if he had always been in command of the ship.

"No, sir," Data said. "I am picking up an increase in intership communication, though. Obviously, they saw our conduit opcn and are trying to determine why."

Kirk saw Spock check the displays on the arm of his chair. "Helm, take us in to the second planet. I believe it is the one I saw when I melded with V'Ger."

But Picard stepped up to Spock. "You said you would depend on our guidance, Mr. Spock."

"I am listening, Captain."

"Save your analysis of that planet for later. Right now, we owe it to the Federation to inflict as much damage as possible on these ships." He pointed at the screen. "That's a Romulan spread-wing formation. They're on the brink of launching into battle."

"How do you propose this one vessel take on such a fleet?" Spock asked, with no trace of rancor.

"These Romulan vessels are clearly working *with* the Borg ships," Picard said. "Therefore, they are tied into the Borg communications system."

Spock understood. "Ah, and this vessel's deflector array is configured to deliver a subspace pulse to effectively blank out all operative subspace transmitters."

"Will that destroy them?" Kirk asked.

"No," Picard said. "But best-guess estimates say it will be fifteen minutes before the Borg are able to reform the collective enough to coordinate their attack. In the meantime, we would be able to proceed, unhindered."

"If you don't mind me asking," Kirk said. "If you have the ability to blank Borg communications, why didn't you do that on New Titan?"

"Because individual Borg recover within seconds. Each ship will reestablish its own internal systems within a minute.

It is the sheer complexity of reestablishing the intership subspace network that will slow the Borg down."

Spock nodded. "It is a logical decision. Mr. Data, prepare to fire the deflector pulse."

Data glanced back at the captains with an expression of surprise. "Captain Picard, I have just realized that it was precisely this kind of pulse which could account for the erasure of all computer records on the world of Trilex."

"I will be quite fascinated to discuss archaeology with you *later,* Data. Now, proceed with Ambassador Spock's order."

"At once, sir."

Kirk looked down at McCoy as the doctor shifted uncomfortably in his mobility chair. "Talking archaeology when we're facing the biggest fleet this side of Utopia Planitia," McCoy muttered. "I still say he has pointed ears."

Spock glanced back at McCoy. "I am sure you intend Mr. Data to consider that a compliment, Doctor."

Kirk grinned. It was good to be back in action, even if he were little more than an observer.

He flinched as a searing pain shot through his legs. The inexorable nanites, still at work. Kirk took a breath to steady himself. Given present circumstances, he reminded himself, it was good to be anywhere.

Salatrel sat beside Tran, double checking all her subcommander's sensor readings. "The ship *has* to be somewhere in the system," she said.

"Most logically, it will attempt to map the Borg world," Vox said. "You should concentrate your search there."

"Why don't *you* concentrate a search there?" Salatrel snapped.

"You remain ignorant of the resources that this armada has consumed for the collective," Vox said. "We are limited in what we can do here."

At one level, Salatrel was pleased by that admission. It was the first time she had heard any Borg admit there were limits to what they could accomplish. If the Federation were able to withstand this armada, the Borg might be defenseless, exactly as Salatrel had hoped.

"Tran—order all Birds-of-Prey into tight orbit of the Borg world. They are to scan for tachyons and fire on any sources."

"But that will break the attack formation," Vox said. "The formation must be maintained to balance its entry into the transwarp dimension."

"We've come this far," Salatrel said. "A few more minutes won't hurt. Unless you want to risk a Federation ship's dropping a few quantum torpedoes on the Borg homeworld."

Salatrel watched Vox carefully for a reaction. The Romulan Speaker for the Borg wasn't pleased. She took that to mean that the homeworld *was* vulnerable to attack.

Perhaps the Borg had become too complacent here, never expecting that anyone could do to them what they did to the galaxy.

"Tran, send the order."

"At once, Commander."

Tran began to change the configuration of his control panel to bring up the subspace radio link that united the armada. "Attention all Birds-of-Prey. For the glory of the Empire, you are ordered to—"

The Warbird rocked as every ODN circuit lining the bridge arced with a power discharge.

Collision alerts sounded.

"Tran! Report!" Salatrel demanded.

How could the Starfleet vessel know enough to target *her* ship?

"That was an extremely powerful subspace pulse," Tran reported. "A useless gesture, if it was the Starfleet vessel. All of our circuits are shielded. No damage."

Salatrel was puzzled. "Then what was the point of . . . ?"

She stopped as she saw Vox bent over, clutching his head and circuitry.

"Vox?"

The Borg-Romulan looked up in agony.

"The collective is gone from our mind. . . . We are alone."

Tran shouted, near panic. "Commander! He's right! The entire Borg communications system has been overloaded. The whole fleet is out of contact."

Salatrel lurched toward Tran. "Then *reestablish* contact!"

Tran shrugged helplessly. "I can't. Every Borg system will respond by moving to a new method of communications. By the time we all match frequencies . . . it'll be too late."

Salatrel spun to the screen. Clenched her fist.

"Kirk," she said.

It was the only answer.

FORTY-NINE

☆

Silent, unseen, the *Enterprise* sped toward the Borg homeworld.

On her bridge, Spock still held the center chair, with Kirk and Picard still beside him, and McCoy to the side. Riker served as science officer, Worf as communications, Data at the helm. Beverly Crusher and Deanna Troi both arrived from the ship's spartan sickbay to witness the historic voyage firsthand. La Forge labored in engineering, guiding the intricate meshing of Borg technology with Starfleet's latest wonders.

And a crew of Starfleet's finest, trained by Shelby and Lewinski for the worst the Borg could throw at them, held their stations throughout the sleek and deadly ship.

The Federation had never faced a more menacing threat than the Borg collective. But if this ship proved worthy of her namesakes, that threat might end, here and forever.

"That is the world I saw," Spock said. "Without question."

"I wonder why V'Ger didn't return with a crew of Borg," Riker asked.

"Who knows? V'Ger was here a long time ago," Kirk said. "Maybe the collective followed different strategies then. Maybe there were no Borg as you know them now." He paused and regarded the new crew of the new *Enterprise*. "What we need to remember is, if this world *is* a single, living creature, then it's doing what all living things do—evolving, growing, learning."

Picard frowned. "Which means that somewhere down below could be the start of something even more deadly and relentless than what we've faced already."

"Destroy it," McCoy said. "While that damn fleet is immobilized, burn away its surface. Sterilize the place."

"If it is a living creature, doctor," Spock said, "that would be a crime against everything the Federation stands for."

"Then we cut it off," Kirk said.

"I agree," Picard added. "The power of the collective is in its organization. If we can make this interruption of its communications system permanent, then we deprive it of its ability to organize its conquest of the galaxy."

"Who knows?" Kirk said. "If we slow it down enough, maybe we can even try to reason with it."

"Reason with the Borg?" Riker asked.

Picard made the argument. "Destroying them will always be an option, Will. But an option we can never go back on."

"Are you sure, sir?" Riker asked.

Picard looked at Kirk. "After what I've been through recently, yes. I am."

"The problem still remains," Spock said, "how do we make this interruption of their communications permanent?"

Picard stepped forward to better see the viewscreen and the

world of light upon it. "From my time with them, I now know that somewhere down there is the Central Node of the entire collective. We must find it. And we must . . . destroy it. Beyond any chance of them reconstructing it."

Picard turned to face Spock. "If you agree, sir. This ship does have that power."

Kirk thought Spock's response was noticeably grim. "Provided we utilize it within the next ten minutes, Commander. If we attempt to act once the Borg and Romulan fleet are functional as a united force, I estimate our useful lifetime in the system at less than two minutes."

Picard turned to Data and Riker. "Gentlemen, I suggest you begin a full sensor sweep of the Borg homeworld at once."

Kirk raised a finger. "Um, I'm not an expert on this ship, but won't our sensors reveal our location to the Borg?"

"Only if they're looking for us this close to the planet," Picard said.

"I would be," Kirk replied.

Picard smiled. "Then I would suggest you take the weapons console."

Kirk moved there directly and found the layout familiar enough to hope he'd have a chance to use it.

Spock addressed the helm. "Mr. Data—estimated time to scan the Borg planet?"

"Eighteen minutes, sir."

"Full Borg communications will be restored in eight minutes."

Data turned to Spock. "Sir, may I try an experiment?"

Even from his position at the weapons console, Kirk could hear McCoy groan.

"Do you believe it will decrease the time necessary to search for the Central Node?" Spock asked.

"I believe so, sir."

"Will you just get on with it!" McCoy snapped. Then he

started coughing uncontrollably, and Kirk smiled as he saw both Dr. Crusher and Deanna Troi rush to McCoy's side.

On the viewscreen, a schematic of the Borg homeworld appeared to one side. On the other side, the schematic of another planet Kirk did not recognize. Though he did find it familiar.

Picard recognized it, though. "Data, that's Trilex, isn't it?"

"Yes, sir. A reconstruction of its landmasses, seas, and population centers, prior to the disaster which claimed its sun."

"Very interesting," Picard said. "But what does it have to do with the situation at hand?"

"Sir, I submit that the organic and machine intelligences of Trilex did not perish in a war against each other. I believe that they were involved in a war against the Borg. Or, at least, the Borg as they existed at that time."

"Go on, Mr. Data."

"The damage that was done to the Trilex computer infrastructure was the result of a subspace pulse similar to what we have just used to temporarily incapacitate the Borg fleet. If we accept that our technique is one which can be independently developed by any who fight the Borg, then the ruins of Trilex could indicate that the inhabitants of that world used a massive subspace pulse to incapacitate a Borg invasion force in their system."

"Mr. Data, are you saying that the people of Trilex, organic and artificial, deliberately triggered the deadly explosion of their sun."

"Yes, sir. They might have thought there was a chance some of the population might survive. But if the Borg were not stopped, then none would survive."

"It would be an act of terrible desperation for a people to gamble the existence of their world," Picard said.

"I find it is an act of hope, sir."

"In what way?"

"What better indication could there be that organic and artificial beings can live together, than by their decision to fight and die together, for what they believe in? Surely that shows they were united in a common purpose."

Kirk had watched and listened to the lengthy exchange between Picard and the android. He felt certain that on his bridge, he and Spock had rarely indulged in such introspection. He wondered if things had moved faster in his day. No one else on the bridge seemed as impatient as he felt with the inaction. He checked the time readout. Six minutes remained before they would come under fire.

"You may have answered the Trilex Question, Mr. Data," Picard continued. "But how does it apply here?"

"The Borg are not imaginative, sir. They follow preset patterns. If we overlay the pattern of destruction on Trilex—" On the viewscreen, the two schematics merged. "—on top of the Borg homeworld, I believe that since the people of Trilex were intending to destroy the Borg center of communication on their world, the area of the worst destruction should line up with the location of the Central Node on this world. Assuming that the Borg followed the same pattern, that is."

Spock turned to Riker. "Commander Riker, if you would scan those coordinates, please."

Kirk watched Riker work with intense concentration. Then Riker looked up, almost in surprise. "Ambassador Spock, we have located the Central Node." Perhaps, Kirk thought, there was a place for introspection on a captain's bridge.

Picard pounded Data on the back. "Well done, Data."

Data smiled. Kirk found it disturbing to see an android exhibit emotions. But when in the twenty-fourth century . . .

"Thank you," Data said. "But we must really thank the people of Trilex, both organic and synthetic."

Spock nodded at Kirk. "Captain, if you would target the Central Node."

With relief at the call to action, Kirk checked the coordinate readouts. With a few commands, he successfully locked the *Enterprise*'s phasers on the center of the target and laid in a torpedo barrage to encircle any backup connections that might be linked into it.

"Target locked," he confirmed.

"Four minutes to reacquisition of communications," Worf announced.

"I'll be damned," McCoy said, slapping his leg. "It's not even close. We're going to make it after all."

And then the *Enterprise* shook as the first barrage hit, sending half the crew to the deck as the ship began to dive.

Tran shook his fist in the air in triumph.

"Direct hit, Commander!"

"Stay on it," Salatrel said. Alone of all the armada she had brought her ship in close to the homeworld. And her suspicions had been correct.

On the bridge viewscreen, she saw the rippling effect of a cloaking field dispersing and knew she had caused considerable damage to the Starfleet vessel, whatever it was.

She turned to Vox.

"See? A single ship is of no concern.".

"Did you not read its sensor returns?" Vox said. "It had located the Central Node. The collective could not hold."

"What about the famed Borg redundancy?"

"There can be only one collective," Vox said.

Salatrel smiled in fierce satisfaction. At last, she knew. The Borg had a fatal weakness after all.

"Fire at will," Salatrel commanded. Then she sat back in her chair and dreamed of victory.

"Where the hell did that come from?!" Riker shouted.

La Forge answered over the bridge speakers. "It's this transwarp drive, Commander. It interferes with our tachyon detection modes."

Worf confirmed La Forge's analysis. The cloaked ship that had attacked them would remain undetectable as long as the transwarp drive was engaged.

"Disengage the transwarp drive," Spock ordered matter-of-factly.

"And pull up," Picard suggested.

Data was already involved in doing just that, leveling out the *Enterprise's* path so she would not repeat the ignominious end of her predecessor by crash-landing on the Borg world.

"As soon as we have a fix," Kirk said, "torpedoes are ready for launching."

Everyone on the bridge worked in perfect balance. The instant the transwarp drive was offline, Riker reconfigured the sensors for maximum tachyon sensitivity. The instant the sensors picked up the tachyon signature of the cloaked ship trailing them, Data transferred the coordinates to Kirk's weapons controls. Kirk launched the torpedoes less than an instant after that.

The *Avatar of Tomed* spun twice on its vertical axis as a quantum torpedo struck its outer starboard hull support.

Only its structural integrity field kept it together.

Only its artificial gravity and inertial dampeners kept its crew from being crushed.

Tran brought the Warbird back into trim and continued its pursuit. But its cloak dissipated as quickly as had the *Enterprise's*.

"It's a Warbird," Data announced as the image of the pursuing vessel appeared on the screen.

"I know that ship," Kirk said. "Can you get a closer image? Give me a name?"

The viewscreen fluttered as magnification was enhanced.

Data read the Romulan script on its raptor prow.

"The *Avatar of Tomed.* A poetic reference to the battle in which—"

"That's her!" Kirk said. "Salatrel."

"Fascinating," Spock commended. "*She* is the one who set all of this in motion."

Kirk punched the controls and fired more torpedoes.

The Warbird swerved to avoid them.

But the moment her port side was exposed, the *Enterprise's* phaser dug into that hull support as well.

"Excellent shooting, sir," Data said as the Warbird wobbled erratically. "Without hull integrity on both supports, it will be unable to withstand the compression of its defensive shields."

The *Enterprise* shook as the *Avatar* struck out again.

"We're going into overload!" La Forge shouted.

"I thought this ship was shielded!" Riker shouted back.

"Not with this damn transwarp drive! All our power curves are off."

Kirk targeted the Warbird's rear hull support, planning to put a shot through the gap between her upper and lower hulls the next time she swerved.

He fired two more torpedoes.

The Warbird swerved as he had anticipated, and he fired.

Plasma streamed out from behind the *Tomed.*

"Direct hit!" Data cheered. "Her shields are fluctuating . . . fluctuating . . . *gone!*"

Spock sat forward in his chair. "Mr. Worf, open a hailing frequency to the Romulan ship."

"They are refusing to answer," Worf said.

"Can they hear us?"

"Yes, sir."

Spock spoke loudly. "Attention, Romulan vessel. Your shields are disabled. If you withdraw, we will not destroy you." Spock looked over at Worf. "Is there any answer, Mr.—"

Spock's answer came as the bridge filled with streamers of power sparks.

"Direct hit on us," Data said in disbelief.

Kirk watched as his control board shut down. "The phaser banks are offline!"

"Good work," McCoy said. "They don't have any shields. We don't have any weapons. What are we supposed to do? Ram them?"

Picard turned to McCoy. "Actually, I have—"

The collision alarms wailed.

On the screen, the Warbird accelerated forward.

"*They* are attempting to ram us!" Data exclaimed. He jabbed his fingers on his controls. "The helm is not responding! We have stationkeeping thrusters only! Too close for torpedoes!"

"All hands, brace for impact!" Riker ordered.

But Kirk left his station to seek out Data. "Data—do you trust me?"

"That is a curious question to ask at this—"

"Then move over!" Kirk said, and slid in beside the android. "Now get me La Forge in engineering and stand by on the cloak."

Data blinked. "Sir, in twenty-eight seconds, we will be spinning debris."

"Trust me," Kirk said.

Then he turned to the board and did the only thing he could.

He changed the rules.

Moments before impact, the *Enterprise* rippled within its cloak and disappeared.

"They've cloaked," Tran reported.

"A meaningless act of desperation," Salatrel said. "They can't go anywhere. Stand by for impact."

"Five . . ." Tran counted, "four . . . three . . . two . . . one . . . impact!"

The Warbird moved smoothly on course.

Salatrel was out of her chair and by Tran in a second. "Where did they go?"

Tran looked at his board in helpless confusion. "Nowhere, Commander. They're so badly damaged, we would have picked up any attempt to leave their position."

"Activate all external scanners," Salatrel said.

Vox stepped up beside her. "We told you James Kirk was not to be underestimated."

"You don't know Kirk is on that ship!"

"Then how does it keep evading us?"

"Luck," Salatrel muttered.

"Luck is irrelevant."

The viewscreen flickered with rapid views of the volume of space surrounding the Warbird. There were no sensor traces anywhere.

"That is impossible!" Salatrel said. "It's not as if we swallowed him whole and . . ."

She stopped talking as the horrible truth hit her.

Tran turned to her in disbelief.

And Vox, through his implants, even seemed to smile.

On the bridge of the *Enterprise,* Picard shook his head as he watched the viewscreen. On it was the back hull of the Warbird's raptor prow.

Kirk had slipped the *Enterprise* between the Romulan vessel's double hull.

"I'm seeing it," Picard said, "but I'm not believing it."

"What's the matter?" Kirk asked. "You don't tell the story of the Trojan Horse anymore?"

"Captain Picard, Captain Kirk—the Warbird is activating its internal sensors," Riker said. "They must have guessed our strategy."

The captains turned to Spock. "It's up to you," Kirk said.

Spock nodded. "Mr. Data . . . on my mark, you will use stationkeeping thrusters to initiate a three-hundred-and-sixty-degree lateral rotation. Drop the cloak to put full strength into the structural integrity field."

"Yes, sir."

Kirk smiled as Spock shifted in his command chair.

"Mark," the reluctant commander of the *Enterprise* said.

Salatrel grabbed the helm as she saw the Starfleet vessel shimmer into view between the *Tomed's* hulls. She knew that in seconds it would begin to rotate and gut them. There was nothing left for her to do.

"This is your fault!" she screamed at Vox.

And this time, Vox did smile. "No. This is all the fault of James T. Kirk. And since you are the one who brought him to us . . ." Vox stopped speaking as he saw something to the side.

Salatrel turned to see Tran aim a disruptor at her.

"You did this," the subcommander raged. "All you old people making wars . . . you make me—"

The bridge groaned.

On the viewscreen, just before the image winked out in a flurry of static, Salatrel saw the starfleet vessel begin its rotation.

The bridge shook.

Salatrel heard the hiss of escaping air.

And with an endless cry of denial, she was sucked out through the rent in the hull, knowing she fell through stars that still shone on Kirk, but which would never shine on her again.

Nestled in between the double hulls of the Romulan Warbird, Starfleet's newest *Enterprise* slowly continued her lateral, lethal roll.

Her streamlined profile and reduced size had made it possible for her to ease inside the Warbird, skirting her prow, to take up stationkeeping above the ventral and below the dorsal hulls.

By rotating within that enclosed space, without having to

fight the force of the Warbird's shields, the *Enterprise* opened the ship like a hatchling splitting an egg.

The shell of the Warbird spun away in a glittering cloud of tumbling wreckage, fogged by a frozen, sublimating cloud of escaping atmosphere.

And from that cloud, like a phoenix reborn, the *Enterprise* broke free and continued on her mission.

FIFTY

"One minute to acquisition of communications," Riker announced. "But we have no weapons left to destroy the Central Node."

"Unless we ram it ourselves," Spock said bluntly.

There was a moment of silence on the bridge. To save the Federation from the Borg, there was no one on board who would not agree to such a drastic sacrifice. But was it the only way?

Kirk left his weapons station. "Send me down, Spock. There has to be a self-destruct mechanism . . . or a power generator I can put on overload. . . ."

"You will be sacrificing your life," Spock said.

Kirk grinned. "You're the one suggesting a suicide dive. Beam me down. I'll take my chances with the Borg."

Picard stepped up beside him. "I'll go with you."

Kirk shook his head. "Don't forget, I'm the one with the nanites eating through me. You have a life ahead of you."

"Not if the Borg are allowed to continue unopposed."

Picard matched Kirk's grin. "Besides, with what you know about the Borg, you're liable to help them *fix* their Central Node and not destroy it."

Kirk studied him in silence, then nodded, sealing their pact.

Picard sought out Crusher at the back of the bridge, still with Troi and McCoy. "Beverly. I'll need the interface in the transporter room. At once."

Kirk stepped out of the armorer's storage room laden with phasers and photon grenades.

Spock and McCoy were waiting for him.

A hundred glib remarks came to Kirk. Light things. Easy jokes. Anything to ease the burden of these last precious seconds. But somehow he knew the time for that had passed. Decades ago.

So instead, he reached out to them, gripping one of their hands in each of his.

"It's all right," Kirk said. "I had a second chance. Not a lot of people can say that."

Even after all their years together, Spock's expression was unreadable. But McCoy's eyes glistened.

"The way I figure it, you're working on your fiftieth chance by now," the doctor croaked. His old-man's voice trembled with unexpressed emotion.

"A second chance," Kirk said softly, realizing the enormity of the gift he had been given: to see his two friends again, even for these brief hours. "And there's still not enough time. Never has been."

"I am . . ." Spock began, then faltered.

Kirk understood. "And always will be . . . your friend."

Then he let go of them, stepped back, fixing them both in his mind's eye to hold them there for the rest of his life. "Look after each other. Never give up." Then he turned and hurried to the transporter room, unable to look back.

* * *

In the transporter room, Kirk found Picard burdened by the same array of weaponry on his own equipment harness. He also held a black carryall pouch which Crusher had given him.

Crusher watched as Kirk stepped up on the platform.

"I can do this myself, you know," Kirk said. "You can tell Starfleet what we've found here."

Picard shook his head. "I have faith in my crew."

Then Kirk saw Dr. Crusher staring at Picard. Suddenly, she ran over to him, hugged him, hard. He eased her away, gently.

The deck rumbled underfoot. A weapons impact. Spock's voice came from the speakers. He was back on the bridge. "We have been engaged by a Bird-of-Prey. Communications capability is returning to the enemy fleet. Please transport at once. We will loop back in precisely eight hundred seconds for an emergency beam-out."

"Energize," Picard ordered.

The cramped transporter room dissolved around Kirk, then reformed as a dark warren of ugly black metal struts and walkways. He tested his footing in the gravity of the Borg world. It was lighter than he had expected.

"Is the whole planet like this?" Kirk asked. The metal framework seemed to stretch to the horizon, lit only by glowing and pulsing emanations from below.

"If we're lucky," Picard said, "we won't have to find out." He glanced around to get his bearings, then headed off to the right. "This way."

"Why not?" Kirk said and followed him.

Above the Borg homeworld, the *Enterprise* went to full impulse, deliberately directing itself toward the densest accumulation of Borg and Romulan ships. Spock had concluded that that was where they would find those few ships which had not yet rejoined the newly restored Borg communications network, and where those that had would be least likely to use their weapons, for fear of hitting allies.

The *Enterprise* flew on toward that mass of ships, swerving as closely as Data dared take them to Borg cubeships and Romulan formations. And because Data navigated with the precise control of a machine, his maneuvers were daring enough to alarm even Spock.

On the homeworld, Kirk and Picard stood outside a massive metal door, at least ten meters tall. It was covered in intricate scrollwork. Writing of some kind, Kirk decided. Faintly reminiscent of old circuit designs. Picard checked his tricorder. "The Central Node is through here. According to the tricorder, the door hasn't been opened for at least two hundred thousand years."

"Good," Kirk said as he drew his phaser. "Then you've come far enough. Wait here for the beam-out. Let me go on."

"And let you have all the fun?"

Picard drew his own phaser and blasted the door's locking device.

It swung open with a gust of foul air.

Picard waved to the dark passageway beyond. With a smile he said, "After you . . ."

Kirk returned the gesture, and the grin. "Oh, no . . . after you. . . ."

With shared laughter, the two captains stepped through together.

The *Enterprise* streaked through space, avoiding those few ships that fired on her. Her restored shields protecting her from the shots that didn't miss.

"The enemy fleet still appears to be in confusion," Riker said. Spock had already deduced that the subspace pulse from the deflector array had been more destructive than Starfleet had anticipated.

Data amended Riker's assessment. "Except for the Borg vessels directly ahead."

Spock called for them to go onscreen.

It was not an encouraging image.

Once again the cubeships were reassembling themselves, not into larger cubes, but into other, more ominous shapes—some long and bristling with disruptor cannons, some resembling vessels with twin nacelles formed as if from a child's set of building blocks.

"They are adapting to us," Worf marvelled.

Spock had no need to check a time readout. "As long as they take more than six hundred seconds to do so, Mr. Worf, we will have a chance to recover Captains Kirk and Picard."

The *Enterprise* flew on. But now the reconfigured Borg ships took up the chase. And the distance between hunter and prey grew smaller.

The dark passageway beyond the ancient door smelled worse the deeper Kirk and Picard penetrated. But at last, no more than two hundred meters later, the passageway opened up into a vast interior space that made Kirk think of the Grand Canyon turned upside down.

A Grand Canyon of black metal and endless pipelines.

But that oppressive technological mass was above them, lit only by gouts of flame, as if oil wells were being vented. Below them, on a lower plaza ten stories deep, a sunken dome stretched away, kilometers wide, its surface pulsing with flashing traces of cold blue light.

The patterns of that light were the same as those Kirk had seen on the ancient door.

There was order here, and purpose. Though Kirk doubted even a Vulcan could appreciate or comprehend it.

Picard folded his tricorder shut. "That's it," he said.

"*Now* why don't you go back?" Kirk asked. "Now that we've found it, I can deal with it."

"But can you deal with them?" Picard said.

Kirk turned to look in the direction Picard looked, along the wide deck that ran from the passageway in a sweeping circle around the glowing dome and sunken plaza.

He saw what Picard saw.

Borg.

Thousands of them.

Marching toward them.

"Coming up on course change," Data announced.

Spock steepled his fingers as the *Enterprise* shook beneath the onslaught of disruptor fire it was taking from the Borg ship in pursuit.

"Commander Riker," Spock said, "have you noticed the delay in the Borg's response to our course changes?"

"Yes, sir," Riker said. "Their ship is more massive, less responsive to sudden vector changes."

"I calculate a three-second discrepancy."

"I concur."

Spock put his hands on the arms of his command chair and held on tightly. "Mr. Data, put us on a collision course with the Borg ship, bearing forty-three, twenty-seven, mark eight. I would like you to pull out at two seconds before collision."

"Yes, sir," Data said. "I believe I would like that as well."

Kirk and Picard crouched behind a power conduit more than five meters thick. It ran down from the wall of the immense interior space, across the wide circular deck, then down the ten stories where it snaked into the side of the dome of flashing light traces.

Picard pointed to a switching lever on the side of the stained and mineral-encrusted metal that formed the pipe.

"This lever will do it," Picard said, confirming his guess with his tricorder. "It will cut the power to the Central Node's core and trigger a feedback surge that will burn out all its circuits." He looked around. "This facility was constructed long before the Borg developed redundancy to the extent they practice it today."

"How can you know all this?" Kirk asked.

"I don't," Picard answered. "But Locutus does."

The mass of approaching Borg was coming closer. Not all of them marched. Some rolled, some crawled, some floated as if on antigravs. But the sound of their approach hammered on the metal plates of the deck, making Kirk think of rolling thunder on a planet which could have no more weather.

"Do you think they're going to *let* us cut the power to the Central Node?"

"That is not within the realm of possibility," Picard said.

"Then we should cut the power now."

"No," Picard said. "We have to time it for the *Enterprise*'s return. That way there's still a chance for us to get out."

"The *Enterprise* is still eight minutes away," Kirk said. "How do we hold them back till then?"

"You don't," Picard said. "I do."

Picard opened the black carryall pouch that Dr. Crusher had given him. Kirk glanced inside. Saw the Borg interface.

Knew what it meant.

To destroy the Borg homeworld, Picard had to truly become Locutus again.

"Collision in ten seconds," Data said calmly.

Spock made a cutting motion with his hand. "Shut off the collision alarms, please, Mr. Worf."

The bridge of the *Enterprise* fell silent.

The screen filled with the chaotic mass of metal pipes and tubes that would collide with the *Enterprise* in a matter of seconds. Directly before them, submodular cubeships formed themselves into a shape that looked like a spear—a spear aimed at the *Enterprise*.

In contrast, the Borg ship that pursued them was spiked and blazed with disruptor fire that converged from three emitters into a single, central, stabbing beam.

Spock had Data hold his course, absorbing hit after hit from that beam.

Data continued his countdown. ". . . four . . . three . . . *course change*!"

The *Enterprise* sidestepped the spear-shaped Borg vessel by fewer than three hundred meters.

And as Spock had anticipated, the pursuing Borg ship didn't miss it at all.

The two Borg ships met, blazing like a new sun, shedding thick golden shafts of light on the tumbling cubeships that spiraled away and dissolved into storms of debris as the power of the explosion reached out to them.

The *Enterprise* banked in that firestorm of plasma. Her shields took all the energy of the dying Borg without fail or complaint.

She had been in transit for four hundred seconds when Spock gave the order to return from where she had started.

His captain awaited him.

Picard drew his hand away from the neural plate now attached to his face. The power cell and subspace transmitter were already strapped to his chest.

"Are you sure?" Kirk asked.

"Is there a choice?" Picard answered.

Kirk pointed out the phasers and the photon grenades laid out before them behind the power conduit.

"These could keep them busy for a while."

"And what if one of that horde gets off a lucky shot? And we miss being able to pull on the lever? And the Node isn't destroyed?"

Kirk put his hand on Picard's shoulder. "Captain—I've seen Locutus. Spock took me in there, inside your mind. I know what it means to you . . . to put that thing back on."

"Spock showed me things, too," Picard said. "As did you." He held up the interface cord, felt for the slots that would guide it into place. "Some of the courage in here is yours. Some is Spock's. The truth is, I'm not any less afraid of the collective, or of Locutus. But it's been so long since I even allowed myself to feel fear, I unwittingly gave it power over me." Picard held the input jack to the neural plate. "You've shown me how to face fear, Captain. And I will return from that encounter—just as you did."

Picard jabbed the jack home. A faint blue crackle of energy leapt along the input cable to the power cell on his shoulder. His hand fell back. His eyes rolled back in his head until only white remained.

Beyond the conduit, the Borg horde advanced.

Picard rose to his feet beside Kirk, facing the enemy as it approached.

Kirk stood as well. "Is it working?"

Picard stared at him as if he were nothing more than the metallic debris that littered this world.

"We are Locutus," Picard said. "We are . . . Borg."

FIFTY-ONE

Kirk grabbed Picard by the shoulders. Shook him.

"Fight it!" he shouted.

Picard's eyes cleared, but just for an instant. "It wasn't . . . supposed to . . . be like this. . . . It's too strong."

Picard's hand scrabbled for the interface cable. Kirk pulled the hand away. "Not yet! You have to send them away!" He twisted Picard around to face the advancing Borg.

Kirk could hear the whine of their servomotors. The awful raspy wheeze of their assisted breathing.

"Tell them to stop or I'll cut off the power now!"

Picard lurched forward, bracing himself against the power conduit. Mouth open. Gasping.

"Resistance . . . resistance . . . *resistance is futile!"* he screamed and swung at Kirk.

Kirk grabbed his arms, held him.

"Picard! You are a starship captain! *Act like one!*"

And Kirk slapped him. Slapped him again.

Slapped him until Picard brought up his hand and caught Kirk's arm in midswing. "I think," he gasped, "you've convinced me. . . ."

Picard faced the Borg, now no more than a handful of meters away.

"Go back," he said. "We are Borg . . . the collective is safe . . . return . . . return to your functions. . . ."

Kirk tensed as he watched the Borg hesitate, swaying back and forth, motors whining.

And then, as one, they turned and moved away.

"It *is* working," Kirk said.

Picard's eyes followed the retreating Borg. "They want me back. And this time they're not asking. They're demanding."

Kirk looked intently at Picard, trying to read his emotions beneath the implant plate.

Picard's answering gaze was firm, unwavering. "And I'm saying . . . *no.*"

"Then go deeper into the collective," Kirk urged in relief. "Find out what we need to know about the power cut-off. How long do we have after we throw it?"

"We don't," Picard said. He held his hands to his head. "The feedback is immediate. The instant we throw the lever, the Node is . . . the Node is. . . ."

Kirk pulled Picard around to face him. "Concentrate, Captain. Look into the collective. Is there any way to pull that lever and still get out?"

Picard shook his head. "Whoever pulls that lever will die." His eyes cleared again. "Resistance is futile."

His eyes began to drift away again. His head turned in the direction the Borg had marched away.

Kirk had heard enough.

He grabbed the interface cable and pulled it free.

Picard cried out.

Gasped as if struck.

Then stared at Kirk.

"How long?" he asked.

Kirk checked his tricorder. "We've got sixty seconds till the *Enterprise* does her flyby."

"I can take it from here," Picard said.

"No, you can't," Kirk argued. "In case you don't remember, whoever pulls that lever and destroys the Node gets trapped in the power surge."

"I do remember. It is my job to do it. You've done enough."

"Jean-Luc, I'm dying."

"Who isn't?"

Spock's voice crackled out of Kirk's commbadge. "*Enterprise* to away team. We are at thirty seconds to emergency beam-out. What is your status?"

Picard locked eyes with Kirk. Touched his own commbadge. "This is Picard, *Enterprise.* Break off your approach. Repeat—"

Kirk pushed Picard's hand away from his commbadge, hit his own.

"Ignore that last order, Spock. Bring that ship in."

"I am not leaving!" Picard said.

Kirk was about to shout back, when he suddenly stood down.

"Did you ever try to save the *Kobayashi Maru* at the Academy?"

Picard watched Kirk with deep suspicion. "Yesss. . . . But it can't be done. It's a no-win scenario designed for cadets."

Kirk smiled. "That's what they'd like you to believe. But there is one strategy that can win it. It's just that nobody in your time seems to do it anymore. Spock tells me it's a lost art now."

"Are you suggesting a compromise?"

Kirk thought it over. "You could call it that."

Well," Picard said. "Go ahead. I'm always open to suggestions."

Kirk nodded. "Good."

Then he slugged Picard in the jaw as hard as he could.

Picard dropped like deadweight.

Kirk dragged Picard away by his collar, until he was well away from the power conduit.

He pulled off his own commbadge, touched the front to activate.

"Kirk to *Enterprise,*" he said.

"Spock here."

Kirk smiled.

He felt better already.

"Keep the ship out of danger, Mr. Spock." He studied the Starfleet delta in his hand. Remembered when it had belonged only to the *Enterprise.* But some things had to change. It was the way of the world. Of the universe.

He was glad to have been part of it.

"Lock onto my signal," Kirk said. "One to beam up." Then he tossed his commbadge onto Picard's chest and stepped back.

Picard reacted to the impact of the badge. His eyes opened. He looked up. Started to speak.

Then dissolved in the transporter as the *Enterprise* once more claimed her own.

Kirk turned back to the power conduit. Grabbed the lever in both hands. Tested it once to see how much force he might need. Felt it move easily.

"A second chance," he said aloud.

Then he closed his eyes.

Squeezed his hands tight.

Pulled.

Heard a sudden, deafening roar of thunder coming from the dome.

Then a scrape as quiet as a footstep behind him.

Kirk turned.

Opened his eyes.

Saw the—

"Dear God," McCoy said.

On the bridge of the *Enterprise,* to which he had been directly beamed, Picard shielded his eyes against the sudden glare from the viewscreen. On it, a blinding column of light shot up from the Borg homeworld, directly from what had been the Central Node.

In the intensity of that destructive light, every surface on the bridge that faced the viewscreen was too bright to look at. Every surface that was in shadow was too dark to reveal detail.

But Picard watched with grim fascination as ripples of explosions began to spread across the homeworld's surface, following the strict lines and angles of circuitry.

Beside him, Beverly Crusher took his hand. Riker stood beside her. Data and La Forge sat together at the helm. At his station, Worf made no effort to hide his eyes from the light. And Picard saw tears roll down Troi's cheeks. He knew the counselor was overwhelmed by the emotions of all who surrounded her, their joy and their grief.

For one crew had been reunited.

While another had at last been torn asunder.

McCoy stepped forward, held up only by his exoskeleton, to stand by Spock's side.

In the flickering of that light, Picard saw the Vulcan rise from the command chair to place his hand on the old man's shoulder. And through it all, Data counted off the uncountable Borg and Romulan ships colliding throughout the system, with no more subspace signals from the collective to link or guide them.

The explosions spread out in a web of fire, encompassing a third of the homeworld as a thousand other cubeships broke from its surface and jumped to transwarp, fleeing the death of whatever this planet had been.

There would still be Borg, somewhere, Picard knew. But not the Borg they had known. Not the Borg that had threatened them in the past.

For today, and with luck tomorrow, the Federation had been preserved.

Because of one man.

Picard rubbed his jaw as he watched the flaming destruction spread over the planet before them. "Perhaps this is a more fitting memorial," he said, "than a simple cairn of stones."

Riker nodded. "A great man died today."

Then Picard saw Spock turn to look at Riker. To Picard, the Vulcan's expression was disturbingly both unfathomable and familiar.

"Captain Picard," Spock said, "Now, I believe, the bridge is yours."

Picard watched in silence as Spock and McCoy slowly left the bridge, Spock supporting his friend, again with no regard for the normal Vulcan aversion to touching and being touched.

When they were gone, Riker turned to his captain.

"Did you see the look on Spock's face?" he asked, astonished.

A flame leapt into life within Picard as he waited for his first officer to continue.

"I've seen it before," Riker said. "At the salvage camp. Spock *still* doesn't believe that Kirk is dead."

Picard looked at the commbadge in his hand.

He remembered fleeting images of what he had seen in Kirk's mind. What Spock had shown him there.

He remembered Kirk's dream. The dream that had always haunted Kirk. Always shown him how he would die.

"There are always possibilities," he said.

The Borg homeworld was a blazing pyre, bringing light to a system that had been dark for a time too long to be measured.

Against that light, a tiny craft came about, its space-black hull catching just a glimmer of that fire, so that all the universe could know its name.

A name which had lived on other ships.

A name which would live on ships still to come.

Triumphant, victorious, in the new dawn's light, *Starship Enterprise* set course for home.

One voyage at an end.

The continuing mission far from over.

EPILOGUE

He fell. . . .

But this time, not alone.

The rocky face of El Capitan blurred past him.

The brilliant sun of Yosemite blazed down on him through the pure blue of Earth's own sky.

He shouted out his challenge to the world that raced to meet him.

He would not *die today.*

And then, as he knew it must, Spock's hand took his ankle in a grip of duranium and held the world—and death—at bay.

That night, by the campfire, three friends sharing shore leave together, McCoy had railed at him. "Human life is far too precious to risk on crazy stunts. Maybe it didn't cross that macho mind of yours, but you should have been killed when you fell off that mountain."

"It crossed my mind."

"And . . . ?"

"And . . . even as I fell, I knew I wouldn't die. Because the two of you were with me."

"I do not understand," Spock had said.

So the falling man had looked into his heart and spoken a

truth he had never shared. "I've always known . . . that I'll die alone."

That night, he stares up at the stars, knowing all their names, but still wanting to know more.

He hears the crackle of the dying fire. Breathes deeply of its fragrant smoke mingled with the green scent of pine and the richness of earth.

In this moment, the falling man once more is immersed in life, content to drift beneath those stars, on the planet of his birth, knowing that his ship waits above him for his return. That there are still many voyages left before the dream that haunts him becomes his final reality.

But then, from the shadows of the trees, a figure robed in white approaches and stands over him.

It is the figure from his dream.

The *dream.*

The figure from whom he has run all his life.

The falling man is troubled, knowing that in some way this *is the time in which his hunter will claim him.*

"Must I go?" he asks.

For the first time, the figure turns back his hood and holds out his hand.

"There will be time enough for rest, later," Sarek says. "But not here. Not now."

The falling man looks back at the campfire, at three friends resting peacefully beside it.

Spock and McCoy and . . . himself.

"You must leave them behind," Sarek says. "They cannot be with you."

"Why?" the falling man asks, bewildered that he does not remember how he came to this place in his past, though he has always known that it would be to this place and to this moment he would return. The moment when he first spoke of his dream with his friends.

"Sarek . . . why has it always been you in my dreams? Even before we met. Before I met your son. Before I left Earth . . . it

has always *been you who comes to take me from my friends and to my death."*

"Because of what we share," Sarek answers. "Or will share."

"My dream? Or my death?"

"As long as a single mind remembers, as long as a single heart still beats with passion, how can a dream die?"

"But what of the dreamer?"

Sarek smiles. "Look to the stars, James Kirk." He takes the falling man's hand as he has always taken his hand in this dream. Sarek's smile fades. "Avenge me."

And then, for the first time, the dream continued. Beyond the shadows.

There would be one last journey for him. One last voyage. One last mission.

And as he had always known he must, James T. Kirk turned his back on the past and rushed to embrace his future.

STAR TREK®
AVENGER

Three is a lucky number. This is the third of a trilogy of novels. And I also have three editors to whom I wish to dedicate this novel: Kevin Ryan, John Ordover, and Margaret Clark, members of the illustrious clan of Simon & Schuster. All good things come in threes. Now just to louse things up, the publisher has asked for another two novels. I've got to find me a couple of editors!

ACKNOWLEDGMENTS

Gar and Judy Reeves-Stevens deserve accolades,
not acknowledgments.
What would I have done without them?

PROLOGUE

Kirk knew it was over . . .

. . . in Yosemite. The rocky face of El Capitan blurring past him . . .

. . . on the Enterprise-*B. The bulkhead of the deflector room ripped away by the unfathomable power of the Nexus, pulling him into space . . .*

. . . on Veridian III. Plunging downward, twisting, in a tangle of torn metal as Picard defeated Tolian Soran . . .

. . . and on the Borg homeworld. The two captains of the Enterprise, *Kirk and Picard, each ready to throw the switch that would shut off all power to the collective's Central Node. The power feedback would be immediate. Whoever threw that switch would die.*

"It's my job to do it," Picard insisted. "You've done enough."

But Kirk's course was chosen. His body was being inexorably damaged from within by the Borg nanites that had reconstructed him and brought him back from that undiscovered country that lies beyond life.

"Jean-Luc," he said, "I'm dying." The nanites would see to that in less than a day.

But Picard would not be swayed. "Who isn't?"

Spock's voice crackled out of Kirk's comm badge. "Enterprise *to away team. We are at thirty seconds to emergency beam-out. What is your status?"*

Picard locked eyes with Kirk. Touched his own comm badge. "This is Picard, Enterprise. *Break off your approach. Repeat—"*

Kirk pushed Picard's hand away from his comm badge, hit his own.

"Ignore that last order, Spock. Bring that ship in."

"I am not leaving!" Picard said.

Kirk was about to shout back, when he suddenly stood down.

"Did you ever try to save the Kobayashi Maru *at the Academy?"*

Picard regarded Kirk with deep suspicion. "Yesss . . . But it can't be done. It's a no-win scenario designed for cadets."

Kirk smiled. "That's what they'd like you to believe. But there is a strategy that can win it. It's just that nobody in your time seems to do it anymore. Spock tells me it's a lost art now."

"Are you suggesting a compromise?"

Kirk thought it over. "You could call it that."

"Well," Picard said. "Go ahead. I'm always open to suggestions."

Kirk nodded. "Good."

Then he slugged Picard in the jaw as hard as he could.

Picard dropped like deadweight.

Kirk dragged Picard by his collar, until he was well away from the power conduit.

He pulled off his own comm badge, touched the front to activate it.

"Kirk to Enterprise,*" he said.*

"Spock here."

Kirk smiled.

He felt better already.

"Keep the ship out of danger, Mr. Spock." He studied the

Starfleet delta in his hand. Remembered when it had belonged only to the Enterprise. *But some things had to change. It was the way of the world. Of the universe.*

He was glad to have been part of it.

"Lock on to my signal," Kirk said. "One to beam up." Then he tossed his comm badge onto Picard's chest and stepped back.

Picard reacted to the impact of the badge. His eyes opened. He looked up. Started to speak.

Then dissolved in the transporter as the Enterprise *once more claimed her own.*

Kirk turned back to the power conduit. Grabbed the lever in both hands. Tested it once to see how much force he might need. Felt it move easily.

"A second chance," he said aloud.

Then he closed his eyes.

Squeezed his hands tight.

Pulled.

Heard a sudden, deafening roar of thunder coming from the dome.

Then a scrape as quiet as a footstep behind him.

Kirk turned.

Opened his eyes.

Saw the shimmer of an energy beam sweep across the floor like a searchlight. Whatever that beam touched glowed as if lit from within, then disappeared.

As if the shimmer were a transporter beam.

Or a phaser set to disintegrate.

The dome above him cracked open with an explosive blossom of energy.

Kirk felt the floor rise up beneath him.

Less than a heartbeat remained before the energy feedback that he had set in motion would destroy the Central Node.

There was no time for Spock's logic. No time for McCoy's emotion. There was only time for action.

And Kirk responded, even in what might be his last moment of existence.

He threw himself forward, dissolving in the beam as all around him was vaporized.

Whatever the beam's origins, whatever it was, Kirk was still alive. *Within it.*

Once more he fell.

From El Capitan . . .

From the Enterprise-*B . . .*

From the Veridian precipice . . .

Alone to his death.

As he had always known he must.

But without knowing why *he knew.*

Or how *he knew.*

Until now . . .

ONE

This was the first time.

When it had all begun.

When it hurt even to breathe the icy air of Tarsus IV.

Blinding snow swirled around him, glistening in the light of the planet's twin moons, covering his tracks as quickly as he made them. He was weak with hunger, shaking with fear and bitter cold as he fled into the darkness, knowing that he could not run forever.

This first time, he was thirteen years old. He was alone and the shadow was behind him. Running even faster.

There could be no doubt. Death pursued him. Relentless. Inescapable.

The boy lost his footing in the snow, slammed into the ice-prickled bark of a daggertree, thudded backward to the ground with a gasp of pain.

He lost his breath. Tasted blood from a sudden cut on his cheek.

Tears ran from his eyes.

His whole body ached with the cold, with frustration, with fear, more than any child, any man, anyone should bear.

Sprawled in the snow, the boy gave up, closed his eyes.

Saw the face of Kodos staring back at him. A face he would never forget.

. . . boy . . . keep running . . .

Jimmy Kirk's eyes flew open. He looked up, startled, expecting to stare into the glowing barrel of a laser rifle. Whoever had just whispered in his ear could only have been centimeters away.

But there was no one near him.

The boy struggled to his feet, convinced he was not alone. But all he saw was the stabbing shaft of light dancing through the dark silhouettes of the trees, coming from the handtorch of his pursuer.

. . . keep running . . .

The boy stumbled forward, sobbing. His toes burned with the cold in his frozen boots.

But he ran.

Eight thousand people had lived on this planet when he had arrived here.

It was a colony world. His parents had friends here. He was to spend a semester with them, then meet his father to travel back home. To Earth.

But the Romulans had done something in the Neutral Zone. His father's leave from Starfleet had been canceled. The shipping lanes closed.

And then the fungus struck.

It destroyed the grain. Poisoned the animals.

Four thousand people survived on Tarsus IV now.

Governor Kodos had killed the other four thousand to extend the food supply.

It was a "necessity," the governor had told those gathered by the open pits that would be their graves.

The boy still heard the lasers. The screams.

And still there was not enough food.

So thirteen-year-old Jimmy Kirk, with no parents to protect him, no ration book to feed him, no one to speak up for him, was selected for the second list.

Out of necessity, said the governor.

A beam of light flashed over him.

The boy almost fell, knowing he had been found.

But the near yet distant voice whispered once more . . . *keep running. . . .*

The boy wavered, confused. It was almost as if he were hearing someone else's thoughts.

A shaft of light locked on to him.

He tried to twist away, but it followed him.

He tensed, waiting for the searing pain of a laser, lost his footing, slipped in the ice and the snow, tumbling wildly, arms waving, screaming out for his father as he fell . . . alone—

—into two strong arms that caught him.

Saved him.

Then a caring voice spoke, calm, reassuring, soothing beyond any rational explanation. The same voice that had whispered to his mind now spoke to him in person.

"Let me help," that voice said, three words which would resonate in the boy's life forever.

The boy stopped struggling. He knew it wasn't Kodos who held him, nor one of the governor's men.

He looked around, suddenly realizing that his run through the woods had led him to the field where the landing pads were.

There was a new ship there, its outline barely visible through the blowing snow. But its viewports and loading bay were clearly defined by the blinding shafts of brilliant light that streamed from them, swirling snowflakes into streaks like stars seen from warp.

Silhouetted against that light, dark figures unloaded crates with antigravs.

Supplies. The colony was saved.

With relief greater than he could express, the boy looked up at the tall stranger who had caught him, half-expecting to see his own father.

"Are you from Starfleet?" the boy asked, his teeth chattering with the cold.

The stranger tugged back the hood of his parka.

The boy's gaze fixed on the points of the man's ears.

"You're a Vulcanian?" the boy stammered.

"I am Sarek," the Vulcan said. "And you are safe now."

For a moment, Jimmy Kirk almost believed him.

But then from behind, Kodos spoke: "The boy was a witness. He must die."

Jimmy Kirk twisted in Sarek's grip to see Kodos three meters away, laser rifle unslung, barrel glowing. There was a handtorch clipped to the rifle's sight. The boy squinted at its brightness.

But Sarek didn't turn away from the light. "No more will die," he said. "We were wrong."

Kodos raised his rifle. "What is it you are so fond of saying . . . ? About the needs of the many outweighing the needs of the few?"

Sarek kept his hand locked around the boy's wrist, to keep him close. At the same time, he stepped forward, placing his body as a shield between the boy and Kodos.

"The experiment must end," Sarek said. "The Romulan action was not anticipated."

"Not anticipated? That was the point of the lesson. Safeguards must be taken. They have to learn. The boy must die, like the others."

Kirk's eyes widened as Sarek drew a compact laser pistol and aimed it directly at Kodos. From the governor's reaction, the sight of a Vulcanian brandishing a weapon was as remarkable to Kodos as it was to the boy.

But Kodos did not lower his rifle.

"We will permit you to leave on our vessel," Sarek said.

"There are four thousand who know me back in the colony."

"We will provide you with a new identity, passage to a different sector."

"And what of the cause?" Kodos demanded.

The boy heard hesitation in Sarek's reply.

"It must be . . . reexamined."

"Vulcanians." Kodos frowned. "Your logic is a mask for your cowardice."

Sarek's arm was like duranium, his aim unmoved.

The boy leaned out from behind Sarek to stare at Kodos. The governor looked directly at him. "Even if I never see any of the colonists again, this boy's heard every word we've said about my leaving."

"He will not remember them."

The boy didn't like the sound of that. Neither did Kodos.

"And if he does?"

"Then I shall be at equal risk with you. Just as I am now."

For long moments, the boy shivered. Then Kodos turned off his rifle, removed the attached handtorch, and slung the rifle over his back. He directed the handtorch downward, at the ground. The shadows cast upward were unsettling to the boy. He did his best to ignore them.

Sarek returned his laser pistol to the folds of his parka.

Kodos moved threateningly close to Sarek, held up his hand in the Vulcanian salute.

"Live long and prosper." The governor's voice was heavy with sarcasm. He stared down at Jimmy Kirk. "If you ever speak about what you've seen here, boy, I'll know. And the Vulcanians can't protect you forever. Someday you'll be alone, and I promise you, that will be the day you *will* die."

Sarek pulled the boy closer. Somehow, at the Vulcanian's touch, Jimmy Kirk felt his unreasoning urge to run back into the woods begin to fade.

"Leave, Governor. We shall not meet again."

"For the sake of the cause, you had better hope you're right."

Then Kodos pushed past them, striding off toward the Vulcanian ship on the landing pad.

Jimmy Kirk stared after him, his shivering almost gone. But not his fear or his anger. "Why are you letting him go?"

Sarek looked down with eyes that seemed far older than the rest of him. "I have a son, only a few years older than you."

The boy never understood the way adults talked about children. What did the Vulcanian's answer have to do with his question? He struggled in Sarek's grip. "He's getting away! You're letting him get away!"

But Sarek's hold was unbreakable. "No one escapes his fate, young human. Neither Kodos. Nor I." Even to a thirteen-year-old whose knowledge of Vulcanians came primarily from schoolboy jokes, the sadness in Sarek's words was unmistakable.

"What about me?" the boy asked with all the bitterness of youth unjustly ignored.

Sarek bit the edge of a glove and tugged it off, baring his hand to the icy wind of Tarsus IV. "No one can know the future," he said.

Then, to the boy, it suddenly seemed as if the two of them were somewhere else, on a blistering desert, or in a quiet forest, or . . . The middle-aged Vulcanian seemed centuries old, sallow and shrunken.

Jimmy Kirk shook his head, clearing his mind of the strange images that had filled it. "I know my future," he said indignantly.

"Then let us share it," Sarek replied. He reached out to touch his fingers to precise points on the boy's face.

"What are you doing?" The boy was nervous. He had heard stories about Vulcanians and their strange mental powers. They could change shape, fly, even—

"Shh," Sarek whispered. "Your mind to my mind . . ."

The touch of the Vulcanian's fingertips was electric. The boy felt his body relax instantly, as if the Vulcanian had drained him of emotions.

For a few moments, he seemed to be observing images through someone else's eyes. He saw . . . the Plains of Gol? A red desert? Words came to him from another language, as if his thoughts were mixing with another's.

"Our minds are one," Sarek intoned.

The boy heard a whispered voice ask his name.

"We are one, James Kirk," Sarek said aloud.

Just then, the boy experienced, felt, saw an image of a Vulcanian boy, a teenager, sharp-featured, with a human woman at his side.

The teenager's unpronounceable Vulcanian name flashed into Jimmy Kirk's consciousness as he suddenly understood that Sarek and he had somehow merged their minds. That desert was on Vulcan! The teenager was Sarek's son! He was seeing through *Sarek's* eyes.

The boy was astounded, amazed, excited. Overwhelmed with alien thoughts and concepts. He wanted more. To see more. To *know* more.

But something held him back.

No, James Kirk, Sarek's thoughts whispered. *This meld is not for knowledge. This meld is to help you forget that which you should never have known.*

No, the boy thought.

Forget, Sarek commanded.

"Never," the boy said aloud.

But the struggle was unequal and the boy's last conscious memory of that night was Sarek reflecting on an unexpected discovery: *How like my son. . . .*

In his mind, in his memory, Kirk continued to fall from the Borg homeworld.

He wondered whose arms would save him this time.

TWO

It was not supposed to be this way.

Picard knew it.

He could sense the same frustration in each member of his bridge crew as the *Enterprise*-E screamed through space, all weapons systems locked on to a sister ship of the Federation. Of Starfleet.

The captain of the *Enterprise* gripped the arms of his command chair, willing himself to stay focused on his mission.

But he felt poised on the brink of a precipice, and at any moment he knew he would slip and fall and there would be no way back.

Not for anyone.

The *Enterprise* shuddered as Data banked the mighty *Sovereign*-class vessel to slip past an asteroid at better than five hundred kilometers per second—a fraction of the speed the ship was capable of achieving, but as fast as the asteroid belt of the Alta Vista system made practical.

The ship's deflectors nudged the asteroid aside, but the imperfect momentum exchange between starship and space rock made the internal dampeners lag, jarring the bridge crew to the side. Ever since the deflector array had been replaced, after Picard's last encounter with the Borg in Earth's twenty-first century, the navigational deflectors remained slightly, though maddeningly, out of phase.

The unsettling vibration that imbalance brought to the ship was a constant reminder to Picard of what all of Starfleet faced: the lack of resources to correct what should have been a simple problem.

The fleet was stretched too thin, and not even the genius of Chief Engineer La Forge could work miracles when he was denied the most basic supplies and replacement parts.

"Coming up on Alta Vista two five seven," Data announced.

Picard gave his order, knowing how useless it was. "Stand by on tractor beams." From the corner of his eye, he saw Will Riker turn in his first officer's chair.

"Using the tractor beams won't work," Riker said.

Picard felt his anger escape, unwanted, so close to being uncontrollable. "I am not prepared to fire on a Starfleet vessel."

Riker did not turn away from his commanding officer. "Captain Picard, we do not have a choice. The blockade *must* be held or . . ."

There was no need for Riker to finish.

Everyone knew what he meant. Picard's orders were clear.

"Or this will spread," Picard said.

On the viewscreen, the asteroid field dead ahead spun dizzyingly as Data rolled the *Enterprise* through a narrow gap between two irregular carbonaceous chunks of stone, each ten times the size of the ship.

Directly beyond them was the nickel-iron crescent of Alta Vista 257—the fifteen-kilometer-long asteroid behind which their quarry hid, her master no doubt hoping to be shielded from the *Enterprise*'s sensors.

Picard set the approach. "One-eighth impulse, Mr. Data.

Course change: bearing mark eight seven. I want to come in from the side."

Data's android fingers moved easily over the smooth control panels of the navigation console. "That is the longest way around, sir. There is a chance the *Bennett* will run again before we lock our tractor beam on her."

Picard felt an inexplicable wave of sadness come over him. At his left, Deanna Troi looked away from him, clearly sensing his emotions but not wishing to intrude upon them. As if there were anything she, or any of the others, could do.

"The *Bennett* will not run," Picard said. They were at the edge of the asteroid belt. There were no more hiding places left in the Alta Vista system. "She has nowhere else to go."

"Coming about on course change," Data said. His tone betrayed that he still had far to go in integrating his emotion chip with the rest of his personality programming, in order to keep some of his feelings to himself. It was obvious that the android did not believe his captain's assessment of the situation any more than Picard did.

For in truth, the commander of the *Bennett* did have one last option open, other than that of surrendering.

"Ready on tractor beam," Riker said.

Lieutenant Rolk acknowledged Riker's orders from her tactical station behind the command chairs. The blue-skinned Bolian security officer was a promising replacement for Worf: brusque, confident, inhumanly competent.

Data swung the ship about. "Coming up on target."

The pockmarked surface of the asteroid flew by the viewscreen.

"Asteroid horizon at eight hundred meters and . . . target acquired!"

The viewscreen flared as the blue glow of the *Enterprise*'s tractor beam shot out through space and locked on the *Bennett*—a *Fernandes*-class cruiser escort, named for one of the great admirals of the twenty-third century.

The viewscreen image instantly expanded to show the smaller vessel, an elongated disk half the size of the *Enterprise*-E's saucer section, with twin warp nacelles trailing from short, tapered pylons.

"We have her, sir," Rolk stated, but with so little conviction that Picard knew they would not have their quarry for long.

"Hailing frequencies," Picard ordered.

"She is releasing additional mines," Data said.

That was what the cruiser escort had done the last time the *Enterprise* had snared her, three hours earlier on the other side of the asteroid belt.

The spherical mines, each a meter across, had been jettisoned into the tractor beam, where they had been swiftly drawn toward the *Enterprise.* As Rolk had taken each out with a precision phaser hit, the resulting explosions had disrupted the beam enough for the *Bennett* to escape.

"Targeting mines," Rolk announced.

"Do not fire," Picard said. "Full power to forward shields."

"Sir," Data warned, "they are antimatter mines."

"And our shields are at one hundred percent," Picard said. Under these conditions, his new *Enterprise* could withstand multiple impacts with minimal damage. The *Bennett* would not escape him again.

Picard stood to address his unseen captive.

"This is Captain Jean-Luc Picard of the *Enterprise—*"

"First impact in two seconds," Data interrupted.

"—requesting contact with the commander of the *Bennett.*"

The viewscreen flashed white and the bridge shook as the first mine detonated against the forward shields.

"The *Bennett's* impulse engines are going to full power," Data said.

"Add auxiliary tractor beams," Picard ordered. "But watch

the *Bennett's* structural integrity. We don't want to crack her hull."

"Two more detonations—"

The jarring thunder of a double explosion echoed through the bridge, replaced by the rising whine of the straining tractor generators.

"—imminent," Data completed.

"Commander of the *Bennett,"* Picard said. "You cannot escape. Please, power down your engines and drop your shields for boarding."

Data turned in his chair to face Picard. "Captain, the *Bennett's* warp engines are powering up."

Riker stood up beside Picard. "He's in a tractor beam."

"Bennett acknowledge!" Picard urged. Other ships might attempt such a maneuver against a *Sovereign*-class vessel and survive, but not a cruiser escort. "If you attempt to go to warp while in our tractor beam, you will destroy yourself."

"Receiving a transmission from the *Bennett,"* Rolk announced.

"Onscreen," Picard said even as the bridge shook with the final cluster of mine impacts and the tractor beam's whine soared in response to the *Bennett's* continued impulse thrust.

When the viewscreen flickered to display the image from the *Bennett's* bridge, Picard's concern and frustration became shock and bewilderment.

How was this possible?

The master of the *Bennett,* the commander who had led the *Enterprise* on a near-suicidal chase and who now held his ship a hairsbreadth from destruction, was a *Vulcan*—young, male, and in a *Starfleet* uniform.

"Captain Picard, I request that you disengage your tractor beam and release my vessel."

The Vulcan's words were calm, unhurried, though every action he had taken this day had been tinged with reckless desperation.

"May I know who I am addressing?" Picard asked. At the very least, a Vulcan could be counted upon to negotiate, if not explain. And, even more important, to listen to logic.

"I am Stron," the Vulcan replied.

Picard read the pips on the Vulcan's collar. "Lieutenant Commander Stron," he began.

But the Vulcan would not let him finish.

"I have resigned my commission. I am no longer part of Starfleet."

"Perhaps you would care to reconsider," Picard said, feeling his way through this inexplicable situation. "Otherwise, you will be charged with the theft of a Starfleet vessel, instead of simply misusing it."

"I will not be charged with anything."

With the briefest of glances, Picard looked past Data's shoulders to check the status of the *Bennett.* Her impulse engines still warred against the *Enterprise*'s tractor beams. Her warp engines were online in standby mode. Picard again spoke. "I must warn you, sir, that as yet I fail to understand the logic of your actions."

The Vulcan's gaze was unwavering as he held up two fingers. "Attend me," he said.

A young human female, also in a Starfleet uniform with lieutenant-commander pips, stepped into the image area. She touched her two fingers to Stron's in a ritual Vulcan embrace between husband and wife. Picard estimated the young woman was six months pregnant.

"There are no prospects for the future in this system," Stron said, as if that explained everything.

"That can be corrected," Picard answered, hoping that what he said might someday be true. "But in the meantime, I must insist you and your family return to quarantine. We will escort you back to Gamow Station."

The Vulcan's mouth tensed in what Picard recognized from experience as a powerful display of emotion.

"The replicators are failing, Captain Picard. Gamow Station was designed to support fifty scientists for the study of solar inversions. It cannot support fourteen hundred refugees."

"We will provide additional supplies," Picard promised.

"How?" There was almost bitterness in Stron's tone. "You already off-loaded all your emergency supplies when you joined the blockade. You have not been resupplied since. No Starfleet vessel in this sector has."

Picard sighed. He hated arguing with Vulcans. "Stron, return to the outpost, submit to quarantine. It is the only way to survive."

"To return is to face certain death."

Picard spoke sharply. "If I let you go, you will spread death to whichever world you visit next."

"No!" Stron's eyes flashed with most un-Vulcanlike anger. "My mate and I have been through the transporter six times—each time with the biofilters set to finer resolution."

"The biofilters are ineffective," Picard said. "The virogen cannot be screened out by the transporter."

Onscreen, Stron and his mate appeared to exchange a worried look.

"Listen to reason, Stron. The finest minds in the Federation are working on this. There will be a solution soon. But we cannot risk spreading the contagion any further."

Stron's mate took Stron's hand in hers, squeezed tightly. It seemed to Picard that some unspoken signal had passed between them.

"I was a communications officer," Stron said, with full Vulcan reserve now returned to him. "I have intercepted and decoded every message Starfleet has sent to you in the past month."

"No. . . ." Picard knew the terrible projections the Vulcan had seen. Knew why they must still be kept classified.

"If we return to quarantine, we will die, Captain. Along with the rest of this sector."

"Stron! There *will* be a solution!"

Stron's mate placed her hand on her swollen stomach, closed her eyes.

"To return to quarantine is to give ourselves over to a painful death," Stron said evenly. "You will release us from your tractor beam, or we will die quickly. Either way, we will be free."

Picard knew conviction when he heard it. He turned to Deanna Troi. Eyes wide with concern, she nodded once, confirming his unspoken question. She could sense the Vulcan's emotional mood, and it was what Picard feared.

"I cannot release you," Picard said slowly, surprised by the strain betrayed in his voice.

"I am now preparing to go to warp," Stron replied.

"No," Picard said. "For the sake of your child, you must have hope for the future!"

Stron's eyes burned from the viewscreen.

"I have seen the future in your Starfleet communiqués. The Federation cannot hold. Hope is not logical."

Picard raised his hand as if he could reach through the viewscreen and save the—

Picard's bridge was caught in blinding light as the image on the screen instantly flicked to an exterior view of the *Bennett*'s destruction.

The *Enterprise* lurched violently forward as the mass she had been holding suddenly vanished, transformed into pure energy.

Red-alert sirens roared and sparks flew from an environmental station as a subspace concussion wave from the *Bennett*'s imploding warp drive slammed against the *Enterprise*'s shields along with the escort's debris.

Riker braced Picard as both stumbled.

"Stron attempted to go to warp," Data stated, quite unnecessarily.

Picard felt himself slip from the precipice as he heard Stron's calm voice whisper in his ear.

The Federation cannot hold.

Hope is not logical.

Picard knew it was not supposed to be this way.

But Stron had spoken the truth. The Federation was dying.

After more than two hundred years, that unprecedented assemblage of united worlds had finally met an enemy it could not overcome.

The Federation itself.

THREE

Eden was dying.

The stranger's boots trod through its ashes, following a path through the destruction and decay that had once been a city, when this world had been alive and the Federation had been secure.

The planet's name was Chal, a Klingon term for Heaven. Once, long ago, that was what this world had been.

It was a water world, on the farthest reaches of the long-disputed border between the Klingon and Romulan Empires. The children of those empires had settled this world. The *chalchaj 'qmey,* the Klingons had called them, the sky's offspring, the Children of Heaven.

For that is what they had been.

Descendants of the Klingons and the Romulans, genetically engineered for youth, and strength, and vigor, possessing the best attributes of both species, then enhanced further with transplanted tissue barbarically removed from living human captives.

They had been created at a time when interstellar war was thought to be inevitable. When the Klingon and Romulan leaders had feared the warmongering barbarians of the Federation would lay waste the worlds of the empires.

The Children of Heaven had been created to live on those war-ravaged planets, so that even if the empires should fall, their offspring could rise up against the Federation monsters and restore peace to the galaxy.

But as diplomatic relations improved between the Federation and the empires, the old stereotypes faded. Surprisingly, the soldiers of Starfleet turned out to be explorers, not babykillers. The warriors of *Qo'noS* placed honor above treachery. The Romulan senate did engage in public debate and comprehended the principles of compromise and cooperation.

Peace flourished—unsteady, uncertain, not always understood. But the arms-race mentality that had created the Children of Heaven faded from history. And left behind a paradise.

Eighty years ago, the stranger knew, the inhabitants of Chal had applied for membership in the Federation. Their world had been forgotten by the empires. They wished to chart their own future.

Though the Federation had responded favorably, certain rumors had to be dispelled. Chal was not a fountain of youth. The genetic vigor of her engineered inhabitants was solely theirs. It could not be shared by breathing the atmosphere or drinking the water.

Still, Chal prospered in the Federation's embrace.

Her legendary isles became a sought-after destination for those desiring respite from the pressures of interplanetary commerce. Cerulean blue waves lapped peacefully at sandy beaches. Soft breezes stirred tropical plants that blossomed with explosions of colors unknown on other worlds. The warmth of twin suns enriched its life. Her children thrived.

But that had been eighty years ago.

Now putrescent waves were choked with massive blooms of

algae. Dying sea creatures littered sand dunes stained by sludge and rotting alien kelp.

The verdant jungles of Chal had withered. Surviving leaves were stunted, obscured by the yellow and brown of decaying vegetation.

It had been more than a year since a flower had blossomed.

And what the collapse of nature had begun, human fear had accelerated.

Hundreds of light-years away, in the security of the Federation's Bureau of Disaster Relief, what had happened on Chal was now called the "evacuation difficulties."

The stranger walked through the aftermath of those difficulties.

Destroyed buildings. Torched hovercraft. The central transporter station little more than a blackened pit.

The only structures that appeared untouched in Chal's main city were those most recently erected by Starfleet's relief mission.

So it was to those structures the stranger went. To find the records of the past. To sift through the ashes of what once had been Eden.

Commander Christine MacDonald swore as the replicator control pad shorted out for the fifth time. The emitter of her molecular welding probe sparked an instant later, its nanotip exploding with a miniature sonic boom that echoed crisply against the stone walls of the supply depot.

"And that was the last isolinear on the planet," Engineer Barc grunted beside her. He snapped his tricorder shut and sat back on the floor, frowning at the smoke that curled up from the replicator's inner workings. His snout twitched in obvious displeasure at the acrid odor of burning insulation.

Christine pushed a lock of curly blond hair off her forehead, unaware of the soot streak her blackened fingers left behind. "That was probably the last isolinear in the sector," she sighed. Chal hadn't had a supply ship visit for almost two months. Overall, Starfleet was six months behind in her relief team's requisition requests.

"So what now?" Barc asked. He was a Tellarite, and Christine could tell from the way his fur was plastered to his snout that the oppressive heat of the main city was gaining on him.

"Why don't you go take a mud bath," she suggested.

Barc's beady black eyes widened for a moment; then he snuffled disconsolately. "Not enough water rations."

Christine pulled back and forth on her uniform tunic, trying to generate some sort of local breeze. Like most of the other Starfleet personnel on this mission, she had long ago given away almost all of her standard-issue clothing to the stricken citizens of Chal, including her sleeveless vests. To face the unrelenting heat of Chal's summer, she had then cut the arms off her uniform tunic. It wasn't regulation, but it helped. "Can't use seawater?" she asked.

Barc tapped a stubby hand against the side of his snout. "As bad as it smells to you humans, it's a hundred times worse to me."

Christine held out her hand and helped Barc to his feet. "If we can get this replicator working, we'll be able to turn out a hundred liters of fresh water a day."

"Rrr," Barc snarled. "And if my grandmother had *snargs* she'd be a *trasnik.* There're just no more parts."

"There're no more isolinear control chips," Christine corrected. She gazed up at the wooden beams of the tall ceiling, trying to reformulate the problem, to see it from a different point of view. "But what if we take two engineering tricorders and set them up to *simulate* a replicator control chip, as if we were running a diagnostic?"

Barc's snout twitched questioningly. "Tricorders aren't made to do that."

"What's that got to do with anything?"

The engineer sniffed the stale air thoughtfully. "I suppose if I increased the power supply . . . ran it through a type-two inverter . . ."

Christine smiled at the engineer. "You're a miracle worker, Barcs."

The Tellarite snorted in derision. "That's what you keep telling me." He waddled for the depot door—no more than a curtain of cloth to block the sun. "I'll be over at the shuttle pads, trying to talk someone out of a tricorder."

Christine smiled to herself. It was amazing what a little inspiration could do for her engineer. And without supplies, inspiration was just about all she had left to offer as commander of Starfleet's relief mission to Chal.

She turned back to the replicator, took a deep breath, then exhaled sharply, straight up, to keep her unruly hair off her forehead. There had to be something more she hadn't thought of. Some way to get the recalcitrant machine to work. She refused to accept defeat. She . . . realized the shuffle of Barc's boots had been replaced by a different set of footsteps.

Christine turned to see the stranger, surprised that he was so close. She decided he must have entered the depot just as Barc left. Either that, or he had walked in as silently as a ghost.

"This isn't a distribution center," she said, adopting a more formal, Starfleet manner. But even as she spoke she realized the stranger hadn't come for food or water. He didn't walk with the round-shouldered stoop of the people of Chal—people who had lived for a year in demoralizing despair. And he didn't wear local clothes. Instead, he was garbed in the simple tunic and cloak of a Vulcan trader—austere, unassuming, the garb of a pilgrim.

"I only want information," the stranger said.

Christine stopped thinking about the replicator and paid closer attention to the stranger. Everyone on Chal was exhausted. It was odd to hear such a measured, forceful voice again, especially coming from a human. If this had been the Academy and she had been an ensign, she would have been inspired to salute such a voice.

"What kind of information, Mister . . . ?"

Other than his beard, she couldn't discern his features, hidden as they were in his cloak's hood. Christine decided that under all those clothes, in this heat, he must be sweating like a . . . a Tellarite.

"There is a graveyard at the outskirts of town. At least, there used to be."

Christine folded her arms, fully aware that the stranger had sidestepped her question about his name. She was intrigued, and on guard. The last thing the people of Chal needed was some smooth-talking swindler offering a way off the planet.

"What about it?" she asked.

"At city hall, they said the maps were kept here."

"Maps? Of the graveyard?"

"A . . . friend lived here," the stranger said, and his voice, for a moment, lost its strength. "A long time ago."

Now Christine understood. Another victim of Chal's misfortunes, in search of his past. She nodded to a wide doorway in the stone wall behind her. "We've got a central library terminal still running in there. That should have what you need. Follow me."

She started toward the doorway, then paused as she saw the stranger apparently transfixed by the open access panel on the replicator. He was staring into its intricate jumble of wires, conduits, and circuitry.

It was such an unusual reaction that she suddenly had an idea.

"You wouldn't know anything about replicators, would you?" she asked.

The stranger snapped his head up, as if taken unawares. "No. Machines and I . . ." He started forward. "No. Nothing about replicators, I'm afraid."

Christine filed his reaction. She never wasted anything. But she decided the replicator's innards must have reminded him of something else. Something important, judging from his reaction.

The room in which the library terminal had been installed was windowless. It was one of the coolest locations in the depot. Christine enjoyed the sensation of the chilled air on her bare arms. She gestured to the chair in front of the terminal.

But the stranger held back. "Please," he said, motioning to the chair. "If you could."

Christine frowned at the stranger. A grown human uncertain about how to operate a computer? What planet had he come from? Literally.

But sensing his extreme reluctance, she set aside her curiosity and took her place in front of the terminal. "You can do most everything by talking to it."

"Thank you," the stranger said, leaving no doubt that he still wanted Christine to do the talking.

She cleared her throat. "Computer: Access burial records for Chal, main city . . . time period . . ." She looked back at the stranger. "When did your friend . . . you know?"

"I don't," the stranger said. "Sometime in the past . . . eighty years."

Christine passed the information on to the terminal. A stream of names flew by. She glanced over her shoulder. "The records are online. What was your friend's name?"

"Teilani," the stranger said, and instantly Christine knew his story.

Whoever the stranger was, whoever Teilani had been, they had been in love. Deeply. And then they had been separated by some tragedy that had kept him from her for almost a century. It was all there, all in the way he had said her name.

Christine turned back to the computer, overwhelmed by the emotions this traveler had nurtured for so long.

She called up a keyboard on a control surface and entered the name in multiple listings, spelling it phonetically in Romulan and Klingon script.

"Teilani," the computer said. "Searching."

Christine thought it odd that the computer even had time to add that statement. Fewer than a million people had lived on Chal in the past century. The search should have been instantaneous.

"Record not found," the computer announced.

"Are you sure she was from Chal?" Christine asked.

The stranger nodded.

"Search all population records for designated name," Christine said. Some Chal would have migrated. Perhaps the grave the stranger sought was on another world.

"Teilani: Speaker to the second Chal assembly. Federation delegate, 2293 to 2314."

The stranger stepped forward. Christine could sense his grief. "Yes," he said.

"Display location of grave."

"Speaker Teilani is not listed as deceased," the computer replied.

"Present location?" the stranger asked, his voice hesitant, as if not quite believing what he had just heard.

"Speaker Teilani is in Starfleet medical facility three, Chal, main city."

Christine caught her breath.

"She's alive . . ." the stranger whispered.

Christine reached out to take the stranger's hand, not knowing how to say what she knew she must.

Medical facility three was a hospice for the terminally ill.

If this Teilani, the love of this man's life, still lived, she was not expected to live for long.

FOUR

Babel had changed in the century since Spock had first come to it.

The neutral planetoid was now almost completely terraformed. Where once beneath oppressive metal domes the warmongers and peacemakers of an earlier age had met to shape the history of this small quadrant of the galaxy, now the diplomats and ambassadors who were their heirs could walk beneath open skies.

Spock wondered if the less fettered environment had an accompanying liberating effect on the treaties and the issues decided here. There was no logic to that concept. But then, in his 143 years of life, he had learned that logic seldom applied in politics.

It seldom applied to anything in which humans were concerned.

But as a long-lost friend had eventually taught him, that wasn't necessarily wrong.

Thus Spock turned his mind away from logic, and concentrated on the songs of the birds in the park before him. He stood on a sweeping, white stone balcony of the assembly hall, framed by fluted pillars, looking over the green, wind-riffled leaves of the arcadia trees. Some had been planted long ago, before artificial-gravity generators had been installed throughout the planetoid, and now towered tens of meters into the air. But their younger seedlings barely topped five meters, though their trunks were nearly twice as thick.

That adaptation pleased Spock's sense of aesthetics.

Both the younger and the older trees were of the same species, yet each had altered itself according to the conditions of its germination. The two generations were different, but apart from their exteriors, they were the same within.

Spock fingered the IDIC medallion he wore, meditating on Infinite Diversity in Infinite Combinations and on the sameness of things. The trees of Babel were a worthy lesson.

In time, he heard Srell's footsteps approach.

A century ago, awaiting someone who might be bringing news of such importance, Spock might have tried to judge that person's mood by the length and strength of his stride, and thereby deduce the information he brought.

But even at the age of thirty, Srell was an adept of the *Kolinahr.* Though it would be years before the young Vulcan would be permitted to undergo the final rituals of that discipline, in which his emotions would be purged in the pursuit of pure logic, Spock had no doubt of Srell's success. Whatever Surak, the father of Vulcan logic, had envisioned as the end result of his dream for his people, young Srell had surely achieved it. It was why Sarek, Spock's father, had chosen the promising student as his aide seven years ago, and why Srell continued in that role for Sarek's son. Spock knew of no finer mind on Vulcan. Therefore he made no attempt to interpret Srell's mood.

As the elder ambassador finished his meditation, Srell waited patiently at his side. Only when Spock had slipped his IDIC back into his robes did he address his young aide, still keeping his gaze on the colonnade of trees stretching out before him.

"I once stood on this balcony with my father."

"Indeed," Srell replied. Admirably, the young Vulcan did not seek to question Spock further.

"A Babel Conference had been held to consider the matter of Coridan's admission into the Federation."

"One hundred and six standard years ago," Srell said instantly. He was an excellent student of history. "I have studied Ambassador Sarek's speech from that session. It was most . . . unexpected."

Spock nodded. He had observed that session himself, heard his father hold forth on the fundamental nature of the Federation, the quest for peace in the face of war, the pursuit of perfection in the knowledge that perfection was never possible.

To hear a Vulcan speak in such illogical terms, soar so close to poetry in his oration, had electrified the assembled diplomats of that conference.

Tellarites had pounded their hairy fists on their tables.

Andorians had hissed with excitement, blue antennae quivering.

Sarek's speech indeed had been most unexpected.

Spock knew that his father had held each of his listeners captive by the power of his words, not emotions, raising his voice only to remind them all of the power of the universal ideals each representative held dear.

That day, Sarek had made Coridan the most important world in the galaxy, because it came to represent the Federation itself.

"This is the moment we have come to," Sarek had concluded that day. "Not to vote on the admission of one small world, worth nothing in the vastness of the space and the stars that surround us. But to say we do this thing not because it will make us stronger, not because it will diminish our foes, but because there is nothing else we can do if we are to be true to those great beings whose words have brought us here today."

Then Sarek had recited the preamble to the great charter of the Federation, and to all in that chamber on that day, it was as though they heard those stirring words for the first time.

Srell politely turned his gaze away from Spock as he said, "I have always been curious about Sarek's strategy in constructing that speech."

"In what way?"

Srell dipped his head a fraction of a millimeter in a perfectly crafted show of Vulcan emotion, letting Spock know that he apologized in advance for any unintentional offense he might cause with his next words. "It seemed so . . . emotional."

Spock straightened his robes. "Some of those who attended that session believed my father to be a passionate man."

Srell nodded thoughtfully. "Then his speech was not born of cynicism."

"I believe not," Spock said. "Though since his passing, we shall never know."

Srell regarded Spock with almost imperceptible puzzlement. "I would have thought that on this matter, he would have shared his mind with you."

Spock sighed, a human affectation that in his latter years he no longer strove to hide. The battle between his Vulcan and his human heritage had ended long ago. "I never melded with my father."

Though the young Vulcan's expression did not change, Spock could see that Srell was shocked speechless. For a father and son not to share a mindmeld was almost unheard of in Vulcan society. Though there was no logic to it, Spock did regret those missed opportunities to know his father's heart and mind.

True, he had shared fleeting glimpses into Sarek's thoughts. The legendary starship captain Jean-Luc Picard had once melded with Sarek when the *Enterprise* had conveyed the ambassador to Legara IV. Two years later, shortly after Sarek's death, Picard had invited Spock to meld with him and experience what Sarek had shared.

Spock had accepted the invitation. The encounter had been appreciated, but frustratingly incomplete. He had felt enmeshed in shadows, seeing only brief glimpses of his father's life. At the time, he had almost felt that Sarek had deliberately masked his thoughts from him, though that was, of course, completely illogical.

Still, the lingering doubts about Sarek's neglect to meld with his own son continued to gnaw at Spock, even to this day, five years after his father's death.

Srell seemed to sense Spock's discomfort in thinking about the past.

"Whatever the ambassador's motives, the speech was a success," the younger Vulcan said politely. "Coridan was admitted."

Spock allowed an edge of irony to color his tone. "To protect the planet's extensive dilithium reserves."

"It was a different time," Srell allowed. Dilithium crystals, so necessary for warp propulsion, had once been the fragile lifeblood of the interstellar community. But now they were easily recrystallized and thus abundant. Today, to start a war over dilithium would make no more sense than to fight over cometary ice. "Coridan's admission set a course for peace in its sector that still continues. The ambassador's accomplishment was most satisfactory."

In Vulcan terms, Srell's comments were gushing, almost fawning praise. But Spock allowed his aide the enthusiasm of youth. He almost found it refreshing.

"I regret I was not able to extend my father's legacy of reconciliation," Spock said.

Srell clearly understood Spock's comment, and that Spock's attention had returned to what had brought them both to Babel. "I suspected you would not need me to deliver the news."

"No," Spock agreed. "The result of the vote was that obvious." That was the curse of logic. Spock had always known that the first attempt to initiate official contact between Vulcans and Romulans would end in defeat. But at least the groundwork had been laid for further attempts. One of them would inevitably be successful. Eventually, Spock knew, even he would be permitted to take his place in the official negotiations, instead of having to rely on the presence of his aide, in order to spare the Federation official embarrassment caused by Spock's unsanctioned attempts to broker peace.

But Srell's next comment exploded Spock's line of reasoning. "Actually, Ambassador, there was no vote."

Spock put a steadying hand on the cool white stone of the balcony railing. "Is the advisory group aware of the danger the Romulan delegation has risked to come to Babel?" The Romulan Star Empire had few official contacts with the Federation. Even fewer with Vulcan. But for more than eighty years, Spock had been working unceasingly to bring the Romulans and the Vulcans together—*back* together. For the Romulans were an offshoot from the Vulcan race. The unification of Romulans and Vulcans had become Spock's greatest dream, and, he was convinced, a political necessity, if lasting peace was to be possible in this quadrant.

"Ambassador, the advisory group is well aware of the extraordinary efforts you have made to bring an unofficial Romulan delegation to Babel. On the surface, it is a historic accomplishment."

Spock heard the qualification. "On the surface?"

Srell adopted an even more formal posture to indicate he

was merely passing on information he had been given, without necessarily believing it himself.

"I have been informed that there are those on the Council who believe the stated reason for the Romulans' presence here is misdirection. They do not believe Romulus wishes to pursue either unification with Vulcan or membership in the Federation."

Spock tightened his grip on the balcony railing. What did the Federation Council believe he had been doing on Romulus for the past eight decades? Everything he had worked for had been aimed at this moment—to finally have representatives of Vulcan, Romulus, and the Federation sit down at the same table, however unofficially, to openly discuss their joint future.

"What other reason could there be?" Spock asked.

"The virogen."

Spock turned away. He placed *both* hands on the balcony railing. "That is"—a dozen Earth terms sprang to mind, but Spock restrained himself in order to be a proper role model for Srell—"most illogical."

"Though the news is being withheld from the public updates, I have been reliably informed that the virogen has now spread to a seventh system," Srell said. "Fully one-third of the most densely populated sectors of the Federation have been cut off from regular food shipments. Starfleet relief efforts are undeniably strained."

"One-third," Spock said, almost in disbelief.

"The advisory group believes that the Romulan delegation's sole purpose in being here is to obtain aid guarantees in the event the Empire's own food-production centers become infected. Indeed, Starfleet intelligence suggests that the virogen has already established itself in the Core sectors, and even in the Klingon Empire."

"How is that possible?"

Srell ignored the question. The details of the virogen's spread from system to system were the target of the greatest scientific research effort in the Federation's history. "For whatever reason, I have been informed that the Federation is unwilling to support Vulcan trade and development guarantees for the Romulan Star Empire at a time when its own resources are so taxed."

Spock turned back to Srell, using all his discipline to keep an appropriate Vulcan demeanor. "Can they not see that it is precisely because of the threat of the virogen to the food supply that we *must* enlarge the scope of the Federation? That we are *all* threatened and must share resources and knowledge to survive?"

"Ambassador, you ask that question as if you expect the Federation Council to be guided by logic. They are not. At this time, their guiding principle is fear."

Spock felt unjustly chastised by his young assistant. Had he not just been contemplating the fact that politics and logic seldom agreed? Had he not achieved a balance between his human and his Vulcan halves, so that he was uniquely placed to understand the motivations of both Vulcans and humans? And yet, he had been completely unprepared for this turn of events.

"Fear," was all Spock could say. More than three centuries had passed since Vulcans had first joined with humans in an unprecedented partnership to explore strange new worlds, to seek out new life and new civilizations. But that insidious monster of the past—fear of the unknown—still threatened to push all that they had accomplished back into the planetary mud.

Then Srell added to Spock's sense of disorientation. "For humans, it is a logical reaction."

"Fear . . . is logical?" Spock asked.

"If quarantine fails, if one more system becomes exposed to the virogen, Starfleet will not be able to respond. History suggests that if Starfleet fails in its mission to protect our food supply from contamination, some beleaguered worlds will secede from the Federation. In some systems, local resource wars will inevitably result. Any one of a dozen local conflicts could escalate dangerously."

The human half of Spock could not comprehend Srell's equanimity as the young Vulcan blandly recited the events that would lead to galactic anarchy. Even a Vulcan should have been appalled at some level by this terrible scenario.

"Multisector civil war is not out of the question," Srell continued. "Especially if any of the Federation's rivals, such as the Romulans, decide to encourage dissent through covert means."

Spock turned his mind back to the calming practices he had learned during his own study of the *Kolinahr.* "You realize you are describing the collapse of the Federation," Spock said.

Completely without emotion, Srell replied, "Unless a cure for the virogen is found and the food supply protected, the collapse of the Federation is a certainty."

Spock reached into his robes for his medallion. But it brought no comfort to him.

Here where he had once shared his father's greatest success, he was poised on the brink of his own greatest failure.

Logic was no guide. Emotion only paralyzed him.

He needed to take action.

But he missed the long-lost friend who could tell him what that action should be.

FIVE

Christine MacDonald stood in the doorway of the hospice, watching the reaction of the stranger beside her. He had seen death before, Christine concluded. Too much of it. Or else he was like Christine, and even one death was too much.

Christine led the stranger along the narrow pathway that ran between the cots on which the dying patients lay. The smell of disinfectant was strong, because there were not enough medical exclusion field generators to go around. The few the mission had that still worked were being used in the nursery. If a child of Chal could survive the first round of virogen poisoning, there was a chance he or she could recover. But once the poisoning had progressed to the secondary stage, as it had in the patients in the hospice, little could be done.

Christine looked to both sides of the pathway as she headed for the doctor's office—a curtained corner in the large room. Before the evacuation, this building had been an art gallery—a large open space with spectacular skylights with holographic windows that kept the sunslight always focused in the center of the gallery. But the skylights had been shuttered to spare the sensitive eyes of the dying. Glow strips hung on the walls now, leaving the gallery's interior in a perpetual twilight, like the fading lives it contained.

Christine rapped her knuckles against the wooden beam that formed a corner of the doctor's office. "Hey, Bones—you in there?"

Christine caught the stranger's reaction of surprise—something to do with her affectionate nickname for the doctor, she decided.

"Keep your shirt on," M'Benga testily replied.

The curtain tugged back and Dr. Andrea M'Benga stepped out, medical tricorder in hand. The sleeves were cut from her blue-shouldered jumpsuit as well, and she wore a bandana of fragile white Chal fabric tied firmly around her broad forehead. The pale cloth contrasted strikingly with her dark skin and close-cropped black hair. She looked sharply at the stranger, then seemed to relax. "Well, you're not a patient, at least." Christine was unable to interpret the expression on the stranger's face as he scrutinized the doctor in turn.

Christine smiled encouragingly at the stranger. "Dr. Andrea M'Benga, this is . . ."

"Dr. . . . M'Benga." A quizzical smile flickered on the stranger's lips. "I'm looking for a patient. Her name is Teilani."

Christine's eyes narrowed. The stranger seemed determined not to give his name.

"Teilani," M'Benga said as she wearily scratched her head. "Yeah. Over in the far corner. You a relative?"

"A friend," the stranger said. "I'd like to see her."

"You understand what's happening here, do you?" the doctor asked.

The stranger gazed into the darkened corner M'Benga had pointed to. "Something's gone wrong."

Christine didn't know if the stranger was being profound or was simple.

M'Benga exchanged a look with Christine. Christine

shrugged. "I'll say something's gone wrong," the doctor muttered. "That damned virogen hit. Went clear through the food chain in less than a month. Humans, Tellarites, most carbon-based life-forms, they get a taste of it and they double over for a week. Intestinal flora shot to hell. But recovery's just a matter of plenty of liquids, salt and sugar to restore electrolyte balance, and—"

"I'd like to see her," the stranger said again, obviously not interested in the doctor's lecture.

"Look, the point is, the Chal aren't like most people. Their genetic structure is artificial in places. Most common medical therapies don't work on them. Protoplasers can't rearrange their tissue, they metabolize drugs before the drugs can help them . . ." Christine could see that M'Benga realized she wasn't getting through to the stranger. "The thing is, your friend's dying, and there's nothing I can do to save her. Understand?"

"Which bed?" the stranger asked.

M'Benga gave up. "This way." She led Christine and the stranger away from her office, along the back wall.

Teilani was in the far corner. Christine had seen enough Chal succumb to the virogen that she could tell the woman had less than a day to live. Once, she had undoubtedly had great beauty, with elegant, pointed Romulan ears and aristocratic Klingon ridges furrowing her brow, but now disease and age had blurred and diminished her.

In human terms, judging strictly by appearance, Christine would place her age at fifty, which for a Chal could make her almost one hundred and twenty-five. But the wasting of the virogen had reduced her honey-golden skin to a patchwork of broken capillaries and purple bruises, shrunken tight to her fine-boned skull. A sterile pad was taped to her sunken cheek, no doubt to cover an open sore, common in the final stages of the virogen reaction. It extended over one eye and Christine guessed she had probably lost some of her sight already.

She knew that she was looking at what had once been a vibrant being, and at the future of every human who would someday succumb to the inevitable destruction of time and fortune. But in the stranger's eyes, there was no revulsion, no pity, and no fear.

Christine watched as the stranger knelt by Teilani's cot and softly stroked her brow, as if this place were still an art gallery and Teilani was the most precious and most beautiful work in it.

The woman's eyes fluttered at the touch, but she did not awaken.

Beside Christine, M'Benga surreptitiously checked her tricorder. Christine's eyes met hers. The doctor shook her head. Time was running out.

"I need hot water," the stranger said, never taking his eyes off Teilani.

"Her liquid balance is fine," M'Benga said gruffly. "We're on strict rations."

The stranger turned to look up at the doctor. "Hot water. Boiling. A single cup."

Christine blinked at the intensity of the stranger's tone.

M'Benga started to protest.

But Christine put a hand on the doctor's shoulder. "It's all right, Bones. Take it from my allotment."

M'Benga's eyes flashed at Christine. The doctor's temper did not welcome opposition. "I hope you know what you're doing."

Christine nodded. M'Benga went to the supply room.

The stranger smoothed out the woman's blanket, adjusted her pillow. Then carefully and deliberately touched several points on her neck, forehead, and exposed cheek.

Christine's attention sharpened. Some of the locations corresponded to Vulcan *katra* points. If she hadn't heard the emotion in his voice, she'd suspect the stranger had pointed ears hidden beneath the hood of his cloak.

"Are you a healer?" she asked.

But the stranger shook his head, as if to dismiss her continued presence as well as her question. He was intent only on the woman who lay dying on the cot.

"Is there anything else I can do?"

The stranger spoke without looking at Christine. "You've done enough."

"No," she said, and she knelt beside him. "Let me help."

The stranger paused, as if she had said something remarkable. Then he looked around, spotted something under the cot, and pulled it out.

Whatever it was, it was heavy, wrapped in Chal fabric. The stranger handed it to Christine, having her hold it as if it were a tray.

Beneath the fabric, Christine could feel a metal plaque of some sort, thirty-five centimeters by twenty-five, a centimeter thick. It was most likely a decorative plate or something similar that had held special meaning for the woman.

The stranger produced a small earthen cup from within his cloak, then a small packet made of some type of . . . paper, Christine reasoned. It crackled like paper, at least.

The stranger unfolded it. Within was a small pile of crumbled brown leaves.

"Is that tea?" Christine asked.

"Of a sort," the stranger replied.

M'Benga returned with a flask of water. The stranger held out the cup to her. The doctor twisted the heater collar on the flask and poured out a stream of boiling water.

The stranger powdered the leaves between his fingers as he dropped them into the water, rocking the cup gently to stir its contents.

Instantly the air filled with a rich green scent. Christine was almost overwhelmed by its fragrance. She had smelled the decay of Chal for so long, she had almost forgotten there were any other scents in the universe.

"Could you at least tell me what that is before you give it to my patient?" M'Benga asked in exasperation.

"What's your prognosis for her?"

M'Benga spoke plainly. "Terminal."

"Then what does it matter?"

He turned to the woman on the cot, gently lifted her head, and carefully let the tea he had brewed trickle onto her lips.

M'Benga sighed heavily and brought out her tricorder again. She waved it over the remnants of the paper packet on the tray Christine held. Then blinked at the readings on the device as if she couldn't interpret them.

"What is it, Bones?" Christine whispered.

"Damned if I know."

M'Benga aimed her tricorder at Teilani. Shook her head again at Christine.

"I'd like to take her from this place," the stranger said.

But M'Benga would have no part of it. "No. I will not have you disturbing my patient."

Teilani moaned. The first sound she had made. Her eyes fluttered again.

The stranger leaned closer to her, touched her *katra* points again.

M'Benga activated her tricorder. Christine saw the doctor's eyes widen. "I don't believe it. . . ."

The stranger stood up by the cot, nodded at the doctor. "I believe she's my patient now." Then he gathered Teilani in his arms, and lifted her from the cot as if she were sweeter to him than life itself.

Christine got to her feet in time to see Teilani's eyes open and turn to focus on the stranger.

Then Teilani smiled, in wonder and in disbelief. Her voice was faint. "James . . . you came back. . . ."

The stranger walked from the hospice, carrying Teilani in his arms. Christine and M'Benga watched him go. The doctor tapped the side of her tricorder to be sure it was working properly. "Her pulse rate is strengthening. Her fever is dropping." She lifted the packet from the fabric-wrapped tray Christine carried and sniffed at it suspiciously.

"James," Christine repeated thoughtfully. At least the stranger had a name now. A human one at that.

She looked down at the makeshift, shrouded tray, then began to unwrap the fabric from it. As she got to the last layer, she could feel that there were letters on the metal object inside. It was some type of plaque.

"Well," M'Benga complained beside her. "What the devil is that thing?"

The fabric slipped to the floor as Christine turned the plaque over to read what was written on it.

She gasped.

In raised and polished letters of bronze, almost glowing in the pale light, were the words

USS ENTERPRISE

STARFLEET REGISTRY NCC-1701-A
SAN FRANCISCO FLEET YARDS, EARTH
COMMISSIONED: STARDATE 8442.5
SECOND STARSHIP TO BEAR THE NAME

". . . to boldly go where no man has gone before."

Christine and M'Benga both turned to stare at the distant entrance to the hospice, just as the stranger disappeared through it, with Teilani in his arms.

"James . . ." Christine said again. For the second time that day, she felt goose bumps rise up on the skin of her bare arms. And not because the air was cool.

It was impossible.

But then, that's just what *he* was known for.

SIX

Picard stared at the empty corner of his ready room.

The original plans for the *Enterprise*-E had called for an environmental unit to be placed there. Some captains chose to install a sleeping perch for a cat, some a terrarium for more exotic life-forms. The designers responsible for the life-support sections of the starship had checked Picard's service records and had specified a cylindrical aquarium, with an Earth-normal saltwater environment that would support an Australian lionfish.

But when Picard had first stepped into the ready room, after the bridge module had been installed, he had immediately asked for the aquarium's removal.

He had come to the realization that space was too unforgiving an environment for innocent life-forms.

Picard had reviewed the sensor logs of the evacuation of the *Enterprise*-D over Veridian III. He had heard the children cry out as they had been herded along, separated from their parents, only minutes away from being engulfed by the explosive fury of a warp-core breach, and still to face the harrowing descent of the saucer through the atmosphere.

Those cries of terror were not what Starfleet's mission

planners had had in mind when the *Galaxy*-class ship had been commissioned.

Picard had no complaint about families being assigned to deep space together. But children and nonprofessionals must always remain out of harm's way.

So he felt reassured that this *Enterprise* had no children aboard her. And though he missed the relaxing comfort of watching the fins of a lionfish undulate in an aquarium's slow current, he was glad that on this ship there was one life-form fewer for which he was responsible.

When he had first gone into space, it seemed to him he had seen only the brilliance of the stars. But now, more than ever, he saw the dark and endless void between them.

The door announcer chimed. "Come," Picard said.

His first officer entered, frowning, a padd in his hand.

"Yes, Number One?"

Riker didn't waste any time. He didn't like the *Enterprise's* current assignment any more than Picard did. That tension was becoming more apparent in all the crew.

"There was no Lieutenant Commander Stron assigned to Gamow Station."

It took a moment for the importance of that statement to register with Picard.

"Was he from one of the other blockade ships?" Picard asked.

Riker shook his head. "I checked every personnel log remotely connected to Alta Vista. There was no Stron assigned to any of the earlier relief missions. No Stron assigned to communications since the station was brought online three years ago." Riker passed the padd across the table to Picard. "In all of Starfleet, there are nine Vulcans with Stron as a given name. The only one within three hundred light-years of this sector is a Captain Stron of the survey ship *Sloane.* And he's one hundred and sixty years old."

"Are the remaining eight Strons accounted for?"

Riker nodded at the padd. Picard scanned it. The duty rosters for all nine Vulcans were complete.

"I confess I'm not certain which surprises me more. The fact that a Vulcan chose to commit suicide, or the fact that a Vulcan lied."

"Given either possibility, sir, we really can't be sure if he was a Vulcan in the first place."

"Is there any record of a pregnant lieutenant commander?"

"Several. But again, none near this sector. None missing. And none matching our sensor-log recording."

Picard stood up and walked to an observation window, staring past his reflection. Almost half a million kilometers away, Alta Vista III was a small, faded yellow sphere, streaked by indigo clouds. A year ago, the clouds had been spectacularly green—fine, airborne colonies of alta mist, a unique epiphytic single-cell plant. But the deadly virogen had taken hold here, as it had in six other systems.

Wherever it had evolved, however it had come to the worlds of the Federation, seen in microscan images the virogen was deceptively simple, even beautiful. Physically, it was a strand of ribonucleic acids, coiled into a single-helix structure, only a few thousand amino-acid base pairs long. By most traditional definitions, it was rightly considered a mere molecule, with far too little material to qualify as living matter. On its own, it was inert, its fragile RNA chain protected by a unique and rigid matching strand of silicon. Though the genetic structure of the virogen was technically exposed in this configuration, without the benefit of a protective wall or capsule, the rigid silicon served as a molecular spine to maintain the virogen's shape and lethality.

In an animal, the virogen's genetic material curiously bonded only to the membranes of reproducing cells, and multiplied as affected cells multiplied, without ever interfering with the cells' own interior genetic structure. Thus, animals served only as factories for the virogen's production, shedding it through exhalations and secretions, all without long-lasting physical impairment in most species.

But in chlorophyll-producing plants, the virogen bonded with the chloroplasts themselves, taking over the plants' own energy-producing mechanisms to fuel its reproduction. Unlike its effects on animals, the virogen's reproduction strategy led to a slow death for each affected plant, as it gradually lost the ability to convert sunlight into energy.

Thus the virogen's effect on Alta Vista III had been no different than it had been in all the other systems it had pervaded. Every form of plant life had been poisoned—become useless as a source of food. Every form of animal life, though largely unaffected by disease, was a carrier. The repercussions for the centers of food production were staggering.

"Why would a Vulcan—or someone altered to appear Vulcan—take on the identity of a Starfleet officer to escape from a quarantined system?"

"And then kill himself and his mate when we cornered him?" Riker added.

Picard turned to face Riker. Riker looked puzzled by the slight smile his captain wore. "Number One, this almost feels like a Dixon Hill mystery."

"Except this isn't the holodeck. Two people are dead."

"Dix would be the first to say appearances can be deceiving."

Riker waited expectantly, if doubtfully.

"If everything Stron told us was a lie, then logically we should not assume that any of his actions were what they appeared to be, either."

"Sir, the *Bennett* took off from Gamow Station without authorization. Stron and his mate were down there. They were clearly attempting to leave the system."

"No. They were attempting to leave the planet and *evade*

us. That's all we can know for fact. What their ultimate destination was, we cannot say."

"Except we know they didn't achieve it."

But Picard shook his head. "Stron and his mate somehow arrived at Gamow Station without anyone discovering they weren't what they claimed to be. In the confusion of the overcrowding down there, that is an understandable, even unavoidable breach of security. But however they managed it, I think we can presume our two fugitives had an equally effective escape route planned."

"Sir, we saw them blow up. That is not what I would call effective."

"What we saw was a warp-core explosion at the same apparent coordinates as the *Bennett.* Then we left the asteroid and returned to our blockade position."

Picard could see that Riker understood where his chain of reasoning was leading.

"Shall I lay in a course back to Alta Vista two five seven?" Riker asked.

Picard nodded. "And prepare an away team," he added.

Riker returned to the bridge. Picard looked back through the observation port again. Less than a minute later, Alta Vista III shrank to a pinpoint as the *Enterprise*-E returned to the system's asteroid belt at warp.

Unfounded suspicions aside, Picard had no idea what they would find there. But the act of looking was far preferable to standing guard over a dying colony.

If the Federation were going to fall, then the captain of the *Enterprise* was determined to go down doing something more than just watching.

Riker felt a wash of vertigo sweep through him as he materialized on the surface of Alta Vista 257. Transporting from the *Enterprise's* artificial gravity to the almost nonexistent pull of the asteroid was more disorienting than simply stepping through an airlock.

The clear visor of his environment suit sparkled with reflected energy as La Forge and Data took form beside him. Simply turning his head to check on their status was enough to set Riker drifting up from the asteroid's space-black surface.

Riker canceled his momentum by giving a momentary tap to the joystick on the control arm of the maneuvering unit he wore. He saw La Forge do the same, with small, precisely controlled puffs of stabiline gas venting from the tiny thrusters on the engineer's own maneuvering unit backpack.

Data, though deceptively slight in appearance, was much more massive than a human, and capable of controlling his movements more exactly. Thus, he alone remained fixed in position on the asteroid's surface. At least, at first. The android reached down to the leg controls for his magnetic boots, and though Riker saw the activation lights switch on, even Data began to float away from the surface.

Data's boot soles, however, bristled with nickel-iron dust.

"There are too many impurities for our boots to function properly," Data said over his suit's communicator as he repositioned himself with his own maneuvering unit. Technically, the android did not need an environmental suit to function in the vacuum of space. But he did have a number of organic components in his system whose chemistry could be temporarily disrupted by prolonged outgassing, and it was more convenient for his coworkers if he could communicate by voice.

"Well, it's not as if we can drift too far off target," Riker said. He glanced through the upper plane of his visor and saw a magnificent view of the *Enterprise* stationkeeping only a few kilometers above him, relatively speaking. "Riker to *Enterprise*. We've arrived at the center of the blast zone."

Picard's voice answered from Riker's helmet speakers. "Do the blast marks appear legitimate?"

Riker glanced around. The *Bennett* had exploded directly overhead, approximately one kilometer above the asteroid's surface. The surface around the away team was striated with raised silvery streaks, all radiating out from a central point. Riker knew the markings were the result of microscopic pieces of wreckage from the *Bennett* hitting the nickel-iron asteroid at close to lightspeed. The kinetic energy of the tiny particles had been sufficient to gouge molten tracks in the raw metal of which the asteroid was formed.

To Riker's trained eye, just as the *Enterprise*'s sensors and viewscreen had initially confirmed, the blast marks did appear to be recent, and consistent with the *Bennett*'s destruction. But despite all the *Enterprise*'s sophisticated equipment, in some cases there was still no replacement for the human presence in space as skilled observer. Or, in the case of Geordi La Forge, a more than human presence.

La Forge manipulated his maneuvering unit controls so that he floated horizontally, only centimeters above the asteroid's surface. Riker knew the engineer's new ocular implants were scanning the blast damage with much finer resolution than the *Enterprise*'s more powerful sensors could be tuned to at a distance.

"Commander," La Forge said. "I'm detecting no trace of space-dust precipitate on the melted impact streaks. These scorches *are* less than a day old. I'm certain of it."

Riker refrained from shrugging. In his suit, it would only disturb his orientation again. "Captain Picard," he reported, being careful to keep his tone neutral. "The *Bennett* does appear to have exploded as we witnessed."

Picard had proposed that the *Bennett* might have used a phase inhibitor to escape the tractor beam, then gone to warp, leaving a second, separate warp core behind, rigged to explode. There was an unexplained subspace burst in the sensor log, followed by a recording gap as the *Enterprise*'s sensors had been overloaded by the warp explosion. It was possible that the deception might have been completed before the sensors had automatically realigned themselves. But being possible and being likely were two different things.

Privately, Riker suspected that Picard was looking for any excuse to relieve the monotony of and his distaste for maintaining a blockade on a Starfleet facility. In fact, he was almost sorry his captain's theory had been proven false. Riker agreed with Picard that the *Enterprise* and her crew were meant for more challenging missions.

"What about organic residue?" Picard asked. If the *Bennett* had exploded, Stron and his mate would have been vaporized, and traces of the carbon isotopes from their bodies should be spread evenly throughout the blast site. Detecting that grisly residue was Data's task.

Like La Forge, Data floated near the asteroid's surface, lightly tapping a molecular probe to likely areas and reading the results from the tricorder display screen built into the bottom of his helmet. "The isotope traces I'm detecting are consistent with machinery only," the android said. "I see no sign of organic remains."

That surprised Riker. "Are you certain?" he asked, forgetting for the moment to whom he was speaking.

"To four decimal places, sir. Which leaves room for some doubt, though not an appreciable amount. In fact, it might be said that—"

"Data," Riker interrupted, as he suddenly recollected another of Picard's speculations. "What if Stron wasn't Vulcan and his mate wasn't human? What if they were altered Klingons or Romulans?"

Data slowly rotated into a perpendicular orientation. "In that case," the android said, "the carbon isotopes of their bodies would indeed yield different fractions, according to the signature chemistries of the worlds each species evolved on. But almost any carbon-based life-form would leave a detectable trace as the captain has theorized."

Over the comm link, Picard joined the conversation again. "In other words, Mr. Data, though the *Bennett* might have exploded as we saw, Stron and his mate were not on it."

"Yes, sir. That is the most likely explanation."

More than anything, Riker wanted to scratch at his beard. But he had to content himself with gazing over the irregular horizon of the asteroid. On the axis length, the horizon was about eight kilometers distant. On the equatorial length, only about three. But aside from the gentle rise and fall of a surface pitted with millennia of deeply shadowed impact craters, there was no sign of a pressure dome or launch facility. Besides, if there had been, the *Enterprise* could have detected either from thousands of kilometers away, along with the machines associated with any underground base.

"Comments, Number One?" Picard asked.

Riker knew he had no choice but to support his captain. Picard had put his suppositions to the test and they had been confirmed. "No doubt about it. We definitely have a mystery here, sir."

"Actually, Commander," Picard replied, "we have two."

For a moment, the implications of Picard's words were like the chill of space moving through the insulating layers of Riker's suit. Could Picard be serious? "Are you suggesting that what happened here is connected to the spread of the virogen?"

In his mind's eye, Riker could almost see Picard settle back into the command chair on the *Enterprise*'s bridge as he contemplated the challenge of a new mission. "Two mysteries in one area of space, Number One? Every instinct I have tells me that the relationship between them is not coincidental."

Riker was aware of La Forge and Data adjusting their positions so they could make eye contact with him. Even in

Data's android features, the emotion of surprise was easy to read.

Picard was not the only one in Starfleet who had theorized that the sudden appearance and spread of the virogen might be deliberate.

But it appeared he might be the first to uncover evidence to prove it.

And if Picard was right again, then the greatest natural disaster facing the Federation might not be natural at all.

SEVEN

Dawn came to Chal. A lone bird sang in the dying jungle. Faintly, plaintively. Alone.

It was the last of its species. The generation to come lost to weakened eggshells that exposed the nestlings to the air before their lungs had fully formed.

The pitiful chicks had perished in their nests, suffocating within an hour of birth, watched passively by their parents, who had never evolved behaviors necessary to cope with the interference of so-called intelligent beings.

When the virogen had first appeared on this world, the first response by the guardians of the environment had been to clear-cut the affected foliage and spray broad-spectrum antiviral agents on the surrounding areas. The results were catastrophic.

The antiviral agents had unpredictably inserted five engineered genes into an amino-acid sequence peculiar to a common flowering bush indigenous to Chal. The combination accelerated the flowering cycle, making whole fields of the plant bloom months before the insect responsible for its pollination had awakened from its dormant cycle.

Three months later, the berry yield on Chal's primary

islands was less than twenty-two percent of normal. Entire populations of birds and insects starved to death. With their passing, the absence of food rippled exponentially through the food chain, becoming more pronounced at every level.

One species of bird resorted to cannibalism of its young. Another was driven to forage among mountain plants far out of its local habitat. That change in behavior exposed the species to a high-altitude, parasitic mite that infested its plumage. Mating levels plummeted. Federation ecologists saw the multiple disasters propagating through Chal's ecosystems and reacted again with well-intentioned alarm to restore the natural order. In order to keep the mountain mite from spreading, terraforming runabouts were seconded on a priority basis to spray insecticides in the traditional habitats of the displaced birds.

The mites died as planned, but the insecticides, developed for conditions on another world, were anything but natural on Chal. They also entered the food chain, where they unexpectedly interfered with calcium absorption by Chal's indigenous animal species.

Within another three months, almost all Chal mammals were delivered stillborn, their fragile, incompletely formed bones crushed by the contractions of birth. Like the shells of birds' eggs, now mammal skulls were paper thin.

This was how a world died.

Doomed by humanity's simple intention to do good, against the realities of an ecosystem more complex than any human mind could comprehend, more dynamic than any computer simulation could model.

One bird singing. Faintly, plaintively. Alone.

Eighty years after history reported him dead for the first time, James T. Kirk heard that last bird sing as the twin suns of Chal broke through the dull gray haze of morning.

He understood the plaintiveness of its cry.

Just as he understood the unquenchable drive that made it sing, even in the face of sure and certain destruction.

Kirk had seen destruction. He had walked the ruins of civilizations that had been old before Earth's sun was born. Seen friends sacrifice themselves for love and duty. Lost loved ones to capriciousness and hate. Watched strangers die for no reason other than ignorance and greed.

Once he had thought he might change that.

In time, he had become bitter as he had learned how little one man could actually do.

Then he had faced death himself. And against all odds, for reasons which he still did not fully grasp, the end had not come.

Sometimes it seemed to him as if all his life was one endless series of second chances. But this time, he knew he had been given more than just another opportunity.

Kirk had come to Chal renewed, reborn.

He had finally learned the one secret that must be treasured above all else in a universe that had never cared about him and his kind, and never would.

He sat by Teilani's side, warmed by the fire he had built near the bare stone foundations and fire-blackened timbers of the building that had once been her home.

She stirred there, on her bed of blankets, smiling as she woke to feel the warmth of the sunslight on her face for the first time in weeks.

Kirk gently stroked her uninjured cheek.

She looked up at him, her one uncovered eye alight with awe. She reached for his hand.

"It wasn't a dream . . . ?" she asked.

"I love you," Kirk said, and it was as if he truly said those words for the first time, at last understanding their meaning. Knowing they were the only words in the universe that meant anything at all.

Tears formed in Teilani's eyes, gleaming as they slowly rolled down to her gray-flecked hair.

"You came back," she said.

Kirk smiled, and it was as if he smiled for the first time as well.

"For you," he said. "For us."

"James T. Kirk?" Barc grunted.

Christine MacDonald showed the Tellarite the padd to which she had downloaded the historical files from her ship's main computer. The display screen showed an image of Kirk recorded eighty years ago, on the occasion of the ill-fated launch of the *Enterprise*-B. "Look at this," the young commander said. "It's him."

Dr. M'Benga peered over Barc's shoulder. The morning sunslight streaming through the window of the Starfleet general-issue emergency shelter tent was bright enough to make the display look washed out. M'Benga held up a hand to cast a shadow on the padd and scowled in disagreement. "He's dead, Chris."

"That's what they said eighty years ago," Christine said triumphantly. "And then guess who showed up on Veridian Three?"

"They didn't have a body eighty years ago," Barc complained. "But two years ago at Veridian, with Picard, definitely a body. Picard buried him. End of story."

Christine flashed a triumphant smile at the taciturn engineer, pulled back the padd, called up another screen, this time of text. She held it for Barc and M'Benga to read.

The Tellarite's snout twitched in curiosity. M'Benga's scowl became a puzzled grimace.

"They left him there?" Barc said.

"With the *Enterprise?*" M'Benga added.

"Do you honestly believe Starfleet would just forget James T. Kirk?" Christine asked.

"Rrr, nothing the admiralty did would surprise me," Barc huffed. "But they couldn't leave the D on Veridian Three. Too many Prime Directive problems if the inhabitants of Veridian Four ever found the wreckage."

M'Benga looked thoughtful. "Or the body of an alien. Kirk's remains would have to be removed from the planet. I'm surprised they didn't bring him back to Earth for burial."

Christine gestured with the padd. "But Starfleet general records hold no information on the disposition of the *Enterprise's* wreckage, or of Kirk's body. As far as I'm concerned, that means they didn't have a body after Veridian Three, either. And the story of whatever happened there after the crash is being covered up."

Barc grunted, unconvinced. "If it's not in the general records, then it didn't happen."

Christine knew better than to argue with the obstinate Tellarite. But M'Benga could be counted upon to see past the facts of a situation, into its heart.

"Your grandfather served with Kirk, didn't he?" Christine asked the doctor.

"Great-grandfather," M'Benga corrected. "And not for long."

"But you know the stories about Kirk."

M'Benga rolled her eyes. "Everyone knows the stories. And if even a tenth of them were true, Kirk's first five-year mission would have lasted *fifty* years."

Christine was becoming annoyed. How could she make her friends see how obvious the situation was? "All I'm suggesting is that given what we know of the man, we shouldn't be surprised that he of all people is someone who managed to cheat death yet again. I mean, come on, Bones—you analyzed the dried leaves he used for that Teilani woman. You've got your lab up on the *Tobias* churning out clone cultures, and the computer says that that tea, or whatever it is, *will* inhibit the virogen's reproduction in the people of Chal. Even you have to admit that's a medical miracle. So why can't Kirk be using some other miracle compound to keep himself alive?"

M'Benga shook her head. "Chris, all I'm hearing is hero worship. If James T. Kirk *had* survived Veridian Three, don't you think Starfleet would have hauled him back to Earth for a hero's welcome? Don't you think he'd be on every update, writing his memoirs, teaching history at the Academy?"

"Except," Christine said, pointing to the padd, "we don't *know* what happened on Veridian Three after the *Enterprise* crashed. The gaps in the general records tell me that Starfleet's covering up something."

"What?" Barc asked with exasperation.

Christine sighed. "Barcs, if I knew, then it wouldn't be a cover-up, would it?"

The engineer paused a moment to consider that insight. In her usual blunt fashion, the doctor went for the bottom line. "Why don't you just *ask* him if he's Kirk?"

"He doesn't want to tell me his name."

"Chris, you're the commander of Starfleet's relief mission to this world. It's under martial law. You have the authority to ask anyone anything." M'Benga allowed herself a small, dry smile. "Then again, maybe he's tired of people telling him he looks like Kirk."

"Or maybe he's got a good reason to want to hide."

M'Benga glanced sharply at Christine. No longer a ship's doctor, but a friend who had shared enough Academy courses to know her commander well. "Oh, no, I've seen that look before."

Christine drew herself up defensively. "What look?"

"You're falling in love with him."

"After five minutes with him? Don't be ridiculous."

Barc threw up his hands as his ear fur bristled in embarrassment. "That's it. I'm leaving. Feel free to keep all the sordid details of human mating habits to yourselves."

But Christine placed a restraining hand on the engineer's

broad shoulder. "Barc, wait. If you see Kirk—the stranger, whatever you want to call him—don't tell him about . . . any of this."

"Don't worry. I wouldn't want him to think I'm crazy, too." The Tellarite pulled back the flap of fabric that was the tent's makeshift door. "I'll be back at the replicators. For all the good it will do." He snorted in disgust as he ducked outside.

M'Benga took a long look at Christine. "Your problem is, you're bored with the mission."

Christine frowned. "How could I be? We're saving a world here. That's why we signed on."

"We're not saving anything."

M'Benga's glum words hung in the silence of the tent.

"I received an alert from Starfleet Medical an hour ago. Two more systems are affected. It's confirmed."

"Dear God, Bones, why didn't you tell me?"

M'Benga shrugged. "Barc's ready to quit as it is. In case you haven't noticed, morale among the other personnel is the lowest I've ever seen in any Starfleet operation. And whatever hope we were holding out for supplies, well, that's pretty well out the airlock. All we've got is whatever's down here now, and whatever's left to cannibalize from the *Tobias.* That's it. We're on our own."

Christine felt as if M'Benga had punched her. The promise of resupply, of new personnel for the relief mission, was all that was keeping her people going. "Does anyone else know?"

M'Benga shook her head. "It was medical eyes only. Starfleet knows how precarious the situation is. The last thing we need is more panic."

"But Kirk's leaves will work, won't they?"

"For the original inhabitants of Chal with their peculiar Klingon-Romulan metabolism, yes. I'm about as certain as I can be."

"That'll be good for morale, then. No more deaths."

M'Benga gazed down at the padd, as if she didn't have the strength to look her commander in the eyes. Christine had never seen her friend so serious. "Chris, a higher survival rate also means more mouths to feed. We're down to less than thirty days' supply of food as it is."

"The replicators . . . ?"

"Barc says your idea about using the tricorders is brilliant, and should last about ten operational hours. That'll give us what? A few hundred liters of fresh water for the children? Maybe buy us a day or two overall?"

Christine yanked the padd back from M'Benga. "I will not accept defeat."

"This isn't personal, Chris. You're the commander of a science vessel, not captain of a starship. The only reason we got this assignment is because the Fleet is stretched too thin to begin with. We weren't expected to win here. Only to hold the line."

"But you're telling me there is no line to hold."

M'Benga seemed to age before Christine's eyes. She pulled a small chair out from a folding table. Sat down, slumping wearily against the table. "I'm a doctor, not a soldier. I will care for these people as long as I am able. But the enemy we're facing here isn't personal, and isn't out to get *you* or me."

Christine leaned forward, trying to energize her friend. "But it *is* personal. It has to be. Otherwise, what's the point of trying to fight this damned virogen?"

M'Benga pressed a control on the padd and slid it across the table to Chris. Its display showed that old image of Kirk again, on the brink of another great adventure.

"You sound like you've been spending too much time reading those books about Kirk."

"He never gave up."

"He lived a hundred years ago. Life was simpler in the twenty-third century. Things were easier."

Christine picked up the padd and brandished it as if it were a talisman to ward off the evil that surrounded her and infused this world. "Don't you think Kirk said the same thing about life in the twenty-second century? Don't you think the people then said the same about Cochrane's era? Don't you think Cochrane was envious of the twentieth century?" Christine felt the surface of the padd deform under the pressure of her grip. "We all say things were different in the past, but they weren't. Every time's the same. And what worked a century ago *can* work today."

M'Benga repeated Christine's words almost with pity. "Honestly, Chris, just listen to yourself—'What worked a century ago'?"

Christine thumped the padd against the table for emphasis. "He *never* gave up. Never."

From behind her, the stranger said, "Who never gave up?"

M'Benga started in her chair, staring toward the tent's entrance. Christine whirled around.

Kirk stood there, still in his Vulcan trader's garb, though with his hood pushed back to lie around his shoulders.

His face held an inquiring expression, as if to tell them that he knew he had interrupted their conversation and wished it to continue.

Christine glanced down at the image on the padd, then looked again at the man before her. He had longer hair than in the image, tied back. There was no trace of pointed Academy sideburns. Instead he wore a neat beard, flecked with white. But the eyes were the same, Christine swore to herself. However he had managed it, she was certain James T. Kirk stood before her.

But why wouldn't he admit it?

"You were saying?" Kirk prompted again.

Christine flicked off the padd and the image of Kirk faded. "Nothing," she said, placing the padd on the table. "How is your friend? Teilani?"

"Much better."

"The leaves," M'Benga began as she rose, "can you tell me where they're from?"

"No, I can't," Kirk said, then paused, correcting himself. "They were given to me by . . . a teacher. I don't know what planet they're from."

"Do you know what they're called? They're working miracles on the Chal."

"I'm glad," Kirk said simply. "It's what I hoped. I can tell you they're called *trannin* leaves, if that helps." He pronounced the word with a guttural harshness.

Christine glanced at M'Benga. "Klingon?"

M'Benga pursed her lips. "I'll have the computer search for references." Then the doctor fixed Kirk with one of her brightest smiles. "Say, has anyone ever told you how much you resemble—"

"Dr. M'Benga," Christine interrupted with the full authority of her rank. "I believe you have morning rounds to make."

M'Benga locked eyes with Christine. Christine did not have to add the words "That's an order" for her intent to be known.

"Whatever you say, Commander." M'Benga picked up her medical kit from a cot, started out, then turned to Kirk. "Good-bye, Mr. . . . ?"

"Good-bye, Doctor," Kirk said, deflecting the unstated request.

Then Christine was alone with James Tiberius Kirk.

A pioneer whose exploits would live as long as there was a Starfleet and a Federation to guide it.

An improbable survivor from another age.

Her personal hero. Perhaps more.

"What can I do for you?" she asked.

Kirk hesitated, as if he had just thought of a topic to discuss at Christine's suggestion. "Teilani . . ." he began.

"Your 'friend'?" Christine interrupted, before she could stop herself.

"Yes, Teilani." Kirk offered no other explanation for his relationship to the Chal woman, though the way he spoke her name revealed his intimate connection to her. "She tells me that what has happened here, to Chal, is happening on other worlds."

"You didn't know?" Christine asked.

"I've been . . . away. On the frontier."

I'll bet you have, Christine thought.

"Officially," she said, "six other systems have been infected."

"Which means that unofficially, the count is higher."

"I'm afraid so."

Kirk glanced around the tent. Christine got the impression he was recording everything he saw, wasting nothing. "It was bound to happen sooner or later, don't you think?" he asked.

"What?"

"Do you have records of how it began?"

Christine felt she was missing something. As if Kirk were making leaps in the conversation she couldn't follow. "You mean the virogen plague?"

"I want to know how it came to Chal."

"You and half of Starfleet."

"Do you have records?"

Christine tugged down on her tunic to smooth it. If Kirk had some agenda he preferred to keep from her, then at least she could choose the arena.

"To thank you for the leaves you've brought, I'd be honored to have you visit my ship," she said. "We receive constant updates from Starfleet on the state of our efforts to track and contain the virogen, and I'd be happy to share them with you."

"You have a ship?" Kirk asked.

"The *U.S.S. Tobias.* A science vessel." Christine didn't understand the blank look in Kirk's eyes. "In orbit," she explained. Maybe the stranger wasn't Kirk after all.

"I'm familiar with the concept," Kirk said gently.

Christine tapped her comm badge, heard it chirp. "MacDonald to *Tobias.* Two to beam up."

The disembodied voice of the transporter chief replied from the comm badge. "Locking on . . ."

Christine glanced hopefully at Kirk. "You know, it would be a lot easier to give you a tour if I knew your name."

Kirk shrugged, as if his name were no longer of importance. "Call me Jim," he said.

Christine allowed herself a brief smile, and was sorry M'Benga hadn't been there to hear that name.

And then the transporter took them.

EIGHT

Throughout his life, Spock had been accepting of defeat. In most cases, it could provide a valuable lesson. Properly understood, defeat in one instance could enhance the prospects for prevailing in a new encounter. Thus, logic dictated that defeat should be experienced without emotion. It was merely a tool that ultimately, if used correctly, would bring victory.

Yet knowing all that, believing all that, Spock still felt angry at what had happened on Babel. Sifting through the reasons for his feelings in his subsequent meditations, he was intrigued, though not surprised, to discover the cause of his anger.

He did not feel betrayed by the Federation advisors.

He did not feel embarrassed by the Romulan delegation's reaction to the cancellation of the vote.

He was just growing older.

The cause of his discomfort was that simple.

For almost a century and a half, he had fought the good fight, and now he was becoming impatient with the struggle. His tolerance for diplomatic niceties was fading. He understood problems more rapidly than he had in the past. He saw solutions clearly ahead of him. There was no logic in waiting to achieve them.

But the absolute key to his emotional state on this day was that he *knew* beyond any doubt that one day the Romulan and Vulcan people would be united, and that he now doubted he would be alive to see that day.

To anyone who watched the ambassador pack his few personal items into a carryall in his austere diplomatic quarters on the Babel planetoid, no trace of his emotional distress would be noticeable.

Displaying all the calm deliberation of a lifetime of discipline, Spock went about his inconsequential tasks without betraying the turmoil that raged within. Though it was his way, recently he had begun to question why it must remain so.

For a moment, Spock paused before pressing the closure tab on the small fabric case on the writing table before him. Any witness might have suspected he was merely reviewing the contents—a personal terminal padd, tricorder, formal robes, toiletries, and two physical books: Surak's *The Art of Peace,* and, for diversion, the timeless Earth classic, Harold Robbins's *The Carpetbaggers.* But the ambassador was in fact caught up in an ancient memory.

Once, more than a century ago on the *Enterprise,* when he had entered the *Pon farr,* he had allowed his discipline to break down to the extent that he had thrown—actually thrown in rage—a bowl of soup across his quarters to smash against a corridor wall.

Spock thought about that irrational act now, and reflected on how unusually satisfying it had been. He wondered if perhaps he should try such an act again. He certainly felt as if he should.

His door announcer chimed. Srell was early, but that was typical of his young aide.

"Come," Spock said.

The door slid open.

But it was not Srell who called upon him.

It was a young Klingon officer in full battle garb.

Spock raised an eyebrow. There were several Klingon delegations currently on Babel, he knew. Though relations between the Empire and the Federation were improving since the Cardassian incident, full diplomatic contact was still to be completely restored. But Spock could think of no reason why a Klingon would wish to seek him out privately.

"What do you want?" Spock demanded. It was the polite thing to say under the circumstances.

The Klingon bowed his head for a moment, then entered Spock's quarters without waiting for Spock's permission to do so. Spock noted that he carried a small diplomatic courier's pouch on his belt.

"Ambassador," the Klingon began. "I have been asked to deliver this to you."

The Klingon took a small holoprojector from the pouch and handed it to Spock. Spock recognized it as a civilian unit which could be used to record a personal message. Its most common function was to serve as a memento of the dead.

"To whom should I offer my thanks?" Spock asked.

"I have fulfilled my duty," the Klingon stated.

"Am I to receive no information about its source?"

The Klingon looked as annoyed as Spock felt. This duty had undoubtedly been forced upon him and he resented being a mere messenger.

"I cannot tell you what I do not know. I will leave now."

In a most Klingon fashion, the Klingon stalked out. The door slid shut behind him.

Spock examined the holoprojector visually. It was little more than a small black base with an activation stud. He placed the unit on the writing desk, then checked it with the small tricorder he removed from his carryall.

There were no traces of explosives. The holoprojector was exactly what it appeared to be.

Spock constructed a mental web of logic to predict the information the projector might contain. Because it was being given to him under covert conditions on the Babel planetoid, he concluded it most likely had something to do with his father. Perhaps an unofficial recording Sarek had once made, which a fellow ambassador had decided should be given to Sarek's son. He activated the projector and a pillar of light formed over the base, resolving into a humanoid form about twenty centimeters tall.

Spock cocked his head, intrigued, as he recognized the figure. Ki Mendrossen. The diplomat who had served as his father's chief of staff in the final years of Sarek's career. He was an officious human, totally devoted to Sarek's well-being, and possessed of an almost Vulcanlike capacity to focus on details. Though Sarek had never commented upon Mendrossen's abilities, the fact that the man had served so long was testament enough to his competence.

Mendrossen's appearance on this projector was unexpected, but Spock felt satisfaction that the message he was about to hear did in some way connect to his father. In some matters, it seemed, his logic remained robust.

As the holographic figure began to speak, Mendrossen seemed much older than Spock remembered him. His shoulders were stooped, as if he had recorded this message while fatigued. Visual static disrupted the projected image as well, as if the recording sensors had not been properly aligned—a sign of haste or ill-preparation, both qualities quite unlike Mendrossen.

"My name is Ki Aloysius Mendrossen, former chief of staff to the office of Ambassador Sarek of Vulcan. I make this confession of my own free will."

The word "confession" startled Spock.

"During my tenure with the ambassador, I reported on a

regular basis to the prefect of Gonthar District. The nature of my reports was to keep Gonthar apprised of the ambassador's work on the following matters: the Amtara reparations, the redrafting of Starfleet's First Contact protocols, the repatriation of the Andorian drallstone, and all discussions relating to thc Romulan unification."

Spock absently touched his IDIC medallion. He was stunned. Mendrossen was confessing to having been a spy in an organization that routinely relied on mindmelds to maintain security and unanimity. How could such actions be possible?

"I offer no excuse for this betrayal," Mendrossen's projection continued. "For the good of the cause, of the revolution, I believed it was, at the time, a necessity. It is only now, as I see the purposes for which my information was used, that I realize the error in judgment I have made."

Mendrossen bowed his head in a human expression of shame. He did it awkwardly, as if his years on Vulcan had made him lose touch with his own human heritage.

"For all that I believed I followed in the path of Surak, my logic was uncertain and I do regret my actions."

His image shimmering erratically over the display base, Mendrossen squared his shoulders. Now his voice took on a more measured tone, as if he were reciting memorized lines. "Some remnant of the Federation will survive these dark days, and it is my wish that what rises from the ashes will be a more evolved association, devoted to the preservation of each world's distinctive nature.

"That the Federation must end, I have no doubt. That it will end in this particular way, is, I believe, more humane than if matters were left to the inevitable currents of history."

Here, the formality of Mendrossen's words seemed to fade, as if he had abandoned his script and now spoke from his heart. "But I do bitterly regret my role in the death of Ambassador Sarek. Of all the actions of which history might judge me guilty, his murder is the one for which I truly beg forgiveness." The small figure held up his hand in the traditional salute. "Peace and long life."

Spock stared with incomprehension as the holographic image of Sarek's chief of staff reached within the loose gray jacket he wore and withdrew a small, green-finished phaser of Vulcan design. Mendrossen twisted the setting ring, then clutched it to his chest, lowered his head a final time, and transformed himself into a quantum mist.

For twenty silent seconds, all the holoprojector displayed was a flickering patch of stone flooring. Then the recording ended and the shaft of projection winked out.

Spock stepped back from the projector until he bumped into the simple bed and sat down upon it, almost falling as he did so.

His mind struggled to find some logical way of dealing with what he had just witnessed. It was absurd. His father had died of Bendii Syndrome. It was a rare illness, to be sure, most often afflicting Vulcans over the age of two hundred. But the way it had ravaged his father's intellect was well documented. There could be no question that Sarek had died a natural death.

But then, there could be no question that the Vulcan diplomatic corps had never harbored a spy. Such a deception was not only unthinkable, it was impossible.

As impossible as Ki Mendrossen's confession to—Spock could barely bring himself to even think the words—Sarek's murder.

Two impossibilities. Reducing the chance of coincidence.

Spock felt his heart race. He knew he was on emotional edge, but this unexpected message from the past was having more of an effect on him than his control could suppress.

It was one thing to have lost a chance to bring Romulans and Vulcans together.

It was one thing to have lost his father to the inescapable ravages of age and time.

But if his father had been *murdered.* If Spock had knowingly abandoned Sarek to the machinations of a criminal who had worked on his staff, without recognizing the danger his father faced. The failure of son to father was more profound than any mere disturbance in diplomacy.

How could such a thing have happened?

How could he have left his father to such a fate?

Without even realizing what he was doing, Spock squeezed on his IDIC medallion until the heavy chain dug into the flesh of his neck, then snapped.

In one quick motion, Spock hurled the metal disk across the room to smash against the far wall.

His cry of outrage, of shame, echoed in the room.

There was no more room in his life for failure.

Or for logic.

It was time things changed.

NINE

The *Tobias* was an *Oberth*-class science vessel with a total volume, including warp nacelles, less than two-thirds of the saucer section of a *Galaxy*-class starship. It was one of the workhorses of Starfleet, with a small engineering hull that sat directly beneath its command saucer. The command saucer itself was attached at both sides to the warp nacelles, with the total effect being as if a more standard starship design had been squashed together, fore and aft. The ungainly though sturdy configuration of the *Oberth* class had changed little in almost a century.

Yet Christine MacDonald was proud to be her commander. Many of the officers whose careers she studied, including Kathryn Janeway, had begun as science specialists, then risen to starship command. Christine viewed the *Tobias* as a way station on her path to taking the center chair of one of the new *Sovereign* ships herself.

Presuming, of course, that Starfleet and the Federation survived.

But Christine was willing to make that presumption.

Like the man who materialized beside her on the ship's

transporter pad, she would never give up, and neither would the Federation.

Christine stepped down from the elevated platform, nodded to the transporter tech behind his console, and started for the door. Only when the doors puffed open did she realize that Kirk was no longer at her side. She turned back to find him still standing on the pad.

"Jim?" she asked. "Are you all right?"

Kirk hesitated before answering, as if clearing his head. "It was . . . an unusual experience," he said. "Transportation."

Christine was mystified by his reaction. Even if Jim weren't the legendary starship captain James T. Kirk, though she was still sure he was, who went into space these days who had not, at least once, been transported?

"Have you never been beamed before?" she asked incredulously.

Kirk stepped lightly from the pad. "It's just been a long time since I concentrated on what the sensations of the process actually are." He smiled reflectively. "Quite remarkable when you think about it."

Christine almost said, "It's just simple matter dematerialization," but didn't, afraid she'd sound rude. However, her desire to confront Kirk about how he had managed to survive the events of Veridian III grew even stronger and harder to suppress.

"Let's go to the bridge," she said. "That's where the most efficient library consoles are."

This time, Kirk followed.

The corridors of the *Tobias* were almost deserted. The ship had been in standard orbit of Chal for almost eight months, with stationkeeping procedures fully automated, and most of her crew of ninety-eight aiding the relief effort on the surface.

The only other time her ship had felt so empty to Christine was when she had toured it in spacedock at Vulcan, during its last refit. Then, it slept like a bulky dragon, full of brute power and potential, waiting to be awakened. But now, it felt infirm to her. Passive, waiting, on hold.

If the Federation fell, she wondered, what would be the fate of the thousands of other ships that served it? Would they end their days in lonely orbits, slowly decaying until inevitable reentry, leaving fiery trails to be incorporated into the myths of the primitives living among the ruins of once great civilizations? Or, would they, centuries hence, be rediscovered in abandoned spaceports, restored, and given a second chance to become the driving force behind a second Federation?

Christine stopped for a moment by the turbolift doors. Unconsciously, she reached out to touch the corridor wall, searching for the vibration of the generators that kept her ship in standby mode.

She became aware of Kirk watching her.

"The ship is quiet," he said.

"She's old," Christine answered, though she knew that wasn't what Kirk had meant. "Refit at least five times."

"You wonder how she'll end."

Unnerved, Christine nodded as the lift doors slipped open. It was like having a conversation with a Betazoid, as if he could read her thoughts.

She stepped into the lift with Kirk. "Bridge," she said. The car hummed to life.

"The ships aren't important," Kirk said.

Christine turned to Kirk, surprised. That's not what a starship captain was supposed to believe. "The ships have to be important," she protested. "They're what keep the Federation alive and growing. They're the lifeblood of our civilization, our growth as a species, our acquisition of knowledge." She flushed, embarrassed at her outburst. She had spoken without thought, only with passion.

Kirk looked at her as if he were a parent humoring a child. Christine was annoyed to feel so foolish, so exposed.

"It's just machinery," Kirk said mildly. "And sometimes, it

can blind us to the minds that conceived it, and the souls who serve it."

Now Christine was sure that that was not anything the James T. Kirk she had worshipped might have said. Perhaps it was time to confront Kirk directly as M'Benga had urged her to do. She had to know what could have changed her childhood idol so dramatically from the way history had recorded him.

But he continued before she could begin.

"It's your crew, Commander. That's what's important. The *Tobias* is only a shell that can take you from world to world. In time, it will wear out, or be destroyed. . . ." Kirk paused, looking away, as if caught up in a memory. "There always will be another machine to replace it. Faster, sleeker, more powerful. But even the newest ship in the fleet means nothing without her crew."

"And her captain," Christine said pointedly.

The lift doors opened on the bridge. Half the stations were dark. Kirk put his hand on Christine's shoulder, to stop her from stepping forward.

She felt the heat of him where he touched the bare skin of her shoulder, exposed by the cut-out sleeves of her tunic. She turned to him, drawn by his close presence.

"I once knew someone who thought being captain of a starship was the highest goal anyone could achieve. But the position is a sentence, not a job."

"I don't understand," Christine said. The air in the turbolift car felt charged. His gaze still held her. His hand was still on her shoulder.

"The captain is the one trapped in the middle, caught between the machine and the crew, unable to be one or the other. It's . . . very lonely."

"Everything demands a price," Christine said, and believed every word. "If I'm willing to pay it, then nothing else should matter."

Kirk slowly took his hand away, as if understanding that he could not change her mind.

"The person I knew, he thought just like that. Believed what you believe."

"What happened to him?" Christine asked, no doubt in her mind as to the identity of the person they discussed. "Did he get what he wanted?"

"He became a starship captain."

"And what price did he pay?"

Kirk studied her, seeming to search through all the words he knew, unable to find any that could answer her question, until: "He couldn't be anything else."

It was the one answer Christine hadn't expected. She stood in awkward silence; then Kirk gestured to the bridge, as if this were his ship and she were the guest.

"This way," she said, and they left the turbolift together.

An hour later, Kirk's briefing had ended.

Christine had placed herself at the computer terminal as before, but this time Kirk asked the questions and read the screens above the science station—the largest bridge position on the science vessel. He assimilated the data in a way that required Christine to struggle to keep up.

When he had exhausted the information available, Kirk sat down in the operator's chair beside Christine. Deep in thought, he leaned back, steepling his fingers.

Christine ignored the questioning glances from the only other crew on the bridge of her ship—Pini at communications, and Changdrapnor at operations. She was intent on hearing what Kirk's pronouncement would be.

"You look like someone who's seen this before," she said.

An expression of anger darkened Kirk's eyes. "Ecological disaster? Breakdown in the food supply? What else is history made from?"

"I meant, personally," Christine explained.

Kirk seemed to think about his answer for a moment. "Yes," he said. "I have." It was the first piece of real information he had given her about his background.

"Where?" Christine pressed him. When Kirk didn't answer at once, she persisted, "Your homeworld? A colony planet?"

"A colony world," Kirk finally acknowledged. "A long time ago." He looked back at the science-station screen, where the sector's main trade routes were displayed. "This shouldn't have happened," he said.

Christine straightened up in her chair. "Hold on, weren't you the one who just told me something like the virogen plague was bound to happen? That it was only a question of when?"

Kirk tapped the display screen. "On those key trading worlds, yes. We've introduced too many different life-forms into too many different environments. We've tried to create uniform ecologies on worlds with different suns, different biological histories. Half the grain-producing planets in the Federation now use the same strain of wheat. That means one disease could wipe out half the agricultural base of the quadrant. The diversity of a thousand worlds is being eradicated more and more every day. We call it efficiency. But it's an act of strangulation. Of suicide."

It was the first time Kirk had spoken with something other than quiet deliberation and careful choice of words. She heard a passion in his tone that was as surprising to her as if a Vulcan had suddenly shouted in anger.

She probed his reasoning. "But hasn't the virogen done more than a single grain disease would ever be capable of? It affects all chlorophyll-producing plants, not just grains."

"That's my point," Kirk said, frustration evident in his voice. "Chlorophyll is only one of nature's solutions to transforming solar energy into plant growth. But the Federation has systematically spread chlorophyll-producing plants to every planet in its boundaries. If native ecosystems had been left intact, this virogen would have affected Earth, Mars, a handful of other worlds with similar plant stocks. Any disruption on those planets could have easily been dealt with, by relief efforts from non-chlorophyll-based worlds. But look what's happened because we wiped out diversity. All we cared about was growth, not stability. And now we're paying the price."

Christine had heard these arguments before, though she was surprised to hear them coming from a man of action like Kirk. And she knew the Federation's terraforming bureaus were quick with counterarguments.

Uncontrolled ecosystems were precisely those in which unexpected mutations and disease organisms arose. By establishing an artificial interplanetary ecology, one that was uniform and understood in near-molecular detail from decades of study and refinement, the Federation's experts maintained that change could be averted and biological security guaranteed. But somehow Christine was certain that even this Kirk would not be swayed by the opinions of the Federation's experts. He would never change that much.

There was another question she did want answered, though.

"If all that you say is true, then why is what happened on Chal different?"

Kirk's eyes flashed with an intensity that Christine could not identify—pain, outrage, despair . . . whatever its source, it had reached the point at which Kirk had lost all patience.

"Chal was a paradise," he said. "Its biosphere was engineered by Romulan and Klingon ecologists."

"Engineered?" Christine said in surprise. "I never read that in the briefings. The background logs say this was just a colony world."

"Then the background logs have been sanitized. Chal was established as a military outpost. Very few of the land-based plants and animals are native." Kirk's tone became scathing. "It is ridiculous to believe that a virogen that affects an artificial ecosystem created with native Earth life-forms could also affect a Klingon/Romulan ecosystem at the same time. One way or another, there has to be time for adaptation and evolution."

Christine's training came to the fore and without thought she pushed away all consideration of her hero's personal mystery. Kirk had just brought a new piece of the puzzle to the equation that affected her job, new information which she was certain even Starfleet didn't know.

"But you saw the latest report from Starfleet," she reminded Kirk. "No one believes that the virogen arose overnight. They believe it existed in a benign or dormant form for years, spread along the trade routes, and only then became active. That accounts for it striking so many different worlds in so short a time."

"They're wrong," Kirk said. "Chal is not on any major trade routes. It is not a net importer of food products. Its ecosystem is artificial. The virogen could never have arisen here by natural contamination processes."

Christine opened her mouth but nothing came out. From the corner of her eyes, she saw Pini and Changdrapnor turn to look at Kirk.

Christine kept her eyes locked on Kirk as well. The conclusion he was advancing was terrifying. She had to be sure he knew what he was talking about.

"Why do you know things about Chal's ecosystem that Starfleet doesn't?"

"Ask the Chal who live in the main city," Kirk answered. "There used to be a . . . museum in the center of town, disguised as a power-generating station. It told the history of the colony in great detail."

Christine turned to the science terminal, called up a map of the main city, and cycled back through the years until she saw a major structure in the town's center. She called up the data on it.

"Power station. Says here the Starfleet Corps of Engineers tore it down about seventy-five years ago, just before Chal joined the Federation."

"It was a military museum," Kirk said. "I was in it."

Christine turned back to him. "Seventy-five years ago?"

"Eighty years ago."

Christine let the improbability of that statement pass. Eventually Kirk would have to confirm his identity and explain how he had survived. Right now, his theory about the virogen was more important to establish.

"You're actually suggesting that the military branches of Starfleet have information which could help the science sections understand the virogen, but which they aren't sharing? I find that difficult to believe."

"Whatever else Starfleet is," Kirk said, "it's a bureaucracy. You work for it. You know how information can become compartmentalized and lost."

"Maybe that's how they did things in the past," Christine said. "But I have more faith in Starfleet than you apparently do."

"It was a long time ago," Kirk allowed. "But it's still Starfleet."

Christine turned back to the terminal, rapidly typed in more commands, then read the resulting text with a shock of understanding.

"Eighty years ago," she read out to Kirk in a low voice that would not be heard by her curious bridge staff, "Chal applied to the Federation for membership. It says here there was an incident of sorts. Klingon vessels were destroyed. The result of the last gasp of the Cartwright conspiracy in Starfleet Command." She narrowed her eyes, looking for any hint of reaction. "Starfleet's C-in-C, Androvar Drake, died in a space battle here."

Kirk gave away nothing.

"The logs say that the person responsible was James T. Kirk."

Kirk's expression was so impassive that Christine was certain he had studied on Vulcan.

"Did you ever meet him back then? Eighty years ago? Jim?"

Kirk stood up, completely unreadable. "James T. Kirk died a long time ago. I don't believe in dwelling on the past."

"I'm going to have to tell Starfleet what you've told me," Christine warned him.

"It's too late to do any good. But when you do, tell them to activate all sealed files on the *chalchaj 'qmey.* The Children of Heaven. That'll bring up the data they need on Chal's ecosystem." Kirk started for the turbolift. "I have to get back to Teilani."

"Jim, wait," Christine said. "I'm going to have to tell Starfleet how I got this information. Why won't you tell me who you are? For the record."

For a moment, Kirk hesitated, as if caught in an inner struggle. "I'm no one," he said at last. "Let it go at that."

Christine wanted to protest that he was wrong, that it was time he step out of the shadows of the past. But something in his face stopped her.

"Please," Kirk said.

Christine nodded, wondering what it would be like to find herself in a new century, with all the old familiar touchstones gone. "But if you remember anything else that might help us. . . ."

"I'm not going anywhere," Kirk said, and this time found an almost wistful smile. "Chal is my home, now. I'd like to keep it that way."

Christine nodded. However Kirk had come to this place and this time, he had clearly decided his days of adventure were over. She could respect that decision, even if she couldn't understand it.

She watched him walk to the turbolift. Once inside, he paused, keeping the doors from closing as he glanced around the bridge.

"It's a fine ship," he told Christine. He met her eyes. "But just a ship."

He stepped back. The doors closed. And he was gone.

Instantly Pini and Changdrapnor got to their feet and joined their commander.

"Who was that?" the diminutive communications officer asked.

"No one," Christine said.

Changdrapnor scratched at the iridescent scales that grew at the edge of his beak. "He looked familiar. Almost like—"

"No speculation," Christine said firmly. "We owe him that much."

Both Pini and Changdrapnor reacted with unquestioning acceptance.

Christine regarded her crew with pride. Kirk had been partially right. A ship was nothing but a shell without a good crew to go with her. And her crew was one of the best.

"Lieutenant Pini," she said crisply, "get me Starfleet Command emergency relief headquarters, priority channel. I want to speak with Admiral Goddard personally."

The communications officer looked wide-eyed in concern. "Commander . . . I'm not sure I can do that. We're just a science vessel."

"Tell his office that we have uncovered evidence that may indicate the virogen plague is artificial."

"We have?" Changdrapnor hissed in surprise.

"Maybe, maybe not," Christine said as she looked over at the closed turbolift doors. "But at least we'll get someone's attention."

TEN

Will Riker's protestations were still ringing in Picard's ears as he materialized in the cramped manager's office of Gamow Station on Alta Vista III. As first officer, it was Riker's duty to take on all hazardous away missions. The captain was too valuable a resource to risk.

But Picard had argued that he was merely beaming into a Federation science station. How hazardous could that be?

Riker had muttered that he hoped they wouldn't find out, and then Picard had dissolved in the transporter's beam, and reappeared here.

The manager, Chiton Kincaid, was an extraordinarily tall and slender woman, almost two and a half meters in height, from a low-gravity Earth colony world. As she rose to greet her visitor, Picard had to look up through his helmet visor to meet her eyes. He hoped he was able to control his expression of surprise at her size as easily as she controlled her reaction to his wearing a hard-vacuum environmental suit. His communications with her by viewscreen had not prepared him for the total impact of her height.

Chiton lightly shook Picard's gloved hand. "I take it Starfleet still hasn't been able to isolate the virogen?"

Picard adjusted his interior comm-link control so he could speak to the station manager through the comm badge she wore on her Starfleet uniform. "Not yet," he said. "Though Dr. Crusher remains hopeful."

Chiton appeared to believe Picard's assessment of the situation as much as he did—not at all. She gestured to a chair by her piled-high desk. "Sit, if you can."

Picard declined. Chiton pushed a stack of diagnostic kits to the side and sat back on the corner of her desk, her thin arms folded against her chest. The movement made Picard think of insect limbs. He suppressed the unsettling thought quickly.

"Forgive me if I don't offer you something to drink," Chiton said.

Picard admired the station manager's ability to find humor under present conditions. The only way her science outpost could support the fourteen hundred refugees who had been brought to it was by abandoning all pretense as to her original mission. The domes in which solar sensors had been deployed to study the inversions of the Alta Vista sun had been emptied of all scientific apparatus. The rocky scrubland that surrounded Gamow Station's pressure domes was littered with hurriedly disassembled machinery and unnecessary equipment. Even so, there was barely room inside the domes for the cots and replicators the *Enterprise* and other relief vessels had beamed down.

But in no way could any of Gamow Station's refugees or science staff be beamed up. Everyone on the station had been exposed to the virogen, and only the strictest quarantine measures could keep it contained. *If it* can *be contained,* Picard thought.

Chiton seemed sensitive to Picard's reluctance to begin. "I'm assuming you beamed down to tell me something in person you can't risk transmitting so that others might hear," she prompted.

Picard appreciated the station manager's effort to make

this easier for him. "Two people from this station may have escaped the blockade."

Chiton frowned. "My staff tracked the chase with our deep-space sensors. The *Enterprise* was the only ship to come back."

"Our sensors might have been fooled as well," Picard said.

"Fooled?"

Picard told Chiton how the *Enterprise*'s chase of the *Bennett* had ended.

"A Vulcan and his pregnant, human mate?" she asked incredulously. "And they killed themselves?"

"Perhaps not. We checked the blast zone and there were no traces of organic residue. I believe Stron and his wife beamed to another location. A second ship, perhaps."

Chiton put a hand on her jaw and sharply twisted her head to one side as she thought over the implications. "Then it was a very well organized escape."

Picard winced as he heard a ripple of cracks come from her elongated neck. His helmet's speakers amplified the sound alarmingly.

"What I am trying to determine," Picard said, "is who among your staff would have had clearance and opportunity, first to keep Stron's presence at the station hidden, and then to allow him access to the *Bennett*."

"Me," the station manager said at once, clearly untroubled that she might be drawing suspicion to herself. "A couple of others in operations."

"Who, specifically?"

Chiton rose to her full height and walked around her desk to the computer terminal half-hidden in the clutter on the surface of the desk. She began typing in commands. "Anyone who maintained individual quarters. In the dormitories, someone definitely would have noticed a Vulcan and his pregnant human mate." Chiton turned the display screen around so that Picard could read it. "These are current medical logs for the station, including all refugees. No pregnancies. Twenty-two Vulcans. No one missing."

"You're certain that all the refugees would have been included in this list?"

"S.O.P., Captain. When the refugees arrived, we still weren't sure what we were dealing with. So everyone was inoculated with broad-spectrum antiviral serum at the transporter pads as they beamed in, or at the airlocks as they transferred from shuttles."

Picard reached for the terminal control surface, then realized he wouldn't be able to input properly with his gloves. "Are all the shuttles accounted for?" he asked.

Chiton typed in the query. "Yes," she said.

"When did the *Bennett* arrive?"

This time, the station manager didn't enter Picard's question. "The *Bennett*'s been here from the beginning. It was part of the original equipment allotment for the station."

Picard stared at Chiton Kincaid, his surprise obvious. "The *Bennett* was a cruiser escort. Why was it assigned to a planet-based solar observatory like Gamow Station?"

Chiton appeared to be equally surprised by his lack of knowledge. "The ship wasn't part of our solar mission. She was part of a terraforming study group."

Picard's puzzlement deepened. "I wasn't aware that Alta Vista Three was a candidate for terraforming. It already has a native ecosystem." Picard was aware that the planet's plant and animal species thrived in an atmosphere with more sulphur and less oxygen than humans could survive in, but he also knew that Federation regulations strictly prohibited the alteration of an existing alien biosphere unless it closely matched Earth norms.

"Most assuredly," Chiton agreed.

"Then what exactly *was* the *Bennett*'s mission?"

The station manager gestured up past the ceiling of her office. "The alta mist, Captain. Those colored clouds are giant colonies of what's virtually an airborne algae. They're epiphytic—absorb all their nutrients from the air. The Federation's terraforming bureaus were interested in engineering the epiphytes to help in seeding other planets with oxygen. The *Bennett* was modified to scoop samples from the atmosphere and transfer them to terraforming pilot projccts."

Picard felt as if he had been struck by a phaser. "Could that be how the virogen was spread?" he asked. Could the answer to the greatest disaster that had ever threatened the Federation be so easily found?

Chiton shook her head. "We thought of that, too. But the *Bennett* never left the system. Once the virogen established itself in the alta mist, that's when the quarantine began."

Picard sighed, briefly fogging his visor. It would have been too simple a solution to connect the *Bennett* and the alta mist with the virogen. But still . . . there was one detail that nagged at him.

"What precisely was the nature of the *Bennett*'s modifications?"

Chiton called up a schematic of the ship. It was a simple warp design, sleek enough for impulse-powered atmospheric flight. The outlines of two large pods mounted on its undercarriage began to flash. "Sampling tanks," Chiton explained. "Pressurized nozzles, venting chambers, built-in transporter links for transfer to holding tanks at the pilot projects. It's a standard modification for biological assay missions."

The pods were like a red-alert beacon to Picard. "Did the *Bennett* fulfill any of its mission objectives?"

Chiton looked annoyed. "As I said, it never left the system."

"But did it ever undertake sampling runs?"

Chiton checked her computer. "Several," she said. "We were using it to track the spread of the virogen around the planet. All the data have been forwarded to Starfleet Medical."

"Then those sampling tanks must have been full," Picard said.

"What's your point, Captain?"

"There was *no* organic residue at the blast site. Even if Stron and his wife had beamed off the ship, the blast site should have been covered with the residue of the alta mist from the sampling tanks. Thus, it must have been beamed off, as well."

"You're saying someone *stole* the alta mist?"

"Under our noses." Picard wanted to contact his ship at once, assemble his team, get Data and Geordi and Will at work on this right away. But he still didn't dare transmit his suspicions over subspace. Who knew who might be listening in?

"But why would anyone do that?" the station manager asked.

"I can't be certain," Picard admitted. "But it must have something to do with the atmospheric spread of the virogen."

Chiton straightened up and put her hands on her hips. Picard could see the skepticism in her eyes and her posture.

"Unfortunately, the virogen arose on several other systems before it appeared here," she said. "That would seem to leave a rather large hole in your theory."

But Picard was certain he was on to something that no one had yet suspected. His voice rose with his urgency. "Starfleet believes the virogen might have been spreading through the sector in a dormant phase, and only last year did it become virulent. But what if it were *engineered* here in the first place? Spread by colonies of alta mist which were released into the atmosphere of a dozen worlds?"

Chiton's angular face tightened. "Captain Picard, I told you: The *Bennett* never left the system."

"But surely other ships might have come and gone before it. And the *Bennett*'s cargo and crew did break quarantine when we chased it. It could be part of an ongoing operation."

The station manager moved around her desk to face Picard directly, towering over him. "You do realize what you're suggesting?"

Picard almost trembled at the thought that this might be the breakthrough all of Starfleet had been waiting for. "Yes. That the virogen is artificial and deliberately spread. A hideous act of biological warfare against the Federation!"

Picard looked up at the manager in excitement and was surprised to see she didn't share his outrage.

"Captain," she said quietly, "I think you're very wise to keep this off the subspace channels."

"But not for long," Picard replied. He felt invigorated, charged with energy. After months of doing nothing, he had an enemy to focus on, a goal to achieve. His findings here could rally Starfleet in its darkest hour. Give the Federation hope.

Then Chiton grabbed his arm so suddenly, he didn't even think to pull away. For a moment, he wondered if he appeared too agitated, if she were going to suggest he compose himself.

He reached for the comm-link control on his forearm. "Manager Kincaid, please . . . I must beam back to the *Enterprise.*"

But from behind her back, Chiton produced a medical protoplaser.

"My regrets, Captain," she said. Then she slashed the protoplaser's cutting beam across Picard's helmet, fusing the built-in communicator circuits in a spray of sparks, and slicing open Picard's clear visor. He felt the rush of Alta Vista air strike his skin an instant before the sizzling heat of a spray of molten transparent aluminum.

Picard collapsed to his knees, gasping in agony, clawing at his helmet, futilely trying to wipe the burning metal from his face.

Then the pain seemed to disappear as he felt the manager's

boot kick him sharply beneath the ribs, driving the air from his lungs, making his vision sparkle with black stars.

He fell back on the floor of the office, his vision swimming as Chiton knelt beside him, still a giant, like a storm cloud above him as he kept falling back into a dark place where all pain would end.

The last image he remembered was the tip of the protoplaser moving closer, glowing, whiting out the manager's face. Her voice echoed in his helmet. "You're not going anywhere."

Then the pain vanished, along with everything else.

ELEVEN

Kirk's hands were raw where blisters had burst. His muscles protested. His knee twinged where he had twisted the wrong way while hefting one of the collapsed beams from the ruins of Teilani's home.

But he had never felt better.

And looking at the small cabin he had constructed and braced between two existing stone walls, he had never felt more satisfied.

He did not know how these feelings had come to be. Over his career, he had never stopped learning. There had always been more capable teachers to follow, more experienced specialists whose examples he could profit by. As the years had progressed, so had his store of knowledge and skills, sometimes in spite of himself.

If anything, he reflected, at his age he should be capable of great and complex accomplishments, using the sum total of his knowledge and experience.

Yet more than ever, it was the simple things that drew him now. Building a cabin instead of exploring a galaxy.

Youth had been for him an explosion of opportunity and

possibilities—a thousand worlds to experience, an infinite number of directions to pursue.

Each direction he had chosen, each challenge he had accepted, had narrowed the focus of his life, until he had come to this time and this place—the crossroads of his existence.

He would not have it any other way.

One home. One dream. One love.

He felt Teilani's arms slip around him as she stood to admire his work.

"It's beautiful," she said.

Kirk tilted his head at his creation. "The door's crooked," he said.

"I understand it's a very popular architectural feature on *Qo'noS.*"

"There're only two rooms."

Teilani leaned her head against his shoulder. He ignored the flash of pain her movement caused his strained muscles. He wanted to feel her head resting against him.

"Who needs more than two?" she asked.

"And without plumbing, I had to dig a ditch out behind the far wall."

Teilani smiled up at him. "That's different. Tomorrow I'll help you find some pipes."

But whatever she said made no impression on him. He saw only her eyes, her lips, the passion they had shared once and which he knew they would share again.

There was nothing he could do but kiss her. Nothing she could do but return that kiss, as if no time had passed in all the years they had been apart.

Kirk lifted her and felt only the fire of youth in his arms. If his knee twinged, it had the good sense to keep its complaints to itself.

He carried her across the threshold he had built, leaving the nightmare of Chal behind.

The second, smaller room held their bed—a mattress made of scavenged blankets, pillows of rolled-up food sacks, a shuttered window casting bars of light and shadow as if it were summer outside and the world and the Federation weren't dying all around them.

He placed her gently on that bed and she did not take her arms from around him.

For a moment, he felt a sense of nervousness. He had been gone so long.

But she whispered in his ear to tell him that no time had passed at all. That in this bed he had made, in this home he had built, the years held no dominion.

He kissed the scar that ravaged her face, touched her hair embroidered with gray, and knew she was right.

Time meant nothing.

All his life meant nothing.

Except for this one perfect moment in the arms of this one woman.

They made love then.

For the first time, for the hundredth. It didn't matter.

After all the years and the light-years he had traveled, all the worlds he had seen, James T. Kirk had finally found what he had sought.

In Teilani's embrace, he was home.

They lay together, letting the breeze cool the sweat from their bodies, watching dust motes spiral in the thin shafts of light that pierced the wooden wall.

Teilani stretched against him. Kirk held her hand, kissed her fingers, felt the tension inside her.

He rolled onto his side, traced the frown she wore. "What?" he asked.

"Spock told me you were gone."

"Shhh," Kirk whispered. He kissed her eye, kissed the

Klingon furrows of her brow, the Romulan tips of her ears. "I didn't die. I was only lost."

"Spock came to Chal to tell me in person. Less than a year after . . . after you left. He didn't say you were dead. I don't think he believed it. But he said you were gone. And I could tell he meant forever."

She turned to touch his chest, stare into his eyes. "I read about what happened on Veridian Three." She gazed at him questioningly, waiting for him to answer next what he must.

"I didn't die," Kirk said, smiling.

"But how . . . ?" Teilani asked.

He held a finger to her lips. Saw her react to the shadows in his eyes. He had wondered how much Starfleet would make public about his rescue by the Borg. About the Borg and renegade Romulan alliance to invade the Federation. Some secrets were best left to history.

"I came back," Kirk said. "Isn't that enough?"

Teilani pressed her head against his chest, held him tight. He was flooded with the memory of where he had gone after the near-destruction of the Borg homeworld. The teachers he had found. The mysteries revealed.

"I'm so afraid you'll leave again."

"Not today," Kirk said.

They made love again. For the first time. For the hundredth . . .

. . . and awoke to the screams of the dying, as Orion fighters blazed through the night sky, raining death and destruction on the last of Kirk's Eden.

TWELVE

For the fifth time that day, Sarek's chief of staff transformed himself into the mist of quantum dissolution.

In the privacy of a Babel conference room, Spock studied his young aide, Srell, for his reaction to the holoprojector's recording.

Predictably, Srell betrayed no emotional response at all.

"It is an obvious forgery," the young Vulcan said.

"Explain."

"Ki Mendrossen is not dead."

"How do you know?"

In the clipped, efficient exchange that passed for conversation among Vulcans, Srell did not hesitate. "Before our arrival at Babel, I reviewed personnel files at the diplomatic corps. Mendrossen's was current."

Intrigued by Srell's comment, Spock reached out and shut off the holoprojector before the recording of the empty floor ended on its own. "Why did you review Ki Mendrossen's personnel file?"

"I anticipated a positive result to the vote on expanding negotiations with Romulus. To fully exploit the opportunity would have required additional workers with expertise in delicate diplomatic matters. Mendrossen's work for your father was most satisfactory. I wished to see if he were available for reassignment."

"Was he?"

"Ki Mendrossen is on leave. I presume he will be available for reassignment upon his return."

Spock nodded, placed his hands behind his back, and began to walk the length of the conference room. The walls of the simple chamber were adorned with the banners of Federation members. Many of them were battle flags—the lesson being that even onetime enemies could eventually sit at the same table in peaceful negotiation.

"What is the current status of Sakkath?" Spock asked as he paced. At the same time Mendrossen had been Spock's father's chief of staff, Sakkath had been Sarek's personal assistant. The Vulcan aide had used his telepathic skills to help stabilize Sarek's emotional control during the final negotiations to complete the Legaran treaty.

This time, Srell did hesitate before answering. "I do not know."

Spock found that a curious response. "Would it not have been logical to ascertain Sakkath's status at the same time you reviewed Mendrossen's?"

Srell remained seated at the table, hands folded before him. Spock now stood behind his assistant's chair. Their different positions and attitudes properly reflected their relation as teacher and student.

"Sakkath is Vulcan," Srell explained. "I did not believe the Romulans would deem him a suitable neutral observer. Mendrossen is human. The Romulans would complain about his connection to the Vulcan diplomatic corps, but in the end, he would be suitable."

"Sakkath is also on leave," Spock said.

Srell turned in his chair to face the elder ambassador. "Then you have checked the personnel files as well."

"No," Spock said. "I contacted a colleague at the corps. My inquiries were unofficial. No data trail exists which possibly might alert remaining spies."

"A spy in the Vulcan diplomatic corps is a logical impossibility."

"Yet Ki Mendrossen has disappeared."

A human might have questioned Spock's assertion. Srell knew better. He simply asked for more information. "Are there indications of suicide?"

Spock leaned past Srell to pick up the holoprojector which still sat on the conference table before the young Vulcan. "This unit contains power cells manufactured on New Malta. Mendrossen's last known communiqué with the corps was from New Malta. He arrived at New Malta on the passenger liner *Olaf Stapledon.* He had further booked diplomatic courtesy passage on the Starfleet survey vessel *Sloane,* to depart ten standard days later. Yet he was not aboard the *Sloane* when it departed New Malta. He is no longer known to be on New Malta. Logic, and this recording, suggest he died on New Malta."

"There are many arguments I could construct," Srell said calmly. "Perhaps Mendrossen went into hiding after creating this fraudulent recording. Perhaps Mendrossen was kidnapped or murdered by an unknown assailant who subsequently manufactured this recording."

"For what purpose?" Spock asked.

"There are insufficient data." The young Vulcan stood up beside Spock. "The most important fact is that Sarek was not murdered. He died of Bendii Syndrome. Thus, however it was made, Mendrossen's confession to participating in your father's murder is also a fabrication."

Spock took a moment to prepare himself before he stated his most shocking discovery of the day. "Srell, I have ascertained that my father was never clinically diagnosed."

For a moment, Srell's emotional control faltered. "Ambassador . . . I assure you I was at his side day and night. His wife attended him. The best healers from Vulcan attended him. You yourself have read the reports of the events at Legara Four when Sarek's emotional turmoil bled through to the crew of the starship he traveled on. Everything unequivocally pointed to Bendii."

But Spock was unswayed. "Observation of symptoms aside, the only definitive diagnosis of Bendii Syndrome is obtained by culturing tissue from the metathalamus. I have determined that procedure was never undertaken."

Spock's young assistant looked stricken. "But . . . that is illogical. How could healers treat a patient without confirming their diagnosis?"

Spock sighed for the many lessons of age that the years still held for Srell. "Even on Vulcan, logic does not always obtain. My father was old, revered, dying. I find it most logical that given the apparent definitive nature of his symptoms, no healer felt it necessary to subject him to the discomfort of a biopsy of his metathalamus."

Srell sat down abruptly, rigidly staring across the chamber at the flag of the Martian Colonies that hung directly opposite him. The flag was stitched with laser holes from the War of Declaration. "I was on your father's staff. I should have known. I might have done something."

"Regrets are illogical," Spock said, though he knew he was not convincing.

In any event, Srell did not appear interested in any wisdom Spock might dispense. "Why would anyone want to kill Sarek?"

Spock sat down beside Srell, no longer a teacher instructing his student. Instead, they were two colleagues mourning a revered mentor. "My father's career spanned more than a century and a half. That is ample time to make enemies.

Perhaps members of the cause or revolution to which Ki Mendrossen referred."

"But to kill him in such a manner," Srell said.

"In what manner?"

Srell glanced at Spock. "To make it appear as if he had Bendii Syndrome, of course."

"Of course. But how could his murderer accomplish that?" Spock asked.

Srell looked around the room at the flags, then down at the table. He found no answer. "I . . . do not know."

"There are three possible techniques," Spock said.

"You conferred with yet another colleague?"

"With a holographic representation of an expert in Vulcan criminal investigations. I availed myself of the holodeck in the health center."

Srell made no pretense of hiding his bewilderment. "How can there be an expert in Vulcan criminal investigations? There is no crime on Vulcan."

"Other than the murder of my father," Spock agreed dryly, "there is very little. Nonetheless, I reconfigured several Vulcan expert systems in sociology and medicine to interface with a fictional human detective. He was quite illuminating in his understanding of motive, opportunity, and technique. Though his violin skills are rudimentary, at best."

"You conferred with a fictional human detective on a holodeck?" Srell said in the Vulcan equivalent of shock. "That is not a technique they teach at the Academy."

"I have learned to be adaptable."

"Indeed." Srell visibly struggled to compose himself, then sat forward in his chair, holding his hands together on the tabletop again, preparing to be enlightened. "What are the three techniques by which Bendii Syndrome might be duplicated?"

"First, telepathic induction," Spock said. "It would require a series of progressively intrusive mindmelds between murderer and victim, with the memories of those mindmelds continually erased. Second, gradual exposure to deuterium, in food and drink, which would build up in Vulcan neural tissue and degrade its function, and which could be detected at autopsy. And third, deliberate exposure to the Bendii Syndrome pathogen."

Srell blinked. "Bendii is not communicable."

"Almost any disease is communicable if extraordinary measures are taken to introduce the pathogen into the body of the victim."

Srell sat in silent contemplation for long moments. "Why was your father simply not shot? Lost in a transporter malfunction? Poisoned in one dose?" Srell looked beseechingly at Spock. "He died almost three years after he was thought to exhibit Bendii symptoms. Why so long?"

"Clearly, it was important to the murderer that no one suspect Sarek was murdered. Perhaps it was enough that his abilities were impaired."

"His stamina grew steadily worse," Srell admitted. "But his abilities, when he commanded them, were as formidable as ever."

"However, as my father's stamina declined, he undoubtedly had to relinquish involvement in many ongoing missions."

"That is true," Srell conceded.

"But not," Spock said, quoting the subjects on which Ki Mendrossen, Sarek's chief of staff, had reported to the mysterious prefect of Gonthar District, "his involvement in the Amtara reparations, the redrafting of Starfleet's First Contact protocols, the repatriation of the Andorian drallstone, and all discussions relating to the Romulan unification."

Srell nodded slowly. "That is also true."

"Thus, logic dictates that the reason for my father's murder is connected to one or more of those ongoing negotiations."

"Sarek was not involved in Romulan unification. He followed that topic only because of your involvement in it."

"Indeed."

"He was . . . pleased with your progress, if not your tactics."

Spock lifted an eyebrow. It was most inappropriate for young Srell to discuss Sarek's feelings with Sarek's son. "My fictional expert pointed out a common element to all three methods of murder," Spock said, changing the subject.

"Ongoing personal contact," Srell said.

Spock noted with approval his assistant's quick and logical response. He decided the youth's earlier, inappropriate comments had merely been the natural result of shock.

"Thus, there are many suspects," Spock suggested.

"His wife, Perrin. Sakkath. Ki Mendrossen, who has confessed—"

"Who might have assisted in the murder," Spock amended, "implying there may have been other conspirators—from the so-called cause or revolution."

"Myself," Srell continued matter-of-factly. "The staff of healers who attended him." The young Vulcan paused. "It will be necessary to obtain a list of his visitors and appointments for the years preceding his death."

"They are being prepared for me on Vulcan," Spock said. Again, he had made the request of the Vulcan archives through a third party—a scholar claiming to be researching Sarek's life for a thesis.

"When will the lists be available to us?" Srell asked.

"When we arrive on Vulcan."

Srell blinked. "I had assumed we would be returning to the Romulan border."

"The Empire will wait. There is no trace of the Klingon

who delivered the holoprojector to me. There is no library correlation to a prefect of the Gonthar District. There is nothing more we can do by subspace. Therefore, whatever answers are to be found are waiting on Vulcan. The scene of the crime, as it were." He stood up, signaling to Srell that their meeting had ended.

Srell immediately stood and smoothed the long, black tunic he wore. "I will make new travel arrangements."

Spock nodded.

Srell went to the door, turned back with a sudden thought. "Ambassador, given the unusual circumstances by which you obtained Ki Mendrossen's confession, have you considered that you yourself are being manipulated into returning to Vulcan to investigate your father's murder?"

"Of course I am being manipulated," Spock said. "It is merely a question of discovering who the manipulator is: Ki Mendrossen, seeking absolution after his death, or a person or persons unknown, for reasons which for now still remain unclear to me."

Srell spoke cautiously. "In regard to those reasons, Ambassador, it could well be that having killed your father, the person or persons responsible might not hesitate to kill again if they fear their crime will be uncovered."

"They are right to be afraid," Spock said.

Srell didn't understand.

"I am only half Vulcan," Spock explained. "Whoever killed my father will have to answer to my human side."

Spock noted with interest the manner in which Srell raised both his eyebrows.

In Vulcan terms, Spock's vow of revenge was obscenely emotional.

But it felt right. And at this moment in his life, that was all that Spock cared about.

Logic and Surak be damned.

THIRTEEN

Kirk leapt from his bed, propelled by instinct, not conscious thought. The whine of phaser hits was that ingrained in his mind.

He ran from the bedroom, pulling his Vulcan cloak around his shoulders. Outside, the low clouds of Chal's night sky flickered and flared with lances of phaser energy from the air, and explosions and fire from the ground.

Teilani was suddenly at Kirk's side, holding his arm, standing unafraid as the scream of impulse engines echoed around them.

"Atmospheric fighters," she said. She pointed up to a sudden streak of blue light high above them. "They're coming in from high orbit."

Kirk calculated the flight path of the attacking ships. "They're headed for the relief headquarters." He turned and ran back inside the cabin, emerged a minute later, fully clothed.

He paused to see that Teilani was already dressed.

"You have to stay here," he said automatically as the ground rocked with distant explosions.

Teilani merely smiled at him. "This is my world, James.

We'll fight for it today the way we fought for it before. Together."

Kirk caught her up in a fierce embrace. Then they ran for the center of the city, the sky on fire around them.

Christine MacDonald dug her way out from beneath her cot and crawled across the floor of the tent, blindly fumbling for her tunic and the comm badge pinned to it.

Her ears rang with the explosion that had thrown her from her sleep. She squinted as blinding phaser flashes struck a nearby building. The midrange orange hue told her she was seeing phaser bursts originating in the atmosphere, not from orbit. If the *Tobias* had not already been taken out by a mothership, then her crew should be able to handle a few fighters.

Another blast slammed into her, flattening the Starfleet tent all around her. She fought against the constricting folds of heavy fabric that pinned her arms to her sides. She gasped for air as the collapsing tent pressed ever more tightly against her face.

Then she smelled smoke. Recognized the acrid odor of the tent's insulation.

I refuse to die out of uniform, she told herself.

She stopped struggling. Forced her arms to relax at her side.

She refused to die at all.

She turned her head in the suffocating fabric.

In one direction, she could feel a breeze along her right cheek. That meant she wasn't completely entangled. There was an opening somewhere.

She rotated her right shoulder, felt the heavy fabric ease up a few centimeters up on her right side.

She ignored the roar of fighters streaking overhead. Did not react to the thunder of the shock waves they left behind, or the growing heat she felt on her left side.

First solve the problem of being trapped, she told herself firmly. Then she could worry about fighting back.

Her bare foot made contact with a blast of hot air.

She bent her leg, kicked, twisted sideways until her right hand was free at her waist. She wriggled down, bracing herself against the ground, straining her neck, her shoulders, until . . .

. . . she broke free of the tent and found herself surrounded by flames.

The relief camp was a war zone. The hospice across the town square was an inferno.

Christine stood in the middle of the destruction, in nothing more than Starfleet-issue T-shirt and shorts, and instantly assessed the situation.

Whoever was flying those fighters, no one on the ground was getting out alive.

She pushed her hair out of her face and looked around. About five meters away, there was a gap in the flames from the ruined tent. If she ran for it, didn't mind stepping on coals with her bare feet, she could make it. Might make it.

But then what?

She directed her attention to the tented landscape that surrounded her. Peered through the billowing smoke and flickers of flame until she made out what had to be the enshrouded outline of a folding chair on its side. It was where she had thrown her uniform when she had gone to bed only an hour ago.

Ignoring the flames rushing closer, she stumbled over the mounds of tent fabric until she stood beside the chair's outline. She felt around for the leg of the chair and rubbed it back and forth against the fabric until the chair leg gashed a hole in the tent. She ripped the gash wider. Reached through the opening. Felt her uniform tunic. Yanked it out. Hit the comm badge.

"MacDonald to *Tobias*—one to beam up *now!*"

And just as an explosion lifted a wall of blazing tentcloth toward her, Christine dissolved in a different fire . . .

. . . and found herself kneeling on the transporter pad of her ship.

She leapt to her feet, tunic still clutched in one hand. Battle stations sounded. Alert lamps flashed.

"How bad?" she shouted at the transporter tech.

Two more transporter columns blossomed beside her. One was M'Benga, brushing out sparks on her pant leg. The other was a young Chal male, still half asleep.

"They're jamming our sensors," the transporter tech shouted back. "But we're punching through to beam up everyone we can lock on to."

Christine grabbed M'Benga and the young Chal by their arms and hauled them off the pad. Another column of energy appeared—another crew member rescued from the carnage below.

"Is the ship under attack?" Christine asked.

The deck lurched with the shudder of buckling shields.

"They're hammering us," the tech said as his hands flew over the controls. "Barc has the conn. He wants to hold orbit as long as we can beam between shield cycles."

Christine ran for the transporter controls. "Set your sensors for human-only readings—no Chal, exclude anyone with a comm badge."

The transporter tech looked at his half-dressed commander in horror. "Commander—we've got to take 'em as we find 'em. They're being slaughtered down there!"

Christine slammed down on the controls and wiped every comm-badge trace off the board. "You're scanning for a human male. He'll be running for the center of the attack."

The tech screwed up his face in incomprehension. "What? Everyone else is running away."

"Then it should be easy to find him"—the deck lurched

again, the lights flickered as auxiliary life-support kicked in—"right, Ensign?"

"Yes, ma'am," the tech said. Sweat dripped from his brow to the console. "Got someone on the move, heading into town. . . ."

"Lock on, mister," Christine said.

"Have to wait for the shields to cycle." The ship seemed to fall a foot beneath them as the artificial-gravity field stuttered. "Barc's not dropping the shields. He's not cycling. . . ."

Christine hit the comm control on the console. "MacDonald to bridge! Lieutenant Barc—drop shields over the transporter waveguides! Now!"

Barc growled back over the speakers. "Commander, we won't last a Klingon second!"

"Now, Barcs! That's an order!"

The engineer's only reply was a Tellarite snarl, but the transporter tech announced that he had an opening.

"Energize!" Christine shouted, and a moment later James T. Kirk charged off the pad, transported in midstride.

He looked at Christine without an instant of disorientation, as if he were transported on the run every day. It was a startling change from his last transport—now he was the Kirk of her history books, and dreams. "There're people down there who need my help!"

Christine ran to him. "I need you on this ship!" Another hit echoed through the transporter room. "We're under attack and my only combat experience is in the Academy simulator!"

Kirk was enraged. "What makes you think I could do any better?!"

She grabbed his shirtfront, refusing to accept any outcome but the one she wanted.

"Because I know who you are, *Captain.* And right now, you're our only way out of whatever the hell is happening here!" She released his shirt. "Report to the bridge! That's an order!"

Kirk's jaw clenched. His eyes blazed into hers. But neither one would give.

Then Kirk looked at the tech. "There was a woman beside me, running in the same direction." He looked back at Christine. "And if she's not on this ship by the time I get to the bridge, so help me I'll fly us all into the suns."

Christine snapped her fingers at the tech. "You heard him! Lock on and energize!"

She stared at Kirk. "Anything else?"

"No. But when this is over, we're going to have a long talk." Then he ran for the doors and they parted before him.

Kirk was awake in a nightmare. He knew it was the *Tobias* that lurched and trembled around him. But he kept seeing the corridors of the *Enterprise*-B as he ran for the deflector relay room. Captain Harriman on the bridge. Scotty at ops, holding her together. And the Nexus a wild beast, tearing at the ship and her shields, clawing through the bulkheads to rip Kirk from his time and—

The lift doors opened and Kirk erupted onto the bridge. A Tellarite jumped up from the center chair. "Chief Engineer Barc, sir. The commander said you have the conn, sir!"

Kirk made his way to the chair, eyes fixed on the main screen. A shaft of phaser energy flashed from an invisible point among the stars and the ship trembled.

"Shield strength?" Kirk called out.

"Forty percent forward. Eighty percent aft." Kirk took a look at the helmsman. He, or she, or it was humanoid, but covered in iridescent blue and purple scales, with a mane of what appeared to be bristling, prehensile tendrils cascading from his shoulders. But one look was all Kirk had time for.

"How many attackers?" he asked the helmsman.

"Just one in orbit."

"Then turn the ship around!" Kirk ordered.

Instantly, the starfield on the screen twirled and the dark disk of Chal's nightside flashed by. Another impact slammed the ship, but the shields' response was stronger.

"Keep giving me readings," Kirk said.

"Aft shields seventy-seven percent, holding strong," the helmsman said.

"Who's weapons officer?" Kirk demanded.

Beside Kirk, the Tellarite nervously grunted. "Uh, this is a science vessel, sir."

The scaled helmsman didn't take his eyes off his controls, but raised a wickedly clawed hand with three jointless fingers. "I have weapons, sir."

"Then give me aft sensors on the screen," Kirk commanded. "I want range, class . . . How many fighters below us?"

"Seven, sir."

Kirk leaned back in his chair, tapped a finger against the arm, then suddenly looked down to make certain he hadn't hit any control he hadn't expected. "That's a standard Orion attack wing," Kirk said. "Any idea who our attackers are?"

A short blond officer looked over from communications. "There was no warning, sir. They refuse to respond to our hailing frequencies."

"Maximum magnification on the attacker."

The viewscreen wavered. A small point of light became a larger point of light.

"They're bleeding energy through their shields," Kirk said as he recognized the visual signature. "Keeps us from identifying their class and targeting vital areas."

Barc glanced at Kirk. "You've seen this before?"

"An old Orion trick. We're being attacked by pirates."

"There haven't been pirates in this sector for at least a century." Kirk noted the skeptical grunt that accompanied the Tellarite's observation.

The bridge rocked and a sensor-control station threw off an arc of sparks.

"You want the chair back?" Kirk challenged Barc.

"No. Sir."

Kirk turned back to the screen. In some small part of his mind, he was troubled that he did not have to think about the possible strategies he could follow. They were as neatly arranged in his thoughts as if they had been programmed. Is this what Starfleet had made him? Would this be the destiny he could never escape?

"That orbiting ship will have to stay in space," Kirk said, an analysis of Orion tactics coming effortlessly to him. "We have to take out those fighters. Helmsman: Weapons status for atmospheric combat?"

"None, sir."

"No torpedoes?"

"None, sir."

"Phasers?"

"Designed for clearing navigational obstructions. We could never cycle them fast enough to take on a fighter."

Kirk leaned forward in his chair. "We *can* go into the atmosphere, can't we?"

The scaled helmsman glanced over his shoulder, and his bristling mane parted so his solid green eyes could make contact with Kirk's. "We can, sir. But we'll have the maneuverability of a brick."

None of that was what Kirk wanted to hear. But there was no time to waste. "Plot a course to the main city. Take us down."

At least the crew of Christine MacDonald's *Tobias* was better than the ship's capabilities would suggest. Almost at once, the stars slipped up the viewscreen as the dark disk of Chal rushed toward them.

Kirk held on to the arms of the command chair as the *Tobias* began to vibrate with atmospheric drag.

"Structural integrity field is holding," the helmsman announced. "Two minutes to target."

Kirk was aware of everyone's eyes upon him. Two minutes to target and then what? Without useful weapons and maneuverability, the *Tobias* would be an easy target for the seven fighters laying waste to the main city. The Orions would not be able to resist attacking her.

Then Kirk saw the way out.

"Track those fighters, helmsman," Kirk ordered. He heard the turbolift doors open behind him. Teilani was now on his right. Christine on his left, back in uniform.

"Situation?" Christine asked.

"We'll know in ninety seconds," Kirk said. "Helmsman, maintain speed at Mach three. Configure shields for maximum displacement of air during sonic boom, but don't enlarge them until those fighters are coming at us."

Kirk knew the alien at the helm wouldn't understand what he was planning, but he was pleased to see the helmsman's claws race over the board, following Kirk's orders to the letter. Christine had trained her crew well.

"Fighters are banking," the helmsman said. "Coming up on intercept course."

"Do not break heading," Kirk told him. "Continue straight for them, drop at the last second, then deploy tractor beams."

The Tellarite stepped closer to Kirk and lowered his voice to a growl. "Sir, at this speed, we'll never be able to hold on to all seven of them."

"We don't have to," Kirk said. "They're atmospheric fighters, dependent on lift. Between the sonic-boom displacement and even a second or two of contact with our tractor beams, the pilots won't be able to maintain control."

"What if they have antigrav backups?"

"Then they'll be as slow as we are, and the first thing they'll want to do is get back into space."

"Fighters are converging," the helmsman reported. "Twenty seconds to intercept."

"Ready on those shields. . . ."

On the viewscreen, Kirk could see seven thin traces of fiery exhaust merging over the black silhouette of the main island. The fighters were rising to meet the *Tobias*.

Then phasers lanced out from the exhaust trails. The viewscreen flared as the forward shields, already strained by atmospheric friction, shimmered on the brink of overload.

"Forward shields at twenty-three percent," the helmsman reported. "Intercept in eight seconds . . . seventeen percent . . . five seconds . . . twelve percent . . ."

Kirk felt Teilani's hand on his. He glanced at Christine. She was grinning as she stared at the viewscreen and he knew she shared his absolute conviction that this would work.

Then the *Tobias*'s bridge angled down as the impulse engines roared and the viewscreen flared and—

—the scaled helmsman cheered!

"Four fighters down! Multiple collisions! We have midair explosions!"

Kirk leaned forward, ignoring the cheers. "Status of the other three?"

The viewscreen image shifted to show flaming debris falling from the sky. An exhaust trail traced a twisting spiral as an intact fighter spun toward the ocean.

"One fighter out of control . . . two others climbing into orbit on antigrav propulsion."

"Take them out, helmsman."

"Aye, sir," the helmsman said uncertainly, and the *Tobias* banked to follow her prey.

For the first time, Christine spoke to Kirk. "They're defenseless. Let them go."

Kirk flashed her a sharp look. She seemed so young to be in command of a ship. There was still so much she had to learn.

"If they make it back to their mothership, they can be

repaired. And I guarantee you they will not fall for this tactic again."

"We are in range," the helmsman said. "Phasers locked."

Before Kirk could give the order to fire, Christine interrupted. "Transporter room, beam the pilots to the brig."

The tech replied over the bridge speakers. "Commander, their shields are up."

Christine hesitated. Kirk turned to her. "You saw what they did to the city," he said.

Christine set her jaw. "Is this how you did things in your century? By butchery and barbarism?"

Kirk had no patience for what it would take to explain the realities of the universe to this novice. He looked back at the screen.

"Fire phasers."

The phasers whined before Christine could countermand him.

On the viewscreen, the small dots of the escaping fighters flared into miniature suns, then trailed in falling fire to the planet far below.

"Sir," the helmsman said, "the mothership is breaking orbit. Going to warp."

Christine spoke very clearly to Kirk. "We are not chasing her."

But Kirk agreed without protest. "Chal needs us." He stood up from the chair, went to Teilani as Christine reclaimed command of her ship and gave her crew the orders to return to orbit.

"Are you all right?" Teilani asked Kirk. Her gaze commanded the truth from him.

Kirk couldn't shake the feeling that he had done something wrong. The adrenaline surge of sitting in that chair, fighting that battle, left him shaken.

"I never wanted to do that again," he said to her. "I'm . . . tired."

Teilani slipped her arm around him. "I'll take you home," she said. They started toward the turbolift.

"Jim, wait," Christine called out behind him.

He paused on the upper deck.

"Barcs said you identified the attackers as Orion pirates."

Kirk nodded.

"Anything else?" Christine asked. "Any idea why they'd attack us?"

Inwardly, Kirk sighed. Sometimes he wished he could forget so many things in his past, but no one would let him.

"Put an aerial view of the main city on the screen," he said. Beside him, Teilani stiffened as the image appeared—the city scribed by precise lines of fire and destruction. "Now overlay a map schematic," Kirk said.

The schematic appeared, making it easy to identify the structures that had been hit.

Christine's chief engineer swore in Tellarite.

"They went after all the communications systems," Christine said. "Every subspace transmitter, every long-range sensor array." She turned to look back at Kirk. "They were trying to silence us. Why?"

"Did you send your inquiry to Starfleet?" Kirk asked. "About the *chalchaj 'qmey* and the chance that the virogen was deliberate?"

Christine's face went white. "Yes," she said.

"Then offhand," Kirk said as he turned back to the turbolift, "I'd say someone got the message."

FOURTEEN

"We've had a bit of a revolt, Commander."

On the main screen of the *Enterprise*-E, Manager Chiton Kincaid of Gamow Station had the decency to appear embarrassed and concerned.

"Protesters broke into the office complex as I was meeting with Captain Picard," she continued. "They opened his suit with a medical protoplaser, and took him hostage."

Riker contained his anger. He had advised Picard not to beam down to meet with Chiton, precisely because the unexpected had a way of springing to life around starship captains.

"If you can drop your shields," Riker said icily, "we will be able to locate the captain and beam him up."

"You didn't hear me," the station manager replied. "Your captain's been exposed to the virogen. He's in no medical danger, but he can spread the disease to plant life-forms, just like everyone else who's infected."

Riker wanted to bellow with frustration. He didn't care if everyone on the *Enterprise* were exposed to the virogen. He wanted his captain back, and he *would* get him, despite

Manager Kincaid's obstructions. It was up to him to figure out how.

But his anger still disrupted his thinking. Behind the command chair, he could hear Deanna talking to Lieutenant Rolk. He turned to tell them to be quiet. He had to concentrate. He had to—

The ship's counselor made a warning gesture, the Bolian security officer hit a control, and Riker saw the viewscreen flicker out from the corner of his eye. The plain, padded wall of the bridge replaced it.

"Deanna?" Riker said, unsure why she had just cut communications with Gamow Station.

"She's lying, Will."

"About what?"

Deanna shrugged. "Almost everything. But I sense the most deception when she talks about the protesters."

Riker went to the heart of the matter. "Is the captain still alive?"

"I believe so. She is concerned about him in some way."

"Then chances are, Manager Kincaid is the one who's holding him captive."

"She is involved," Deanna said. "Absolutely."

Now Riker felt sure and composed. His voice rang out crisply. "Counselor, stand out of scanner range where I can see you. Lieutenant Rolk: screen on."

The virtual viewscreen re-formed and Chiton reappeared. "Is there a problem, Commander?"

"It's the new viewer," Riker lied smoothly. "We're still working out the bugs." He settled back in his chair. "Manager Kincaid, I am going to beam down an assault team to blow your forcefield generators from the ground." He glanced over at Deanna. She gestured imperceptibly that Chiton Kincaid was perturbed by Riker's decision.

But on the screen, the station manager conveyed only

compassionate concern. "Commander Riker, that's a valiant idea. But destroying our forcefield generators will put the whole station at risk from meteorological disturbances. And the protesters have said they will kill your captain, and their other hostages, if any rescue is attempted."

"Don't *they* want to be rescued?" Riker asked, frowning. His mind rapidly considered the possible motives of Picard's abductors. Why else would they have captured him?

"They apparently realize there is nowhere they can go. Their demands are merely for more supplies."

At the side of the bridge, Deanna mouthed the word "lie."

Riker leaned forward in the command chair. "Tell the protesters that we are willing to meet their demands for additional replicators, and whatever other matériel we can provide, on the condition that we speak with Captain Picard to ascertain he is still alive."

"I will do my best, Commander. But . . . conditions down here are . . . somewhat unstable."

"Inform the protesters that however 'unstable' conditions are now, when this ship blows holes in your pressure domes and exposes everyone inside to a poisonous sulphur atmosphere, they will discover the true meaning of the word."

Riker did not need Deanna's Betazoid abilities to register the alarm in the station manager.

"You would risk the lives of fourteen hundred innocent civilians?"

"I want my captain back, Manager. To rescue him, I am prepared to take any means necessary. *Enterprise* out."

Deanna approached Riker. "She believed your threat."

"Good," Riker said. "Only it wasn't a threat."

He could see Deanna sense the truth of what he said. "Will, what do you think is really going on down there?"

Riker stood. "The captain went down to uncover any reason which could explain how Stron managed to hijack the

Bennett, and who might have helped him orchestrate his escape. I believe the captain found the answers to those questions."

"You suspect Manager Kincaid was involved?"

"I'll know that when I have a chance to speak with her, face-to-face." Before Deanna could question his decision, Riker added, "Counselor: You have the conn." He strode toward the turbolift. "Data, Rolk, you're with me." He touched his comm badge. "Dr. Crusher: Report to transporter room two, combat field kit."

Deanna gave him a concerned smile. "Good luck, Will."

But Riker returned the smile with a grin as Rolk and Data joined him. "I don't need luck," he said. "I've got the *Enterprise.*"

Picard awoke in darkness. His face felt numb. He tried to touch his eyes to see if they were covered or if he were blind, but his hands were tied, as were his legs.

He strained every muscle at once.

He was in a chair. Completely immobilized.

"He's awake," a female voice said. Another deeper one, male, responded, "We'll begin."

Picard felt his head pushed from side to side. Something was being removed. Then light exploded into his eyes.

His eye.

He realized he had sight in only one.

The other half of his face was tight with bandages.

He felt groggy, couldn't focus.

"I'll hit him again," the first voice said. Though female, Picard could tell, it wasn't Chiton Kincaid's.

He braced himself for the blow.

But instead, the cool tip of a hypospray touched his neck. He heard it hiss. Felt his lungs respond reflexively as he drew in a huge gasp of air, as if they had suddenly doubled in capacity. Then everything snapped into focus and he was fully alert.

Staring directly into a face he recognized.

Stron.

The Vulcan who had lied.

But who had not, after all, killed himself.

"I am impressed," Picard said. He heard himself slur his words. Half his face was frozen, under some type of neural block, he assumed. The molten aluminum from his visor. It must have inflicted considerable damage, requiring the bandages.

"So am I," Stron said. The Vulcan no longer wore a Starfleet uniform, only a civilian jumpsuit such as a shuttle worker might wear. His was the deeper voice Picard had heard.

With some difficulty, Picard looked to one side, then the other, to find the source of the female voice he had heard.

Stron's human wife, still pregnant, though now in drab civilian clothes. She was the one who had given him the hypospray.

"So not everything you told me was a lie," Picard said.

"Vulcans never lie," Stron replied stiffly.

"Except when there is a logical reason to do so."

Stron made a show of ignoring Picard's comment. Picard's unobstructed eye scanned the room. Some type of supply storage area, he guessed. The light panels on the ceiling were too dim for a regular working area, there were no windows, and from where Picard sat, he could see no door. The unfinished walls were lined with shelves, stocked with small-part trays. From the standard Starfleet inventory stickers on the trays, and the milky smell of tetralubisol, Picard concluded they were in a storage bay attached to Gamow Station's shuttle launchpad.

Stron positioned himself on a chair in front of Picard. "I

must ask you some questions," he said. His manner was formal, as if their meeting were not that of abductor and hostage. "As a Starfleet officer, your first duty will, of course, be to refuse. However, as a reasonable being, you know that no one can resist a Vulcan interrogation."

Picard couldn't quite believe what Stron was implying. "You would mindmeld with an unwilling subject?"

"Did you discuss the *Bennett's* modifications for gathering alta mist with any of your crew?"

Picard's pulse quickened. He felt vindicated by Stron's question. It meant there *was* a connection between the alta mist and the virogen. But he also realized the Vulcan's question was a ruse. Under other circumstances, Picard would have been tempted to say that his whole crew knew about the modifications, so that Stron would believe there would be nothing to gain by silencing Picard. But these were not other circumstances.

"Manager Kincaid was the one who informed me of the modifications," Picard began. "As you know, I have not been in contact with any of my crew since I beamed into her office."

Stron tried another trick question. "Who else among your crew are aware of your suspicions that the *Bennett* did not explode over asteroid Alta Vista two five seven?"

"But the *Bennett* did explode," Picard said calmly, matching the Vulcan's air of detachment. "The only suspicions I shared with my senior staff were that you and your mate were not aboard."

"Are you aware of how that was accomplished?"

"There are anomalous readings in our sensor logs of the explosion," Picard said. "My science department heads are analyzing them in detail."

Stron reached out and pressed two fingers into the side of Picard's neck, somehow creating a lance of pain that burned through Picard's body.

"That was a lie."

Picard's eye watered. He blinked to clear it. "If you already know the answers, you are being illogical to waste time and effort in questioning me."

"The alta mist is already en route, Captain. We have an abundance of time."

Picard strove not to react to that information. "My officers will not rest until they have found me. You have far less time than you imagine."

Stron glanced at his wife, then pulled his chair even closer to Picard. "Then we shall accelerate the process at the cost of your intellect. I have yet to meet a human with the discipline necessary to survive a forced meld unimpaired."

The Vulcan reached out to Picard's face, aligning each fingertip with a *katra* point.

Picard spit in Stron's face.

Without a hint of emotion, Stron again touched a nerve point on Picard's neck, in what was obviously not a Vulcan technique.

Picard made no effort to ignore the pain that touch created. He let it fuel his rage. Let the Vulcan deal with that if he could.

Stron's wife came to Stron's side. She had a medical kit. "Let me try the drugs first," she said.

Stron sat back in his chair. "He is a Starfleet officer. They are trained and conditioned to resist most forms of interrogation." He glanced at Picard with apparent disinterest. "Is that not correct?"

"You want answers," Picard growled, relishing the way in which Stron's wife started in surprise. "You come in and try to take them!"

Then he rocked back and forth in the chair, shouting, snarling, doing anything to keep his emotions at fever pitch. He would pit his emotions against Vulcan impassivity any day.

Stron leaned forward and locked his arm around Picard's neck, immobilizing his head. Picard struggled to bite the Vulcan's fingers.

"Hold him," Stron commanded his wife.

Picard felt inordinately pleased at the hint of exasperation he detected in Stron's voice.

Stron's wife now wrapped her arms around Picard as well, pressing on his neck, keeping his head bent forward and down, making breathing difficult.

Picard felt Stron's fingers again stab into his face, forcing the contact.

The Vulcan spoke the incantation with implacable determination. "My mind to yours, Jean-Luc Picard."

Picard thought of his brother and nephew burned alive in the fire that had swept the château. He thought of the Borg, strapping him down, drilling into his flesh, violating his identity.

He saw his ship, the *Enterprise*-D, consumed by flames as it plunged through the atmosphere of Veridian. Saw James T. Kirk die before his eyes.

Picard fought to fill his heart and his mind with hate and rage and sorrow and channeled it all at the Vulcan who dared invade his mind.

Stron's howl echoed with Picard's as those emotions shot back into the Vulcan's own mind.

Picard felt the woman's arm tighten around his neck. His breathing stopped. Blood hammered in his ears, each pulse a phaser burst of unbridled emotion.

And then, as if he had been plunged into a sea of cooling water, the hate and pain were gone.

My mind to yours, the Vulcan whispered in his mind, as he overcame Picard's defenses.

"Never," Picard croaked.

Then a sudden stream of alien words and oddly familiar

images flashed through his thoughts and he felt the assault abruptly cease as Stron pulled himself away in amazement.

Picard twisted away from the woman's grip, gasping for air.

She knelt by her husband where he had fallen to the floor.

"What's wrong?" she asked urgently. "What happened?"

Stron gazed up at Picard in awe, frighteningly stripped of any attempt to maintain Vulcan composure.

"He has melded before," Stron said. "With the leader."

Stron's wife stared at Picard with equal shock.

Picard trembled, still bound in the chair. He did not understand their reaction, but knew what Stron had found within him.

The echo of a long-ago mindmeld with a different Vulcan.

Ambassador Sarek.

Their leader.

FIFTEEN

Smoke curled up from the fuselage of the Orion fighter, each thin tendril incandescent in the dawn's first light, dissipating only slowly into the dying yellow leaves of the jungle canopy above.

Kirk walked around the wreckage, surefootedly finding a path among the twisted roots and scattered branches outside the acrid burn zone of charred vegetation. What had crashed here was little more than the life-support and control capsule of the fighter—a battered, tapered cylinder no longer than a small shuttlecraft, and only about half its thickness.

The stubs of the fighter's forward-sloping wings trailed control linkages and ODN wires, indicating the wings had been torn off on landing, and not by phaser bursts. Judging from the orientation of the fighter, Kirk guessed the pilot had retained some sort of control until the end, struggling to bring what was left of his craft in for a landing.

Kirk checked the line of broken tree limbs and shredded foliage to the east. On other terrain, the pilot might have walked away from this one.

Christine MacDonald stumbled a few meters behind Kirk,

showing little interest in the wreckage, keeping her attention on her tricorder.

"This is only about half of it," she said as she caught up with Kirk.

But Kirk already knew that. "The main drive units are usually designed to explode away from the pilot's cabin. It's a safety feature."

Christine aimed her tricorder at the knot of crumpled, blackened metal ten meters distant. "Not that it did him a lot of good. We've got a body in there."

Kirk sighed. Of course there was a body in the wreckage. The *Tobias* had not detected anyone ejecting, or drifting to safety on an antigrav chute, from any of the fighters they had downed. He wondered if he had ever been as struck by death as Christine was. Or had he simply encountered it too often in his life?

For a moment, Kirk and Christine stood in silence, watching as Barc lumbered toward the wreckage in an isolation suit. Volatile lubricants and hydraulic fluids had been sprayed around the impact area. Anyone not in protective gear had to remain well back. The vapors could be corrosive, and interfered with most tricorder readings taken at a distance.

Finally, Kirk's curiosity got the better of him. "When did you know?" he asked.

"About who you were? I mean, are?"

Kirk gave her a look of skeptical forbearance. What else would he mean?

"Back at the hospice. The plaque. You gave it to Teilani, didn't you?"

Kirk nodded, remembering. He had taken the plaque from the *Enterprise*-A before he had left his ship to her fate in the fires of Chal's twin suns. Then he had given it to Teilani at a time when he had not been able to give anything of himself. When he had had to return to Earth, and the launch of the *Enterprise*-B.

"That's when I looked up the records," Christine explained. "Saw the resemblance between you and . . . you."

"And you didn't tell anyone?" Kirk asked. He felt touched that she had respected his unspoken wishes to remain anonymous in this new age.

"I tried to. But no one believed me."

Kirk nodded again. So much for respect.

"You know," Christine began, "I studied you in—"

Kirk held up a warning hand. "I do not ever want to hear those words again. Understand?"

Christine bit her lip. Looked uncomfortable. "I only meant to say you've been—"

"An inspiration," Kirk completed.

This time, Christine nodded.

Kirk had heard it all before. He sometimes wondered, with all the attention that had been paid to the *Enterprise,* if Starfleet had ever had any other starships on missions in his day. "I know," he said. "I'm what made you decide to join Starfleet."

Christine wrinkled her nose as she thought that over. "Well, joining Starfleet, that was mostly because of Captain Sulu and the *Excelsior."*

Kirk opened his mouth to say something, then thought better of it.

"My dad used to read me stories about Sulu at bedtime." She looked at Kirk and didn't appear to know how to interpret his expression. "But once I got into the Academy, and started reading the old history tapes . . ."

"'Old' history tapes," Kirk repeated.

Christine began to falter, as if sensing how deep a hole she was digging for herself. "That's when I started reading about you . . . and the . . . old . . . days. . . . How *did* you manage to survive what happened on Veridian Three anyway?" she suddenly asked.

Kirk didn't know whether or not to be thankful for the change in subject.

"I mean, it was all over Starfleet. Captain Picard finding you, bringing you out of that temporal anomaly . . ."

"I've had quite enough of temporal anomalies, thank you," Kirk said.

"But then . . . his log did say he buried you."

"He did."

Christine stared at Kirk for a few moments. "And . . . ?" she said.

Kirk gave her a tight-lipped smile to let her know this particular topic of conversation was at an end. "He obviously didn't do a very good job of it."

"Right." Christine patted her hand against her tricorder as she studied the wreckage. By the flush on her cheeks, Kirk knew she knew she had been rebuffed. "I take it you fought Orions before. Back in the *old* days," she added pointedly.

"They've been mercenaries for as long as they've had spaceflight," Kirk said, trying to ease the sudden awkwardness that had sprung up between them. "I've had my run-ins with them."

Christine kept her eyes on the wreckage. Barc was scanning it at close range, using a tricorder modified for his bulky fingers. He seemed to keep resetting the device, as if he were getting a reading that made no sense. "Any idea why they'd respond this way to an inquiry about the virogen?" She asked the question with no hint of tension or embarrassment. Kirk approved of the professionalism it indicated. Knew it meant she'd go far.

"They were paid to respond," Kirk said. "So we wouldn't be able to connect the attack to the people who intercepted your communications with Command."

"By attacking, though, aren't they confirming what we thought? That the virogen is artificial and deliberately spread?"

"There weren't supposed to be any survivors, Commander. Whoever sent the Orions to attack Chal were expecting their only opposition to be the overworked crew of a science vessel."

"And not the legendary Captain Kirk."

"Jim," Kirk said. "The name is Jim."

Christine threw professionalism aside. "Look. Get it through your head—you're a legend, all right? You can't pretend your career never happened. So . . . move on." She slammed her tricorder shut and stared at him as if she were ready to wrestle him to the ground.

Or embrace him.

Completely unexpectedly, Kirk's first instinct was to kiss her. Fast. He knew that passion he sensed in her didn't come just from her devotion to Starfleet. He had felt the attraction spark between them from the moment he had stepped into her tent at the main city. He had seen the way she watched him when she thought he wasn't paying attention. Her response to him, physically.

He admitted to himself he had watched her the same way. Felt the same pull.

There was such energy in her. All the promise of youth, the excitement, the adventure, the universe waiting for her to reveal it. The way he had once felt.

Kirk knew that same drive and force still existed within him. He knew it would roar into renewed life with just a kiss of her soft lips, a caress of her smooth, unmarked skin. There was a part of him that knew he could be reinvigorated just being at her side, accompanying her on her grand adventure.

But it would be *her* adventure.

And his own still continued.

Teilani waited for him at the main city. She was working with M'Benga, to restore hope and order to her world. His world.

That was Kirk's adventure now. One world. One dream. One love.

He had chosen his path and he knew it was the right one.

But his eyes remained fixed on Christine's.

She moved closer to him.

"Jim . . ." she said.

Kirk knew what was coming.

How wrong would it be to feel her in his arms, knowing that nothing more could come of it?

How wrong would it be to kiss her?

He knew what he should do. He also knew what he felt. Would the two ever be reconciled?

He felt her hand on his shoulder. Knew in the same instant how she would feel pressed against him.

He turned to her, to—

Barc squealed in alarm from the wreckage.

Whatever else Christine and Kirk were, they were both products of Starfleet. Without a moment's hesitation, they ran toward the Tellarite, giving no thought to their lack of protective gear. Because they were needed.

Barc was caught on something by the fighter's shattered canopy, struggling to get free.

Kirk reached him first, half-expecting to see the engineer's isolation suit snagged on a shard of metal.

But something *held* the Tellarite. Gripped his forearm.

A blackened claw of a hand.

Barc's oversized helmet visor was misted from his rapid exhalations. Even without a comm badge, Kirk could hear his husky voice.

"It's alive," the Tellarite snarled.

Kirk grabbed the engineer's shoulder for purchase, grabbed the wrist of whatever it was that held him, and pulled the two apart.

Two screams cut through the morning mist—Barc's as he

fell back from the fuselage, and the fighter pilot's as he rose from the mangled cockpit.

For an instant, Kirk was frozen by the apparition. Half the pilot's flight suit had been fused by flames to his body. Half his helmet had also melted, making his head appear misshapen, half-missing.

The visor was clouded by soot and multiple fracture lines. Kirk could see no trace of the pilot within. But he knew from the condition of the flight suit and the wreckage that the pain the pilot endured would be unbearable.

The pilot, still shrieking, jerked his charred and blackened arm away from Kirk. Kirk let it go, feeling the flakes of plastic and flesh still clinging to his hand.

The pilot's other arm emerged from the cockpit. It held a small green weapon. Too late Kirk realized what was going to happen. He had miscalculated, allowed shock to extend his reaction time.

He wasn't going to make it.

And then he felt Christine roughly shove him aside as she leapt up to plant both feet on the pilot's chest, sending the pilot flying backward from the cockpit.

As Kirk fell sideways, he saw the green weapon spiral through the air above him, its metal finish gleaming in the morning light.

He rolled once and sprang to his feet, ready at least to make the second charge if it was necessary.

But Christine stood poised on the wreckage, looking down on the other side where the pilot had fallen. She was prepared to attack again, though there was no need. She checked over her shoulder to be sure Kirk was safe, then nimbly jumped down on the far side.

Barc got to his feet beside Kirk. Together they circled the wreckage, to join Christine, who kneeled by the unmoving pilot, her fingers working the helmet locking-ring release.

Something new caught Kirk's eye. A more subtle detail

hidden in the charred pressure suit and flesh of the pilot's burned arm.

Each crack was marked by a glistening line of green.

Not the green of Orion skin.

The green of copper-based blood.

Christine grunted as she tugged the pilot's helmet free and let it roll onto the burned vegetation. It carried with it a flap of skin, fused to the melted frame of the visor. But despite the damage to the pilot's face, the missing skin, the exposed muscles and raw cheekbone, enough remained intact to reveal a pointed ear, an arching brow.

"A Romulan?" Christine asked.

But Barc answered with a growl as he played his tricorder over the pilot's body. "No. I can't detect the genetic drift. That's no Romulan," he said.

Kirk understood.

The pilot who had tried to wipe out Chal and keep the secret of the virogen from spreading was not the enemy anyone had expected.

Barc looked up from his tricorder. "He's Vulcan."

To Kirk, that meant only one thing.

This time, the Federation was under attack from within.

SIXTEEN

"Any questions?" Riker asked.

On the transporter platform, Data, Crusher, and Rolk stared through their blast shield visors and shook their heads. All seemed tense in their bulky, black phaser armor. Then Data took a second look at the four hexagonal cargo containers on the opposite side of the pad and apparently reconsidered. He raised his hand. "Actually, I do have one."

Riker stepped up beside his crew and tightened the straps holding his equipment harness to his phaser armor. "Go ahead."

"Has this ever been tried before?"

"You're the one with direct access to the ship's computer," Riker said. He snapped down his blast shield and adjusted the sound level on his helmet speakers.

"That is what concerns me," Data replied. "I am unable to find any reference to this type of maneuver at all."

Riker clapped his hand against Data's shoulder. His armored glove clanged dully against Data's armored chest plate. "Then I'd say we're about to make history." He winked at the android. "Again."

Riker gave a thumbs-up signal to the transporter chief. "You know what you have to do."

The transporter chief nodded, trying to match Riker's hearty enthusiasm, though few on the ship could come close.

"Stage one," the chief said. "Energizing."

Riker looked to the side and saw the cargo containers begin to dematerialize. When they had almost completely vanished, stage two began and the transporter room seemed to evaporate all around him.

A moment later, Riker's boots made contact with the solid metal dome of Gamow Station's generating complex, one hundred meters above the ground. He instantly dropped to his knees, braced his helmet with his arms, and before he could close his eyes, the dome metal flared with overhead light and an explosive concussion threw him flat against the metal.

As he rolled to his feet again, Riker saw that Data was the first one standing. The android was helping both Crusher and Rolk to their feet, as well.

Riker glanced up. About thirty meters above him, against the streaky, pale yellow sky of Alta Vista III, he could just make out the rippling blue distortions in the forcefield that protected the dome. The ripples were what was left of the explosive interference caused by his ship's attempt to beam the four cargo containers into the airspace bisected by the energy screen. For approximately three seconds, exactly as Riker had calculated, the energy of the quasi-solid containers and the dome's forcefield had been the same. The result had been four zones of zero-energy through which Riker, Rolk, Data, and Crusher had been successfully beamed.

As soon as Riker and the others had solidified, the *Enterprise* had reversed the transportation of the cargo containers. The forcefield had snapped back to full strength, simultaneously obliterating a handful of container atoms that had not been beamed out in time. Riker trusted that the explosions that had erupted on the surface of the field would be interpreted by the dome's personnel as an impact by a flock of birds, or whatever passed for birds on this planet.

Data appeared to be the most impressed by Riker's tactic. "It is unfortunate that this method of penetrating a forcefield with a transporter beam can only work on relatively low-powered meteorological screens."

"For now," Riker said. "I'm sure you and Geordi will come up with improvements."

Data's facial expression blanked as he rapidly began working on the problem.

"I meant later, Data," Riker cautioned. He unhooked a projectile gun from his harness and fired a fusion piton into the dome. The piton flared as it melted into the metal plating. Riker pulled on the carbon-fiber cable that trailed from it. The line was secure.

Riker snapped the line to the induction clip on his belt as the others did the same. He pointed to the north. "That direction to the generator conduits. Dr. Crusher, start scanning for the captain as soon as we hit ground."

Riker began running down thc gently sloping curve of the immense dome, playing out the line through his induction clip until he was almost horizontal. Then he gave a push and rappelled down the rest of the dome's nearly vertical wall, pushing off every five meters until he touched down on the gravel around the dome's foundation.

As he disconnected the line, he watched with approval as Crusher and Rolk expertly rappelled behind him. Data, on the other hand, simply kept running straight down at full speed, obviously capable of maintaining a perfect balance between his own forward momentum and the rate at which his line played out.

Two meters from the gravel, Data abruptly swung upright

as if he were doing spacewalk maneuvers, and stepped onto the gravel as lightly as if he had merely stepped around the corner.

"Very smoothly done, Mr. Data," Riker said.

"Thank you, sir. According to terminology associated with the new experiences afforded by my emotion chip, I could say it was quite a rush."

Riker had no idea what Data meant. The term sounded like yet another one of the archaic slang expressions Zefram Cochrane had been so fond of using back in the twenty-first century.

"Whatever." Riker held out his hand. "Antimatter charges."

Data slapped two finger-sized tubes into Riker's glove. Riker headed for a thick conduit that snaked from the wall of the dome and disappeared beneath the gravel. It carried power to the buried forcefield generators that protected Gamow Station's exposed sensors and dome plating from Alta Vista III's sulphurous rain and acid hail. Two antimatter blasts and the forcefields would be down. Less than thirty seconds later, Captain Picard would be located and beamed to safety. *This is going to be simple,* Riker thought.

That was when the first sniper blast hit him and the ambush began.

In the storeroom, Stron's wife held the phaser on Picard. Stron seemed too upset to do much of anything. Whatever trace of Sarek's mind he had discovered in his attempt to meld with Picard, it had clearly unnerved him.

"When did you meld with Sarek?" Stron's wife demanded. Her accusing tone revealed her disbelief that the leader could ever have chosen to meld with Picard.

"Release me," Picard said. "Then we can talk."

Stron and his wife exchanged a questioning glance.

"We can't," she said.

"But he only melded with those who were part of the cause," Stron argued. He stared at Picard with an expression of near fear. "Have you been to Gonthar District?"

Picard had no idea to what the Vulcan referred, but he recognized a weakness to exploit when he saw one.

"You can ask me that when you have the temerity to tie me up like a common outsider?"

Stron looked at his wife. "He must be one of us." He started toward Picard.

"Stay back," the woman warned Stron. She raised the phaser until it was trained at Picard's head. Her death-dealing gesture seemed in cruel juxtaposition to her life-swollen belly. "These are dangerous times for the cause," she reminded her husband. "You know each cell must remain unknown to the others to avoid betrayal. We must do nothing to risk our mission."

"You risk betrayal by keeping me from my ship." Picard hoped he was playing his part correctly. "If Starfleet investigates my disappearance, I will not be able to protect any of us."

Picard could see that Stron wanted to untie him at once. But Stron's wife was not convinced.

"Give us the proper countersign," she challenged Picard. "*Have* you been to Gonthar District?"

Picard had no choice but to brazen it out. "That code is obsolete. My cell has not used it for years."

The woman studied him for a moment, then lifted the phaser in salute. "I acknowledge your courage. Farewell, Captain."

Her intent was clear. Picard did not flinch.

But Stron pushed his wife aside. The phaser beam missed.

The struggle was over in seconds. Now Stron held the weapon.

"My mate is correct," the Vulcan said. "It is illogical to

believe you are part of the revolution." He spoke to his wife. "But he *has* melded with Sarek. And that we cannot ignore."

The woman wrapped her arms around her stomach, cradling their unborn child. "We have to kill him, Stron. For the sake of the future."

Stron gestured to the medical kit on a nearby shelf. "We'll use the drugs first. Then I'll meld with him again. Whatever reason Sarek had for linking with him will be easier to find."

Stron's wife pulled a hypospray from the kit. "And then we'll kill him," she said firmly.

Picard watched her approach. He was out of options. He knew that whatever dose of whatever drug she was about to give him would be too high.

"Think of your child," he said. "Don't do this."

"It is for our child that we do," she said.

She raised the hypospray.

Then the supply room was plunged into darkness.

Riker flattened himself behind one of the exterior support ribs of the dome as phaser beams whined only centimeters away from him. Fortunately, their attackers' weapons were not set high enough to risk puncturing the dome itself, so the ribs provided adequate protection.

Crusher and Rolk were five meters farther back, flattened behind another support rib. Data was beside Riker, setting his hand phaser to full stun.

"Where did they come from?" Riker muttered. He had his own phaser in one hand, the two antimatter charges in the other.

"The odds favor them not believing the power fluctuations were the result of birds flying into the forcefield," Data said pleasantly. He leaned forward and fired three precise bursts.

Riker winced as an orange beam hit Data and threw him back against the dome with a solid thud. "Are you all right?" he asked.

Data shook his head as if to clear it. "My phaser armor is operational," the android said. "However, I must warn you that our attackers' weapons are set to kill."

"How many are there?"

"There were eight. But now there are five," Data said proudly. He pantomimed blowing smoke from the barrel of his phaser. "I am a purty good shot, pardner," he drawled.

Riker rolled his eyes. Data's emotion chip could still be unsettling at times. Though the android now generally understood humor, he was still struggling with the concept of when it was appropriate.

"If I set a short timer on the antimatter," Riker asked, bringing the android back to the dangerous situation that faced them, "can you throw one at the conduit?"

"They are precision charges," Data said. "They are meant to be in contact with whatever they are to destroy. Otherwise, we might rupture the dome."

Riker fired at a figure that darted behind a small rise about twenty meters away. A puff of smoke went up from a rock, but Riker couldn't tell if he had hit the runner or not. "We've got to try, Data. Otherwise they're going to surround us and pick us off."

Data slapped his phaser against his harness. "I must estimate the distance to the conduit," he said, then leaned out for an instant and withdrew as another beam missed.

"Set the timer for one point three five seconds."

Riker twisted the dial on the charge. "I can only set it for complete seconds. Take your choice: one or two."

"Two then. I will alter the trajectory accordingly."

Riker handed Data the first charge. "Please do."

Data pressed the activation switch, leaned out again, and threw the charge like a knife.

An orange beam caught his shoulder and spun him around into Riker just as a massive concussion thundered through the air.

Riker hit the gravel beside Data. He heard running footsteps behind him, rolled to see five figures in protective gear charging at him, phaser rifles lowered.

Riker tore his own phaser from his harness, aimed it without checking its setting.

Two figures flew back as the wide beam hit them.

The three others returned fire.

Riker felt himself slammed back into Data and the dome. His armor crackled with dispersed energy, but the concentration of firepower was too intense.

A temperature alarm beeped in his helmet. "Suit destruction in three seconds," the familiar, standard Starfleet comm voice said.

In those last few seconds, Riker tried to fire again, but his phaser was blasted from his hand. He couldn't breathe. He only hoped the captain had been found alive.

Then a glittering curtain of energy filled his dimming field of vision.

He had been right about not needing luck.

Not when he had the *Enterprise.*

SEVENTEEN

Picard jerked his body to one side so the hypospray couldn't reach his neck. But the move had been too violent and he felt his chair topple sideways.

The storeroom was without any source of light. He couldn't judge the angle of his fall. His head struck the flooring, making him gasp.

"He's right in front of you," Stron called out.

Picard felt the woman's foot hit his leg as she tried to find him in the darkness. "Open the door and get some light in here," she cried. Her hand grabbed Picard's boot. "I've got him!"

Picard tried to roll again, flopping the chair onto its back so he looked straight up.

He saw the woman looking straight down at him, encased in an indigo glow.

Picard's first thought was that Stron had found the lights.

But then the woman's eyes widened in shock as she and the storeroom were obscured by the familiar sparkle of the transporter.

A moment later, Picard was flat on his back, still tied to the chair, on the deck of a shuttlecraft.

Picard glanced around. "Hello?" he said, wincing as his movements set off a new burst of pain from his burned face. But no one answered. The shuttle was deserted. Then a shimmer of blue light reflected from the ceiling as another transporter beam materialized in the cabin.

Beverly Crusher was kneeling at his side. She wore phaser armor, blast shield pushed up, medical tricorder already open and working.

"Beverly?"

"Commander Riker shut down the station's forcefield," she explained. "You've been beamed directly to the *Galileo.*"

The *Galileo* was one of the *Enterprise's* shuttles, Picard knew. But that wasn't answer enough for his unspoken question. "Where, exactly, is the *Galileo?*"

"Shuttlebay One," Beverly said as she held a hypospray to Picard's neck. "The bay has been decompressed. We're in vacuum."

The pain in Picard's face faded instantly in response to Beverly's ministrations. "We're in quarantine, you mean."

Beverly smiled as she lightly prodded at the bandages Picard wore over half his face. "That's right. We've been exposed to the virogen."

Picard understood what the doctor had just done for him. "You mean I've been exposed to the virogen," he told her. "And you've been exposed to me."

Riker raced onto the bridge of the *Enterprise,* followed by Data and Rolk. Though he and his team had been plucked from the ground before the attackers had succeeded in overwhelming them, the beamback had been rough.

Operating under Starfleet's strictest quarantine protocols, Riker and the others had been transported to a point in space one hundred meters off the *Enterprise's* bow. Then, with precision focus, they had been beamed out of their armor and onto the ship.

The contaminated equipment they had worn was left in space. It would undergo the ultimate sterilization process as it burned up on reentry. But Riker, Data, and Rolk were free to return to the general areas of the ship, uncontaminated.

Picard and Beverly were a different matter.

"Put the *Galileo* onscreen," Riker said as he took the conn from Troi. "Then get me Manager Kincaid."

On the main screen, Crusher stood up in the cabin of the shuttlecraft, safely isolated by vacuum in the shuttlebay. Since contamination was no longer an issue with her, she had been beamed directly to Picard's side and was still in her armor.

Riker felt relief as he watched her help Picard to his feet and direct him to the copilot's chair.

"Welcome back, Captain," Riker said.

Picard lightly touched the sparkling antiseptic bandage he wore over one eye and cheek. "Well done, Will."

"Thank the chief," Riker said. "Transporter control had you located and locked on to ten seconds after the forcefield dropped." He leaned forward in his chair. "What did you find out down there?"

Picard took a breath to steady himself and Riker knew that his captain had been badly injured, more than he allowed to show. He was glad Crusher had chosen to go into quarantine with Picard. Strictly speaking, it hadn't been necessary. She could have beamed in and out in biological isolation garb. But onsite personal care was infinitely preferable.

"Stron and his wife are still alive. They are working with Chiton Kincaid as part of a . . . cause, or revolution, that is somehow connected with the virogen and the alta mist."

Riker sat back in his chair, stunned by the significance of Picard's revelation.

"By whatever means Stron used to escape from the *Bennett,* a shipment of alta mist was also transferred from the vessel and is somehow already in transit to an unknown location. The blockade has been broken, Will."

"And Chiton Kincaid is in on it?" Riker asked.

"She attacked me with a protoplaser. When I regained consciousness, I was with Stron and his wife."

Riker clutched at the arms of his chair in cold fury. "I understand, sir. I'll get to the bottom of this."

On the screen, Picard forced a smile. "That would be most gratifying, Number One."

Riker turned to Troi. "Counselor, I'll want you standing by for interrogation of Kincaid, Stron, whoever else is involved. Riker to transporter room two: Stand by for—"

Rolk interrupted. "Sir, I have Manager Kincaid."

"Onscreen, and feed it to the captain in the *Galileo.*"

The main viewscreen flashed from an image of Picard to one of Chiton. Beside the station manager, Riker saw Stron and his wife, both barely as tall as Chiton's shoulders.

"Manager Kincaid," Riker began, "under the provisions of the Federation's emergency disaster relief provisions of stardate 35333, you are to consider yourself and your accomplices in custody."

"We do not recognize the Federation's authority over our actions," Chiton Kincaid responded.

"You don't have a choice."

"What do you propose to do, Commander? Beam us aboard the *Enterprise* and contaminate it and your crew?"

"There are quarantine measures that can be taken."

But Chiton shook her head. "Quarantine implies separation, Commander. And that concept does not exist. All worlds are connected. All life is one. And until the intelligent beings of the galaxy realize that, all efforts to establish an interstellar community are doomed to failure, with the lives of billions at stake."

"I suspect those lives are at stake because of actions you

yourself have taken," Riker said. "You will be held accountable for that."

"Would you be willing to sacrifice your life for the life of your crew, Commander?"

Riker didn't understand the question. "What does that have to do with—"

"I attended the Academy," Chiton said, her voice rising with emotion. "I know a commander's duty. Her life for her captain. Her life for her crew."

Riker stood, sensing he was losing control of this conversation. "I know my duty, Kincaid. You've betrayed yours."

But the station manager ignored Riker. "Where does that duty end, Commander? Your life for five hundred others? Your ship to save a world? The Federation is dying! Its end is inevitable. Would you condemn trillions of beings to hideous lingering deaths if by sacrificing only a few billion you could insure that suffering would not come to pass?"

"A few *billion?*"

Troi stepped close to Riker. "She's working up to making some kind of decision, Will. You have to get her out of there."

On the screen, Chiton continued passionately. "We know our duty, Commander, just as you know yours. The symmetry of all things must be preserved. You differ from us only in degree."

"Riker to transporter control: I want—"

"The revolution will prevail," Chiton exulted. "Those who survive will come to praise us for our sacrifice!" Then she leaned forward and touched a control.

The image winked out.

"Will—" Troi's voice faltered.

"Massive energy release on the planet's surface!" Rolk said.

"Orbital view," Riker ordered.

When the image changed again, where Gamow Station had been was only a blazing fireball, rising slowly into the superheated air above it.

Troi staggered back and fell into her chair, ashen. "They're . . . all gone . . ." she whispered in empathetic agony. "I felt them die . . . all fourteen hundred. . . ."

Riker looked at Rolk for confirmation.

"They shut off the restriction fields in their matter-antimatter reactor," the Bolian said. "Complete annihilation. No survivors."

Picard came back onscreen, looking as shaken as Riker felt.

"There was nothing you could do, Will. They were fanatics of the worst kind."

Riker stared imploringly at Picard. Fourteen hundred innocent lives lost. *Was* it because of something he had done? Or failed to do?

"Did you hear what she said?" Picard asked. "Just before the end? About 'the symmetry of all things'?"

Riker didn't know what he meant.

"They're Symmetrists, Will. After more than a century, they're back."

EIGHTEEN

Spock breathed deeply of the air of Vulcan. Of home.

He had played in the red-tinged desert stretched out before him on the Plains of Gol, when he had been a child and was still permitted to play. It was to the Llangon Mountains in the distance he had retreated, when he could not face his father's disapproval. But it was to this mountain villa that he had returned each time.

Even when he had been reborn on Mount Seleya, it was to this home he had come.

He closed his eyes. Smelled the faint cinnamon dust of this world. Could almost hear his mother, a fragile Earthling, doomed to age and die before even half a Vulcan lifespan had gone by.

Spock bowed his head. What would Amanda think of him, knowing he had left his father unprotected when Sarek had needed his family most? Needed his son.

"Do you recall the name Tarok?" Srell asked.

Spock was startled from his reverie. He had not heard his young aide approach. He wondered if his Vulcan senses were diminishing with each day he allowed his human emotions greater reign.

Spock turned to see Srell at the edge of the wide stone plaza that joined the various buildings of his family's villa. Spock still wore his ambassadorial robes, though his young assistant had opted for a more functional, long-jacketed suit.

Srell carried a small computer interface. One of Sarek's antiques. It was a thick pane of transparent crystal that had little of the capacity of a modern padd. But it served adequately to link with the villa's computer system and Sarek had seen no need to replace it.

Srell handed the crystal to Spock. Spock angled it to more easily read the Vulcan script that glowed within.

"I found the database where Perrin said it would be," Srell explained. "And I have cross-referenced it with the lists your contacts provided. Of all the visitors and guests Sarek entertained in his final months here, only one name does not have a corresponding preference file in the home system."

Spock read the name. Tarok.

"There would be no need for a file," Spock said. "He is an old family friend."

Spock remembered sitting at Tarok's knee as the Vulcan scholar had told him wholly inappropriate stories from before the time of the Vulcan Reformation. There were tales of fierce battles, jealousy and greed. Passionate romances, cruel betrayals, kingdoms lost to forbidden love, sons sacrificing all to avenge the wrongs done their fathers.

As a child, Spock had been fascinated by that earlier age in which Vulcans had not controlled their emotions. Sarek had voiced his disapproval—as he so often did—complaining that it was he, not Tarok, who had to deal with his young son's inevitable nightmares after hearing those stories. But Amanda had been a co-conspirator with Tarok, encouraging the story sessions, and keeping them secret whenever she could.

In human terms, Tarok had been Spock's uncle, though there was no kinship by blood.

"It might be possible that Tarok's file was erased," Srell suggested, "in order to divert suspicion from him."

Spock was puzzled that Srell persisted in suggesting Tarok as a suspect. "Tarok and my father were friends when they were boys. My parents knew all his preferences. A file would not be needed."

Srell was not dissuaded. *"Amanda* and Sarek would have known him well, then. But what of your stepmother, Perrin? She told me these files had all been updated after her marriage to Sarek, to help her organize the diplomatic functions held here."

Spock stopped to consider Srell's observation. His father's most recent wife, Perrin, was currently on Earth, continuing her work with the Vulcan diplomatic corps as a cultural attaché. She had been most helpful in providing Srell with the passwords and codes necessary to activate the villa's system.

"You raise an interesting point," Spock conceded. Amanda and Sarek had entertained Tarok so often, had him and his associates as guests here so frequently, that any preferences he had would be well known. But of course a new file would have to have been created for Perrin when she had taken over the villa's organizational duties.

"Tarok now resides in Gonthar District," Srell added.

"Indeed."

"And, he also is afflicted with Bendii."

Spock instantly squeezed the corner of the crystal that changed it from a data display to a communications window. "Please arrange transport to Gonthar," Spock said.

Srell folded his hands behind his back. "I have already done so."

Spock nodded, remembering when he had been as sure in his logic as Srell was now. In fact, Srell reminded him of himself at a similar age.

Spock wondered if that was why Sarek had chosen the youth as his aide. Had he also seen an echo of another time, an opportunity to replay history, to have a son who would not run off to Starfleet?

Spock thought of second chances as he placed a communications inquiry to Tarok's estate.

Of all he had been given in this life, a second chance with his father had been the one thing denied him.

The inquiry went through. An aide answered. Spock made his request.

Though he did not reveal his own reaction, Spock was amused by Srell's less than perfect attempt to control his response to his first sight of Tarok's nurse.

She was a Klingon.

Young, dressed in a tight-fitting version of pale green Vulcan healer's garb, but savage of brow, of hair, and of attitude.

"nuqneH?" she snarled as Srell and Spock stepped from the small antigrav flyer they had taken to Tarok's forest estate.

Srell was clearly at a disadvantage. His thoughts did not need to be stated. What Vulcan would entrust his well-being to a Klingon?

But Spock understood, all too well. Tarok would have hired a Klingon nursing staff for the same reason he told bloodthirsty tales of the Reformation to impressionable youngsters. Too many Vulcans believed that control of emotions meant they should have no emotions at all. But Tarok had always reveled in his, clearly understanding the difference between public comportment and private enjoyment. In its way, Tarok's unorthodox philosophy was most logical.

"I am Spock, child of Sarek, child of Skon," Spock said. "This is my aide."

The Klingon bared her teeth at Spock. Slowly she looked Srell over, coolly assessing more than his emotional detachment, apparently gratified by what she perceived to be his nervousness.

She angled her head toward the large wooden doors leading from the landing drive. "This way," she growled.

She spun around and walked away, the tightness of her uniform accentuating each taut curve of her well-exercised flesh. Despite the seriousness of their mission, Spock could not resist commenting to Srell, "I believe she likes you."

Srell kept his eyes fixed on the nurse's head and nowhere else as he followed her. Spock wondered if he himself could possibly have been as mirthless as Srell when he had been that age. He decided he probably had been. He was going to enjoy visiting with Tarok again. It might be good for Srell, as well.

As Spock and Srell were ushered into Tarok's sitting room, they found that their host awaited them, picking at a corner of the white robes he wore, his lips moving in a soundless monologue. Attending him was a second Klingon nurse, in a healer's uniform as revealing as that of their escort's.

Tarok was much smaller than Spock had remembered him. The elder Vulcan, 205 standard years old, had withered with age. His short white hair stuck up in odd tufts, his cheeks were hollow, but the lines on his face still conspired to make him appear as if he constantly smiled.

Tarok sat in a padded chair, a concession to his age and infirmity, in the low-ceilinged, wood-paneled sitting room, which was adorned with mementos of his career in interstellar commerce. Where Sarek had gone into diplomacy, Tarok had joined the Vulcan trade mission. It was Tarok's keen intellect and illuminating logic, more than any other being's in the Federation, that had formulated the current economic environment in which money was no longer necessary. Spock understood that effigies of Tarok were burned during holidays on the worlds of the Ferengi.

"Takta," the second nurse said respectfully. Spock was not surprised that she used a diminutive for Tarok's name that was by tradition reserved only for the use of children. "Your visitors are here."

Tarok looked up at the nurse, blinking as if trying to recall who she was. The first nurse leaned in closely to Spock. "You are aware of the symptoms of Bendii?"

"I am," Spock confirmed.

The nurse dropped her voice to a harsh whisper. "He is a great man. Treat him with respect, or my sister and I shall gut you and feed you to the *norsehlats*. Understood?"

Spock was not concerned by the Klingon's threat. "He is my uncle," he said. "When I was a child, I called him Takta, as well."

"That is the only reason we have allowed you to see him." The nurse snarled at her sister and they left together, though Spock had no doubt they would be watching everything that transpired on a hidden scanner.

Spock approached the elder Vulcan. "Tarok, I have come to see you." He spoke more loudly than he normally would, hoping to cut through the haze of Bendii.

Tarok peered up at him from within the enveloping billows of his robes. For a moment, his eyes seemed to clear and a childlike smile spread across his face. "Sarek?"

Spock sat in the chair the nurse had used. "I am Spock, his son."

"Ahh," Tarok said, as if everything were explained by that. He blinked at Srell. "And this young man . . . ?"

Srell carried another chair forward so he could sit at eye level with Tarok. "I am Srell, child of Staron, child of Stonn." But that association meant nothing to Tarok. "Aide to Sarek, and to Spock," Srell added.

"Sarek . . ." Tarok sighed. He reached out to take Spock's hand, a terrible breach of Vulcan etiquette because of the low-level telepathy all Vulcans possessed. Direct physical contact was rare on social occasions, and only with consent. "Is Amanda well?"

Spock automatically called on his training in the *Kolinahr* to clear his mind and keep his emotions at a level that would not upset the old one. "My mother died, many years ago."

"Ah, yes," Tarok said. "Human. Such a loss."

"I would like to talk to you about my parents," Spock said.

"Fine people. Sarek so unbending, though. At the meetings, much too serious. The humans didn't like him. Trusted him. Didn't like him."

"When did you last see Sarek?" Spock asked gently, trying to keep the old Vulcan focused. With Bendii, Tarok's recollections might well skip from one decade to another, blending all his memories into one seamless tapestry where everything happened at once.

"Tried to warn him," Tarok sighed. He squeezed Spock's hand as he studied him. His other hand reached out to touch Spock's *katra* points but Spock lightly warded off the attempt. It would be dangerous for them both to attempt a meld with Tarok's symptoms so strong.

"What did you try to warn Sarek about?" Spock asked. He had no idea if this would be a useful line of inquiry. Sarek and Tarok would have had uncountable dealings in the past. Diplomatic agreements were almost always accompanied by trade relations.

"They were coming back, you see," Tarok said.

"Who were?"

"We thought it was over. We had ended it." Tarok's voice quickened as if he were caught up in an intense memory. "At your home. You weren't there, of course. Always going off to the mountains." He took a deep and rasping breath. "Your father was so worried. But I knew why you went." He patted Spock's hand. His voice slowed, trembled. "Your Takta knew."

Spock resisted the sudden impulse to expose his emotions to Tarok. He wanted him to know how much he had appreciated the time they had spent together, the guidance he had been given.

He glanced at Srell, but the young Vulcan was correctly impassive, merely an observer.

"What did you 'end' at my home?" Spock asked.

Tarok took his hand away. Smoothed his robes. He now spoke with the energy of a younger man. "You were not to be part of it. Your father made that clear."

"Part of what?"

"He knew what it meant. No chance to meld. A terrible burden between father and son."

Spock straightened in his chair, not certain what Tarok's words meant but anxious to learn.

"We could not risk it," Tarok continued. "None of us. We could meld only with those who were in the cause."

"What cause?" Spock asked urgently, forgetting all pretense of holding his emotions in check, forgetting that Srell was a witness to his loss of control.

Tarok looked at Spock for a long time. His eyes dimmed, as if he were looking beyond Spock to a different time. "I never had a son. Sometimes, when I told you stories, I could almost imagine that you were mine. Flesh of my flesh, riding forth as in the days of old, a son to avenge his father's fate. That is what they did then, you know. Long, long ago. . . ."

"What cause?" Spock insisted.

"I was so proud of you when you went to the Academy. But that proved Sarek had been right. What if we *had* told you? Your duty would have required you to report us."

"Tarok," Spock said. "Forgive me. . . ."

Tarok's eyes cleared. Became neutral. "Forgiveness is not logical, Spock."

It might have been Sarek speaking. Spock leaned forward, disturbed, impatient. He would no longer have secrets kept from him. Impulsively, he placed his hands on Tarok's face and began to meld.

A torrent of images, emotions, experiences, chaotic in the

throes of Bendii, mixed with glimpses of his father, of his mother, an incoherent ocean of other minds, other thoughts, drowning out Tarok's cries of confusion as Spock violently burst into his mind and—

Spock felt himself fly back through the air to hit the floor. Before he could move again, one of the Klingon nurses was kneeling on his chest, holding a *d'k tahg* knife to his throat. The outrider blades sprang open as she forced it against his skin.

"Have you no honor?" she spat.

Still struggling to make sense of the images he had experienced, Spock stared past her and saw Srell in the armlock of the other nurse, another knife at his throat. Tarok had collapsed in his chair, hands fluttering at his face. His ragged sobbing tore at Spock's heart.

"You must go now," the nurse hissed in Spock's ear. Then she hauled him to his feet as if he were a sack of trillium.

Spock wrestled against the Klingon's grip. "Tarok! Who is the prefect of Gonthar?"

From across the room, Tarok looked up, tears spilling from his ancient eyes. "I told your father they would kill him if the codes were known! I told him they were back!" The old Vulcan suddenly looked to the side. He held out a shaking finger. "There! It's all there!"

Spock followed Tarok's line of sight, even as the nurse began to drag him to the door. The aged scholar was pointing to a table beside the doorway. The table held an antique IDIC medallion, a scroll, and a handful of other artifacts of great antiquity and cultural value.

But among them, the black base of an ordinary, civilian holoprojector, just like the one Spock had been given on Babel. Completely out of place.

Still in the implacable grip of the Klingon nurse, Spock shouted: "Tarok! Who killed my father?!"

Tarok staggered painfully to his feet, trembling, hands held forward in supplication. "Forgive me, my child. Surak forgive us all. . . ."

Then the room shook with the first explosion and Spock was swept once more into a maelstrom of fire and memories that were not his own.

NINETEEN

Spock awoke in darkness. In the distance, he could hear phaser fire, the crackle of disruptors. Another explosion erupted nearby. He tried to get up.

But Srell pushed him down.

"The estate is under attack," Srell said.

"Where is Tarok?" Spock asked.

"The two Klingons took him. We have to get back to the flyer."

"No! It is imperative we locate Tarok!"

Spock felt Srell back away from him, no doubt alarmed by the raw emotion in Spock's voice. He sat up and looked around, eyes gradually adapting to the darkness. He was still in the sitting room. Only moments must have passed. But he could smell smoke. The estate building was on fire.

"Why is Tarok important?" Srell asked. "Did *he* kill your father? Is that what you saw in his mind?"

Spock got to his feet, slipped off his robes so he wore only simple black trousers and tunic. "I saw my parents there," he said. "As they were years ago."

Srell joined Spock as Spock moved quickly to the doorway.

"They were Symmetrists," Spock said.

"The cult?" Srell asked, faint distaste evident in his voice.

"It was never a cult. It began as a political movement. When it spread to other worlds, they called it a revolution."

The hallway beyond the doorway was also in darkness. The power lines in the estate must have been cut. Spock listened carefully. He could hear people running and tried to estimate how many attackers there might be.

"That is what Ki Mendrossen spoke of," Srell said. "In his recording. 'For the good of the cause,'" the young Vulcan quoted. "'For the revolution.'"

"The Symmetrist cause was repudiated almost two centuries ago," Spock said. The attacking force seemed to be coming from the woods at the rear of the estate. There might be a chance to get back to the antigrav flyer at the front drive. But he didn't want to leave without Tarok. He had no doubt that was who the target of this attack was.

"Then Tarok is wrong," Srell said. "He was thinking in the past."

Spock pointed down the hallway toward the main entrance of the building. "Go to the flyer. Wait for me there. I will find Tarok."

"Let me," Srell said. "You are too valuable to Vulcan. And to Romulus. You must not let your work end here."

Spock appreciated the logic of Srell's request. But what he had to do was personal.

"If I cannot save Tarok, I might have to meld with him again, so that his knowledge does not die. You go forward, Srell. You make the dream of unification a reality."

Srell seemed to recognize his place was not to argue with Spock's logic. "Peace and long life," he said. "I am honored in my work with you."

"Live long and prosper," Spock replied. "Now, go!"

Srell hurried down the hallway. Spock headed off in the opposite direction, to where the sound of fighting was loudest.

He came to a smaller hallway that, from what he recalled of seeing the estate from the air, was a connecting structure between two larger buildings. The fighting seemed concentrated around the second structure.

Spock suddenly wondered who was fighting. Tarok obviously had a staff greater than two Klingon nurses. He also wondered why anyone who wished to kill Tarok didn't just use a quantum explosive to wipe out everything within a kilometer.

Too easy to trace, Spock decided. A simpler approach would be more subtle.

But he still couldn't reconcile that strategy with the increasing sounds of all-out armed combat. Unless the attackers had been completely surprised by the size of Tarok's home security force.

Spock moved silently along the narrow connecting corridor, toward the second building. He could see flashes of orange and blue energy reflected in the tall windows. Some of the phaser fire seemed to match the wavelength of standard-issue Starfleet sidearms. He assumed Tarok had many friends in the service.

At the end of the corridor, a large atrium flickered with the firefight being waged outside. Spock judged the distance to a sizable tree in the center of the large room, and estimated he would have eight chances in nine of reaching it undetected. He had no doubt that the fighting was centered on whatever stronghold to which Tarok's Klingon nurses had taken the old trader. Perhaps he could create a diversion by attacking from behind.

Spock turned his mind to improvising a weapon as he began his sprint toward the tree.

But after he had gone a single meter, he tripped over an unseen obstacle and fell to the tile floor with a grunt.

Before he could roll over to defend himself, an attacker had leapt onto his back, then jabbed a knuckle punch under his ribs.

Spock's breath exploded from him, but he rammed his elbow upward and had the satisfaction of hearing an answering grunt as his attacker slumped to the side.

Instantly Spock was up on his hands and knees, then his feet, and then—

—down again as his assailant swept his legs out from under him.

Spock gasped for breath. It had been almost a century since his last round of intensive, hand-to-hand combat training. His stamina was down. But not his skill.

He kicked out at the approaching silhouette of his adversary and caught him in the stomach. He heard the body tumble to the floor and launched himself toward it, rolling over twice before bringing his hand down to deliver a fight-ending nerve pinch.

His fingers hit armor.

A fist hit his face.

Spock rolled again.

His attacker jumped him.

Spock's hands closed around his assailant's throat—an intemperate move, because it allowed his opponent to do the same.

Now it came down to who could hold out the longest before succumbing to suffocation.

Spock wheezed as he put all his energy into closing his fingers into fists.

His assailant wheezed just as heavily, as if he weren't a trained soldier either.

Spock felt his strength failing.

But his opponent's strength was failing just as rapidly.

Something was wrong.

A sudden phaser burst smashed through an atrium window and hit the tree behind Spock. Dried foliage burst into flames, and in the flickering light of the explosion, Spock at last saw his attacker's face.

And for one of the few times in his life, Spock screamed.

TWENTY

Kirk's scream was easily a match for Spock's.

He couldn't have been more surprised if the firelight had revealed he was fighting a Gorn.

He jumped away from Spock.

Spock gaped at him.

"Jim?"

"Spock?"

Then Spock smiled broadly as he reached out to grab his friend by his shoulders. "I knew it! I knew you escaped the Borg homeworld!"

Kirk ducked as another phaser burst shattered more atrium glass.

Spock took his hands away, tried to collect himself. "What are you doing here?"

"Looking for you," Kirk said. "What are *you* doing here?"

"Trying to save the man who knows who murdered my father."

"Tarok?" Kirk asked.

Spock looked at Kirk through narrowed eyes. "Why am I not surprised."

Kirk leapt to his feet and angled a thumb toward an atrium

exit. "My crew's outside. There're at least five attackers with phasers coming out of the woods."

"Your crew?" Spock asked as he jumped up beside Kirk.

Kirk chuckled. "Listen to us trying to catch our breath."

"I am out of practice," Spock said.

"Then let's make up for lost time."

Kirk ran for the exit, Spock at his side.

That simple fact alone made Kirk feel at least a century younger. Maybe even two.

The battle outside was short and to the point.

Spock unerringly located each attacker from the angle of the phaser fire. Kirk's crew kept the attacker pinned down. Kirk unerringly slipped through the forest and surprised the attacker. Spock used the nerve pinch to end each fight. They used the attackers' own jackets to tie them up.

Kirk was troubled that all five of them were Vulcan, but he wasn't surprised. The involvement of Vulcans in the events surrounding the virogen was precisely why he had come to find Spock. He was fortunate that the Vulcan diplomatic corps kept such careful track of Spock's travel plans, and had deigned to reveal them to the commander of a Starfleet vessel.

By the time the final attacker was neutralized, both Kirk and Spock were wheezing uncontrollably, but Kirk wouldn't have it any other way.

"You know," he gasped, as he leaned over to catch his breath, hands on his knees, "if you had asked me an hour ago . . . I would have said I missed this kind of nonsense."

Spock leaned against a tree, gasping just as deeply. But he clearly had other matters on his mind. "How *did* you . . . survive the partial destruction of . . . the Borg homeworld?"

Kirk glanced toward the estate as he saw shadowy figures run toward him. "There'll be time for that later." Then Commander MacDonald, Engineer Barc, and Dr. M'Benga were upon them.

Kirk made the introductions. The two young officers and the Tellarite stared in openmouthed awe.

"Kirk *and* Spock?" Christine said.

"What did I tell you?" Kirk warned her. Then he took M'Benga's medical tricorder and fiddled with the unfamiliar controls. He pointed to a smaller building that stood alone. "C'mon, Spock. You said you were looking for Tarok."

Kirk ran off, the others at his side. He was amused to hear how both he and Spock struggled to control their breathing with an audience present.

The small building was a meditation chamber. Kirk read two life signs inside, both Vulcan, one very old. Again, not a surprise.

He eased open the ornately carved wooden door. Inside the austere chamber, candles were lit, adding a warm glow to the surreal violence frozen in place.

Two Klingon females were sprawled on the floor, pools of thick pink blood surrounding them. In the far corner, a young male Vulcan cradled an old male Vulcan.

Kirk quickly checked the tricorder's display. The old Vulcan was fading quickly. M'Benga snatched the tricorder from Kirk's hand as she rushed to the dying man.

"Anyone know the history of this man?" the doctor asked urgently.

Spock pushed past Kirk. "Bendii Syndrome," he said. "I must meld with him."

But M'Benga stood in Spock's way. "He's dying, sir. And with Bendii, not even his *katra* can be claimed at this stage."

"You don't understand," Spock said. "He is the only one who knows—"

"It is over," the young Vulcan said.

Kirk was hurt to see how his friend seemed to collapse at that pronouncement, as if the old Vulcan had been the most important thing in his life.

Kirk went to Spock's side. "It'll be all right, Spock. We're both on it now."

Spock straightened his shoulders. The young Vulcan stood up. "Srell," Spock said formally, "may I introduce James T. Kirk."

Srell stared at Kirk for several long seconds, then raised an eyebrow in an all-too-familiar expression.

Kirk smiled at Spock. "Friend of yours?"

"My aide."

"A pleasure," Kirk said, knowing better than to extend his hand. "I wish the circumstances were more agreeable, but I have the feeling we'll be working together."

Srell still said nothing.

Kirk was used to that reaction, especially since the repeated reports of his death. He turned back to the Klingons. M'Benga was kneeling by them.

"How did they die?" Kirk asked.

"Disruptor fire," the doctor said, but didn't sound convinced. "I don't often see bleeding when that happens. Could be close-range stun, but . . ." She stood up, adjusted her uniform. "We'll have to wait for the authorities to conduct an autopsy."

"I do not believe it would be wise to contact the authorities," Spock said.

Everyone in the meditation chamber stared at him.

"At this stage in my investigation," he explained, "I am not certain if we can trust them."

"Spock?" Kirk said. "We can't trust *Vulcan* authorities?"

Christine stepped up beside Kirk. "He might have a point, given who was in that fighter on Chal."

At last Srell spoke. "You were on Chal?"

"Five days ago," Kirk said.

"But," the young Vulcan came close to stammering, "that is one of the systems infected with the virogen. If you were there, you have exposed Vulcan to it."

M'Benga answered for the crew of the *Tobias.* "We're clear of it," she said. "Jim brought us a compound that removes it from animal cells."

"A cure?" Srell asked. Kirk noted that he seemed disoriented. If that was possible for a Vulcan.

But M'Benga shook her head. "A way to slow down its spread, but not a cure. At least the quarantined systems can be opened up after proper treatment."

Kirk knew the technical discussions could wait. He trusted Spock to make the right decision about what strategy they must follow right now. "It's your world, Spock. What do we do?"

"For the time being, I believe we are on our own."

"Suits me," Kirk said. *Some things never change,* he thought. Kirk looked at the bodies of the Klingons and Tarok. "Let's send down a forensics team to clean the place up and create records for the authorities for when the time comes to involve them."

"A forensics team?" Spock asked.

"From Commander MacDonald's ship. You think I flew here on my own?"

"Under the circumstances, that would not surprise me either," Spock said. With an imperceptibly slight trace of a smile, he added, "And that would explain your fatigue."

Kirk saw the look of confusion on the faces of Christine, M'Benga, and Barc.

"Did I hear right," M'Benga asked gruffly, "or did a Vulcan just make a joke?"

"You mean, tried to make a joke," Christine said with a smile.

Srell regarded them stonily, hands behind his back. "I assure you, Vulcans never joke."

"Rrrr," Barc growled, "then you haven't seen how they can translate technical manuals. They're responsible for the most confusing ones in my collection."

Kirk glanced over at Spock. "Is it just me, or do they remind you of anyone?"

Spock looked thoughtful for a moment, then raised an eyebrow and said, "It is just you."

Kirk grinned. He had forgotten just how much he had missed his old friend. He fumbled with the Starfleet comm badge on his civilian shirt.

"Kirk to *Tobias,*" he said as it chirped. "Six to beam up."

Now that his team had been assembled, it was time to get to work.

TWENTY-ONE

☆

Except for the whisper of the environmental systems, the observation lounge of the *Enterprise*-E was quiet. At their chairs, La Forge, Data, Lieutenant Rolk, and Riker watched the slowly rotating surface of Alta Vista 257 beyond the large ports, or stared across the conference table at the display case of golden *Enterprise*s of the past. No one talked. They were giving Counselor Deanna Troi a moment to compose herself.

Though not a full Betazoid, Troi had been focusing her empathic ability on Chiton Kincaid, Stron, and his wife, at the moment of their deaths. And of fourteen hundred others.

The awful wave of emotion that had flashed from Gamow Station in the horror of the reactor explosion still reverberated within her, leaving her shaken and detached.

Riker did not think it was necessary for her to be present at this briefing, so soon after the disaster, but Picard had insisted. He had his reasons, he had told Riker, for wanting all his senior staff available.

The somber mood in the room was suddenly broken as the new virtual viewscreen shimmered into life in front of the far bulkhead.

Picard and Crusher appeared there, their images transmitted from the *Galileo.* The captain and the doctor were still in quarantine on the decompressed shuttlebay deck. Riker was relieved to see that Picard wore a smaller dressing on his facial wound and seemed more rested. Crusher's treatments were having some success.

"I feel awkward at having to address you in this manner," Picard said, "but Dr. Crusher has confirmed that I am now a carrier of the virogen."

"As am I," Crusher added.

"No ill effects?" Riker asked.

"Mild," Crusher said. "Slight fever. Intestinal upset. But we're both following the typical thirty-hour curve of symptoms. We'll be fine by morning, though still contagious."

Picard began the meeting. "Lieutenant Rolk: Have you had any response from Starfleet?"

As the Bolian security officer frowned, the fleshy ridge bisecting her blue face stiffened. "Sir, I've been having difficulties establishing a repeater link with Starbase Seven-eighteen." Rolk didn't wait for Picard to ask the obvious question. "All the ship's systems test out, but I'm not receiving a signal confirmation. None of the ships in the blockade can."

"Is it some type of subspace interference?" Picard asked.

The Bolian looked over at Riker. They had already discussed the situation and Riker could see she was feeling out of her depth. He took up the report.

"Captain, it could just be subspace chatter, but there have been unconfirmed reports of . . . a riot at the starbase."

Picard looked grim, yet offered no response. At any other time, such a thing would have been impossible. But for months now, the signs of growing strain in the infrastructure of the Federation had been clearly increasing. Full-scale food and resource riots were breaking out on the most badly affected worlds. But for a Starfleet installation to suffer the same fate was a serious matter, and an alarming indication of how rapidly the situation was deteriorating.

"I have not been able to confirm that report," Riker added. "But given that no ship in the immediate sector has been able to raise Starbase Seven-eighteen for the past seven days, it seems reasonable to assume that something . . . disruptive has happened there."

Riker was familiar with the stoic expression that now came to his captain. Whatever Picard's personal thoughts on this escalation of the virogen's impact, he would keep them to himself. First and foremost, he was a starship captain.

"Lieutenant Rolk, you are, of course, establishing contact with Command through other links in the subspace relay network," Picard said.

"Yes, sir," the security officer confirmed. "The fleet system is . . . suffering sporadic overloads and shutdowns because of the unusually high level of emergency traffic, but I will establish contact within the next day."

"A fast transport can travel more than five light-years in a day."

Riker knew what the captain meant.

They had finally discovered how Stron, his wife, and the alta mist samples had survived the destruction of the *Bennett*—they had beamed to the asteroid designated Alta Vista 257 during the suspicious burst of subspace static from the *Bennett's* deflector dish, only instants before the warp-core breach had begun. That static had been the source of the previously unexplained reading.

Picard had suggested the possibility of a surreptitious transport once it was determined that no organic residue of Stron and his wife could be found. But there had been no other ships within transporter range, and the *Enterprise* had been unable to detect any sign of an artificial structure or even a portable life-support shelter on the asteroid. Because there hadn't been one.

Instead, the crew and the cargo of the *Bennett* had been beamed *into* a naturally formed bubble in the nickel-iron asteroid, 2.8 kilometers below the surface, completely contained, with no physical link to the outside. Data had explored the bubble after Picard had ordered the *Enterprise* to return to the asteroid for a more thorough search.

The bubble, frozen in the metal when the asteroid had cooled from Alta Vista's planetary-accretion disk more than eight billion years ago, was one of hundreds in the object. The roughly spherical chamber was approximately twenty meters across, and had been lined with an insulating foam and outfitted with glow strips, a cargo tank for the alta mist samples, and a small life-support unit used to fill the bubble with an atmosphere and warm the contents above the asteroid's normal interior temperature of −357° Celsius.

When Rolk had detected the faint though anomalous hot spot in the asteroid's interior, he had transported a remote sensor array to scan the bubble. Then Data beamed in to help recover the equipment that had been installed there.

Only now, days after the *Bennett's* apparent destruction, was it clear to Riker and the others what had happened. Based on the replicator load Data had calculated from the life-support unit's consumables supply, the android had reported that Stron and his wife had hidden in the bubble for only a few hours. At that time, a second ship from outside the system came to the asteroid and beamed the two of them out along with the alta vista from the holding tank. Residual amounts of the one-celled, airborne plant cells still remained on the inner surfaces of the tank. The level of virogen contamination within it was exceedingly high.

How that second ship then returned Stron and his wife to Alta Vista III and left the system, Riker wasn't sure. But Rolk confirmed that while in orbit, the *Enterprise* had made no special efforts to scan for the tachyon signature sometimes associated with cloaking devices. Thus, Riker did not find it impossible that one small, fast, cloaked vessel might have successfully passed through the quarantine blockade undetected.

Which meant that that same ship could already be dozens of light-years distant, taking the contaminated alta mist to an unknown destination. And as the captain had pointed out, each hour's delay took that unknown vessel and its deadly cargo even farther away.

"With the destruction of the Gamow Station," Picard told his assembled senior officers from the viewscreen, "maintenance of the blockade in this system has become moot. In the absence of orders from Command, as senior ranking officer, I am freeing the blockade vessels to move on to other vital assignments."

Riker asked the question he knew would be on everyone else's mind. "What will our new assignment be?"

"That is where I am going to need your advice," Picard said. "It is my opinion that based on the events we have witnessed here, the virogen plague that is threatening the stability of the Federation is a deliberate terrorist attack, conducted by the organization known as the Symmetrists."

"Who, or what, are the Symmetrists?" La Forge asked. "I've never heard of them."

"Few have," Picard explained. "They grew out of an environmental movement begun on Vulcan more than two centuries ago, just after the founding of the Federation."

"In fact," Data unexpectedly continued, "the Symmetrists considered themselves a political response to the Federation's formation. They were the equivalent of the isolationist parties on Earth, which lobbied to keep that world from joining the Federation. The Symmetrists felt that logic demanded Vulcan and her colonies remain independent."

"Data, you sound as if you've studied the movement," Crusher said from the screen.

"I am endlessly fascinated by the differences of opinion

that arise among Vulcans. For a people who follow logic, they exhibit many of the same tendencies of other, more emotional races, to fragment into different political factions which—"

"I'll take that as a yes," Picard said, to stop the threatened lecture. "However, on Earth, the various isolationist groups were the last gasp of twenty-first-century regionalism, swept away in the Reconstruction that followed first contact. There was never any serious opposition to the Federation among the members of Earth's world government. But on Vulcan, those who opposed the Federation were not driven by political motives. Rather, they perceived a threat to the galactic ecology."

With that phrase, Riker abruptly remembered an obscure history course he had taken in his second year at the Academy. The idea of a galactic ecology was still widely debated among exopaleobiologists. Certainly, evidence clearly established that many worlds shared related life-forms. Some of this was due to the interplanetary exchange of bacteria and viruses fueled by violent meteoric impacts. In Earth's own system, life on Earth, the underground bacteria of Mars, the oceans of Europa, and the ice viruses of Mercury all shared common origins.

Exciting similarities between more distant worlds, such as Earth, *Qo'noS,* and Vulcan, were then proven, in part by this very crew, to have originated as the result of the genetic seeding of dozens of planets by the first humanoid race to evolve in the galaxy, more than four billion years ago.

But where the experts still disagreed was in accepting the existence of a natural, interplanetary web of connectedness throughout the galaxy.

The majority view held that any such theory was based on inaccurate observations and flawed reasoning. To those who controlled the scientific status quo, each life-bearing planet was a separate storehouse of biological riches to be exploited at will, with the confidence of knowing individual worlds existed in a natural quarantine enforced by the cold, radiation-filled vacuum of interstellar space.

But on Vulcan, a vocal minority said it was the majority who were mistaken. Just because a web of connection could not be rigorously demonstrated by the science of the day did not mean that the web did not exist, in a form unknown, and perhaps unknowable, to human observers.

These scientists, the forerunners of the Symmetrist movement, said that each planet was a link in a chain of life that had evolved according to the rhythms of the galaxy's natural ebb and flow of matter and energy. To those who accepted the Vulcans' postulates, the galactic ecology could be perceived as a single organism, indescribably vast, operating at a timescale in which the birth and death of stars passed in an eyeblink.

To interfere with the natural state of that galactic ecology, by traveling between the distant worlds on warp-powered ships, subjecting delicately balanced planetary biospheres indiscriminately to the shock of alien microbes, plants, and animals over the course of years and not eons, was a crime. An ecological crime.

As the newly formed Federation began to codify the rules and regulations of an organized, concerted effort to explore all the worlds of the galaxy, it was on Vulcan that the scientific opposition to this strategy became most vocal.

That opposition argued that intelligent beings must be stewards of the galactic ecology, not exploiters. Humans, Vulcans, Tellarites, Andorians . . . the citizens of all space-faring civilizations had a responsibility to recognize and preserve the symmetry of all things.

The highest ideal of that symmetry stated that the galaxy was no different from a living being.

Therefore, if the Federation accepted the sanctity of an

individual's right to exist, which it did, then the Federation must also accept the sanctity of all life, including that of the galaxy itself.

Led by some of the most noted biologists and philosophers of the day, the Symmetrists pleaded with the Federation to amend its charter so that strict quarantine protocols would be followed on each world discovered to have a native biosphere, and that colonization and terraforming would occur only on those worlds that were completely lifeless.

Logic demanded no less.

But, Riker recalled, the Federation had rejected the Symmetrists' arguments as unfounded and unproven, and perhaps, more importantly, as potentially expensive and capable of bringing galactic exploration to a standstill.

Only if the concerned scientists could return with the hard data necessary to prove their far-fetched view of the galaxy would the Federation Council deign to revisit their proposals.

But until then, the Council ruled, the Federation would continue to regard the galaxy merely as a resource that belonged to everyone.

"When the Vulcans who opposed the Federation's ambitious exploration plans were rebuffed," Picard continued, "the Symmetrist movement began. At first, they were a loosely knit academic group, committed to compiling the data necessary to prove their case to the Federation Council. Eventually, the Symmetrists became aligned with other scientific groups on other worlds, and the scope of their activities expanded."

"That was about the time of the hostage incident on Deneva," Riker said.

Picard looked pleased that another member of his staff shared his knowledge of history. "Precisely, Number One. At the time, Deneva was considered one of the most beautiful worlds in the quadrant. Its biosphere was fully developed,

Earth-normal. Exactly the kind of world the Federation sought to colonize. And exactly the kind of world the Symmetrists said must be kept isolated and untouched."

"More hostages," Deanna Troi said softly.

Everyone at the table looked at her with concern.

She kept her eyes on the tabletop. "As part of my counselor's training, I've taken part in the Deneva incident in a holosimulation. A group of radical environmentalists from Alpha Centauri said that any attempt to colonize Deneva would end in disaster. To prove their point, they took over the first colony ship, set it with explosives while it was still in orbit, and threatened to blow it up with all colonists aboard, unless the Federation withdrew."

Troi looked up at the captain on the viewscreen, and Riker could see how she was forcing herself to regain control of her emotions, to serve her ship and her fellow crew. "The radicals said it was necessary for the Federation to be taught a lesson. Rather than letting the colonists die due to environmental collapse over decades, they felt the authorities would take more notice if all the colonists died at once. So the Federation couldn't hide from the tragedy and would be forced to reevaluate their policies."

"How many colonists, Data?" Riker asked.

"Six hundred and fifty. Of which four hundred and eight died when an assault team from the *Archon* attempted to board the colonists' ship. Thirty-two Starfleet personnel were lost, as well as all of the radicals."

"The frightening thing is," Troi continued, "is that in all the simulations I tried, I couldn't get a better result. It was before subspace radio had been invented. There was no support from Command. No contact with other ships." She sighed, as if the deaths of all innocent hostages throughout all time were her personal responsibility.

"The radicals at Deneva were fanatics," Picard said sharply. "They had no intention of ever letting the colonists go. They had a point to prove. A lesson to teach. And they would let nothing stand in their way."

Riker could see what Picard was thinking. "Do you think that's what's happening today? With the virogen?"

"I do," Picard said. "The virogen and its effect on the agriculture of the Federation is precisely the type of ecological disaster the Symmetrists warned us of."

Rolk had a question. "But were the Symmetrists responsible for what happened on Deneva?"

"A radical offshoot of their organization claimed responsibility," Picard said. "For the next fifty years or so, the Symmetrists existed almost as an underground community of scientists, trying to make their concerns known, but thwarted as extreme elements among them enacted schemes of ecological terrorism."

Data clarified the timeline. "Records show that by 2248, Symmetrists had ceased to exist as an organized group, completely discredited by their more radical followers."

Riker wasn't convinced. "Captain, that's one hundred and twenty-five years ago. Are you suggesting descendants of the Symmetrist cause have been working as an underground group all this time?"

Picard's face hardened into a mask that told Riker his captain was not revealing everything he knew. He spoke his next words carefully. "You're forgetting, Number One. The Symmetrist movement came out of Vulcan. There are individuals alive today who could have been founding members of it almost *two* centuries ago. And judging from the participation of Stron, it seems likely that whole new generations as well have been drafted into the cause."

La Forge gave a low whistle. "Are you saying that this whole virogen plague is nothing more than . . . than some *lesson* the Federation is being taught? By a group of *Vulcan* terrorists?"

Riker tried to determine what it was Picard wasn't telling

them. Normally, when the ship was not facing immediate danger, the captain encouraged his crew to question his conclusions. Consensus was a valid operating principle for something as complex as a starship. But to Riker, it appeared as if Picard considered this time to be one of immediate danger, and La Forge's attitude was not welcome. Was it possible the captain had knowledge of an individual Vulcan who might be linked to the Symmetrists today?

Riker tried to catch La Forge's eye, to suggest the engineer ease off, but Picard responded too quickly.

"I am saying, Mr. La Forge, that the virogen plague *resembles* other acts of environmental terrorism carried out by the Symmetrists in the past, though on a vastly larger scale. And my questions to you are, *if* that is the case, then why is the alta mist an important part of that act of terrorism, and where would the Symmetrists be taking it?"

Riker could see that La Forge felt sufficiently chastised by the captain's tone. The engineer rubbed at his eyes, an unusual sight to Riker, who still hadn't completely adjusted to the replacement of La Forge's VISOR by eerie, blue-circuitry ocular implants. "The alta mist is how the plague is spread," La Forge said, with a tinge of desperation. "That's got to be it."

"No," Picard said. "The alta mist exists only on Alta Vista Three. Starfleet has conducted extensive bioassays of every affected system. If the alta mist had been found anywhere else, we would have known about it six months ago."

"Perhaps all the Symmetrists wish to do is measure the extent of the virogen's spread," Data suggested.

"Again," Picard said, "unlikely. When we captured the *Bennett,* Stron said he had intercepted all Starfleet communications. Certainly, that is not beyond the capabilities of any group so well prepared as the Symmetrists appear to be. And if that's the case, then they have no need to conduct their own surveys of the virogen's spread. They can simply eavesdrop on Starfleet's own findings."

Riker smiled ruefully at the captain. "In other words, we now have *three* mysteries in the same region of space."

"And all connected," Picard agreed.

Dr. Crusher appeared to have a sudden flash of inspiration. "What if we skip over the mystery of the alta mist for now, and ask ourselves the critical question—if the Symmetrists are somehow involved, where're they located?"

Just as Worf might have done, Rolk offered the most obvious answer. "Somewhere safe."

"A valid point," Picard agreed. "Though true Symmetrists would be the first to say that no place in the Federation is safe."

Troi suddenly straightened in her chair. "Fear," she said. All eyes turned to her. *"That's* what was missing!" She turned to the viewscreen. "Captain—when Kincaid destroyed the station, I felt her fear, even the fear of Stron and his wife, and . . . everyone else caught in the explosion. But . . . when we captured the *Bennett* by this asteroid, I felt only . . . tension coming from Stron. He knew he was in a difficult situation, but he did not consider it a life-threatening one.

"I assumed his emotional response was deadened because he was a Vulcan. But when we discovered the life-support bubble in the asteroid, I realized Stron's emotional response was correct. He *knew* there was a way off the *Bennett.* He *wasn't* in a life-or-death situation."

Troi paused. Though Riker knew everyone else in the room, and on the *Galileo,* was eager for her to continue, no one dared interrupt whatever chain of thought and emotion the counselor was following.

She spoke again. "I'm certain of it, sir. In all the conversations I witnessed with Stron and Kincaid, in every mention of the virogen and its effect on the Federation"—her dark eyes gleamed as she stared intently at the viewscreen—"I never felt the fear of death."

Silence ruled the lounge as the import of Troi's observation made itself known.

Then Picard stated the obvious conclusion, his face flushed with the excitement of discovery. *"They* weren't afraid of the virogen, because somewhere, somehow, the Symmetrists already have a *cure."*

For Riker, the shock of that statement brought both relief and tension. There was a chance that the virogen was not the Federation's death knell, that the disease could be controlled. But where would the Symmetrists be keeping it? With two quadrants of the galaxy to search, how could one hiding place ever be found?

Fortunately, the captain had already considered that question, and reached a decision.

"If we're to find that cure, we must first find the Symmetrists. And to do that, the best place to begin is where they themselves arose."

Riker stood at once, not even waiting for the order to be dismissed. The captain's logic was unassailable.

Less than two minutes later, the *Enterprise*-E tore open the fabric of space, and blazed through warp for where it had all begun.

And where, Riker hoped, it would all end.

The *Enterprise* flew to Vulcan.

TWENTY-TWO

"Please state the nature of the medical emergency."

In the sickbay of the *Tobias,* Kirk literally jumped back into M'Benga as the ship's Emergency Medical Hologram resolved before him.

"What the hell is that?" Kirk said.

For a hologram without a personality, to Kirk the EMH looked distinctly annoyed. "I beg your pardon?"

"It's a backup medical program," M'Benga explained. "I don't have a large staff, so he comes in handy when I've got a lot to deal with."

Kirk glanced around the sickbay. It was small, even by the twenty-third-century standards of his own *Enterprise.* But it was hardly crowded. M'Benga was treating Spock for a few cuts and scrapes. Christine MacDonald was cleaning herself up at a sink that had folded out from a wall. And then there was Kirk and the holographic doctor.

It was not what Kirk would consider a medical emergency.

"What, exactly, do you have to deal with?" Kirk asked. He was winded from the fight and the chase at Tarok's estate, but the exhilaration of the physical conflict had left him feeling much better than he had after the purely mechanical confrontation in the skies of Chal.

Fighting the Orion attack wing, he had been little more than a puppet master, pressing buttons, ordering changes in vectors and velocities with all the passion of a computer.

For all that starships had opened up the galaxy to humanity, there had come a time in his career when the emphasis had seemed to shift from technology as a tool to technology for its own sake.

Perhaps more than any other person in the Federation, he knew the horror of the limits to which that worship of the machine could be taken. He could still recall the inhuman sensation of the nanites moving within him, infesting him, reworking his flesh according to their own unknowing program.

The Emergency Medical Hologram was a disturbing reminder of what had happened to him after his escape from the Borg homeworld. Especially since he could see no use for the program's presence at the moment.

But Dr. M'Benga apparently had another view of the situation.

"What I have to deal with," she said, "is you."

"Me?"

M'Benga stopped running her instruments over the cut on Spock's forearm. Green blood had crusted around the minor cut, but the flesh beneath was already being pushed together by the medical treatment field.

"Vulcans I can handle," the doctor said.

"Like great-grandfather, like great-granddaughter?" Kirk asked. He remembered the M'Benga who had served so well on his *Enterprise.* That M'Benga had been one of the first human specialists in Vulcan medicine.

"It runs in the family," the doctor agreed. "But you're another matter."

"I feel fine," Kirk said. "Never better."

M'Benga harrumphed in response, reminding Kirk of another doctor who was not inclined to have his patients talk back. "According to records, you're one hundred and forty years old. How you 'feel' and how you actually are is a bit out of my experience."

Christine joined the conversation. "Bones, there was the little matter of the temporal anomaly Picard reported."

"Thank you," Kirk said.

But M'Benga held her ground. "There was also the 'little matter' of you dying."

Kirk didn't know where to begin. So he did what he had found always worked best in these awkward situations. "Spock, explain it to them."

Spock carefully brushed off the last of the dried blood on his treated arm. "I cannot," he said.

"Spock?"

"Captain . . ." Spock paused. "Admiral . . ." That still wasn't right. Then he had it. "*Jim*—we last met two years ago on a mission that to my knowledge has remained classified at the highest levels of Starfleet. Even if we were at liberty to discuss it among present company, I have no idea what has happened to you in the ensuing two years."

Kirk realized there was only one way out—fight back. "Dr. M'Benga, classified matters aside, I am not one hundred and forty years old. When the *Enterprise*-B was launched, I was sixty, and that's how old I was when I helped out Captain Picard on Veridian. It's two years later. I'm sixty-two." He stared belligerently at the EMH. "And I don't need a hologram to give me a physical."

M'Benga shrugged. "All right. Sixty-two I can handle. Take off your clothes."

Kirk didn't like the sound of that. "Don't you people have . . . scanners? A medical tricorder?"

"Think of me as an old country doctor," M'Benga said with

a predatory smile. She pulled a pair of isolation gloves from a supply drawer, giving them an alarming snap. "I prefer the hands-on approach."

Kirk knew when he had been outmaneuvered. For whatever reason, the doctor of this vessel wanted a medical report on him, and he had long ago learned that not even a starship captain could fight a ship's doctor and win. "On second thought, I'll go with the hologram."

"How nice to be wanted," the EMH said.

M'Benga knew she had won and let Kirk know she knew with a sarcastic smile. "Thank you for your cooperation." She gestured to the others. "Why don't we give our guest some privacy."

M'Benga, Christine, and Spock began to leave. But Kirk called Spock back.

"We should talk," Kirk said. "About what happened."

Spock remained as the sickbay doors slipped shut. Kirk saw Christine turn to glance back at him, and he held her gaze for just an instant before he and Spock were alone.

The EMH came at him with a medical probe. "Say 'ahhh,'" the hologram told him.

"Is there any way to turn you off?" Kirk asked.

"Several."

"I don't suppose you could tell me the best one."

"Not a chance."

Kirk opened his mouth and said "ahhh." Then, as the hologram busied himself with other readings, Kirk turned his attention to Spock, apprehensive about the answer to the question he knew he must ask.

"How's . . . McCoy?"

For a moment, Spock looked uncomfortable, and Kirk feared the worst. But the answer was not what he had expected. "I attended the doctor's one hundred and forty-sixth birthday party on Wrigley's Pleasure Planet."

"Wrigley's? What was the doctor's . . . pleasure?"

Spock seemed even more uncomfortable. "Dancing girls. I told the doctor it was most unseemly for a man of his years to be comporting himself in such a manner."

"And . . . ?"

"The good doctor informed me that in his considered opinion, the mere fact that a man of his years could comport himself in any manner, let alone still draw breath, was reason enough to celebrate in whatever fashion he chose."

Kirk grinned as he thought of his friends still bickering after all these years, knowing that each argument served only to bind their friendship closer. "I'm sorry I missed the party," Kirk said, and he meant it.

"He has something special planned for his one hundred and fiftieth birthday," Spock said. "He will not tell me what it is, but no doubt we will both be invited."

Kirk winced as the hologram pushed his arm through a series of twisting bends. "Do people really live that long in this time?"

"In Dr. McCoy's case, he tells me he does it to spite me."

"Oww!" Kirk said as he felt his shoulder blade click painfully. He pulled his arm from the hologram's grip. "You're supposed to make people feel better."

"I see, you're telling me how I should do my job? And how many years of medical training have you had?"

"You're a hologram," Kirk said. "How many have *you* had?"

"Combining the years of training of all the medical experts who contributed to my programming, one thousand seven hundred and eight." The hologram sounded far too pleased with himself for Kirk's liking. "What? No snappy comeback? Has the great James T. Kirk been bested by a mere machine who—"

With a flash of light, the EMH suddenly winked out.

Kirk turned to see Spock standing by a medical computer, one finger still on a button.

"Fascinating," Spock said. "An Off switch."

Kirk sighed with relief. "You've done it again."

Spock waited patiently for clarification.

"Saved me," Kirk said.

"I would not go so far as to characterize the act of switching off an emergency medical hologram as a—"

Spock stopped in response to Kirk's upheld hand.

Kirk glanced around the sickbay. "Do you suppose this place is *fully* stocked? The way McCoy would stock it?"

Spock nodded in understanding, and began opening supply cupboards with Kirk, until he found a bottle of Jack Daniel's. It was from Manozec XII, but the label said the oak casks were made with wood cloned from the original forests on Mars. At least it was the right solar system.

Kirk poured two glasses.

Spock joined him in a toast without protest.

"To absent friends," Kirk said.

"And Dr. McCoy."

For a moment, the two men stood in silence, their lives and their careers so closely aligned that it was at times as if they were one force moving through the universe. Kirk was glad to be back. He had no idea how many more second chances he might be given, so he intended to make the most of this one.

The most of every day remaining.

Kirk looked at the whisky swirling in the glass he held. "So what now?" he asked his friend.

"For now, we must wait," Spock answered. "Srell is directing the forensics team at Tarok's estate. At the same time, he will attempt to obtain data from the estate's computers that might guide us to other people linked with Tarok, my parents, and what he referred to as 'the movement.'"

"'The movement.' What's that?"

"I do not know." Spock told Kirk the story of the holographic recording of Ki Mendrossen he had received on the Babel planetoid, of how it indicated that his father had been murdered. And how Spock and Srell had followed a chain of evidence that led back to Vulcan, to Sarek's villa, and finally to Tarok's estate, looking for any clues to a possible conspiracy—what Spock took to be "the cause" that Tarok had mentioned.

"As you can see," Spock concluded, "without additional data, I am at a loss."

"'The cause,'" Kirk repeated. "Why does that sound familiar?"

"It is a generic description for any manner of undertaking," Spock said. "Little information is contained in it." Cautiously, he sipped at his whisky.

"You never used to like alcohol all that much," Kirk observed.

Spock took another sip. "You have yet to tell me how you escaped from the Borg homeworld, and rid yourself of the nanites."

Kirk found a chair, pulled it over to the desk. Spock did the same.

"I take it that Picard told you what happened in the Central Node."

"Up to the moment you 'slugged' him, was the way he put it. Then had him beamed aboard the ship. Quite against his will, he informed us."

"He's a good man," Kirk said. "Carries on the tradition well. He's just, I don't know, too . . . by-the-book."

"The 'book' says little about fellow officers slugging each other in the jaw."

"Maybe not in the twenty-fourth century."

"The Borg homeworld," Spock said, recalling Kirk's attention to the topic at hand. "You were in the Central Node. You had Picard beamed out. And then what? Did you pull the lever?"

Kirk braced himself for what was to come. As much as he

was a man who lived in the present, always traveling toward the future, there were times, he knew, when he must return to the past.

This was one of them.

"I pulled the lever," Kirk said.

It was time to tell the story.

TWENTY-THREE

It was a transporter beam that had claimed him, and that had ripped him from the Node.

Kirk knew all that the instant he re-formed in darkness, felt the physical burden of reality return to him.

Then he had dropped a full two meters.

Into mud.

He opened his mouth for air and the stench of the mud choked him.

It reeked of sewage. Of death.

He struggled as the heavy, freezing sludge engulfed him. From instinct more than thought, he strained to keep his head above the suffocating grasp of whatever held him.

He had no idea where he was.

An ordinary transport lasted scant seconds at most, accompanied by a slight vertigo, a glittering spray of light, and then solidity again.

But an ordinary transport could beam matter only twenty-five thousand kilometers.

This transport had lasted longer than any he had experienced before. Long enough that he had actually been conscious of his immaterial state.

There were other technologies possible, other rules, Kirk knew. Once his ship had intercepted a transporter beam that had originated from across the galaxy.

But how far had Kirk been transported within *this* beam? And by what or whom?

Then any thoughts as to where he might be, how far from the Borg homeworld he had come, and who or what might be responsible were vanquished by the sudden incredible pain that convulsed his body, nearly submerging him in the odiferous mud.

The nanites were still at their work in Kirk's body. Submicroscopic machines of Borg and Romulan origin. The machines that renegade Romulans had used to reconstruct his body according to the template laid down in his own DNA. Once activated, the nanites could not be stopped, or removed. They would continue their work of restructuring him until they had played out their function by accelerating the genetically programmed apoptosis that brought death by aging to all living beings.

When Kirk had pulled the lever in the Borg Central Node, he had had only hours to live. And though he had escaped the explosion that devastated the Borg homeworld, he was not going to escape his fate.

Kirk contorted in agony as he felt the organs of his body shift and twist in response to the burrowing, cutting, rearranging nanites. His fingers spread into useless claws to dig against the clinging mud.

From the surrounding darkness, he could hear the groaning sounds of other struggles. And in the distance, the rumble of vast explosions and unceasing machines.

He lay back, half-buried in the muck, gulping for air.

Whatever part of Kirk that had lived in him as a child and had made him think there might be something under the bed or lurking in the closet, it whispered to him now.

He was *dead.*

This was *hell.*

And it was here he would spend *eternity.*

The nanites ate away at him as the eagle tore at the liver of Prometheus. But in the void, he chose neither the comforts of mysticism, nor the escape of desperate fantasy.

Instead, a single word emerged from Kirk's frozen, mud-caked lips.

". . . no . . ."

He was *not* dead.

There was *no* hell.

But there *was* an explanation. There must *always* be an explanation.

He was somewhere in the universe. Somewhere physical. Therefore real. And he was—

". . . still alive . . ." he whispered.

Then, through force of will alone, he smiled fiercely, drawing his lips back from chattering teeth.

Because high above him, the sky was growing lighter.

The *sky.*

Low gray clouds lit by a sun that rose unseen on the horizon.

He was on a planet, exactly as he had believed. The explanation had been found.

He thrust himself up to assess his surroundings.

He was in a field of mud.

Far in the distance, he could see dark shapes moving closer, like the roiling clouds of a storm front or peaks on a slow-moving wave, something within them sparking with red and blue fire. Somehow, he knew they were the source of the machine rumbling and explosions.

But he ignored them for the moment, because they were still far off. And because the mud so much closer to him . . .

—moved.

At first he thought it was alive. The very mud of this planet a living creature hungrily gnawing at him, as inexorable as death, drawing him deep within itself to be consumed.

But as the light continued to increase, as day broke on this new world, Kirk saw the nightmarish landscape around him. Writhing, twisting, stretching out, reaching out, caught as he was caught, dying as he was dying.

Wherever he was, however he had come there, James T. Kirk faced the last hours of his life, trapped in a field of fellow sufferers.

He was surrounded by thousands upon thousands of dying Borg. . . .

"Fascinating," Spock said.

Kirk knocked back the last of his whisky and poured himself another shot. He swallowed that as well, letting the heat of it take away the memory of that horrible place.

"Fascinating my ass," he said. "I was in a garbage dump, Spock. A Borg garbage dump."

"Then the transporter beam you leapt into . . . ?"

"Was part of the homeworld's evacuation system. Our ships have escape pods, so maybe the Borg have escape *beams*. They punch through transwarp space so their range is virtually unlimited, and they enable Borg units that are still connected to the Collective to regather and re-form whatever branch they're from."

Spock looked thoughtful. "Last year, a Borg vessel attacked Earth. It was defeated, but during the unusual events of its attack, Captain Picard encountered a most interesting Borg individual whom all records indicate had perished years earlier in the destruction of another Borg cubeship. Perhaps these escape beams offer a possible explanation for that individual's survival."

Kirk shook his head. "Individual survival isn't what the Borg system was set up for."

Spock looked at Kirk with immediate understanding. "The machines on the horizon," he said.

Kirk nodded. "They didn't stay on the horizon for long."

Whatever sun this planet circled, its glow seemed to surge through the clouds in uneven jumps.

The machines on the horizon did the same, lunging closer in manic advances each time Kirk closed his eyes.

He could see them more clearly now—moving walls of multilayered metal, propelled by treads that rose a hundred meters in the air, each monstrous machine with a deep slot at its base, large enough to swallow a runabout, filled with grinding, gnashing blades, and lit by flashing beams of fusion fire.

The mechanical beasts swept over the mud as voracious devourers of all they encountered. Borg by the thousands were swept into their jaws, to be torn apart, reclaimed, and reassembled.

Kirk located the machine that was bearing down on him, still kilometers distant. He calculated it would reach him near sundown. Though he doubted the nanites would let him last that long.

He had to laugh at the irony of his end.

On the literal garbage heap of galactic history.

But still, somehow he could not give up. He found himself wondering what the insides of those machines might look like. He set himself the goal of surviving the nanites long enough to be swallowed by the machine.

Hadn't that, in fact, been what had happened to him ages ago, when he had taken the center chair for the very first time? When the starships had swallowed him, making him little more than another plug-in component in a cosmic machine?

"I'm ready for you," Kirk whispered to the monster that drove for him. And time and again, the sun jumped in the sky as the monster leapt forward.

In his lucid moments, Kirk realized the strobing effect meant he was lapsing in and out of consciousness. He forced himself to concentrate, to keep himself alert until the end. Determined not to waste a moment of life.

But all that came to him was a scattered vision of the bridge on Veridian III. Then, like now, he had been certain that death had claimed him, inescapably.

That day beneath the Veridian sun, after his fall, after the Nexus had passed, he had seen again the dark shape that had chased him all his life . . . felt that he was finally alone, how he had always known he would die. He had stared up into that mystery for what, in his final thoughts, he had believed would be his last moment of awareness . . .

. . . and seen Sarek?

Reliving that moment, Kirk muttered to the mud and the Borg that lay round him. As little more than an observer of his own fate, shut off from the horror around him, some still-rational part of his being decided that this must be how the human brain died. Cut off from oxygen. Brain cells making up hallucinations to hide the face of impending extinction. Floods of endorphins released to ease the suffering. Creating a white light that drew him forward.

But in that light . . .

. . . he saw Sarek once again.

For a time, it seemed to Kirk that he now stood beside himself in that field of mud, Sarek next to him, silent.

Only they weren't in the field of mud.

They were in a forest. At night. Beneath a sea of stars. Kirk recognized the setting.

Yosemite. Fragrant smoke from a crackling fire mingling with the green scent of pine and the richness of earth.

"We've been here before," Kirk said. He looked around and saw three people in sleeping bags, resting by the fire. Spock, and McCoy, and . . . himself.

Then Kirk recognized the time.

It was the day he had fallen from El Capitan. Plunged to certain death. The day when, against all reason, he had felt no fear.

That night by the fire, after Spock had rescued him, after McCoy had scolded him, he had revealed to his friends what he had never told another soul.

I've always known . . . that I'll die alone.

"Yes, Kirk. That is the key," Sarek now told him.

Kirk closed his eyes and heard the rumbling of the machines, the cries of dying Borg. He opened his eyes, and saw the forest, Sarek beckoning to him from within the trees.

"You must leave them behind," Sarek called out. "They cannot be with you."

Kirk wasn't ready. He needed to know why. "I've had this dream before," he said.

But Sarek gave no answer. His robes seemed to glow, billowing about him as if caught in a breeze that Kirk couldn't feel.

Memories flooded into Kirk then, each one about this dream, this hidden knowledge of his death.

And as always happened when this occurred, he was filled with the knowledge that he had had this dream before.

As long ago as he could remember.

And always it was the same.

Always it came with . . .

"Sarek . . ." Kirk pleaded, "why has it always been you in my dreams? Even before we met. Before I met your son. Before I left Earth . . . it has *always* been you who comes to take me from my friends and to my death."

Sarek now was only a light in the forest—shafts of radiance lancing out from the dark trees and branches.

"Because of what we share," Sarek said. "Or will share."

"My dream? Or my death?" Kirk asked.

Sarek's voice came from all around him, a roll of thunder in the air. But Kirk already knew the words Sarek spoke. They were always the same.

As long as a single mind remembers, as long as a single heart still beats with passion, how can a dream die?

Kirk held his hands up to the night, imploringly. "But what of the dreamer?"

Look to the stars, James Kirk.

Kirk felt Sarek's hand on his arm.

Just as Sarek had taken his arm that first time . . .

That first time on . . .

But once again that final link in the chain would *not* come to him, no matter how hard he tried to bring it forth, as if a portion of his mind and memory were lost to him, as if hidden behind some barricade to the truth.

Long ago on Tarsus IV, here again in Yosemite, there on the field of dying Borg . . . Sarek kept his hand locked around Kirk's wrist, to keep him close.

And the words he spoke electrified Kirk.

As they always did.

Avenge me.

Kirk closed his eyes in the agony of lost knowledge, lost time, lost life.

And even as the dream evaporated and the machine loomed above him, there was still a hand holding on to his wrist.

But the dream was over. Kirk looked up into the untroubled eyes of a young female humanoid, streaked with filth, naked except for a mud-caked loincloth. Beneath the filth, her skin was a quilt of brown and white.

". . . who are . . . you . . . ?" Kirk gasped, his throat almost closed by the ravages of the nanites.

The youth looked over at something Kirk couldn't see. "This one is operational," she shouted.

Barely conscious, Kirk felt the thunderous pulse of the approaching machine blend in his body with the unceasing waves of pain from the nanites. His death would be violent. He felt as if the end must come in mere moments, when his body could no longer take the stress and would simply explode.

A second humanoid joined the first. This time, a male, as mud-coated and as lightly clothed as the female, also with the same odd patchwork pattern of skin, this time white and pink.

The youth knelt down beside Kirk, felt his pulse, briefly touched his mud-darkened fingers to points on Kirk's face that called up the whisper of forgotten memories.

"He is not 'operational,' " the youth said to the female. "He is alive. Just as we are."

Roughly, the youth lifted Kirk's head from the mud. The towering wall of metal was visible above him, only a minute away from claiming them all.

"What is your designation?" the youth asked.

Time stopped for Kirk. He rallied himself to identify his existence before it ended forever.

". . . Kirk," he whispered. ". . . James . . . Tiberius . . ."

The youth stood and, with no sign of exertion, hoisted Kirk to his feet.

Kirk could not feel his legs. He remained upright only because the two young people supported him. Effortlessly.

"Welcome, Kirk James Tiberius," the young male said. "My name is Hugh."

"Hugh?" Spock said. "I have studied Captain Picard's detailed accounts of his encounters with the Borg. Could that have been the same Hugh who was infected with individuality? And who then was part of a revolt against the Collective?"

Kirk stretched back in the chair in sickbay. He was feeling hoarse after so much explanation. Another shot of whisky eased the irritation in his throat. "I have no idea, Spock. Half the people in the clan that found me were called Hugh. It was a common name, as if it had been passed on to them from other branches."

"The clan?"

Kirk shrugged. There were still events from those first few days on that world that weren't clear to him. "They were Borg," he said. "Or, had been Borg. Apparently, they'd renounced their implants."

"Everything we know about the Borg suggests that is impossible."

"If a Borg named Hugh can be infected with individuality and then revolt against the Collective, then I'd say the different branches of the Borg are capable of evolving their own, unique modes of organization. And the Borg who found me had access to unique forms of biotechnology."

"That would explain many inconsistencies in their behavior."

Kirk stared at his friend. "Spock, is that all you can say? That what happened to me explains Borg inconsistencies?"

"What would you have me say?"

Kirk put his glass down on the table. Despite his Vulcan heritage, Spock *had* to see the irony in what had happened. "Don't you see? I was . . . recycled."

From Spock's expression, Kirk could see that his friend didn't see the irony at all.

"I was beamed by a Borg emergency escape transporter to a planet where damaged Borg components were sent to be broken down and reassembled. A clan of Borg who had abandoned their cybernetic implants found me, detected the nanites, and assumed I was like them. So they *processed* me, Spock. By whatever means they used to rid themselves of their machine parts, they took the nanites from me. I was . . . cleansed. Recycled. Made human again only by being treated like . . . a *product.*"

Spock regarded Kirk for long moments. "You say you had a vision of my father?"

Kirk sighed. "Why do I even bother?"

"I am trying to understand," Spock assured Kirk. "And I am fascinated that you claim to have had dreams about my father even before you met him. Though that is a common aftereffect of mindmelding, and you and I have melded often enough in the past that you undoubtedly acquired and retained early images of my father, based on my own memories of him."

Kirk thought that over. "You know, I melded with your father once myself."

Both of Spock's eyebrows shot up.

"In San Francisco," Kirk said. "After . . . after what happened with Khan. When you . . ."

"When I died."

"Your father came to me, searching for your *katra.* He didn't know you had placed it in McCoy."

Spock looked as if Kirk had just slugged him instead of Picard. "You never told me this," he said, but it was as if his words were not meant for Kirk. "It is no wonder that you have dreamt about Sarek. You have not been trained in the methods of controlling the residual effects of a meld."

Kirk was puzzled. "You mean, I *haven't* dreamt about your father since I can remember? It's all been some sort of false memory?"

Because they were friends, because they were alone, Spock spoke gently, trying to lighten the blow, Kirk knew. "Unless you melded with my father when you were a child, the dreams you experienced were merely a result of the effect of my father's more disciplined mind on yours."

"No different from the hallucinations of a near-death experience?" Kirk asked.

"An illusion," Spock agreed.

Kirk tapped his fingers against the table, considering

Spock's analysis. As always, it seemed logical. It just didn't seem right.

"But my memories of Sarek seem so clear," Kirk said.

"Then I envy you, Jim. For I never melded with my father."

Kirk was surprised by the emotion in Spock's voice. He knew that Spock had just revealed something of great importance to him. As important, perhaps, as Kirk's own feelings about coming so close to death.

What could one friend say to another after such a revelation? So much time had passed between them, yet when they were together, it was as if no time had passed at all. There must be something Kirk could say. There must be—

Every unsecured object in sickbay—including the bottle of Jack Daniel's and the two friends in their chairs—was hurled to the side as the ship's hull creaked in protest. Kirk caught the whisky bottle just before it jumped from the table.

An instant later, red alert sounded.

Kirk looked around for a wall communicator. But Spock beat him to it by pulling a comm badge from within his shirt.

"Spock to bridge. Are we in difficulty?"

Commander Christine MacDonald's young voice replied. "It depends on your definition of difficulty, Ambassador. We have just been grappled with tractor beams by Vulcan patrol ships. It seems they wish to question us about an incident at Tarok's estate. Our forensics team is already in their custody and is being beamed aboard."

"That, Commander MacDonald," Spock said, "fits my definition of 'difficulty' to perfection."

TWENTY-FOUR

Vulcans were nothing if not efficient. Within an hour, the *Tobias* had been escorted to a civilian spacedock, her entire crew was in custody, and her senior officers had been assembled to face a Vulcan magistrate in the spacedock's justice facilities.

In the magistrate's antechamber, deep within the spacedock's administration levels, Kirk squirmed uncomfortably in his new uniform. Like Christine's, it was black with gray shoulders. The pips on the command-red shirt he wore under the tunic gave his rank as lieutenant. He ran his fingers behind the small metal disks, trying to stretch out the collar fabric. He glanced at Spock. "The longer I stay in Starfleet, the lower my rank gets. Think someone's trying to tell me something?"

Once more in the company of Christine, M'Benga, Barc, and Srell, Spock had reverted to his more usual stoic behavior, as well as changed back into his black robes. "If this charade is to work, 'Lieutenant,' it will be necessary for you to appear comfortable in that uniform, as if you have always worn it."

Kirk let his hands fall to his sides. "You honestly think we can fool a Vulcan magistrate?"

The doors to the magistrate's office slid open.

"There are always possibilities," Spock said quietly. Then he, Srell, and the officers of the *Tobias* followed the directional lights on the wall and, in single file, entered the office.

As the legal preliminaries were under way, Kirk took the opportunity to glance around and was surprised to see that the Vulcan style of architecture and decoration had changed little from his age to the next. An exquisitely etched glass panel was the centerpiece of the simple room, showing the IDIC symbol in the muted earth tones and deep reds so common to all of Vulcan's art.

Even the proceedings had changed little from Kirk's day. The magistrate was a middle-aged Vulcan female, dark-skinned, in a simple robe adorned by only a few polished gemstones. She had four padds on her desk, and shifted her attention easily from one to the next, each no doubt connected to a different database relating to the complex case before her.

Under normal conditions, Kirk doubted that anyone could deceive the Vulcan legal system, though he was certainly willing to give it a try. But Spock maintained that because of the virogen's impact on interstellar communications, conditions were anything but normal.

The magistrate's aide, a stern Vulcan male in an understated brown suit with a simple jeweled clasp, stood by her desk and read the names of all present for the hearing—they were not yet called prisoners. For the purposes of this appearance, Kirk had assumed the name of Lieutenant Adrian Plummer.

The real Lieutenant Plummer had served on the *Tobias* for fourteen months, and was now with the sixty crew members who had stayed on Chal with Teilani, to carry on the relief mission. However, Christine had altered the ship's records to show that Plummer had remained aboard for the journey to Vulcan, and she had replaced all of Plummer's medical and identification files with Kirk's. Spock had felt they would have quite enough to explain, without sidetracking the spacedock inquiry by revealing Kirk's identity. No matter how disruptive the threat of the virogen, anyone, like Kirk, who had a connection with the Borg would be seen as an even more immediate concern to the Federation's security. Spock was adamant that they could not risk the extra level of scrutiny Kirk's presence would immediately bring.

After formal identification of those present, the magistrate seemed to decide that the only person in the room worth talking to was Spock. She addressed him with deference.

"Ambassador Spock, I am pleased to meet you in person. Your services to Vulcan, the Federation, and the cause of galactic peace are most remarkable, and bring honor to Vulcan and the teachings of Surak. However, I would be remiss if I allowed your reputation, and the debt which all Vulcan owes you, to influence any dealings with this office."

"Your position is most logical," Spock assured her.

"Thank you."

"You are welcome."

The magistrate's aide cleared his throat. "There are many other matters we must attend to this day," he said.

The magistrate took on a more neutral demeanor. "Ambassador Spock," she began, "current Starfleet records show that the *U.S.S. Tobias* is assigned to relief efforts on Chal. Yet it is in Vulcan orbital space. Is this a dereliction of duty on the part of its commander?"

Kirk would never have accepted that kind of charge, and he was glad to see that Christine wouldn't, either. She instantly stepped forward to protest. "Your Honor, I am here on a matter of utmost—"

"Kroykah!"

Whether Christine understood the Vulcan word or not, she recognized its intent and stopped speaking at once.

"I apologize for Commander MacDonald's interruption," Spock said sincerely. "However, I must point out that you will not find the *Tobias's* current assignment on the open Starfleet channels, as we are engaged in a classified mission."

Kirk hid his smile. Technically, Spock hadn't lied. But he had managed to convey the impression that their classified mission was somehow connected to Starfleet.

"At what level of classification?" the magistrate asked.

"Above the level of this office," Spock said firmly.

The magistrate eyed him carefully, clearly understanding that Spock was challenging her authority to hold him. "Therefore, if this office were to make further inquiries to Starfleet, we would be told nothing?"

"I believe the cover story Starfleet would be required to relate to you would state that the *Tobias* was still on duty at Chal."

The magistrate moved one padd to sit atop another, as if shuffling old-fashioned papers. "Therefore, whether the facts you present are accurate or not, the response from Starfleet will be the same. You present me with an intriguing paradox."

"That is true," Spock agreed.

The magistrate shifted the padds again. "Then there is the matter of three unnatural deaths in Gonthar District: Tarok, and two of his staff—Klingon nationals, whose involvement contributes another level of complexity. As does evidence of multiple-weapons discharge in violation of local codes."

Kirk marveled at the smoothness of Spock's reply. "We were attempting to gather evidence of those crimes to present to the authorities when the authorities arrived."

"Are you, or any of those present, responsible for the deaths?"

"We came to Vulcan attempting to stop them," Spock said.

At that admission, Kirk cringed inwardly. Spock had just given the magistrate an opening for charging them with a crime. How could he have made such a mistake?

"Therefore, you had previous knowledge of a potential crime, yet you did not report it to the proper authorities?"

Spock hesitated before answering, as if acknowledging his guilt.

"That is true, Magistrate."

"Are you aware that as a Vulcan citizen, your act of omission is considered a breach of the public good?"

"I am."

The magistrate looked at Srell. "As are you?"

"I am," Srell said contritely.

The magistrate turned her attention to the others in the room. "For the rest of you, though you are not Vulcan citizens, you are Starfleet personnel, and as such, bound to the laws of this world by the articles of Federation. Therefore, you are equally subject to charges in this matter."

Barc huffed noisily and Kirk could see the Tellarite's ear fur bristle. Fortunately, though, the engineer knew enough to control his temper. In a Vulcan court, emotional outbursts had severe consequences.

The magistrate picked up a small baton and tapped it against a tiny hanging metal plate, no larger than a hand. An electronically produced gong note sounded, and Kirk recognized the small device as a symbolic version of the larger ones used in important ceremonies on Vulcan.

"The Vulcans, Spock and Srell, the Tellarite, Barc, and the humans, MacDonald, M'Benga, and Plummer, are remanded to protective custody, pending investigation of charges to be brought, concerning violation of Vulcan laws. The prisoners will be beamed to a custodial facility on the surface, and—"

Kirk was surprised as Spock interrupted the magistrate's recitation. "Magistrate, that would not be wise."

The magistrate gestured with the small baton. "Are you

aware of the penalties involved with the obstruction of justice, Spock?"

"Please check your records," Spock said. "The crew of the *Tobias* have been on active duty on Chal. They have been exposed to the virogen."

The magistrate dropped the baton on her desk.

"Though they claim they are uninfected, it would be prudent to test them for exposure before beaming them to the surface."

Though the magistrate's expression was unchanged, even Kirk could see that her composure was no longer perfect. She turned to her aide. "This spacedock is now in quarantine. The prisoners are to be placed in detention cells in this facility. Medical workers are to be dispatched at once, to test them for exposure to the virogen." She rose, staring at Spock with all the intensity her Vulcan impassivity would allow. "You have exposed this facility and threatened our homeworld, Spock."

Spock was unperturbed. "Your charge is not logical. You brought us aboard spacedock without first ascertaining the duty status of the *Tobias*."

Kirk thought the magistrate was going to suffer apoplexy, at least in a Vulcan fashion that would be undetectable to untrained observers. "You did not warn us, Spock."

"I did not expect to have a vital Starfleet mission interrupted by so junior a functionary."

Kirk and Christine exchanged a glance. Spock had just called the magistrate an incompetent novice. In a time before the Vulcan Reformation, his head would have been cut off and on a pike before he left the magistrate's presence.

"I will conduct a full investigation into your claims," the magistrate said in a voice of iron.

"I welcome it," Spock said. "As I welcome your presence in the detention cells once our government realizes what you have done."

The magistrate fumbled for the baton, then hit the small gong once more. "Take them away," she ordered.

As Kirk and the others were shepherded away through another door, Kirk thought he heard the sound of the baton being snapped in two just as the office doors slid shut. Such an act would have been an unthinkable display of emotion for the magistrate. But then, Spock could have that effect on humans. Perhaps he did the same for some Vulcans.

The prisoners were now in a utilitarian corridor that gradually curved to match the spacedock's circumference. The lighting was distinctly redshifted, matching normal illumination on Vulcan. The magistrate's aide led the way. Two Vulcan security guards, with no obvious weapons, had emerged from another door and now marched behind the full party.

Kirk fell into step beside Spock. "Was that necessary?" he asked in a low whisper. "You just made a powerful enemy for us."

"I assure you, the animosity of a spacedock magistrate is preferable to being placed in custody in a Vulcan jail," Spock said. "Escape is not possible. At least in a spacedock detention cell, we will have a chance to get back to the *Tobias.*"

"Is that why you slipped up by admitting you didn't warn the authorities about the attempt on Tarok's life?"

"It was not a 'slipup,'" Spock explained. "If the magistrate had continued to ask us questions about our presence, she would eventually have determined that Srell and I arrived separately from you and the *Tobias.* That would imply that we were not part of a Starfleet mission, which would have raised her suspicions even more, and quite possibly have brought in a higher rank of investigator. If we are to continue our own investigation, this is by far the least difficult facility from which to extricate ourselves."

Kirk felt relieved that Spock had not made a mistake after

all. It was in matters of strategy and diplomacy that he had come to depend on his friend the most. "So, how *do* we escape from a Vulcan detention cell?" Kirk asked.

Spock looked at Kirk. "I have the utmost faith in you, Jim. It is precisely in these situations that I have come to depend upon you thc most."

Before Kirk could say anything more, the magistrate's aide stopped by a forcefield frame, then placed his hand on an identity scanner. The forcefield winked out. The detention cells waited in the blind corridor beyond.

Kirk was encouraged to see that the doors of each cell were solid, not forcefields. Solid doors meant there would be locks; locks meant there were computer controls; and computers were meant to be outsmarted.

Kirk was further encouraged when Christine and Dr. M'Benga were ushered into one cell. It would be much easier for them to plan an escape with a partner. Unfortunately, Kirk saw he was going to be given the wrong one. Spock and Srell were being directed to the next cell, with Kirk and Barc obviously intended to share the last.

Kirk knew he had to be paired with Spock. Between the two of them, there was nothing they could not accomplish.

"Human, Tellarite, in here," a guard said, indicating the cell across from Spock and Srell.

Kirk looked at the Tellarite. There was only one way out.

He sneezed.

"You can't lock me up with a Tellarite. All that fur . . ." Kirk looked apologetically at the guard, rubbed his nose, squinted his eyes. "I'm allergic."

Barc snarled and Kirk guessed what he had said was considered an insult. But he couldn't turn back now.

"I'll need my medication," Kirk continued. "Otherwise, my throat swells up, I can't breathe. . . ." He sneezed again in the guard's direction.

The guard looked at Spock and Srell.

Kirk saw Spock subtly step back, knowing full well what Kirk was attempting.

The guard pointed at Srell. "You, with the Tellarite."

Srell and Kirk changed places.

Spock and Kirk walked into their detention cell together.

When the solid door slid shut, Kirk quickly examined the cell. It was surprisingly large, about four meters square, but had nothing in the way of chairs, benches, or beds. It was just an empty cube of a room.

"How Vulcan," Kirk said with a wry smile. Then he looked at the door, checking its outline to find some indication of its locking mechanism. There was a small control panel by the doorframe. It would be a good place to start. "But between the two of us, we should be out of here within the . . . Spock?"

Kirk reached out to grab Spock's arm as he felt the floor slip beneath him, angling dramatically as the outline of the door seemed to blur, then spiral away.

The sense of disorientation had been too sudden. Both Kirk and Spock stumbled to the ground. Kirk recognized part of the sensation—the artificial gravity field in the cell had cycled swiftly through multiple areas of central attraction.

When he looked up from the floor, trying to locate the door again, he recognized another trick of technology.

He and Spock now appeared to be in a garden.

The sky was Vulcan red above them. Leaves in a nearby glade of trees rustled in the gentle breeze. Birds sang. And a small plot of meditation stones to their side, artfully placed among furrows of red and brown sand, compellingly invited their contemplation of the infinite.

"It's a holodeck, isn't it?" Kirk grumbled as he stood up. The metal deck beneath him now seemed to be made of interlocked clay bricks.

"Apparently so," Spock said. "It would appear to be a recreation of the meditation gardens surrounding the Surak Memorial in ShirKahr." Spock pointed into the holographically simulated distance. "You can see the dome of the memorial through those trees."

Kirk felt all his encouragement evaporate. He knew the walls of the detention cell were no more than four meters away in any direction. But he also knew that if he started walking in what he thought was a straight line, he could probably continue for what would seem kilometers. Between the holoprojectors creating the scenery, and the forcefields and gravity control that could alter his path without him realizing it, he was trapped.

It was the ultimate prison cell because it had no walls to climb and no locks to pick.

He found it far too logical, but he had to admit that the Vulcans had known what they were doing. For the first time in his life, Kirk wondered if he was in a trap from which there could be no escape.

TWENTY-FIVE

"Well, Spock," Kirk said as he brushed holographic dust from his uniform's trousers, "I'm certainly glad we're not in a jail on the surface. I've heard those are tough."

"This *is* what jails are like on the surface," Spock replied. "I was not aware the spacedock facilities had been upgraded."

Kirk looked around, trying to ignore the pang of desperation he felt. The illusion of being outdoors on Vulcan was staggeringly detailed. Somewhere, perhaps even within arm's reach, there was an exit that led to the spacedock's corridor. But it might as well be on another planet. "I don't suppose you have any Vulcan tricks up your sleeves."

Small specks of dirt and grit crunched under Kirk's boots. The sun gleaming off the golden dome of Surak's memorial was a pinpoint of blinding brilliance. He could scent the water from the fountain that splashed a hundred meters away.

Spock didn't grace Kirk with a reply.

Then Kirk took a second look at Spock.

In the midst of all this simulated detail, how could he know if Spock was even Spock?

"Is something wrong, 'Lieutenant'?" Spock asked.

Kirk narrowed his eyes at what might or might not be his friend. Could Vulcan logic be that devious? Would the justice authorities go so far as to make two prisoners seem to share a cell, them separate them holographically with simulated duplicates that might elicit a confession?

Technology made it possible.

But Kirk would bet on the human touch every time.

"It's all right, Spock. We're alone. You can call me by my real rank."

Spock's expression remained detached. But he idly scratched an earlobe. "Unless there is something you have not told me, as far as I know, your real rank is that of lieutenant."

Kirk had to think it through. That might have been the response of a holographic duplicate fishing for information. Or, Spock might have said that, knowing that everything they said to each other in the cell was being monitored. Is that why Spock had scratched his ear? In warning?

"Just checking," Kirk said. His mind worked furiously as he tried to figure a way around Vulcan logic—both that of his captors, and Spock's. It was worse than trying to figure out temporal anomalies. And it was giving him a headache.

"Ah," Spock said. "You believe I might be a holographic duplicate intended to elicit details of your crimes."

Kirk frowned. "Spock, we committed no crimes."

Spock, if it were Spock, spoke in a low voice. "I was speaking for the benefit of the listening devices which even now might be recording everything we say."

"Is that legal on Vulcan?" Kirk asked.

"Until we have been tested for exposure to the virogen, I think we may assume we are under the jurisdiction of one of the planetary defense bureaus. As a member of the diplomatic corps, and with you as a member of Starfleet, our civil liberties are severely constrained by the oaths of duty to which we both attested."

Kirk frowned at Spock. With conversation like that, how could he tell the difference between a computer-driven version of a Vulcan and a real Vulcan? Especially if the real Vulcan didn't want to reveal any important information that might be used against them in future legal proceedings?

It would have to be something trivial, Kirk decided. Some small detail that would be known only to Spock and himself, unavailable in any database.

Kirk scratched at the side of his jaw. He had it. "Spock, do you remember when we were on that planetoid in the Gamma Canaris region? Do you remember who we found there?"

That was a safe question, Kirk knew. In Gamma Canaris, he and Spock and McCoy unexpectedly had come upon the human inventor of the warp drive, Zefram Cochrane himself. Cochrane had survived his own era because of the influence of a mysterious alien he called the Companion. When Kirk, Spock, and McCoy were ready to leave, Cochrane had asked them to promise never to reveal his existence to anyone else. He wanted to remain with the Companion undisturbed, to live out the remainder of their lives in peace.

Kirk had kept his word. Spock and McCoy were the only two people who shared that secret with him. If this Spock was a hologram, he would have no idea to what Kirk referred.

But Spock's reply revealed a third possibility. "I am afraid you are mistaken. I was last in the Gamma Canaris region on stardate 3219.8; one hundred and six years ago. Clearly, you had not been born at that time."

Kirk stared up at the simulated sky. Of course. In this detention cell, for the benefit of their Vulcan captors, Kirk was Lieutenant Plummer. Spock's reply could have come from a holographic duplicate, or from the real Spock, determined to keep Kirk's identity a secret. Whatever question

Kirk asked, it would have to be based on more recent events. He cleared his throat.

"Ambassador Spock, when we were on Tarok's estate, I asked you if the crew of the *Tobias* reminded you of anyone."

"No," Spock said. "You asked me if the senior officers of the *Tobias* with Mr. Srell reminded me of anyone."

Kirk closed his eyes in relief. No one else had heard him ask Spock that question.

"And I told you they did not," Spock added.

"Thank you," Kirk said. "I'm convinced you're you."

Then he realized that now Spock was giving him a questioning look.

"Don't tell me," Kirk said as he understood the reason for Spock's expression. "Now you're wondering if *I'm* a hologram."

"Someone else might have overheard you ask that question, and then related it to an interrogator for inclusion in a holographic simulation," Spock said.

"So, ask me something, Spock. Something that only I would know. That would never have been input into a database or told to anyone else."

Spock looked thoughtful for a few moments. "Once, I and a mutual physician friend of ours had to access the personal safe in your quarters on . . . your vessel."

Kirk thought frantically. The mutual friend was certainly McCoy. The unnamed vessel had to be the *Enterprise.* But when had Spock and McCoy gone into his safe? It was something they would have done only if they thought he had died in the line of duty, and they required copies of his final orders. And the only time that had happened was . . . in Tholian space?

"Just a minute," Kirk said indignantly before Spock could finish. "At the time of the incident to which you're referring, I specifically asked you and . . . our friend if you had looked at the orders in my safe, and you told me you hadn't."

"We lied," Spock said blandly. "Returning to the safe. What was the combination?"

Kirk didn't have to think. "Five three four," he said. They were the birth months of his brother, Sam; himself; and his nephew, Peter—certainly not trivial. And certainly not anything he would ever forget.

Spock nodded. "I am satisfied. Only the real . . . Lieutenant Plummer would have known that code."

Kirk still couldn't get over Spock's earlier admission. "You lied to me."

"It was the doctor's idea," Spock countered.

Kirk was getting tired of standing. He took a few steps toward the low wall surrounding the meditation garden and sat on the gold-colored, metallic ledge that topped it. It was difficult to believe it was only a holographic illusion, but his feet felt better. "So what now?"

Spock joined Kirk on the ledge. "I am open to suggestions."

Kirk drew in a deep breath. The illusion of being on Vulcan was so complete that he could even detect the faint scent of cinnamon that seemed to perfume the dust of the planet. "The magistrate said we were to be tested for exposure to the virogen. Is that something that can be done by medical scanners?"

"No. The test will require blood samples."

That gave Kirk a starting point. "Then we'll have company any time now. A medical technician. Probably a guard."

"That would be logical."

And if they can get in, Kirk thought, *they'll know the way out. How's that for logic?*

"We should keep our eyes open," Kirk said. "Try and see where they come from."

Spock looked skeptical. "Though I am willing to be open-minded, it *is* a Vulcan prison. You can be sure there are countermeasures for every strategy you can devise."

Kirk reached behind himself and ran his fingers over the sand in the meditation garden, disturbing the precise alignment of two channels of red and brown. The deception was so perfect, he could even feel small particles of sand cling to his fingertips.

"Since we have nothing else to do at this time," Spock said, "perhaps you could continue your story."

"Story?"

"About . . . our friend," Spock said. "Who last found himself being helped by Hugh's clan."

Kirk took a handful of holographic sand and let it fall from his fist. It feathered into a wispy plume in the artificial breeze.

"Why not?" Surrounded by the artifice of technology, it seemed the perfect setting to explain how it came to be that he had freed himself from it.

Or, at least, how he had tried.

The female's name was Miko. She and Hugh had carted Kirk through the mud, past the dead and dying Borg, letting his useless feet drag behind him.

To Kirk, it was as if he floated over a war zone, the aftermath of a battle waged by demons.

Looking back on it, perhaps it was a suitable way to think of the life he had lived up to that place and time—a war of demons, out of control.

Perhaps it was time that control finally emerged.

Eventually, the rapacious monsters that cleansed that battlefield were left behind, to scoop up and dismember the remnants of whatever Borg bastions had fallen.

In time—how long, he couldn't tell—Kirk was aware that Hugh and Miko were carrying him across solid ground.

They climbed a worn path hacked out of obsidian stone, flecked with glints of red and silver, bearing him up a mountainside shrouded in the low-lying clouds of this world.

The cold, cloying mist enveloped Kirk as they climbed.

He felt the nanites burn within him. The pain now unceasing. All the peaks and surges of it joined in one continuous wave of agony.

He knew he would never live to see this journey's end.

And then, they passed through the clouds, and the sun of this world blazed down upon him.

But it was not a sun.

Kirk trembled as he saw the vision that awaited him.

Its beauty was so overwhelming that he did not know when Hugh and Miko had lowered him to the ground.

For it was not one star that shone on him.

It was thousands, *millions,* all the stars that he had ever seen in his entire life, brought together in some way to shine their light on him alone.

Long after, he would come to understand that what he saw was a galactic core—a dense collection of stars so closely packed that supernovae flared among them in a cosmic chain reaction, creating a star-strewn ball of luminescent fire that filled a quarter of the sky.

Kirk stared up at that fire and that brilliance, seeing wisps of matter and energy dance with incalculable energies, and knew he was no longer in the galaxy of his birth.

Removed beyond all reason from everything that he knew, he cried with the joy and the pain of facing death while beholding such beauty. To know such transcendence only in the final moments of his life seemed both miraculous and cruel, a gift desired but acquired too late.

Had he really come to take the universe for granted?

With all that he had been given by fate, with all that he had earned by effort, had he really grown so inured to the wonders he had encountered that he had forgotten there were wonders more, still to be discovered?

Kirk raised his hand to that vast assembly of stars, longing to reach them, to touch, to go on.

He *had* forgotten.

There was still more to do.

But his realization of that simple truth was far too late. The nanites were almost finished with their work.

Kirk's vision shifted from the infinity of stars to his own tattered flesh. Blood welled from a thousand microscopic cuts on his arm as the nanites at last reached the surface of his skin and burst through.

Blood dimmed his vision as he lost all sense of feeling and fell up to those stars . . .

. . . only to feel the gentle pressure of Miko's hands, holding him back, soothing his wounds with a smooth, fragrant salve.

Then Hugh and Miko brought him to a stream that gushed into a hollow in the slick, black rock.

They plunged him into the icy depths and it was as if his flesh froze and shattered and he was plucked from within it, new, and whole, and cleansed.

Kirk lay beside that stream as Miko wiped the mud and the salve from him. He did not know it at the time, but when she was done, the nanites were no longer within him. The salve had lured them out and neutralized them with plant-based pheromones and genetic markers that the nanites' voracious programming could not resist.

Thus had technology succumbed to its own selfish appetites.

It might have been days later. It might have been months. But when at last Kirk felt sensation return to him, all he could see on his skin was a faint pebbling of tiny scars.

"The nanites?" he asked.

Miko drew a cloth across his brow. "All that was machine has been taken from you. Just as it was taken from us."

He stared at her then, and saw the logic of the brown and white skin that covered her.

She had been Borg, but now, wherever Borg implants had been taken from her, new brown skin was in its place. White skin showed where she had remained untouched at the time of her assimilation.

"How?" Kirk asked.

Hugh took Kirk's hand as he led him from the water. "We will show you," he said.

And Kirk went with them from the mountain to the village of the clan.

"An actual village?" Spock asked.

"It's the best word for it," Kirk said. "Some of the dwellings were carved from the rock walls. Some were wood. And the whole of it was filled with . . . others who had been reclaimed from the Collective. Humanoids, aliens, skin, fur, scales . . ." Kirk shook his head at the memory of it. "Every day, that galactic core would blaze like a sun. And every night, the sky burned with transwarp transporter beams, bringing in reclaimed material from . . . from wherever a Borg installation had failed but was still in contact with the Collective's backup systems." Kirk rubbed the grains of sand between his fingers. "It gave me . . . it gave my *friend,* the feeling the Borg were everywhere. Not just this galaxy, but . . . everywhere. As if the fusion of flesh and machine were . . . inevitable."

Spock regarded Kirk intently. "It appears to have been a profound experience. For your friend."

Kirk grinned for a moment, marveling at Spock's gift for understatement. Then he gave up any pretense of trying to make possible eavesdroppers think he was relating a tale told to him by someone else. He doubted the Vulcans would know what to make of his story anyway. It was one purely of emotion, not logic.

"Spock, in the true sense of the word, I had become Borg. Not like Picard. Not with implants. I hadn't been assimilated. But figuratively, metaphorically, if you want, I had allowed myself, in the way I had lived my life, to become . . .

absorbed by the objects and the things around me." Kirk tossed the sand away, not bothering to see where it would fall. "I lost *myself.* Everything else was just trappings. My career in Starfleet. Whether I could have that chair again. Whether there'd be another mission for me. Maybe falling into the Nexus was the best thing that could have happened to me. To die on Veridian, to finally be cut off from history . . . really, it ended up freeing me in a way I'd never have expected."

"Yet," Spock said, "you have returned. You could have stayed with Teilani, out of sight, undisturbed, like our mutual friend in the Gamma Canaris region."

"I'm not who I was, Spock. For what I did in the past, I've no regrets. And maybe, if the Federation survives, somehow I'll keep on doing what I've always done. But *why* I'm doing it, and *how,* that's different now. To lose everything, and then to have a chance to get it back, that experience makes *everything* different."

"Is this what you were taught?" Spock asked.

"It's what I was shown. It's what I came to know."

Miko had stayed with him, in a shelter made of wooden beams and woven fibers that had never seen a replicator.

She took him to the fields where the clan grew the crops that fed them. She took him to the forests where the clan hewed the wood that sheltered them. She took him to her bed, where she let sensation rule him, driving out the need for thought.

When his strength had recovered, Kirk had joined Hugh in the clan's work. Moving through the reclamation fields to find those who could be saved from assimilation. Hugh showed him how to touch those precise points on a being through which the life force could be sensed.

Kirk recognized the placement. They were the same as those Vulcans used in mindmelds.

Hugh agreed. He knew about Vulcans.

The Borg had assimilated thousands of worlds, tens of thousands of cultures. Though Hugh and his clan had abandoned the machine, they retained the knowledge that had been absorbed by the Collective.

"That knowledge is the same," Hugh said. "That spark of life that fills the worlds of all the galaxies, it is the same everywhere. A necessary part of existence. As sure as the fusion of hydrogen or the orbit of a star."

Kirk took other Borg to the stream to cleanse them of their implants. Miko showed him the secrets that would free and redeem them, secrets that had been learned only here, known only to the Borg who were brought to this world.

The transwarp transporters brought everything here—Borg, and machinery, and clumps of soil from worlds throughout the universe.

Some of the clan sorted through that soil, to find green shoots and seeds. These they grew on the mountain slopes. These they used to make the salves and dried compounds that would ease the pain of those who were reclaimed.

Kirk learned well. Held the Borg down as their implants were rejected. Applied the medicines that would heal their wounds.

Since he had not been Borg himself, it was simpler for him to handle those implants, to gather them together, some still moving with a macabre machine-echo of life, and take them to the dumping grounds where they could never be recycled by the all-consuming machines.

It was there Kirk found the Borg scoutship.

Intact.

And he realized the time had come for his journey to continue once again.

TWENTY-SIX

"It was as simple as that?" Spock asked.

Kirk was irritated by the question. "Spock, it wasn't simple at all. I spent two years with Hugh and his people. My wounds healed. I lived with them. Celebrated with them. Learned from them. But they had all been Borg. The life they led there, it was what *they* needed. I had my time with them, and then it was time for me to move on with what I had to do."

"How did you know how to operate a Borg scoutship?"

"I didn't have to. The clan knew. Some of them, who weren't afraid of the machine, they operated it for me."

"And brought you where?"

Kirk smiled. "Heaven. Chal. If I were really going to have a second chance at life, I knew I had to lay my old life to rest. It didn't matter how Teilani and I had met, that we'd both been manipulated by Drake, I knew I loved her. I had to see her grave. To say good-bye."

Spock nodded. "But she hadn't died."

"A second chance," Kirk said. "After all the things this universe has taken from me, it finally gave me something back. Something I know how to treasure now."

Spock stared far away, as if this false garden really were Vulcan, as if this really were his home.

"I understand the irony now," he said. "The universe has given you a second chance at life, at love, and yet the Federation, the very thing that makes your life possible, is on the brink of ruin."

"We've saved it before," Kirk said.

"From its enemies. Hugh told you the spark of life was intrinsic to the universe. It could well be that the virogen confronting us is a natural by-product of the Federation's own unprincipled growth. I do not know how we might save the Federation from itself."

"When has not knowing stopped us before?"

Spock rose to his feet. He seemed offended by Kirk's attempt at humor. "My father was murdered. I was not there to protect him." Spock pointed at Kirk. "What *I* want from the universe is a chance to set that right."

Kirk stood up slowly, alarmed to see his friend actually begin to tremble with what could only be rage. He reached out to touch Spock's arm. "Are you all right? This isn't like you at all."

But Spock tore away from Kirk's grasp.

"I am tired of 'being like me.' I am tired of control, and denial, and the blind, Vulcan acceptance of everything that is wrong in this world!"

Kirk stared at Spock as if he were watching a transformation at work. As if some shapeshifter had taken Spock's form. Because what Spock was saying simply could never come from him.

"Spock, this isn't the time or the place for—"

"It is! It is what I feel! And I will not deny it any longer!"

For an instant, Kirk's instinct was to slap Spock, to focus his attention, to break the momentum of whatever had caused his friend's startling loss of self-control. But before he could act, a new voice called out in the cell.

"Do not move from your positions!"

At once, Kirk and Spock both turned their heads toward the direction from which the voice had come.

Two Vulcans stood two meters away, as if they had stepped out from the air. One was a spacedock guard. The other, from her pale green cloak, was a healer. She held a medical kit and had obviously come to draw blood samples.

Both Vulcans stared at Spock with disquieting intensity. They had obviously witnessed his most uncharacteristic outburst.

The healer broke the silence. "Are you well, Ambassador?"

Spock smoothed his robes. "I say again for the benefit of the magistrate, you are interfering in vital Starfleet affairs."

The healer approached Kirk. "The magistrate is attempting to contact Starfleet Command to confirm your assignment. In any event, this test is necessary in order to insure the safety of Vulcan's biosphere."

The healer took Kirk's arm and motioned for him to roll up his sleeve.

"Where is your logic?" Spock complained. "We have already been down on Vulcan. Do you really think I would allow my home to be placed in danger?"

The healer drew a sample of Kirk's blood from his inner elbow. "The magistrate is aware of that," she said calmly. "There are many aspects to your presence and your actions here that trouble her."

Kirk rolled down his sleeve as the healer deftly placed the ampule of his blood into her kit. He saw four other ampules there. One green, one purple-black, two dark red. Vulcan, Tellarite, and human. "Are our friends all right?" he asked.

The healer looked at him as if a trained monkey had addressed her. "The others are as you last saw them. Their blood will be tested for the virogen, as well." She looked away from Kirk as if he had ceased to exist. "Ambassador, please expose your arm."

Kirk watched as Spock chewed his lip, as if debating the healer's request.

"Ambassador, this is a serious matter. I am authorized to have you stunned in order to obtain a sample."

Spock wrenched his sleeve up and thrust his arm at the healer with a barely restrained expression of anger.

When the healer approached Spock with her syringe, Kirk sensed her caution. "Sir, I am a healer. Is there anything else I can do for you?"

Spock fixed his eyes on the ampule that filled with his green blood. "Release me."

Once she had obtained her sample, the healer stepped away quickly. "I am sure the magistrate is doing everything in her power to expedite your request."

She rejoined the guard. Kirk watched them closely, hoping to see them step through the doorway that was hidden by the holographic imagery.

"Good-bye, Ambassador," the healer said. "May your journey be without incident." Then she nodded at the guard, he touched a control on the belt he wore, and both Vulcans appeared to take on the colors and details of the scenery behind them, then faded from view.

Kirk fixed their exact location by counting the bricks between him and where they had last stood. He looked at Spock. "What happened to them? Don't they have to step through an arch to get in and out?"

"That is on a standard holodeck," Spock said, as if annoyed that Kirk was speaking to him. "In the event your attention has been elsewhere, this is a prison."

Kirk regarded his friend with concern, but did not move toward him. He was determined to keep his feet in exactly the same position they had been when the Vulcans had faded into the background. It was the only way he could be sure of what constituted the real volume of the holodeck.

"Spock, I don't know what's happened to you, but if you

want to get out of here, you're going to have to work with me."

"What leads you to believe you can possibly escape a Vulcan cell?"

Kirk was appalled by how much Spock sounded like a petulant child. "Because you said you had faith in me," he snapped. "Now get over here."

Reluctantly, Spock walked over to Kirk. Both their backs were to the meditation garden. Kirk maneuvered Spock into position and had him place his feet in Kirk's own footsteps, one foot after another. "All right, now don't move. You're going to give me a lesson in holosimulations."

Kirk ran a few steps to the meditation garden, leaned over the low wall, and scooped up two handfuls of sand. "First thing, where does the sand come from?"

Spock sounded totally disinterested. "It is replicator matter. Everything physical with which we can interact is some form of replicator matter combined with precision forcefields."

Kirk started a trail of sand from the toe of Spock's boots, on a direct line toward the bricks where the guard and the healer had been standing. His first handful of sand ran out as he reached that brick. He kept going, checking to make sure he was keeping the line of sand straight. When he was finished with the second handful, he had a trail of sand at least eight meters long.

Kirk stood at the end of the sand line. "We're now farther apart than the room is wide. Explain to me how it works," Kirk called back to Spock.

"It is, of course, a logical impossibility," Spock said, still irritable. "As you walked away from me, sensors in the floor tracked your footsteps. As you neared the wall, forcefields in the floor began moving like a treadmill, giving you the physical sensation of walking, even though you remained in place. The OHD panels lining the cell projected holographic images to keep the scenery moving to match your apparent physical progress."

"But you *look* as if you're eight meters away, Spock."

"What you are seeing from your vantage point is a holographic image of me in forced perspective. In actuality, I am no more than three or four meters from you, as logic demands."

"So the real you is hidden behind a holographic screen," Kirk said.

"Until you come within a logical visual range of me. Then the plane of the holographic illusion will pass over me, allowing you to see me as I really am."

Kirk walked back along the line of sand. In his mind's eye, he pictured the bare cube of the holodeck, filled with a series of virtual-projection screens that changed their position according to the position of the two people within the cell. The trick was to get behind one of those screens. And Kirk knew how to do it.

He stood on one foot and pulled off his boot. Spock watched him with a frown.

"I assure you, the tactile response works on feet as well as fingers," Spock said.

"That's not what I had in mind," Kirk told him. "Watch. And listen."

Then Kirk threw his boot as hard as he could, straight along the line of sand.

About three meters away, he heard a faint thump, as if the boot had hit something solid. But visually, the boot seemed to sail another five meters before tumbling onto the ground.

"Let *me* tell you what just happened," Kirk said. "My boot, which is not replicator matter, hit the wall of the cell somewhere between here and the end of that trail of sand. But what the holoprojectors did was to create an image of the boot continuing on its trajectory, while at the same time putting a holographic screen over the boot as it fell to the floor against the wall."

"Exactly," Spock said. "So."

Kirk looked down at the blank spot on his uniform where his comm badge had been fastened. Unfortunately, it had been removed by the guards before he had been brought before the magistrate. "So, my friend, the trick is, we need to know exactly how far the wall really is."

"I fail to see how that information could possibly be useful."

"I don't suppose they let you keep your comm badge? We need something hard."

Spock fingered his IDIC medallion. It gleamed in the artificial light of the artificial garden. "Would this suffice?"

Spock handed the medallion to Kirk.

"May I throw it?"

Spock shrugged. "I have."

Kirk didn't bother to ask for an explanation. "Close your eyes," he said. "You have to listen for the medallion hitting the wall, and then tell me how far away it is."

Spock closed his eyes.

Kirk hurled the medallion like a miniature discus.

Though it appeared to soar far away, he heard the metallic impact of it striking the wall only a second after release. A section of the background scenery even wavered for a moment, as if one or two of the OHD panels had been broken.

Kirk turned to Spock. "How far?" he asked.

"Two point six meters," Spock answered. "And you broke the medallion."

"I'll get you another. How're your arms?"

Spock instantly knew what Kirk had in mind. "You cannot be serious."

Kirk was hurt. "Did I miss something about how this holocell works?"

Spock followed the line of sand with his eyes. "Two point

six meters," he repeated. "It will have to be done with sufficient force to strike the wall before touching the floor."

Kirk nodded. "Exactly, so the forcefields on the floor will lose track of me."

Spock looked dubious.

"It worked for the boot," Kirk said, "and the medallion."

Spock took off his robe and dropped it to the holographic bricks, then cupped his hands and adjusted his stance. "You will have to do it without running, to take the program by surprise."

Kirk put his bootless foot in Spock's cupped hands and braced his hands on Spock's shoulders. "What if we're being watched?"

"Then I trust the guards will be entertained," Spock said. "On the count of three?"

Kirk counted off, setting their timing.

On "three," he pushed up and forward as Spock pivoted and threw him in the same direction.

For an instant, Kirk saw the meditation garden swirl around him, and then he felt the jarring shock of hitting an invisible wall.

He slapped his arms against it, trying to absorb some of the impact, but he had miscalculated and felt his breath explode from his lungs as his chest was momentarily paralyzed.

Fortunately, the jolt against the floor as he slid down the wall relieved the symptom. He could breathe again, almost.

"Are you all right?" Spock called out.

Kirk raised his head from the floor and looked in the direction of the sound of Spock's voice. Beneath his hands, he could feel, and more importantly, *see* the bare floor of the cell, not holographic bricks. He ran his fingers along the dark metal, confirming the texture of the miniature OHD panels that lined it. He was out of the illusion!

Spock was less than three meters away, but appeared to be

little more than a splotchy collection of coarse pixels, shimmering with out-of-phase color and motion.

"Spock! It worked!" Kirk shouted. He was *behind* the holographic screens. The program running the simulation had treated his thrown body as if it were an inanimate prop. "What do you see?"

"You appear to have rolled onto the bricks about four meters away," Spock called out. "I suggest you hurry, before the program's heuristics realize what you have done and trigger a restart."

Kirk got to his feet and turned to face the wall, keeping in as close contact with it as possible. He looked to both sides. To the left, he saw the outline of the door. He edged toward it, pressing against the wall so that he wouldn't slip back into the holographic illusion.

It was better than he had hoped. He easily found the small control panel by the door which he had noticed the first time he had looked, just before the simulation had begun. The panel had only two control surfaces. He pressed the one on the left.

The door slid open onto the corridor, no exit code needed.

Kirk could understand the simplicity of the mechanism from a Vulcan's point of view: Why bother to lock a door that the prisoner would never find?

He pressed the control on the right, confident of what the result would be. Sure enough, there was a flashing flurry of lights behind him, and when he turned again, Spock was standing in the center of the bare holocell, his robe on the metal floor beside him.

"Pick that up, would you?" Kirk pointed to his boot lying against the wall. "I'll hold the door." Then he stepped halfway through the doorway and glanced down the corridor.

Christine and M'Benga were running toward him.

Kirk stared at them. "How . . . ?"

M'Benga rotated her shoulder with a tight-lipped expression of pain. "Chris had this bright idea of throwing me against the wall."

"It worked, didn't it?" Christine said.

Spock appeared in the doorway and handed Kirk his boot. Kirk pointed across the corridor. "Barc and Srell are in that—"

They heard a dull clang of metal and a Tellarite's grunt of pain. A moment later, the cell door slid open to reveal Barc shaking his head. Srell stepped out from behind him.

"Did everyone figure out the same flaw?" Kirk asked incredulously.

Srell adjusted his jacket. Kirk realized that Srell and Spock were the only two who hadn't seen the way out. "When Vulcan prisoners are placed in a holographic re-creation of Surak's meditation garden," Srell said loftily, "they are expected to meditate and reflect on their wrongdoings. These are new facilities, and I imagine the authorities will augment the simulation to take into account the actions of non-Vulcans."

"A logical assessment," Spock said. "And now, I believe we should continue our escape."

"Of course," Srell said.

But it was a blind corridor. Kirk pointed toward the only exit. "Forcefield," he reminded everyone. He reached down for his boot.

Barc merely growled and waddled toward the forcefield frame. In seconds, he had popped a wall access panel with a powerful punch. Then, boot forgotten, Kirk watched in amazement as the Tellarite used his seemingly clumsy hands to pick the metal pips from his collar, tie them together with a thread he pulled from his tunic, and dangle them inside the access port. He pushed his head half inside, one eye closed, the tip of his broad tongue sticking out from the side of his snout in an expression of rapt concentration.

Barc grunted to himself once or twice; then he pulled back

his hand, and the forcefield frame shorted out in a gratifying display of static and sparks.

Barc shook his fingers back and forth. The fur on his knuckles was smoldering.

"Next," he said with great satisfaction.

Christine thudded him on his shoulder, making him rock. "You did it again, Barcs!"

"Rrrr, that I did."

Kirk looked up from pulling on his boot. "Am I the only one who wants to know what's keeping the guards?"

Srell gingerly passed his hand through the forcefield frame, confirming that the field was down. "Until the blood samples confirm that we are free of virogen contamination, there will be no guards assigned to this section."

Kirk walked through the frame. However the Tellarite engineer had managed to shut down the field, there wasn't even a residual static charge left. Very impressive. But the forcefield couldn't be the only security measure in use. "Why aren't they using scanners in the corridor?" he asked.

"That would not be logical," Spock said. "Since no one can escape from a holocell, there is no need to look for escapees."

Kirk saw Barc turn to Christine and M'Benga. "It's still too easy if you ask me."

Kirk agreed, but wasn't inclined to join the debate. "Why don't we just keep moving," he suggested. "After all, when on Vulcan. . . ."

He turned and began to jog down the corridor, away from the magistrate's office, in the general direction of the turbolift banks that served the spacedock's umbilical docking levels. He was gratified to hear the others quickly catch up behind him.

Kirk had long ago learned that when faced with an apparently complex problem, it was sometimes better to make a quick decision, rather than remain immobile while trying to determine the correct one.

But even with his decision made, he still wrestled with himself to determine if he was doing the right thing. Because Barc had been right. Vulcan obstinacy aside, this escape *was* too easy.

Which meant he could be leading his team into another trap, even worse than the last.

Wouldn't be the first time, he thought. And with no other options before him, Kirk did the only thing he could.

He ran faster.

TWENTY-SEVEN

Picard had never felt so frustrated.

All around him, he could feel the pulse and the rhythms of his ship. Even in the vacuum of the shuttlebay, the vibrations traveled through the deck plates, through the landing skids, and brought the hull of the *Galileo* to resonant life. The life of a starship.

Yet because he was in quarantine, Picard could not be part of it.

Beverly placed a cup of Earl Grey on the work surface that folded out from the *Galileo*'s main instrument panel.

"This is quite maddening," he said.

"The tea?"

Her smile was enough to ease some of his tension. Her presence, even more. He returned the smile gratefully. The week they had spent in the close quarters of the shuttle had been a reminder of the rare treasure of time spent in each other's presence, free of the ever-present responsibilities both took so seriously.

"Certainly not the tea," Picard said as he savored the aroma. "Nor the company. But . . ." He gestured wistfully at the small navigational display on the instrument panel.

Upon it, the planet Vulcan, in all her stern and crimson majesty, was reduced to little more than a dull red disk on a ten-centimeter screen.

The flight deck of a shuttle was never meant to be the bridge of a starship.

Beverly sat on the arm of Picard's flight chair. "We won't be in here forever."

"Does that mean you have faith in my supposition that the Symmetrists' cure can be found on Vulcan?" he asked. "Or are you about to tell me you've discovered an antivirogen yourself?"

Picard had asked that last question almost in jest. He still hadn't dared share with anyone Stron's startling identification of Sarek as the Symmetrists' leader. That possibility, if true, was the key reason why Picard believed Vulcan might hold the answer to the mystery of the virogen's creation and purpose.

"As a matter of fact," Beverly said, "Starfleet Medical may be making some progress. Three days ago, they completed a simulated clinical trial using an old Klingon herbal treatment for certain types of food poisoning. Dried *trannin* leaves, of all things.

"Apparently, when the leaves dry, they exude a resin containing a compound that binds perfectly to the virogen's silicon spine, so its RNA can't cleave. That stops reproduction of the virogen, *and* tags it so antibodies can form. The simulator trials indicate that the *trannin* compound can reduce the virogen load in a typical animal model to zero within thirty hours."

"That is most encouraging. Can the treatment be applied to plants as well as animals?"

"Not yet. The compound is a macromolecule—too large to efficiently penetrate plant cell membranes the way the virogen does. But if the compound really does test out, and it can be synthesized *and* replicated, then we have a good chance of stopping all animal transmission. Which means, we can get out of this shuttlecraft."

"Are you in that much of a hurry? It's so peaceful."

"I could erase the medical logs," she teased. "We might have to stay here for years."

Picard made a show of thinking the possibility over. But one detail stopped him. "How did Medical ever come up with the idea of testing an old Klingon folk remedy for a new disease organism?"

"Well, technically, the virogen isn't an organism. And the idea came out of a medical log filed from one of the affected systems. Apparently, a doctor assigned to a relief mission reported positive results on some of her patients and recommended the leaves for further study. I only read the abstract, but I gather she got the leaves from some sort of Klingon folk healer on the planet."

"How fortunate for us all."

"I'd say it was time something fortunate happened in all of this." Beverly's smile faltered. She glanced away for a moment, looking through the shuttle's forward viewport at the deserted bay. "Jean-Luc, the latest figures from Medical put the number of affected systems at nineteen."

Picard was stunned. "That's more than double what it was a week ago."

"Between emergency transport of food supplies, relief missions . . . Starfleet no longer has enough ships to adequately maintain the quarantine. Blockades are being run everywhere. The contagion's spreading."

Picard sat forward to enter his access code into the shuttle's communications system. Instantly, all command bulletins he had received from Starfleet over the past seventy hours appeared onscreen. Picard had read them all as they had been received, but he checked their subject headings again. "Beverly, my command updates report only nine affected systems."

Beverly leaned forward to read over Picard's shoulder. She found the reason for the discrepancy at once. "Look at the stardates. These were already four to five days old when you received them."

Picard expanded the most recent update and accessed the routing information embedded in it. It was horrendously complex—a hopelessly inefficient web of starbases, subspace relay stations, and even ship-to-ship transmissions. A message which normally should have reached the *Enterprise* in less than half a day had taken five.

Picard traced the data on the screen with his finger, astounded by the revelations contained within them. "The whole subspace network is breaking down. There are missing starbases, retransmissions . . . How can Medical's communications be so far ahead of Command's?"

Beverly input her access codes to call up her own most recent medical bulletins on another display. The routing information contained in them explained part of the reason for the timing differences. "The Command bulletins are originating from Starfleet Headquarters on Earth. The medical bulletins originate from the Virogen Task Force Headquarters at Starbase Five-fifteen."

To Picard, it made perfect sense that in this emergency Starfleet would decentralize its command structure to insure a more rapid response, and he knew from personal experience that the medical facilities at 515 were superb. But according to the time delays indicated in the routing information, Starfleet Headquarters and Starfleet Medical were no longer in direct communication with each other.

"They're not coordinating their actions," Picard said. "They've lost the capability. . . ." He sat back in the flight chair, rubbing his hands over his face in exhaustion. "Beverly, even if we find the Symmetrists' cure on Vulcan . . . or even if those Klingon leaves were found to be a total cure for every expression of the virogen, animal and plant, if this communications breakdown continues to spread, Starfleet won't be able to disseminate its discoveries." Picard looked up at the doctor. "And if the virogen's range continues to double every seven days. . . ."

Beverly didn't need him to complete the calculation. "In less than three months, every home system, every colony, every world in the Federation will be contaminated."

Picard stared out the viewport, overcome by the escalation of the disaster's scope. "Why didn't you share your medical logs with me, Doctor?"

He could see Beverly stiffen defensively at his use of her title. She replied in an equally brittle tone. "Because, *Captain,* I had no reason to suspect that Medical's updates were appreciably different from Command's."

Picard immediately regretted the severity of his question. He wondered how often in the past week this same conversation had been enacted on starships and starbases throughout the Federation, as the extent of the communications breakdown became apparent.

"Beverly, forgive me," he said. "That didn't come out the way I had intended."

Beverly understood. She put a hand on his shoulder. "The Federation has faced worse, Jean-Luc."

"And so have we," he said.

She was too close, too caring, the home of too many memories.

He reached up and placed his hand around hers.

She leaned down, her lips close to his.

"Captain?" On the display beside Vulcan, Will Riker suddenly appeared.

Beverly straightened up so quickly, she almost fell from the arm of the flight chair.

Picard replied to his first officer with equanimity, as if he and Beverly had just been conferring as usual. "Yes, Number One?" At any other time, Picard would have expected to see at least a hint of a smile play over Riker's face, for having caught his captain in so human a moment.

But Riker continued seriously, as if he had seen nothing out of the ordinary, or as if he didn't have time to deal with it.

"Sir, we've arrived on orbit, but none of the Vulcan orbital authorities has a record of our arrival notice."

Because of what he had just seen in his own updates, Picard knew why. Upon leaving the Alta Vista system, he had filed the *Enterprise*'s new flight plan through regular Starfleet channels. Given what he'd just learned about the state of the fleet's communications system, it was most likely the message hadn't even arrived at Earth for processing. "Have any of the support vessels we requested arrived?"

Riker shook his head. "Lieutenant Rolk has contacted all other interstellar Starfleet vessels in the Vulcan system. There are fifteen in total, none larger than *Miranda*-class. Eight are here on other Starfleet assignments, and their commanders have offered whatever support they can provide to help us search for a Symmetrist base. Six are in transit under urgent orders connected to other relief missions, and must decline."

"What about the fifteenth?" Picard asked.

"That appears to be a troubling matter, sir. The ship is currently impounded at a civilian spacedock."

Picard let his expression of surprise ask his next question.

Riker continued. "Rolk has put through a formal request for information from the civilian authorities. But, unofficially, sir, a local magistrate has forwarded a report to Starfleet recommending a possible mutiny investigation. The impounded ship is listed as being currently assigned to relief duties near the Klingon-Romulan border. She shouldn't be anywhere near here."

"What ship, Number One?"

"The *Tobias,* sir." Riker looked offscreen to check his own data display. "Commander Christine MacDonald's ship."

Picard knew of the *Tobias,* a standard Starfleet science

vessel that had been in service for decades. But he was unfamiliar with her commander.

A hundred questions came to Picard then. Why had the *Tobias* abandoned its duty? More importantly, why had an allegedly mutinous vessel come to Vulcan, instead of trying to escape to a nonaligned system? Still, Starfleet maintained considerable resources on Vulcan, and the question of the *Tobias* must properly remain with the local command. Especially if it was up to Picard alone to convince the Vulcan authorities that the Symmetrists might be behind the virogen outbreak.

"Has there been any further word on the possibility of riots at Starbase Seven-eighteen?" Picard asked. Mutiny was a virtually nonexistent crime in the fleet. But if the rumors of riots at Starfleet facilities were true, how long could it be before dissent and fear did incite mutiny on individual ships?

Riker frowned and Picard suddenly realized how haggard his senior officer looked. Locked away in the *Galileo,* Picard felt increasingly out of touch with his crew as well as his ship.

"Seven-eighteen's sector is in a complete subspace shutdown, sir." Riker's response left no doubt that there was more bad news he had to report.

"What else, Number One?"

"I've been trying to sort out all of this . . . confusion with local command. But Admiral Strak and his staff left on the *Intrepid* five days ago, and—"

"Left the Vulcan system?"

"There's an emergency situation at Bajor. It's the Cardassians and the Dominion, sir. With the fleet spread so thin, they appear to be testing our defenses and response times. Intelligence has also reported a buildup of Romulan ships just off the Neutral Zone. The alerts are coming in from everywhere."

Picard stood. "Why am I just hearing this now, Commander?"

Riker gestured uselessly. "As far as I can tell, sir, these alerts haven't been relayed out of Vulcan command. Rolk says Starfleet facilities here are operating with about ten percent of their normal workforce, with most replicators already shipped out for emergency duty, and no spare parts."

Picard braced himself on the work surface that still held his untouched tea. All starship captains were prepared to carry out their missions while out of contact with Command. It was the nature of the job. But those situations arose only on the farthest reaches of the frontier. To be cut off within the heart of Federation space, in the Vulcan home system itself, was unthinkable. And in this time of crisis—unacceptable.

Picard concentrated on controlling his voice. Anger had no useful role to play in what was happening. He *had* to arrange a full planetary search for a hidden Symmetrist base. And only Starfleet Command could give him the necessary influence to persuade Vulcan civilian authorities to allow such an unprecedented intrusion into the planet's security. "Will, with everything you're reporting, is there a Starfleet presence in the Vulcan system at all?"

Riker hesitated, as if recognizing the absurdity of his captain's question. His reply was cautious, but definitive. "Sir, as far as I can tell, all starbase facilities in the Vulcan system are intact and operational, staffed by skeleton crews of support and administrative personnel who have not been transferred to relief duty. But, if you mean, is there a Starfleet *command* presence here . . . sir, I'd have to say, no. Except, perhaps, for the *Enterprise,* and you."

For a moment, Picard was overwhelmed by a feeling of being completely powerless. He couldn't help thinking that if he were not confined to the *Galileo,* if he were only back in his command chair, that he could seize full control of the situation.

But control required information.

He and his ship were but tools of the Federation. They had

duties to perform, capabilities to unleash. Yet, without direction, without consensus, even the *Enterprise* could be rendered as ineffectual as if it had been hit by a quantum mine with all shields down.

The situation was intolerable.

And Picard would not—*could* not—allow it to continue.

With deliberation, he slowly sat back in his flight chair. Beverly now stood at his side.

"Commander Riker, in light of the extraordinary circumstances surrounding our presence in Vulcan space—specifically, my belief that the virogen plague is a deliberate attack on the Federation, an attack that has already crippled our lines of communication and supply—I am, under Starfleet Wartime Regulations, initiating a Code One alert."

Picard could see that Riker understood the seriousness of his decision, but the first officer showed no sign of protest.

Cut off from Command, the captain of the *Enterprise* had just issued a declaration of war.

Picard reached for his tea. "Have Rolk alert the commanders of the other Starfleet vessels standing by. I would like to have them gathered in the observation lounge within the hour, and I will brief them via viewscreen to coordinate our search of Vulcan. We'll need to contact senior members of the Vulcan government to attend as well, but their presence will be merely as observers. Stress that, Will. We will make the search as unobtrusive as possible, but we will be conducting it on a war footing."

"Aye, sir."

Picard was about to sign off, when he felt Beverly's hand on his shoulder.

"Excuse me, Captain," she said. "But if we really want to conduct high-resolution scans of Vulcan as quickly as possible, perhaps we should see about getting the *Tobias* released from impound and staffed with personnel from the other ships."

Picard didn't even have to think about the suggestion. As a science vessel, the *Tobias* would have permanently configured sensors that could be used at once.

"An excellent suggestion. Follow up on that as well, Number One."

Riker nodded. "At once, sir."

"I'll be standing by to talk to whichever Vulcan representative wishes to lodge the most serious protest to our presence here," Picard added.

At that, Riker finally smiled. "I'm certain there will be considerable competition for the honor." Then his image winked out.

Beverly sat in the second flight chair as Picard stretched back in his. He could see from the corner of his eye that she was watching him.

"Yes?" he said.

"For as long as I've known you, you've always shown respect for the system, the chain of command. I've watched you in crisis situations and seen someone who enjoys the interplay, the challenge of being part of a team."

Picard turned to face her. "Are you being a psychiatrist now, Doctor?"

Beverly smiled. "Off the record, if I didn't know better, seeing you right now, cut off from Command, with no support from Starfleet, the chain of command broken . . . I'd almost say you were enjoying yourself even more."

"Acting unilaterally can be rather exhilarating. And it certainly gets things done faster."

Beverly's smile faded. "What about acting correctly? Shouldn't that be the overriding concern?"

Picard understood what she meant, from both sides. But the key to survival was adaptability. It was a lesson he had learned only after years of unbending rigidity and devotion to rules and regulations written to serve an organization that might not exist in the next three months.

"Absolute certainty requires time, Beverly. That is a luxury we and the Federation no longer have."

She had no reply for him. Instead, she watched the tiny disk of Vulcan slowly rotate on the screen.

Picard decided to enjoy the silence. Once Riker made contact with Vulcan and the other vessels, he knew it wouldn't last.

He sipped his tea.

It was cold.

So, as he had so many other things in his life, he set it aside.

And waited for the Federation to fall.

TWENTY-EIGHT

The problem was insoluble.

Kirk, Spock, and Srell, and Christine MacDonald, M'Benga, and Barc, were trapped in a thruster repair chamber on one side of the spacedock's cavernous cargo bay. The circular chamber was narrow, but stretched twenty meters above them—high enough for disassembling most impulse-thrusters, including the one that currently towered overhead on the central work platform.

Outside the chamber's half-open personnel doors lay the cargo bay, and the turbolift station at which Kirk and the others had arrived. The incessant thrumming that pulsed from the bay was a combination of noisily vibrating antigrav loaders, cargo containers slamming into each other and the deck, and the shouted commands of the stevedores.

A full half-kilometer distant was the bay's far wall, inset with several multilevel viewports. Through those viewports, Kirk could see the even larger expanse of the spacedock's enclosed docking area, where a handful of ships rested in webs of umbilical tunnels, and were serviced by darting maintenance shuttles.

The closest of those ships was the *Tobias.*

Which was where the problem lay.

Between the repair chamber and the far wall of the cargo bay, there were just too many customs patrol points, safety inspectors, and ID stations. The six escapees didn't have the slightest chance of reaching the airlock doors that led to the *Tobias*'s umbilical. And even if they could make it that far, the two Vulcan security officers guarding the airlock were an effective last line of defense.

"We're done for," Barc growled. "There's no way through."

"There's a way through everything," Kirk said. "It's just another *Kobayashi Maru."* Kirk knew the Academy still ran that supposedly unbeatable scenario for its students. He looked expectantly at Christine, waiting for her to argue with him. Then he'd be able to explain how he had defeated the test's no-win scenario, and enlighten her about looking at problems from a different perspective.

Christine carefully studied the layout of the bay outside. "Unfortunately, there're no computers to reprogram out there."

Kirk stared at Christine. "You know how to beat the *Kobayashi Maru?"* He had been the first cadet to do it—the first to ever win.

Christine shrugged. "Who doesn't? Figuring out new ways to change the parameters is the whole reason for the test. How else could anyone win?"

Kirk consoled himself by deciding he had blazed the path. But it appeared Christine might not need as much instruction as he had thought. He turned to the Tellarite engineer.

"Barc, you know how these docks are built. Are there any Jefferies tubes running under this chamber and the cargo bay deck?"

Barc nodded his understanding of what Kirk was after. "You're thinking we might tunnel our way out."

"It'd be a good start," Kirk said. "Provided we don't take a detour into hard vacuum."

Barc scratched at the fur around his snout, then glanced around the narrow chamber. "If I had a tricorder and an anaphasic jack for the floor plates . . ." He lumbered over to an equipment pod, still muttering to himself.

Christine caught Kirk's attention and pointed to a diagnostics display screen on a nearby section of the wall. "We might need a few other strategies to fall back on. According to the schedule up there, the next shift is due here in eight minutes."

Kirk felt a twinge of embarrassment. Christine had noticed a critical factor in the situation which he had overlooked. Quickly he glanced around, saw a row of storage lockers on the far wall. "Let's see if we can find some engineer coveralls. Maybe try a disguise." He led Christine and the others across the chamber to began the search.

"I still say we're better off talking to the Vulcans," M'Benga grumbled as she followed them around the thruster platform.

Srell dismissed her suggestion. "You are not being logical, Doctor."

M'Benga glared at the presumptuous Vulcan, but allowed him to explain himself without interruption.

"If we were to turn ourselves back in to the authorities, we would no longer be simply held for further disposition. Instead, they would deliver you and your crew to Starfleet security, and arrest Ambassador Spock and myself. Split up, our capability for action would be diminished. Additionally, we would undoubtedly be incarcerated at a greater distance from the *Tobias,* further limiting our ability to escape."

"That's where you're losing me," M'Benga said. "If we tell them the truth, it'll be clear we're not guilty of anything, and we won't have anything to escape from. Logic your way out of that one." M'Benga looked pleased with herself for having set a logical trap for her maddeningly self-assured adversary.

Kirk and Spock exchanged a glance as they arrived at the

lockers. Kirk knew the answer, but he was curious to see how well Spock's young protégé could handle himself.

"Consider the reasons which have brought the ambassador and me to Vulcan," Srell began. "We are searching for a sophisticated, likely criminal organization, which apparently is capable of infiltrating the Vulcan diplomatic corps and murdering our planet's most revered statesmen. Our search took us to another elder Vulcan who might have shed light on the circumstances of Sarek's death. Yet at the very time we visited Tarok, assassins struck and he also died. I submit that those responsible for Sarek's death therefore might also be capable of intercepting private communications and of infiltrating other Vulcan organizations. That would explain how our presence at Tarok's estate was known, as well as the relatively early arrival of the peacekeeping forces who took our forensics team into custody."

As Kirk and Spock began searching through the first pair of lockers, Kirk listened nostalgically for M'Benga's response. The doctor and the Vulcan were bringing back memories of another unlikely pairing of friends, and he wondered what the future held for these two young adversaries.

M'Benga and Srell continued their debate as they searched through a second pair of lockers. Beside them, Christine searched a third set.

"All right," M'Benga said, "I'll grant that covers you and the ambassador, but what about Commander MacDonald and the crew of the *Tobias?* We're not involved with you or your search."

"My good doctor, may I remind you that whatever brought you to Vulcan also had the misfortune of bringing you to Tarok's estate at the time of the assassins' attack."

M'Benga's eyes narrowed. "I wouldn't exactly call it misfortune. If it weren't for Jim and Christine and Barc and me, the assassins would've won."

In the first locker, Kirk had found nothing but old tools, a few water bottles, and a pair of scanner goggles. He looked up at the diagnostic display. Six minutes to shift change. In the few minutes left to them, he needed everyone working on a way out of the chamber, but Srell might be onto something.

"Mr. Srell raises an interesting point," Kirk said. "The crew of the *Tobias* came to Vulcan for virtually the same reason. We're also looking for a sophisticated, definitely criminal organization of Vulcans—one able to intercept Starfleet communications. Only the crime is different. The group we're after might be responsible for murdering millions, if not billions, of people by releasing the virogen."

From the next locker, Spock looked over at Kirk. "At Tarok's estate, you said you were looking for me."

Kirk shut the door of the locker he'd been searching. Still nothing that could be a disguise. "Who better to investigate a Vulcan terrorist group? You mention the possibility to most people, and all they'll say is that Vulcan terrorists *can't* exist."

"They cannot," Srell said.

"Yet, here we are," Kirk pointed out, "all talking about Vulcan murderers and criminals as if they're as common here as everywhere else."

M'Benga looked thoughtful. "You don't suppose we're looking for the same people, do you? I mean, it's pretty remarkable to be thinking there's even one group of Vulcans that's capable of murder. But *two* groups? The odds would have to be pretty low."

Kirk glanced at Spock, but it was Srell who gave the inevitable response. "I believe the odds would be roughly on the order of . . . 10,126,582,300 to one."

"'Roughly'?" M'Benga asked with a hint of contempt.

Kirk saw Srell stiffen, as if he didn't realize the doctor was leading him on. "The calculation is based on the total number of Vulcans who have lived on the planet since the Reformation, and assumes that any effective terrorist organization would require a minimum of ten individuals. I thereby calculated the odds that any twenty Vulcans at random from the total population would happen to be alive in the current generation, and divided by the number of Vulcans who, since Reformation, are known to have engaged in terrorist acts. Given the understandable ambiguity surrounding population figures for the first few hundred years following the establishment of Surak's peace, I do not believe I am off by more than a factor of two. Hence, the modifying descriptor, 'roughly.' "

"Are you saying that Vulcans *have* been known to participate in terrorist acts in the past?" Kirk asked his question before M'Benga could torture Srell with another provocative remark. The math didn't interest Kirk. Srell's startling revelation did. For the moment, the search of the lockers and the impending arrival of the next shift of workers could wait.

Srell looked pained, as if he had just given away a planetary secret. "Not counting those individuals whose violently antisocial actions resulted from alien mind-control, disease, or physical injury to the brain, a total of three hundred and twelve Vulcans are known to have committed terrorist acts in the past millennium."

Kirk looked at Spock for confirmation. "That is correct," Spock said.

Kirk was astounded. He had assumed that the Vulcans they were looking for were modern aberrations, perhaps unduly influenced by alien upbringing on a Vulcan colony world. Yet now it appeared that Vulcan actually might have a history of such criminal behavior. In all their many discussions of Vulcan, Spock had never admitted to Kirk that his planet had had such problems. But then, after the incident with Balok and the *Fesarius,* Spock had become quite skillful at poker.

"What could possibly make a Vulcan think it was logical to commit an act of terrorism?" Kirk asked.

Christine pointed to the display again. "Four minutes," she warned.

But Srell did not make use of her warning as a way to avoid

answering. Especially when Spock nodded at him, as if to say the teacher condoned the student's report of hidden knowledge. "Terrorist acts on Vulcan have been rare, generally limited to expressions of extreme political theory and, in the past, to sporadic attempts to return to the violent philosophies that ruled our world in the days before Surak."

Kirk could see a possible connection forming. "If the terrorism came out of politics, then that implies it was organized, correct?"

"It does," Srell conceded.

Kirk could tell that even with Spock's approval, the young Vulcan was uncomfortable to be discussing what must be, for him, an embarrassing facet of Vulcan history.

"Is there a chance," Kirk persisted, "that any of those political terrorist groups might exist in some form today?"

Srell fumbled for an answer. "Within reason, anything is possible. That is to say . . . any number of political groups . . . but if they are secret . . ."

"Good Lord," M'Benga said. "Just spit it out. Yes or no?"

"Yes," Srell said, clearly displeased.

Kirk gestured for the young Vulcan to hurry. "What groups? Their goals? Who are the most logical ones to remain active today?"

Srell glanced up at the distant ceiling of the thruster chamber. "The Adepts of T'Pel," he began, as if reading from a hidden list. "They are a guild of assassins dating from the time of Surak. Some say they continue their secret traditions among the Romulans today."

Kirk quickly looked to Spock. "What about it, Spock? Could there be a Romulan connection to all this?"

"I am doubtful. The majority of Romulans know that a strong Federation is necessary to keep the Klingon Empire in check. It is not in Romulan interests to destabilize the Federation, and certainly not with a biological weapon that could spread to their own planets."

Kirk looked back to Srell. "Who else?"

"The Kahrilites. A small group that fought for the independence of a southern district more than three centuries ago. They were given independence and the movement quickly died." Before Kirk could prompt him, Srell continued. "The Followers of the Cupric Band. Their mistaken logic led them to reject the concept that intelligence is possible in beings with non-copper-based blood. They were active at the time Vulcan's first contact protocols were formulated."

Kirk could see Spock's interest was piqued by that. "What is it, Spock?"

"In his holographic confession, Ki Mendrossen said he reported on my father's activities regarding the redrafting of Starfleet's first contact protocols. But as one of one hundred and fifty Federation member worlds, the question of first contact as it applies to Vulcan is moot. We are a fully interplanetary society. The Cupric Band is not applicable to this situation."

"The Binaries," Srell continued. "Opposed the introduction of duotronic computer circuitry. The Traxton Compound. They follow a school of logic that does not focus on Surak, believing the concentration on the individual to be in conflict with the attainment of *Kolinahr.* The Central Source. Aggressive opposition to financial policy and the abolition of money as a means of exchange." Srell paused, then unfolded his hands, ending his recitation. "In addition, a handful of other violent individuals acted on their own for reasons best described as politically unsound. To the best of my knowledge, that is the extent of terrorism on Vulcan."

Kirk felt his excitement fade as he realized his first guess must be closer to the truth; that the Vulcans who might be involved in the spread of the virogen were a relatively recent group, diverted from peaceful Vulcan ways because of alien influences. But Spock's next statement changed all that.

"Srell," Spock said, "you did not mention the Symmetrists."

Srell seemed unperturbed by the omission. "They were not politically motivated. And whatever acts of terrorism they are alleged to have committed, historians disagree as to the extent to which Vulcan Symmetrists were responsible for the actions of non-Vulcans."

As long as there was a single pathway to explore, Kirk was not ready to abandon a possible connection to an existing group. He checked the display again. They were almost out of time. But he had to know. "Tell me about the Symmetrists," he said to Spock.

Spock kept his gaze on Srell. "More than two centuries ago, they began as a group of noted scientists concerned about the ecological ramifications of the newly formed Federation's plans for exploring other worlds."

"They were environmentalists," Srell said. "Not political activists."

Kirk noted, with interest, the difference of opinion between Spock and his student.

"An interesting distinction," Spock said. "But the environmental issues they addressed were defined by the political process."

Christine raised her hands. "This is all very fascinating, but we've got precisely two minutes to come up with something here."

M'Benga looked back at the personnel doors. "Can't we seal those doors? Buy us some more time?"

Kirk and Christine both spoke at the same time.

"They'd just transport in a repair crew . . ." Kirk began.

"Not with so many transporters in this . . ." Christine said.

Kirk and Christine looked at each other, sharing a single thought. Then they looked up at the thruster assembly towering above them. It was far too large to have entered the chamber through the personnel doors.

And the doors were the only way in or out of the chamber.

"Barc!" they both shouted.

The Tellarite looked out from behind the central platform with an answering growl.

"The platform!" Christine called out.

"It's a cargo transporter pad!" Kirk added.

Barc almost danced as he waved everyone over.

They ran to climb up on the platform as the Tellarite scurried to find the transporter controls.

But Kirk hadn't forgotten what had brought them this far, nor how much farther they still had to go.

"Quickly, Srell—what acts of violence did the Symmetrists commit?" he asked as he and his team reached the platform.

"Please bear in mind that at one time, they were respected scientists," Srell said as he looked for a handhold to begin climbing. Kirk marveled again at the Vulcan's emotional control, even in times of crisis. His own heart was pounding, but Srell revealed no concern. "Only later did off-planet factions take up violence in the Symmetrists' name. And the subsequent public outcry led to the cause being abandoned on Vulcan."

Kirk felt electricity shoot through him. "The 'cause,'" he repeated. "Spock—*what* did the Symmetrists do?"

Kirk could see that Spock sensed his excitement, though he couldn't know what fueled it.

Spock pulled himself up onto the platform beside the thruster, and reached down to help M'Benga complete the climb. "If memory serves, the Symmetrists would board colony ships and take hostages in order to 'save' pristine planets from ecological contamination. They poisoned water sources and food supplies to force colonies to relocate. They—"

Kirk jumped up beside Spock on the platform. "Kodos!" he said.

Srell stared at him blankly. Spock seemed intrigued.

"Kodos the Executioner? Of Tarsus Four?" Christine asked as she climbed up behind the others.

"Tarsus?" M'Benga added. "That was one of the first systems hit by the virogen."

"When Kodos was governor, the colony's grain supply was infected with . . . a fungus," Kirk said, overwhelmed by the memory of what he had seen when little more than a child. "He butchered four thousand colonists. A lesson, Mr. Spock?"

"It is an intriguing hypothesis. Subsequent to Kodos's death on the *Enterprise,* I researched the events at Tarsus Four. No cause for the fungal infection was ever found, thus sabotage could not be ruled out. As policy, emergency food supplies were maintained only to support the colony for a three-week period, which was the normal shipping time from the closest port worlds. However, at the time the colony's grain stores were infected, the Romulans constructed several outposts at the outer boundaries of the Neutral Zone. Fearing a new outbreak of hostilities, Starfleet closed all shipping lanes. Resupply of Tarsus Four was impossible, and only an unsanctioned relief mission undertaken by ships of the Earth Forces managed to avert the total loss of all colonists."

Kirk looked at Spock closely. "Earth Forces? Weren't the Vulcans involved in the rescue mission?"

Spock thought a moment, then shook his head. "There was no mention of Vulcan involvement in the records."

Kirk frowned. "That's odd. I thought I remembered . . ."

But Kirk's memories were cut short as a blue light abruptly began to flash in the thruster chamber, accompanied by the echoing of buzzers from the cargo bay beyond the doors.

"Is that a prisoner alert?" M'Benga asked with sudden worry.

But Barc flailed up onto the platform beside the others, an engineer's remote-control padd in one hand. "It's the shift change," the Tellarite grunted. "We've got sixty seconds."

Kirk eyed him. "*Is* this a transporter pad?"

Barc's tiny black eyes sparkled. "*Rrrr,* that it is." He held up the padd. "And I've set it for a one-minute delay to give me time to get up here with the rest of you."

M'Benga gave the Tellarite an inquiring look. "You *are* sending us to the *Tobias,* right?"

Barc bared his teeth. "No, Doctor, I'm beaming us back to the magistrate's office. What do you think?"

"It's a cargo transporter," M'Benga said. "And we're not cargo."

The Tellarite smiled. "If that's what you're worried about, let's just say I've made a few small adjustments to the resolution buffers."

M'Benga seemed relieved. They waited.

Christine stepped closer to Kirk. "Are you thinking Kodos was a Symmetrist? And that what happened on Tarsus Four was just . . . a trial run for what's happening across the Federation? I mean, Bones is right—that world was the first to collapse because of the virogen."

Kirk wanted to answer, but there was a memory just beyond the reach of his consciousness. Why was he so certain that Vulcans had been part of the relief mission to the colony?

"Jim was at Tarsus Four during the crisis," Spock explained. "He was one of nine eyewitnesses to the first wave of executions by the governor."

Christine put a hand on his shoulder, misunderstanding the reason for his concern. "Jim, I'm sorry. Was your family . . . ?"

Kirk brushed her question aside. "They were on Earth. My mother was, at least. My father was on his ship. Spock, it was something Kodos said."

"His notorious address to the colonists he selected for execution?"

As if he were a boy of thirteen again, Kirk heard that harsh voice in his mind. He spoke aloud the words he could never forget. "'The revolution is successful . . . but survival depends on drastic measures. . . .'"

Spock broke in. "Of course—Mendrossen referred to the revolution in his confession. 'For the good of the cause, for the revolution,' he said."

Kirk pounded a fist into his hand. "Spock! That's it! It wasn't what Kodos said on Tarsus Four—it was what he said to *me* on the *Enterprise!*"

M'Benga looked nervously around. "Didn't Barc say we were on a sixty-second delay?"

"That I did," Barc confirmed. He held up his padd. The time display on it counted down the last five seconds.

Across the chamber, the personnel doors slid open and the voices of the arriving crew of technicians became clear over the din of the cargo bay.

"You *spoke* with Kodos?" Christine asked Kirk.

Kirk heard the initiating hum of the transporter circuits start up. He took Christine's hand.

"It'll have to wait," he said as the first glimmer of golden light began to shimmer around them.

But even as Kirk vanished in the transporter beam, he knew he had found the answer to what had happened.

All that remained was to prove it.

TWENTY-NINE

"You will forgive me, Captain Picard, if my logic is uncertain, but you have apparently had Starfleet declare war against Vulcan."

At any other time, Riker would have laughed. But the tension in the observation lounge was at a dangerous level.

He and Data shared the table with eight starship commanders and three representatives from the Vulcan planetary government. Each of the Vulcans was more than a century old, their robes resplendent with the polished gemstones of their office.

Solok, the most senior of the three, steepled his fingers as he fixed his green eyes on the virtual viewscreen on the far wall. The observation-lounge lights gleamed from his hairless, black scalp. He was framed by the crimson mass of Vulcan that filled the observation ports behind him. Somewhere over the equator, storm clouds flashed with hidden lightning.

From the viewscreen, Picard returned the Vulcan's patient stare. "With respect, Representative Solok, the time for debate is at a later date. I have merely invoked a condition of war. I have not stated who our enemy is."

Solok tapped two fingers together. "Captain, you have

issued a Code One alert. It is a declaration of war. You then inform the Vulcan government that a fleet of nine Starfleet vessels will englobe our world and subject it to a full-spectrum sensor sweep at maximum power and resolution, with the intent of locating the base from which your 'enemy' is thought to operate."

Beside Solok, Representative T'Pring continued the statement. Her stark white hair was cut short to reveal her dramatic ears, accentuating her sharp features. "Your search of Vulcan under these conditions is a violation of our sovereignty, will interfere in numerous scientific and industrial endeavors, will reveal the nature of Vulcan planetary defenses in a way that third parties might exploit, and cannot logically be expected to yield positive results."

The third representative, Stonn, concluded the statement of the Vulcans' position. Riker had escorted Stonn and T'Pring from the transporter room, and had learned they were husband and wife.

"Captain Picard," Stonn said, "all other matters of sovereignty and interplanetary law and treaty aside, the fact remains that you believe the enemy you seek is on Vulcan. Therefore, the enemy is Vulcan. Therefore, you have declared war on Vulcan."

Solok delivered the summation. "The situation is unsatisfactory. Permission to search our world in this manner is denied."

All eyes turned to the viewscreen and Picard's response.

"I agree," Picard said, and Riker could tell how the captain struggled to maintain a reasonable tone. They had expected reticence on the part of the Vulcan government, but not outright refusal. "The situation is *most* unsatisfactory. But it is your position that is without logic."

Riker checked. None of the Vulcans reacted. But the Starfleet commanders were fully on Picard's side.

"We are facing the gravest threat our worlds have ever known. You have seen the figures provided by my chief medical officer. The lifetime of the United Federation of Planets can be measured in *days* unless a cure to the virogen is found. Does not logic demand that every means must be undertaken in order to find that cure?"

Solok carefully folded his hands in his lap. "Your tales of the long-forgotten Symmetrists are sheer speculation, not logic. It is impossible to conceive of a group so clever, and so secretive, that they could operate on Vulcan without attracting the scrutiny of our peacekeepers."

"We submit," T'Pring continued, "that you have access to information which you are not sharing with us. That suggests that you have an ulterior motive for your desire to subject Vulcan to such an unwarranted intrusion of its fundamental rights as an independent world."

"And that," Stonn said, "suggests that for some reason, you have declared war on a sister member of the Federation. Either that or, as certain developments suggest, you and the ships you represent no longer speak for Starfleet, and have mutinied."

All the commanders began to protest at once, but Picard cut them off with an authoritative command for silence. This time when he spoke, he wasn't concerned with hiding his anger.

"I submit to you that your reluctance to participate in an operation that could save the Federation suggests that you are also in possession of information that you wish to keep secret."

Solok's steely gaze did not waver. Yet Riker noted that Solok avoided directly looking at Picard. "To use an Earth term, Captain, that statement is preposterous. And unless you can provide some evidence to support your incautious accusations, this meeting will end and you and your vessels will be served formal notice to quit our system."

Solok, T'Pring, and Stonn exchanged quick glances, then rose as one, their decision made.

"I know who the Symmetrist leader was," Picard said.

That stopped the Vulcans.

"Was?" Solok asked. He still looked away from the viewscreen, as if Picard still offered nothing of interest or importance.

"He died five years ago. But given his renowned abilities and accomplishments, his role as leader could explain the ability of a secret organization to exist on Vulcan without detection."

Solok smoothed his robes. "You are prepared to share the name of this 'leader' with us?"

"Ambassador Sarek."

Everyone except the Vulcans reacted with stunned silence. But even Riker could see the effect that name had on them.

Solok finally stared at Picard. "Sarek . . . of ShirKahr?"

"Yes," Picard said.

Solok raised a hairless eyebrow as he considered that information.

Riker saw Stonn and T'Pring lean close to each other so that T'Pring could whisper in Stonn's ear.

"Did you know the ambassador?" Riker asked, hoping to break up their private conversation.

T'Pring addressed Riker as a queen might address a commoner. "All on Vulcan knew Sarek. That he would be involved in the Symmetrist cause is . . . absurd."

"Do you have evidence to support this accusation?" Solok asked.

Picard touched his temple. "I have the evidence of what I learned in a mindmeld on Alta Vista Three. I invite you to meld with me, and know I speak the truth."

Stonn pushed his chair back, ready to depart. "You would have us expose ourselves to the virogen based on your improbable theory?"

Beside Picard, Dr. Crusher spoke. "Representative Stonn, Starfleet continues to make progress on a treatment for animal exposure to the virogen. If you, or some other member of your party, joined us in quarantine, I feel confident you would not be confined for more than a few weeks."

"Is that not a small enough price to pay for the truth?" Picard asked.

Solok hesitated, as if prepared to seriously consider the captain's argument. But T'Pring would have no part of it.

"It is also a clever pretense for a trap," she declared. Then she turned to Solok. "The Federation is in danger. Of that there can be no doubt. But surely part of the problem is Starfleet itself. Recent developments in our own system prove that Starfleet has already been destabilized. We cannot trust them, Solok. As long as we keep our world free of contamination, Vulcan can survive the collapse of the Federation. Therefore, it serves no logical purpose for us to sacrifice our world for a spurious argument from an emotional being."

Riker saw his captain reflexively straighten his tunic, as if getting ready to issue an ultimatum. He saw that this meeting was about to fall apart. He saw a way out.

"Representative Solok," Riker said, "what if Captain Picard is correct? Even if there is the smallest chance, is that not worth a few more minutes of your time?"

"To what purpose?" Solok asked.

"Let's find out about the mutiny on the *Tobias.*" Riker looked at T'Pring and Stonn. "That is what you're concerned about, isn't it? That whatever happened on that ship might be happening on the *Enterprise,* and on all the ships represented here?"

Before T'Pring could reply, Solok said, "That is a reasonable request. How do you propose to proceed?"

"The crew was called before a magistrate on one of your spacedocks. Let's contact that magistrate, review the crew's statements. Even interview the crew if we have to. Whatever it takes for you to be confident that we are not involved with them. Then we can arrange a mindmeld with Captain Picard."

Solok nodded gravely, and sat down. "Given the stakes, I will wait." He looked up at T'Pring and Stonn. Reluctantly, they sat as well.

On the viewscreen, Picard gave Riker a small nod of approval. Then Riker tapped his comm badge and put Rolk to work on the bridge, setting up a communications link to the civilian spacedock where the *Tobias* was impounded.

It took less than a minute. The virtual viewscreen shifted so that Picard and Beverly in the *Galileo* appeared on one side, and a stern female magistrate appeared on the other. She hid her reaction well, Riker knew, but the presence of Solok, T'Pring, and Stonn surprised her.

Riker got to the point at once. "Magistrate, we are most interested in learning more about your request that the crew of the *Tobias* be investigated for possible charges of mutiny."

The magistrate cleared her throat, as if she were not used to speaking with government representatives of the rank present here. "The *Tobias* is not where orders require it to be. Her commander could not give adequate explanation for her presence here. Three people are dead, perhaps because of actions taken by her crew. And in an alarming breach of all Federation policies, her crew may have exposed our world to the virogen."

This time, Riker noted, even the Vulcans at the table reacted.

"Did the commander of the vessel give an explanation for her actions?" Riker asked.

"She did not. The explanation given was that her ship was on a classified mission at Starfleet's behest."

Solok abruptly stood. "That is all I needed to hear." He glared at the viewscreen, and at Picard. "Are you satisfied,

Captain? A classified Starfleet mission to expose this world to the virogen? Your mutinous ruse has been penetrated."

Stonn and T'Pring rose beside Solok. Riker realized that all control had been lost. He had no idea how to reclaim it.

But apparently Data did. "Representative Solok, may I ask your patience for one final question of the magistrate?" the android asked.

Solok gave no answer, but he remained where he was, giving Data tacit approval.

Data addressed the viewscreen. "Magistrate, you stated that the ship's commander did not give an explanation for her actions, but that an explanation was given, nonetheless. May I ask who gave that explanation?"

The magistrate looked uncomfortable. "This is a delicate matter." She looked to Solok for guidance.

"It is also crucial," Solok replied. "We await your answer."

Riker looked at Data. His machine memory and attention to detail might have come through for them again.

"The explanation was given by Ambassador Spock," the magistrate said.

Riker saw Solok's grip on his robes tighten. "Spock, child of Sarek?"

"The same."

"Indeed," Solok said. "Is it possible you have a recording of Spock's statement?"

The magistrate seemed relieved to be excused from assuming further responsibility in relating what had happened. "I will play it for you at once, sir." She adjusted some controls out of scanner range; then her image was replaced by a log tape of her office.

Riker watched as the time and date codes slipped by in Vulcan script. Then, onscreen, two carved wooden doors in the office slid open, and a group of six people entered the magistrate's office, four in Starfleet uniforms, one of them a Tellarite.

Spock was unmistakable, his distinctive features known to half the Federation on sight. To one side was a young Vulcan civilian, to the other a Starfleet lieutenant. Though, Riker thought, the lieutenant seemed mature for what was a relatively junior—

"Sacre merde!" Picard sputtered. "Computer—freeze frame! Enhance grid section twelve!"

On the viewscreen, the image from the magistrate's office expanded into coarse pixels, then resolved into finer detail until the Starfleet officer beside Spock filled the screen.

An instant later, Riker felt the hair on his neck bristle as he saw what Picard saw.

That was no lieutenant.

It was James T. Kirk.

THIRTY

With unerring accuracy, Barc had placed them on the bridge of the *Tobias.*

Seconds after the transporter effect had faded, Kirk watched as Christine spun around, quickly assessing the status of every station. He recognized the fire in her eye, the territorial gleam.

This was her ship.

"You did it again, Barcs," she said.

The Tellarite was already making his way to the engineering station. "I always do," he growled.

"Only one problem," Kirk said.

Christine nodded. More than half the bridge stations were dark. "We've been powered down and placed on umbilical supply from the spacedock."

"And any surge of power drawn through the umbilical is going to raise someone's suspicions," Kirk said.

"Therefore, we should disconnect the umbilical," Srell suggested.

"Which would also raise suspicions," Spock said. "And would leave us in the precarious position of powering up the vessel while a security team came to investigate."

Kirk looked around the circular bridge. The basic design had changed little, even from the days of his first five-year mission. But who knew what advances hid behind the sleek control surfaces? "How long will it take to get a ship like this up to full power?"

"With a full crew," Christine said, "we've drilled at one minute, eighteen seconds."

"And under present conditions?" Kirk asked.

Christine looked over at Barc. "What do you think, Barcs? We reset the main power buses throughout the ship manually, leaving the final connections isolated to the bridge controls, then we detach the umbilical and throw all the final switches at the same time from here?"

The Tellarite rubbed his thick fingers along his snout. "Maybe thirty minutes to set up the buses. But then no more than ten seconds to bring us up to full shields and impulse."

"How long to warp capability?" Kirk asked.

Barc checked the readouts on the engineering station, and huffed approval at what he read. "At least they had the good sense to keep the core on standby. I'll get you warp three minutes after we have power."

"Sounds good," Christine said. "Here's the breakdown—"

But before she could continue, Srell interrupted. "A question. Once we are powered up and have warp capability, where, exactly, do you propose to take us?"

Christine looked at Kirk and Spock.

"If you're right about the Symmetrists, where *do* we go?" she asked.

Kirk was surprised Spock didn't respond to Christine's question, as if he didn't have the answer. But only one answer was possible. He was sure of it. "You get this ship powered up. I'll get us where we need to go."

"Good enough for me," Christine said. If she was curious about their ultimate destination, she held whatever questions she might have in check. Kirk appreciated her professional acceptance of his command of the mission, if not of her ship.

Christine began to describe the sequence by which the *Tobias* would be brought to life. Barc would begin in engineering, with M'Benga helping Christine set the power conduits in the deflector and shield control rooms.

Since Srell had no experience with ships of any kind, he would remain on the bridge with Kirk and Spock. Kirk and Spock would watch the individual station boards as internal connections were set throughout the ship. They would be responsible for placing the bridge switches on standby, so they could be activated when the umbilical joining the *Tobias* to the spacedock was disconnected.

Then Christine, Barc, and M'Benga were gone, using the interdeck ladders instead of the turbolifts to avoid drawing noticeable amounts of power.

Kirk and Spock positioned themselves by the science vessel's engineering and deflector stations. Srell studied the blank main viewer. For now, all they could do was wait.

Kirk took advantage of the few moments of respite. He closed his eyes, rubbed the bridge of his nose, and again reached back into the past. Once more he was on the *Enterprise* of old, face-to-face with the acclaimed Shakespearean actor Anton Karidian, a man whose history began only where that of Kodos the Executioner ended.

When the supply ships had finally reached Tarsus IV, Governor Kodos had disappeared. A burned body had been found in a crashed orbital transfer shuttle, a body so badly charred that not even DNA analysis could be performed. But the craft had been Kodos's personal transport and the search for him was called off, the case closed.

Twenty years later, the Karidian Company of Players had come aboard the *Enterprise,* and Kirk had learned that the actor and the executioner were one and the same.

Kirk went to the actor's quarters to confront the monster from his past, not knowing if he were searching for justice as a starship captain, or vengeance as the victimized boy he had been on Tarsus IV.

But instead of a monster, Kirk had found a confused old man whose memory had grown dim. Kodos did not hide from his past, nor deny it. He was *tired* of it.

At the time, Kirk had been a young man, and could feel nothing but contempt for Kodos. The old man's point of view was beyond Kirk's understanding.

"Here you stand, a perfect symbol of our technical society," Kodos had said. "Mechanized, electronicized, and not very human."

Kirk had had no interest in an old man's demented ramblings, but the words had somehow stayed with him, and they came back to him now with surprising clarity.

"You've done away with humanity," Kodos had said accusingly, as if Kirk and not he were the guilty one, "the striving of man to achieve greatness through his own resources."

Full of himself, his mission, and his youth, Kirk had discounted Kodos and all that he was or believed.

"We've armed man with tools," Kirk had answered. "The striving for greatness continues."

Kirk paused in his recollection, rehearing his own words of so long ago, wondering how he had survived those early years, understanding so little of what life was about.

For part of what Kodos had told him was true. Kirk himself had said as much to Christine MacDonald when he had stepped aboard her ship at Chal—that her generation placed too much emphasis on the machinery of their lives, and not enough on the spirit; paid too much attention to the starship, not to the crew.

Kirk wondered if Christine saw him as he had seen Kodos: unable to comprehend, let alone meet, the challenges of modern life; no longer relevant; old.

He wondered if Kodos had seen him as he himself now saw Christine: a distant reflection of what he had been once: headstrong; talented, though unseasoned; young.

Was this cycle of the generations bound to continue forever?

Had Kirk come all this way in his life's journey only to discover the unthinkable—that the worst monster from his past, Kodos the *Executioner,* had in some cold-blooded way been *right?*

Uneasily, Kirk now remembered being on the bridge of the *Tobias* over Chal, ordering the destruction of the Orion fighters. Ordering their pilots to their deaths to prevent more deaths in the future.

Had *he* become Kodos?

"Are you well, Jim?"

Spock's concerned voice broke Kirk from his reverie. He quickly checked the engineering board. The status lights were still out. Barc had yet to complete his tasks.

"Sorry, Spock. I was just remembering."

"What Kodos said to you on the *Enterprise?"* Spock asked. It was what they had been discussing before they had been transported from the spacedock to the *Tobias.* Spock forgot little.

" 'I was a soldier in a cause,' " Kirk said, quoting what Kodos had said in his quarters more than a century ago. "There were things to be done. Terrible things."

Spock nodded, then turned to Srell. "After consideration, I concur with Jim. It is possible Kodos was a Symmetrist and what happened on Tarsus Four can be considered a model for what's happening throughout the Federation."

Kirk saw Srell's reaction to what Spock had said.

"Objections, Mr. Srell?" Kirk asked.

"Three," Srell said promptly. "First, the Symmetrists, at least those who embraced violence, were not reserved about claiming responsibility for their actions. Yet they made no claims about actions on Tarsus Four. Second, there was no Vulcan involvement in Tarsus Four. Third, though a case can be made that the colony's grain was exposed to a fungus in order to halt a colonization program, there is no support for the theory that today's spread of the virogen is a political action. The intelligent mind searches for patterns, Mr. Kirk, with the danger that patterns are often seen where the data do not support the conclusions."

"I beg to differ," Spock said, and Kirk could see something in Spock's face that told him his old friend was about to say something that he was reluctant to share, but felt obliged to state.

"If I am in error, I would be pleased to be corrected," Srell replied stiffly. Not even Kirk was convinced the young Vulcan meant what he said.

"My parents were Symmetrists."

Both Kirk and Srell stared at Spock in surprise.

"Sarek?" Kirk said. "A Symmetrist?"

"I learned of it only recently myself," Spock explained. "In my mindmeld with Tarok, just before his death."

"I must protest," Srell said. "Sarek's belief in nonviolence formed the core of his reputation and personal beliefs. Consider the source of your information, Ambassador—the confused recollections of a diseased mind."

An expression of concern came to Spock. "Do not misunderstand, Srell. My parents were not terrorists, and as Surak and logic demand, they denounced violence as a means to any end. But it does explain much about my childhood."

Kirk could see that Spock was now retreating into long-buried memory, just as he himself had done moments earlier.

"The conversations that would stop when I entered a room," Spock said. "My father's unexplained absences when he was not on diplomatic assignment. So many inconsequential yet perplexing occurrences are now so obvious. For quite legitimate reasons, Sarek and Amanda were members of an organization the galaxy abhorred because of acts of violence committed by others in the Symmetrists' name. It is quite a profound discovery to make about one's parents after so many years."

Kirk asked the necessary question. "Spock, do you think your father's tie to the Symmetrists could be the reason he was murdered?"

Spock considered the question for long moments. "Logic suggests—"

"Logic suggests *nothing,"* Srell interrupted. "How could you even conceive that someone like Sarek, whose every move and appointment were rigorously scheduled, could have the time to consort with criminals?"

Spock looked at Srell as if the young Vulcan were a misbehaving child. "Srell, I said my parents *were* Symmetrists. Quite clearly in Tarok's mind I saw that their group disbanded, long ago, when I was a youth, when they realized that their beliefs were being distorted and their influence misused."

Something about Spock's reference to his being a youth prompted Kirk to ask, "How long ago?"

"More than a century."

"I mean, how old were you?"

"In standard years, sixteen, I would suspect."

Kirk did the conversions from stardates. "That would make it . . . 2246."

Spock angled his head as he made the same connection. "Fascinating."

Srell folded his arms in a show of Vulcan impatience. "I fail to see the significance of the date."

"Twenty-two forty-six," Kirk said. "Spock was sixteen, I was thirteen. And Kodos was governor of Tarsus Four."

"And at about the same time, my parents withdrew from the Symmetrists."

Kirk took the chain of logic to its ultimate conclusion. "Because someone had used whatever information the Symmetrists had developed about ecological disaster to deliberately engineer the events at Tarsus Four."

Srell was as close to sputtering as a Vulcan could ever get in public. "Are you seriously suggesting that Ambassador Sarek was *responsible* for the events there?"

"Not directly," Kirk said. "But it seems clear he had some connection to them. A connection that led to him withdrawing from the Symmetrist cause after what happened. And a connection that might have led to his death in this age."

Srell confronted Spock. "Ambassador, are you going to let this . . . this human besmirch your father's name?"

"He has done no such thing," Spock said. "My friend has simply pointed out a series of logical connections between uncontested historical events. You would do well to reconsider your reluctance to accept that logic."

Srell reacted as if Spock had slapped him.

Then four power-supply panels lit up on the engineering board and Kirk knew the time for reflection and discussion had passed. Somewhere in engineering, Barc had manually reconnected all the power couplings, with the final break in the circuit routed to this board.

The theory was the same as in Kirk's cadet days, and he quickly touched the standby controls on the board. "That's impulse, environmental, gravity, and internal power," he said.

Spock was already pressing the controls on the deflector board, responding to what Christine and M'Benga were doing in their sections of the ship. "We now have navigation, shields, sensors, and deflectors on standby," Spock reported.

Kirk and Spock swiftly rotated to other dark stations, placing additional systems on standby as Christine, M'Benga, and Barc ran through the ship.

Fifteen minutes after they had left, the commander, doctor,

and engineer scrambled up the ladder in the emergency alcove off the bridge.

Christine was flushed, her blond curls stuck to her forehead, but there was no sign of exhaustion in her. Kirk recognized the cause of her excitement. When her ship came to life again, so would she.

She hurried to the ops console to check the ship's status, gratified by what she saw. "Barcs did it again. We took less than half the time he thought!"

Kirk glanced at the bulky Tellarite as he stepped up to the engineering board. "Or else he thought it would take fifteen minutes to begin with, and multiplied by two," Kirk said softly.

Barc glared at Kirk and drew back his lips in a subtle warning snarl.

Kirk smiled as he relinquished the engineering station to him. "Your secret's safe with me." Then he went to join Christine.

"All we have to do now is drop the umbilical," she said as the main viewscreen switched on, showing the forward view from the leading edge of the *Tobias's* command saucer.

On the screen, Kirk could see two viewports in the cargo bay wall. Beyond them, the cargo activity was unceasing, normal. More importantly, there was no sign of security forces conducting a search.

"Can't we just back out?" M'Benga asked as she stood at Kirk's side. "Why give them any warning?"

"We might rupture the airlock," Christine explained. "Too many people could get hurt."

"In my day," Kirk said, "most spacedock umbilicals had manual release locks with physical timers, so computer error couldn't cause an accidental disconnection."

"This spacedock was built in your day," Spock said dryly.

Kirk grinned. "Then we shouldn't have a problem disconnecting, should we, Spock?"

"I take it I have volunteered, again."

"Some things never change. Let's go."

As Kirk and Spock headed for the emergency ladder, Srell joined them.

Kirk stayed out of what he thought might become a confrontation between Sarek's devoted defender and Sarek's son. But Srell wasn't looking for conflict.

"Ambassador, I would like to do something concrete to assist us in our . . . escape," the young Vulcan said.

"Your help will be most appreciated," Spock replied.

Between Vulcans, that was all it took. Kirk saw that an apology had been made and accepted. He jumped onto the ladder, hooked his feet around the outer poles, and slid from the bridge.

Only when he had reached the first full deck and swung out to the corridor did he suddenly realize he wasn't on a *Constitution*-class ship. He had no idea where the umbilical airlock was.

Spock and Srell swung out from the alcove seconds later. Spock instantly grasped Kirk's dilemma. Ever discreet, he pointed helpfully down the corridor. "Starboard, outer corridor, section four."

"Thank you, Mr. Spock." Kirk began to run, the Vulcans keeping up beside him.

When they reached the airlock, it was open. It led to a circular umbilical tunnel that extended ten meters to a matching airlock that opened onto the cargo bay. Kirk was pleased to see that the inner doors there, the ones that opened directly onto the bay, were closed. Back in the impulse repair chamber, he had looked across the cargo bay and noted the two Vulcan guards posted at those doors. But as long as the airlock remained closed, he wouldn't have to deal with them.

Kirk led Srell to the edge of the *Tobias*'s airlock. "All we have to do is go through this tunnel, keeping low so no one can see us through the umbilical's viewports. When we get to the cargo-bay airlock, you close the outer doors so the cargo bay will be sealed off behind both sets of doors, then run back here. Spock and I will set the timers on the manual releases and follow."

Srell nodded, but Kirk thought his eyes were a bit too wide.

"You do know how to close an airlock, don't you?"

"I have undergone basic safety training on transport ships."

"That is adequate," Spock said.

Spock's confidence was good enough for Kirk. He started along the umbilical tunnel, crouching low to avoid the small viewports that studded both sides every two meters.

At the cargo-bay airlock, Kirk and Spock positioned themselves at the manual release levers that physically clamped the umbilical collar to the airlock. Srell continued inside.

"Press the control, then run," Kirk reminded him. "You'll have . . ." He looked at Spock.

"Fifteen seconds," Spock said.

Srell nodded. He pressed the control.

And the inner doors began to open.

"Get out!" Kirk shouted as a small gust of wind blew through the tunnel and the atmospheric pressure between the cargo bay and the *Tobias* equalized.

He ran into the airlock just as the two Vulcan guards appeared between the still opening doors. A Vulcan green warning light flashed overhead to indicate the umbilical was open at both ends.

Kirk pushed Srell back as he hit the Close controls for both sets of doors.

A Vulcan guard grabbed him.

Kirk whirled around and kicked out, hard, connecting with the guard's chest, sending him into the airlock wall. Both sets of doors began sliding shut. Fifteen seconds left.

The second guard swung at Kirk. Kirk ducked. As he came up ready to swing back, the second guard's body was already crumpling to the floor, Spock's fingers pressing on the key nerve points in his shoulder.

"I'm sorry!" Srell said, revealing far too much emotion. "I activated the incorrect controls."

"Don't apologize!" Kirk told him. Ten seconds left. He pointed toward the tunnel. *"Move!"*

Kirk and Spock rushed through the half-closed doors to the umbilical. Eight seconds. But two meters into it, Kirk realized he couldn't hear Srell behind them.

Together, Kirk and Spock turned to see—

—Srell still in the airlock, in the grip of the first guard.

And the first guard had a phaser.

Small, green gleaming metal.

Ten centimeters from Srell's chest.

Five seconds.

"No!" Spock said.

He started forward.

Kirk grabbed Spock's arm, pulled him back. "Get to the ship!"

Srell looked out at them, the doors almost closed. Three seconds.

"I'm sorry!" he cried.

And then Srell grabbed at the phaser as if to push it away and the weapon discharged. A bolt of blue phased energy blasted Srell's chest. His eyes glowed. A gout of green blood burst from his mouth and he flew back from the guard's grip against the wall as—

Zero seconds. The airlock doors shut and sealed.

"Srellllll!" Spock's shocked cry sounded human.

"Spock, no! We have to get back! We've set the timers!"

Spock looked at Kirk in crazed despair. In all their years of friendship, Kirk had never seen Spock so disturbed, even when Spock had been in the violent throes of the *Plak-tow,* the Vulcan blood fever.

Kirk heard the hiss of the first umbilical collar releasing. He yanked Spock forward by his robe. "Run!"

But it was Kirk who did the running, dragging Spock who stumbled behind him.

Five meters from the *Tobias,* the second release hissed.

At three meters, the ship's umbilical detached.

At two meters, a hurricane blasted Kirk as the *Tobias* decompressed.

He nearly fell, sucked into vacuum.

Spock nearly tumbled back and out of his grip.

But Kirk had not come this far to fail.

He defied the raging wall of wind that tore at him. Step by step he leaned against it, pulling Spock with him until he could push his friend through the outer doors of the *Tobias*'s airlock and stagger through himself.

He braced himself on the airlock frame and used every ounce of strength he had to lift his arm against the howling wind to press the airlock control.

He heard the pressure sirens wailing in the *Tobias,* almost inaudible above the raging storm.

But the doors began to close.

The wind diminished.

The umbilical tunnel deflated behind him and already he could see that the *Tobias* had begun to drift away from the cargo-bay wall.

Then the airlock door thunked shut and the rush of air ended.

And beneath the mad howl of the sirens, Kirk heard a sound he had never heard before.

Spock weeping.

Kirk drew his old friend near, knowing too well the burden of guilt Spock felt, but not comprehending how it had so thoroughly shattered his Vulcan training.

He slammed his hand against the airlock comm panel.

He was tired of death. Tired of the price that had to be paid.

He was beginning to understand what Kodos had felt.

What Kodos had meant about being *tired.*

And it frightened him.

"Kirk to bridge," he said. "Get us the hell out of here. . . ."

THIRTY-ONE

There was pandemonium in the observation lounge of the *Enterprise*-E. Half the starship commanders were on their feet, arguing with each other or trying to get Picard's attention. But it was Representative Solok's resonant voice that rose above the confusion.

"That cannot possibly be *the* James T. Kirk."

Again Riker resisted the urge to laugh. "Oh, yes, it can be," he said.

It had been two years since Riker had last seen Kirk, a traveler out of time. Afterward, the Borg homeworld had been devastated; at Starbase 324, the engineers responsible for devising anti-Borg weaponry were now closing in on a new understanding of the secrets of the Borg transwarp drive; and an alarmingly unexpected alliance between the Borg and renegade Romulans had been totally defeated. All because of James T. Kirk, a man who had died twice. At least, twice that history knew of.

"It appears you were right, Number One," Picard said from the virtual viewscreen.

It took a moment for Riker to understand what his captain meant. Then he remembered: Two years ago on the bridge of a *Defiant*-class starship that had unofficially been christened the *Enterprise,* he'd watched a pyre of destruction erupt from the Borg homeworld. At the time, he'd been certain that the spectacular fountain of flame was Kirk's final, fitting memorial.

But beside him on that bridge, he also remembered seeing the expression on Ambassador Spock's face. It told him that Spock did not believe that Kirk was dead.

Riker had shared his observation with Picard. Somehow, the captain had understood what Riker could only suspect. The mindmeld Picard had undergone with both Kirk and Spock at the same time had left him with a deeper sense of Kirk's fate. Something to do with an echo of Kirk's mind that told Picard that Kirk had always known how he would die.

The Borg homeworld was not the time, and not the place.

"There are always possibilities," Picard had said.

"We both were right," Riker now told Picard. He raised his voice to be heard over the other conversations in the observation lounge. "Along with Ambassador Spock."

"Captain Picard, the government of Vulcan demands an explanation," Solok said.

"I wish I had one to give you," Picard answered. "But believe me, Representative, I have no more explanation for Kirk's presence on that ship than you have for Spock's." Picard reached down to touch a control out of the scanner's view. "Magistrate," he asked, "what is the disposition of the people you took into custody?"

On the viewscreen, the unlikely image of Kirk in Starfleet's latest uniform rippled away, to be replaced by the stern magistrate.

"Spock, his aide, and the crew of the *Tobias* were placed in detention cells awaiting Starfleet's response to this office's request for investigation."

Riker looked up at Picard and saw in his captain the same amused skepticism he felt himself.

"Magistrate," Riker asked, "how long ago did you place Kirk and Spock in detention?"

"Two point three hours."

Riker gave her a smile of commiseration. "Magistrate, if you check your detention cells, I believe you'll find you've had a breakout."

"Impossible."

Riker shrugged. "Not if history is to be our guide."

A green light suddenly began flashing beneath the magistrate's face. She looked down and Riker saw the unmistakable hallmark of Vulcan surprise—a slowly raised eyebrow.

Then Riker's comm badge chirped.

"Bridge to Commander Riker." It was Lieutenant Rolk.

"Riker here."

"Sir, we've received a distress call from a civilian spacedock. The impounded Starfleet vessel . . . it seems it's being stolen."

Riker kept his eyes fixed on Solok, trying with difficulty not to gloat. "I take it you're referring to the *Tobias?*"

"Aye, sir."

Riker addressed the senior representative. "That would be the ship on which Kirk and Spock arrived." He looked at the magistrate. *"Are* your prisoners in their cells, Magistrate?"

The magistrate folded her hands inside her robes and took on an air of unnatural calm. "We appear to have suffered a systems malfunction. That is the only explanation."

"Don't bet on it," Riker said softly. "Captain Picard, should we intercept the *Tobias?"*

"Take us to the spacedock, Number One, and have Rolk open communications."

Riker got up and gestured to Data. "Mr. Data, please take over."

Data glanced around the observation deck. Noisy confusion still reigned. "Of course, sir. But take over what?"

"You'll think of something." Then Riker hurried out to the

bridge. Behind him, above the excited babble, he was glad to hear Representative Solok's sonorous voice cut off in midsentence as the observation lounge doors slid shut.

"Helm, take us to the spacedock," Riker said as he took the center chair. He touched a comm switch on its arm. "Counselor Troi, Commander La Forge, to the bridge."

On the main screen, the scarlet arc of Vulcan rolled beneath them as the *Enterprise* changed orbits. By the time the turbolift doors opened and Troi and La Forge arrived, the impressive, elongated mushroom shape of the spacedock was already coming into view.

"Where is the *Tobias?*" Riker asked.

Behind him, at the security station, Rolk said, "Still within the main enclosure, sir. Traffic control reports spacedock doors are closed and locked."

"Not for long," Riker said.

Deanna Troi slipped into the chair to Riker's left. "Are we transferring crew to the *Tobias* for the search?" she asked.

"The *Tobias* already has a crew." Riker watched for Troi's reaction to what he said next. "It includes Ambassador Spock and James T. Kirk."

Her mouth opened in shock. "Will . . . you're joking. Aren't you?"

"You should have seen the look on the Vulcan representatives' faces when they saw him."

La Forge stood beside Riker, watching the spacedock grow on the screen. "Kirk and Spock back together? Now, this I've got to see." Then he looked down at Riker. "But you didn't call me up here to watch, did you?"

Riker shook his head. "This is the situation. Almost three hours ago, Kirk, Spock, a Vulcan aide, and three members of the *Tobias*'s crew were placed in detention cells. They've escaped—"

"That's a surprise," La Forge joked.

"—reclaimed their ship," Riker continued, "and are now attempting to leave the spacedock."

"Do we have any idea what they're after?" Troi asked.

"That's what the captain would like us to find out." Riker shifted in his chair to look behind him. "Rolk, put the captain on the corner of the screen, and keep feeding our main sensor view to the *Galileo.*" He turned back to La Forge. "Geordi, the spacedock doors are closed, but I have no doubt that Kirk will get the *Tobias* out. When she's clear, I want you ready to stop her with absolutely minimal damage."

"You've got it, Commander." La Forge moved forward to replace the ensign filling in for Data at ops.

On the screen, the visual feed from the *Galileo* appeared in the upper right-hand corner. Both Picard and Beverly were there.

"I trust you've reached the same conclusion I have?" Picard asked Riker.

"Sarek was the leader of the Symmetrists, and Sarek's son is now present on Vulcan under unusual circumstances," Riker said. "I'd say that's *four* mysteries to deal with, which means they're all connected."

"The only wild card is Kirk," Picard agreed. "But if he's involved with Spock, I'm certain he can only be a benefit to what we must do."

Beside Riker, Troi leaned forward. "Captain, I think we should remember that the last time we encountered Kirk, he was infused with Borg nanites. There's no way to predict what his condition is today."

Suddenly, the bridge was sharply illuminated by a web of flickering energy discharges arcing from a section of the spacedock's outer hull. As the discharge faded, Riker saw two massive doors begin to slide open.

"Stand by, Mr. La Forge. I believe Kirk is right on schedule."

Rolk cleared her throat behind Riker. "Sir, spacedock is reporting a power surge in all their computer controls. The doors are opening in response to an outside signal."

"I'll bet they are," Riker said. "Helm, head in to block the *Tobias,* hold at five hundred meters and dip our bow. I'd like the people on that ship to know who they're dealing with."

On the viewscreen, the *Tobias* eased out from the spacedock doors, probably at the exact instant the doors were open wide enough to allow her to pass, Riker guessed. If Kirk was known for anything, it was his timing. Then the image of the small science vessel grew to fill the screen as the *Enterprise* moved into the path of the *Tobias.*

The observation lounge doors opened again. Riker was pleased to hear that the sounds of heated argument had diminished to a less-confrontational murmur. Riker saw Data leading the three Vulcan representatives to the side of the bridge. Then Data approached Riker.

"I am sorry," the android explained, "but the Vulcans are within their rights to insist on monitoring Starfleet activity in their system."

"That's all right," Riker said. "I guarantee they'll find this interesting."

"Commander," La Forge reported from ops, "the *Tobias*'s warp core is powering up. She'll have warp in . . . ninety seconds."

Riker stood up from the center chair and faced the screen. "Open hailing frequencies, Lieutenant Rolk, and patch through the captain."

"Aye, sir," Rolk replied. "Going to visual."

Riker smiled with anticipation. He wished he were in a position to see the Vulcans' faces this time. Because, as the Vulcans might agree, Riker was certain the next ninety seconds should be . . . fascinating.

THIRTY-TWO

Kirk and Spock stepped onto the bridge of the *Tobias* just as she cleared the spacedock doors.

Christine MacDonald was in the command chair, Barc at the helm, M'Benga at ops. Kirk supposed he should go to the engineering station, to make certain the warp-core power-up was proceeding correctly. But he didn't want to leave Spock. His friend looked dazed. The death of Srell clearly weighed heavily upon him.

Barc glanced back at Kirk. "I wouldn't have believed it, but that override command sequence worked," the Tellarite engineer said. "Once I updated it, of course."

"A little trick I learned from one of your colleagues," Kirk said. He helped Spock to a chair at one of the science stations.

"Ninety seconds to warp," Barc announced. "We could be using a heading sometime soon."

Kirk took a final concerned look at Spock, then went to the helm, just as a huge white disk swept up on the main screen.

A collision alert siren roared.

"Full shields!" Christine ordered. "All stop!"

Kirk grabbed the back of Barc's chair as the bridge lurched. Then he saw the name and number emblazoned on the disk.

"The *E?"* he said. "What's wrong? Has Starfleet run out of names?"

"It's the new one," Christine said from behind him. "The tradition continues."

Then the image of the *Enterprise* cut out, to be replaced by a familiar face.

"Jean-Luc," Kirk said with a wary grin, "what a surprise."

On the screen, Picard returned the smile, a bit too warmly. "Jim, a pleasure as always."

Kirk nudged Barc aside and slipped into the helm position. "I'd love to talk, but we are running late. I don't suppose you'd like to move out of our way?"

Kirk checked his board, saw the distance to the *Enterprise,* gave a nudge to the stationkeeping thrusters to give the *Tobias* just a few meters per second of relative forward motion.

"Talking sounds like a grand idea," Picard said. "Why don't you come aboard, and we can . . . catch up on old times?"

Kirk shot a quick glance toward M'Benga's ops board. A display of the *Enterprise's* online defenses showed that her shields were set for low-risk orbital navigation, holding steady at ten meters from the hull. She was not expecting any trouble. Always a good sign for the other side.

The *Tobias* kept drifting forward.

"Jean-Luc, trust me. We don't have the time. The Federation doesn't have the time."

The ships were three hundred meters apart. Two ninety. Two eighty.

"I believe we can help you," Picard said.

Kirk saw with satisfaction that the *Enterprise* was now drifting back as well. The larger ship was taking measures to avoid collision, probably assuming that with only a handful of people on board, the *Tobias* was not under full control.

"Help us do what?"

Picard's polite smile vanished. Kirk saw that a line had been crossed. "You are not the only one who is running out of time. You are here because of events involving the Symmetrists. Yes? Or no?"

Kirk was aware of Spock moving to stand behind him. With the *Enterprise* backing off to match the *Tobias's* forward drift, the ships were holding at 285 meters separation.

"What do you know of the Symmetrists?" Spock asked.

Picard's expression became even more serious. "Ambassador Spock, I am truly sorry we meet again under these circumstances. I regret even more to inform you that in investigating the spread of the virogen, I am forced to conclude that its spread is the result of a deliberate attack on the Federation, and that your father was a part of the organization responsible. The Symmetrists."

Kirk felt Spock's hand tighten its grip on the back of his chair.

"That is true," Spock acknowledged. He sounded exhausted. Despairing.

Kirk could see that Picard was hesitant, as if uncertain how to deal with a Vulcan who appeared to be expressing his emotions. "Ambassador, please give careful consideration to what I am about to say. I believe the Symmetrists' base is hidden on Vulcan. I believe that at that base we will find a cure for the virogen. To find that cure, Starfleet must subject Vulcan to an intensive and intrusive sensor sweep. And to do so, we will need the permission of the Vulcan government. Three representatives of the government are on board the *Enterprise.* Will you talk to them? Will you help me do what must be done?"

Spock said nothing. Kirk checked the board. Warp power would be online in thirty more seconds.

"Put the representatives on," Kirk suggested.

Picard vanished. Three Vulcans appeared on what was

apparently the *Enterprise*'s bridge. Kirk recognized Commander Riker and Counselor Troi standing behind them. He took a closer look at the Vulcans. Two were familiar.

Spock raised his hand in the traditional greeting. "Peace and long life, Representative Solok."

The dark-skinned Vulcan returned the salute. "And to you, Ambassador."

But then Spock turned his attention to the other Vulcans. "Representative T'Pring, Representative Stonn, I bear unfortunate news."

T'Pring? Kirk thought. *Stonn?* No wonder the two Vulcans were familiar. The woman had been Spock's betrothed. Stonn had been her suitor. Kirk had almost been killed in hand-to-hand combat with Spock in the machinations that had surrounded T'Pring's new choice of husband.

"Your grandchild, Srell, has died."

Kirk half rose from the helm, then pushed himself back in position. Srell? The grandson of the woman who was to have been Spock's wife? Kirk had seen Spock treat the young Vulcan as if he were his own son. Was *that* the reason for Spock's unprecedented loss of self-control? Was Srell the son Spock felt he had never had?

Kirk suddenly thought of his own lost son, David. For all that Kirk and Spock had shared, Kirk now wished he could spare Spock the pain that would never lessen. Of a future never realized.

On the screen, both Stonn and T'Pring remained emotionless. "Do you carry his *katra?*" T'Pring asked.

"I do not," Spock said. He lowered his eyes. "His death was unanticipated."

"Regrettable," Stonn said.

That appeared to be the extent of the grandparents' mourning.

Kirk kept one eye on the screen as he entered a warp

heading for the *Tobias.* The new *Enterprise* was undoubtedly faster than Christine's ship. But if he timed his next maneuver properly, he was certain he could get an appreciable head start. And if Picard was convinced he would find the Symmetrists' base on Vulcan, then more power to him. But Kirk already knew where that base had to be, the only logical place it could be, and those were the coordinates he fed into the helm.

On the screen, Solok stepped in front of T'Pring and Stonn. Kirk noticed that in the background, Deanna Troi was whispering something into Riker's ear. Riker looked even more intent than usual, his attention fixed rigidly on Srell's grandparents.

"Ambassador," Solok said, "Captain Picard has made troubling charges in regard to your father. He uses them as justification for an unprecedented violation of Vulcan's security. Can such charges be true?"

"Regarding my father and the Symmetrists, yes," Spock said. "I believe it was for that very reason that my father was murdered."

Kirk saw the barely perceptible expression of shock on Solok's face. Stonn and T'Pring gave no reaction. But then, neither had they responded to the news of their grandson's death.

"Spock," Solok said, "that cannot be possible."

"If I had time, I could relate the logic of it. But it is true."

Solok licked his lips in what was almost a gesture of nervousness. "Is the rest of it true? Can the Symmetrists be found on Vulcan?"

"Some, undoubtedly," Spock said. "But not their base. And as for a cure for the virogen, of that I have no knowledge."

The bridge scene disappeared at once, to be replaced by Picard. Kirk suddenly wondered where exactly Picard was.

His surroundings looked more like a small flight deck than anything else. But for whatever reason, if Picard were removed from the center of the action, even longer delays in his response were likely.

"Ambassador," Picard said urgently. "Do you know where the Symmetrist base is? I guarantee you the cure will be found there!"

"Captain Picard, I know you are an honorable man." Kirk was surprised to hear Spock almost slur his words, as if overcome by a sudden exhaustion. "But the truth is, I can no longer trust the Federation. Not under present conditions."

Kirk saw the look of puzzled hesitation on Picard's face as he assessed Spock's condition. Kirk seized the advantage. The time was right.

He punched the forward impulse controls and the *Tobias* jumped forward.

Instantly, the main screen blazed with the energy discharge as the *Tobias*'s shields impinged on the *Enterprise*'s.

But Christine had ordered her ship's shields set to full power. The *Enterprise*'s were on low.

The physics of the situation were clear in any age.

David beat Goliath.

Kirk reached back to brace Spock as the *Tobias* pushed through the *Enterprise*'s navigational shields. Spock seemed disoriented and slipped from Kirk's grasp. Then the *Tobias*'s own shields made violent contact with the bare hull metal of the huge new ship, before rebounding away as the *Enterprise*'s shields finally responded automatically and cycled to full power. The impact sent shudders through the small science vessel, and Spock fell to the deck.

By then, the *Enterprise* was spiraling away from the *Tobias,* her crew obviously aware that any rapid response to correct her course might lead to a collision with the spacedock.

Onscreen, the stars, Vulcan, the *Enterprise,* and the spacedock spun rapidly around a central point as the small science vessel rolled. Adjusting for that could come later, Kirk knew. For now, he hit the warp controls and all other objects were gone in a heartbeat, replaced by the comforting passage of stars seen from warp.

As Kirk used the attitude controls to level the *Tobias's* orientation, M'Benga jumped up from her chair to attend to Spock.

"How are we doing, Mr. Barc?" Kirk asked.

"Warp five point eight and climbing," the Tellarite answered. "We'll get you nine point two and then some."

Kirk checked that M'Benga had Spock in hand, then faced Christine, who still sat in her command chair, little more than a passenger at the mercy of Kirk's maneuvers. She wore an expression that was equal parts bemused delight and apprehensive confusion.

"How fast is the new *Enterprise?"* Kirk asked.

"If she's still in one piece after that little trick, she's fast enough to catch us for breakfast."

Kirk checked the automated heading indicators. They were on course. He got up and went to Spock. "That's *if* Picard decides to chase us. He seems convinced that what he's looking for is on Vulcan."

"Let's get him to sickbay," M'Benga said as she took hold of Spock's arm and helped him up from the deck. Kirk took hold of his other arm and they guided him toward the turbolift.

Christine watched as the lift doors opened. "If the *Enterprise* were my ship and you did that to me, there's no way I'd be staying around Vulcan."

"But the *Enterprise* isn't your ship," Kirk said as he entered the lift with Spock and M'Benga. "She's Picard's. And he likes to look at the big picture." Kirk studied Spock.

The Vulcan hung his head as if unaware of his surroundings.

"Our job's to look after our own," Kirk said. "We won't be seeing Jean-Luc Picard anytime soon. Trust me."

"As if I have a choice," Christine said as the doors began to slide shut. "You haven't even told me where we're going."

Kirk looked again at his friend. "Would it make a difference?"

THIRTY-THREE

☆

As the collision alarms blared, Riker pushed himself up from the deck of the bridge and ran for the helm. "Geordi! Pursuit course! Maximum warp!"

But La Forge slammed his fist against the console in frustration. "No good, Commander! We've got physical damage to the forward saucer!" The engineer looked at Riker in amazement. "He actually *hit* us. *Through* the shields."

"Can't the structural integrity field compensate until we make repairs?" Riker asked.

"Sure, but we can't risk warp until we've done a visual inspection. We're stuck here for a couple of hours at least. He knew what he was doing, all right."

Riker threw his hands up in defeat. "He's had a hundred and forty years to practice," he complained.

Troi joined Riker at the helm. "Will, you were the one who was so positive he'd escape the spacedock."

"But from the *Enterprise?*"

Picard appeared on the screen again. "How are our passengers, Number One?"

The Vulcans were on their feet, apparently unperturbed by what had happened. Solok stepped forward.

"Captain Picard, in light of Ambassador Spock's confirmation of your charges linking his father to the Symmetrists, logic suggests we allow your request to search Vulcan."

"We are in agreement," Stonn added.

Picard seemed surprised by the Vulcans' acquiescence. "The emotional content of Spock's confirmation was not alarming to you?" Picard asked.

Solok looked noncommittal. "We have seen such behavior before, Captain. We prefer not to comment on it. If you could beam us to our assembly, we shall begin making preparations for your task."

Riker had Data escort the Vulcans to the transporter room. The individual Starfleet commanders still in the observation lounge had their own ships beam them directly from that part of the upper deck.

Ten minutes after the *Tobias*'s remarkable escape, Riker was reduced to sitting in the command chair, tapping his fingers, waiting for La Forge's damage-control team to certify the *Enterprise* for warp travel. The *Tobias,* whose last speed had been edging up to warp nine, was long gone from sensor range. Instead of a chase, it was now going to be a search.

Troi came over to Riker with a cup of replicator coffee. "Come into the observation lounge with me," she said.

"Are you going to show me the stars?" Riker asked.

"I believe I already have," Troi replied, then headed for the lounge.

When Riker and she entered, Picard and Beverly were back on the virtual viewscreen. Riker was still not used to dealing with the captain at such a remove.

"The counselor told me what she reported to you about the Vulcans' emotional response to Spock's revelations," Picard said.

Riker took a chair beside Troi and warmed his hands around the coffee cup. Troi's report had been little more than a whispered warning in his ear as the Vulcans and Spock had conversed by viewscreen.

"I just checked the records about that," Riker said. "There was another emotional dynamic at work. Spock used to be, I suppose the word is 'engaged,' to T'Pring. She chose Stonn, instead."

"No, there was something more present," Troi said. "I sensed no emotions relating to any previous entanglements between Spock, Stonn, and T'Pring. Instead, it was the absence of emotion I felt."

"They're Vulcans, Deanna. Of course there was an absence of emotion."

But Picard interrupted from the viewscreen. "No, Number One. That's too simple an explanation for what the counselor sensed."

"It was Solok who reacted emotionally to the news of Srell's death," Troi said. "On the surface, he showed nothing, but inside he experienced . . . sadness. Yet T'Pring and Stonn, they felt nothing, Will. And I sensed that same absence of feeling in Stron and his mate when the *Enterprise* confronted the *Bennett.* They were not afraid because they knew they had a way to escape us. And I propose that Stonn and T'Pring felt nothing about the death of their grandson because they do not believe he's dead."

"I don't know, Deanna. That's quite a leap."

"Go on, Counselor," Picard said.

"I sensed an even stronger emotional response from Solok when Ambassador Spock began . . . having difficulty speaking. Solok became alarmed, and again, very sad. But at the same time, Stonn and T'Pring seemed pleased that Spock appeared to be experiencing a problem. It was almost as if they were expecting it."

Riker took a sip of his coffee, giving himself a moment to think. "I think I see part of what you're getting at. You're suggesting that Stonn and T'Pring have information about Srell that Solok doesn't. And if they're not surprised by Spock's behavior, then perhaps . . ." He shook his head. "No. I don't see the connection. Especially since we have been given permission to search Vulcan."

"This is the connection," Beverly said.

Riker glanced up at the viewscreen and beside Picard, he saw the doctor holding up a medical padd.

"When Spock and the others from the *Tobias* were placed in detention, they were given blood tests to determine if they had been exposed to the virogen. Fortunately, the virogen tests came back negative, which means Vulcan has not been exposed, and neither has the spacedock. However, the magistrate was concerned by what she thought was Spock's overly emotional behavior at the hearing. She ordered additional tests."

"And . . . ?" Riker asked.

"Well, the only conclusive diagnostic test would be to culture tissue from his metathalamus, but Ambassador Spock's blood shows antibodies suggestive of the presence of Bendii Syndrome."

Riker went on alert. "That's the disease Sarek died of."

"Officially, yes," Picard said. "But remember what Spock told us. He said his father had been murdered because of his connection to the Symmetrists."

"Bendii is a disease of extreme old age," Riker said. "How can someone be murdered by it?"

"I'm not an expert on Vulcan medicine," Beverly answered, "but I presume that measures could be taken to introduce the pathogen directly into the victim's body."

"And in the case of Spock," Picard continued, "I think we have proof that that is exactly what happened."

"I don't understand," Riker said.

Beverly explained. "Bendii is very rare, and almost entirely limited to Vulcans over the age of two hundred. Spock is a hundred and forty-three years old. That either makes him the youngest Bendii sufferer in the entire history of Vulcan, or a potential murder victim, just like his father."

Riker stared across the table at the collection of earlier *Enterprise*s. He picked out the simple, geometrical lines of Kirk's ship. Spock's ship. Two of them, actually. The first, and the A.

"You're right. That's the connection," he said at last. "Stonn and T'Pring are Symmetrists. They're killing Spock, or they're at least aware of the attempt to kill him, for the same reason Sarek was killed."

"And," Picard concluded, "they no longer protest our proposed search of Vulcan."

Riker understood. They had been manipulated from the beginning. "Which means," he said, "that what we're looking for is obviously not on Vulcan, and they don't want us going off anywhere where we might find it."

"Precisely," Picard agreed. "And it is my order that we not reveal that conclusion to any member of the Vulcan government, or to any other member of Starfleet present in this system."

"You think the Symmetrists are that powerful?" Riker asked.

"If they have survived the centuries with the power to infiltrate the Vulcan government, to kill her most revered citizens in an indetectable manner, and to bring the Federation to its knees, I think they are more dangerous than any foe we have ever faced before."

Riker was having a hard time accepting the inescapable conclusion. As members of the Federation, Vulcans had been among its greatest and most valuable supporters. To now imagine them as enemies was to see the Federation dead.

"Kirk knows, doesn't he?" Riker asked, as he put the final pieces of the puzzle together. The final picture was appalling.

"I believe so," Picard said. "I believe he was the one

element that Vulcan logic could not predict. The Symmetrists conceived what they believed to be a perfect plan. Sarek's murder, committed without a hint of suspicion, is more than enough proof of their ability to make perfect plans that cover every eventuality."

"Except for one," Troi said.

Riker straightened his shoulders. Their next move was obvious. "Shall I lay in a pursuit course, sir?"

"Exactly, Number One. And contact Virogen Task Force Headquarters at Starbase Five-fifteen to let them know where we're going. We'll need a full medical support team when we arrive."

"Excuse me, sir," Troi asked, "but where are we going?"

"We follow Kirk," Picard said. "To the source."

THIRTY-FOUR

Spock sat in silence in his quarters on the *Tobias.* He kept the lighting dim, the temperature Vulcan warm. At any other time in his life, he would have meditated.

But he could no longer see the point.

What was the sense of discovering inner peace when the universe tore itself apart in chaos all around him?

Too late he realized that chaos was the goal he should have sought. To fight the forces of existence with logic was to build a fortress of reeds. The storm did not care about aesthetics. Only about wiping the worlds clean.

Spock put a hand up to cover his eyes. He lowered his head. He wept.

For Sarek. For Srell.

And for himself.

In time, his door announcer chimed.

He looked up, unmindful of the tears that streaked his face. "Come," he said, not caring who was on the other side.

But it was Kirk.

He carried a tray of food, though Spock wasn't hungry.

Kirk seemed to sense that. He put the tray on a dresser at the side of the room, pulled up a chair, sat next to his friend.

"It wasn't your fault," Kirk said.

"Does it matter?"

"Sadness is one thing. Guilt is another. You have no cause to feel guilty."

Spock looked away. "I have no cause to feel anything. Yet I do. I always have. And I have never understood why."

"Spock . . ."

But Spock wasn't ready to listen.

"How much time have I wasted, Jim? I thought . . . I believed I had conquered this war inside me."

"It's not a war, Spock. You've told me yourself: It's a balance. Harmony. You found it once. Not the harshness of total logic. Not the . . . the madness of total emotion. But the blending of the two."

Spock looked at his friend with haunted eyes. "Have you found it? Can it ever be found?"

Kirk returned Spock's thoughtful gaze. Got up. Went to the tray of food. Returned with the black base of a commercial holoprojector.

Spock stared at it, bewildered. "Ki Mendrossen's confession?" As far as he knew, the holoprojector containing the message that had shattered his life was still on Vulcan. He had left it at his family villa.

"M'Benga found this in one of the onboard labs," Kirk explained. "When the peacekeepers at Tarok's estate took the forensics team into custody, they beamed everyone back to the *Tobias,* along with everything they'd collected. I suppose the authorities didn't want to move it again until they were certain it hadn't been contaminated."

Spock took the black base from Kirk, turned it over. It was the same model as the one that had contained Mendrossen's recording.

"The notation on this one said Srell collected it personally," Kirk added.

"I remember," Spock said. "I saw it in Tarok's sitting

room. It was on a table with . . . quite rare antiques. Objects of great value. It seemed out of place."

"Maybe not," Kirk said.

Spock didn't know what his friend meant. "You have seen it?"

"So should you."

Spock hefted the base in his hand, wondering if there was any reason he should ever care about anything again. There was nothing this projector could do to repair his past. Nothing it could do to restore his future. If he had the superhuman strength required, he would have been tempted to heave the base through the viewport and follow it gladly into the oblivion of space.

"Play it, Spock."

Spock sighed. He'd play it. If not for himself, then for his friend.

He placed the holoprojector on the low table beside him, and touched the switch.

A shaft of rose-colored light grew from its center.

Spock waited to see his father's image resolve from that light. It was the only logical explanation for Kirk's insistence that he watch the recording.

But Spock was wrong.

There was another explanation. One that had little to do with logic.

And everything to do with emotion.

The figure was Amanda.

Tears stung Spock's eyes, as once again he heard his mother speak.

"Oh, Spock," she said, her long-silent voice like magic to him, "I've waited so long to tell you this, and I know your father's right and that even after I've made this recording, it might be years before you hear it. But you must hear it. And I must say it. Because we . . . I . . . have not been honest with you.

"Just yesterday, you left for Starfleet Academy, to learn to sail the stars. How I envy you. How proud I am of you. And even your father, in his way, feels the same.

"Oh, I know you're not speaking. I know that you know why your father objects so forcefully to your joining Starfleet. And I know all about the Vulcan traditions between fathers and sons so I am not going to try to use this to bring you back together. That is something only the two of you can do.

"But there is one small part of your father's decision that you do not know. Something you have to know. And maybe it will help you understand.

"Spock, I know what's gone unspoken between you and Sarek. And I know that you especially feel that if only your father could touch your mind, he could feel what you feel, understand what you need and desire.

"And I know the Vulcan pride that keeps you from asking for that contact.

"Believe me, Spock, it is not Vulcan pride that keeps your father from offering you that joining of minds. He only wishes to protect you."

Spock looked at Kirk but Kirk pointed back to the glowing, radiant image of Amanda. She held her hands together, above her human heart, speaking to a son she didn't see, and now would never see again.

"Spock, I am going to give this recording to Uncle Tarok, and he will see that you get it . . . when he thinks that enough time has gone by." Spock understood the hesitation in his mother's voice. For some reason, she did not intend for him to hear her words until both she and Sarek were dead. "When you see this, go to Tarok. He will answer all the questions I know you'll have when you hear what I have to say."

Amanda placed her hands at her side, glanced down, as if preparing herself to make a confession, just like Ki Mendrossen. The light that formed her image sparkled through Spock's tear-misted vision.

"Years ago, when we were young, your father and I believed our worlds, Vulcan and Earth and all the other planets of the Federation, faced great danger. We were members of a group called the Symmetrists. And you must believe me when I say we intended no harm toward anyone. We only wished to gather information, to make others see the unifying symmetry of all things the way we did, and then use those insights to solve the problems we faced, together and in peace.

"But others, whose identities we do not know, took up our cause without our knowledge, and corrupted our ideals, committing hideous crimes in the name of our cause. And so we, and Tarok, and our friends have abandoned our organization.

"We have done nothing wrong, Spock. But the false Symmetrists have. And your father is fearful that if you meld with him, and see these secrets in his mind, then your duty as a Starfleet officer will force you to denounce him. And your own connection by birth to such a group could end the career that even your father knows means so much to you.

"Someday, I know he hopes to explain this to you himself. I know he longs to share his mind with you as his father did with him. But for now, he cannot. And for his sake, I ask for your understanding and forgiveness.

"I love you, Spock. And so does your father.

"Never forget that. Never."

Then, like the fading luster of a comet's tail, the rose-colored image from the past diminished, its light swallowed by the darkness of the room, and the years.

Kirk and Spock sat in the dim light and the silence together. There was no need for either to speak.

Presently, Spock straightened in his chair, wiped the tears from his face. When he spoke, his voice was stronger, more assured.

"I was eighteen when I joined the Academy," he said. "My father and I did not speak again until. . . ."

"The Babel Conference," Kirk said. "About the Coridan admission. That was when I met your . . ."

Kirk paused, looked into a far dark corner of the room.

"Jim?" Spock said.

Kirk shrugged. "That mindmeld confusion," he said. "I know I never met your father until he came on board the *Enterprise* that time. But . . . Spock, those dreams of your father seem so real."

Spock carefully took the holoprojector in his hand. "Answers sometimes lie in unexpected places," Spock said.

Kirk smiled at his friend. "Then you admit that there *are* answers?"

Spock nodded. "I am afraid I have not been myself. I have been . . . a burden to the mission."

"Never," Kirk said. He hesitated again. "That's what I told your father . . . ? Never forget . . . no! He told me to forget? I said never?" Kirk closed his eyes, grimaced in his efforts to remember. Spock grew concerned. Kirk stood up, held out his hand as if to grasp an answer from the air. "There was something your father told me, Spock. Something important. But . . . what? And when?"

Spock was glad to have something other than his own pain to focus on. "Do you remember the context?" he asked.

Kirk's comm badge chirped. Kirk touched it, gingerly, still becoming used to his new environment. "Kirk here."

It was Christine reporting from the bridge. "We're coming up on orbit, Jim."

"I'll be there," Kirk said. He looked at Spock. "What do you say? One more mission?"

Spock allowed just the hint of a smile to form, almost as if he were himself again. "At the very least."

Kirk touched his comm badge again. "We'll both be there," he said.

THIRTY-FIVE

Kirk and Spock stepped onto the bridge of the *Tobias.*

It didn't matter that it wasn't an *Enterprise.*

It didn't matter that it wasn't even Kirk's ship.

It wasn't the machinery that was important, it was the people. And with Spock at his side, with Christine, M'Benga, and Barc, Kirk knew he was ready for what would come next.

For what he knew had been waiting for him all his life.

If only he could remember *why* he knew. And *how* . . .

He stood by Christine's chair as the small disk of their destination grew against the stars. The last time Kirk had seen this world, it had been a sweep of equatorial green and purple vegetation with milky blue seas, bordered by bands of snow in the temperate zones, and wreathed in misty clouds.

Now, except for the white of the swollen polar regions, it was black, and brown, streaked with red, its waterways clogged with eruptions of strange yellow formations that resembled spreading colonies of mold.

"Coming up on standard orbit," Barc said from the helm.

Christine leaned closer to Kirk. "You're sure about this? This planet's so far gone we didn't even have to run a Starfleet blockade."

"I'm sure," Kirk said as the dead world filled the screen and scrolled beneath them. "It's where it started."

Spock nodded. "And where it will end."

"Standard orbit," Barc growled. "Welcome to Tarsus Four."

Christine pushed herself up from her chair, nodded at Kirk. "You take the conn. I'll be more useful at the sensor stations."

Kirk looked at the empty chair. "I can't," he said. He had to put those days behind him. "I'll take the helm."

Christine didn't argue, told Barc the conn was his, then moved to the main science station to prepare for the first sensor sweep. Spock joined her there, to offer assistance. Kirk could see she was alert to Spock's change of mood.

Kirk took his place at the helm. M'Benga was beside him at ops. "Why here?" the doctor asked.

Kirk's eyes stayed on the screen. He could see the outlines of landforms and lakes and mountains he had memorized as a child, when coming to an alien world for a summer trip from Earth was to be the greatest adventure of his life.

"Logic," he said. "The Symmetrists tried an experiment here before. It worked."

M'Benga's dark eyes flashed with outrage. "Kodos executed four thousand innocent people on this world, and you say the experiment 'worked'?"

Kirk understood her reaction, but for him, the outrage of Tarsus IV had passed into history, when he had seen Kodos die to save Kirk's life. The executioner had been executed by his own daughter—the final step in the old man's efforts to forget the past of which he had grown so tired. Outrage meant nothing in the face of that. The memory of boyhood terror remained. But he had nothing left to feel about Kodos the man.

"Because of what happened here," Kirk said, "food distribution policies changed throughout the Federation. Crop diversity was mandated to prevent another case where a single disease organism could wipe out a colony's entire food supply." He glanced at the doctor. "Of course, that was when I was a teenager. By the time I graduated the Academy, those rules had all been rewritten or forgotten."

"So, you think the Symmetrists came back here to try again, but on a bigger scale?" M'Benga asked.

"I don't know," Kirk said. On the viewscreen, he saw the main continent of Tarsus Four coming up. In the central plain would be the main city, where the first colony had been founded. Where the mass graves remained as a memorial, in mute testimony to the madness that had come to this place. "Maybe they never left. Maybe they felt they could make a stronger point if this became one of the first worlds to be infected by the virogen. History repeats itself. The lesson reinforced by blood."

"That doesn't sound like logic," M'Benga said. "It sounds like emotion."

"When you get right down to it," Kirk said, "there's not a lot of difference between the two. It's just a question of finding the proper balance."

M'Benga eyed him skeptically. "You're the same Jim Kirk who stole your old starship from under Starfleet's nose, risked war with the Klingon Empire, blew up the *Enterprise,* and hijacked a Bird-of-Prey to rescue Spock? And you talk about *balance?"*

Kirk saw his control boards change configuration as Christine switched sensor control to the helm and ops. "Dr. M'Benga, all I can say is, at the time, it seemed like the logical thing to do."

M'Benga had the decency to laugh. She obviously knew when she was being set up, and understood the game.

"Coming up on main city," Kirk said.

M'Benga asked quietly, "Did it ever get a name?"

"New Haven," Kirk said. "But after Kodos, they just called it the city."

Kirk brought the sensors online and the first returns were depressing. Frequency of viable life-forms was less than eight percent of the figure given in the Starfleet database from the last planetary survey only two years ago.

"No sign of any colonists," Kirk said.

"That's probably why there was no blockade," Christine said from her station. "The evacuation was completed."

"You'd think they'd keep at least one ship on station," Kirk said as he kept scanning the sensor returns. "If only to keep Orion pirates from looting the place."

"Acquiring main city," Spock announced.

Kirk reassigned sensor sensitivity to search for humanoid life and industrial installations. Both should be present if his theory was correct.

"Picking up sensor scatter," Spock said.

Kirk saw it. "Looks like there's a forcefield operating in the city."

"No life signs," M'Benga reported.

"Someone's got to be keeping that shield going," Christine said. "Going for high resolution on the surrounding area. Putting it onscreen."

The dying continent that slowly moved below them was replaced by a false-color enhanced image of one small section of the main city. The widest thoroughfares were familiar to Kirk. They were the same ones laid out when the colony had been founded, the same streets he had walked when he had been a boy.

Near the intersection of two of the largest streets, a large amorphous shape pulsated—indicating the area protected from sensors by forcefields.

"Jim," Christine asked, "any idea what that installation is?"

Kirk frowned. "If that's the old center of town, it's about where the Starfleet administration center was. But that was more than a century ago."

On the screen, a map overlay appeared, labeled: CITY PLAN, NEW HAVEN, TARSUS IV.

The Starfleet delta was positioned directly over the sensor-opaque area.

"Looks like it still is the Starfleet center," Christine said. "Bones, any chance there's a team from Medical down there we don't know about?"

"Not without a support ship on orbit," M'Benga said.

Christine made her decision. "Then that's it. We've found your base, Jim. What happens next?"

Kirk didn't have an answer right away. He hadn't expected the base to be so easy to find. Either the Symmetrists were overconfident, or—

Kirk's hands flew over the helm and reconfigured the controls for warp flight. "Brace yourselves! Get ready for—"

The viewscreen blasted the bridge with blinding white light as the ship screamed and spun to the starboard, throwing the crew from their chairs.

Kirk scrambled back to the helm as Barc squealed and every alarm on the bridge clanged, wailed, and beeped at once. Shadows danced crazily from all the flashing warning and overload lights. An irregular vibration pulsed through the deck.

"Damage reports!" Christine shouted over the cacophony.

The screen cleared slightly, enough to show the planet below them, and then a golden sparkle of light appeared and—

The *Tobias* seemed to fall as artificial gravity failed in the impact of another explosion. Kirk hooked his feet under the console and pulled M'Benga back into position. If they got hit again before gravity was reestablished, inertia would smash them against the ceiling, deck, or bulkhead.

"Barcs!" Christine shouted. "Inertial control! Full gravity now! What are they hitting us with?!"

"Transporter mines," Spock said. "They are being beamed directly into our path from the surface."

This was exactly what Kirk had suddenly realized. For the Symmetrists' base to be so obvious meant they had to have exceptional defenses.

"Barcs! Forget the environmentals! Get us out of—"

"New mine materializing, fifty meters astern," Spock said.

Kirk braced himself, but he knew it would do no good. When that mine went off, the *Tobias* would lurch forward at hundreds of kilometers per second, while the inertia of her crew kept each person at relative rest until the back wall of the bridge hit them and reduced them to little more than organic paste.

Kirk stared at the screen, at Tarsus IV below him, knowing it was not supposed to end this way.

It didn't.

The transporter mine didn't detonate.

"Spock?" Kirk called as he twisted to look behind him. "What's happening out there?"

But Spock, anchored to the science station beside Christine, merely pointed forward at the main screen.

Kirk twisted back.

Just in time to see the enormous but familiar white disk of a starship's command saucer eclipse the screen.

He didn't even have to wait to see the lettering on the hull to know what ship it was, and who commanded her.

So much for thinking Picard would stay behind to search Vulcan instead of following the *Tobias.*

The screen flashed once, and a direct visual communications feed began.

Jean-Luc Picard appeared, inexplicably still in his small flight deck, but most definitely the captain in control.

"Greetings, *Tobias,*" Picard said with a smile. "I was wondering if we might offer you the services of a slightly larger vessel?"

Kirk hit the comm switch on his console. "Just so there're no misunderstandings, we have a mission to perform here. And you're not taking us back until we're done."

"I don't think you're in a particularly strong position for stating your terms, Jim, but we have no intention of taking you back. In fact, since we both have missions here, perhaps we could work together, instead of trying to ram each other out of space?"

Kirk slowly settled back into his chair as Barc brought the gravity online again. He could only guess that the *Enterprise*'s shields or firepower or both were keeping them protected from the transporter mines.

"What, exactly, is your mission?" Kirk asked.

"You're here for the Symmetrists," Picard said. "We're here for the virogen cure. And as far as our sensors are concerned, we'll find both directly below us."

"You've got yourself a partner," Kirk said.

Picard smiled. "You're welcome."

THIRTY-SIX

☆

Beneath the dark clouds that covered the main city, the Great Seal of the Federation was fifteen meters across, carved from the distinctive bluestone of Tarsus IV, and inlaid with a mosaic pattern of minerals from each of the fifty-two worlds who were members at the time it was dedicated.

As a teenager, Kirk had stared up in awe at the monument outside the Starfleet administration building. But now the seal was cracked, the top third fallen off, most of the mosaic stones missing. Like the Federation it represented, the monument was crumbling in the aftermath of the virogen.

Kirk materialized before that monument, still in his new Starfleet uniform, though now with a jacket and a hand phaser. Spock, Christine, Barc, and M'Benga resolved beside him. Barc and Christine carried phaser rifles. M'Benga a hand phaser and a medical field kit.

Kirk studied the cracked seal for a moment, but quickly dismissed it as a mere symbol. Throughout history, people had been obsessed with creating similar icons, imbuing them with power, rallying around them, going to war for them. But not Kirk. There had been other symbols in the past, there would be new ones in the future. The Great Seal of the

Federation was not the reason he and the others were here today. The ideals from which those symbols arose were far more important.

Kirk leaned out from behind the decaying monument and checked the state of the Starfleet installation beyond.

A domed forcefield rippled around it, enclosing it safely and completely, impenetrable to everything except limited wavelengths of visible light.

Kirk tapped his comm badge. He was beginning to appreciate how convenient this type of communicator was. "Kirk here. The buildings inside the forcefield appear to be intact."

Riker's voice responded. "Can you see any guards?"

"None visible," Kirk said. He glanced around at the rest of what he could see of the main city. Burned-out buildings, crashed flyers, signs of looting. Scans from orbit had failed to pick up a single life-form in the ruins larger than a rat. He thought of Chal and Teilani. "I don't think there's anything left to guard."

"They've got to know we're coming," Christine said as she slipped in beside him. "They targeted the *Tobias* precisely, so they must have seen the *Enterprise.*"

"Commander MacDonald's right," Kirk said as he touched his comm badge. "If the Symmetrists have guards at this installation, then they'll all be inside, waiting for us."

"Then let's not keep them waiting," Riker replied. "Stand by. *Enterprise* out."

A moment later, two new columns of transporter energy appeared by Kirk's team. They resolved into Picard and Beverly Crusher.

"Nice of you to drop in," Kirk said. "But I thought starship captains were supposed to mind the store these days."

Picard looked around, his grip on his phaser rifle almost casual, as if he did this every day. "Beverly and I have already been exposed to the virogen, which makes us perfect volunteers for this mission."

"I hate to disappoint you," M'Benga said, "but I can eliminate the virogen from animal carriers."

Beverly looked at M'Benga in delight. "Dried *trannin* leaves?"

M'Benga returned the smile. "You read my report?"

The two doctors excitedly introduced themselves to each other, shook hands. "Medical's already sent out the replicator programs for your compound," Beverly said. "It's a brilliant piece of work. And how fortunate that Klingon folk healer was on your world."

"Klingon . . . folk healer?" M'Benga repeated. She glanced at Kirk. He shook his head, not wanting the attention. "Right. A real mystery man. Never did catch his name."

"A shame," Beverly said. Then she looked around, saw Spock. "Ambassador, may I have a word with you, please?"

Spock looked surprised. "Dr. Crusher, this is hardly the time."

But Beverly insisted. She motioned for Spock to step away from the others with her.

"Is something wrong?" Kirk asked Picard.

"A medical matter," Picard said.

"Bendii Syndrome?" Even as he finally said those words, Kirk hoped his suspicions were incorrect.

Picard was impressed. "How did you know?"

"I've known Spock for . . . forever. The way he's been behaving these past few days, it hasn't been like him at all. But I read the reports of Sarek's death—the official results. The symptoms seemed the same."

Kirk and Picard watched Spock and Beverly in whispered conversation. "Bendii can't be confirmed without specialized procedures," Picard said. "But blood tests suggest he has been deliberately exposed to the same pathogen that killed his father."

Kirk felt a wave of inexpressible sorrow pass over him. "Is there any chance of a cure?"

"It might not even be Bendii, Jim. Just a poison that mimics its effects."

"Any idea how he was exposed?"

"Not yet."

Beverly gave Spock an injection from a hypospray.

"That will help him maintain control," Picard said. "For a little while at least."

Spock returned to the group, his face revealing nothing of his conversation with the doctor.

Kirk allowed his friend his privacy. "What now?" he asked Picard.

"Now, my first officer and my engineer will show off a new technique they're quite proud of."

"A new technique for what?" Kirk asked. "Shouldn't we be starting a bombardment to wear down that forcefield?"

"Welcome to the twenty-fourth century," Picard said. Then he tapped his comm badge. "Picard to *Enterprise.* You may begin."

Instantly the air filled with a powerful transporter harmonic. Picard gestured to the others to look past the protection of the monument at the forcefield.

Kirk was startled to see what appeared to be an umbrella of . . . cargo containers? They were materializing along the precise boundary of the domed forcefield.

Interference patterns formed, sending ripples of energy disturbances across the field, so bright that the low dark clouds were illuminated from below. Kirk squinted to bring the scene into clearer focus.

"Watch your eyes," Picard warned him.

Then at least two dozen Starfleet personnel in black phaser armor materialized *within* the forcefield on the dead lawn of the administration building.

"Punch through!" Barc snarled. The Tellarite beamed in delighted approval. "Interference disruption and transporter punch through! Absolutely brilliant! Not that there aren't twenty different settings I could make to stop it from ever happening again," he added.

"It works best on atmospheric shields," Picard said. Then he ducked and a moment later Kirk saw all the cargo containers disappear, followed by a series of explosions that covered the forcefield's surface.

Some of the troops in phaser armor stumbled under the force of the overhead blasts, but they were all quickly up on their feet and running for the building.

The surprise and the novelty of their attack had been so unexpected that fully half of them had burst into the closest building before the first shots of defensive phaser fire were directed at them. There *were* Symmetrist guards hiding inside.

Picard tapped his comm badge as the last of the armored crew dived into cover. "Picard to *Enterprise.* The second team is in. No casualties."

Kirk could hear Riker's grin in his reply. "All transporters standing by, sir."

Then, from far away, Kirk could hear muffled explosions, the whine of phaser fire. No more than a hundred meters away, the troops from the *Enterprise* were fighting the Symmetrist defenders—fighting and dying, and for what?

Kirk could almost hear Kodos's reply: *Survival depends on drastic measures. . . .*

Then a larger explosion rumbled through the ground. Kirk saw the forcefield shimmer, then wink out.

Riker's voice came from everyone's comm badges.

"The shield is down. Third team is beaming in now. We will transport targets out at will."

Picard nodded at Kirk as he hefted his phaser rifle. "Right now, minding a store doesn't seem like a bad idea."

Kirk smiled. He suspected that he and Picard were more alike than either of them knew, or would admit.

Then the transporter claimed them again and the real battle began.

THIRTY-SEVEN

Christine's ears popped as she materialized in a dark underground room, somewhere in the lower levels of the old administration building. The blueprints from the main computer libraries of the *Enterprise* had shown that this building had originally been equipped with deep shelters for the city's population. Tarsus IV was close to the Neutral Zone, and the colony's founders had decided to be prudent.

In the attack's planning sessions, conducted while the crippled *Tobias* had been unceremoniously towed from orbit by two of the *Enterprise*'s shuttles, Spock had reasoned that the underground shelter complex would be the perfect setting for the antivirogen installation Picard expected to find. Thus, Picard's team had been chosen for the deepest penetration into enemy territory.

Christine swung her phaser rifle up to cover the area as Kirk and Picard, Spock and Barc, and the two doctors took form beside her. Crusher and M'Benga were crucial to this part of the operation. Both Kirk and Spock agreed that the Symmetrists would have outfitted their installation with self-destruct charges. The two doctors would be responsible for locating and isolating samples of the antivirogen before those charges could be detonated. Picard and the others would be responsible for getting everyone out alive.

An explosion rumbled from somewhere many levels overhead.

"Was that a phaser hit?" M'Benga asked nervously.

Picard shook his head. "An explosive. And my people aren't carrying any."

Christine understood what that meant. Kirk and Spock had been right about the self-destruct charges, and they were already being activated.

"The Symmetrists are fanatics," Picard reminded everyone. A second explosion thundered from far away. "If they're destroying this installation, they'll do it methodically, whether they feel they can escape or not. We only have a few minutes at most."

Dr. Crusher moved her medical tricorder back and forth, then pointed toward a narrow doorway in a distant corner. "Diffuse life signs," she said. "Plant-based. Maybe in a growth medium."

Picard motioned ahead with his rifle, exchanged a tight smile with Kirk. Together, they ran to the doorway. Spock ran with them.

Despite the gravity of the situation, Christine had to fight down a sudden rush of elation. She was on a mission with Kirk and Spock, *and* Picard. The Symmetrists, however fanatical, didn't have a chance.

Another explosion shook the floor. This one was closer. Christine told Crusher and M'Benga to run ahead, she'd follow with Barc.

"Feels like we're making history, doesn't it?" she asked the engineer as she ran beside him.

"*Rrr,* I'd rather be juggling antimatter in a variable gravity field."

As they reached the doorway behind the others, an even closer explosion cracked the air around them. "Careful what you wish for, Barcs." Then she and the Tellarite ducked through the door and ran on.

Ahead of them, a pipe-lined corridor stretched about fifty meters. Crusher and M'Benga used their tricorders at every closed door on either side, but all readings indicated the strongest life signs came from straight ahead.

That was where the corridor opened into a large, well-lit storage chamber, at least three stories high, with white-tiled walls, holding five enormous, spherical white tanks ringed by catwalks, plastered with warning placards, and attached to diagnostic pressure displays.

Kirk and Picard ran to opposite sides of the storage chamber, checking each likely hiding place among the alcoves, computer stations, and stacks of packing crates. Since the main lighting sources were centered in the ceiling, there were impenetrable shadows everywhere—under the tanks, under catwalks, even on the catwalk ringing the top level of the chamber.

Crusher and M'Benga cautiously approached the tanks with their tricorders. Each tank was positioned on thick metal legs that raised it high enough for workers to walk under it. From a protected position between two large packing crates, Christine peered into those shadows.

"This tank is full of virogen culture," Crusher announced from the first tank. She read the results of her scan from her tricorder. "This must be where they were growing it in the first place."

"Virogen," M'Benga confirmed at the second tank.

Barc slung his phaser rifle over his shoulder and pulled out his own engineering tricorder. He started scanning for explosives.

Christine peered up at the highest reaches of the chamber. There were shadows enough in each corner of the catwalk to hide two or three watchers, or soldiers with weapons.

"More virogen cultures," Crusher said from beside the third tank.

"Dr. Crusher," Christine called out to her. "Could you sweep those balconies for life signs?" She indicated the shadowed areas with the barrel of her phaser rifle.

"Certainly," Crusher said. She adjusted the setting on her tricorder, pointed it up, and began to move it.

Then she screamed as an orange disruptor bolt blasted her back into one of the tank's support legs and sent her tricorder flying.

Instantly Kirk's and Picard's voices echoed in the chamber. "Everyone down!"

Christine saw where Picard fired to try and pick off whoever shot Crusher. Christine began firing to the right and left of Picard's target zones.

"Over there!" Barc suddenly shouted.

Christine saw where the Tellarite was pointing—at the catwalk circling the fifth tank—and fired at a moving shadow just as Picard fired again.

But another disruptor bolt shot down and hit Barc, throwing him squealing across the floor.

Christine wheeled as Kirk leapt to cover beside her. She was surprised to see he hadn't drawn his phaser.

"There are two of them," he said in a low voice. "On tank five, and on the catwalk up in that corner. M'Benga's safe under the fourth tank. Picard's standing by in the far corner. I'm going after Dr. Crusher and pull her under the tank for safety. When I draw fire, you go for the one on the catwalk, Picard goes for the one on the fifth tank."

"When you draw fire?" Christine said. "You're not a target!"

"Someone has to be." He gave her his phaser. "And I can't do this anymore." He got ready to run into the open area.

"Jim, wait!" Christine said.

He turned, just for a moment, to face her.

It was now or never. She reached out for him, kissed him.

He was startled. Pulled back. "This isn't . . ." he began.

And then it was too late.

Christine shoved the phaser rifle into his hands, pushed him down between the packing crates, and charged out across the chamber floor, heading for Dr. Crusher.

She heard the crackle of a disruptor bolt hit the floor behind her, but she kept pumping her legs and arms, never slowing.

Phaser whines screamed behind her, from two different sources. She smiled, knowing that Kirk was doing some of the shooting.

A scream rang out, but it came from the wrong place to be either Kirk or Picard. It had to be one of the two other shooters. The Symmetrists.

She dived behind a stand of pipes at the base of the third tank and slid in beside Crusher. The doctor was conscious, barely, and Christine jammed one arm around her and dragged her to shelter beneath the tank.

She blew her hair up off her forehead and peered back the way she had run.

Kirk was kneeling where she had left him between the crates, phaser rifle in his hand, perfectly positioned to pick off more attackers.

She felt proud of herself for having outmaneuvered him. She wondered if Kirk would forgive her the kiss.

And then she felt the cold emitter of a disruptor dig into the back of her neck.

"Resourceful," a familiar voice said. "For a human."

Christine turned around as a powerful hand gripped her hair and sharply tugged her off balance to keep her from trying anything sudden.

But she already knew who had captured her.

The voice belonged to Srell.

THIRTY-EIGHT

Kirk breathed heavily, from exertion, from anger, he didn't know which.

He could still hear the scream of the man he had shot on the catwalk. The man who had then fallen three stories to certain death on the chamber floor.

But he also still tasted the unexpected softness of Christine's lips on his.

Life and love in the face of death. The juxtaposition had been enough to let her take him by surprise.

She had changed the rules. On him.

He didn't know whether to be angry or proud.

He decided to think about it later. He touched his comm badge. "Kirk to *Enterprise.*"

No response. He could hear the hiss of a jamming device in operation. The Symmetrists had been thorough in the defense of their installation.

Then he heard another explosion roar from the corridor that had led to this chamber. If a communicator signal couldn't get through, he knew the *Enterprise* could never lock on a transporter beam. From the sounds of the explosions, all the exits were being shut down, so there would be no physical way out, either.

He tapped the comm badge again. "Kirk to Picard."

"Go ahead," Picard answered. The communicators still worked over short distances.

"I picked off the one on the catwalk." There was no pride in Kirk's voice. He had merely done his job.

"The one on the tank didn't show himself," Picard said.

Kirk was relieved that Picard didn't ask why Christine, and not he, had made the run to Beverly. "Do you think he might have left the chamber?" Kirk asked.

"There's one way to find out."

Kirk knew what Picard had in mind. Another run across the chamber to draw a sniper's fire. But then the loudest blast yet detonated on the level three stories directly overhead. Tiles and chunks of extruded silicon rained down from the ceiling. Overhead pipes burst and water sprayed in one corner, gushing forth and splashing like a waterfall.

Kirk checked on Barc. The Tellarite was unmoving in the center of the chamber floor, but he hadn't been hit by any debris.

A new voice came from Kirk's comm badge. "Spock here. If the explosions we have been experiencing are following the pattern I have discerned, then the next sequence will begin on the level directly above us. And the sequence after that, on this level."

"Do you have a suggestion, Mr. Spock?" Picard asked.

"To proceed with dispatch, Captain Picard."

Kirk laughed silently. If Spock wasn't careful he might become a comedian in his old age.

Then Kirk's laughter froze as he saw Christine stumble out from beneath the third tank, a dark figure holding a disruptor to her head. When the figure spoke, Kirk's heart froze as well.

"Kirk! The rest of you! Reveal yourselves or the commander loses her head!"

Kirk didn't stop to think. He was on his feet at once, striding forward, ready to use the weapon in his hand, ready to use his hands alone if he had to, to rip out Srell's throat.

"That's close enough, Kirk. Drop the phaser."

Christine gasped as the young Vulcan jammed the disruptor against the base of her skull.

Kirk threw the phaser rifle away as if it were a spear. It clattered noisily among the debris that had fallen from the ceiling.

"Where is the logic in betrayal?" Kirk demanded.

"Spock!" Srell shouted to the chamber's ceiling. "I need your counsel!"

No reply.

"You're too exposed where you are," Kirk said, taunting Srell. "There are at least three other weapons pointing at you right now. Give up and you'll live."

Srell was unimpressed by the threat. "You're not from this time. Otherwise, you would recognize what's behind me."

Kirk saw that Srell stood close to a display panel. "So?"

"We are not dealing with the modified phaser that led you to believe I had been killed in spacedock. If a misplaced phaser bolt hits that panel, the tank explodes." Srell shouted again. *"Spock!* All you others, come forth now or I shall kill the commander *and* Kirk."

"Save your breath," Kirk said. "They're not coming out." He took two more steps toward Srell. They were only three meters apart. "This is a war. Soldiers die."

"Without knowing the symmetry of all things, you cannot understand the meaning of death," Srell said. He tightened his hand on the disruptor. "But I shall be your teacher."

Time stopped for Kirk. This time he had no doubt.

Srell was going to fire.

Christine was going to die.

He started forward, knowing he could never reach her in time.

And then, like some dark avenging angel, Spock dropped from the sky, from the catwalk on the tank above them, and landed on Srell as Srell's weapon discharged.

As if in a low-gravity ballet, Christine spun away from Srell's grip and the two Vulcans tumbled to the floor.

A halo of disruptor energy shimmered endlessly through Christine's hair, setting it ablaze.

Then time snapped back into place. Kirk threw himself at her and caught her in his arms as they both fell to the floor.

He gasped as he felt a sharp crack in his ribs, but his outstretched arms broke her fall.

He pulled himself up, gathering her close in his arms.

He couldn't speak as he felt how limp she was.

He touched her face, so young, still warm. Turned her head to see the ruin of scorched hair and charred skin that blackened her scalp.

But just a small part of her scalp.

Kirk spoke her name.

Touched her neck.

Felt a pulse.

Christine opened her eyes.

Smiled at him despite the pain he knew she felt.

". . . not bad for a hundred and forty . . ." she rasped.

He squeezed her hand, unable to speak. Then M'Benga was beside Kirk, pushing him away. A glittering medical instrument already whirring in her hand.

"She'll be okay," the doctor said. "Just give me room."

Kirk stumbled to his feet, holding his arm around his chest where his rib had cracked. Then he saw Spock and Srell locked in combat on the floor.

Spock lay on his back. Srell held him down, squeezing Spock's neck with all the ferocity of youth.

Kirk saw Picard running forward, aiming his rifle, ready to take his shot.

But this wasn't Picard's fight.

Spock was in danger. And that meant Srell belonged to Kirk.

Kirk charged forward and kicked at the youth's head as hard as he could.

The violent impact threw Srell from Spock. The young Vulcan's body hit the floor, rolled, then lay still.

Picard skidded to a stop. "It's under control," Kirk said, each breath a victory over the stabbing pain that lanced his side. "Beverly needs you."

Picard ran on to the *Enterprise's* doctor. She was sitting on the floor under the tank, cradling her head, still shaken by the disruptor blast she had taken.

Kirk held out his hand to help Spock to his feet.

Spock rose and looked at him. Eyes blank.

"Spock, it's all right."

But Spock shoved Kirk aside and went to Srell, lifting him one-handed by his neck. Then Kirk watched in disbelief as Spock struck the youth, keeping him upright by clutching the front of his tunic, not letting him fall.

"Spock, no!" Kirk shouted. But then he coughed weakly as his cracked rib robbed him of breath.

Spock's closed fist struck Srell again. One of Srell's eyes was closed, dripping with green blood.

Kirk caught Spock's fist to stop another blow.

"Think what you're doing, Spock."

Spock glared wildly at Kirk, breathing through his mouth in spasmodic gasps. "This is what I *feel,"* he raged.

"It's Bendii! Picard told me! You've been poisoned. Infected. This isn't you!"

Spock spoke through clenched teeth. "Dr. Crusher has treated me. Perhaps Bendii affected me in the past. But not now." He stared at Srell with murderous intent. "Now I am in perfect control."

He wrenched his fist from Kirk's grip.

Then a gigantic explosion burst through the far wall of the

chamber at the second-story level, causing a hailstorm of pulverized tile and shards of stone. Fire crackled along two exposed power conduits, sending sprays of sparks to hiss in the spreading water released from the already broken pipes. The main lighting flared, then dimmed. Low vapor began to form against the floor.

Spock lost his balance in the concussion of a second blast, releasing Srell.

The youth fell heavily to the floor, tried to push himself up. Could barely move.

"Get up!" Spock spit at him. He swayed on his feet, one arm half-raised as if ready to strike again. Both Vulcans were near total collapse. Srell, physical. Spock, emotional.

Srell stared up at Spock with contempt. "Kill me here. Finish your assignment."

Spock dropped to his knees, looked at Srell. The clipped style of Vulcan speech returned to him. "Explain."

Srell sneered at him, all pretense at control lost in the primal emotions of their conflict. "You have known all along." He coughed up green blood, spit out a clot of it on the chamber floor. "You were manipulated, Spock. Just as you said on Babel."

"Why?"

Srell raised a shaking hand to his swollen face. "It was so logical. The lesson had to be taught. The ecology is weak. The systems too complex." Srell stopped to taste the blood on his cracked lip. "Our projections showed the Federation would collapse on its own in less than thirty years, beyond the power of anyone to stop. The virogen was a necessity."

Spock's voice was deep, congested. "But the Federation is collapsing now, precisely because of the virogen."

"Because today, it *can* recover on its own. But thirty years from now . . ." Srell's gaze was locked on Spock. "The fall of a galactic civilization, Spock. Can you imagine the waste?

The horror?" Srell turned his head toward Kirk. "That is the death you must understand! Billions! Trillions! On your hands!"

Kirk stood over Srell. "How can the Federation recover?" His voice was commanding, compelling.

"We're . . . we're making an antivirogen here."

Kirk widened his eyes in shock. "You released the virogen *without* having a cure?"

Srell opened and closed his mouth like a drowning fish. "We *had* a cure. But . . . the virogen mutated. Our cure doesn't work. That's why we needed the alta mist. A new mode of delivery." Srell looked up at them both, madness growing in his eyes. "It is the symmetry of all things. . . ."

Kirk felt near to collapse himself. The Symmetrists had sought to teach the Federation a lesson about the complexity of the environment, without first understanding that lesson themselves.

"Why manipulate *me?*" Spock asked, seeking understanding of his own.

Srell doubled up with a violent cough. Green blood bubbled at the corner of his lip. Kirk looked over to see M'Benga still treating Christine. Picard was still assisting Beverly. Medical attention for Srell would have to wait.

"You were to test us, Spock. Your fine mind put to our use, to find the weak parts of our plan. And I was to follow beside you on your investigation. The dutiful student. Correcting any errors that you found. Obscuring any clues that others might discover. As long as we could be sure you would not report what you found to anyone but me, the plan was perfect. Even to the perfection of you seeing me die so I would never be suspected of betrayal."

"Not logical," Spock said wearily. "Eventually, I would have to tell someone else."

Srell shook his head. Blood dripped from his mouth to the

floor. "Mendrossen's confession. The holoprojector the Klingon brought you. The first time you touched the switch to play it."

"Bendii," Kirk said. *"That's* how you infected him."

Srell stared up at Kirk with almost an expression of admiration. "Not exactly Bendii, Kirk, but a poison so close that no doctor would suspect the difference."

"Your plan was flawed from the beginning," Spock said.

"My plan was perfect. It worked on Tarok. It worked on Sarek. It—"

Too late, Srell stopped, as if just realizing what he had said.

Spock lurched forward, raised a fumbling hand for Srell's tunic. *"Explain."*

Srell tried to crawl away but couldn't escape Spock's grip. "Sarek knew the Federation was doomed," he gasped. "More than a century ago. His work gave our cause the scientific basis we needed to proceed here."

"Here?" Kirk asked. "On Tarsus Four?"

"The lesson must be taught," Srell whispered. "If anything is to survive, an example must be made. But Sarek denied the logic of the fate that awaits us. He knew the time had come for the Federation to experience its future while steps could still be taken to avoid collapse. But he wanted to stop us."

"What did you do?" Spock demanded.

"I was a soldier in a cause!" Srell muttered. "There were things to be done. Terrible things!"

Spock raised trembling hands to reach for Srell. *"What did you do to my father?!"*

"I killed him!" Srell said. *"For the good of the many—Sarek had to die!"*

Spock covered his mouth with his hand, stifling the terrible sob that tore through him.

But something other than anguish for his friend tore through Kirk. Long-buried memories broke free. Finally unleashed.

There were things to be done. Terrible things . . .

For the good of the many . . .

Sarek . . .

Here, on Tarsus IV . . .

Kirk lifted Srell to his feet. He grabbed Srell's hand, spread his fingers, thrust them against the *katra* points of his own face.

"Show me," Kirk said. "Show me, damn you!"

And in fear, in terror, and, at last, in relief, Srell revealed his final secret, and opened his mind to James T. Kirk.

THIRTY-NINE

At first in Srell's mind, there was pain.

But Kirk knew pain. The nanites had brought him that.

Then there was Srell's fear of death.

But Kirk had died. There were no mysteries there.

Confusion came next, terrifying for a Vulcan like Srell for whom logic and order were the cornerstones of life, built on the sand of the universe's indifference.

But confusion was a necessary part of being human, and Kirk knew it well. He willingly accepted all of Srell's youthful failings, his pain and fear, because he had felt them all before.

What Kirk sought in Srell's immature mind was unexpected wisdom.

Brought there by the touch of other minds.

Older minds.

With the disciplines he had learned from Hugh and his clan of reclaimed Borg, with the secrets culled from a thousand assimilated worlds, Kirk controlled the meld. It was not his power that drove it, for that ability belonged only to Vulcans. But it was Kirk's will that harnessed Srell's talent and forced it to his own purpose.

Kirk moved through Srell's thoughts like a whirlwind.

He saw Stonn and T'Pring, knew they were secret conspirators with Srell. He saw a dozen other minds he did not stop to identify. For he only sought one.

And he found it.

Sarek.

My mind to your mind, *Kirk told Srell, peeling back the layers of the youth's experience to reveal that which Kirk sought.*

And then Kirk touched Sarek's mind again. But not for the second time.

For the third.

Because the second time had been in San Francisco. And the first had been here. On Tarsus IV. When Kirk had escaped from Kodos only because Sarek had saved him.

Kirk saw it all, felt it all, knew it all—every memory that Sarek had taken from him that night was now returned. And Sarek's memories came with them.

Kirk saw how Sarek had calculated the effects of disruption in the galactic food supply.

Kirk saw how others had taken Sarek's scenarios for destruction and had chosen to demonstrate them.

Understanding the horror of what he had wrought by accident, Sarek had risked his life and his career to brave the Neutral Zone and lead the relief forces here. He had saved thirteen-year-old Jimmy Kirk on the night he had arrived. And to insure the boy's safety, he had entered his mind to bring forgetfulness.

How like my son. . . .

The echo of that thought was here as well, poignant, bittersweet, brimming with emotion that Sarek could never express.

That night on Tarsus IV, Sarek had touched Kirk's mind as a father to a son, and had opened the boy's mind to the call of the stars. And Kirk in turn had touched Sarek's mind, sharing with him his youth, his wonder, his dreams for the future, all the possibilities that Sarek would never touch and know in his own son.

Filled with understanding, slowly Kirk withdrew from the mind of Srell, taking all that was there of Sarek and that night.

He heard Kodos's threats again in the swirling snow. He knew now why he had always felt that he would die alone—because that is what Kodos had told him. He knew now why he had always been pursued by the dark shadow through his dreams—because that was how Kodos had chased him.

Now, closer to the end of his life, Kirk had reached back to its beginning, and at last seen and understood how each part fit into the next in turn, and how the beginning had defined what would be the end.

That was why it had always been Sarek in his dreams.

That was why he knew his duty now.

The duty every Vulcan son had shared since before the Reformation.

Avenge me, *the voice of Sarek cried.*

And so Kirk prepared to be what he had always known he must become.

His father's son.

Avenger.

FORTY

Kirk tore Srell's hand from his face, the knowledge of what he must do burning in his mind, and in his blood.

Another explosion tore apart the far wall. Debris thudded against the first tank, making its metal groan. Sparks flew, flames erupted, vapors swirled above pooling water.

But nothing could distract Kirk, or change him from his course.

Srell scrambled back from his pursuer, slipping on the wet floor. He stared up at Kirk, his eyes reflecting the chilling knowledge that he had no secrets from him.

Behind Kirk, Spock still knelt, trapped by the onslaught of emotions he had denied too long, not knowing how to escape them.

Picard moved quickly over to Kirk and Spock, Beverly at his side. "We have to leave. The next explosions will take out this entire level."

Kirk kept his eyes on Srell. "We need a sample from tank five," he said. He had seen the purpose of this installation in Srell's mind. "It has the alta mist they've engineered to carry the antivirogen."

Picard's face lit up. "Then they do have a cure?"

"Get the sample," Kirk said. Explanations could wait. There was little time left. Picard and Beverly ran for tank five.

M'Benga and Barc half-dragged Christine toward Kirk, Spock, and Srell, through the billowing white vapor that covered the floor. The commander of the *Tobias* was dazed, but alive and on her feet. Barc listed, as if Christine were supporting the Tellarite as much as he was supporting her.

Kirk took M'Benga's phaser before she could think to stop him.

Its controls were simple.

He set it to kill.

Picard and Beverly returned on the run. Picard held a small pressure cylinder from Beverly's medical kit. "We have it," he said.

From somewhere on this same level, a new blast made the air snap past them like a sonic boom. When the echo died, Kirk was aware of Picard's intense gaze, directed at the phaser he held.

"Kirk, whatever this man's crimes, we will need him for questioning."

"No," Kirk said.

"You're a Starfleet officer!"

"Not anymore."

"You have a duty to the Federation!"

But Kirk ignored him. "I've done my duty. More than enough."

In a lightning move, Picard grabbed Beverly's phaser from her side and swung it up to Kirk's head—

—just as Kirk swung his phaser to Picard.

They froze there, eyes locked, weapons held only centimeters from each other's neck, so close even a stun blast would kill, each only a finger twitch from oblivion.

No one else in that chamber dared move. Not even as the explosions continued, coming closer, growing louder.

"I will not allow you to kill that man," Picard said through clenched teeth.

Kirk's answer was equally to the point. "Then logic dictates that I kill you first."

Sweat glistened from each man's brow. The phasers they held kept their aim with unshaking precision.

"Listen to the words you're using," Picard pleaded. "You've shared another's mind. Someone else's thoughts are influencing you."

"Put down the phaser, Jean-Luc."

"You first."

Seconds passed, with neither man so much as breathing.

Then slowly, and deliberately, Kirk moved his phaser from Picard to Srell. "Then kill me," he said. "If you can."

Kirk waited then, his weapon locked on Srell. Until he heard, as he knew he would, the slow escape of breath from Picard. The captain of the *Enterprise* was an honorable man. He couldn't kill Kirk. "Jim, please . . ." Picard said. But that was all the protest he could make.

Kirk leveled his phaser at Srell. Somehow he knew the words he must say in an ancient Vulcan tongue he had never studied, or even heard of. *"Terr'tra stol nu, kRen jhal."*

. . . *and so I avenge my father's death* . . .

But Srell threw back his head, defiant. "You forget, Kirk—even as you looked into my mind, I looked into yours."

Kirk's phaser wavered as his hand trembled.

"Keep running, boy," the young Vulcan said mockingly, echoing Sarek's words to thirteen-year-old Jimmy Kirk. "Run as you've always run. From your past. From your failures. From yourself."

Another explosion, nearer, closer, louder, slammed into the chamber. But Kirk didn't flinch. It was as if he drew strength from its fury.

Because, however harsh they were, however damning, he heard the truth in Srell's words.

He *had* spent his life running. From his past. But not from failures. He had run from what he knew lurked deep within him, that hidden part that drove him to always find another path, a different solution, a way to change the rules.

Because at the heart of every confrontation he had faced, he had known there was always one simple answer: to release the beast that lay in the heart of every human and let it lash out and destroy all that was wrong.

Destruction and chaos whirled around Kirk and for the first time in his life, Kirk embraced it.

Let this base be blown to dust. Let the Federation fall. Let all the stars of all the galaxies be thrown into oblivion.

Nothing else mattered except this time and this place. This intersection of all the events of his life when he at last stopped running.

Kirk leveled his weapon at Srell and the Vulcan became for him the focus of all that was evil in his life, in his universe.

"Look into my mind," Kirk challenged him. "Tell me what you see *now.*"

Completely unbidden, a wave of primal anticipation erupted in Kirk as he sensed the first weakness exposed in the youth's contemptuous Vulcan armor of superiority.

Whatever secrets Srell had seen in Kirk's mind, he was at last beginning to understand them, even as Kirk did. And Kirk could see that Srell at last recognized what he had freed.

The Vulcan raised his hands uncertainly. ". . . no . . ." he whispered.

But his final word was lost to the noise of the base's destruction. Lost to the raw fury of Kirk's unrestrained emotions.

Kirk thrust out the phaser before him as if it were a thunderbolt to be hurled from the heavens.

He shouted a cry that came from a place so deep within that it seemed to stop time.

And in that infinite instant Kirk at last threw off the final vestiges of his outer shell and became what he had struggled all his life to hold in check.

Pure passion.

Srell stumbled back, his eyes filled with the terror of total understanding of what was to happen next.

And it did.

Kirk fired.

And at the same instant the chamber reverberated with a sequence of escalating explosions that caused the closest tank to blossom like a dying flower, releasing a torrent of gelatinous growth medium in a solid wave that engulfed Srell even as the phaser's beam lanced toward him.

He vanished in the mist the phaser blasted from the thick swirling liquid, gone forever.

Kirk breathed deeply as time resumed for him. Whether he had killed Srell, or the liquid had consumed him, he might never know. But his intention had been clear. And that unexpected knowledge was enough.

Kirk let the phaser slip from his hand, to fall into the ankle-deep sludge of the growth medium that flowed across the floor, hidden by the billows of white vapor.

From somewhere far off, he heard Picard call for the *Enterprise.* This time, there was no answering hiss of a jamming device. Riker responded.

Then Picard's stern voice eclipsed the dying convulsions of the chamber and the Symmetrists' dreams.

"Six to beam up," he said.

Swept up by the ship they had all served, Kirk and his

fellows escaped destruction, just as the chamber blew apart around them.

But Kirk was not concerned.

He felt . . . clean, free of pain and doubt.

Sarek's death had been avenged.

As had Kirk's life of denial.

Even in the midst of destruction, Kirk was, at last, at peace.

FORTY-ONE

Kirk closed his eyes, and saw the flames of Tarsus IV.

Cleansing. Purifying. Costly.

The battle to take control of the Symmetrists' base had been brutal. Fourteen of the *Enterprise*'s crew had been killed, along with fifty-two Symmetrists, half of them Vulcan. Another eight crew members were in sickbay, in intensive care. Only twelve Symmetrists had been captured, all so badly wounded that they had not been able to kill themselves. They were being treated in triage areas set up in the shuttlebay, under constant guard.

Even now, a full day after the battle, the collapsed administration buildings in the main city still burned. Kirk had seen the conflagration only from orbit on the *Enterprise*'s main screen, but he could picture how those flames rose into the night, illuminating the crumbling monument that had been the Federation's great seal. In that image, he saw the future.

Federation's end.

"I've finished my preliminary report to Starfleet," Picard said.

Kirk opened his eyes. He had been sitting at a workstation Beverly Crusher had set up for him in an alcove off sickbay.

Before him, he had laid out all the herbs and leaves Hugh's people had given him when he had left their world. La Forge's repair crew had recovered the botanicals from his quarters on the *Tobias,* and he catalogued them, recording what he knew of each, to be sure his knowledge wasn't lost. Though he knew that all anyone was interested in were the *trannin* leaves that had saved Teilani and the children of Chal.

Picard stood in the alcove entrance, still waiting for Kirk's reply. Behind him, at least twenty medical personnel worked at consoles and lab tables. A few were from the *Enterprise.* But most were specialists who had come in the emergency flotilla launched from Starbase 515. More medical vessels were arriving every hour as word of what had happened here spread through the stars.

"It will be a useful addendum to the reports we've received from Vulcan. Stonn and T'Pring have been arrested. They have confessed to the Symmetrists' complicity in Sarek's murder, as well as Tarok's. And they have named other members of the movement. Apparently, now that their plan has failed, they are eager to explain the . . . logic of their beliefs."

Picard held Kirk's gaze for a moment, as if deciding how he should continue. "My report states that Srell died when the tank burst," Picard said.

"That's not what killed him. I did."

"You can't know that for certain. The tank burst. Srell's body was swept away intact."

"It doesn't matter," Kirk said. "I fired the phaser. I wanted him to die."

Picard glanced over his shoulder, as if to check that no one in the work area behind him could hear what he said. He stepped into Kirk's alcove.

"I've read your biographies, Jim. I've worked with you. On Veridian Three. The Borg homeworld. Now Tarsus Four. And everything I've learned about you tells me that if what you say happened *is* true, then it was an aberration. A shockwave from an explosion made you reflexively press the firing stud. Or you weren't aware that the weapon was set to kill."

Picard was grasping at straws. Kirk knew it. He could see that Picard knew it as well.

"People change, Jean-Luc."

"Rarely so profoundly."

Kirk rested an elbow on the work surface, rubbed his face with his hand. How could a life like his be explained in a handful of words? "You're right. I take it back."

Picard looked intrigued by that admission.

"People don't change." He remembered what Kodos had told him, alone on the *Enterprise.* His *Enterprise.* "But after enough time has passed. After they've seen enough of the atrocities that make up our civilization, . . . they become tired, Jean-Luc. Impatient. And as I've grown older, I've found that . . . I no longer want to wait for the things that are important in life."

"Why would that young man's death have been important to you? For *honor?"*

"For vengeance," Kirk said, though he could see that Picard didn't understand the emotional wellsprings from which that answer had come. At least, not yet.

"Some people," Picard said, "would argue that a civilized society has no place for vengeance."

"And while those people argue, civilizations fall. I don't have the patience for arguing anymore. Time is the ultimate nonrenewable resource, and we are rapidly running out of it."

Kirk could see that Picard wanted to question him further, but Spock stepped up behind him, disturbing the moment.

Like Kirk, Spock had returned to his civilian garb, setting aside his ambassadorial robes. Instead, he wore an unadorned black tunic. One sleeve had been rolled up to allow for the small inducer pump on his forearm, through which his blood was continually filtered.

Beverly Crusher had finally identified the contact poison the Symmetrists had used to mimic Bendii Syndrome. It would take a month of treatment to cleanse Spock's system of it, but the total length of his exposure had been limited, and Beverly expected a full recovery. Though Kirk knew the scars of Spock's emotional outbursts, caused by the poison that had robbed him of his self-control, would take far more than a month to heal.

"Excuse me, Captain," Spock said to Picard. Then he looked at Kirk. "Dr. M'Benga is ready for you, Jim."

Kirk stood up, and smoothed the Vulcan trader's clothes he once again wore. He felt their simple design was preferable to the new uniform he had worn on the *Tobias*. And all the other old uniforms he had worn in the past, as well.

"Do you think this will be it?" Picard asked as Kirk stepped past him.

But Kirk had no answer. Only time would tell.

FORTY-TWO

Kirk, Spock, and Picard went to a lab off the main sickbay. All the parts of the puzzle were laid out on the large worktable at its center: a pressurized container of alta mist, whose importance had been discovered only by Picard's dogged pursuit of the mysterious destruction of the *Bennett;* a tray of replicated *trannin* leaves brought to Starfleet's attention only by Kirk's unexpected return; and a beaker of pure virogen culture obtained from Tarsus IV, the planet Kirk had identified as the Symmetrists' base, a base only Picard's *Enterprise* could have subdued.

It wasn't symmetry that had brought all these elements to this one place and time, Kirk knew. It was *tapestry,* the subtle interweaving of individual threads to create a picture greater than the whole.

Spock brought the tray of *trannin* leaves to Kirk. The Vulcan was the puzzle's final piece. For if not for Spock's pursuit of his father's murderer, then Kirk and Picard might never have been brought together.

"All right, everyone," Dr. M'Benga said to Beverly Crusher and the five other Starfleet doctors and technicians in the lab. "Watch carefully."

Feeling just a bit self-conscious at having to perform such a modest task, Kirk picked up the dried leaves and began to fold them in his fingers, feeling them crack, then crumble, exactly as Miko had taught him on the world whose sun had been a galactic core.

He let the fine leaf fragments fall like coarse powder onto a clean patch of filter mesh. After he had created a mound about three centimeters across, he stopped.

"See," M'Benga said. "That's the consistency we need. We have to crack it along the leaf veins to expose the resin compound without contaminating it with stomatic residue."

Kirk stepped back from the lab table to let the experts go to work with the sample he'd prepared. In principle, he knew what M'Benga and Beverly and all of Starfleet Medical were now working toward. The *trannin* compound could stop the virogen's reproduction, but it was useful only in animals. Alta mist was fine enough to circulate through a planet's entire biosphere, drawing nourishment only from the air, thus not interfering with existing food chains.

The medical team believed that if they could somehow insert the *trannin* compound into the alta-mist cells, so the cells would generate the compound and spread it as they reproduced, then Starfleet would have an antivirogen that could move through plant populations as quickly as the virogen itself, cleansing whole worlds just as the inducer pump cleansed Spock's blood of poison.

But thus far, no matter how precisely Kirk had prepared the leaves, no matter how rigorously the technicians had attempted to artificially re-create the compound's molecular structure at a smaller scale, the two critical components Kirk and Picard had discovered—the *trannin* leaves and the alta mist—had not yet joined together.

And with each day of failure, more systems fell prey to the destabilizing virogen contagion and the Federation moved another step closer to total collapse.

Kirk watched as a technician agitated a sample tube in which the *trannin* and the alta mist had been mixed. Beverly ran her tricorder over the tube. Shook her head. Still no progress.

"What exactly is the problem?" Kirk finally asked. How difficult could it be to mix two biological substances that should have a natural affinity? Especially for twenty-fourth-century science?

"We have to establish a precise degree of permeability for the membrane of the alta-mist cells," M'Benga said. "If we leave the cell walls too rigid, the *trannin* compound can't penetrate them. If we leave the walls too permeable, then the *trannin* gets in, but the cell's chloroplasts and nucleii can migrate out."

"The frustrating aspect of it," Beverly added, "is that the possible solutions to the problem are almost infinite. We just can't work fast enough to try all the different variations in a reasonable time."

M'Benga suddenly looked over at her colleague. "Dr. Crusher, maybe there's a way we can automate the process. Do you have an EMH?"

Beverly scowled. "Yes," she said, and to Kirk it sounded as if she were confessing to a particularly embarrassing crime. "I suppose that as long as I'm not letting it work on my patients, I can't really complain." She sighed. "Computer, run the EMH."

There was a flash of light and a holographic doctor took form beside Kirk. It looked exactly like the one he had seen on the *Tobias*. "Please state the nature of your medical emergency," the hologram said, as if even a technological illusion had more important matters to attend to.

Beverly and M'Benga briefed the nameless doctor on the tasks they wanted him to perform: the rapid trial-and-error mixing of different alta mist and *trannin* combinations.

"You consider that a medical emergency?" the doctor

asked. The irritation in his voice made it clear that his program certainly didn't recognize it as such. Not for the first time, Kirk wondered whether personality chose profession, or if it were the other way around.

"The fate of the Federation may rest in the successful completion of these experiments," M'Benga explained.

"Well," the doctor said reluctantly, "if you put it that way." Then he began rearranging the equipment on the lab table in order, he said, to make his work more efficient.

Kirk glanced over at Spock. Much of the twenty-fourth century wasn't so very different from what he was used to. But some of it was simply peculiar. "So where does that thing get its personality?" Kirk asked. "What there is of it, I mean."

"I believe it is a simulation based on its original programmer, augmented by a database of all the different medical experts whose specialized knowledge and experience were combined to produce—"

The hologram suddenly looked across the lab table at Kirk and Spock. "Do you two mind?" he said. "I'm taking critical measurements and your voices are causing minute vibrations."

Kirk gave Spock a bemused look. "Did a computer just tell us to shut up?"

"I'm a doctor, not a computer," the hologram muttered.

Kirk thought about that response for a moment, then walked around the table to Beverly, ignoring the hologram's sharp look of annoyance.

Kirk whispered a question into Beverly's ear. She nodded in agreement, though not understanding, then took Kirk to a medical display screen where she called up a list of all the medical personnel who had been modeled as expert systems and combined to create the EMH.

At the display screen, Kirk scrolled through the list until he found the one name he knew had to be there.

He typed in a command to isolate a single visual and

personality subsystem from the EMH program, then turned to watch in satisfaction as the image of the holographic doctor rippled. In moments, the prickly bald doctor in the black and blue uniform transformed into a prickly white-haired doctor in an old-fashioned wine-colored uniform . . .

Medical expert Leonard H. McCoy. Age seventy.

"Well, what the blazes are all you people just standing around for?" the simulated McCoy groused. "We've got a galaxy to save. As usual."

Kirk walked back to Spock with a grin as McCoy barked orders to doctors and technicians alike. M'Benga was assigned to clean sample tubes. Beverly measured *trannin* samples. McCoy completely rearranged the lab-table equipment into an ungainly, though apparently even more efficient configuration. "I'm a doctor, not an interior designer," he complained.

Kirk saw the look of affectionate amusement in Spock's eyes, and the sadness. Though the Bendii poison was being leached from his body, its emotional effects were obviously still present.

"Now that's what I call a simulation," Kirk said.

Spock agreed. "I think I would like to help it."

"For old time's sake?" Kirk said.

Spock tilted his head to one side, as if not comprehending the question. "To save the galaxy from collapse," he said earnestly.

Kirk watched with anticipation as the simulated McCoy looked up to see Spock. For a moment, the program paused, as if it had just received input which it could not categorize.

"Do I know you?" the program asked.

In an act of pure illogic, Spock said, "Yes."

"Well, then, haul your pointy ears over to the sterilization unit and set up a sterile field around the alta mist. You amateurs have so many contaminants mixing into these samples, it's no wonder you can't get the same answer twice."

Eventually, the simulated McCoy got around to ordering Kirk to keep the table wiped down. And within the hour, instead of facing an infinite number of possible mixing combinations, McCoy had narrowed the possibilities to a limited range. Instead of months of work, M'Benga said they were now within days of a solution. If the Federation could last that long.

By the time another hour had passed, a medical debate had broken out. Spock, Beverly, and the simulated McCoy were arguing about which strategy to follow for the next round of tests. M'Benga had removed herself from the discussion—it was outside her area of expertise. But she reminded everyone that because of the equipment configuration that would be needed, choosing the wrong strategy could delay the project by an additional day.

"Why are you people so dead set against harming the alta mist organism? That's what's holding you back," McCoy said. "I say, harm the beast, but then give it the tools it needs to repair itself *after* the *trannin* has been absorbed."

Spock rose to the challenge. "The alta mist is a one-celled plant, Doctor. It wouldn't know what to do with 'tools.'"

"Now don't get smart with me, you green-blooded hobgoblin. Stop trying to force everything in such neat compartments."

"It is called logic."

"Well, I call it a waste of time. Life has a logic of its own, and I suggest we use it."

Kirk was ready to wade in and break up the argument that was paralyzing the medical team. But it was a medical matter, and Beverly Crusher assumed the role of mediator before he could act.

"Dr. McCoy," she began. "Could you please explain your approach? What do you want to do here?"

The hologram rolled his eyes in exasperation. "I thought you'd never ask. I simply want to exploit the existing signal pathways for general defense and tissue repair in the alta mist cells," he explained, as if it were the most obvious thing in the universe. "We'll use elicitors: oligogalacturonide fragments of pectin polysaccharides; the *18mer* peptide, systemin; *and* fatty acid derivatives including jasmonic acid. The cells will repair themselves like that!" The hologram snapped its simulated fingers.

"That's it, do it the hard way," McCoy said.

Kirk blinked. The holographic simulation had just spoken, but its mouth hadn't moved.

"If you want to keep the wound repair process under control in plants, then forget all that fancy gene expression crap and stick to salicylic acid. Plain old aspirin."

Kirk suddenly realized that though the holographic McCoy was in front of him, the familiar gruff voice was coming from behind. Kirk decided it must be an equipment failure. But then he noticed everyone else in the lab looking behind him, even the holographic McCoy.

Kirk turned—

—to see Admiral Leonard H. McCoy, age 146, gaping right back at Kirk with as stunned an expression of surprise as Kirk knew was on his own face.

Starfleet's greatest doctor was frail, and moved with the aid of exoskeleton braces on his legs and the support of Data's arm. But there was no mistaking the brightness in his eyes, and the quickness of his smile.

"Hell. I thought you were dead, Jim."

"I thought you'd run off with some dancing girls from Wrigley's."

McCoy winked. "These days, they can run faster than I can."

With deference and great care, Data escorted McCoy into the lab, where the medical personnel stared at a legend in the flesh.

Then Kirk saw Data react to the presence of the holographic McCoy across the room. The android smiled delightedly at Kirk. "Given the present conditions," Data said, "I think we might say that I have on my arm the *real* McCoy."

McCoy peered up at Data as he pulled his arm away. "Since when did you get a sense of humor?"

"Two years, two months, six days, eight hours, three—"

"Good Lord," McCoy muttered. "And I thought Spock was bad."

McCoy made his way to the lab table on his own, his exoskeleton braces humming as his legs moved with slow, deliberate steps.

He steadied himself against the table, then looked around at everyone who was looking at him.

"Well, what do you think this is? A picnic? I'm a doctor, not a sideshow. Someone mix up an aspirin solution, get me a chair—"

The holographic McCoy stepped forward. "In my opinion, the proper strategy is to *elicit* cell-repair functions, not degrade them."

"And somebody shut that damn thing off," McCoy snapped.

Two technicians ran toward the medical control panel and an instant later the EMH faded from view.

McCoy flashed a triumphant smile at Kirk. "By God, it's good to be old." Then he turned to the rest of the workers. "Well, don't just stand there—let's get this show on the road."

They did.

Two hours later, McCoy had the cure.

FORTY-THREE

In a violent and uncaring universe of chaos and uncertainty, there were still some absolutes that were never meant to change, and never would.

It was with that thought that Kirk stood with Spock and McCoy on the bridge of the *Starship Enterprise*. For just one perfect moment, he heard Teilani's words, that time had no dominion.

But from bittersweet experience, Kirk knew that moments had a way of passing, and that this new *Enterprise* belonged to a different crew: Picard in the center chair, Riker and Troi to either side of their captain. Data at ops, La Forge at engineering, and Beverly Crusher at the main science station.

Kirk gazed approvingly at the new team. All at their posts, so intent on their mission.

As he had finally come to know from all his voyages, it had always been the crew who had mattered most, and in this new team he saw the best of his own.

But then he looked to the main screen, and wondered if even they would be worthy of the challenges that lay ahead.

Challenges not just for them, for Starfleet, and the Federation. But for all the people of the galaxy: Earthling, Vulcan, and Klingon alike, humanity in all its colors, shapes, and chemistries.

"Coming up on terminator and planetary dawn," Data said.

Kirk looked to his friends. Spock stood with his hands behind his back, his expression at peace, hiding the inner turmoil that Kirk knew still ravaged him. McCoy rested his hands on the belt of his exoskeleton support, thoughtfully chewing his bottom lip.

A wash of golden light filled the bridge as the sudden flash of the Tarsus sun lit the thin shell of its fourth planet's atmosphere. An arc of that dying world slowly grew, glowing in the early dawn.

"Beginning sensor sweep," Beverly announced.

No one spoke. Kirk didn't have to be a Betazoid to sense the tension on the bridge.

Three days ago, after the *Enterprise* had replicated enough of McCoy's antivirogen to fill the auxiliary propellant tanks of five terraforming runabouts, the first full-scale assault on the Symmetrists' plan had begun.

For twenty hours, the runabouts had circled Tarsus IV, streaking through its stratosphere, releasing their cargo as a fine mist.

McCoy had said the effect would be noticeable within fifty hours after exposure.

If the antivirogen worked.

On the screen, a wedge of sunlight grew across the planet's surface as the *Enterprise* flew through her orbit. But the world that light illuminated was still black and brown and dying.

Then Kirk peered more closely at the screen. He pointed at the lower left corner. "Spock . . . do you see that?"

"Dr. Crusher," Spock said, "scan the southeast quadrant of the landmass directly below us at full resolution, if you would."

"Full resolution," Beverly confirmed.

The image on the viewscreen expanded until Kirk could see the shadows that individual clouds cast on the ground.

Green clouds.

"There!" Kirk said.

"By the mountain range!" McCoy directed.

Beverly's voice rang through the bridge. "Sensors detect *chlorophyll!* It's pure, uncontaminated alta mist! The antivirogen is working!"

As one, the bridge crew stood up from their stations and turned to McCoy. Their applause thundered.

"I'm getting returns from all over the southern continent," Beverly said, ecstatic.

McCoy grinned proudly at Spock. "Hear that? They're applauding *me* for a change."

"Doctor," Spock replied, "I am pleased that you think so."

Kirk cupped a hand to his ear. "Is someone applauding?"

McCoy's grin faded as he looked back to the screen. "I liked you both better when you were dead."

As the crew returned to their duties with elation, Picard joined the *Enterprise*'s honored guests at the side of the bridge. He smiled broadly as he spoke.

"Dr. McCoy, this is indeed a monumental achievement. I've instructed Lieutenant Rolk to begin broadcasting the antivirogen's complete replicator code on all subspace frequencies, Starfleet and civilian. Even with the current communications difficulties, within two weeks every affected system in the Federation will be able to begin combating the virogen."

But Kirk shared none of Picard's optimism, and for good reason. He drew Picard aside. "You mean, every system that's maintained an operational subspace communications system," Kirk said. "You saw what Tarsus Four was like. The city was torn apart before the evacuation was completed. How many other worlds are there like this one?"

Picard dropped his smile. "We shall find them all, Jim. Starfleet no longer needs to maintain quarantine blockades. Our ships are free to patrol our borders, to make contact with any world or colony that may have succumbed to. . . ."

"Anarchy," Kirk said flatly. "It's what happens when the system doesn't work."

"But the system *is* working," Picard insisted. "Food supplies are already arriving at their destinations. Because of what you and Spock and McCoy have done here, we are now able to release seed stores to agricultural centers without fear of contamination. And with the threat of further contagion eliminated, the unaffected sectors of the Federation *can* and *will* reach out to those in need. Jim, you should be proud of what you've accomplished. What we've all accomplished. The Federation *is* secure."

"For how long?" Kirk asked. "The Symmetrists did this because they wanted to teach us a lesson. Did we learn it?"

Contempt shaded Picard's reply. "The Symmetrists were terrorists, not teachers. Tens of thousands have died because of what they've done."

"And billions more may have been saved."

Picard's body stiffened. "Are you *condoning* what these maniacs have done?!"

"Of course not," Kirk said. "But that doesn't change the fact that *they are right!"*

"That's absurd."

Kirk gestured at the viewscreen. "Look at that world, Jean-Luc!" Despite the promise represented by the small patches of green alta mist that again floated in the air of Tarsus IV, the world below bore the scars of ecological collapse, and would for decades still to come. "That could have been Earth, or Vulcan! Unless we learn our lesson, someday it will be! And what's the Federation doing to *change* that future—*nothing!"*

No one else on the bridge spoke. The only sound was the background hum of the instruments.

Picard flushed with anger. "The Federation Council is holding emergency sessions around the clock. At this very moment, it is reviewing its colonization and expansion programs in order to identify and insure the integrity of the entire galactic ecosystem. New committees will be formed. New studies begun."

Kirk held out both hands to Picard. "Don't you see? That's what they did in my age. They haven't learned, Jean-Luc. They can't see what's coming."

"And you can?"

Kirk heard the reproach in Picard's question, and understood why it was there. Kirk wasn't a scientist. He had no special skills as an environmentalist or biologist. But he did have the capacity to learn from those who did have the skills and the knowledge that the future needed.

"I can see what's coming," Kirk said, "because I've seen through better eyes than mine. Experienced the thoughts of better minds. Sarek saw the future. There're a hundred other scientists throughout the Federation who know what he knew about how much more expansion and exploration and colonization the galaxy can absorb."

Picard stared at Kirk, and Kirk knew what he was thinking. It was one thing for two starship commanders to have a difference of opinion.

But Sarek was another matter.

"Thirty years," Kirk said. "That's it. You look at the statistics. The growing pattern of complexity. There are other virogens waiting out there, other environmental disruptions that we can't even imagine because we have no real conception of our interstellar environment and our place in it. Thirty years, and it won't be fanatics trying to teach us a lesson. It'll be the real thing. A complete and total interplanetary collapse."

Picard shook his head. "Thirty years is a long time, Jim. Surely, someone will solve this problem before then."

"But who?" Kirk asked softly. "I've done all I can. Now . . . it's up to you."

Picard held Kirk's gaze and did not look away. Kirk knew the challenge had been issued and accepted.

Picard held out his hand. Starship captain to starship captain.

"Somehow I feel that we will meet again," Picard said. A truce declared, despite their differences.

Kirk shook Picard's hand in turn. "When we do, let's hope we're still on the same side."

Later, Data escorted Kirk, Spock, and McCoy through the corridors of the *Enterprise,* on their way to transporter room two. In matching orbit of Tarsus IV, the newly repaired *Tobias* waited to receive her passengers. Commander Christine MacDonald had been given her orders by a grateful Starfleet Command: She would take Kirk, Spock, and McCoy wherever they wished to go, then return to collect the rest of her crew on Vulcan.

Also, in light of the result of her unauthorized mission to Tarsus IV, questions concerning matters of disobeying orders and outright mutiny had been set aside. A personal note added to her orders from Admiral Strak of Vulcan, suggested that Commander MacDonald might wish to discuss the historical precedents for this ruling with one James T. Kirk.

The doors to the transporter room slid open as Kirk and the others approached. Data stepped to one side and stood at ease. "I will wait while you say your good-byes."

Kirk, Spock, and McCoy looked at the android.

"To whom will we say these good-byes?" Spock asked.

Data looked from Kirk to Spock. "This is the transporter room. I assumed that after you two left, I would escort Admiral McCoy to a shuttlecraft."

"The hell you will," McCoy said. "I'm beaming out with my friends."

Data blinked in confusion. "My apologies, Admiral. But I recall that you do not like the transporter as a mode of transportation."

"Hell, son. At my age, if my molecules get scrambled it can only be an improvement."

McCoy laughed. Spock frowned. Kirk shrugged at the android. "I can't take them anywhere," he said.

The three friends started into the transporter room.

But then McCoy stopped and turned back to Data.

"Son, you remember what I told you when you headed out on that last ship of yours?" he asked.

"I do, sir," Data replied. "You specifically told me to remember what you said."

"Well?"

"You said, 'You treat her like a lady. She'll always bring you home.'"

McCoy gave Data a cautioning look. "You keep remembering that, son. And take *care* of this one for a change, all right?"

Kirk smiled at the android's bemused expression.

"C'mon, Bones," he said. "It's time to go home."

FORTY-FOUR

Mount Seleya beckoned, and this time Kirk heard her call.

He stood with Spock and McCoy on the windswept mountaintop, the crimson Vulcan sunset bathing them in the alien color of human blood, human passion.

In the distance, they could see the sprawling temple in which Spock had been returned to life so long ago, his *katra* rejoined to his reborn body.

But the temple was not their destination this night.

Instead, they stood before the *fal-lan-tral*—the Passage of All Mysteries.

A worn path paved with ancient blocks of dusty red stone led up to the opening of a cave in the mountain's side. Within, in a labyrinth of hand-carved tunnels and passageways which none but Vulcan eyes had ever seen, waited the *tral katra*—the keepers of the spirits of the past.

The secret of the *tral katra* had never been revealed to outworlders. Some rumors said they were enormous crystals which held the wisdom of the Vulcan departed. Others claimed the *tral katra* were Vulcan priestesses who sat in yearlong meditations, each holding the *katras* of a thousand dead.

But all that was known for certain by non-Vulcan investigators was that beyond that dark entrance into the cave lay the repository of Vulcan souls, the place to which each *katra* was returned.

That fathomless cave was Spock's destination. And, as Spock had said, it must also be Kirk's.

"Can you feel it?" Spock asked.

Kirk pulled his cloak closer as the mountain breeze cooled with the approaching night.

Spock was right. He could feel it. Somewhere in the darkness beyond, Sarek's *katra* was in repose—all that Sarek had been, all that he had known, saved from extinction by the power of the Vulcan mind.

"We must go together," Spock said.

But Kirk shook his head.

Spock put his hand on Kirk's shoulder. "You are his son as much as I am."

Kirk stared at Spock. Deep within himself, he acknowledged the special bond that had formed between himself and Sarek. He knew it explained so many things about his past, his present, and his future.

But Kirk also knew what Spock truly meant, and desired at this moment.

Absolution.

"You didn't abandon him, Spock."

Spock looked out at the fiery Vulcan sun as it touched the horizon, only minutes from setting. "Then help me tell him that."

"*You* go to him, Spock. Touch his mind. He'll understand."

Spock hesitated. "I find, with age, my emotions are no longer my own, Jim. I need yours to guide me."

Kirk knew Spock's confession had been difficult for him, but the truth was that time had eroded Kirk's own ability to experience his emotions, just as it had eroded Spock's ability to control his. "Spock . . . you're being illogical."

"But it was you who avenged my father's death."

"There was more to it than one man's life," Kirk said. He thought of the pilots he had consigned to death above the jungles of Chal. He thought of his decision—his *desire*—to fire his phaser at Srell. Was either action different from what Kodos had done? Or what the Symmetrists had attempted? Is this what age had brought him to? "It was my duty." And so complete was Kirk's catharsis that to himself, his voice was as devoid of emotion as a Vulcan's.

"Good Lord," McCoy suddenly said. "Is this what it's come down to?"

He had been their silent witness, wrapped in a long admiralty coat against the rising wind.

"Have you two grown so close that you've managed to switch sides? With Spock too full of confusing emotions, and Jim cut off from what makes him human?"

"Your point, Doctor?" Spock asked coldly.

"What is it that stops you two from seeing yourselves as you really are? Spock, Jim may be cut off from what makes him human—but he's *still* human. It's the way he was born. But *you*—you had a choice, and you chose to be Vulcan. And I'm going to hate myself for telling you this, but you're damned good at it. No matter how old you are."

The three friends stood together, huddled against the fall of night, before the cave that led to mysteries unexplored.

Above them, the stars of Vulcan slowly brightened, shimmering through the growing crimson twilight.

"Have we changed?" Spock asked.

Kirk held out his hand to Spock. He had been asked that question before. He knew the answer.

"Not us," he said. As the two friends clasped hands, Kirk was struck by a stunning bolt of clarity. He recalled his first glimpse of Spock, not when they had met, but the image that had been in Sarek's mind that night on Tarsus IV, when Spock had been a youth, no different from himself.

How like my son, Sarek had thought.

Kirk finally understood the ultimate mystery that had united them.

He *and* Spock were Sarek's sons.

And in that moment, Spock understood as well.

"You are my brother, Jim. I, of Sarek's flesh. You, of Sarek's mind."

"Go on," McCoy told them. "You have to." His coat fluttered around him like resting wings. On the horizon, the last spike of day flared against the fall of night. He smiled. "Don't worry. I'll still be here when you come back."

Above them, day had ended. Night was absolute.

Spock looked to Kirk, as if uncertain what to think about what would happen next.

Kirk looked to Spock, uncertain how he should feel.

But he *was* certain that the answer was just ahead. There was always an explanation to be found.

And with his friends, his family, at his side, those things without which no life has meaning, he was not afraid to take the next step on his journey.

Into his future.

Into the *fal-lan-tral.*

FORTY-FIVE

The *Tobias* blazed through space, the stars a rainbow in her wake.

On her bridge, Christine MacDonald held the center chair.

She ran her fingers along the inside of her uniform's collar. Counted the four metal disks that were now affixed to it.

Captain MacDonald.

Her final passenger smiled at her. She smiled back, realizing she had been caught.

"I know," she said. "It's not important. Just more trappings."

But Kirk shook his head.

"It was important to me when I was your age. It should be important to you." He looked ahead to the viewscreen, watching the stars pass, thinking of the cycle of the generations.

Christine reached out and took Kirk's hand, held it close. She spoke diffidently, but her true emotions were apparent.

"I don't suppose you're looking for another ship? There's still a lot of galaxy left out there."

Kirk felt the eyes of every member of her crew upon him. Barc and M'Benga, the blond communications officer whose name he'd never learned, the blue-scaled helmsman whose species he'd never seen. This crew would take her far.

But not where he was going.

He gently slipped his hand from hers, and turned away from the stars to look at her in her chair—*the* chair—to remember one last time how it felt. "Explore it for me. And if you ever pass this way again . . ."

On the viewscreen, the stars stopped moving as the *Tobias* fell from warp, coming up on her destination—a world where blue oceans and white clouds beckoned once again, a planet healed.

"I'll know where to find you," Christine said.

Below him, Chal waited. His world. His dream. Teilani.

Kirk had come home to stay.